LOST KINGDOMS

Also by Phillip H. McMath

Fiction
Native Ground (1984)
Arrival Point (1991)
The Broken Vase (unpublished)

Drama
Dress Blues

LOST KINGDOMS

Phillip H. McMath

PHOENIX INTERNATIONAL, INC.

FAYETTEVILLE

Inquiries should be addressed to:
Phoenix International, Inc.
17762 Summer Rain Road
Fayetteville, Arkansas 72701
Phone (479) 521-2204
www.phoenixbase.com

Library of Congress Cataloging-in-Publication Data

McMath, Phillip H., 1945–
 Lost kingdoms / Phillip H. McMath.
   . p. cm.
 Sequel to: Arrival point.
 ISBN 978-0-9768007-3-6 (alk. paper)
 1. Arkansas—Fiction. 2. Domestic fiction. I. Title.
 PS3563.C3865L67 2007
 813'.54—dc22

                                                        2006101527

This book is dedicated to the memory of my maternal grandparents
—great Mississippians who taught me to love a good story—
Jimmie Belle Vance Phillips (1883–1964)
and
James Fair Phillips (1881–1967)

And I will overthrow the throne of kingdoms, and I will destroy the strength of the kingdoms of the heathen; and I will overthrow the chariots, and those that ride in them; and the horses and their riders shall come down, every one by the sword of his brother.

—Haggai 2:22

Author's Comments

Lost Kingdoms, although it stands alone, completes a trilogy begun in 1976 at a cabin on the Buffalo River and finished in 2006 at a house in Little Rock. The first two novels appeared as *Native Ground* in 1984 and *Arrival Point* in 1991. But it would be wrong to imply this has been a continuous project of some thirty years, as there have been several breaks and lots of fits and starts. For example, I had the pleasure of writing and acting in a play, *Dress Blues;* I was privileged to help my father with his autobiography, *Promises Kept;* and I have shared the last four years with writing *The Broken Vase,* a historical novel about the Holocaust.

In what I enjoy calling "The Lost Kingdoms trilogy," an attempt is made to weave a thread of historical continuity around the Shaw family, living as they have in their fictional Delta place of Wattensaw County, Arkansas. So what was a kind of brooding back-story presence in the first two books now comes center stage in the Lost Kingdoms of Arkansas and the South—or what the Spanish tagged "La Florida"—the lower half of that colossus we have come to know as the United States. I have imagined this narration, if you will, as a great wheel with Arkansas the hub and all else as spokes radiating out to the world's rim. Accordingly, I have tried to encircle it with the lives of various characters and families so as to provide the subjective intimacy necessary for the story's more objective historical context.

In this regard, to the extent that facts are known, I have remained faithful; where in dispute or unknown, I have chosen the version I prefer or taken the liberty of inventing them. I have never seen a bibliography for a novel, but in this book the reader, I think, should be aware of several major sources. Samuel Eliot Morison's *The European Discovery of America: The Southern Voyages* was relied upon for the early exploration of La Florida and the West Indies. For that overlooked conquistador, Hernando De Soto, Charles Hudson's *Knights of Spain, Warriors of the Sun* has been invaluable.

As to the French and Indians in Arkansas, Morris "Buzz" Arnold's magnificent

Poste aux Arcs trilogy is without question the best work ever crafted about that subject; indeed, it is one of the greatest pieces of Arkansas history ever written. Then there is John Gould Fletcher's autobiography, poetry, and history; and in touching upon the Civil War in Arkansas and the misnamed "Trans-Mississippi," James Woods, *Rebellion and Realignment,* Tom DeBlack's *With Fire and Sword,* Carl Moneyhon's *The Impact of the Civil War and Reconstruction on Arkansas,* Mark Christ's *Rugged and Sublime,* Ed Bearss's *Steele's Retreat from Camden,* Curt Anders's *Disaster in Damp Sand,* and Shelby Foote's three magisterial volumes have proven indispensable. For J. O. Shelby's march to Mexico, I have ridden hard upon two very strong horses—Daniel O'Flaherty's biography and Conger Beasley's finely edited *Shelby's Expedition to Mexico* by John Edwards—and a handy little pony that has carried me far is *Fallen Guidon* by Edward Davis. The self-told adventures of Mrs. Susan Bricelin Fletcher and the wonderful diary of Virginia McCollum Stinson have delighted me—her sketch of Steele's occupation of Camden is priceless. There have been numerous biographies of all the major historical players that have proven useful. Of the autobiographies, Grant's is justly considered a masterpiece, but an underappreciated one that I found of particular brilliance is Richard Taylor's *Destruction and Reconstruction.* And if Von Clausewitz was right in saying that war is "the continuation of politics by other means," then the American Reconstruction proves the opposite is also true. Anyone with something approaching a serious interest in that subject should be familiar with Eric Foner's *Reconstruction* and Brooks Simpson's *The Reconstruction Presidents.* As for Reconstructing Arkansas, Kenneth Barnes's *Who Killed John Clayton?* is essential.

One will readily see that the thematic nucleus of the novel is occupied by the tragedy of race and slavery for which Hugh Thomas's *The Slave Trade,* Orville Taylor's *Negro Slavery in Arkansas,* and Eugene Genovese's *Roll Jordan Roll* and *A Consuming Fire* are of critical importance. The best thing this researcher can find on Haiti and its slave revolution is Laurent Dubois's *Avengers of the New World.*

Looking even further southward beyond the great river, hypnotically good are Hugh Thomas's *Conquest* and *Mexico* by Enrique Krauze. Krauze is that rarity, a historian with a touch of the poet, and this history reader can't find anyone who knows more about the "New World" than Thomas.

The South (La Florida) has traditionally been a unique place—a kind of country within a country—and, as such, has borne a very different and somewhat misunderstood relationship not only with Britain, but also with Spain,

France, Mexico, the West Indies, and of course Africa. It is for this reason a narrative eye has been cast upon some aspects of this history that a few readers might find surprising. I hope so.

Philosophically speaking, Nicolas Berdyaev has made an impression. His *The Meaning of History* is worth looking at, if one can find it.

I want to thank my beloved wife Carol for something like a lifetime of patience, encouragement, and editing. Without her a book might get started but it would never be finished.

Also, I am grateful to John Coghlan of Phoenix International and to Debbie Self for helping put on the final touches for publishing. Finally, many thanks go to my dear friends Buzz Arnold and Chuck Woodard for suggesting, encouraging, and error spotting.

In a word, *Lost Kingdoms* is woven from the mint of memory, work, and time, and I hope the reader finds it to be indeed a "good story."

Phillip H. McMath
Little Rock, Arkansas

BOOK ONE

CHAPTER ONE

All I could see from where I stood was three long mountains and a wood.
—Renascence, *Edna St.Vincent Millay*

Elizabeth Shaw, fifty and childless, found herself more and more alone. The big clock struck five, but she had been up since three, waiting for the sun. Conrad slept. He had leased his land and now lived in the easy comfort of a fallow retirement. He would be up soon, dress, drink coffee, offer an official kiss then be gone.

It was cold. Elizabeth pulled on her sweater. Perhaps Conrad would build their first fire. It was almost that time, but he seemed to wait longer and longer, deeper into the winter. Now, too, instead of cutting his own, he bought wood from an old man in dirty overalls, with hands like bark, who smelled of smoke and drove a truck with broken springs. He would come, then it would freeze, as if it had waited.

November—the trees in the Bayou Blanc bottoms turn red and a dull, soft, wet-looking brown and gold, their leaves layering in the mud, sinking through the dusky swamp water, like little capsized boats, curling and twisting from trees seemingly a darker-gray and whiter-white, withering themselves into December. In the morning fog, the trees peer through like intruding ghosts, holding hands with rooted fingers, intertwined under the soil—leaves, water, then ice, a smoking mirror connecting the trees in a glass skirt. Elizabeth would break the ice with a small black stick—it was her favorite time—a relief from summer.

She gazed out the grand kitchen window but it was still dark—windless—quiet—nothing, not even a cry from the dead. Why hadn't there been another child? We bring them for ourselves, she thought. The house was too large. Why hadn't one come? She had waited so long. Why? Conrad wanted to adopt, now in the late autumn of life. But could she? Maybe it was the thing that was needed, but it seemed so hard, so tardy, so out of harmony with the nature of things. But he would have an heir—something to pass on—hold—permanent.

She moved, stepped away, opened a drawer, took out a heavy black pan. She set it down, sighed, stood, stared, then made coffee and waited. He would be down soon, shuffling and coughing. She could hear him cough through the wall.

There had been a boy. The one who asked her first. It had been so odd, his asking, his desperate, tormented insistence. It had frightened her so she had gone to church and prayed, kneeling when no one ever did. Then there was the funeral with the weeping woman leaning over the open box, caressing the body of a girl, mumbling and fumbling with her hands. It was then, seeing the old woman, that Elizabeth knew, decided, that she could not marry the boy, wondering how she would tell him, and why, seeing the coffin and the old woman's grief, she knew what she must do—not marry but send him away.

The clock was ticking in its long wooden box in the hall … like a coffin … clocks are like coffins, she thought. She tried not to listen, but still it ticked. When her mother died they covered hers with black cloth. Someday they would cover this one in black … release her from time at last. She had often wanted to break the clock … or burn it … she imagined a great pyre … consuming … consumed. But Conrad loved this clock, it was his, a gift to her but somehow still his, like most things he gave. Conrad had no sense of eternity, not really, only clock time. When his mother died, Elizabeth had stopped the clock, taken out the pendulum, covered it, too, in black, black crepe—9:17, on a Wednesday evening, June 6, 1955. Conrad thought her foolish, but she wanted to leave it for a year. It had moved twelve minutes—9:29. Static electricity, Conrad said, but Elizabeth wondered and was afraid to touch it. Conrad reset it—to tell time, he said simply. Elizabeth did not want really ever to tell time and Barrel, the Negro hand, said it was bad luck to reset the clock, and she believed him.

Now Elizabeth lit the stove, set the pan over a low flame, put in bacon—white strip by white strip—peeled out and laid delicately in neat rows. She pressed and arranged, watching its fat whiteness against the black pan turning into bubbling grease. Her mother had let her fix it as a child; she had been proud that her mother was proud and never cooked bacon without thinking of her and their cooking together, learning the things of the kitchen, their joy, a thing shared.

But then there had been that boy. He was not only love, but also freedom. They would run away in a "grand adventure"—somewhere—anywhere—to the other side of the world—such a heart she had for him, and he for her. They would escape the slavery of want, work, and duty and fling themselves into a "journey of devotion and romance," she had said aloud one night looking out her window at Venus. She would lie awake looking through that dark glass, dreaming. Even now she could see him clearly as she stared at the bacon, not seeing it at all, but seeing the boy's face with his almond-brown eyes and black, almost blue, thick hair. Elizabeth smothered a sob, a choking, a swelling of grief for that boy. Yet unshed tears swam in her eyes, while she turned the bacon and pressed it down a little too hard, ignoring the popping grease that burnt her hand and wrist, losing the boy's face and trying to conjure it again. Then she saw him—a forlorn figure standing in a tepid rain, smiling at her like he had done before they had made love.

The grease was bubbling, popping like that rain—close your eyes and you can't tell the difference, she often thought. He is dead, Christopher and the boy, both are dead. Another boy had come, a Yankee boy with a funny German name, a friend, he said, looking for a friend of Christopher's. "Had he come visiting?" he had asked. He had lost contact with him and was "trying to find him." She told him she had not seen him since Christopher's college days when he had come as a brief visitor—but she hardly remembered him, in fact. The German boy was polite for a Yankee, and he stayed for dinner, chatted, then went on his way to New Orleans, he said, to keep looking for this young man named Poltam. But he promised he'd stay in touch, and a letter had arrived yesterday. She had read it hurriedly then set it aside to read again in a leisurely way—she would take it with her today.

Strange how it all worked, she thought. Little dramas swirling everywhere, close by and we don't even know. Blind we are and blind we remain—blind to those closest to us, blind to the truth, others, and ourselves; we live as the blind in a half-blind world. The depths and shadows always stand nearby, in and out of the lives and souls of others, and we never know or see them.

What did Conrad think about when he stared into the fire or moaned in his sleep—speaking unintelligible words out to the night like a whispering shibboleth to some other world, as we all do—that he would not or could not share. And there was, of course, a world that she did not share with him. They had shared Christopher, who was their lost flesh, their last world. But there was, to each, another world unto themselves that they did not share and it was this place they kept secret in their sleeping and waking dreams which she thought about now like that boy who was dead also and who had wanted and finally had her— the first—and asked her to marry him but she had rejected after being in the church that strange day seeing the old woman weeping over her daughter in the box that reminded her of a big pendulum clock that wouldn't stop ticking.

She was seized almost by terror and turned the bacon to ward it off. But still she shuddered as she pressed the bacon down with the spatula, grease sputtering around the edges. She flipped it out on a paper towel, watching the hot liquid fat relaxing in a gray circle like a living thing come at last to rest.

The clock swung on and on in louder undulating ticks, louder than before, louder and louder. Each day's sun dawns but once, and she looked out again into the darkness in anticipation. There once had been her son's face almost against the window before he started out to hunt with Conrad, once the face of a horse that had gotten out during a storm, peering in at her with an ominous stupidity, the blazed dark face lit by a white flashing light, like the lightning blaze down his face, melding fields and trees together in a shimmering instant; the black gelding staring into the kitchen shortly before Christopher's death, an omen, making her scream till Conrad came to lead the creature away through the rain, thunder, and forking light.

But now Christopher was backhoed into the earth, in his oblong little cell. She wanted to free him, let him run and breathe and laugh.

She thought of the school poem.

> I know the path that tells Thy way
> Through the cool eve of every day;
> God, I can push the grass apart
> And lay my finger on Thy heart.

Elizabeth cooked eggs and toast, then poured her coffee.

> … push the grass apart
> And lay my finger on Thy heart.

She would do that today, go and push the grass apart and lay her finger on his heart.

Conrad did not like her to go so often, so she simply did not tell him, going secretly, sitting quietly alone in the shade. There seemed no clocks there; seconds, minutes, hours, days, years, which hold us like little chips of wood, turning us through time's fingers, till we drop away, one by one, piece by piece, our turn into the ground.

> Thou canst not move through the grass
> But my quick eyes will see thee pass. …

She sipped the coffee as the rhyme went round again and again through her memory, obsessively repeating the refrain in fragments.

Now it seemed to lighten a bit in the fields, the sun would soon break over the trees. It would be a warm day, yet cool enough, a good day to go. Then her mind returned to the poem, repeating it as her lips burned from coffee and her thoughts began to accelerate and clear with the breaking light. An outline was pulled across the horizon by the rising sun and the trees appeared as backdrop to the bare fields. It was the Bayou Blanc bottoms, deep and long, beginning there as the entryway to the big woods, numberless sloughs and backwaters, where a small, brown, little brother of a river merged into a much bigger one that ran finally into the Mississippi, the father river, accepting it for its final, slow, inexorable surge down the Arkansas Delta, past Lake Village, then Greenville, Vicksburg, Natchez, Baton Rouge, New Orleans, and on to the sea. New Orleans, where Christopher's strange friend, Poltam, might have gone and where the nice Yankee boy, Kroner, had also gone in search of him and had finally sent a letter back, like a message from the dead.

There was a noise—Conrad entered.

So it had always been. So it had been for mothers and grandmothers and their mothers and grandmothers—numberless. To make company for some lonely God, her grandmother had said. He was lonely so He made the world—and man was lonely, so He made a woman. The same God had made Grandma Nora ... who moved back to west Tennessee ... who hated Yankees because a Blue soldier had stolen her blanket when she was a girl and the men were away at war.

They took a horse, too, but the blanket was what she could not ever forgive—they stole horses and mules all the time—but that blanket was personal. Stealing a blanket in a bad winter from a little girl who needed it seemed to say something about Yankees and their world—all that she, or anyone, needed to know about such folks. Anyway, that's what she said all her life, repeating it to Elizabeth over and over, her youngest grandchild. What kind of country sends soldiers to steal blankets from little girls? It wasn't *her* country that would do such a thing. The South was *her* country, Arkansas and Tennessee, it was all the country she would ever want or need or understand. Country was something you "felt in your bones," Grandma Nora had said, not something you really had to think about.

"Why," Elizabeth asked, "did God make Yankees in the first place? Come to think of it, why had He created a world of Yankees, horseflies, rattlesnakes, ticks and chiggers, chicken pox, and such, anyway?" Well, horseflies and ticks fed the birds and rattlesnakes ate mice, but she was perplexed about the need for pox and Yankees, answered her grandmother. Maybe it was the price of the Fall, she offered. Then Elizabeth asked what that was and never got a good answer from her grandmother or anyone else. The Fall was something she would never understand—a strange contradiction between God's will and man's choice, all of which somehow got laid at the doorstep of simple folks who had no choice at all—it would remain a mystery, for sure, that's all one could really say about it, and so she let it drop.

The coffee was bitter. Elizabeth stirred in sugar. How easy it had been to make. Her mother had to grind the beans with a crank. Elizabeth remembered getting up shivering to help in the dark, laying the stove, then her father stirring, up without speaking—a certain resistance. In winter, his laying the fireplace fire exactly the same, going out, coming in with logs, doors slamming, dogs barking, darkness pressing hard against the windows, sometimes frost around the edges; going out in the late stars or early moonlight, usually before sunup, unless there was a storm or rain; or, if there were, the trees would be awake and shake and shimmer—upset by the weather, fearful of the wind—tossing and throwing their sticks in agitation against the window; limbs and nuts hitting the roof with a shot-like bang, the light flicking inside, dancing along the walls like apparitions—like her grandfather's fingers playing over a lantern in the barn, a game he enjoyed entertaining the children with. The smell of wood smoke so common that her clothes always smelled of it like the old man who now brought Conrad his bought wood, smelling him, reminiscent of father's Ozark house, the next set of mountains over; her father's family coming west from Virginia to Kentucky to Tennessee to Arkansas, from poor-farm to poor-farm, dropping their dead along the way—pathetic packages of interrupted time—into little scratched-out holes in the ground, mourned, then forgotten in lost thickets of cockleburrs, dog fennel, and wildflowers. But still having more children, almost by the litter, and having them die litter-like of diphtheria, smallpox, whooping cough, croup, pneumonia, blood poisoning, bullets, snakebite, worms, tick, swamp, and scarlet fever—plus a thousand causes unknown, all now "in heaven with the Lord," folks would say, being born and dying over and over, loving, working, singing, and dying like the phantoms playing against the barn wall from grandfather's old crooked but agile fingers, the smell of hay and manure burning deep into your nostrils with a curious kind of pain; fingers playing lightly their magic like the now dead boy's over young Elizabeth's undressed white body and the small, soft breasts that summer night in the thick green of the cemetery grass, the only place to be alone near the church. His entering her for the first time while they moaned over the unvoiced dead; sex, birth, and death, merging for one moment of delight in the luscious, grassy darkness under a cloud-chased, tumescent moon, the happiest moment of Elizabeth Shaw's life, except when she gave birth to

Christopher—love and birth, the Janus-face of the ecstatic other. And, had she known the word, *le mystère,* running between them like an electric, connecting current.

From that night forward she had shared her father's mute rebellion, his unspoken, half-desperate resistance, and each morning she had newly arisen in a kind of pain, no longer a child but a grumpy and quietly defiant young woman looking for her own way, the way to repeat what she thought was unique to her—the love, birth, and death cycle that had brought her here this morning, standing in her big kitchen on what amounted to one of the richest plantations in the Arkansas Delta, watching the new sun light her fields for what would be for her another afflictive day unless she could find her way to a certain place; her whole life, in a sense, being the search for that special thing set among the witless sun's everyday turning, finally finding her way free of time.

There was another noise. He was coming. It was lighter out. The sun was swinging around; no, the earth was turning to meet it—she never could remember just which. Once again, it would come around, over and over, whether she understood it or not, whether she lived or not, it would come around and light the hard ground; and mothers would rise up and children cry, dogs bark and men lay fires, and it would all begin once again.

It would all happen like yesterday, and the day before, and the day before that—on and on—the sun swinging round, vanquishing our small shards of time, then shaping new ones to repeat it all again and again.

There had been the drama of Elizabeth's youth, her parents' struggle, the boy, then Conrad, Christopher, his death in Vietnam, and now their final days; yet she was still trapped in the now and everyday, with all its routine, the chronological and the necessary, which, because of its very immediacy, obscures, blinds to everything but the urgent and practical, never seeing the important till it is past, making the past, finally, mysteriously, essential.

Then there is the grave, or the boy-lover, or the story about the Yankee who stole the blanket from Grandma Nora when she was a little girl, or her little brother, Homer Joe, who everyone inexplicably called "Virgy," who lay sick with fever in the winter of 1863–64, when it got to zero. The big river froze so Yankee wagons could cross; why would God do that? she wondered. The past stopping the sun, stopping Grandfather's dancing shadows, stopping everything—for a moment—stopping it all.

Now there was a deep cough. It came through the wall; there was something about such a cough coming through a wall.

Conrad entered. Mumbled, coughed again, said good morning and asked how she slept. Then squatted, laid the fire, struck a match, paused as it went out, strikes another. There was a blaze and so another day began.

Driving along a graveled road canyoned by tall green pines, Elizabeth slowed behind a logger's "billet" truck, its timbered trees skinned of limbs exposing shiny yellow wounds that bled sap through barkless trunks broken and bound by rusty chains seemingly on the verge of bursting. It moaned out dirty smoke into a blinding black-brown dust until she could accelerate around in a rush.

Then a pickup appeared around the next curve forcing her to flash an automatic greeting—a custom of the back roads—a right hand thrown up, with a quick smile—warding off envy and resentment—dropped just as quickly without much caring whether it was seen or not, like the mechanical tipping of a hat or a nod of the head—a kind of talisman of the rural South where every human emotion is checked behind the routine of courtesy.

She had packed a lunch of cheese and crackers, canned peaches, slices of ham, and potato salad. There was suet for the birds, a thermos of hot coffee, and an old blanket she kept in the trunk, all for a picnic under a tree in the graveyard—alone, she hoped. If anyone was there she would drive by, waving and smiling, but going by, to wait, then circle furtively back in search of solitude—under a tree.

There was another curve before a straight stretch with an old man walking in the same direction, quickly turning, to frown and stare at the intruder in the same way she feared someone would intrude upon her. It was Mr. Fox, the hunter, now too old for serious hunting, wearing overalls and a tattered brown coat with holes in the sleeves. Recognizing her, he waved with a slight smile, tipped his red hat, and turned away, resuming a frown as he stared at the hard brown earth, ignoring Elizabeth's dust as she sped by with a wave and smile— animals, horses, mules, and wagons giving way to machines—intruding— binding everything in a new way—a new slavery.

Elizabeth glanced back as Mr. Fox was swallowed up. He had hunted with Christopher and Conrad—happy autumns now fled—falls being a way of counting. She resolved yet again to stop trying to dissect past from future, as Mr. Fox disappeared, his image erased, the thought intruding as she gripped the wheel. The past, bringing it forever forward, fixing it fast, locking it against future's door—her knuckles sweating as she thought of this.

It would be the same—the ongoing slipping away of seconds—she would build it up all into one motionless, self-conscious effort—the obsession of trying always to hold, grasp, arrest its steady inching into memory—into a past that she must then need recall, transform, and hold hard again against an unwanted and unyielding tomorrow.

Was there some mysterious power at work, she wondered, lurking like a river's current beneath the surface or a horse running in a rain—coming to our side—either too strong or not quite strong enough, working dumbly without knowing, yet cleverly knowing all.

Elizabeth came to this at Queeny's funeral. The Black church with its country graveyard behind. It was long and white, set over wet soggy ground, the building sagging into a buckle like a wooden ship at sea, hanging suspended between waves. A tiny foyer opened into an oblong room with a slightly raised podium, and a cardboard picture of Jesus, and a box for the choir. It rocked with the power of their voices. The riddle of the South was in the inexpressible power of those African voices; something deeper than the throat or bone or flesh or muscle there, something deeper than mind or thought or words; something beyond the mere ineffability of music; something that rises out of night and rivers and forests and time and fields and levies and moonlight over the tops of thick dark trees and even more time so long and deep as to be longer and deeper than anything, including Man himself; something buried in the hopelessness of all thought or any puny words on paper; something lifting itself out of darkness, out of eons of flesh, blood, and the rhythms of life that mock and uplift those who listen.

Finally, burial in the back, under a hovering oak, older than the oldest grave, amidst other largely forgotten, unmarked lumps of ground. The coffin brought round in a stumbling, shuffling procession of Black men whispering—swinging and laying open at the quarter-top, a small mound of head of short gray curls, emerging like a black island from a white sea of ersatz silk—the pulling away of a folded piece—the last look—a pathetic toy placed by an arm—a picture of a little boy—a flower thrown in—sobs—the closing. The last-minute hammering of a wooden cover; a last service, and the lowering. Voices, tears, a shriek, a milling, and a confused, slow, embarrassed, self-conscious, half-reluctant wandering away—Black and White—mingled yet separate, always that, inching away from the mystery; standing mute yet like a dark, knowing laughter—Blacks and Whites—Africa and Europe—thrown together in a unique blond and black juxtaposition that is unthinkably, incomparably, the American South with its never more than half-understood intuitions in the dark will of souls—the same and different—that sameness and difference being their tragedy and salvation—mingled and apart—loving and hating—thrown together and separated—existing above a small slit in the earth that marks the exit and the entryway, the only such, from their Southerness and from their history. It was this egress, this trapdoor to eternity, this departure, that Elizabeth had known then and come for today—to stand over the now-sealed entrance for a moment, with Christopher closed behind the wall without a cough, a voice, a cry, but in so doing, escaping at last from the infernal ticking of Conrad's clock, sitting in the hall like an upright coffin.

She looked ahead for a moment and then back again. Mr. Fox was gone in the dust as she knew he would be. Even while he was there his going had been with him so that in his being there had also been a kind of going.

She had looked at her father in the same way—looked and he was there—then turned away and he was gone—kissed him—then turned to go, did not look back—then he vanished, too. How can people do that? She did not, could not, believe that they really did that—simply vanished—escaped—through a slit in the ground, then closed the earth behind; like on hinges. She would simply stand outside, wait, until her time—the South, death, race, history, Grandma Nora, Grandfather's fingers, her parents, the boy entering her, Conrad, Christopher, Barrel, Queeny, the clock in the hall—all at last would be transformed.

She drove to the graveyard on a slight hill and stopped behind it in a small clearing, looking around, she could see nearby a fire pit, blackened with burned-out timber strips and a few broken stones in a rough circle where last year's loggers had parked their worn-out trucks, stood to talk, curse, laugh, urinate, spit, and smoke while hitching and unhitching tree-skidding mules along the road. They had, of course, littered: paper, cans, spilt oil, rusty and broken tools, worn-out tires, split timber, cigarette butts, broken auto parts, and shards of old clothes—shreds of shirts, used-up gloves, and even a black half-burnt leather boot with no sole. The mules had gotten into the cemetery so the ladies cleaned and manicured it before putting up a fence—new silver wire around old graves.

Elizabeth got out and went to the gate that was latched but never locked. A small white sign said, announced, in bold black letters, "Ephesus Cemetery, Wattensaw Cemetery Association, Ashley Drew Griggs, President." Elizabeth stepped in. She knew everyone—kin, friends, or friends of kin. Trees crowded on three sides, the fourth a ditch and the road.

"We have been cured forever of any notions of progress," she once said sententiously to Conrad.

"What?" he asked, baffled.

"Progress is a Yankee notion," she added.

"You mean roads and dams and such?" he said, blinking like a man awakening—she said the damnedest things, he thought.

"No, not really that … before the war, maybe, but after that … no … I think we were just silly romantics then," she persisted, knowing that he wasn't following, but just wanting someone to say it so she could hear it with an outer rather than an inner voice. "Really, after that, I think … that was the turning point … after then, don't you agree?"

"You think too much," he said, shaking his head.

"Maybe not too much but too well …," she replied, adding, "progress stops here … at Ephesus Gate. There you just find rotting leaves, grass, mud, everything … all mixed up … bones … hopes … but no progress, whatever that is."

Conrad could only stare.

Today, at Ephesus Gate, outside the fence, there was an admixture of manure from the mules and leaves among the murl and grass. Elizabeth ignored this as she stepped through and walked among the graves. She was at home in an odd, half-unanticipated way—at least for now—today—this late fall morning warmed by the sun with a slight, surviving but ephemeral coolness in the air, which for her had a certain soul-saving serenity.

Sometime she thought that her entire life had been a preparation for some unspoken, important, wonderful something that would inevitably happen but had not, and now wasn't going to happen at all, at least not in the way that she ever imagined. But things never happened as imagined, she had learned that. What that something was didn't involve ordinary life but in an enigmatic, inscrutable, way was here—this collection of bones resting upwards just below a crust of earth; lying supine in box-like couches, roofed over with earth sprouting trees, grass, leaves, worms, traces of dry, decaying dung, and a few songbirds flitting in and through the shaded chiaroscuro of sun and shadow under which she strode in hard black leather and very sensible shoes, wearing a cotton dress, sweater, and hat with a basket over an arm.

But maybe Elizabeth Shaw had finally arrived at that great thing that was finally to happen after all. It was the last thing—being—in a world of becoming, which, river-like, had denied itself altogether till now and, through the relentlessness of the world, had imprisoned everything and everyone in an endless agitation.

"While we live yet we are …," the thought trailed off as her eye traced over each tombstone. She was standing among her dead at last, herself but a fugitive, alone and lost in this dark wood mixed with light: not fully knowing but striving to know, not with her mind, but with all her heart to understand, as she clung in desperation to the riddles of Faith, Family, and Place. Elizabeth removed her hat, sat against a tree near her son's grave, and ate a peach.

CHAPTER TWO

Must commerce be cemented with the blood of innocents?
   —Captain Balthazar de Villiers, Commandante of Arkansas Post,
   1776

Elizabeth knew that the South was dying. She could see it all around, thrashing out its life like a wounded animal. It soon would be dead like Christopher, her only son and child, killed by Vietnam, another civil war that made less sense in dying for than anything that could come to mind.

Her Christopher was dead. The South, something she had once half thought of as a thing immortal, and which she never conceived of as not, till now, was nearly dead. She couldn't really say what the South, as a living thing, actually was. But it was, indeed, something living—in the soul. Like loving someone it was something in the flesh, too deep to think of as not being there—but mortal.

But the loving was never easy—the child's conception in 1619 announced by one John Rolfe, a Norfolk planter, who wrote: "About the last of August came a Dutch man of war that sold us twenty Negroes."

When that Dutchman, its white sails luffing off Virginia, tacked into view, it was by all accounts a bright, fair day, the small ship coming about, silently shortening sail, working its rattling rigging quietly upon an easy, rolling, sunlit sea. The first slaver, sliding in, wharfing, then delivering her survivors from Guinea—the "land of the five slave rivers," as it was then called: the Benin, the Río Reale, the Cross, the Old Calabar and the mighty Niger, draining like dark brown blood from the slave coast into the ocean "making the green one red."

> Beware and take care of the Bight of Benin;
> Few come out, though many come in.

So went the slavers' sailor's song. It was not a healthy place, they said of the Bight of Benin.

But soon there would be others coming from there to touch the colonies: the *Treasurer* (1619), *James* (1621), *Margaret and John* (1622), and the *Swan* (1623). *Desire* (1637) was the first slaver to lay her timbers in America, built at Marblehead, Massachusetts, registered at Salem, she took the quicker route to the West Indies, returning with slaves for sale in Connecticut.

It had all begun with the Portuguese, slipping mostly over to Brazil, but soon the Spanish, going to their empire, then the French, Dutch, British, and finally, the Americans, who went everywhere. Eleven million humans captured and sold, usually by African kings, then shipped to the Americas, from 1492 to 1870, on a voyage that, had Dante known, he could never have written it in the *Inferno* without canceling his *Paradiso*. Chained side-by-side in a dark, head-stooping hold, smelling eternally of vomit, urine, and excrement (Alexander Hamilton said you could smell slavers at more than a mile), sounding the rolling timbers with sobs of suffering incessant, fever, thirst, and death; then bodies, often half-living, splashed over from ships the Spanish and Portuguese named for saints and virgins—the English, Americans, and Dutch, for women and men who were anything but virgins and saints—the French for abstractions or their creators, the *Voltaire, Rousseau, Nouvelle Société,* and *Égalité,* feeding the steadfast ones swimming patiently for Satan, as Melville reports in his great novel, "Sharks … are the invariable outriders of all slave ships crossing the Atlantic, systematically trotting alongside …"

The Portuguese baptized (no one should venture to Brazil without it). They gave each convert a Christian name smudged out on dirty paper, then touched every head with holy water and every tongue with salt, finally sermonizing their minds with a catechist's admonishment: "Consider that you are now children of Christ. You are going to set off to Portuguese territory, where you will learn matters of the Faith. Never think anymore of your place of origin. Do not eat dogs, nor rats, nor horses. Be content."

Slaves of all colors had built the pyramids of Egypt and Mexico, the Parthenon of Athens, the dams of China, practically everything in Rome—that great empire using up half a million per year as the Rabbi Jesus preached brotherhood. Germans or Saxons were considered among the best. Verdun was the finest slave market in all of Europe, some said, noted for its fine blond eunuchs who fetched a very high price.

It was a world of slaves and masters. Approved of by the Koran, the Caliph Muqtadir, we are told, owned 300,000 taken in war. Muslim slaves, owned by Christians, built the Cathedral of Santiago de Compostela, honoring St. James, as Christian ones built the great Mosque of Kutubiyya in Marrakesh, to honor Allah. The Bible, Aristotle, and Sir Thomas More's *Utopia*, all approved. So did the entire Renaissance. Oddly, the first voice against it was a soldier's, writing of war—Fernão de Oliveira, a Portuguese captain and military intellectual, who, in his *Arte da Guerra no Mar*, 1554, described it as an "evil trade" with the heart of a "slaughterhouse butcher."

In Europe, it was replaced by feudalism—a more efficient form of exploitation, till that in turn was supplanted by slave wages, the improvements being incremental. But Black slavery remained while the American Indians died or were murdered ("ethnically cleansed," as we would say), so that Europe sweetened its tea with white sugar, Black sweat, and Blacker blood as modernity's capital.

Balzac put it best, echoing young captain De Villiers, "For every great fortune, there is a great crime."

America's greatest city is named for one—the Duke of York (1660), stockholder of the Royal Adventurers, the slave company later supplanted by the Royal Africa Company, who took the town from the Dutch in the trade, Harlem, for slavers' interests. Her capital, Washington, is named for her most famous slave owner; for ty of our first forty-eight presidents, including the first two after Lincoln, were owners; and, of course, there was the regicide Jefferson, the champion of the guillotine and "Unalienable Rights." Too, his mentor of liberty, John Locke, was heavily invested, as was Isaac Newton, Alexander Pope, much of parliament, the House of Lords, the King and family, including the Queen Mother and all the Royal Bastards. (The word "guinea" became British money slang for "pound.")

The early slave capitalists of America were mostly New Englanders—whalers doing a brisk side business, many of them Quakers. It was said in 1687, "That there's not a house in Boston, however small may be its means, that has not one or two slaves. There are those that have five or six."

Great families of Massachusetts got their egg money in the trade—the Belchers, the Waldos, Faneuils, and also the Cabots. It always seemed to be "a thing of families." The de Wolfs, the Browns, the Leylands, and the Hobhouses built estates and fortunes so their heirs could be well-heeled characters in James and Wharton. James de Wolf called his palace "Mount Hope," while John Brown's mansion in Providence is considered "one of the best in New England" and he even built a liberal university that took his name. (Not to be confused with the abolitionist of greater fame but lesser respectability, the Brown whose body is "a-moldering.")

In time, Newport supplanted Boston and New York, as Nantes did Bordeaux, and Liverpool did Bristol and London. But the Portuguese remained tops till 1730 when the British pushed them off by financing an Empire in which the American South was a rich stepchild in its West Indian family.

It was the slaves of all the great Sugar, Rice, Rum, Tobacco and Cotton Kingdoms that bankrolled Britain's fortune—Lancashire repaying slavery in its rich perpetuation. In 1810 Britain consumed 79 million pounds of cotton of which 48 percent came from the South, in twenty years it was 248 million and 70 percent, in 1860 a billion and 92 percent, making cotton America's king export picked by two billion dollars' worth of golden slaves—ten times the Federal budget at the bombing of Fort Sumter.

Thus slave-capital fed the greatest economic revolution in history, building its cities, railroads, and "satanic mills" over the English countryside, consuming iron, steel, coal, and labor without cease. The entire edifice of "Upstairs-Downstairs" England was laced up by Louisiana, Lancashire, and Luanda—propping up its *Mansfield Park* world of cocked, and later, top-hat society of silk stockings, periwig balls, barouches, and painted, pushed-up white bosoms on the great estate and drawing-room stage of England. Abolition came, but not before a *Bleak House* capitalism shocked those who could employ half a brain for half an hours' thought into some form of radicalism, which meant, of course, there were relatively few radicals.

So, it was in that quiet but portentous moment, then, in 1619, that everything changed. America's history took another lurch as Virginia accepted the admixture—Anglo, Celtic, African—into an unconscious infusion; painfully giving birth to a new ineffable thing of Elizabeth's lament—known as "The South," christened in time by Whitney's diabolic mechanism that bred more machines for Manchester and today for Manhattan.

The South, tragic, yet somehow thought of as comic, too—a place to laugh at or despise; a place with a shabby misunderstood perspicacity born of a slow-burning suffering; never easily tongued; more felt, or just known in a vague soul-touching, poorly articulated, way—an idiot genius born into first British, then American bastardy. This was the half-known thing that Elizabeth Shaw loved and wanted very much to understand fully—to embrace its angels while trying to defy its devils that came at her arm in arm from the hell and heaven of her own personal history—loving while trying not to hate.

Sun in snow—ice with flame—a commonality producing something never yet seen. Black and White, as said, the same yet different—the sameness and difference always there—the same yet different. I will take your language and make it different and give it back to you and it will become common but different, salt it with a lilt of sympathy, kindness, beauty, and strangeness—the same but different. I will take your land and make it different and give it back to you and make it fruitful. I will take your children, nurture, and make them like me, the same yet different, always giving them back to you, like all the others but different—changed—I will change everything.

I will take your music, transform it, give it beat and syncopation and a thing called "soul" because of where it arises. I will change music forever—the same and yet totally different. I will take your religion, change it, give it empathy and a sad, dark power, and will sing such songs of praise that have never been heard in the midst of such suffering that I will touch an unknown part of you, a part you did not know was there, lying hidden under centuries of your artificial civilization, explore the depths that you have never known, convert everyone, when all else is falling away into ruin—the same yet different. I will win the world and convert it—and teach forgiveness.

I will take the South and change it, make it the same yet very, very different, a part of America yet always very different. The South will be my home, and your home and we will live there together and cease to be Europeans or Africans and become in time something the same, yet very, very different. You will fight to keep me a slave but you will never want to leave the land that I have changed for you and made unique. The lost war won't matter because our roots will sink with your blood and our bodies will mix into a new fertility of Southern ground in a way only known by the heart, always the heart, that in the end can't be suffocated by the machines I will help make and the cities and science I will help build, though I never wanted it. Our Black-White soul, our European-Anglo-Celtic-African soul, is the same yet different. Not like anything that ever was or ever will be seen again. The same yet different— containing a greater truth than can ever be beaten by any such lost war and all its defeated armies and all its Lost Kingdoms.

CHAPTER THREE

I'm hungry.
——*Nora Pilgrim*

Grandma Nora, in telling the story of the blanket, was always fond of bragging to Elizabeth about how she had been practically raised by slaves, explaining how well she "understood the darkies." They had owned several families, she would say proudly. (You had to be well-off in Arkansas to own any.) When Nora was but a girl of six she lived on the Pilgrim plantation of several hundred acres with the great, grand name of Arcadia. Here the Whites lived, together but separately, with a roughly equal number of Blacks for the raising of cotton, corn, cows, and chickens.

The Whites lived in a two-storied "Big House" and the Blacks in cabins behind, both huddled in a little clearing west of the "Rock," a frontier town sleeping on the long, ever-winding Arkansas river, about one day's ride away. Little Rock was of no real significance to anyone except those five thousand or so souls who were fated to live there, but, as a Confederate capital, it had come of late to enjoy an unexpected prestige as a "center of rebellion," as it was called in the Northern press. Soon, it began to romanticize itself into a kind of modern Troy or Athens——both slave-owning societies, everyone said. Somehow Rome seemed too grand and this comparison was reserved for Richmond or Atlanta, while Little Rock became a lesser but equally brave city-state, indefatigably fending off barbaric hordes, in the name of light and goodness against darkness and an evil with which all Yankeedom had become associated——the Hun, Tartar, Vandal, or Philistine coming readily to mind.

But Arkansas, like her Upper South sisters——Tennessee, North Carolina, and Virginia——had not really wanted out at all and, between South Carolina's exit and Fort Sumter, had, in fact, voted to stay in. But after Sumter, the "fat was in the flame ... and that black Republican, Mr. Lincoln, had put us the question," as Medora was fond of saying, by demanding from all states a levy upon their young White men. Arkansas could not raise her sword against her

Southern sisters—honor dictated disobedience. Secession then passed the convention with but one dissent, that of Isaac Murphy, a mountaineer, who caught a bouquet from a lady in the balcony and the eventual Union governorship from Lincoln for his pains. Thus the Upper joined the Lower, while the Border neither quite joined nor ever really remained but held itself suspended as a perpetual battleground of bloody ambivalence.

Titus, Medora's husband, said he'd seen it all coming and "the sooner the better." Like most slave owners he wanted to go with the Lower part, had ridden half a day to vote for Breckinridge in '60 to bring it about, then served in both conventions to vote "yes." "If she hadn't thrown those flowers, I thank Murphy would'a been killed," he told Medora that evening at the hotel across the street.

Into the cauldron were thrown Nora and her older sister, Iphigenia, or "Ephey," fourteen, and their fever-infected, ten-year-old little brother, Homer Joe, or "Virgy," as he was called for some unknown reason by the slaves and practically everyone else. Two babies had been born and died between Homer and Nora—they were buried under slanting white crosses nearby in a newly made and well-tended cemetery, a fenced-off clearing among the trees, much like the one where Elizabeth was sitting now drinking coffee out of a thermos top, leaning against a tree, remembering her own dead while thinking, too, of the dying of the South.

But when the Yankees came for Nora's immortal blanket, the children were living with their mother, Medora Covington Pilgrim, and two remaining female "house" slaves—Aunt Essie, who was getting old, gray-headed, and a little stooped, and Rose-In-May, called "Rosamay" or usually just "Rosy," who was not yet twenty. The two families of "field" slaves had followed Stancil, a massive, very black slave in his early thirties, who handled horses and mules like large puppies and could, it was said, "make cotton grow on the head of a pin"; they all had run to freedom behind him like their Moses as soon as the Yankees came within walking distance.

That year General Steele had come marching virtually unopposed west from Helena while his opposites, Gray generals Marmaduke and Walker, dueled among themselves about whose fault it all was. Steele crossed the river into the Rock, flanking Marmaduke, who escaped with great sound but little fury, except for the fatal shot fired into Walker's breast on the other side. So it came about on a very hot, late summer's day in September 1863, that a half-empty, sullen town of women, children, old men, runaway Blacks (called "contraband" by the

Yankees), and a few White dodgers waited upon the entrance of the "Huns" from Minnesota, Illinois, Ohio, Iowa, Indiana, and Missouri. These marauders were mostly farm boys in dusty blue uniforms with heavy dark packs and bedrolls laced diagonally across their chests as was fashionable in the Western Federal army. Their regiments marched quietly over a rickety pontoon bridge to a drummer boy's slow, steady but diminutive rattle, only hours behind the chattering Confederates, no longer much in gray but an army of tatters whose bare feet meandered through the town in a broken, ill-disciplined column, pausing to accept water ladled out of tin buckets with long spoons from helpful ladies and girls, drunk with a kindly "thank ye, mam" or poured into a floppy, sweaty hat for cooling of the heated head.

One such pourer was little Adolphine Krause, aged nine, fluent in German and piano, future mother of the poet John Gould Fletcher. She said that some scarecrow of a Confederate announced loudly as she poured: "Well, goodbye, girls. We've got to be going on, but we're coming back soon to fight for you." But they never did. Not there anyway.

Rose-In-May, a "high yeller" born on a Mississippi plantation with an uncomfortable resemblance to her owner, was sold along with her mother, on insistence of his consort, to a trader in Memphis named Forrest. From there, they were passed by several hands to Arcadia, only for Rosy to be orphaned by the same fever that now gripped Homer.

Rosy had a tendency to wander, and after she heard about Steele at the Rock, she ran again but came back crying and wouldn't tell anybody what she was crying about, what had happened, or why she had come back at all, not even Aunt Essie, to whom she told everything.

"She jes cain't git Stancil outa of her hade," pronounced Aunt Essie with great authority.

"Why didn't she jes run when he did?" Medora had asked.

"Stancil know Rosy ... she cain't keep no secrets," said Aunt Essie. "He done run an' lef' her."

The patriarch of this house, father, husband, and master, was one Titus Heaton Pilgrim, Colonel, C.S.A., proud owner of Arcadia. He had gone south on his fine gray riding gelding, Pegasus, with what remained of his regiment. Some soldiers were with Lee, but more than half of Arkansas's Confederates, men and boys, were either in the south of the state—the "bottoms"—a fever-infested wilderness that would kill more Yankees in Arkansas than musket, cannon, or saber—were paroled from Vicksburg, or were fighting with the Army of Tennessee under the heroic Anglo-Irishman, Patrick Cleburne, and his mentor, Hardee, both Delta gentlemen serving under a proud idiot named Braxton Bragg, who was despised by everyone but Jefferson Davis.

Simply put, there were no more men and boys to be had. "Arkansas was picked thew," as Colonel Titus had said. Only the dregs remained: criminals, dodgers, bushwhackers, traitors, and guerrillas. Of course, there were lots of women and children. Or, as one Yankee soldier put it, "Arkansas is short of everything but poverty and disease." He might have added widows and orphans to his list of "plenty."

As for General Steele, Medora never tired of comparing him to Lucifer, saying the "devil hath the capacity to assume many forms ... and now right yar in Arkansas, he's got his black boot own our necks ... we gotta bargain as we can with ever'thang but our souls," she would thunder.

"Why has God let this happen?" asked Nora innocently, one solemn evening by the fire.

Thinking for a moment, her mother answered, "Lincoln and this war have come from God as punishment fur our sins."

"What sins?" asked Nora.

"Not following God's law," said Medora, adding, "God scourges them He loves."

"Why? Why would He do that?" she asked.

"For not followin' His law," said Medora. "To make us do better ... honey, it's a mystery."

Nora thought. "Maw, are we bein' scourged 'cause of the darkies?"

"Now they got nothin' to do with it ... that's jes abolitionist lies. Slavery is ordained by the Lord," she said. "Jes read the Bible ... it's full of struggle, sin, and slavery ... obedience is what God demands ... just look at Abraham and Isaac ... salvation is in the next world, not yar ... yar, there's only the folly of a fallen world ... awl souls are equal afore God ... that's our salvation, honey, ... our only hope ... and it lies in eternity. Yankees're from the Devil," she would say, with a kind of wild, mad fire in her eye when she got her blood all up, usually taking a dip of snuff to settle things.

Their "Big House" sat before a jutting hill in a small valley facing south. The place was well tended for what had so recently been frontier. There was a white fence around the front with a big barn and "out" buildings behind in addition to the slave quarters. The house's parlor was furnished with St. Louis furniture, and there was a dining table with chairs and a few other expensive things chugged by steamboat up the Arkansas from the Mississippi.

But '63 was a bad year and promised to get worse. They were a small group of "calvry," that is, they were riding horses, all seven, led by a surly, red-headed sergeant from southern Illinois.

"Out to have some fun!" he bellowed, rocking back on his heels with that lusty melodramatic, destructive vitality of all barbarians, age-to-age.

Then, after little ado, they proceeded to sack Arcadia—impulse slipping the ever-stretched leash of civilized control—looting the smokehouse and burning the slave quarters. Then, the soldiers busied themselves with stealing the horses, mules, a cow, and whatever else they could load.

Drunkenly, they taunted Medora, saying they knew her colonel was fighting with the Rebs and, "We come to see you paid your Reb tax. Yep, today you pay!" they laughed.

Aunt Essie and Rose-In-May had run off with Nora and Ephey to hide one of the milk cows, keeping one eye on her and another on the looters.

Ephey raised the musket, resting it on a limb, sighting in on the sergeant's golden breast button.

"If he so much as raises a hand to Ma, I'll shoot," she whispered.

"You gonna kill that Yankee, Ephey?" asked Nora, standing nearby, shivering with cold and fear.

The soldiers had been struck by an odd odor in the room where Homer Joe lay crumpled in the bed. Doc Flippin had ridden over the day before from Saline County to say what everyone already knew, that Homer Joe had "the fever." He poured down calomel, but it did no good.

"He needs medicine I cain't give," he mumbled. "Take him to Little Rock an' ask the Yankees fur hep ... they got all yew need thar ... at that hospital over at the Arsenal. If yew don't, he'll die, Mrs. Pilgrim. I done all I can."

Then Flippin got on his worn-out horse, tied on his black bag, and rode off—to another sick house, he said, and they all believed him because folks were dying everywhere.

"Arkansas is full of houses, cabins, and farms, run by lonely widder women, nursin' ailin', half-starved sick orphans an' skeered darkies that don't know whether to run nor stay," Flippin had said.

The sergeant had laughed again at Medora, looking down upon the pale boy. "Why, that's just too damned bad, ain't it, Mam ... you folks done started this here war and now you're a-losing it. Your niggers done run off and now you got to hew the wood, haul the water, and pick the cotton all by your lonesome ... so here it is ... the Devil's to pay and I'm here to collect his tax, Mam ... so you best step aside," he said, touching his cap in mock deference.

With that, the sacking of Medora's home rose to a perfervid pitch with Nora's immortal blanket making its appearance as it was thrown over some tools, silver, pots, pans, even lamps—plunder piling up the back of a U.S. Army wagon pulled by as fine a team of fat horses as anyone had seen in a while.

Then the sergeant, rescuing Medora's St. Louis Sunday hat from the head of a private, propped it on a fence post and began strutting back across the yard like a blue rooster. Standing unsteadily he took some more whiskey swigs and began firing his revolver at it.

Medora Covington Pilgrim, however, whose ancestors had fought British oppression in Virginia and savages in Tennessee, was not cowed by the godless.

"Cain't see whur yew so much as hit a red feather," she said, as he thumbed in a reload.

He then turned and shot Calvin, a runt of a hound complaining under the front porch, striking him between his long ears, hitting him just behind a white spot.

"I'm a great friend of silence in dogs," announced the sergeant with that fatuous pride nearly unique to ignorant men.

An unexpected quiet descended, but Medora found her tongue again, giving him its edge. "Well, sergeant, ye got lucky own that one ... I'll give yew that. Yew know, sir, there's a rat-killin' cat named Luther hidin' out in the barn ... why don't yew see if ye cain't land one between his eyes as a topper? What say ... reckon you're up to it? Or do ye need more liquor in your gut to attack defenseless women and their pets?"

"You're a clever one, ain't you?" said the sergeant.

"Not as clever as a drunken, thievin', dog-killin' Yankee, I warrant," Medora said spitting at his feet.

He struck her with the back of his hand.

As Ephey pulled the trigger, the front sight blade was bobbing nervously up and down with every diastole and systole of her fluttering heart. She had squeezed on the down beat, as the blade touched a sun-lit copper button sitting like a pumpkin on a fence post, but there was only a loud click.

"Damnation!" she said, fiddling in a new match as Medora, now standing with hand to face, humbled them all with her silence. In that moment, some nubbin of moral training seemed to reassert itself, and the soldiers were ashamed, if not sobered.

Gradually, the sergeant growled and cursed his little mob back into the saddle, his "foraging expedition" moving off, consisting now of a wad of men, two unsaddled horses, three mules, a clinking, loot-loaded wagon with a reluctant mooing cow roped behind, looking more like gypsies than any of Mr. Lincoln's finest, slowly merging into the trees.

There was a quiet pause, then, like scattered quail, everyone coveyed up. Aunt Essie and Rose-In-May led the children and the cow from the woods. The untouched hat was removed and carefully put away; things were gathered, recovered, straightened, and returned to something passing for normal. Now they had little food and were short of Sally the milk cow, some good mules, all the horses, and, too, Calvin the hound, lying dead in the dirt since no one had the heart to move him yet, a pool of blood exuding from his mouth like a long red tongue.

But the gods had been merciful in their strange way. Ulysses, a mule left at the pleading of an Iowa private, remained standing, immutable, stock-still among the manure-strewn lot—a solitary, stoical figure, his long face exuding a solemn, unspoken perplexity about the sacking of Arcadia.

One can be sure that deep in the recesses of his mule mind was a growing realization that something important had happened, but unlike Calvin who was Reb to the bone, Ulysses was totally apolitical; and with a wisdom unique to his race, he would worry about it in a half-comic, half-serious way, then lay it all aside as one more insignificant piece in that great puzzlement of human folly. Surely the essence of mule wisdom is acceptance.

A highbred, high-hellion horse like the colonel's Pegasus could almost never accept anything—good or bad—turning each new thing into a kind of compounded form of trouble or crises. Ulysses, however, had a powerful inner need for serenity, and he wasn't about to let a bunch of Yankee thieves interfere with that. So, aside from swinging his large black head to the left and raising his massive ears up to full stretch, he showed almost no reaction to the barking, yelling, shooting, mooing, clanking, and cursing that had occurred over the better part of an hour only a few feet away.

Ulysses he was and Ulysses he'd remain, and that was that. He was, in fact, convinced that all things were destined to be by some force, or higher power, much greater than himself, and he was damned if he was going to fret over any of it.

His master, Colonel Titus Heaton Pilgrim, fancied himself a "classicist," and fretted over even this rather cheap Missouri mule bought off a neighbor who didn't feel like pulling him all the way to Texas. Titus had always wanted something or someone named Odysseus, having read lots of Homer, a little Latin, and lots more of Walter Scott. Everyone laughed, especially the slaves, but Ulysses was pushed through by force of the master's will. It did not matter, for the slaves, as always in such matters, prevailed, calling him "U'sses," which in a twinkling became "Useless." It was a blessing. And, it stuck.

"Ulysses" (Titus was the only one who still called him that) would've become an odious name, indeed, as everyone but the colonel agreed, given the rise of that monster of an oxymoron, Ulysses S. Grant—that strange contradictory bundle of slave-owning Unionist—heroic and mundane, ordinary and unusual, who managed to become at once despised and admired by nearly everyone. A mule Grant and a thoroughbred Lee—a Bluish Ulysses and a Grayish Pegasus— but no one, not even Titus Heaton, saw this, though Medora got close when she pointed out that the mule mind was much closer to Grant's than to Homer's. After all, she said, having a mule named for you was not the most wonderful thing in the world—you would never name a mule George Washington, for example, or Shakespeare. She almost added Moses but was glad she had not since naming a mule Moses seemed somehow to fit; she liked it and about half-decided that her next mule would in fact be named Moses. They all knew that the naming of mules, horses, cows, cats, and dogs was like the naming of children and slaves, a serious business and the subject always of great reflection, debate, and even prayer. But as for this one, Useless it was and Useless it remained.

With the coming of Steele, Colonel Pilgrim had flown off proudly on his magnificent winged Pegasus, called to glory in the "bottoms" of south Arkansas, while Useless was granted a quiet *de facto* reign over Arcadia. The ironies were endless.

Anyway, they buried Calvin in the family cemetery, marked by a large, almost completely clear, Ouachita quartz stone. Medora comforted them at the little funeral by saying, "Calvin was a good dawg, but he was predestined to die at the hands of that half-drunken Yankee sergeant, clearly the instrument of the Devil and all his works. God's will be done."

They all went to bed tired and fell promptly and hopelessly into an almost sleepless desperation. Lying there staring at the ceiling, Ephey couldn't put tongue to it, but she didn't feel comforted at all. She couldn't understand how or why the Almighty would've gone to all that much trouble on the very first day of Creation to think and plan for Calvin to be shot dead by a drunken Yankee in her front yard several million years later. Or why He'd bless them with Arcadia and then send a bunch of sorry damn Blue-bellies to sack it. But, too, she couldn't figure out why He had "cursed the world with awl them other evil things either." It was indeed puzzling. Here were the puzzling, perpetual questions, handed down from generation to generation.

The reason for things like killing fever and Yankees was hard to figure. If she could get rid of one of them forever, it wouldn't be a tough choice—it'd be the Yankees. They came from the Devil, for sure. And the Devil must have some peculiar power in the world that the Lord couldn't do much about. But how could the Lord be powerless in the world, she wondered? She didn't know. But one thing she was sure of, though she couldn't prove it, and that was "God didn't have a durn thing to do with Calvin getting shot by a no-good, low-down, thievin' soldier" in her front yard. She was converted in that very moment to a lifetime of defending free will. That was all man's doings and no one else's.

But she knew also she could never tell Medora what she thought. Medora was a stomp-down Predestination believer, and she, her family, and anyone else she liked were among the Elect. Ephey would never waste time talking to her about it, but she was consoled by the sure and certain hope that all abolitionists, every last one of them, would pay a heavy price on Judgment Day for the evil they had visited on everybody, including Calvin. "Freeing up the darkies" was just causing trouble, and she was comforted by the certainty that "all jay-hawking-Yankee-abolitionist sinners would burn in hell for what they done."

Anyway, all this confusion came from being Presbyterian. She was determined to become a freewill Methodist—and as soon as possible. She'd marry a freewill Methodist to make it stick, and then she'd buy a fine place just like Arcadia and fill it up with lots of kids, dogs, cats, cows, horses, mules, and "good darkies," even if she had to pay wages; and she'd have as little to do with "godless, Baal-worshiping, abolitionist shopkeepers and complicated Presbyterians as possible." That was her plan and her comfort as she untangled these thoughts, thinking of Calvin's little grave piled over now with fresh black dirt like an upside-down hog trough.

She was certain that she'd make it past everything this war would visit upon her. Anyway, that was what she decided that day, considering brave little Calvin, who had died for his "kith-and-kin" just as well as any Confederate soldier. Then she said a prayer for his wonderfully sweet soul, even though she believed in free will and wasn't sure that the Almighty interfered in things even if you asked for them. Somehow praying seemed to help. "It cain't hurt none," she whispered.

It was, indeed, a long hard, very cold night. In fact it snowed some and Homer Joe started "chilling" again, "salvating" and shaking and generally going out of his head, saying all kinds of crazy things. Aunt Essie said, "He done been takin' by de spirit an' is talkin' in tongues." It was like he was possessed by some demon or other, and Medora resolved then and there that she had to go into Little Rock the very next day and find a doctor.

"There's nothin fur it, I gotta go," she declared, rubbing her hands nervously, then standing up after sitting by him, nursing him as best she could with Aunt Essie, Rosy, and "the girls" helping.

The Yankees might be evil but they had better doctors. In fact, they had better of just about everything, and everybody knew it.

While she was at it, Medora added, she'd buy what food and staples she could with the money she'd hid in a rusty tin box under a stump. After the defeat at the Elkhorn, she figured she'd need it. She would have to travel alone. Arcadia needed looking after and she would leave both Aunt Essie and Rose-In-May with the girls. If she took Rosy, she might just run away again—the hope of finding Stancil and freedom would be all together too much. Besides, she'd be gone only about three or four days, she told them.

The next morning she rose before light, hitched up Useless, built a big fire and fed everyone as best she could, then loaded Homer Joe on a mattress under several blankets along with what else she needed in the wagon.

"Homer Joe, I've done the best I could fur ye ... yew'll be comfortable enough back yar. Just yew hang own, son, till we git to the doctor, yew yar?" she said over him, lying as he was in the bed of the wagon.

"Yessum," he mumbled, closing his eyes, turning away.

"Ephey," she said quietly, tucking the blankets around him yet again then climbing into the wagon seat, "like I said, we're gonna lose Virgy if'n he cain't git doctored soon, so, I've got to go ... there's jes no two ways about it."

"Yessum," said Ephey, her hand resting gently on the brake.

"I'm a-leavin' yew an' Aint Essie in charge," she commanded louder, taking the reins with Useless standing stone still at the other end. "Like I done told ye ... yew got to take care of thangs ... jes run back to them ole woods an' hide in that thicket if any more Yankees come back, which I don't thank they will ... there ain't much lef' for'em to come back fur ... but you're a young an' purtty, and thangs could get rough, that's for shore, too, so, take the musket to the woods with Nora, Aint Essie, an' Rosy ... and let them soldiers have run of the place ... burn it, if they must, we'll rebuild, don't worry 'bout saving nothin ... don't stand and fight ... hear me, honey? Don't shoot nobody 'less they're about to hurt ye ... un'erstand? Leave me a note under a rock over own Calvin's grave if yew have to leave fur any reason ... otherwise, jes stay yar an' wait till I git back ... won't be more'n a few days ... but I gotta try an' save our dear sweet Virgy ... there's plenty of split wood an' some vittles."

"Yessum," said Ephey quietly, with Nora, Aunt Essie, and Rose-In-May standing behind with long, sad faces.

"I've gotta go now … I'll git back as soon as I can. It ain't that far, though I gotta git a Confederate pass from General Fagan first … to git thew our own lines, that'll take some time, o'course … don't rightly know how I'll get thew them Yankee lines, but I'll manage … but I'll git back as soon as I can, yew yar?"

"Yessum," said Ephey, tears filling her blue eyes.

"I gotta go now," said Medora, turning away and whipping Useless, who only swung his head back and eyed Medora in disbelief.

"Gittup!" yelled Aunt Essie, walking up and striking him hard with the flat of her hand. Useless swung his head back forward but still did not move.

"Gittup, Useless, you worthless devil!" Medora yelled louder, hitting him hard on the flanks with the reins.

"I'll fetch a switch, Miss Medora," yelled Rose-In-May as she ran and peeled one off a sapling.

"It's the only thang that works on this ole sorry mule," explained Aunt Essie.

Rose-In-May ran back and struck Useless a merciless blow.

Useless now swung his head round at Rose-In-May.

"Gittup! Gittup! Damn your lazy hide!! Feed you all winter long! Gittup!" yelled Medora, standing, slapping him with the reins.

Rose-In-May struck again. "Snap!" popped the switch on Useless's flesh as it jumped and quivered like a horsefly sting. "Snap!" went the sapling again, this time coming from a wind-up that uncoiled in a gray blur upon him till he flinched, quivered, swung his head forward again, and gathered himself all in one graceless mule motion. Then, pausing for half a beat, he lurched forward, jumping into a rough, fast-stepping walk like plowing corn, raising his tail, farting, and dropping green turds as he herky-jerked Medora and Homer Joe out the front gate toward Little Rock.

Rose-In-May ran along, joyfully teasing him with the switch, then tossing it to Medora at the last moment. Medora leaned over, touching Useless with the sapling's bitter-end with one hand while holding the reins in the other. The four females ran behind, waving, crying their goodbyes, and watching as Useless, Medora, Homer Joe, and the wagon disappeared. At last they stood silently before the gate, feeling abandoned, then they meandered into the Big House to look for something to do.

Nora went to bed sobbing, and the others did what small chores they could find. It was a gray-cold day and began getting grayer and colder with the coming night.

Aunt Essie and Ephey built a fire while Rose-In-May cooked some pork fat soup and cornbread. It got dark early so they lit the coal oil lamps and gathered in cold shadows around the kitchen table.

"Y'all sit with us," Ephey announced.

"No, Miss Ephey," protested Aunt Essie.

"Sit? Together?" asked Rose-In-May, standing shyly behind her chair.

"Y'all sit. I'm not some abolitionist, yew understand, I ain't that by a damn sight … but thangs is different now … we've got to face that. Come on, y'all sit with us."

Everyone sat.

"Miss Medora skin us alive … she get back," said Aunt Essie.

"What's gonna happen, den?" asked Rose-In-May.

There was no answer from Ephey.

"Is we free now?" asked Rose-In-May.

"No," said Ephey, her lips going straight.

"Den how come we is sittin' together?" Rose-In-May asked.

"We jes sit together till Mama gits back," said Ephey.

"Where I gonna go, Ephey? I don't knows nothin' else," added Aunt Essie.

"Ya'll just keep workin' here, that's all."

"You gonna pay us now?" asked Rose-In-May.

"Sure, Rosy," said Ephey. "We'll pay."

"But y'all is ruint … dis waw done ruint ya'll fo' sho … y'all cain't pay us nuddin' … cause y'all ain't got it … dats what Stancil say …"

"Don't you worry none, Miss Roseamay … we'll have plenty of money when Paw gits home … but now yew is kinda family … see … we'll jes take day by day till then. Now come on ya'll, let's eat this soup before it gits cold," she said, picking up a big spoon and dipping it.

"Yessum," said Aunt Essie, "'Cause I don't have no folks but ya'll … my people's is all dayed or gone … dis is all I gots … I's too old to run awf no wheres."

"Let's eat," said Rose-In-May, dipping the spoon, dragging, lifting, and blowing all in one smooth motion.

"Ain't yew gonna say de blessin', honey?" asked Aunt Essie. "I cain't eatin' nudin' widout dankin' de Lawd, honey … bring bad luck ifn we don't an' we cain't stand no more of dat … we done had nuff to las' till next yeah."

"Oh, yes, thank yew, Aint Essie … let's all bow our heads," she said, dropping the spoon into the soup, folding her hands, and leaning her head forward.

Nora sneaked some cornbread off the big blue plate and shut her eyes, squeezing them till they hurt. Aunt Essie always said it was "worserer luck to do no kinda peekin' when dey is talkin' to de Man-Upstairs." And Nora figured their luck was something that definitely needed changing so she decided not to push it.

Ephey began to pray.

"Lord," she prayed loudly, as if she was trying to get His attention off something else. "Please, dear God ... please, hear our prayer."

"Amen," said Rose-In-May.

"Yeah, amen," said Aunt Essie, "hear dis prayer, dear God!"

"Lord, we know you're busy," continued Ephey, "but I'm here today, me, little Iphigenia Pilgrim, only fourteen years old, head of this yar plantation awl of a sudden ... with our dear Paw away a-fightin' nem evil Yankees and Maw gone awf to Little Rock to try and save our little sweet Virgy's life from fever ... ye know ... a-lookin' fur one of them high-toned Yankee doctors. Yew need to know that it's just us four females down yar awl alone at Arcadia, jest a-settin' around this table a-askin' yore divine blessin' on this yar food that Rosy done cooked and ..."

"Amen," interrupted Rosy, glad to hear her name. "We needs yo' divine guidance, Lawd ... sho do ... and yo blessin' ..."

"Amen," echoed Aunt Essie. "Lawd hep us."

"Yes, Lord, hep us, hep us to know thy will and to live accordin' to thy plan and not accordin' to our own self-will ... jes learn us to turn it awl own over to thee ... let thy will be done ... not our will ... 'cause we jes mess thangs up a-doin' it our own way ... jes turn it over ... that's what we got to learn ... but it's hard Lord and we ... and we need yore hep."

She paused and shifted smoothly into a new subject, "And bless little Virgy and deliver him from sickness and death ..."

"Bless him ... and deliver him from deaf," said Aunt Essie.

"Oh, yes, Lawd, don't let little Virgy boy die," cried out Rose-In-May, "no, no, uh, uh, deliver him from de angel of deaf, please, Lawd."

Ephey was at first surprised by these interruptions, but now she welcomed them—they let her gather her thoughts. She resumed, "Lord, bless us ..."

"Oh, please, Lawd, bless us," interrupted Rose-In-May.

"And bless little Virgy," plunged in Ephey before anyone could say anything more. "And hep him to git well and not to die ... and please hep Maw ... hep her in her long, per'lous journey to Little Rock ... jes like yew heped the chil'ren of Isra'l and all ... hep her to find a good Yankee doctor and some real good medicine. And bless Useless, too, Lord ... he's not our bes' mule, Lord, we know that yew know that, but he's tryin' hard and I thank he's good down deep in his ole dumb mule heart. And bless Sally, the milk cow the Yankees done stole … and Josephus, our bes' mule, we sure hate losin' him, Lord … we miss him and … and …. bless the horses and stock they done took too and keep-'em from harm. 'cause I'm worried sick what's gonna happen to'em awl. And don't forgit to bless Paw in his battle against the evil Philistines, Lord, we know yew know that, but please don't forgit us in our hour of need … and hep Paw smite them … like in the Old Testament when the enemies of the chil'ren of Isra'l had to lick them Yankees that plagued them so bad and awl … yew know, coming 'round awl the time a-stealin' their land and cattle and mules and dark-ies and such … when they was jes tryin' to lay the crops in and be good and awl … tryin' to follow the word and do thy will … then them ole Philistines who worship the golden calf'd show up and steal ever'thang and do turble evil unto them … jes like them damn Yankees is a-doin' to us rat now. Smite them, Lord … smite'em rale good … for they are shore nuff godless and don't keep your laws none; they only serve the Devil and must be held to account and let plagues be sent down hard upon'em; let your vanjange roll down upon that Blue host like a mighty river, seein' they gone and took up with the dark one and awl his evil angels of death, which we awl know they done."

Ephey was worked up.

"And, too, Lord," she said, catching her breath, "bless Pegasus, Paw's prize saddle horse who carries and serves him … don't let him stumble nor be weary … lighten his load and give him courage to ride Paw into battle like a mag-nificent stead and knight of the olden times and ride own to glory and victory. O' Lord, put thy mighty sword of victory into Paw's hand. Lord, does he love that horse and would jes be sick if anythang happened. So, please, Lord, pro-tect both of them and don't let nothin' turble be visited on nem like yew let happen to poor ole Calvin yesterdee … who we buried with your blessings … now lying a-moldering 'cause of them shopkeepers."

"Amen," said Rose-In-May. "Lawd … please … please protect Massa Titus and his big hoss, Pegasus."

Nora mumbled a little prayer of her own, "Oh, Lord, let Ephey finish soon." Her stomach growled a second to that.

"And, too, Lord, bless Rosy and Aint Essie, our faithful ones … our servants who stayed with us in our hour of need …"

"Amen," said Rose-In-May. "God bless us."

"Bless you, chile," said Aunt Essie, glad of hearing her name again. "And bless us darkies, too."

"Thank you, Lord, for them, and bless and keep these our faithful servants and try not to be too hard on the darkies that's up and done run awf … they done left us … yew know that … when the crops wasn't in yet … and times was extree hard … I know that yew'll brang your wrath down upon their heads without mercy for that. But, Lord, still and awl, try to remember that they were jes field darkies … and didn't really know what they was a-doin' … they's jes that-a way … they cain't hep it none … ever'one knows that … so, don't be too hard on nem … we still have a place in our hearts for 'em awl … each and ever one … so, jes make it clear to 'em they done wrong. The flesh is weak and they jes cain't resist a-runnin' off to Little Rock when that host of godless shoe clerks got thar … awl ready to corrupt them. It was jes too much for 'em to bear, and like Maw says, 'they succumbed to the power of evil.' But awl that glitters is not gold, as ye know, and nem Yankees don't hold nothin' but a false hope for 'em, we know, but Lord temper your vanjange with mercy … some day they'll be back and if you cripple 'em up too bad they won't be fit for nothin'."

"Ephey," whined Nora.

"What, Nora?"

"I'm hungry."

"Okay, okay, but it's not right to talk while I'm talkin' to the Lord."

"Hush, chile!" said Rose-In-May. "Miss Ephey is gitting thangs right with de Man-Upstairs … and we gonna need him fo sho … soon … fact-of-the-bidness, honey … we needs 'em rat now!"

"But I'm hungry," whined Nora louder.

"Okay, Lord, yew know what's goin' own down yar and ever'thang, so, I gotta kindly wind thangs up … so, please bless us and guide us and thank yew fur this bounty. Amen."

"Amen," said Nora, taking in half the cornbread with one bite.

After Monday's initial burst of sapling-sponsored energy, Useless was intent upon converting a two-day journey into three—at best—and so he soon settled into a deadly slow stroll. Indeed, Medora, after obtaining passage through Confederate lines, could only manage the Union pickets by late morning of Wednesday. She had inched along a cross trail then hit the Benton road leading to Little Rock.

The "Rock" sits on the south bank of a very long, usually lazy, mostly brown river that meanders from the Rockies across Colorado, into Kansas, then Oklahoma before nosing into the land of her naming. It quickly pushes the

Ozarks and Ouachita mountains to either side, north to south, then passes inexorably hard upon our little town.

As might be expected, there is, indeed, a rock on the southern bank—the last going down, the first coming up—a permanent demarcation between Delta and Mountain, Lower and Upper South—a harbinger—an *avant-propos* of permanent change. But our river does not tarry, or pay obeisance, but she scurries past, through the Delta, summoning the White River like a lost little brother, as the two then quickly embrace the older Mississippi, searching for the mother sea like bereaved orphans—leaving an alluvium of stranded sea shells, fish fossils, and ancient water worms, exposed upward by her passing skirt to dry in the eons of father sun.

Men came from the west, Red, walking over from Siberia, following the woolly mammoth, giant horse, and great stag, slaying them all, then following the buffalo, the elk, and the deer south to here, eventually calling themselves the Caddo, Choctaw, Osage, and Quapaw. Then other White men came from the east, from Europe, explorers and trappers. Two Frenchmen, among the first, Marquette and Joliet, trader and priest, came in 1673 paddling the Mississippi looking for the other but wrong part of mother ocean—the Pacific. Instead, they found an old Indian who could speak bad news in broken Algonquin. They were in Arkansas, he said, "down river," as the word meant, not California, so they canoed back to Canada.

Those who came later would say, "Meet me at the small rock on the left." It was tagged with the grand name of *Petit Rocher* by exploring Frenchmen. But as noted in writing in a letter of 1774, Arkansas had been long since claimed for Louis the Bourbon, sovereign of a faraway Kingdom called France.

This France did not leave fossils or worms or sea shells in Arkansas, just blood and words—blood in the Indians and names upon the land: Petit Jean, Bois d'Arc, Fourche La Feve, Cache, St. Francis, Forche l'Anguille, Bayou Bartholomew, Maumelle, Cosatot for Casse-Tete, and Ozark for Aux Arkansas, all imprinted by men with names like La Salle, De Tonty, La Metairie, Joutel, Mallet, Bossu, and Dumont. France could have left more for she once owned it all but a small strip in the east: from Quebec and Montreal, to Sault Saint Marie and St. Louis, from the Michilimackinac to the Mississippi, from New Orleans to *Poste aux Arcs,* for a time it was all hers.

Traveling with La Salle, Dumont explored for the legendary "Emerald Rock." He wrote:

> If in this expedition we had not the good fortune to discover the

emerald rock which gave it rise, we had the satisfaction of traversing a very beautiful country, fertile plains, vast prairies covered with
buffalo, stags, deer, turtles, etc. We saw rocks of jasper marble at the
foot of which lay slabs cut by nature's hand, others of slate and talc,
very fair for making plaster. I have no doubt there are gold mines in
the country, as we discovered a little stream that rolled gold dust in
its waters.

There have always been such legends—of gold hidden at a site scratched
out upon a hide and glory for those who searched for it. Before Plymouth and
Jamestown, and five years before Francis Xavier entered Japan searching for
souls, De Soto entered Arkansas (1541) searching for treasure and his bit of
fame. He ravaged through the tangles of virgin wilderness with his half-starved,
sick Spaniards, with enslaved Indians, and beribbed horses and swine—conquistadors—following a whisp of stories along the endless trail of illusory
renown.

Arkansas has always been infected with such kinds of hunger—a restless
sort of threadbare ambition; like a small, half-forgotten volcano it has been
alternately quiet, explosive, noisy, powerful, threatening, feeble, and absurd.
Spanish gold seekers; name-giving, trapping, trading, fornicating, soul-saving
Frenchmen; striding, slave-freeing, Blue-bellied Yankees, and prancing,
drunken, knife-wielding, frontier Anglo politicians—all have found ample
range for a kind of shabby glory in this wild, romantic, feuding, dueling out-
land that, like a half-suppressed impulse, remains in the heart of itself a wilderness which values only the rude honesty of her mountains, swamps, rivers,
forests, and a frontier's violent freedom.

Coming in the Union as the seat of the Texas Revolution; going out as a slave
Kingdom in 1861; then invaded and occupied in 1863, as Medora McDade
Pilgrim, herself a half-wild, stomp-down "secessh," liberty-loving, slave-
owning, Scots-Irish very proud descendant of the Virgin Queen's Tudor colony
of Virginia, daughter of the Revolution, child of Tennessee Indian fighters, wife
of Colonel Titus Heaton Pilgrim, CSA, who at this very moment was riding
astride his mighty Pegasus flying over the mosquitoes, moccasins, and mud of
the Moro Bottoms—as Medora wagoned her lonely way into *Petit Rocher* at a
pace only slightly faster than a Frenchman's up-river canoe and most assuredly
faster than De Soto's floundering Rosinantes and flourishing Razorbacks.

This same Medora—mistress of Arcadia; mother of Iphigenia, Homer Joe,
Nora, and two dead and buried children; West Africans Aunt Essie and Rose-

In-May; the future great-grandmother of Elizabeth Shaw and great-great-grandmother of her son Christopher, lieutenant, USMC, who would die in another civil war trying to take a small, insignificant hill on a beautiful, bright sunny day in 1969, within sight of the South China Sea in another Lost Kingdom of France. This same Pilgrim ambled toward the Rock astride the frozen mud of the Benton road, wondering how she might get through enemy pickets with a very sick boy and a fairly worthless, tired Missouri mule named for a classical hero of war and wandering.

So she came defiantly with her feverish son, and this half-asleep and more than half-starved, worn-out Ulysses, pulling their burden of fragile defiance toward the mightiest of armies; herself, her mule, and her sick son, lying under his now smelly blankets, symbols of a proud but death-thrashing Southern nationhood—half-ludicrous, half-magnificent—making a heroic stand against the ineluctable forces of modernity now represented by a pink-faced private standing before her in a blue uniform, new boots and leather, holding a fine black musket with silver bayonet across his chest, very much at the ready.

As she had approached, nearing the "Carriage House," or inn, just south of our famous little town, Medora was challenged. It came in a made-up, to her ears, flat-sounding, not quite gruff, voice of this soldier boy in blue; musket and soft, hairless face, all focusing up for her; a conquistador from a small farm in Iowa, where he was sorely missed. After all, it was January 1864, and, while Little Rock may have fallen, Atlanta and Richmond showed no signs of it—yet, to be sure, folks were ready for the end. It had all started so gloriously but now seemed so endless.

In fact, unknown to any, the worst was yet to come.

"Halt! Who goes there?" came something sounding like a shout.

This was a question for which Medora had no ready answer.

Useless, however, even though the Germanic sounding word "halt," spoken in a strange Iowa cornfield dialect, was alien to his long "Boot-Heel" Missouri ears, guessed its meaning. He stopped. Swinging his head round, he stared at Medora for reassurance, swung it back again, looking intently into the blue eyes of this farm boy turned soldier who spoke quietly to him now, shifting his musket to his right and with his left hand scratching between these massive ears, touching some special mule-deep spot with gentle searching fingers. This boy obviously knew something of mules. Useless relaxed, nodded his head a dip or two, then shook it, rattling his tack, shifting from curiosity to gratitude. He was tired. He liked the boy. He knew, too, they had pretty much gotten to where they were going, so he raised his tail and relieved the pressure from behind.

Medora leaned forward, set the brake for no obvious reason, and dipped a little snuff—her one permissible vice. She was, after all, a Presbyterian.

"Can I hep yew, sir?" she asked, pushing the snuff out a bit as a means of making herself look more formidable.

"Your pass, mam?" said the boy, leaving Useless and walking up within inches of her ankle-high, tightly laced brown leather shoes.

"Beg your pardon?" she asked, as if a little deaf. Her Confederate pass was worthless, and she knew it.

"Pass, mam ... you have to have a paper saying you can cross through these here lines ... gotta have one, or I can't let you through ... it's orders." She was silent, so he added, "Sorry, mam, but there's a Reb army down that road and you just come from there ... we can't have no spies coming and going back and forwards ... so you gotta have a pass."

"Where's a body to git one of them, son?"

"Gotta make an application."

"How do I do that?"

"At headquarters ... in town at headquarters ... the Arsenal ... at the Provost's, he'll give you one there."

Medora thought, then said, "Well, I suppose yew'll let me pick one up temporary-like while I'm a-doin' my business, is that right, while I'm in town, so I can go by this ... what was it yew said?"

"Provost's."

"I'll go to the Provost's and git one."

"No, mam, can't let you through without no pass."

"Then how in God's name am I to git a pass to git thew to git a pass from the Provost at the Arsenal, jes tell me that, if ye please?"

The boy leaned the musket against the wagon and pushed his cap back, saying, "Well, mam, I don't rightly know ... we was being a might slack up to now ... a-lettin' folks do jes that but they caught this here Reb spy a-trying to sneak through right after Christmas ... without no pass nor nothing ... caught him red-handed ... not far from jes this here spot we're at now ... took him to that stage house over yonder."

He pointed to the two-story building across the road about fifty yards away that was surrounded by horses and milling Union soldiers and civilians.

"Is zat so?" she replied.

"Yessum, he was riddin' a mule, kinda lollygagging in and out-a our lines ... writing stuff down he seed in a code book ... he'd been a Morse operator once ... but when he come up to one of our pickets again, Sergeant Miehr ... of the

First Missouri ... he caught him ... sure did ... found his scribbling paper and everything."

"Yew don't say."

"Yessum ... turned out he was sure enough a spy ... gonna hang him tomorrow ... way they talk. Brought'em in right there," he said, pointing again. "I seen him when Lieutenant Storpal was questioning him and all ... inside. He's younger'n me even ... can't hardly grow a beard ... the Johnnies is getting younger and younger, seems like ... but he was a Reb for sure ... without no papers, except a Confederate pass from General Fagan, a pistol, and lots of secret spy scribbling in a black book ... for all them Johnny friends of his down in Camden ... all 'bout our positions here, numbers of cannons, units, and the like. So, we gotta check real good now ... everybody, mam ... no exceptions ... I'm sorry, but they'll be two hangings if I let you through without no pass."

"What's the boy's name?"

"David O. Dodd, mam."

She thought.

"Never heard of him ... who is he?"

"The son of a secessh sutler from Texas is all I know ... Rebs to the bone, they say."

Medora leaned over a little, straightened her calico, and said softly, "Look yar, son, where's home?"

"Me, mam?"

"Yeah, yew got a home somewhures, don't ye, boy?"

"Well, yeah, sure ... Iowa, mam."

"What'd yore people do?"

"Do?"

"Yes, son, do ... for a livin'?"

"Farm, mam ... we're farmers."

"Yew come from good stock then ... I can tell ... yew ain't no Yankee clerk from Chicago or nothin' like kat," she said, leaning back again.

"No, mam ... just God-fearing farmers."

"Well, boy, we're the same—God-fearin' farmers ... tryin' to git own in a fallen world ... yew understand, son, jes folks, jes tryin' to make it like y'all ... ain't no real difference, see? Yew know about that, don't ye?"

"Know about what, mam?"

"The fallen world ... yew heard of the fallen world even up in Ioway, ain't ye? Or is it still part of the Garden of Eden?"

"Oh, yes, mam ... we're Lutheran ... know all about the fallen world."

"Good, I like Lutherans ... good Christians ... most of 'em," she said, spitting tobacco, then adding, "Look in the back of this yar wagon," she said, nodding her head at Homer Joe, who was just a small clump under a stack of blankets, asleep.

He hesitated then looked quickly and came back, saying, "I wondered what you was hauling."

She said sternly, "That's my son ... he's bad sick ... with the fever ... if I don't git him medicine rale soon, he'll die. Doc Flippin says so ... but he didn't have none ... said to come yar and git it as soon as I could ... yew understand? I'm trying to save my son's life ... that's why I'm yar ... why I've come awl this a-way ... it's nothin' to do with the war or nothin'. I ain't no spy, see?"

"Yes, mam," said the boy, hanging his head.

"Yew understand that, don't yew?"

"Yes, mam."

"Yew don't want such a thang put on your account on the Final Day, do yew? Homer Joe a-dyin', I mean, because yew turned us away and awl, huh? ... when yew had it in yore power to do rat and hep us; don't want that laid on against yew by God, do ye, son?"

"No, mam," he said meekly.

"That'd sure be worse'n any ole hangin', now wouldn't it?"

"Yes, mam, I reckon so."

"There ain't nothin' nobody can do to yew for eternity in this ole world ... yew know that ... only yew can do somethin' about eternity yoreself ... ever thank about that?"

"Yes, mam ... I mean, no, mam, I ain't never, not really, not in them words like ... thinking about eternity is not something I do very good. I don't rightly know how. Now my pa ... why he was real good at it ... he thought about eternity a lot. He'd be a-plowing along a thinking about eternity ... you know, I could tell because he'd get this certain kinda queer look on his face and all ... kindly staring ahead into the distance for something that wasn't really there yet ... but expected any moment ... his brow all wadded up into a knot over his old long nose ... a-stepping like a sleep walker kinda behind them mules of his. And I'd say to myself ... there's Pa a-thinking about eternity again. But me? Mam, I never did quite get the hang of it ... see, eternity ain't nothing that's really easy for me a-hold in my mind for very long ... after a spell it kindly gives me a headache. That is, if I a-work at it for very long I begin to get real uncomfortable, so, I decided long ago to let Pa do all the thinking about eternity that needs doing ... it just comes natural to him and seems to give him some kinda peace of mind doing it."

"I understand, but now yore yar and yore Paw is way up thar in Ioway ..."

"Yessum ... I see where you're a-going but I can honestly say since I've been in Arkansas I been able to get through my days without thinking about eternity so much as once ... and, to tell you the truth, I ain't missed it none neither."

"But yew know the rat of thangs, don't ye, son? Yew have larnt that much, ain't ye?"

"Yes, mam ... I reckon so."

"An the rat of thangs will lead to eternity, don't ye see that?"

"But, yessum, but there ain't much I can do about eternity, mam. It's all I can do taking care of today ... and right now I am just standing here on this here frozen muddy road in Arkansas a-checking folk's passes."

"Son, you've heard of Bartimaeus, haven't yew?"

"Who?"

"Bartimaeus."

A pause.

"Ain't he in the Bible somewhere?"

"He is fur a fact."

"Well, I must've heard something about him ... you know, at church, but I can't rightly place him, to be honest, mam."

"Well, let me tell yew. He was a blind beggar own the road to Jericho ... he didn't have nothin' ... lived kindly hand-to-mouth ... a beggin' from folks as they come along this yar crossroads ... it wuz a good place to beg ... nice and busy and awl ... with lots of folks and soldiers and wagons, horses and mules and sech, see ... then, Jesus come along one day with the disciples and a crowd of followers a-preachin' the word. Well, he, Bartimaeus gits up and starts a-followin' nem because he'd heard that this particular praycher can work miracles and he wanted to be healed of his blindness ... so, he started a-yellin' as loud as he could ... and a-wavin' his arms and sayin', 'Jesus, thou son of David, have mercy upon me!'" Saying this, Medora started yelling and waving her arms. "Over and over ... he keeps a-doin' this ... a-yellin' and wavin' behind this big wad of folks, see. Well, this kindly irritated nem around Jesus, as ye might 'spect, nem that was feeling kindly self-important 'cause of thar relationship with Our Lord and sech like ... yew know like people gits when they're self-righteous and awl ... yew seen folks like that, even in Ioway, I reckon, and they didn't want to be bothered by no loud mouth blind beggars, so, they got tard of Bartimaeus in a hurry, and the good book says 'many charged him that he should hold his peace.' I think that puts it politely … I mean, I figger some other words wuz used … but he wouldn't hush nor nothin', and Jesus finally heard him and commanded that he come unto him … and it wuz so … and then Jesus asked what he wanted and Bartimaeus said he wanted to be healed of his blindness. Then Jesus restored his sight and said, 'Go thy way; thy faith has made thee whole.'"

Medora spit again then leaned back in satisfaction, rising against the wagon seat for the boy's response. He rocked back on his heals a little then steadied himself with his musket like a crutch but gave no signs of knowing what to say. There was a very awkward pause.

"Do yew know the moral of that parable, son?" asked Medora, finally.

"No, mam," he said quietly, dropping his chin a bit, "I can't say that I do."

"Well, Bartimaeus wuz honest see … honest in his desperation … just like we are … and the Lord seen that … and heped him 'cause of it."

"Yes, mam," said the soldier, raising up his head again, "but you still need a pass … Judgment Day or no Judgment Day … Barteus or no …

"Barti … mae … us."

"Barti … mae … us or no Barti … mae … us … I mean, I understand what your a-saying and all, mam, I do … and I surely don't want to go burn in hell for all eternity or nothing but I don't want to hang neither. See what I mean? And that's for sure what's gonna happen if I let you through here without no pass … you can understand that, can't you, mam?"

Medora gathered her breath, shifted the reins from one hand to the other, reflecting, spitting some more snuff, then said, "How about Rahab of Jericho, if yew don't know Bartimaeus maybe surely … you remember Rahab of Jericho?"

"Rahab of Jericho, mam?"

"Yes, son, Rahab of Jericho."

"No, mam … don't reckon I know that one neither."

Medora sighed, then said, "Well, she, Rahab of Jericho, wuz commanded by the evil King to deliver unto him the sons of Isra'l … who she had in her power to hep … so he could put them unto death … but she said to the King's soldiers that the men'd done gone away … which was not true … she'd hid'em … up own her roof … and then she let'em git away with the scarlet thread and awl … yew know about the scarlet thread, don't ye, son, you're not ignorant of that, surely to goodness yore not?"

"Scarlet thread, mam?"

"Yes, Rahab lowered them to the ground outside the walls of Jericho with it ... and they told her to leave it in her winder to save her and her family in return for a-savin' nem ... when they come back to sack the place and awl ... the scarlet thread, son ... yew know, the blood of the Lamb ... her connection to our Redeemer ... our Lord and Savior, surely yew know that?"

"Mam," he said, trying to interrupt.

"Well, she was a harlot, Rahab wuz, and this means nobody is too bad for God's love, if they do right for a change ... and see ... yew are in the same fix a-bein' a Yankee invader and awl ... I don't mean it personal nor nothin' ... yew cain't hep it, I know that, but it's the same ... and yar we are outside our own Jericho and the evil King has commanded yew to do evil unto us ... to kill my son, Homer, yar, who is in great danger of a-losin his life ifn I cain't get into Little Rock and find one of them good Yankee doctors, see? So, I'm a tryin' to hep yew find the scarlet thread ... so yew can save us as well as yore own precious immortal soul, son. Yew see that now, don't ye? Yew understand what I'm a-tryin' to do for yew, am I right? I mean yore lucky I come along 'cause I'm a-carryin' the Word to ye. God speaks to us thew other people and that's just what's happenin' to yew today ... rat now ... this minute ... God is a-talkin' to yew ... what's yore name boy?"

"Arlo ..."

"Arlo? What kinda name is zat?"

"I dunno ... it's just the one they give me after they done got me dried off good ... Arlo Bonar ... that's my name."

"Arlo Bonar?"

"Yessum ... Arlo Obadiah Bonar ... if ye need all of it, mam ..."

"Well, Obadiah ..."

"Arlo, mam ... folks never call me Obadiah ..."

"Alright, Arlo ... son, yew got a real big chance now, that's for shore ... the Lord is a-givin' ye a real chance to avoid perdition ... hell far for awl eternity ... not a drop of water will be placed upon your tongue ... see? ... not one..."

"Mam," interrupted Private Arlo O. Bonar, "mam, a-begging your pardon ... but, you gonna have to have a pass..."

"You cain't put into your mind Jericho and Rahab and what I been tellin' yew and awl?"

"Mam, generally, when I put Little Rock to mind ... Jericho and Rahab don't naturally follow."

"Well, yew need to git in the habit of a-puttin' nem together, son. That is, if'n you plan to make any progress toward a-savin' yore immortal soul."

He scratched his head, then said, "Well, yessum, it does seem like Little Rock some ... now that you mention it ... your talking about it so does bring it to mind ... weren't all them fellas Rahab helped spies?"

Medora stared at him hard. "Well, the situation ain't exactly the same ... see ... yew need to ponder own the main point." She spit again in an end-over-end tobacco blob as a means of gathering her thoughts.

"The main point is you ain't got no pass, mam."

"But yew could make a special case ..."

"I can't think how ..."

"What can yew do for me, son?" she interrupted. "We need hep ... pure and simple, see ... yew gotta hep us," she said, sounding a note of desperation.

"It's real hard but it's real simple too ... you need a pass, Judgment Day or no Judgment Day, or I can't let you through."

"And if'n ye turn us away and my son dies ... do yew thank the Lord is not goin' to hold ye to account? Huh? On the Last Day do ye thank God ... the creator of awl thangs heaven and earth ... the master of the universe ... who made ye, Arlo ... and us awl ... and loves ye and is concerned about yew a-bein' lost to damnation ... which is own the very verge of happenin' this very minute as we sit yar in the middle of this yar frozen, rutty ole road ... do ye thank He is a-goin' to be pleased that yew followed General Steele's commands and not His? Huh? Son, which command is more important?"

"Mam ... you're sure making this real hard ..."

"What can yew do for us ... you cain't jes turn us away?" she said quickly.

There was another long pause.

"My sergeant is a real hard man for shore, mam, and he don't like Private Arlo Obadiah Bonar a-bothering him about secessh folks trying to get through here without no passes ... jes turn'em back, he says. He gets real out-of-sorts when I bother him with such ... but because of that sick boy of yours ... I'll tell him about your a-wantin' a doctor and all ... maybe, he'll get the lieutenant when he hears that."

"I'd be powerful grateful," Medora said, shifting her weight on the seat.

"I'll be right back directly," he said, leaning the musket against the wagon.

"Bless you, Arlo," she said as he walked about half way to the stage house then hesitated and returned.

"They'll hang me if I leave this," he said sheepishly, retrieving the musket. Walking slowly away he disappeared into a large wad of men and horses. Shortly, he reappeared with a burly, dark bearded sergeant, sporting pistols on each hip and wearing muddy, high-top boots.

PHILLIP H. MCMATH

"Yes, mam, can I hep you? I'm Sergeant Zahn," he said in that can't-be-bothered tone of all petty officialdom.

"Yes, sir, Sergeant Zahn, my boy yar is bad sick with the fever and if I cain't git him to town rale soon I'm gonna lose him … but I don't have no pass … can yew hep me, sir?"

The sergeant sauntered over and raised the blankets off of Homer Joe.

"He ain't of military age is he?" he asked, still holding up the blanket, studying him.

"Not unless yore a-takin' twelve-year-olds."

"You Rebs'll take anything," he said, dropping the blanket, then looking over Useless, now relaxing with a delicious cascade of yellow steaming over the ground.

"Listen, Sergeant, I'm jes an old woman with one tard mule and a turble sick boy … I ain't a threat to yore Union."

"Naw, but you'd like to be … I can see that ready enough," the sergeant said, pulling himself up to his full height, letting the blanket drop.

"What I'd like don't matter none, now, does it?" she said. "This yar damn war is lost and ever'body knows it. I'm just tryin' to live and hep my boy to live … that's awl I'm a-thankin' about … yew don't want his death on yore soul do ye now, Sergeant?"

"Mam, boys is a-dyin' ever day … I don't reckon one more'll matter none. I've kilt my share … and if one dyin' was wrong, they all are, is the way I fig-ger it. But you pull over there out of the road and I'll be back in a minute. Stay in your wagon and don't go nowheres till I get back, understand?" he said, then strided off without waiting for an answer.

"Thank ye, sir," Medora said to his back, whipping Useless and pulling under an oak just off the road. The sergeant disappeared into the crowd but returned in half an hour with the pass.

"This here is a temporary three-day pass, mam, signed by the lieutenant," said the sergeant, handing it to her, but still holding it as she closed her fingers around it, saying, "hang on to this no matter what … and come back through our lines right here in this same spot before your time is up, see? We're a-fix-ing to hang a Reb spy not much more'n your own boy's age and we don't won't to have to hang no old ladies besides," he added with a wry smile, then let go of the folded white paper soiled by his thumb as she grabbed it.

"I'm much obliged," she said, hiding the paper in her coat, then asking, "Tell me, Sergeant, ain't St. John's been made a hospital? I need medicine…"

"Yessum, the whole damn town's been made one big hospital, pretty near

… but that's where the hangin's at tomorrow … might wait till they're a-done stretching that young Reb's neck … folks won't be doing much else but watching him face his last hour … you won't be able to stir them with a stick over at St. John's …"

"Thank you, sir. You'll be rewarded on the last day," she said with grim sincerity.

"My a-hepin' you ain't gonna be near enough, mam," he said laughing. "A-sides, all I've likely done is jes save a Reb for us to kill later …"

At this Medora turned away whipping Useless like he was a team of six, weaving around the stage house, falling behind an army sutler wagon inching into town. Glancing back, she saw Arlo standing by the cannon, his musket cradled in his arms again, staring down the Benton road—she wanted to wave but he was looking south, intent upon a small group of civilians approaching at a walk, without passes no doubt.

There was no Grant in Arkansas, just this man, Steele, prancing with all his Sergeant Zahns—striding, strutting, and striving like little uniformed boys, playing upon the stage; marching, invading, and killing—as much as fate would allow. But, after Vicksburg, it didn't really matter. Yet the dying would go on in the bottoms and the backwoods, but it was indeed lost, Medora knew that. But now she was going to save her Homer Joe, if she could, get word to Titus, and scurry back to Arcadia to her brood—save what she was able and live the best she knew how.

It was in the end, like she said, all God's will—her freedom and His will—a contradiction she never bothered to straighten out. "Let the darkies be free, maybe that's God's will, too," she sighed, as she stared at Useless's rear end bobbing dutifully, the faithful, wise old Useless, like her, putting one hoof in front of the other, taking it all as it came. Medora had long since decided that mules, except when lost and running around crying in the wilderness like a lost baby, or being stubborn or kicking the brains out of honest folks, were maybe the wisest creatures on God's green earth—no fear of Yankees or death or even the Final Day—when all that is known will pass away and all that is unknown will be revealed. Useless seemed content—maybe she should be as well, she decided, spitting again, just to emphasize the point.

Then something struck her gently in the face—it was snowing.

CHAPTER FOUR

"O, wonder! How many goodly creatures are
there here! How beauteous mankind is!
Brave new world that has such people in it!"
—The Tempest, V, i

If one drew a line west from where Elizabeth Shaw sat at *Ephesus Gate* eating a peach while communing with her dead, one would only have to turn a little north to find a young White man named William Kroner sitting under a Ponderosa Pine looking for the dead son's living friend. Cross-legged with a scoped rifle across his lap, he searched through binoculars to his left across the Río Grande valley at the Sangre de Cristo Mountains, and, then in a wide sweep, to the San Juans the other way, the northern most reach of the conquistadors.

Nuevo México, the conquest of Francisco Vásquez de Coronado, whose march into this land was paralleled to the east by one Hernando De Soto, born in Extremadura, Spain, in 1500, and, like so many famous *Extremadurados,* Vasco Núñez de Balboa, Francisco Pizarro, Hernán Cortés, Pedro de Alvarado, Pedro de Valdívia, and Francisco de Orellana, De Soto came to the New World for gold and glory. Arriving in *Castilla de Oro* (Panama) at age fourteen, he fell under the tutelage of a monster of a man known as Pedro Arias de Ávila, shortened to Pedrárias, a master of cruelty who taught his charges all the exquisite horrors of Spanish imperialism—burning Indians or throwing them to the hounds—a man who, in a fit of jealous rage, rewarded his son-in-law Balboa for finding the Pacific with his African slave Nuflo de Olano and a pet dog, that is for joining the Isthmus of America to the India of Asia, by unjoining his now immortal head with an axe in the plaza.

This "unforgiven" had at last linked Europe, America, and Africa to Asia in 1513, September 29 (Michaelmas), as two men, Black and White, each from different worlds, waded across sandy flats and into the gentle green rolling surf of a bay soon named San Miguel, which Balboa, sword in hand, claimed for a

Habsburg somewhere by witnessing for God and Man under the happy eyes of his treading hound.

And this Pedrárias, murderer of son Balboa, soon made De Soto, his captain, the *alcalde* of Nicaragua. But De Soto wanted more and soon fell in league with a new mentor, another malicious *Extremadurado,* Francisco Pizarro, master of Peru, who, seeing talent, made De Soto *his* captain, stole him from Pedrárias, as it were, and, through the device of terror, theft, and treachery, privileged him with the blood-pleasures of the looted Incas—silver and gold—enough for De Soto to return to Spain as the king's creditor, accepting Cuba and *La Florida* as collateral—another Cortés—another Pizarro. He would race with Coronado in the west for a greatness of his very own; he would be marquess of a daring new dominion—greater than *Nuevo México* (where William Kroner now sat against a tree, lately come from De Soto's old Lost Kingdom). And, after celebrating mass at the great cathedral, on April 7, 1538, St. Lazarus Day, De Soto had sailed from San Lucar, Spain, with his army, crew, and entourage of a thousand—foot and cavalry, knights and squires, gentlemen and knaves, servants and slaves, pages and priests, matrons and mistresses, horses and mules, pigs and dogs, tailors and carpenters, caulkers and ironsmiths, swordsmiths, and shoemakers, and sailors—all crammed in anticipation over the rails of eight ships, weeping, waving, and wondering; led by his resplendent flagship *San Cristóbal,* whose pennants wafted behind him like long colorful ribbons streaming gracefully from the golden hair of a virgin, drifting upon the folding and unfolding curls of a soft wind that lifted white seabirds in complaining circles; and upon whose quarterdeck a rapacious strutting De Soto received the noble farewell of tears, trumpets, and *te deums,* salvos, salutes, and standards, waving noisy sad *adiós* to an always romantic, lately medieval super-power, Spain, that he would never ever see again.

This great fleet, enlarged with the company of twenty-five merchant treasure ships bound for the pillage of Vera Cruz, was convoyed this day by a fine sunny breeze that gently billowed out their red Maltese Cross—marked white sails until they were swollen like the unsullied belly of *Santa María,* mother of God and Spain, pregnant with her wanton New World, launched forth finally upon a fair sea and swell—bound with the bountiful blessings of God, King, and Man—for *La Florida.*

Arriving in Cuba at Santiago, De Soto sent his ships tacking westward on a forty-day storm plagued loop around *Cabo San Antonio,* through the Yucatan Channel to the Gulf, while he, with a small army, paraded pompously to join them, strutting and hacking in proud circumstance across and along his mountainous, pig-trailed, mosquitoed, jungle island Cuban Kingdom to the little outpost of some seventy houses—the humble of thatch, the wealthy of stone—a village called Havana where he found that only Santiago, from which he had just marched, could boast a modest monastery or even a church. Cuba wasn't Castile nor even Santo Domingo, but it was nevertheless his. So he waited a year, constructing the timbers of his dream—five more ships, two caravels, and ten bergantines—boarding half a thousand Spaniards, half a hundred African slaves, and half as many hobbled horses with a diversity of dogs and a swarm of swine for a glory to equal half again his hateful envy of Cortés and Pizarro.

Yet his winter was worried. Word came of Coronado's gold quest to the fabled *Seven Cities of Cibola,* the Zuni Pueblo, in *Nuevo México.* De Soto must hasten to *La Florida,* a land previously thought a great island, a discovery which Ponce de León had purchased by death from an Apalachee arrow so that another *Adelantado* could issue to *hidalgo* Pánfilo de Narváez, *"Governador de La Florida, Río de Palmas y el Río Espíritu Santo."* This hidalgo touched Tampa with an army that purchased fame with misfortune—six hundred men and five ships— in time to explore the twin disappointments of deception and defeat. The first by his fleet, scudding back to Havana, and the second by the Apalachee, who shot a bow so tall and strong that no Spaniard could pull it, bloodying his band by back-stepping them into the sea.

Narváez ate his horses, that is, all but their hide, from which he fashioned five little boats and paddled away from *Bahía de Caballos,* named for those skinned in gratitude (St. Mark's Bay), hugging his way along the Gulf Coast in the aching, arching hope of eventually hailing Mexico.

They drowned. All but four—Cabeza de Vaca, Captains of Infantry Alonso del Catillo and Andrés Dorantes, and his African chattel, Esteban, whom we herein honor as the first Black slave to grace the future Confederacy. This little group, naked as the sons of Adam, wallowed dazed upon the warm sands of today's Galveston, in Texas.

Seeing these strange ones, the tall, red-bearded Cabeza and the enormous, Black Esteban, the Charucco Indians preferred to think them shaman rather than meddlers landing from the moon.

They were treated to a semi-arid walkabout, sustained with nuts, roots, prickly pears, the generosity of Indians, and lots of conjuring.

> Our method was to bless the sick, breathing upon them, and recite a *Pater Noster* and an *Ave María,* praying with all earnestness to God our Lord that He would give health and influence them to make us some good return.

Caliban and Prospero in league with Gonzalo and Sebastian, wayward, stranded pranksters.

> "O, wonder! How many goodly creatures are there here! How beauteous mankind is! O brave new world that has such people in it!"

They took a wandering southwestward path with hundreds, sometimes thousands, of worshiping Indians. Of this Cabeza would write, "Throughout this country we went naked and cast our skins off like serpents." And of the Indians, he said of these "heathens," who had never heard of Jesus, that they fed them "with kindness and goodwill, and were happy to be without anything to eat, that they might give food to us."

In this way they meandered over the Colorado River (below Austin), then across the Pecos, and were slowly guided "through more than fifty leagues of mountains" into northern Mexico where they chanced upon a rescuing expedition of slave-stealing Spaniards.

In the city of Mexico, eight years after the sea swallowed *Adelantado* Pánfilo Narváez, Castillo and Dorantes drowned themselves in a sea of colonial privilege, but Cabeza de Vaca returned to Spain to labor out a bestseller, *La Relacíon que Dio Álvar Núñez Cabeza de Vaca de lo Acaescido en las Indias en la Armada Donde Iva por Governador Pánphilo Narváez,* or simply, *Relacíon,* printed, published, and praised in time to wreck a very wealthy but bored De Soto. Later, Esteban, known famously as Estébancito ("Little Steve"), at the very moment De Soto searched out the Caloosahatchee River (Fort Myers) before nosing into Tampa, Estébancito found himself leading *Adelantado* Coronado toward the Shangri-la of Cibola in New Mexico—a free man insatiable for life on the edge—walking well ahead of his warriors and women.

"Let me live here forever!"

Shaman for life.

But De Soto found, with the initial good fortune frequently granted the ill-fated, a Narváez survivor—a half-mad maroon, one Juan Ortiz, gone native and speaking Indian dialects so well he had nearly lost his Spanish. It was upon Ortiz's tongue that De Soto would ride fluently across *La Florida* to his ruin.

The tactic was not so much "search and destroy" as "search and consume." Gold was the goal but corn a necessity. The Spanish captured, demanded, took; like insatiable tormenting vermin, they glutted along like a restless plague sent by some inscrutable God. Most Indians submitted, but some fought. First to resist were the Apalachee, who lost their luck bravely at a place called Napituca (Live Oak, Florida), from which they never recovered. Three hundred were enslaved.

Traversing north, De Soto crossed the Suwannee River and waded swamps, harassed by residual Apalachees, till he plundered their town at Anhayca (Tallahassee). Here he wintered before moving into Georgia and on to the chiefdoms of Capachequi, Toa, Ichisi, Altamaha, Ocute, and Cofaqui, crossing rivers with names like Ocmulgee, Oconne, and the Savannah, going eventually into South Carolina—the land of the Cofitachequi.

At Ichisi a question had been put: "Who are you? What do you want?"

The reply was the conquistador's *Requerimiento:* That he was the representative of Christ and the great king of Spain and that they must acknowledge the former and obey the latter.

Cofitachequi was too exhausted for either obeisance. At the confluence of Pine Creek and the Wateree, the Whites found four braves at the river's edge. De Soto spoke Spanish to Ortiz, who spoke Mocozo to an Indian guide, who spoke Muskogean to the Cofitachequi. "Who are they and what did they want?" came the question again.

They were greeted by the chieftess, described royally as *La Señora de Cofitachequi,* who suddenly appeared, floating in a grand canoe, paddling over, seated upon large cushions. She welcomed the representative of her new sovereign, giving them gifts of skins, cloth, and pearls.

Impressed, but ever unsatisfied, the Spaniards asked for gold and silver. They were given mica and copper. They then asked for the sacred things and were led to a great temple centering the village. It was elevated, with vaulted ceilings of cane, and guarded by fierce warrior statues—a mortuary. These dead were soon looted of pearls, beads, shells, furs, moccasins, feathers, and deerskin by these emissaries from Christ upon earth.

But Cofitachequi had already suffered another plague, had little corn, and had fewer people—towns had been abandoned. There was hunger—so the Spaniards ate what remained and moved on, taking *La Señora* as a hostage—indulging her with a coterie of women slaves to ensure respect among the tribes.

Themselves now encumbered by hunger, they entered North Carolina, into the area of Chalaque (Charlotte), Anglicized as "Cherokee." It, too, was poor and the Indians fled. Northward the Spaniards crossed the Catawba River at today's town of Hickory, and proceeding northwest arrived at Xuala at the base

of the mountains (north of Morgantown). Here De Soto camped on a confluence of trails—one north-south that ran into the Tennessee Valley, another to
the east through the Piedmont into Virginia, and one west to the French Broad
River.

There was corn and copper, which, through satiation of one hunger, merely
reawakened another—the gold gluttony—driving them into the high country,
along the Nolichucky to such places as Chiaha, Canasoga, Coste, and Tali.

At Chiaha, in Tennessee (Dandridge)—a fortified town—well situated on
an island in this French Broad, the Spaniards and their horses grew fat; the men
swam in the river and played Indian games. But soon bored, the men demanded
women so the people fled; De Soto gave chase, destroying their cornfields and
cornering them on a river island. Here he accepted five hundred porters,
pearls, and reports of rich lands elsewhere, as with tears of feigned contrition,
the Chiaha people propelled De Soto south—first through the towns of Coste
and Tali in the Valley of the Little Tennessee, then back into Georgia, crossing
the Cooswatte River at the town of Coosa (now at the bottom of Carter's
Lake), where, despite their cooperation, he placed the chief in irons as his
hostage. (*La Señora* had escaped, pretending to squat but sneaking away with
her lover-slave instead, disappearing from history's unhappy page into a much
sweeter oblivion.)

De Soto forded the Etowah, touching Talimachusi, following past Itaba, into
Alabama, along the Coosa River, past Tuasi and into Talisi, near Tallasseehatchee
Creek where he found a large town, surrounded by other towns, prosperous
with abundant fields of corn. Here he released the Coosa chief, now out of his
territory, and in his place ordered the Talisi to pay homage. They did, kow-
towing, giving the necessary corn, women, and porters—telling De Soto of a
great village to the south known as Tascaluza.

Chief Tascaluza's son soon appeared in retinue—a man taller than any a
Spaniard had ever seen. He would guide them to his great father, he said. First,
they rested, then followed through smaller towns, down the trail and across
the Tallapoosa River, camping a little short of Atahachi (Montgomery), where
Chief Tascaluza reigned over one of the greatest of all the Indian Lost Kingdoms
in *La Florida*. De Soto found him waiting in front of a house set upon a large
mound facing the plaza. He sat upon cushions, wearing a cloak of eagle and
hawk feathers, with a cloth round his head like a Muslim. He was indeed
large—perhaps seven feet—with the soft brown "eyes of an ox," they said, and
there were armed guards in a semicircle, while a retainer held a great parasol
to hide him from the sun.

De Soto spoke a few words through a translator, then to impress the king, commanded his horseman to gallop about the plaza. Tascaluza viewed this impassively, some said with a contempt. In return, he ordered food and dancers to appear, which pleased the Spaniards immensely.

Then De Soto demanded women and slaves. Tascaluza demurred, saying he was not given to obeying orders, so De Soto locked him in chains and told him his freedom was at an end—that he must provide porters and women. He got four hundred porters and promise of women from the next village—Mabila. As a hostage, Tascaluza rode with De Soto along the Alabama River, his great legs nearly touching the ground. When two Spaniards came missing, De Soto told Tascaluza he would be burnt if they were not returned. The chief said De Soto would find them at Mabila. Then the Spaniards built rafts, floated the river, and camped (near Selma) where they learned that Mabila was arming for war.

In this the Europeans had the advantage with their horses, dogs, armor, crossbows, pikes, lances, and halberdiers. Wisely the Indians had not fought since the Apalachee—trying appeasement, compromise, and generosity. But the boiling point can always be reached, and De Soto had himself little by little turned up the flame to induce such a boil.

The Spaniards marched along on Monday, October 18, 1540, a pleasant south Alabama day, approaching with horse and infantry as assorted porters, slaves, priests, cooks, friars, and a medley of native hangers-on tagged behind—a motley mob.

They found Mabila to be a fort, encasing a village, with two great gates, east and west, and a palisades of embrasures, out of which the chief appeared, giving De Soto gifts, inviting him in for a feast. De Soto was wary but prideful, so, with a guard of infantry and his baggage, he followed the chief's entourage of dancing musicians into Mabila's large plaza where hundreds of Indians swayed and sang a song of salutation to the swaggering Spaniards.

Tascaluza, De Soto's royal hostage, unshackled for appearances, pretended to casual conversation with lesser chiefs, then vanished into a great house. De Soto sent word for his return, but he refused, saying De Soto should leave in peace. De Soto then sent two men, Gallegos and Moscoso, but there were soon shouts—a struggle—quickly arrows pinged off Spanish armor in the plaza, as, surrounded, the Whites were compressed into a desperate wad that crabbed a slow back-to-back, bloody retreat, fighting rearward through the plaza. Abandoning baggage, dead, and wounded, they slashed their way gradually to the closed gate.

Moscoso and Gallegos had slithered over the opposite wall to rally the cavalry that came forward, penetrating just in time. De Soto mounted a horse, brought by his brave Black slave, then galloped out of arrow shot, gladly accepting the lives of horses and men in exchange for his own, but inadvertently freeing his porters to join Mabila in a taunt of the Spanish devil—yelling from the palisades. It was the first reverse: casualties, horses, food, communion chalices, wafers, and worst of all, the pearls lost—the only loot—swallowed by Mabila in her moment of gleeful revenge.

But Mabila was undone, when, as if on cue, De Soto's remaining infantry arrived. Counterattacking from four directions, they thrust through, were expelled, thrust again, were yet expelled, came in again and again to be expelled; till finally in for good, they separated the Indians into the desperate embrace of a nine-hour, house-to-house, hand-to-hand obstreperous death.

Then a fire awoke as from a sleep, grew and grew, leapt from house to house, wall to wall, insatiating the town in a lust of flame that was quenched only by a mournful moon slowly lifting her face over slain Mabila—a charred body lying prostrate in simmering ruins.

Of her children all were killed or fled except a few surrendering to slavery, while the Spanish felt the pain of 22 dead and 148 wounded. Since Cuba, 1 in 6 had perished for burnt pearls and this heap of charred flesh, but news soon came of ships now waiting at the coast. "Let's go!" they cried. "Home to Spain, Cuba, or even Mexico!" *La Florida* is a land of grief without glory. "Let's go!" they shouted. "There is nothing here but suffering!"

De Soto said no. Abandoning rescue, he turned his reluctant legions to the northwest, marching in a sleeting rain through new wilderness, crossing the Apafalaya River (Black Warrior) into Mississippi, wintering at a place called Chicaza, after a tribe of that name, west of the Tombigbee (Columbus), where he foraged and traded through an uneasy peace that inexorably collapsed under the weight of his habitual cruelty into an inevitable war.

The Chicaza struck them at night, crawling silently in four equal columns, attacking with flaming arrows, burning out the makeshift hovels, stables, and pig sties, stabbing horses, frying swine, and killing twelve in a shouting circle of fire, losing but one, then retreating under the false fear that the panicked horses were cavalry.

De Soto's adventure should have ended at Chicaza on the Tombigbee. But he pressed on, stayed till spring, fought and won another battle with people called the Alibamos. He marched across that country which in another man's tale would be called Yoknapatawpha, fording its slow rivers, streams, and creeks with names like Little Tallatchie and Tippah, exchanging pine for a hardwood forest that inched down from Tennessee and Kentucky as a vast untouched monument. Chestnut, poplar, and oak—surprising our explorers by revealing a wide, well-worn trail leading west into what is now De Soto County, part of a floodplain greater than anything a European had ever thought to walk across. Through and into another forest they described as more towering still, standing in an unsullied silence for hundreds of miles on either side of a flow the French would call *Girardeau* at the top, and *Nouvelle-Orléans* at the bottom, draining a continent bigger than anyone imagined the erstwhile isle of *La Florida* could ever be, attended by the great but lesser lords named Missouri, Ohio, Arkansas, and Red, who served their one great master the Indians called Father, Father of Waters—the Mississippi—which, despite its greatness, had hid from the prying Promethean eyes of Europeans for a short eternity. De Soto found it at last, just past a small village named Quizquiz, immense and daunting, suitable only for and by a god, so God's name it must have. De Soto deemed it the divine presence—*Río de Espíritu Santo.*

Then, like everything new he found, he gave it like a patch in unencumbered fee-simple to a puny Habsburg sitting upon a throne, as Balboa had done with a world's third, likewise, to such a mortal, conveying the sun. We but rent our graves—illegible uprooted stones eventually stacked against a sepulchral wall. But a river? An ocean? A God? How can we lay claim to these?

The Quizquiz sent six braves with gifts of skins and blankets, saying, to De Soto's shock, that they had been expecting him—that there was an ancient tribal legend that White men would come from the east and conquer them. De Soto demanded to see the chief—he wanted more—food, slaves, canoes—submission. The emissaries went away, their chief never came, no canoes were given and the people melted back into the great forest. Then Quizquiz was ravaged of its corn, as the Spanish settled in to the building of boats—*piraguas* for the crossing.

Shortly, four Indians appeared in dugouts from across the water, got out, faced east, paid slow obedience to the sun by bowing deeply, and west to the moon with a lesser bow, then turned to the great Spaniard and bowed quickly to him. They said, pointing, they were from the other side, from a magnificent civilization, that their chief was the glorious Aquijo, and that on the morrow he would come and talk with the White lord. Then, without waiting, they turned and paddled away.

Next day, De Soto, expecting some few canoes with a chief and his entourage, got something else. Riding down the current, swinging in toward him were seven thousand warriors—archers colored in bright red ocher, beads, and feathers—vivid, bright, unique—in two hundred dugouts lined with bright banners and shields; some so large one would later write the word "*galera*" (galley) in the recollection of it; with the grandest, appropriately, floating Aquijo, a chief sitting under a canopy of bright blue—a king crowned with eagle plumes, paddling toward the European knight standing in a helmet of iron.

Aquijo's fleet hove-to, eddying within earshot. De Soto strode among armed soldiers on a bluff slightly above, and Aquijo shouted that he had come to be of service to "the greatest Lord on earth" and inquired as to what De Soto wanted. There was a pause as this trekked through Ortiz's translation. De Soto then offered an invitation to come parley. Aquijo floated in silence for a moment—thinking. The pause continued, then, with the slightest of nods, he propelled three smaller canoes forward with gifts of feathers, fish, and persimmon bread. These were accepted gladly but with beckonings to come ashore. Aquijo paused longer, floating almost still in the eddy, idling amidst his seven thousand, calmly sitting, studying these strangers standing astride his tomorrows.

It was as if he knew, on this nice warm day, the great brown river rolling quietly in backdrop like a subconscious force, that a critical moment had been touched, traversing its weary way through time till now—the European touching the Mississippian. No doubt, within this armed White mass, leering at him in an enticement of trust, Aquijo sensed an evil thing. He ordered a slow, back-paddling withdrawal. Now the Spaniards shot—killing and wounding—but the fallen were quickly replaced; and with a smooth discipline, the Indians slipped the range, pausing to yell threats and taunts, before disappearing on the western shore.

At the river's edge, the Spanish patiently worked on their four *piraguas* that were large enough to float horses, dogs, swine, and men; but every afternoon at about three, a hundred Aquijo canoes would appear to whistle arrows up in a great black wind—lifting, arching them gracefully in a swift eclipse of the summer sun, while Janus-like a shadow followed faithfully underneath the darkness, slipping quietly over the water and across the golden-brown beach and, bending up the bank, dropped in a loud rattle upon the carapace of shields covering the holes of these stranded but ever-busy amphibians.

For twenty-seven days this was done. Again and again, in ritualistic impotence, Aquijo arched his arrows across the face of the sun, as if to awaken it against this unearthly sound hammering at him across the water.

Finally, at about 1:50 in the darkness of June 18, 1541, De Soto, allowing for the current, maneuvered upriver to a place (Memphis) the Spanish would eventually name *San Fernando de las Barrancas*, to launch his fleet, steering it to the southwest, floating it in soft swiftness under a slice of a late spring moon that rose in sad defiance of Aquijo's silently setting star, till at last he nudged to a sandy spot opposite Quizquiz.

Sixty-six years before Jamestown, eighty-seven before Plymouth; while Henry VIII still slept in marital bliss with his second Catherine; while Michelangelo worked in Florence, Luther in Wittenberg, and Calvin in Geneva—De Soto crossed the river to violate Aquijo's Kingdom.

U-gakh-pa, "Quapaw," "down river people," was the word the Indians called themselves, whereas, "Arkansas," is what the French called the Quapaw because that is what the Illinois Indians called them but morphied around the European tongue as Akansea (Marquette, 1673), Acansa (La Salle, 1680), Accanceas (Joutel, 1687), Akanssa (Hennepin, 1698), Acansea (Gravier, 1700), Arkansas (Pénigaut 1700), Alkansas (La Harpe, 1720), Akansaes (Coxe, 1741), Accances (La Potherie, 1753), Arkansaw (Pike, 1811), Arkensaw (Schermerhorn), and officially back again to Pénigaut's name—so would run the conjugation of a pearl placed as one of the fairest in *La Florida's* crown—a land of rivers (almost ten thousand miles)—Mississippi, Arkansas, Illinois, Saline, Ouachita, Buffalo, Cassotot, Cache, White, Red, Little Red, and Black; of bayous, creeks, and swamps; a land of mountain ranges, the Ozarks, the Ouachitas, and the Bostons—of lifting hills, of prairie, of forests, and a Delta that would be cleared into some of the finest farmland on the planet; a land of great beasts: bison, elk, and deer by the herd; the black bear, panther, and red wolf; a land of infinite furs which shed their hides for the cold and ungrateful shoulders of shivering Europe; a land of the eagle, hawk, and osprey; of ducks and geese, gliding south, swarming in black settling clouds over these same swamps, rivers, and bottoms that always awaited their return like lost children; a land whose artist wind flung color as from an easel, parakeets in their now-vanished millions smudging the virgin sky with green and yellow streaks like paint streaming from God's brush.

"If you ever wear out a pair of moccasins in Arkansas, you'll never leave," said the *coureurs de bois* who came from France.

De Soto marched to Aquijo, finding it "a league and a half to the north." Expecting an army he found only spies staring from thickets and lurking around towers of trees. He captured fifteen who told him their people had fled, they said. De Soto confirmed this truth, riding into the disappointing quiet of Aquijo—two imposing dirt pyramids with mounds, temples, and houses circling a ghostly silent plaza.

Connecting the river by a horseshoe lake the town was also a port, so, the Spanish floated up their *piraguas* to be unloaded and disassembled.

After Aquijo was "sacked," when they found no gold, silver, or pearls, no slaves and little food, their prisoners propitiated them with stories of a great and wealthy city to the west, called Casqui. So, like a famished wolf, De Soto left the carrion carcass of Aquijo to hunt for Casqui, loping deeper into this new Kingdom, plunging quickly into a concave of swamps between the Mississippi and St. Francis Rivers—the most difficult in all of *La Florida,* it was written.

They struggled through these vast flooded stands of timber, till, by evening, they reached a natural levee short of what's now named Crowley's Ridge, finding a cluster of villages along the St. Francis—Casqui.

The land was now more open and showed cultivation of walnut, persimmon, and pecan trees, as well as corn.

Surprised, the people did not resist, and the Spaniards galloped their horses over the open country, taking prisoners, food, and skins at will, but soon these things were offered freely. The conquistadors would leave one town of about forty houses only to gain sight of another. It was the most complex society they had yet seen: a village and fields, then more villages and fields, on and on in succession—a civilization. There must be gold and silver as in Mexico and Peru, they said with glee; they had found what they were looking for!

Finally, the Spanish came upon the town of Casqui itself, sitting just below the confluence of the St. Francis and Tyronza, as they are now known—ancient children of their immortal father, the Mississippi. Casqui was spread as a rectangle upon seventeen acres, with a moat on three sides and a fourth wall hard against the rivers on the west, ten feet above the water and floodplain. Walking through the eastern gate, De Soto was transfixed by the sight of a temple set facing him, lording itself twenty feet above its brood of houses huddling in semicircular homage around a very broad central plaza.

Then a gray-headed chief of about fifty emerged. He brought two blind men behind, imploring the conquistador to heal them since he was from heaven and therefore divine. De Soto demurred, speaking instead of God and Christ and the Christian promise of immortality. The old man listened intently then asked if De Soto would make it rain, saying there had been a drought and his people were about to perish. De Soto said he would return with a sign and left.

At noon the next day, De Soto returned to the chief, now weeping a supplication against any delay, so De Soto ordered his Italian carpenter to cut an immense tree to form a cross, which, peeled of bark, was stood on the great mound, towering in magnificent whiteness over a river that would be named after the man from Assisi who did not want gold, or silver, or pearls, and had given all his fortune to the poor. Then De Soto and the chief formed a procession as Indians streamed from the surrounding villages, merging with the Spaniards now camped outside of Casqui, converging behind priests and friars chanting Latin liturgy and singing hymns—a slow dirge of a thousand marching into town, gathering in a great mass before this magnificent cross.

De Soto paused, then fell to his knees and kissed the foot of the cross. The chief followed, then the priests, and friars, and a thousand in turn, kneeling and kissing, while by the river St. Francis hundreds of Casqui cried, wept, and wailed to heaven. The Spanish were moved in a surprising way and touched to tears. But, at last, the priests and friars harmonized into a steady "Te Deum Laudamus" and returned the flock in a slow shuffling movement to camp and village from which no one stirred, as a strange quietude descended over a windless afternoon that, in turn, faded slowly into a hushed darkness.

Then, at midnight, it rained.

El Milagro De Soto quickly sprouted his name in a longed-for apotheosis by this midnight rain. Not one Indian had been tortured, burnt, lanced, or chained; yet the Casqui were now De Soto's most loyal vassals. But these new vassals, as vassals always will, brought new and unwanted problems, one of which they pronounced as "Pacaha"—a fierce enemy to the northeast who pestered them out of slaves and corn. Would De Soto now grant victory as well as abundance? Would he subdue the Pacaha as he had the drought?

Marching with his mixed Euro-American army, De Soto found Pacaha to be formidable, set on a ridge above a bayou called Wapanocca, also well fortified with walls, towers, and wide moats that egressed Pacaha's long canoes to the Mississippi. It seemed impregnable, and, remembering the unforgettable, De Soto's band fell once more into a kind of Mabilian despair.

But the Pacaha, seeing their enemies conjoined with creatures with horses' heads, panicked and fled. Their Casqui slaves, fettered by the Indian device of a sliced heel, wept in joy as they limped after the few stragglers they herded into a pathetic huddled lump, while urging murder as prologue to the rape of the town.

So, seemingly, the same luck or lord that broke the drought now granted the Casqui the curse of revenge, as, first, the chief's house was sacked, then the greater buildings looted and burned. Casqui's joy was embittered with the sight of smiling heads of kinsmen staring like sentries in an impaled semicircle about the temple, but with their new prisoners, they quickly made the switch to fresh guards who slowly drooled their watch of blood upon the sacred sticks.

In rapid violation, the reliquary relinquished its sacred Pacaha bones, which were strewn, defiled, then torched, while the town traded skins, corn, and shells for the limitless ecstasy of the Casqui's lust. Still insatiate, they spilled themselves into the belly of attendant villages lying in helpless clusters like huddled children. On into the limitrophe of today's Missouri the Casqui ran their final, orgasmic, lunging pleasure till all of Pacaha was erased. De Soto swung away in ennui—there had been no stone nor metal nor pearl—his conquests did not conceive and his rapes were always barren.

So our victor rested, refitted, ate fish, probed to the north and east, but when told of even greater cities to the south plunged deeper into Arkansas. Downriver, below Casqui, he found the largest culture yet in *La Florida*—Quiguate, on the lower St. Francis. Again, the people panicked and De Soto rode pridefully into their empty city, quartering himself in one half after burning the other.

The Indian people streamed into the forests, lurking, spying, weeping, wondering, sending first gifts, then a counterfeit chief as hostage to repeat the question for which there never seemed any answer: "Who are you? What do you want?" The reply came with raids, killing, prisoner taking, and, in time, the impostor's master seized and enslaved in his own house. Slowly the Quiguate returned, bringing more gifts, food, and endless supplications. They brought a new weapon also, one that always worked, stories of a magnificent Shangri-La ripe for destruction, to the west in the mountains, a fantastic empire called Coligua—a greater Kingdom to conquer than humble Quiguate. "Go there!" they said pointing, saying that in Coligua the people lived on buffalo and elk, not fish and corn, and will guide you to the vast western sea and the riches you seek.

De Soto, hearing mention of mountains, thought only of gold. Bored with his easy violation of Quiguate, he would have Coligua next—feel her soft fluttering heart beneath his power—become at long last another Cortés—another Pizarro. He was certain that with one more march and battle, one more triumph, one more Kingdom Lost, history would at last tremble at his name.

He would go to Coligua.

But there were murmurs, orders disobeyed, and grumblings in the night. His men wanted something less grand; they wanted home.

"Why do you want to return to Spain?" De Soto shouted into the darkness, his sullen sleeping army listening to his half-sane rage, burning into their hearts like Lucifer's benediction to his angels.

> Did you leave family estates there to enjoy? Why do you want to go to Mexico? To disclose the baseness and littleness of your souls? Possessed now of the power to become lords of such a great Kingdom as this where you have discovered and trodden upon so many and such beautiful provinces, have you deemed it better to go and lodge in a strange house and eat at the table of another when you can have your own house and table with which to entertain many? What honor do you think they will pay you when they have learned as much? Be ashamed of yourselves and bear in mind we all must serve His Majesty, and none shall presume to absent himself because of any pre-eminences he may possess, for should he do so, I will strike off his head, be he who he may! And be undeceived, for as long as I live, no one is to leave this land before we have conquered and settled it or all died in the attempt!

With this jeremiad De Soto burned his words into the hot wax of his fate. By late August the expedition was following a Quiguate guide into the flatness of western cypress (a little north of Wattensaw County), plunging across four saddle-deep swamps alive with alligators, snakes, and mosquitoes, fording uncountable streams, creeks, and rivers some day called L'Anguille, Bayou de View, and Cache.

Then, at last, they slogged up against yet another great river, one more of the Mississippi's half-children, the Coligua, which Anglo settlers, ever prosaic, would name simply the White, that slipped its way east and south of Ephesus Cemetery slithering through its own silent stretch of time like a giant water serpent.

Here the Spanish found a faintly worn trail leading north, down which Union general Samuel Curtis, victor at Elkhorn Tavern (sometimes called Pea Ridge), in the summer of 1862, would terrorize south from Coligua (Batesville), torching Sherman-fashion before Sherman ever did in Georgia and stealing in "such scenes as cannot be described but will last with me while time lasts," as one Federal private wrote; the Union river escort, the *Mound City*, ambushed as it nosed slowly round a bend like some primitive amphibian, exploding and sinking with one hundred and five men scalded as a prelude to drowning, a boiler unpressuring from the intrusion of a Napoleon's nosey ball; Curtis flinching at Parley's Plantation under the sharp blade off Gray-backed general Albert Rust's sword—his mounted division of wild Arkansawyers and Texans turning a sharp fight south along the Cache into a deflection of Curtis to where the Blues were then besieged and trapped with a thousand "contraband" runaways and soldiers mixed together in a fever sump not called Helena, Arkansas, but "Hell in Arkansas."

Up this same White De Soto marched, till the land changed to hill hickory, pine, and oak leading him, as if by the hand, to the promised high ground that lifted up his men's weary down-looking eyes in relief, to an endless gargantuan rising waves of green September summer forest which would roll from the French tongue as Aux Ark (Ozark)—and which, in time, would, like a rock in a stream, split the great western American migration north to south while itself remaining in impervious, splendid, but, temporary, isolation to all things modern.

But Coligua itself was little more than a five-acre disappointment of huts. There were no precious stones or pearls, no Montezuma or Copan, no temples or pyramids. Not even buffalo. Perhaps they were searching for the Kingdom of the Cayas to the southwest, the chief said, who greeted them, pointing at the sun setting behind a hill. "Go there! To the sun! Go to the Cayas! You will find what you seek there!" he said.

So, this monomaniac from Extremadura, afflicted by that most painful of diseases, a half-realized ambition, who had gained enough to engender an unending hope and had lost enough for a lingering despair, now turned his half-mad visage toward the next illusion and trudged to the southwest, skirting the mountains, crossing clearer rivers and coming to more towns with names like Palisema and Quixila, till reaching Coligua's older brother, the River of the Cayas (the Arkansas), of which the old man had spoken, camping wearily on its banks at a place called Tanico, among the Caya Kingdom in the Cadron bottoms, a few miles upriver from where our *Petit Rocher* is to be.

But still there was no gold, no silver, no pearls. "Go up river to Tula!" said the Caya chief, pointing yet again to the same sun setting over a pair of mountains that trappers would mouth as "*Mamelle*" (Maumelle)—which was what French paddlers would see as the lifting breasts of a *jeune fille* lying upon her lonely back as an unfulfilled dream of their desire. "Go there!" he said, "To Tula! It will give you what you want! Follow the golden sun!" (In time Anglos would build a fort west of Tula called Smith—gateway to the "Indian Territory"—a camp for Renee, Christopher's lover and their Eurasian child, refugees from America's Vietnam Kingdom.)

De Soto went to Tula. Up the valley down which General Van Dorn's Army of the West would some day trek after disappointment at the Elkhorn, retracing the same sad Spanish trail to the Mississippi; just in time to be late at Shiloh, but not for Corinth and Iuka, or Holly Springs, where he fell from victory's belated embrace into that of a cuckold's wife to find first a kiss and then a bullet; but only after upsetting another household and baggage train, ruining the Grants' march to Vicksburg as well as his Julia's day as she and her slave of that same name fled with their master's army back to where De Soto had crossed against Aquijo at Memphis.

Up this long valley our conquistador went, his now-vanished army following today's highways, railroads, towns, and villages through forests that are today's farms into valleys with vineyards, forever facing the same terrible star, a sliver of which now is in part and temporarily enslaved in a upside-down atomic hour glass set by still-blue water, athwart the old trail, its fissioned energy dripping hotly through a squeezed middle, then running out in long languid lines over the once unvanquishable mountains; silver giants (towers) standing coldly with spreading Promethean arms of fire, lifting all that's gone before into increasing irrelevance.

Armies! Lilliputians! Why do you march?

Up this same sun ensnared valley Christopher Shaw would drive with Marianne Marsden a mere two winters before finding death waiting in the Vietnam Kingdom on a little hill, past a village and a rice paddy, before his Saigon lover escaped to Tula as he lay freshly made in front of his mother's immortal downriver oak in a grave before which she now ate a peach.

Lovers! Why do you embrace?

Where are the children of the Apalachee? The Aquijo? The Cayas? Whither those Kingdoms of the Mabila? Casqui? Pacaha? The Tula? Tell us, where have they gone and why they ever were?

But the Tula, Oklahoma buffalo hunters who had small fear of large beasts, were fierce, spearing the Spanish horses and fighting with an unyielding desperation that, though defeated, turned De Soto's last western hope into a final and unremitting Southern despair. The Tula forced De Soto back over the river, retracing him down the other side, pushing him through a new range, the Ouachitas, and under a sacred mountain, then called Pisgah, that looms like Arkansas's natural cathedral along the south bank of the Caya, but which Louisiana buckskins would romanticize, not for a god but for a girl—

a charming hair-cropped Viola-like favorite passing as a boy in her newfound Illyria as *Petit Jean*. De Soto crossed under her grave to be, an outcropping shrine, the stone-covered bones arranged over a sacred Indian valley where he camped. The victorious but defeated Spaniards pushed along and down and across Arcadia where Medora, Christopher's great-great-grand-dame, and her brood of females—slaves and children—a dog named Calvin and a cat named Luther—would someday stand bravely in Tula-like defiance of all Yankee inevitability.

The Europeans were now, in a groping, half-realized way, looking no longer for splendor but simply for the sea. They camped at Quipana on the Fourche Le Fave, then at Anoixi, at Quitamaya, and at last on a stream they hoped would lead to the Gulf but instead led them back to the Cayas among the Utiangue people. Finally, on the Cadron, just north of *Petit Rocher*. Here the Utiangue were settled thickly in clusters along the Cayas from the rock to its mouth, as plazas, temples, and mounds were towned together on either side in a long river-dependent culture. They, too, asked De Soto the ubiquitous questions, "Who are you? What do you want?"

He answered by staying and building a fort, and to meet winter's siege, he ate swine, rabbits, dried corn, beans, nuts, and prunes (*ciruelas pasadas*) till he outlasted the blockade of snow melting in the spring of 1542's new warm sun of yet another year.

It was to be a busy one: Catherine Howard, by trying to cure sterility with adultery, would exchange Milady's bed for His Majesty's block; the first Spanish ship would sail from the sands of Acapulco for the Indies and find Waikiki instead; Calvin would obey God's will by burning witches predestined since the Garden to infect Geneva with the plague; and Cortés, languishing in Oaxaca, would buy Africans for conversion in his sugar mill, while De Soto would kill his last Indian infidel in Arkansas.

Reduced by half and with forty half-comical, half-pathetic, be-ribbed horses looking more like Rosinantes than Pegasuses, and burdened with a following of frightened slaves and a swarm of ever-copulating swine, whose increase seemed inverse to the decrease of all else, De Soto wound down the twisting Cayas searching for a final release from ambition's afflictive grip.

As all mighty actions arise from vanity, all mundane ones from necessity, and all mean ones from fear, so driven by this world's ruthless trinity, our

Spanish knight terrorized his way through the Utiangue toward the *Río de Espíritu Santo,* praying to God, hoping in Christ, and swinging his sword at the ever-illusive specter of disappointment.

It was not easy. Swamps and stumps, gnarls of cypress roots kneed out of the mud to trip and impede all but the ever-fecundate, agile pigs. Only they, it seemed, took to *La Florida,* led by the *porqueros* who herded them along, omnivoring up acorns, carrion, snakes, plants, and fruits; anything a rooting snout could churn they ate. The number of pigs increased even while the number of dogs, horses, and men declined, the pigs copulating themselves well past any kind of piglet mortality, snorting at De Soto through the village of Ayays, swimming ahead of the *piraguas* that crossed the Cayas into the face of a returning bout of winter that froze the stirrup-deep water into sheets of sharding ice. De Soto, soldiers, slaves, priests, friars, horses, the few miserable surviving dogs, and the thousand thriving swine, all moseyed along with that rattling miscellany of marching men and trudging animals, when, after three torturous days, they came at last upon a town called Tutelpinco that they had not expected then swam a stream to be called Bayou Meto, in which, it is dutifully reported, Francisco Bastian, from Villanueva de Bacarrota, promptly drowned.

Crossing here, they happened upon the town of Tianto where they learned of the greatest city of all—Anilco—memorialized by Hernandez de Biedma as the most populous and "best" in all *La Florida.* They were now but a hawk's flight south of Elizabeth's tree, slogging between hope and despair, with little thought of gold or silver or of another *Shangri-La* to scourge—only the greenness of surf and sea would satiate them now as they plunged ahead, much more sensible of salvation than success of any kind at all.

The city of Anilco would prove fateful. In 1686, Henri de Tonty, would palm off his mentor, Robert Cavalier de La Salle, as a personal seignreury, and settle in to trade at a stockade soon called *Poste aux Arcs*—the oldest in Louisiana (older even than New Orleans) and, for a time, the only White place west of the great river as the Pueblo's revolted the Spanish out of *Nuevo México* and, for a moment, the West was Red again.

But then the *Poste* was deeded to the *Compagnie d'Occident,* a creation of a notorious, promoting Scot, one John Law, who, reasoning like De Soto that Arkansas had everything so it must have gold, advised Regent Philippe d'Orleans to back it with *billet d'état* so to run things up from zero *livres* to twelve thousand and back down again, crushing Parisian speculators under their double share of avarice into mobbing itself into greed's self-defeating alarm.

Arkansas's insolvency thus played over *l'Ancien Régime* as a gin-up for her Revolution—coming like Manon Lescaut's overture of revenge for a noble death in a wilderness far from the ignoble Parisian stock exchange.

Poste aux Arcs was, indeed, a place for the *habitants* to die in the wonderful romantic wilderness, free of everything but fever, fracas, and fatigue (one child in four never crying into a second year); yet, too, all classes finding it a place to live, "knights, gentry, merchants, farmers, hunters, laborers, slaves—*voyageurs*," as one would write, and so it became the capital of the French, Spanish, and, lately, Anglo Arkansas; raided by Indians, besieged by British, sacked by Sherman—the people and the name "Anilco" forgotten now because of what was about to happen, the fleeing Red people leaving a false chief to expose their enemies, the Guachoya, living to the south across the Cayas, the Spanish recrossing it, finding the evil Guachoya camped on Bayou Macon (MacArthur), which in that time looped to the bigger river they called the *Tamaliseau* and which the Spanish honored as the Holy Spirit for an unholy alliance against Anilco.

Here De Soto bivouacked, parlayed, hesitated, and for the first time was at a loss in this forest he had worked so hard to find. Finally, he sent one Juan de Anasco south with eight horses. They waited anxiously for a belated return that came tonguing out with the lines for our hero's denouement. The land was impassable, Anasco said. There was a great chiefdom called Quigualtam there, stretching from the Yazoo to the Natchez Bluff, and they would fight them by water, all the way down to the ocean. In other words, they'd never make it.

At this news our conquistador turned and found his bed. From here he dictated messages to this magnificent Mississippian, Quigualtam—first exhortations, then curses, then threats. He would rise soon, cross the great water, and teach Quigualtam who was lord over *La Florida,* he shouted, really at no one, shaking his fist at the vacancy of the air above his feverish head.

The chief of Guachoya paid obeisance but De Soto could not stand. "Why does not Quigualtam come?" De Soto asked, lying on his back, staring hollowed-eyed as if in nothingness.

"He is afraid," said the chief. "Why don't you attack him?"

"I will attack your enemy Anilco first," De Soto announced weakly and closed his eyes as if to sleep. So it was done. With Guachoya's help, Anilco was sacked—the six thousand who had returned were scattered, killed, their houses burnt, the women and children enslaved. The screams were louder than anything the Spanish had ever heard as the Guachoya murdered sons, fathers, husbands, and brothers, lancing and swording them till Anilco was no more.

Then Quigualtam was decreed as next, but De Soto could not move, much less rise, so it was spared. Inert, he whispered his will to a priest: Luís de Moscoso was to be his successor, he said, and then he thanked his men, prayed quietly, took confession from the Father who gave him unction, asked mercy of the Holy Trinity and the intercession of God's Holy mother, solicited Christ's compassion and, with his last sigh, beseeched God for entry into paradise for his service upon the earth, then died.

Moscoso first burnt the clothes, then weighted the body with stones, sinking his leader's mortality into the brown god of the great Mississippi—fire and water—nature's final oxymoron converting him into oblivion.

And so it came to pass that Hernando De Soto of Extremadura, the mighty conquistador, *Adelantado* of Cuba and *La Florida*, successor to Cortés and Pizarro, victor of Napituca, Chicaza, Mabila, Quiguate, Tula, and Anilco, discoverer of the *Río de Espíritu Santo*, creditor to a Habsburg, His Royal Highness, King Charles V of the Holy Roman Empire and Catholic Spain, the greatest monarch of the greatest Kingdom on this earth, this same magnificent De Soto, on May 21, 1542, bequeathed his flesh to fishes, his soul to salvation, and all his vast fortune to his friends—three steeds, four slaves, and seven hundred thriving swine.

Luís de Moscoso y Alvarado, successor to De Soto, took a vote among his captains. No one knew how far it was to the Gulf, or whether there was a great waterfall, or if they could find food. They had no boats, and, once built, they would have to fight through Quigualtam, then build ships and sail without a pilot across an uncharted sea. So they decided to walk—all the way to Mexico.

Turning round, they marched along the south side of the Cayas, north of Bayou Bartholomew, came to today's Pine Bluff and turned to the southwest, crossing the Saline River, and entered the Caddoan territory. They came upon the town of Chaguate at the confluence of the Ouachita and Caddo Rivers where they made peace, rested for six days, collected supplies and salt, and sent a patrol to take the baths in the volcanic healing waters at a place settlers would someday call Hot Springs.

They broke camp and, meandering through the Ouachitas, disturbed the Indian towns of Aguacy, Pato, and Amaye before wading the Red River to Nisohone on the Sulphur.

On they slogged into the abyss of timber, creeks, thickets, and swamps of east Texas, across the Cypress, Sabine, Angelina, Neches, and Trinity Rivers, till at last they reached the Brazos in October.

The land slowly changed—drier and less plentiful of food. Here the Indians did not parley, give gifts, or make peace, and they lived more and more on the move, "like Arabs," forever hostile, surrounding these strange intruders, screaming at them during the night and fighting a guerrilla war as resistance to each step they took.

On the banks of the Brazos, Moscoso at last called a halt and took another vote. The captains wanted to go back. Mexico was too far, they said, the land too poor, the Indians too fierce. So, after resting briefly, they turned around. Marching once again back to and through Arkansas, the ever-weakening, diseased men and horses dying along the way, wasting while their flourishing swine swelled with weight and habitually escaped into ever-larger razorback bunches, breeding, then spilling, as if out of their pockets, into the flooded bottoms of the Cayas on the way to Anilco, now only a Golgotha, crossing the river again and camping for the winter at Aminoya (Desha County), about "a league" from the Mississippi.

Soon a Guachoya shamaness, as if waiting for them, appeared mysteriously out of the deep forest, saying the river would make a great new year's rise; so, she told them "you must build boats and float away." There was about her that ineffable aura of truth, and, anxious for a sign, they gathered food and built bergantines, trusting in this prophetess to raise the water.

Then, as if on command, the river slowly rose, stretching out from Aminoya to Anilco, gathering unto itself these twenty-two horses and three hundred and twenty-two men, as the expedition made its last escape from Arkansas, steering seven ships into the powerful middle current, slowly abandoning their five hundred waving and weeping slaves to the wilderness.

Of course, Quigualtam was waiting. A hundred canoes with warriors dressed for battle, chanting songs and paddling in broad strokes, came as Moscoso sent forward a foray of dugouts, easily overwhelmed by a sky of arrows and swimming Indians who taught the Spanish to swim in body armor, surfacing and flipping them into their Adelantado's lap waiting for them in his tomb.

Quigualtam's braves came closer, singing and shouting as a coda of each song. The arquebuses had been hammered into nails for the bergantines and the Spanish could only paddle, hide, and shoot crossbows. It continued for two days, like Grant would do running his boats down to the old slave who handed him the keys to Vicksburg and the war, landing the Blue army at a place called "Hard Times" where Grant unlocked the Confederacy. So, too, the Spanish now ran quickly past the Yazoo basin, landed, tended the wounded, ate their horses, fought yet another battle, then splashed along an ever-widening river into today's Louisiana where they found Indians so tall and dark they called them the "Philistines."

According to a remembering slave, one of these giants stood very erect in a canoe echoing a final judgment over the water: "Thieves, vagabonds, and loiterers who without honor or shame travel along this coast disquieting its inhabitants, depart!!"

With this blessing the Spanish escaped from *La Florida*, bobbing at last into the brackish brown salt sea of the Gulf.

Three hundred and eleven reached Mexico. They brought no horses, no dogs, no gold, no silver, no pearls, nor could they boast of seeing pyramids or the plunder of a *Shangri-La*. They were nothing but bereft, half-naked beggars, appearing to the surprise of a stunned Europe assuming them lost and dead to the last.

But they had bequeathed a great deal—they gave more than mere cruelty and conquest could—so often the mason and mortar of immortality—they also gave a thousand tiny, invisible things inhaled from friendly cats, cows, and chickens—unseen things—smallpox, measles, typhoid, diphtheria, and mumps—which they traded with the Indian people of *La Florida* along with corn and colored glass.

So in 1673 as Marquette and Joliet claimed the Mississippi for France they did not find the Casqui, Pacaha, Quizquiz, Aquijo, Anilco, or the great Quigualtam. They did not find the great Indian towns nor were they met by the great fleets; did not hear the war songs nor see the red feathered riverine braves of the magnificent Mississippians.

BOOK TWO

CHAPTER FIVE

Sincerely don't suffer anymore for us
You must take into account
That the gods are not infallible
And that we have come to forgive everything.
—Padre Nuestro, Nicanor Parra

As De Soto left Spain for the sinking brown oblivion of the Mississippi, tracing his ruthless path proximate to Elizabeth's tree, searching for death, his *entrevista con muerte,* so, forty years later, 1581, did three Franciscan friars, Rodríguez, López, and Santa María. The friars came up the Río Bravo del Norte, as the Río Grande was then called, into a land to be named New Mexico, honoring that great city conquered by Cortés.

Escorted by a small group of soldiers making them twelve—nine for this world and three for the next—they hoped, as always, for *almas y oros.* Discouraged, the soldiers returned but the friars persisted till they found God's paradise, like De Soto, but not from the muddy swirling of a river god but from the swarming Red Tiwas, who favored them with martyrdom.

But this did the Tiwas no real good. Spain soon returned in the flesh of Don Juan de Oñate, *Adelantado* for King Phillip II and his benevolent Catholic faith. Convinced of finding a new Canaan, Oñate claimed a Promise Land on the feast day of the Ascensión—April 13, 1598. He knelt and prayed in a small sanctuary of cottonwoods along the bank of the Río Grande, about three hundred miles south of Kroner's big pine, near the river's present bifurcation of El Paso from Juárez. The prayer was reduced to a proclamation nailed on a cross, then hung in a cottonwood, saying:

> Cross, Holy Cross that you are, divine gate of heaven, altar of the
> one essential sacrifice of the body and blood of the Son of God, way
> of the saints and means of attaining glory, open the door to these
> heathens, establish the church and altars where the body and blood
> of God's Son may be offered, open to us the way to security and

peace for their preservation and ours; and give to our King, and to me in his royal name, peaceful possession of these realms and provinces for his blessed glory. Amen.

Oñate named it *La Toma,* the taking, echoing Joshua, as Fray Angélico Chávez has said, where God said to Joshua, listening on the banks of the Jordan, "I have taken the shame of Egypt away from you."

To be sure, shame can be removed by grace only to be just as surely restored by greed. God's promise was desecrated by the Indians' enslavement in the *del oro* mines. The rebelling Pueblos expelled the Spanish, leaving *Poste aux Arcs,* as the most westward foray of the White Kingdom. But in *Nuevo México,* this fire raged with such cruelty that only a cooling alchemy of racial admixture could at last extinguish it, creating a new people from the old.

Now a descendant of this smothering emerged smoothly from the forest, silently, unexpectedly, almost magically, if you will, as if from a hole in the earth, like his ancestors believed—humanity sprouting up like corn. He was medium build with bandy legs and long black hair nearly touching his shoulders. He wore old tennis shoes, faded jeans, a red pullover and carried a scarred-up lever-action 30/30 rifle with "iron sights." He was christened Antonio Lopez, but Cripple Bear was his tribal name and most folks simply called him Tony. His blood blended across the earth, Siberia to Iberia, Scotland to the Southwest. He was, in a word, a New Mexican.

It had been cold, but now warm noon air mixed with the smell of piñion as the wet snow melted into a medley of muddy patches which Cripple Bear tread round, up to the tree.

"Here you are, my friend," he said, sitting and catching his breath. "Sleeping?"

"Almost," said Kroner, hardly opening his eyes.

"See nothing?"

"Nothing ... nothing but the Río Grande, the Sangre de Cristos ... the valley ... the world ... you coming out of the forest like a ghost ... nothing ... that's what I see ... nothing ... nothing at all."

Cripple Bear laughed then leaned against the trunk, his shoulder touching Kroner's. The valley stretched below, green along the Great River—it was a darkly crimson string seeping through the desert into the insatiable maw of Albuquerque's downstream water supply.

"I like it here," Kroner said. "It's nice."

"Sure," said Cripple Bear quietly, closing his eyes, relaxing.

A pause.

"Saw a bear track back a ways," said Kroner.

"Yeah?"

"Fresh."

"He's around."

"You hunt 'em?"

"No."

"Why not?"

"Bear is sacred ... skin one and he looks like a man. If I kill him, I gotta go through a purification ceremony and everything ... it's a bitch, man ... you wanna hunt bear ... I'll get you a White guide."

"Not interested."

"Good."

"Lots of deer, huh?"

"Oh, hell, yes ... lots of 'em ... deer everywhere ..."

Almost noon, it had gotten hotter, and the slight breeze, the sun and clean air made them sleepy, so they napped. A large bluejay came and sat on a twig, eyeing them; then a coyote circled furtively around their smell and the bear crossed the mountain into the next valley without being seen.

"We gotta be careful," said Cripple Bear quietly, waking after a time, moving slightly, making the jay fly.

"Why?" asked Kroner, his eyes still shut.

"Well ... there's a sacred buck with a white stone in his neck in these mountains ... when he's killed the end of the world will come."

"That right?" Kroner said, turning, looking at Cripple Bear.

"Sure ... no doubt about it, man."

There was another pause.

"How do we know it's him?"

"He'll have a certain look."

"A look?"

"Yeah ... a look."

"What kinda look?"

"I dunno, just a look."

"Special, huh?"

"Yeah, I've hunted the Jemez all my life, man ... forever ... since I was a boy ... with Grandfather ... and he seen him more'n once. He told me and everything. I mean, like, I can feel him around sometimes ... the deer ... around me or something ... just feel him, see. I know when he's around and all. But I ain't never seen him or nothing like Grandfather done. But I never want to kill him … we got to be careful and everything … real careful … up here … hunting deer like this because of him …"

"How?"

"How what?"

"How are we careful about not shooting the sacred buck with the white stone in his neck?"

"Oh, don't worry, William, just don't shoot nothing you kinda gotta a special feeling about … it'll be all right … fine … just keep the sacred deer in the back of your mind all the time. … kinda like … and it'll be okay for sure, man."

Kroner laughed.

"It's true, man."

"Okay."

They sat quietly, Kroner not knowing quite what to say. An eagle circled, and they watched it soar in the up and down drafts without once moving its wings, then disappear into the light blue nothingness over them. Cripple Bear talked about the eagle some, then fell silent again.

"Tell me about your grandfather," said Kroner, after the eagle had disappeared.

There was a pause then Cripple Bear spoke. "He was a father to me … like the eagle there," Cripple Bear said pointing up to where the eagle had vanished. "My real ole man was a drunk … bad … we never done nothing together … only Grandfather … he never drunk nothing … not ever … and he took care of me real good and all."

"I see," said Kroner.

"I come into the world all pissed-off, see," said Cripple Bear, shifting his weight and picking up a rock that was hurting his hip, throwing it in the brush, making a doe that they never saw move down the arroyo, stop, look back and into the next valley.

"You don't act pissed-off," said Kroner.

"No? Well … not anymore, but that's the way it all started. Like, I didn't understand why the Great Spirit, the God of my understanding, made my ole man a drunk and everything … like almost every other Indian on the damn reservation. I mean, why was I an Indian at all? See? Why did he whip this Indian trip on my ass, that's what I wanted to know."

"I see …"

"Life on the reservation … it was just a pile of shacks the government done give us sitting in dust and dog shit. That's how I got started in life … living like that. Why? I seen how the Whites lived in town and around and, like, every damn morning when my eyes popped open I'd seen the way we lived and I'd think about it and wonder what I done to deserve it. It was my morning prayer in them days. Why'd you do this to me, Great Spirit, why? I'd ask. But I didn't wake up in no bed or nothing, 'cause we slept on the dirt floor rolled all up in blankets ... like goddamn dogs. I'd wake up and wonder why I wasn't White like all them rich Anglos in Santa Fe I seen doing so good. Most of 'em weren't that rich really ... some was ... most weren't ... they just seemed rich to me."

Kroner stared into the distance.

"I never did get no answer from the Great Spirit. See, I expected a loud-damn booming voice coming out of the clouds or something ... you know, like fucking Moses and all that stuff ... but that ain't how it works ... not at all ... you know that?"

"I don't know how it works."

"I wouldn't expect you to. See, the Great Spirit talks to us through other people ... that's how it works ... like me talking to you now ... but, I didn't know that then. I was just a stupid little puke and I was all angry, scared, and mixed up. I mean, I hated my damn life. Like one time my ole man come home drunk and all ... beat my mother up real bad and then beat the hell out of me when I tried to stop him and I got away and run off up here in the Jemez and hid for 'bout three days ... built a fire and didn't eat nothing hardly but a candy bar or two ... you know, and done a lot of thinking about stuff. While I was up here and all, I asked the Great Spirit to take my life ... just lift it from me ... let me leave this hell ... asked him to do that, but he wouldn't. The Great Spirit won't let you die when you really want to ... you know that ... unless it's the end and your time has really for sure come or something. So, he let me live and I didn't know why ... why he wanted me to live, I mean. So, I come home but the ole man was gone off again. He never did get sober ... died drunk like a stray gut-shot dog ... you know, howling and whimpering and shit ... puking up blood and cursing and crying and all that good crap that drunks'll do when the end has finally come down on their sorry ass ... and the bill's gotta be paid and all.

"After we buried him, I didn't know what was going to happen. I felt all alone and everything. I mean, my ole man was a no good tongue-tied drunk and it was good to get rid of him, but still I felt alone ... and sad ... sad for him and me ... like maybe I could have done something to help him and didn't ... because deep down in my guts I blamed myself and hated him and loved him and knew he couldn't help it and wondered maybe if I could-a made it right and all ... everything might of been different, you know ... but I didn't have no idea what'd be … but I still felt that way … all crazy and mixed up like. I didn't know what to do, so, I kinda hung around … helping Mother and Grandfather but I still didn't know why I was allowed to live … why the Great Spirit … had done give me this damn life in the first place … what I was supposed to do with it. That's what really bugged me … that question of why he let me live … nothing made no sense."

Realizing that they weren't leaving right away, Kroner shifted the rifle off one leg and on to the other and listened intently.

"Then one day Grandfather asked me to go into town with him in the wagon and all. I mean Grandfather was always good to me and spent time and taught me stuff … how to hunt … how to live in the wild … how to make drums and be aware of the sacred deer and the Great Spirit and everything. So, I was real glad to go with him and run and hitched our old horse to the wagon and we started out for Santa Fe together … just the two of us. Grandfather always told me stories and learnt me our language and never talked in English … just Pueblo. He was very old, even then, and he remembered the old days … even some buffalo … the last of 'em … lots of good things like when the Indian people still lived in the old way and everything … the real way, he said. I didn't have no father except for him. I remember us riding that day, up the dirt road where that damn freeway is now … the old road was better … it took all day and there was not no hurry or nothing … not like now when it's all hurry and you're still late no matter how damn fast you're going … then it was slow and good … you saw folks and waved … dogs barked at you and trotted with you for a while … you seen things then … smelled 'em … like the grass and the sweat from the ole horse … the leather … heard the harness jingle … the flies buzz and watched the clouds float across the sun real soft-like.

"Well, we finally got up to the Plaza and tied up and Grandfather went in to buy supplies. Well, I got away when he wasn't looking and went into that store that had everything. It's gone now, but then it was just off the Plaza. Course I didn't have no money nor nothing, but I just wanted to look at all that stuff in there. It blew my little Indian mind, it really did, looking at all that shit. I never got tired of looking at it all … them fancy clothes … and shiny new rifles and knifes … food … toys even … everything I wanted … I thought. Then I seen it. Candy. Red-and-white striped … like is common … you know how a kid is about candy. I mean, when it come to candy in them days, I was strangely insane."

Cripple Bear laughed. Kroner welcomed the opportunity and laughed too, though he wasn't sure why.

PHILLIP H. MCMATH

"What happened?" asked Kroner.

"Hell, I stole it," laughed Cripple Bear. "Then run out as fast as I could go. I never stole nothing before in my life, but man I wanted that damn candy something terrible, so I just up and stole it ... simple as that ... Jesus."

"And?"

"And, well, when I got back to the wagon, I hid in the back and stuffed it inside my shirt. Then when nobody come, I got up and sat on the seat like nothing was wrong till Grandfather come back. Which he done and we loaded up and headed home. When we got back, I snuck outside to eat it ... you know ... like an egg-sucking dog ... or coyote that done killed something and is trying to hide hisself ... you know tail down, ears back, and that humble shit-eating look on their face ... that was me ... see? But wasn't long before Grandfather missed me. I mean, he knowed me backards-and-forards and he felt something was up when I disappeared all of sudden ... like, see, I was always hanging around, so much he called me horsefly."

"Horsefly?"

"Sure, 'cause I was always buzzing around ... couldn't get rid of me."

They both laughed again.

"Well, anyway, I run and hid in a ditch near the house and started eating that damn red-and-white candy ... but Grandfather ... he come and found me in no time."

"What happened?"

"He was mad as all hell, I could see that clear enough, but he don't say nothing ... just takes it away and then tells me I'm a disgrace to the Indian people and everything; that we're an old and honorable tribe and that I had to make amends to them damn Whites. Boy that was tough! Wow! He meant to that shitty ole White man. I had to go into town and tell that ole bastard what I done and ask his pardon or I never would be free of it, he said ... it would never be right."

"That sounds tough."

"It was tough, William ... tough as hell ... but he was right, of course; it was the right thing. Grandfather knew how to live, how to do it right and all ... it was natural to him. Me, hell, I had to learn everything the hard way. But, really, that wasn't the worst part, the worst part was his shunning me."

"Shunning?"

"Yeah, shunning."

"Gosh."

"See, I didn't want to do it and said I wouldn't. Doing the thing we need to do is always hard ... at first ... it can be a simple thing, but we hate to do it. But he knew what I needed even though I didn't, so, till I'd made it right he wouldn't say nothing, like I was contaminated or something, like killing a bear, and needing purification and everything. Till I'd done gone through the purification, he wasn't having nothing to do with me ... like I was filled up with evil spirits. I mean, I wished he had whupped hell outta me and gotten done with it. This shunning and amends stuff was a thousand times worse, but he never done that ... he never whupped me or touched me in a mean way at all ... never ... not once ... my ole man done that and I resented the hell out of it ... but Grandfather always done things the right way ... he just knew how ... always knew the right thing to do and how to do it just right ... I wanted to be like him and do things that way too ... that was what he was trying to teach me, see, how to live ... that's the hardest and most important thing there is ... just learning how to live, you know, William, is the only thing that's really important in this damn world."

"What happened?"

"We left the next morning ... early ... to go back and say I'm sorry to that goddamn White man. I lay awake all night dreading it. Jesus ... it was terrible ... no shit. Then we got up just before daylight and hitched the ole horse up again, like we done the day before, but this time in quiet. He wouldn't say nothing, just hitched the horse ... without no words ... the horse seemed sad, Grandfather was sad and I was sadder'n hell, I'll tell you that much. Then we set out for town. No flies buzzed, no dogs barked, no other kids come out and yelled at us nor nothing ... even the clouds seemed gray and sad and all ... and the horse walked like he was tired before we even got started ... like he knew all about it and everything. I mean it was like a damn funeral or something. I ain't never felt that bad in my whole life ... not even later when I got drunk and woke up in jail or face down in my own vomit feeling like warmed-over-dog-death ... worse even than that ole tired shit. I loved Grandfather more than anything in this world and knowed I'd done let him down and all. You ever felt like that, William?"

"Some."

"Yeah? Well, that's what the hell it's like, man, hurting someone you love and feeling like because of it you done ruined it all and they aren't going to love you no more ... killing their love ... getting drunk and sick and screwed up is a piece of cake compared to that."

"I believe you."

"Good, I'm glad you do."

"So ... what happened?"

"Well, we finally got to town and all ... I mean, it took a hundred forevers ... see, 'cause all I wanted was to get it over with, man. But, when we got there and all, well, I asked Grandfather if he'd go in with me but he wouldn't ... no-way-José ... said I had to do the amends all on my very lonesome ... there was no choice. Boy did that scare the living shit out of me, no kidding. See, I thought all along he was going in with me and back me up kinda like ... but he wouldn't do that no matter how much I begged him ... man, did I beg ... but no dice, I had to go it alone. I wanted an easier, softer way, see, but he says I stole the candy on my own and would just have to return it the same way ... the hard way is the best ... always is ... it's real simple but real hard ... but it's the only way that works ... really."

There was a pause.

"And?"

Tony shifted his rifle a little, then said, "Shit, I had to go in...with Grandfather waiting in the wagon while I went, you know, real slow and painful like, then I go through this creaky old door ... but there wasn't nobody there or nothing, which kinda surprised me, nothing ever really happens like you think it's going to and like I thought there would be a gang of bad-ass Whites in a posse ... or something ... awaiting just to string my Red ass up with a rope. I thought that maybe they'd hang me from the rafters. I could see myself, clear as day, a swinging back and forth with a big yellow noose around my neck ... my eyes a-popping out like blueberries and all, a-pissing and shitting on myself as they choked the life out of one more sorry-ass goddamn thieving Indian. But there weren't nobody there, and I just walked around a long time and couldn't find nobody ... could've stole the whole damn store and even thought of going back and lying to Grandfather but I knew he'd know ... you couldn't fool him about nothing. Finally, I found this old bastard. Man, he was ten feet tall, ugly, and meaner'n shit, just waiting for me and he come over with this bodacious goddamn look on his face and looks down at me and says, 'Well, whattaya want, Injun?' Hell, I just about messed my pants ... couldn't say nothing ... just froze ... the words choking back down inside me and everything ... and he asks again ... still, I couldn't say nothing ... words just wouldn't come ... so, I holds up this half-eaten, sick-ass-looking piece of red-and-white-striped candy in the palm of my dirty little Indian boy hand ... he looks at it for a moment and then yells lounder'n hell, 'Damn you! You little Injun son-of-a-bitches stealing again!' Then he snatches at the candy like it was gold or something and I jerked back as quick as a rattlesnake and the candy hit the floor and the old bastard tried to sock me but it's too late 'cause I was beating feet ... and him after me and I could feel his nasty breath and knew he was reaching for me with his big ole harry-ass paws so he could cut me up with a knife and feed me to his Indian-hating dogs or something. But I'm too scared ... out run him ... hitting the door in a panic till I get to Grandfather and I run and jump in the wagon and try to hide but he makes me sit up there with him because he says there ain't no reason to be scared or ashamed no more. And the old White man come out and rants and raves and cusses like the roof of hell done caved in and he's an escaped devil or something ... shakes his fist and makes all kind of damn threats ... but Grandfather he just ignores him and we ride slowly outta town with me sitting there by Grandfather."

Without asking, Cripple Bear reached into Kroner's day pack, rummaged around until he found the canteen, unscrewed the top, drank, then handed it to Kroner, who did the same.

"Then what happened?" asked Kroner.

"Well, I started to cry, you know ... mad and afraid ... and I guess a little relief too about having the whole damn thing over with, but Grandfather told me not to ... that we'd done right ... that we'd done it for us and not for really anyone else ... that he didn't really care at all what that old bastard thought, or anyone else for that matter, but that we had to get rid of it and the only way to do that was what we done ... and it was then that I understood and quit crying and got happier and happier because I realized that Grandfather was right ... was pleased with me and loved me ... that I was forgiven. It was good trip back ... the sun come out and things buzzed around and kids yelled at us and even the ole horse seemed to pick up. I got prouder each step he took ... swelling with pride and feeling good. I was like I had been took into town for a hanging and was given a pardon at the very last damn second ... you know, just when they're about to string a guy up and a miracle happens. William, that was the greatest moment in my life."

Kroner smiled.

There was a long silence, then Cripple Bear said, "Guess we better go, huh?" and stood up.

"Sure," said Kroner, following his example.

"We'll eat, then head for the Frazier canyon this afternoon ... okay?"

"Fine."

"There's some monsters in there, man," said Cripple Bear, turning, walking slowly into the trees, disappearing down a faint trail through the forest.

Kroner stood, hurriedly shouldered his pack and rifle, glanced into the valley, then turned and followed.

PHILLIP H. MCMATH

The jay flew from out of nowhere, hopping down to where they had been sitting, looking at the spot curiously.

The brakes seemed to squeak an octave near the upper range of human hearing as the battered pickup inched down the mountain. The road was a series of dirt curves winding between a thousand-foot drop on the right and "The Dome" (a mountain peak like the bald head of an aging giant) on the other. Cripple Bear pumped the brakes, talking incessantly, wrestling the steering wheel then pulling the gear shift into low range as the Dodge moaned like a wounded beast. The grinding of the gear box was a counterpoint to the brakes, like a base complementing a soprano in a screeching out-of-tune duet.

"Yeah, well ... later, I got drafted right outta Indian School," yelled Cripple Bear, resuming his story without any prompting.

"Drafted?" asked Kroner, yelling back.

"Hell yes ... I didn't know what they done to me."

Then he seemed to lose control, the wheel spun away and the truck lurched toward the cliff, the right front tire hanging partially in the air. Cripple Bear jerked it back, cursing.

"Jesus Christ!" shouted Kroner.

"No problem," said Cripple Bear.

Kroner fished nervously around in his pack for the pint of *Ancient Age*, took a slug, then offered it to Cripple Bear, who waved it off.

"Not today."

Kroner took another hit and put it back.

"Shit ... like I said ... I got drafted right out of damn Indian School and all ... didn't know what they done to me or nothing, so I carried them papers up to the Indian Agent and he says, 'Tony, your soul may be God's but your ass is Uncle Sam's.'"

He laughed.

"Shit, William, I had to ask who Uncle Sam was ... but they snatched me up, man ... just like that," he said, taking a hand off the wheel and making a noiseless snap of the fingers, then quickly gripping the wheel again.

"The next thing I knowed, I was prime inspected U.S. grade-A, I was."

Kroner wished the whisky would hurry as he looked over the edge into the canyon.

"Put on the bus to Albuquerque ... a proud member of the U.S. Army."

"What did you do then?" asked Kroner.

"The first thing I done was go to a crazy-ass head-shrinker doctor ..."

"A psychiatrist?"

"Yeah, they thought I was fucking nuts. I kinda was, but not the way they figured," Cripple Bear said, laughing with wry satisfaction.

"Why'd they do that?"

"Well ...," said Cripple Bear, gearing up then back down, as they lurched too fast around a curve, with the valley now looming up like an airfield. Kroner's stomach turned and he fumbled for the bottle again.

"Anyway ...," said Cripple Bear, as he straightened out for the last sharp incline, reduced power, and glided in. "It's just that I ain't never slept on no bed like that before ... you know ... one of them real soft whatchamacallits ...."

"Whatchamacallits?"

"Yeah, thing you sleep on ... softer'n hell?"

"Mattress?"

"That's it ... mattress ... one of them ... I couldn't sleep on it ... no way ... too soft, man, so I slept under it ... under the bed ... you know, on the floor and all."

"Under the damn bed?"

"Right ... on the floor ... it was fine ... slept great."

"You slept on the floor ... under your bed ... on the concrete?"

"Sure ... it was just like at home. We didn't have none on the reservation and it was just too damn soft ... so ... I slept on the floor ... to get some rest ... I mean I had tried the ... whatchamacallit."

"Mattress."

"Sorry, I only got two brain cells left ... one for running my innards and the other for talking to you."

Kroner laughed nervously.

"Any for driving?"

"What?" yelled Cripple Bear.

"You got a brain cell left for driving?" he shouted over the engine noise.

"Oh, yeah, musta miscounted ... I must have three. But I done tried it and couldn't do it. So, they sent me to this weird-ass goddamn head-shrinker fella."

"What'd he say?"

"He made a few passes over me real cool and everything ... like they'll do and all, you know ... then asked me some stupid-ass questions and everything like whether I'd rather sleep with my mother or my sister ... sick shit like that ... then he told me I wasn't crazy or nothing after all but they was going to think I was unless I learned to sleep on the whatchamacallits."

"Mattress."

"Yeah ... mattress."

"Did you?"

"It took some doing, but I done it. I was beat-to-shit for the longest, though, you know, snoring in them classes and everything like that. I couldn't get no damn sleep," he said as the wheels touched down to a smooth landing, coasting along a dusty road billowing yellow dust behind like a great exhaust.

Cripple Bear now shifted into high and sped up, steering with two fingers, elbow out the window, as they sped through the desert. Suddenly it was hot.

"Then ... well, after I done learned to sleep on that bed thing ... they took me out and asked me to look at stuff ... you know, out in the boonies, all covered up and camouflaged. Man, I seen it all. Then they asked me if I wanted to be a Green Beret. Hell, I'd never heard of it, so they told me it was a way of making more money. I said 'why not' and the next thing I knowed I was jumping out of airplanes with a wad of silk on my back. Then they figured out that I could learn a language since I talk Pueblo, English, and some Spanish, so they sent me to this school and learned me Vietnamese ... which I done pretty good ... then ... shit, I turned around and found myself in Viet-fucking-Nam working with them little ARVNs ... you know, looking like kids in them damn helmets we give'em that was way too big for 'em and all ..."

"Vietnam?" asked Kroner, interrupting.

"Yeah ... you make that one?"

"No ... a touch too young."

"When I got there things was just kindly starting. I was an advisor. It was okay ... no shit, not that bad ... out in the boonies a lot. I kinda liked it ... you know, away from all the army Mickey Mouse and everything. Then one day we got off by ourselves and got fucking ambushed ... me and three other Berets and a bunch of worthless Marvin-the-ARVNs ... got our asses handed to us in a big way. I kept trying to tell'em we was fixing to buy the farm, man. I could feel it in my Indian bones. One Beret died in the fight and the rest of us got captured. The gooks killed our wounded captain, 'cause he couldn't keep up, took him off in the bushes ... we heard the shot ... boy was that a bastard ... him screaming and everything ... pleading with them commie bastards. Shit, I'll never forget that ... got drunk lots of times over them screams. But after walking for a couple of million days they put us in a hooch in the jungle near Laos, some-fucking-place ... then me and this Navajo from Arizona escaped. I hid a piece of wire in my boot and got away by sawing through the bamboo at night. Two of our Anglo Beret buddies got out with us. But we split up. We never seen them fellas again … never heard nothing. But me and my Navajo buddy went for days hiding and snooping-and-pooping. We was pretty good at it.

"One night a gook patrol come right by us … we could hear 'em talking and all … smell 'em first. The little shits smell like sardines … strong as hell, man. Then finally … we run into a bunch of trigger-happy Marines. They seen us … you know, two skinny-ass Indians in black pajamas … they come within a deuce of blowing us away. No shit, that was the first time we'd been shot at since we run off. Boy, was I yelling all kinds of crazy shit that only an American would know … about baseball, movies, and shit like that. We finally got them all settled down and everything … they was scared as be-Jesus … and their officer, a lieutenant, he heard our story and he said we was heroes and all … and then we got back and the army sent me to another weird-ass shrink-doctor and this time he said I was crazy sure nuff. It may sound funny, but I was kinda relieved, you know. I mean, this time he was right.

"I got shipped home … got a medical, had some money and pretty much stayed drunk and had to check in the VA time or two … you know, to detox … shaking like a dog shitting plum seeds; then I got sober and went off to Alaska. I worked on the pipeline … that was good money and good work … but I got drunk in Fairbanks … don't know why really … just wanted to drink … it's nuts, man, this alcoholism trip … blacked out … lost my money… boocoo dollars … thousands I'd made. It wasn't nothing new for me. I was always spending money I didn't have on shit I didn't need, you know … on folks I didn't like. I come home broke … had to borrow money to get back … then got a little job in Santa Fe … stayed sober … but got drunk again and lost the job. I could stop for awhile … drinking that is … I could always do that … stop, I mean … I stopped about five times one morning. It was the starting that was getting me."

Kroner laughed and Cripple Bear laughed, and they both laughed together.

Then he resumed. "I couldn't stop starting … see … you can always quit … but how about the starting? That's the hard part, so, shit, I basically stayed drunk … all the damn time … wound up in the VA a couple more times … with the fucking DTs, man … then out again … then in again … doing the same ole shit over and over but hoping for different results. I resented every-body and everything. It was all their fault, see … always them … blamed all of them for everything … but nobody was as bad to me as I was. If someone'd been as bad to me as I was to myself, hell, I'd killed 'em. My buddy the Navajo was still drunk, too … off in Arizona … I wanted to get sober but didn't know how. I was lost. I 'bout died wanting to get sober. I went to see him and he was dying wanting to get sober. I could see it. Jesus, all we done and gone through in 'Nam ... just to die drunk ... didn't make no damn sense. Then I realized, dying drunk is terrible but living drunk is worse. He died that way... drunk I mean ... and I wanted to die, too, and couldn't ... so, shit, I just kinda give up ... surrendered ... figured I had to live ... couldn't fight no more. The shit had whipped my Red ass, man. So, started going to them meetings in Santa Fe and all ... boy, I didn't want to ... never wanted to do that shit ... but I didn't have no choice. Today I'm sober. I mean, I didn't get it at first or nothing ... it took me a while, slipping in and out and all, it was hard for me ... it's real simple but real hard too ... but I done it. It's a lot easier living sober than trying to get sober. I never want to have to do that again ... not sure I got another one in me ... so, I done everything they said. It was simple but at first things didn't get no better, don't misunderstand, but I did ... in time ... I got better ... worked hard at it because I wanted it more than anything in the goddamn world. I got a little job again ... took up guiding Anglos like you who want to fish and hunt and selling shit to tourists at rip-off prices in town ... and here we are my friend ... driving along talking about it. Ain't it strange how it all works? Ain't it strange?"

As they drove with dust blowing in the open windows and desert heat replacing the cool mountain air it was hard to remember being so cold only that morning. The Dodge leveled off at about sixty miles an hour, seemingly its top speed. Another truck full of waving, smiling Indians passed, going in the opposite direction, disappearing into an impenetrable cloud of brown dust.

Then Cripple Bear turned to Kroner.

"Man ... I'm sorry ... hope I didn't bend your ear too hard."

"Well," said Kroner, not knowing what to say, "now it must seem better to you, though, huh ... the past is the past, right?"

"No, man ... I long since quit trying to have a better past."

Kroner looked away for a time, then back, asking: "What are your plans for the future?"

"Plans? Man, I don't never make no plans. That's something I ain't got ... and don't need ... you want to give the stars a big laugh, go out there some clear night, high on a mountain somewheres, like on the Dome over there," he pointed out the window, "go by your lonesome and everything and share your plans with them stars. Ha! They'll run laughing all the way back to goddamn China and tell the sun just to make his day ... and the moon'll fall right in behind, splitting his sides. Today is all I can deal with ... or need ... today ...

me and you hunting … and me sober … them's my plans. Today is tomorrow's yesterday and I don't want to regret it by worrying about tomorrow. I stayed drunk one day at a time. I can live sober one-day-at-a-time, too. Plans I ain't got, my friend, except maybe for lunch 'cause I'm getting hungry … how about you?"

"Yeah … sure."

"The women should have something ready when we get there."

There was another long silence. Kroner had the uneasy feeling that everything he said, Cripple Bear had heard somewhere before and had an answer, like a good hitter who had seen all the pitches.

"I told you my story … how 'bout yours?" Cripple Bear said finally.

Kroner laughed nervously, facing Cripple Bear, saying, "It's not as interesting, I'm afraid."

"They're all interesting."

Kroner pulled himself up, paused, then said, "Okay … well … I was … am … was … a farm boy from South Dakota … long line of mostly Germans … farmers … who came there after the Civil War looking for land. I didn't want to do that … farm, that is … I wanted to see the world, as they say. I had what my father would call 'romantic ideas and such' … he was always saying that … 'and such' … 'such as that' … used to get on my nerves … anyway … I had, according to my tough old man … a stubborn Dutchman, as I sometimes heard said of him … even though he wasn't Dutch but German. He said I had such ideas and he was right. I wanted to get off the plains … away from that hard damn farm work … away from the snow stuff … you know the dream … see the world. I went to college, then did some graduate work in what they call 'Asian Studies,' from there I signed on with the government."

"Doing what?"

"Foreign service … consul's office … in Hong Kong … my first job … boy was I excited about that," said Kroner, wistfully. "Seems like a couple million light years away."

"Jesus!"

"Yeah, you went to Viet Nam and I went to China … or a piece of it."

"Doing what?"

"Bureaucrat … messing around with tourists mostly."

"Like it?"

"Hong Kong?"

"Yeah … your job?"

"For a while," said Kroner.

"Then what?"

"I burned out."

"Burned out?"

"Right."

Pause.

"It didn't take long," said Cripple Bear.

"No ... it didn't."

"Something happened, huh?"

"Sure."

There was another pause.

Cripple Bear held the wheel with his left hand, shifting down quickly with his right, going around a curve, then shifting up again, saying, "I know what you mean ... about burning out and all ... that's what happened to me ... about everything ... got sick-and-tired of being sick-and-tired."

"What'd you do?" asked Kroner.

"Changed."

"Me too."

"Oh, yeah? How'd you do?"

"I quit," said Kroner.

"Nothing else?"

"That was enough."

"You sure?"

"It was for me," said Kroner, sticking to his guns.

Pause.

"Nothing changes till things gets real," pronounced Cripple Bear.

"That's true ... I like that."

"The pain's gotta get bad enough ... no pain no change ... right?"

"Right," agreed Kroner.

"Everything is like that ..."

"I just did what I had to ..."

"That's always better than doing what you can ... doing what you can is never enough," said Cripple Bear with self-assurance.

Kroner paused again, like he had just struck out. It was obvious he was over-matched. But he bored back in. "Well, I came home and fooled around some ... then thought I'd come out here and do a little hunting. So here I am, Tony ... riding along with you talking about it all."

Kroner turned, smiling at Cripple Bear, who seemed to be concentrating on the road.

"What are you hunting for, William?" asked Cripple Bear, finally looking at Kroner as they hit a straight stretch leading to the top of a small mesa set like a giant table across the horizon. "I don't think it's deer."

"A man," said Kroner quietly. "I'm looking for a man."

"I thought so," Cripple Bear said quietly.

Another truck whirled by. Cripple Bear waved. Then they topped the big mesa. The village was below, squatting on a little rise just west of the Río Grande behind which the Sangre de Cristo Mountains lifted their snowy-white heads to meet the sun. It reminded William Kroner of a painting he had seen somewhere and couldn't quite place.

BOOK THREE

CHAPTER SIX

"The dead govern the living."
—Comte

There had been a house on a hill in northern Mississippi, in what people there sometimes call "the hills" (Yoknapatawpha), not far from western Tennessee where Nora had moved from after the Civil War and her marriage to grandfather. Elizabeth had thought her grandmother's house large when it really wasn't. But to a little girl it was indeed large. In a town of few stores and houses, a dilapidated gin, a filling station, and a white-framed Baptist church, the house sat under a large oak that was green in the summer and bare and gray in the winter. There was a gravel road leading up, circling another tree making a loop at the top like the open end of a gigantic lock to which only her memory held the key. A car stopping at the top of this loop was but a step from the front door on one side and a small sandbox on the other. The sandbox was pushed against the tree—two-by-fours propped at angles with its golden sand in the middle—half sunken in its dunes were toys—an old green, metal tractor with rubber tires surrounded by plastic cowboys with broken arms or legs and Indians with broken feathers, raised tomahawks, and missing arrows. There was a rusty shovel and a pale to pour sand and a pink, naked doll with a missing plastic eye—things from the five-and-dime in a larger town nearby where the courthouse was, the movie show, the dentist's, the doctor's, the square of stores, and a funeral home.

In August 1932 Elizabeth's grandfather was laid out and made-up with rouge and powder, which she tasted when she kissed his cold head, bitter and not like his taste or smell at all but just a painted-up doll; when she finished, a Black man came dressed in clean overalls and polished black shoes. The next day he was at the church, too, waiting outside the fence in a warm rain, till they carried her grandfather-doll into the graveyard and covered him with mud. Then the Black man left and she never saw him again. (She remembered his cigar, hidden outside on a wall, unlit, soggy; left from courtesy, then picked up on the way out.)

If you stepped out one side of the car you stepped into the sandbox, if you stepped out the other, you were at a side-door—screened with a worn-out spring that managed to snap shut and you had to walk through without a porch. Here, at the door, it smelled strong and green in the warm months.

There were always hedges and flowers and that smell—especially then. There was something about the heat that brought out this odor in a strange, pungent, sweet way that flowers have.

Elizabeth's grandmother always worked hard on the flowers and hedges, on her knees with a little spade, wearing a pink straw hat like a sombrero. In fact, she worked hard all the time it seemed, just like Elizabeth's own mother, her daughter. Getting up before first light to cook, serve breakfast, wash, do chores, cook, do more chores, work in the flower or vegetable gardens, then cook and serve, eat and go to bed after reading the Bible, just like her daughter would do later, and just like Elizabeth swore that she would never do, marrying a rich planter and having servants who became her only real friends, working and talking together, living every day, then getting old herself and working just for pleasure and habit, but not like her mother or grandmother had worked, not like that. She never wanted to work like that—and didn't.

Once you were inside you entered what to Elizabeth was a secret world—titanic and indestructible. It was a living room that had no hall, which made you realize you had come through a wall, with a few wooden chairs turned round a stone fireplace and tattered couch. There were a few books and magazines stacked over against a piano stuck in a corner where her grandmother would play hymns on Sunday. It was always a little dark and it smelled warm and like Grandfather had smelled when he was alive. She could still smell him there—sweat, tobacco, and a hint of sweet—a cheap lotion from Memphis mixed with coffee, sugar, and some nice something from the local store. It seemed he was still there somewhere, would walk in any moment or come through the door and pick her up and kiss her; she would smell his hot neck and feel his rough bare, but always slightly whiskered, chin against her soft face—not under the clay where she couldn't find him anymore—before they made him into a doll—where she looked for him still, not there, but here, where she would take him by the hand and show him off to her friends who came and to others, explaining that was not what happened to people at all, that he was still there because she could still smell him.

People do not just disappear Elizabeth decided, and she would teach everyone, indeed, the whole world, that this was true. People did not just vanish at all—that couldn't be, no, not at all, that couldn't be at all. She would find all the dead and bring them to life again, which she vowed would be her life's great task.

PHILLIP H. MCMATH

Above the fireplace was a picture of a half-naked Indian scout sitting on a pony, straddling a dark red blanket, staring over a plain out West somewhere. Elizabeth would sit on the couch and watch the scout for hours and wonder what he was thinking and would talk about him with Grandfather. She never solved the secret of the Indian's mystery as he sat on his paint, astride a blanket, moccasined legs hanging down from it—maybe one like the Yankee cavalry stole from Grandmother Nora during the Civil War, when she was a little girl growing up on Arcadia. The Indian brave staring over the evening horizon of the plains—a country vast and empty except for some strange lights in the east. She wondered about the lights and what they meant—perhaps they were the key to the puzzle. Someday she would go out West and understand the mystery of the Indian's mind. And when she did she would find Grandfather and tell him—explain it all—they would sit and talk again like they had when she was a little girl, and she would sit on his lap in the big house, and he would tell her stories, about his boyhood, playing a game with Choctaws, using sticks, speaking their tongue in a melodious low chortling voice, like he said when she asked what they sounded like—like water running in a stream, he said, running softly over rocks. He talked about hunting in the virgin timber of the Mississippi Delta, "putting by" his cotton crop and going off into the big woods with a team of mules, a wagon, and a friend, living for a month or more and searching for those legendary Delta deer and black bear that grow grander and more legendary with time like everything else in the past—living like the Indians who had hunted in that paradise for an eternity before it was ruined by the Whites when De Soto came through and everything was changed forever. He told about the time he got lost and had to drink swamp water and eat squirrel, rabbit, and duck till he found his way back to camp with the help of a young man who wandered around those woods in overalls, barefoot, hunting, who knew the way—and she would ask him endless questions, kiss those cheeks with the strong smells of cologne, tobacco, and the something else she could not describe and never smelled again but always searched for.

Once, after Grandfather had died, Elizabeth wrote him a letter on her fourteenth birthday—sentimental, the kind a girl her age would write to a dead loved one.

> Dearest, Precious Grandpa,
>
>   It's my fourteenth birthday and my second without you. It's not a particularly special day to miss you even though it's my birthday and you always remembered it, because I miss you just as much every

single day of my life. And every day that passes I miss you and feel my love and grief for my loss of you. You gave me so much and have made my life so happy because of the gifts that you gave me that I wanted to write you and thank you for all these wonderful things. What happiness I have comes from you—thank you, thank you, thank you, Grandpa.

I try to have faith and believe with all my heart that you are somewhere safe and happy and that you are aware of things and content with them and can read this letter. I don't know how, really, but I feel that this must be true or things just don't make any sense, so I believe this with all my heart for your sake and mine and everyone's sake too.

I remember our time together, those last years at your home in Mississippi, in that big old house that you and Grandma Nora had under the green shade tree on a hill with a driveway and sand box out front and cows and chickens and a barn out back, when we used to come visit and especially in the summer—what fun that was and how happy we were together then as a family and Mama and Dad were young and you and Grandma Nora were healthy. It was a special time and when I marry I want to find a man just like you and if he's not like you I won't be happy, but then I will have grandchildren and will love them in a special way like you loved me and I will somehow pay my debt to you, Grandpa. I owe you so much.

I'm doing good in school—and I know you would be proud. I'll show you my report card when I get it soon. I have to go now. I love you.

Your Loving Granddaughter,
Elizabeth

She would write many such sentimental letters until she was married and somehow the having of her family changed things. But she still had them, the letters, and would look at them from time to time, but could not bring herself to read. It seemed odd to her that she should write to her dead grandfather, and she was a little bit embarrassed and kept it a secret, but then she found out that others did this and that she was not crazy after all and sometimes she would share this, not the letters which she showed no one, but that she had written them.

A friend had allowed that this was good "therapy" for her, but she never thought of it in that clinical way. Somehow that word did not seem to fit. So she clung to the belief that the letters were read by Grandfather even though she simply put them away and kept them hidden in a small white shoebox under her bed, and now in a closet, in shoeboxes—too painful to read or to throw away.

Her grandparents' house was like an old theater that had closed and was boarded up over the tatters of faded playbills. She returned but it was not the same—nothing was. The structure was there. It sat in the same place under the big green tree, but it was not there. Not even the tree was really there. Everything had been folded up by some unseen hand and put away in the musty trunk of memory. Everything was like that. Hands gathered them up, held the colored props before the mirrors of the mind in a shimmering image—reflecting back before an eye that wanted desperately to touch them, reaching out but touching nothing; having them tricked away like smoke—a thousand fires of heat and smoke drifting away in a magic theater of mirrors, then hidden again.

To the right of the door was a dining room, big to her, but really small, with a large brown wooden table and chairs around and shelves behind Grandmother Nora's empty chair. That day the table was covered in food, enormous plates of it, everywhere, a room filled with people eating, people in the kitchen, in the living room, and out on the front screened-in porch—talking and eating—talking, eating, and laughing.

Through the dining room was the kitchen and in its cupboards were knives, forks, dippers, spoons, plates, pans, pots of all shapes, a bone saw with heavy ragged teeth like a great shark. There were endless cans of vegetables, corn, flour, spices, butter, bread, jam, grease, and sorghum in sealed silver paint buckets from cane ground by a circling mule, walking slowly round and round in a patch of timber, not far from a cornfield, a spring and another little stand of "scrub oak" and cotton fields and the sharecrop "Nigra shacks."

On one side of the kitchen was an iron monster—a black, greasy, sooty stove that sat dormant like a cold, dead star—inert for eons. It was wood-burning and would glow with so much heat that Elizabeth could scarce stay in the kitchen as it consumed forest upon forest inside and flesh on top for people who talked and laughed when she thought they shouldn't to sustain their flesh—flesh to flesh—flesh sustaining itself with flesh—life to death—death to life—a kind of immortality.

To the right of the woodstove was a sink, white with chips of black, hip level beneath a window presenting a view of the backyard, the meadow, and the barn. A tree shaded the south and defended the house from the sun. Between the sink and stove a door led to a hall and out the front or back, to the barn or to the porch where people stood and laughed and talked over a little girl's grief.

In the hallway, a stairway led to an attic—a dark place with a large bed, narrow passageways, crammed-full closets, half-known corners, overflowing boxes, and unexplained, supernatural sounds. Elizabeth would never go there alone and refused to sleep there with anyone but a parent. By day it was filled with a quiet foreboding and by night it exuded a dark terror unbroken even by a nightlight or any other kind of grown-up rational assurances. Elizabeth knew ghosts were there—living here among the living and she wanted to talk with them.

Ascending the stair was for her a passage from one world to the next—the world of light and life to that of darkness—breaking the close.

Down the attic stair and into the hall she fell under the gaze of a deer head, taken from those Mississippi Delta forests, hanging with its sad but frighteningly ironic brown-marble eyes, footing the steps like a spirit of transition. Would it show her the way? Mark the line between what was both feared and wanted. Elizabeth saw it as a frozen angel or spirit—a horned-head wraith that was standing watch—disturbing—listening to her very thoughts. Sometimes she saw its face when she shut her eyes and would open them yet still see the horned face smiling at her and listening. If she had known the word "exorcise," she would have used it. She would have absolved herself of these terrible feelings and urges within her heart that seemed to be growing stronger and stronger with each day—emanating from the animal's ineffable power. She was vaguely aware that something was slowly taking control of her, and she was afraid but glad.

Elizabeth came to feel more and more that she was governed by some great fatality, or force without a name, rushing over her like an unseen storm, blowing everything in one direction, taking her along in the darkness, revealing the bare roots of regret in the morning sun of each's day's awakening. It would be the boy—the field—the passion—the dead daughter lying in a box, cold under her mother's smothering kisses. But the deer knew the thing's name, could see it but would not tell her, smiling with his terrible knowledge ironically, looking like a seer in the service of some mysteriously powerful deity.

Coming through this day she watched the creature watching her and fled into the bedroom where she was startled by a black dress crumpled on her grandmother's bed—it was inert, lying there in a curl like a sleeping cat—visible in the shadows of this half-lit room. It was, indeed, her grandmother lying in a Sunday dress, sleeping it seemed, but she knew it wasn't so, that she was not sleeping, merely wishing for sleep, as her brown and flecked-gray hair fell in over the pillow, hiding her face and neck in a wave of grief.

Elizabeth slipped by, tiptoeing till she reached a small room which was through the opposite corner door. She threw herself on the bed, resting on the starchy pillow, staring at the ceiling. To her this was a rich house, a mansion, and she always felt very special here, like a princess in a story, even now on this funereal afternoon. As she looked at the ceiling she vowed that someday she would have a grand house too—all her own—for her children to grow up in and feel special about.

She rolled over and looked out the window. The morning had come and gone with a sweltering rain—it was a hot afternoon. Flies hit the screen gently, lazily, as if for their own amusement—a slight breeze stirred in the shade tree standing between house and garden. It was a big garden and sometimes Grandmother would have a Negro come with a mule and plow it in the spring. He would be barefooted, wearing baggy blue overalls and no shirt, handling the plow like a toy and bending the mule to his will like a large docile dog. Elizabeth loved to hear him talking to the mule in a low, easy voice like a father to a child, calling him by name, "geeing" and "hawing," clicking his tongue, lifting and lowering the plow, making the tack rattle, man and animal working in a steady, efficient harmony. The garden was fenced to keep out chickens, turkeys, cows, various town curs and other varmints. Sometimes a snake would get in or a possum—once there had even been a red fox slinking behind the cabbages, stopping, their eyes meeting, transfixing her with a look she would never forget as if he knew the thing the deer knew but would not tell her either.

Grandmother always raised corn, greens, tomatoes, squash, peas, okra, turnips, beans, and fox-hiding cabbages. There was a milk cow and eggs from chickens and usually a hog or steer killed, butchered and brought from Grandfather's farm that was not far—just over the hill—past a patch of woods and down a dirt road. Mother told Elizabeth that was where they had lived when they got married. So, this big house was considered "new," even though it seemed so very old.

Mother was in another room talking with the others. The laughter had been hers. Elizabeth stared through the window at the back fence. She smelled the manure mixed with the yellow bitterweed mingling all together in the air, seeping through, gently touching her face, and it felt good.

Grandmother Nora was bedded with her sorrow and the others were laughing and talking while Elizabeth smelled the slight, sticky breeze and listened to the flies hitting the screen. There were always flies. There was a barn and everyone was careful with the screen doors, but barns meant flies.

Then somebody's dog barked nervously in the distance, a chicken clucked under her window while just out of sight a car ground over gravel, stopped, then darted across the road.

Did Grandfather hear these things? How could he not? The flies were real, the breeze was real, the dog, the chicken, and the cow were all very real, so why couldn't he hear them and smell them just like Elizabeth did in this moment? She inched closer to the screen, almost touching it. She thought she could smell the hen that clucked even louder. Elizabeth looked down till her eyes hurt but she could not see the chicken.

She closed her eyes, felt the breeze and the sun, heard the hen—then the world vanished into nothingness.

The sound of the chicken and the buzzing, ever-assiduous flies at last dropped her into the sweet arms of sleep. Breathing heavily she drooled slowly on the starched pillow and everything faded away—the flies went away, the chicken, the sun and the breeze, everything simply vanished. The house, even the black Model-T they came from Arkansas in—Grandmother Nora, whose blanket was stolen by those evil Yankee soldiers that terrible day at Arcadia; the people laughing in the next room; her puppy at home—even her grief—all were gone—absolved. Her father and mother, their house in the mountain woods, the woods themselves, even the mountains, the rusty bucket, the toys in the sand and the broken, one-eyed pink doll with beautiful golden hair—all would fade.

But, awake, today, as it always did, for a moment at least, everything seemed real: Conrad, the cemetery, her son's grave, the bottomland forest and its heavy smell; all were real, as Elizabeth Shaw sat on a blanket, leaned against the oak, stared at a gravestone, ate the peach, and read yet again the inscription.

CHRISTOPHER M. SHAW
1945–1969
Killed in Action—Vietnam
1st. Lt.-USMC

And his epitaph:

> For now we see through a glass, darkly;
> But then face-to-face: now I know in part;
> But then shall I know even as also I am known.

CHAPTER SEVEN

"I will soon be out of this world of sorrow and trouble."
—David O. Dodd

Useless inched Nora's mother and brother into Little Rock. He plodded them along the Old Coach Road, a segment of the Southwest Trail, linking St. Louis with Texas. The railroads played little part in this frontier system of trails, cuts, tracks, fords, ferries, improvised crossings, bypasses, and bewildering, half-seen pathways meandering through mountains, heavy woods, placid swamps, and clear, fast-moving creeks and muddy rivers, finding or losing themselves into the spilling squalor of small but ever-growing towns, farms, flatland plantations, and mountain log cabins of Civil War Arkansas.

In a word, it was steamboat, stage, horse, and foot country. The "Rock" was little more than a village, a collection of slatternly buildings perched on a patch of high ground above a long, turgid, now totally frozen, eastward-moving Arkansas River.

There were, of course, offices, hotels, saloons, shops, stables, and stores squatting around a T-shaped pair of streets. Markham was at the top, enjoying herself as a small but busy bend in the Trail, squirming along south of the river, where she begat wharves, docks, and warehouses, all spilling forth in the service of steamboats, barges, and an assortment of boats darting around like busy waterbugs. Nearby, a polite but superior neighbor, Main Street, thrust forward supporting the roof of the T like a center post, opening it up for horse, stage, and foot traffic. At the base of the letter, there grew up a more respectable neighborhood of freshly painted pretense: new grand Greek-columned mansions trying to look old, and many, larger, but somewhat less grand, gabled houses, more modern than Greek, with a hint of German, shaded by ornate porches, with high ceilings, winding stairways, quiet bedrooms, spacious living and dining rooms—partially fulfilled nouveau riche dreams, standing guard in front of outdoor privies, slave shacks, and barns; all mingling with an eclectic scattering of churches—Presbyterian, Lutheran, Baptist, Methodist, Episcopalian, and one Catholic. All existing in the presence of a small smattering of half-assimilated, untempled Jews who assuaged the Christian Sunday tedium of Southern church going society in their own way by singing, praying, or silently sitting at home.

But while Medora made her way along the muddy, winding road, her only thought was for her son. To be sure, thousands had died for "The Cause," more from disease than bullets, various "fevers" and measles mostly; and, though it never occurred to her, Homer Joe, not being a soldier, could never have the honor of joining the list.

Besides, she didn't really know what "The Cause" was—nor did anyone else much, if the truth be known. It was a deeply felt, but vague abstraction that nobody had successfully put tongue to. Of course, slavery had started it, but that was not really what it was about, most insisted in the South, not really. Robert E. Lee was opposed to slavery, as were many others. Patrick Cleburne, the great Anglo-Irish general from Helena, had circulated a petition urging emancipation in exchange for loyal service of the freed slaves. Grant, everyone pointed out, owned slaves and never freed them. In fact, Julia, his wife, kept a slave as a *femme de chambre* by the same name, Julia's Julia as she was called, who went with the Grants during the Vicksburg campaign. General George McClellan, Generalissimo of the Potomac, opposed abolition and was so angry at Lincoln's proclamation of it that he threatened to lead a coup d'état.

So, it was not as simple as slavery. After all, what poor White man, who owned no slaves, would die for a rich man's property? And didn't the Confederate constitution outlaw the slave trade?

It was all very complicated. And it was all very simple. A quarrel had started about slavery. There was secession, and many Northerners, caring not a fig for abolition, were against disunion, so, there was an invasion, and many Southerners who cared not a fig for preservation of slavery said, "You have invaded my homeland and I will fight—slave or no slave." So it went—so it goes still.

Yet as Medora whipped Useless up and he jerked and took two, noticeably quicker steps and just as quickly settled back down to his maddeningly slow walk, as only a mule can, trudging along that freezing January day in 1864, the worst fighting of this quarrel lay ahead for everyone. But it was nevertheless useless to hurry a useless mule named Useless, and he, like the war itself, would carry forward in his own, useless plodding way. Medora knew that, too, but couldn't help herself. She wanted it all finished now—to save her Homer Joe, Titus, and the others and go home to Arcadia to live in peace—to be finally done with it.

And, although, she was not a woman easily given to fear, she had grown up too hard for that, now she was very much afraid. She had lost children before. Too many. It was common—not half would survive till the summer of their lives—Black or White—in those days. Something always seemed to carry them off. If they survived the borning, then it was swamp fever or pox or measles or tick feve, or bad milk or infection from a bad cut or any number of accidents and unknown things for which there seemed no ready cure.

They would dress them up all pretty in a Sunday suit or white lace skirt and place them in the ground like one of God's special angels waiting to be reborn to paradise. They were always so beautiful and so perfect and so peaceful that it was hard to believe that their flesh would fall away—the worms—Medora tried not to think of them—tough as she was. She just thought of them as they were—in a state of grace. Death had a curious radiance when looked at in that way, she decided. Still it was hard, hard even for hard people, and she wasn't sure she could go through it again with Homer Joe.

Medora heard Aunt Essie say once, "Dey is de lucky ones ... dem little Black and White chillen dat is gone so early ..."

"Why?" Medora had asked.

"Miss Medora, dey is a-sneakin' pass dis ole devil of a world ... slippin' pass a room full of troubles with des sweet little bare feets ... and some day an angel of da Lawd is gwanna swoop down and carry dem off to heaven ... sho is ... de angel is gwanna fly down afta Gabriel done blow his mighty trumpet and tap de graves," she tapped the table where she was sitting, "he gwanna tap ders firs' and dey gwanna rise up to glory ... sho is. Oh, Glory!" Aunt Essie said, raising her hands up to heaven.

Medora believed this—she had to. But standing over the graves of her children, it made for little comfort. "God's not easy; God's hard," she would say. The idea of God being easy was a foolish one. But she wondered if maybe she was being selfish, that she just wanted to keep Homer Joe for herself and for some unknowable reason wasn't supposed to. She wouldn't console herself anymore with having more children—she would have to find another escape— another comfort.

Besides, she needed Homer Joe. The girls would grow up, marry, and she'd be alone. Titus was never far from danger, but she felt that he would go on to the very end. Surely all was lost. Hope was reticent after the Elkhorn and Shiloh—silent after Vicksburg. Then there was that distance thing in Pennsylvania where Marse Lee had gone off in sacrifice of the West—all for his precious Virginia, which everyone knew was the only thing he really cared about. He didn't care a "ten penny nail" for Arkansas, or Louisiana, or Mississippi, or any of the others, just some aristocratic notion about duty to Virginia. No, there was no hope for "The Cause." But maybe there was hope for her family—Titus, Ephey, Nora, and Homer Joe, Aunt Essie, and Rose-In-May.

She knew, too, that Rosy would run away again. She was still uncertain about what happened that last time she did.

So, Medora tried to cling to her Calvinist beliefs. What was to be was just going to be and the only freedom was in accepting that—what she referred to constantly as "God's will." Acceptance was the key to everything—peace of mind, most of all. Whether there was freedom to reject that divine will was not something she ever considered. But Medora was certain that this idea of acceptance was the key to her troubles—she had learned that much from Useless, he accepted everything. The odd thing was, mules were really a dual creation—of God and man together—perhaps that was the way it all was supposed to work—the hand of man in freedom and God's in fate all coming together in the great insight of making the mule of acceptance.

Homer Joe was very quiet. She didn't like that. Why would the Almighty want to harm her boy? The thought repeated itself obsessively, but she wouldn't let herself become angry with God; she couldn't afford it, she decided yet again. But she did begrudge that it was a father and not a mother who played out the Abraham-Isaac drama. The mothers did the bearing and the burying, so the Bible had it wrong. What about Isaac's mother? She was made to sit at home and worry and fret.

But maybe, too, Aunt Essie was right after all; the "blessing" was in the leaving and not in the staying. It's always back to God's will—inescapably, she thought as she contemplated Useless's rump riding up and down in an increasingly slower rhythm. Medora whipped him once more till, with the slowness of all mule time, they at last turned a corner and inched down the half-thawed avenue leading to the first shabby outcroppings of Little Rock.

As they pulled unnoticed into the heart of this little capital, Medora was shocked. The sleepy frontier village she had once known had transformed itself into a veritable hive of a commingling new world: the coming and the leaving—the bearing and the unborn—the made, the unmade, and the yet to be made, all living together in their desires, dreams, and despairs; the upright with the downtrodden and the in-the-middle; the fleeing and the found—Confederates, Contrabands, and Carpetbaggers, all were seen walking side-by-side along the muddy streets with Blue soldiers of all ranks, brushing past orphans, beggars, whores, ladies, and Reb deserters. Horses and mules—

wagons, carriages, drays, and buggies—all were seen sorting through what for Medora, ever thinking back on Arcadia, was as near as she'd get to pandemonium. She had never seen so many people and half of them Yankees and free Negroes!

Gradually she stopped, then "jeed" Useless off the Main Street to her relation's house—a cousin of Titus, Philomena Tottenburg, married to a wealthy merchant and "stomped-down" Unionist named Hans from St Louis and, God forbid, a German Catholic.

The house she was looking for was a refurbished two-storied, freshly painted green and white wooden structure on a tree-lined back street near the river. Trees were everywhere, trees of every sort along avenues, in yards, and on the sides of western hills and parks—oaks, maples, pine, cedar, and dogwood—so plentiful that it seems as though every soul in Little Rock had a tree assigned at birth. A child is born and a tree pushes its way out of its seed—a death occurs and another falls, dies in a storm for ready firewood—trees always coming in a balance of rebirth.

Medora "whoaed" in front of Philomena's magnificent one-hundred-year-old, winter-bare oak and got out as Useless fell instantly into a grateful, head-drooping doze. Philomena Tottenburg would certainly understand her coming suddenly without warning or invitation. She was nothing if not a Christian "even if she has suffered the error of conversion … you know Protestants always make the best Romans," Titus had said.

Indeed, Medora had found herself more and more in the position of making allowances—Contrabands, Carpetbaggers, and now Catholics. Where would it end? she wondered, setting the brake and getting out.

"An old maid should always be forgiven a late-found husband," she had replied, "even if he is a St. Louis Dutchman who kneels."

Philomena embraced her with a squeal of delight. Her "butler," now a wage-earning Contraband named Marcello, whom everyone called Marcel, stabled Useless while Philomena, Medora, and two servants bedded Homer Joe upstairs.

"We're quartering officers so we'll have to put little Virgy in our bedroom …"

"But, dear Philomena, you cain't do that … please …"

"We'll sleep in that little room behind the kitchen … you know … for time being. It'll be fine, honey, just fine. It's been empty since we're short of help," Philomena cooed.

"But that's a slave room," Medora said.

"There aren't any slaves, Medora, that's all finished now ... but it'll do while you're here ... we don't have so many Negras now we pay wages, dear ... just cain't afford it."

"Payin' wages?" Medora said in shock.

"That's the way it is, honey. But they're cheap ... so many have lost their White families or just run away ... they been coming into this town by the droves ... with no work nor means ... nobody knows what to do with them, really ... they've been coming every day ... poor things ... it really is pitiful."

"They should be returned," said Medora.

"That's impossible now ... even our new legislature is planning to officially outlaw slavery."

"Traitors from the hills and Scalawags every one!"

"They have the Union army behind them, honey, and Mister Lincoln."

Medora gave up the debate. She needed her host's goodwill, so she turned the conversation to settling in Homer Joe.

Soon the feminine touch of order and cleanliness mixed with the warmth of a rising fire as Homer Joe was washed, nightshirted, and propped on two clean linen pillows. Revived, he came round enough to hold his mother's hand.

"Where am I, Ma?" he whispered.

"Why, my sweet, you're at Aint Philly's ... in Little Rock ... in her nice warm house, and we're gonna find ye a good doctor real soon, so don't ye worry none ... hear?"

"In her house?"

"Yes, son, in her grand house ... in town ... in her room."

"Thank you," he mumbled and fell asleep again.

A heavy Black "Mammy," called Aunt Bertha, the Southern "Butler," the courageous, diligent, faithful, sensible, and wise middle link of a stratified society, came in and tended to things—fluffing pillows, closeting fresh sheets, arranging medicine bottles, giving advice and orders.

"Oh, Miss Medora, dis boy gwanna be jes fine yar ... my chile come off'n dis same debil of a fever las' year ... but I nursed him to hef ... sho did ... with da Lo'd's hep. We can do de same for yo Homer chile, too. Uh, huh, sho can, jes trus' in da Lo'd ... but don't do nothin' dat tempt him ... be careful 'bout dat ... no false pride ... no nothin' smackin' of sin and de Lo'd'll pull this chile thew like one of his very own special angels, sho will ..."

"Thank you, Aint Bertha," Medora said, hardly interrupting an unceasing chatter. Aunt Bertha either talked, sang, prayed, or instructed but was rarely silent.

"Yessum," Aunt Bertha said, beginning a deep-throated spiritual.

"All the doctors worth their salt are out at St. John's, my dear," said Philomena, tucking in Homer Joe yet again, smoothing the clean sheets and feeling his feverish head for the second time and frowning.

St. John's was a Masonic boy's school—an ugly three-storied thing east of the Arsenal, now serving as a hospital for both sides' sick and wounded.

"General Steele has forced them to work in 'his hospital,' as he calls it ... seems to think the whole town is 'his hospital' ... they're sending wounded here from all over the West. St. John's wasn't big enough, so they've built long white barracks running like spokes, you might say, from a wheel from the main building ... all to care for more wounded and dying men. I could send for ole Doc Yell ... but he's no good ... not really ... and there's one or two more around, too ... but they're all drunks that I wouldn't want to doctor a dog. Maybe Doc Yell'll come ... at least he'll give you medicine if anybody can ... I don't know. Your best chance, honey, is to find a good army doctor at St. John's and ask if he'll see the boy ... just as quick as you possibly can. I can only make him comfortable ... that's all I can really do," Philomena said, looked knowingly at Medora, then glancing away to accept another cold press from Bertha to place it on the boy's forehead.

"I'll get 'em now," said Medora.

"It's late, I know ... but do go now ... tomorrow ... tomorrow there's a hanging and you might not get through."

"A hangin'?!"

"Yes, looks like the general is gonna hang that poor O. Dodd boy."

"The one caught over by Ten Mile house?"

"You know about it?"

"Comin' in ... from the soldiers ... came right by it ... they told me."

"He ain't done nothing, not really. Oh, they found some scribblings in a book ... no doubt he wanted to impress Fagan when he got back down to Camden ... but it doesn't amount to anything ... not enough to hang anyone over, much less a fuzzy-chinned boy of seventeen."

"How about Hans? Cain't he do something ... what with his Yankee connections and all?"

"He did what he could and Mrs. McAlmont ... bless her soul ... she even got up a delegation ... met with the general who was polite and even gracious. Nobody thinks the fate of the Union is resting on that poor boy's neck ... nobody ... but General Steele told the ladies that the Military Commission has tied his hands ... but everybody knows he could save the poor child with just a few scratches of blue ink. Nobody feels right about it, I can tell you that, honey ... nobody at all."

"Why," interrupted Medora, "he's just a Pontius Pilate ..."

"Medora, that's putting it a little strongly dear, the boy is a spy, after all ... but there's not a Union man calling for his blood ... not a single one. It's like an evil thing nobody wants but don't know how to stop. I'm not sure Steele wants it himself ... not really ... but he seems transfixed ... trapped ..."

"It must be the Lord's will," Medora said.

"I cain't believe the Lord wants the boy to hang," asserted Philomena. "Man is free, and this is his doings, not God's. I cain't accept it any other way."

Medora started to retort that God could stop it if He wished, but at this moment a little boy about Homer Joe's age walked into the room, holding Bertha's hand. He wore a clean white shirt, and knee britches and Aunt Bertha had brushed his hair in a slick black wave to one side.

"Oh, Henry, dear, honey no ... don't come near this sick boy!" said Philomena with a shrick, waving him out. "Auntie Bertha, take him away at once!" she added, lunging toward her son.

"Mam, I wa'n't gwanna brang him none too close ... jes to see his cousin ... jes from de doe ..."

"No! No!" said Philomena as she led Henry out with Aunt Bertha following behind mumbling a stream of unintelligible protest while the boy's cries echoed in the hall.

Homer Joe's eyes filled with horror and his lips moved as if to speak at the vacancy where his cousin had been.

"Goodbye, Henry," Medora, said with a wave, trying hard to be nonchalant.

Philomena returned, affecting a sudden out-of-breath calm, saying, "I think seeing Homer was a bit of a shock for Henry. Aunt Bertha's youngest boy nearly died last year of the fever ... they were playmates ... then no sooner got well than Henry lost a little White friend from it too ... down the street ... the Morgans' boy ... God rest him. Henry's been terrified ever since. He's a very sensitive child, I'm afraid, Medora ... not a strong constitution ... I simply can't be too careful ... forgive me, dear."

"Yes, I see, Philly, well, he'll grow out of it ... in time ... these things are always harder at that age ... he'll be fine ... and Bertha is so good with him. I can see that readily enough. But, dear, I must go ... before it's too late ... I must find that Yankee doctor this very evenin' ... if I can ..."

"Oh, yes, you must ... I'll get Marcel to hitch the carriage for you," she said, leaving for a moment to do this then returning to rush Medora into some fresh warm clothes.

The sun was almost touching the trees as Medora passed the State House, a box-like miniature Acropolis, with four front columns, flanked by large east and west wings with two, smaller, covered porches themselves posted with "dwarf colonnades," as they are called.

Here, prodigal Arkansas had voted to come in, then out, and this year would, at bayonet point, come back in again. ("A bickering, drunken rabble of traitors and trash," Medora would say.) Backing the river, this capitol reinforced its north wall since "cannons are on gunboats, my friends," as the builder had insisted. Indeed, a ball had already trespassed the roof.

The "Old State House," as it came to be known, still maintains a certain "color." Its wonderful winding stair was once ridden up by a drunken lawmaker on a sober horse; its hall the scene of a legislative Bowie knife murder over a wolf pelt law; its balcony was the place from where Mrs. Trapnall threw her bouquet to Isaac Murphy; and its yard, as a barricade in Reconstruction, would host a great deal, including a happy follow-on war. "Brooks-Baxter" (a coup d'état between two Republican governors screaming usurpation). This little drama was scripted first as opera buffa but was quickly revised as tragedy by one King White, a red-headed Kentuckian, erstwhile trooper of Morgan, CSA cavalry raider of legend, he said, who mounted a coffee-colored stallion to lead his Black Baxter "mercenaries" in a marching, singing, drunken diversion from the joys of the sharecrop economy in a cheering political parade until the shooting started.

As if on cue, that day, a mounted Federal colonel raised a yellow-gloved hand so that one D.Y. Shall ("Shawl"), an elderly church-going gentleman, prevented a musket ball from shattering his hotel window by thrusting his curious skull out just in the nick of time.

President Grant said enough after a nearly hundred deaths and Baxter walked in but left the door unlocked behind for "Redemption" and the Democrats. But these glories were to come.

But now one can see in time's eye, on January 7, 1864, Medora Pilgrim riding past a split-rail fence of the Capitol's front where was quartered Steele's favorite regiment, the Third Minnesota, privileged by him in pontooning across the water into the Rock first, ahead of the others, rattling its steps past the little Krause girl who stared at them with an empty ladle in her hand on a hot day of the past fall of '63 before this new year's winter had turned off cold as Medora sped past the barracks with her sick son, her buggy pulled by a high-stepping on-loan roan driven by an erstwhile slave, bringing her finally to the grandest edifice of them all—the Ashley Mansion.

She pulled near the mansion facing it from the southeast corner of Scott and Markham. Grand even for the antebellum South, it was a two-storied white creation of six columns—the manifestation of one Chester Ashley's specula-tor ambition, which he also turned, with help from well-tended legislators, into a U.S. Senate seat, but his home was now requisitioned away from his widow, Mary, by the very government he once served, in the person of General Steele, as the imperial palace of Union Arkansas for his command, staff, and personal quarters.

Medora admired the fifty or so well-fed Yankee horses standing rump-to-rump, their tethered heads blowing frost-fire like mythical steeds pulsating over the Widow Ashley's white picket fence. Today it's a parking lot where people rummage for coins to feed a box. But on Medora's day, death dictated the great business of an always very busy place. Reb generals Price, Fagan, Shelby, and Marmaduke were forgotten, pushed off the little exalted Trans-Mississippi stage by a sutler's son caught riding a tired, half-lost mule along a country road, while pocketing a few ciphered notes about cannons and pickets.

Had she the time, Medora might have settled matters there and then by marching through the big guarded door straight into the general's office, up to his grand desk, and in that gesture saved her son, the O. Dodd boy, and maybe by some miracle all the other boys and men soon to die. Instead, she and Marcel wound their way on toward St. John's—the school turned inside-out—from Gaul to gauze to gallows.

Arriving at the "Arsenal," which blocked her way to St. John's, she saw it looming at the far edge as a red brick and white frame of two stories centered by a single, castle-like tower sprouting east and west wings.

Standing up, Medora saw everything: the Arsenal, a headquarters to the Union legions camped in a circling mass of tents; stretched over many acres, like a languishing leviathan of many arms, legs, spines, fangs, and claws—supplies, new rifles, cannons, horses, mules, wagons, and thousands of healthy fairly well fed men milling and drilling in rigid lines made even more blue by the reclining sun's reflection upon the whiteness of fresh snow—hanging a lad tomorrow and slaying the South the day after—that was why they were there in their hordes.

"Show our boys this and the war'd be over in a snap," she said to Marcel, who replied with a polite nod.

Medora realized now the immense power of the Thing arrayed against her country. It was not just numbers, powder, and ball, but the weight of a great, modern something, long in gestation, finally loosed upon the world. A tectonic shift had occurred, leaving a brave but largely irrelevant people no other recourse but to submit or be swept aside—the South, and all else besides.

Faulkner would say it best a little later. "Yankees were not a people nor a belief nor even a form of behavior, but instead were a kind of gully, precipice …" A Thing, he might have added.

It had never really been a question of this or that battle being won or lost, Medora now realized, of this or that being done or not done; of freeing the slaves or not freeing the slaves; of pressing ahead at Shiloh; of Lee not ordering a charge in Pennsylvania, of Stewart getting lost, or Davis not relieving Vicksburg, or not getting rid of that idiot Bragg earlier. None of that mattered because it had all been ordained by some greater force—the South would be vanquished by one means or another—war or peace—the Thing would have its way, here and everywhere, she could see that plain enough now.

Wars are nothing more than just a bloody way of making something already decided, official. Sherman had said when it started, "You must surely lose." Grant-Sherman was this Thing's tooth and claw and Lincoln its head and tongue, but Lincoln, in his own way, had, like the South herself, sprung from an innocent past—a dying America. He was not so much the future as people thought, as he was the past's appeal to it.

Lincoln was a kind of link to what remained—a means of stepping from one to the next—a temporary disguise for the Thing to exercise its incipient, inexorable dominion. Lincoln was not so much modern as modern enough. He would soon be cast away—doomed—just as the South was doomed and Medora now felt somehow doomed as the sun touched the tallest trees, settling the scene into stark semi-tones of light and incipient night, as the fires burned larger and the cold began to bite as men cooked and gathered for the familiar evening rituals of camp. These camp sounds drifted up to Medora and Marcel like a distinct murmuring wind blowing from the mouth of Faulkner's image—the "precipice"—a kind of unnatural inhuman hummmm rising to her ears as she rubbed her hands in the frigid air.

But, too, she felt a deep, inexpressible attraction. All of what she saw before her would be changed into the Thing itself or, if resisting, destroyed—Indians, Spanish, South, West, farms, villages, animals, the earth, and finally the world, all would be subordinated to its will and image, replaced, and, finally, ultimately, destroyed and made into something else. But what she knew not.

Yet Medora felt that God somehow was granting her a special glimpse, not of fire and torment, as always imagined, but something more deeply disturbing—something offering a better way, exchanging a diminished power of the soul for the increasing power of the flesh, and, once lost, bargained for, never reclaimed. Yet it was to this Thing that she herself had come. In the same way Marcel and the slaves had looked to the Thing for their freedom—it had its gifts; its special way of making things better. She would not turn back, she would make her devil's bargain, too.

Marcel threaded the carriage through and around tents, baggage, wagons, curious, milling soldiers and camp followers, crossing the half mile to St. John's. Built before the war, this odd structure was supported in front by two large square turrets with battlements seemingly more suitable for scalding heads than hosting minds or healing bodies and looked something like a three-story Gothic church without flying buttresses. Someone described it as typical of "the castle-lated Gothic order of architecture." It was, indeed, a brickish-looking brute. And around it, long, thin, white painted temporary hospital barracks spoked outward like filaments from a spider's web.

As a school, it had always been more Spartan than Athenian. A prewar syllabus proclaiming:

> The Board are pledged to support the faculty in upholding, under all circumstances, a high standard of scholarship. The discipline will be of the military form—The dress must be neat, manly, economical and uniform. The fall and winter dress of students in the preparatory department must be a blue roundabout coat, with a single row of bright buttons in front, blue military cloth cap, with a brass button on each side, and blue pants with drab stripe down the leg.

Such was the school honoring an apostle whose name means, "God has been gracious," and who some say was Christ's cousin; others, the son of Salome. He authored five books of the New Testament, including Revelation, and, it's generally believed that John lived long, taught love, fought heresy, and preached till buried in an Ephesian tomb commemorated by the Emperor Justinian.

But today, in a lonely space before its giant entrance, stood a freshly built gray wooden gibbet, which, back-lit by the distant fires of gathering men, anchored the base with a darkly looming shadow and, like the face of death, dominated the world with a ubiquitous, silent, secret power not long or easily gazed upon.

It was here that Medora, come to save a son where another mother's son would surely die, creaked up in her carriage, rolling gently over snow-powdered ground, stopping before St. John's gallows, pausing with a shuddering, chilling fear, before descending to the frozen ground. She gathered herself, then stepped toward the monstrously grand door for help from the very Thing she so abhorred.

Dr. Linderman was a sad-eyed man of medium build. He had silver-black salt-and-pepper hair dropping into a small beard and, over a major's uniform, wore a disheveled dirty white physician's frock freckled with blood.

The war had greeted him at Shiloh, near the landing, in that little toe-hold of Union-held ground on the riverbank, a swampy bulge of raised mud along the Tennessee, between Lick, Snake, and Owl Creeks. Here he sawed away in the hospital cabin, just past the ten thousand Yankee skulkers huddled in a hard rain. He whacked off young men's legs and arms, letting them fall into a kick-bucket till it filled, was taken out, and emptied into a pile that rose into a little pyramid of mounting, discarded flesh. The screaming, rained-on men lying under thundering black lightning-lit skies were illuminated till the fields themselves writhed to life. That's what everyone said who saw it: that the fields seemed alive with the twisting and rolling welt of the dying men left behind, lit by bursts of brightness exposing hogs feasting at the Bloody Pond and Peach Orchard, blending with the staggered, thudding explosions from gunboats anchored in a turgid, dark, rising ribbon, more a brooding presence of blood, flooding as if all the gore of war were unleashed, swelling and rushing past, than of a simple, broad rain-lifted river—ponderous bombs lobbing from it through blackness with red sparking tails, comet-like, as from outer space, dropping, bursting, falling, mostly among Union wounded, and just a little shy of the Confederate lines.

The Gray-backed men, hunkering in exhaustion, just that morning, a "lifetime of time," they would all say later, had plunged out of the timber by a little white country church with the Hebrew name for peace, on a hot, sticky sunrise in April, 1862—thirty thousand Confederates staggering forward in three yelling, uneven lines of ten each—crashing out of trees and brush, running behind bounding deer, foxes, rabbits, and assorted varmints, breaking up the leisurely breakfast of Sherman's Blues, who never saw them coming till it was way too late.

That night Dr. Linderman sawed and sawed to a chorus of shrieks that were too much for Grant standing outside in the rain because he couldn't stand it any longer, but, as always, stolid and inscrutable as the man who loved horses, whiskey, and Julia, and not much else, including war, but which he understood better than anyone except Sherman, who understood it best of all because it wasn't just war he understood but *this* war. The ever-laconic Grant, whose ambition had been to teach math to boys, thought instead, as he stood in the storm that night saying to everyone that "we'll lick them in the morning;" the Southerners winning only to lose as they always seemed to, the Blue reinforcements finally up, Lew Wallace at last found, Buell at hand, and their Reb friend, A. S. Johnston, fortuitously dead because he sent his surgeon to help the enemy so he could not be found to stop the bleeding of a boot-filling leg wound.

"Man proposes and God disposes," Grant was fond of saying. And, with God's help, he had stayed mostly sober, except for one famous slip at Vicksburg, and perhaps one more in New Orleans when his horse fell and the whisperers said he was drunk again, but Dr. Linderman, unburdened by fame, frequently soothed his soul with bourbon—the mutterers having long since been silenced by the accomplished fact.

It had taken Medora awhile to find him, wandering the halls of the dimly lit school, among the wounded, asking orderlies and nurses, then waiting, sitting upon a hard cold bench outside a ward where boys' voices had once echoed Latin in Southern tones—Virgil, Livy, and Caesar—the glories of Rome, Punic Wars, the conquest of Gaul, *veni, vidi, vici,* and *vi et armis,* now crammed with hallow-eyed boy/men missing arms, legs, and eyes from a more recent glory.

She rose as the doctor shuffled over.

"Yes, mam?" he asked with quiet resignation.

Medora introduced herself. He took the offered hand, nodded, then dropped it without speaking.

Staring into his flushed face, smelling the whisky which she knew he used to fight the fatigue she saw in his eyes as much as anything, and seeing sadness there too, she knew if anyone could help it would be this man for whom suffering was such a steady, endless irritant.

"My son is dying," she said, admitting this for the first time, surprising herself with this confession. "I need help," she added in almost a whisper.

Medora Pilgrim had not given herself permission to weep, but now, with this simple statement, she almost did.

Seeing this, Linderman sighed deeply.

"What of?" he asked.

"Fever ... swamp fever ... malaria, I think ... I don't know ... but he's got a fever that won't break."

"Where's he now?"

She told him and asked him to come.

"I can't ..."

"But you must, Dr. Linderman, sir, you must!"

"Mam, I have a hospital full of dying ... I can't leave ..."

She saw he meant it.

"Where's Doctor Yell? Maybe he can come."

She had asked of him before but all said, "Talk to Doc Linderman."

"Yell's gone to Fort Smith," said Linderman.

"Fort Smith?"

"Yes, there is an outbreak there ... the Reb bushwhackers've keep'em penned up ... now there's an epidemic. The general sent him. Bring your boy tomorrow ... after the hanging ... I'll have to tend to that first ... the O. Dodd boy ... after that, then I'll look at ..."

"Homer Joe."

"Yes, bring him after the hanging."

"Yes, sir," she said quietly. "Thank you, sir," she added.

"What are you doing for him now?"

"Calomel ... he's salivated."

"Don't give him anymore of that stuff ... just control his fever with cold compresses ... best you can ... that's all you can do."

"Yes, sir."

"Bring him tomorrow ... after they choke the O. Dodd lad."

"Yes, Doctor, thank you."

"But you'll have to come to the provost's and sign the oath of allegiance first ... you know that, of course? The office is here ... on the second floor," he said, pointing upstairs.

"Oath of allegiance?"

"Yes, mam," he said, irritated for the first time. "You're a Rebel ... I can't help you until you swear allegiance to the United States ... bring me that paper or I can't help you ... understand? We're not supposed to help traitors, mam."

"But my good sir, my husband is Colonel Titus Pilgrim," she said, swelling up to her full five feet four, "and he and all his brothers are with our army in the south ... at Washington ... my brother died serving with Pat Cleburne at Shiloh ... I ..."

"Shiloh?" he said, stiffening.

"Yes, sir … we still haven't found his body but that's where he died, sir … in the service of his country."

"We buried the Rebs in a common ditch, mam, you'll never find him."

"So I've been given to understand …"

"I don't care," he interrupted quickly before she could add her disapproval. "None of that makes a damn now … sign their piece of paper … then bring it with the boy or I can't help you … it's a regulation. Get here early, otherwise the provost'll be busy with the hanging."

There was a pause.

"But it'll be a falsehood, my good sir," she said, looking Linderman in the eye.

"I don't care … it's up to you, just bring me the piece of paper so I can tend to your son … otherwise you might lose him."

She thought for a moment.

"I came to you as a Christian, sir."

"You're a Christian today, mam, but a Reb tomorrow … besides, there's not much Christian happening in this war … not that I've seen. Now, if you'll excuse me," he said, turning away.

"Doctor Linderman!" she said, reaching out for him.

"Yes?" he said, turning back to her.

"Thank you, sir."

"Bring me the paper … now good evening, madam," he said, walking off.

"Thank you, sir," she said again as he disappeared into a room followed by two dour nuns, their habits making a ghostly rustle.

As she stepped outside a scream propelled her into the carriage. It was snowing hard as they made their wordless return through the winding, mostly empty, and very dark streets to the Big House on the river.

Medora stayed the night with Homer Joe. She slept fitfully, leaning forward in her chair, her head resting on the sheets, holding his hot hand. He became delirious, turning, withdrawing the hand, waking her. She stared into his face flushing in the candlelight. She felt his forehead over and over—placed cold compresses—wept quietly—paced the room—sat—prayed—got up—sat again—got up—paced some more—then went to the window looking out at the great river clearly visible in the near distance. The snow had stopped, the frozen, moon-shadowed river loomed broadly like a strangely pristine white highway—silently powerful—foreboding—posing a question for which she had no answer.

PHILLIP H. MCMATH

The next morning, Marcel lifted Homer Joe onto the back seat of the carriage and thickly layered him with blankets. Medora took the back seat herself, holding her son tightly into her warm body as they were jerked forward by a fine, fresh, high-stepping brown gelding whose feet lifted smartly on the snow-softened cobblestones leading from the stables to the street.

"God speed," Philomena said, waving at the front gate. A sad, plump figure, made even sadder and plumper by a heavy fur coat and round pink cheeks that contrasted with Aunt Bertha's, standing as she was beside her with her own cheeks so black that they looked like fine new sable.

"I'd go with you, my dear," Philomena had said earlier, glad of an excuse, "but I just caint bear to see that poor lamb hang ... it all grieves me more than I can ever say ... it's downright criminal is what it is."

They all waved as the carriage pulled off on its journey arriving there just as the sun touched the treetops. Medora went hurriedly to the provost office, only to find it closed. She asked everywhere but it was always the same, typified by a lieutenant who said, "He's a-working on the hanging, mam. Come back tomorrow. Ain't nothing gonna get done today about no oaths or nothin' ... jes' breaking that Reb spy's neck is all that they can think about."

Medora then looked through the tent city.

"Halt!" said one bundled-up beardless boy, about the same as Arlo, holding up his bayoneted rifle, the saber catching the sunlight, making Marcel pull up to a stop.

"Cain't go no further, mam," he said, walking up, addressing her, ignoring Marcel.

She explained her problem yet again. Homer Joe moaned. The soldier leaned over and looked under the blanket.

"I'll do what I can," he said, leaving and returning with a sergeant who listened and went away only to return quickly with a captain. After Medora repeated her dilemma yet again, the officer took his turn looking at the sick boy, felt his forehead, and stepped back to say, "You're willing to take the oath, mam?" he asked, even though she had already said she would.

"Yes, sir, I am," she said yet again.

"Well, you can put him in my tent ... till it's sorted out ... it's warm ... at least there's a stove in there and you and your Negro can tend to the boy till we can get Doc Linderman. He's very busy just now, but I'll get him here when I can. It'll be awhile but that's all that I can do ... understand, mam? Just stay in the tent, you understand, till all this is over."

"Oh, bless you, sir! God bless you. I knew that I'd find a Christian some-where!" she said.

Bedded in the tent there was nothing to do but wait and watch Homer Joe sleep, but the commotion outside proved too much and they were irresistibly drawn to it. They would take turns looking out and reporting to the other as the crowd was swelled by the hour, and, as the morning slipped into afternoon; that is, by three, a throng of some six thousand pressed against three walls of Blue infantry and a fourth of cavalry that formed into the four straight lines of a square around the scaffold. And, behind the four-deep horses was a battery of artillery, its gunners set at attention, staring menacingly at the people who herded around them in a buzz.

In a letter to Titus, Medora described it all:

> There were men and women in their best Sunday clothes, holding children by the hand or lifting them upon their shoulders to see, while young White men and Negroes hung from the trees and others at the school sat in the highest windows or even in the turrets like soldiers of a Walter Scott novel defending a castle.
>
> A last minute reprieve had failed, it was said, but others were certain it would come upon the scaffold from Steele himself—and some even believed that General Fagan would ride suddenly into the city like he had promised, save the South's hero and free us all, as well as that poor boy, from Tyranny.
>
> The Yankees must have believed this, too, because they had their entire army out and armed and ready, all starched and dressed in their very best blue uniforms. It was quite a sight to see.

It was known that O. Dodd in a letter to General Steele had maintained his loyalty as a good Unionist, so many, as Medora reported, indeed, had hope right up to the end that he would be spared.

> That I have been born in the South, though it be the chief cause of overstrained suspicions, injurious to me; is nevertheless a simple decree of Fate. That I have thus far lived in the land of Rebellion, is accounted for by my minority, which subjects me to the control of others.

Who were these "others?" That's what Steele wanted to know but the boy would not say, so his letter had done no good, and one, Charles Lake, a hospital orderly about O. Dodd's age, squinting through a telescope from atop St.

John's north tower, described what he saw in a letter of his own to his mother:

> I sat for a long time viewing the countenances of the vast crowd,
> and occasionally took a look over the arsenal at the prison ... My
> eye caught the gleam of steel glistening in the sunlight, and upon this
> I turned my glass—as it came nearer I could make out the figure of
> a carriage, closely guarded. I turned my glass upon the man seated
> upon his coffin. His countenance was a little pale—but perfectly
> composed. The condemned cast his eyes to the rope and seemed per-
> fectly composed and indifferent. He sat looking at the crowd, just as
> calm as could be.

Had young Lake looked, he could have seen Marcel and Medora return to
their carriage and force it through the crowd to the infantry line. Then they
stood up, side by side, the reins hanging slack in Marcel's hands while Medora
balanced with her long fingers by touching the brake.

Medora wrote to Titus, and, after telling him the news about Homer, added:

> Suddenly there was a strange sound, kindly a change of pitch, then
> a roar, as the mob turned its heads to the left. I could see nothing at
> first, then I did. It was a figure gliding over the crowd, as if by some
> mysterious force he seemed to fly above them. It was very strange
> and almost impossible to believe, then there was a slight break in the
> crowd as he turned toward me, and then I saw him clearly, riding
> upon his coffin! He wore a fresh new suit with black western tie
> neatly bowed under his fair white throat, and his hair was combed
> and brushed slickly, as if by his mother, you know, just to look his
> best, like for his wedding or for church.
>
> He passed slowly towards me till I saw him seated upon his pine
> box in the back of a wagon pulled by two, fine matching horses. The
> cold sunlight hurt my eyes so I shaded them with my hand and then
> I saw the poor boy's pink face which had drawn all twelve thousand
> eyes to it like a magnet.
>
> He had such a fine look. Dearest, I know it's blasphemy to say this,
> but Lord forgive me, but I imagine our Lord must have had the same
> sense of serenity. I tell you, he shamed us all! I mean, I was embar-
> rassed for us everyone, but most of all for Steele and his army—all
> those poor lads standing there in the freezing cold—they must have
> felt like Pilate's legions with more men than the Romans to hang that

child. They were permanently stained by his blood, they sure were, you could just see it, even as they stood at attention with that terrible look of shame upon them.

O. Dodd had also written a letter home, that very morning in the quiet of his cell, to his parents.

Military Prison
Little Rock, Jan. 8 10:00 a.m. 1864

My Dear Parents and Sisters,

I was arrested as a Spy and tried and was sentenced to be hung today at 3 o'clock. The time is fast approaching but thank God I am prepared to die. I expect to meet you all in heaven, do not weep for me for I will be better off in heaven. I will soon be out of this world of sorrow and trouble. I would like to see you all before I die but let God's will be done not ours. I pray to God to give you strength to bear your troubles while in this world. I hope God will receive you in heaven. Mother I know it will be hard for you to give up your only son but you must remember it is God's will. Good by. God will give you strength to bear your troubles. I pray that we may meet in heaven. Good by. God will bless you all. Your son and brother.

David O. Dodd

The buzzing roar Medroa reported fell suddenly away into an eerie silence as the wagon turned and smoothed its way under the knot. Encircled by soldiers—erect, gripping black muskets with silver bayonets, facing outward— a little group of men huddled uneasily on the ground near the noose.

Medora's eye sorted through them for Titus:

There was my Provost Marshal, a Lt., someone told me later, I had found him at last. Only now he was too busy to help me save our Virgy; too busy hanging one boy to preserve the life of another! He was standing by a minister, one Reverend Dr. Peck, I heard someone mutter. They said they couldn't find nobody else and had to settle for this Reverend Peck fella, kindly at the last minute. I never did find out his church but he was too nervous to be a Presbyterian. The way I figure, he must of been some kind of freewiller who wasn't sure he was doing the right thing. He kept reading from his Bible and muttering prayers no one could make out. I could see his hands trembling as he turned the pages and lifted his hands to heaven from time to time. Then, next to him, but off a step or two, like he wanted to separate himself from it all, was Doc Linderman. I liked him, even though he was a gruff Yankee and a drunk. I think he wanted to help and he didn't much care if that oath meant something to me or not. He was a little unsteady and I think he must of had a belly full of the good Cincinnati whiskey they say he drunk. He slouched and looked away, wore a great army coat with his hands thrust in his pocket, like he was saying he wasn't going to take no hand in the matter and wore an odd looking army cap, hard billed that looked like a short beaked bird perched and nesting on his long black hair. I don't think he ever looked at any of the others so much as once but kept his head turned away and kindly cast down.

Then, my dearest, there was Major General Frederick Steele hisself! I could have hit him with a rock. He was standing at attention, all funny looking, with a long grayish-black beard he had combed real neat and all, dressed up uncomfortable looking in his starched uniform of blue with gold braid. He was trailing this saber around, and standing almost right under that noose with a plume of a feather in that fancy hat that almost touched it.

Titus, not a one of them could ever bring hisself to look up square at that boy. That godforsaken Provost moped like a whipped dog, with his eyes always glued upon the general, following his every move but breathing heavily—smoking from an infernal fire, it seemed, though, of course, it wasn't a thing but the ice cold air.

And Steele, with his dress uniform, medals, braid, sword and red sash and funny hat and all, looked like he was in some borrowed costume and trinkets for a make-believe play that he had done dreamed up. They'd been funny if they had been doing almost anything else. Well, they didn't seem to know what to do, there was some confusion then the Provost caught a nod from the general and signaled to a teamster who had brought in the wagon and was still sitting in the seat holding the reins. But then he dismounted and came round to let down the wagon gate serving as a trap door. They had to use it because no one had taken the trouble to build a proper scaffold and so they just pulled that wagon gate under that rope.

Then, Titus, something happened that I never will forget. That poor boy, who had been jest setting there so still as you please, perfectly calm, not moving a muscle or nothing, suddenly stood up. He surprised everyone when he done this, I tell you. I mean, it weren't expected. He just stood up from off his coffin seat, and when this happened the folks, I mean all six thousand, let out one big moan. It was like all of them were in shock and soon, after that great moan, they was quiet again and froze into silence. No one said a word. You could have heard a whisper, a whisper! I tell you!

There he stood there without moving, calm as ever, stock still, and, I promise you dearest, had he not moved again they never could have hung him. They was froze by him into doing nothing. Then, without no word said to him by nobody, he just steps onto that gate and stands beneath the noose a-waiting for them. I'll never forget it in all my borned days. He just waited as pretty as you please for them to put that horrible noose around his young neck.

But nobody seemed able to do nothing, they was so froze. But then that teamster took it upon hisself to say something to that Provost and it kindly woke him up like. He looked over at the general who seemed like he nodded and then the Provost scrambled hisself up beside the boy, caught his breath, cause he was breathing hard in that cold air, while the boy's breath couldn't be seen at all and he fumbled his rope out of his coat pocket and bound that poor child's hands and legs. Then he rummaged his pockets again real nervous like, said something to the general still standing upon the ground; fumbled some more, and it was clear to all he couldn't find something so then in desperation he turned sheepishly to O. Dodd saying, just above a whisper, "I sorry, sir, but I cannot seem to find the blindfold."

I'm certain of them words as I am of heaven cause I heard them just as clear as a bell. See, it was still so very quiet and that crowd they was just holding their breath and couldn't say nothing even if somebody had wanted to. It was plumb froze up by what it was seeing.

Then that poor child looked at him like he just couldn't believe what he just heard and then when it had sunk in good, the boy said quietly, "You will find a handkerchief in my coat, sir."

I heard that just as clear as the others. How come him to have that handkerchief I don't know, guess he thought he'd need one but he sure had it.

PHILLIP H. MCMATH

Then that Provost searched the boy's pockets till he found the clean white linen and then tied it around the boy's eyes.

Then he fumbled around some more and found the official paper, unfolded it, and put on some wire specks to read the sentence so quickly a body could hardly understand it but ending with a loud "Death by Hanging."

He looked over at Steele who seemed mighty unhappy and was frowning but without really saying nothing, then the Provost grabbed the noose and slipped it over O. Dodd's neck and tightened it. I have to say he done that pretty good. It was the only thing he done without being all-thumbs about it.

Then nothing happened. I mean, it seemed like an eternity passed and no one wanted to happen what seemed about to happen. Then one of them ambulance horses broke the silence by snorting, raising his tail, making another noise from that end and doing his business upon the snow, then he jerked his head up and down, sneezing and rattling bridle and harness, then he neighed and swung his devilish big black head from side to side, shaking and chewing his bit like a horse, a horse out of Revelations. Then that teamster come round, gripped the halter, holding him, whispering something in his ear till that horse quieted down

Titus, I don't know how long they all made that poor boy stand there with that noose around his neck but it seemed like another eternity. Then the Provost stepped back and the Rev. Dr. Peck scrambled his awkward self up on their little stage. He closed his book, raised his right hand and droned out a prayer that I swear was the longest anyone ever heard and I don't have to tell you as a church-going Presbyterian you know I've heard some prayers that would stretch from Arcadia to Jerusalem. Well, this one Peck done went there and back again. But I promise you I can't remember a word that man said. And I started to kindly get the feeling that he was doing it to maybe save the boy, that if he could do it long enough it wouldn't happen, that somehow they just couldn't go through with it. I'll give the old Reverend that much. But finally, he run out of words and crabbed backwards real awkward like bumping into the coffin that was behind him given the angle he was trying to leave, nearly tripping him off that gate. I swear if he had fell maybe that would have been what it took, but he caught hisself and the crowd gasped again, the first sound they had made since that boy had done stood up like he done so calm like and all.

Then Steele, with the help of a hand from an officer, some kind of colonel, I think, he climbed up there right beside the boy. Now that was a sight. That general all done up with braid and saber and all a standing there by that boy dressed up like for church and everything with his mother's comb lick fresh upon his hair. Then the general leaned over real slow like and, like that teamster done with that horse, whispered something in that boy's ear. The words are not known. No one could hear them. And the general wouldn't tell no one. Folks say he'll take them words to his very own grave. But everyone says he offered the boy his life for the names of them that put him up to it—betrayal bartered for life—that's what he wanted—a Judas! But he said not a word, their faces were no more than an inch apart and they stood there together in silence. I tell you it was something to see!

Then I could see straight off that Steele was disappointed, but he stood there a moment longer looking into that innocent young face and O. Dodd not moving, calling the General's bluff, then Steele he turned and stepped to the ground. And when he done that the others followed leaving O. Dodd up there on that wagon gate with that infernal noose around his neck all alone once again upon them boards—froze and blindfolded—his hands and feet tied, not moving a muscle.

Then the Provost sheeped a look at Steele and he nodded then the Provost tripped that gate latch. My dearest, Titus, what I seen then I can't hardly write to you about. My Lord! That poor child fell and there rose a moan from six thousand throats which very few humans have ever lived to hear. Them was watching as that boy jerked, choked, and swung toeing hisself along the ground.

That's right! As the Lord God is my witness! He was toeing along the ground! The rope was too long! Them Yankee idiots hadn't measured it right and his neck weren't broke proper. Them folks all seemed to see this at the same time and a moan of that six thousand turned to a scream!

Then that stupid Provost grabbed at his legs but he missed as the boy danced away from him choking and twisting. I could not pull my eyes off of him but soldiers fell with the clatter of their muskets hitting the ground, others turned their backs, and women fainting in big heaps and lots just run away. Marcel hollered he said, but I didn't hear him, because he said I was screaming, too, he said later, but I swear I don't recollect making a sound.

Then that teamster, the one who had quieted the horse, he jumped up on that gibbet, shimmed out there and reached for the swinging rope, tugging it upwards with both hands till he pulled that poor boy far enough off the ground to choke him to death and he was finally still at last.

I sat down and Marcel drove us away back to Homer Joe's tent where I stayed with our beloved son through the night. But I couldn't get no doctor at all because I couldn't ever get that god-forsaken, devilish piece of paper to sign. No one could find that Provost and Doc Linderman was so drunk he couldn't walk, folks said, even if I had swore allegiance with it to the singing of a thousand angels to their idea of a Union all wrote down on some heavenly parchment, it wouldn't have done no good

Then one of them German nuns come in without being asked, and said, "I will sit with you. I do not need any piece of paper."

That kindly nun sat with me till we lost Homer Joe, about dawn it was—just a little afore sunrise. I never thought I'd hold hands and pray and cry with a Catholic and a Negro but that's just what I done. The three of us, me and Marcel and that nun, just standing there in that tent by our Homer Joe, holding hands and praying. We prayed for his sweet soul and for that poor O. Dodd boy, too. I'll tell you, my dear, Titus, I loved and miss our boy more than anything in the world, as I know you do, but he's in a better place, I know that for sure. He is with our other lost children now, and at least he didn't have to die the way I seen with the O. Dodd boy, God rest his soul. I hope never to see nothing like that again in all my borned days. I pray for all of them ever night.

I love you and miss you and pray ever night you'll be spared.

Yours In Christ
Your loving wife,
    Medora

CHAPTER EIGHT

The Hanged man. Fear death by water.
I see crowds of people, walking in a ring.
Thank you. If you see dear Mrs. Equitone,
Tell her I bring the horoscope myself:
One must be careful these days.
　　　　　—The Wasteland, *T. S. Eliot*

As Homer Joe's lid was hammered down shut, O. Dodd lay couched "in state" on Dick Johnson's Rock Street front porch, till dawn. Then his cortege, followed by half the town, dirged its way along Main to Mount Holly while O. Dodd went down and Medora went up the road to Arcadia.

Generals, preachers, alcoholic doctors, provost marshals, and gawkers do at last all pass away. The Blue beast of six thousand likewise vanished as the gallows was struck and quickly tossed aside into broken sticks and burnt.

After the war, the school also flamed away like the gallows, each like their executed boy, equally coming to nothing. But today a kind of cinder block remains, just on the back streets of Eleventh and what used to be McAlmont (named for a doctor whose wife tried to save O. Dodd; until now named for a governor), across and south from the ruins of a slattern of an old church, one sees a chain fence guarding a parking lot. Here, in a patch of grass, a modest obelisk is famously ignored. Yet, look closely, its inscription mentions a name, describing it as the "Boy Hero of the Confederacy. UDC, 1926."

To the east and south, an interstate wraps behind in a coil of cement and zoom, humming and slithering, squeezing like a double-bodied serpent—gripping tighter, in an ever-increasing, suffocating constriction of the city. To the west is a park, named for Mac Arthur, "America's Caesar," future Generalissimo of Japan; his birth place, the Arsenal, barracks then, today a museum where Medora first went in search of her useless piece of paper, stands as home to a society of ghosts—the more famous being a young woman who appears in a white gown, holding a lit candle, searching for someone, they say;

and a well-dressed young man is sometimes seen relaxing in the second-floor hall, her friend or son, it is supposed. Folks from the next to last century, they are, hanging on, refusing to leave the Little Rock ladies who meet downstairs for hundreds of years at a time for tea to "come and go, talking of ..." well, of ... things—oblivious to their old friends upstairs.

There are, of course, too, the trees—oaks and elms, as old or older than the common—an Arts Center near a large pond—with grass for lovers, drunks, addicts, and tramps to sleep, walk, embrace, and wander aimlessly about seeking some solitude or even a little peace.

Seemingly unseen by either, to the northeast, recessed girls and boys from a Catholic academy, spiritual children of our good nun, sing and laugh, while skipping their way through time in clean blue and gray uniforms not unlike their distant fathers who fought there; playing out their innocence only a corner away from where the scaffold was set; near the interstate that merges with their school's street, swinging south to touch the edge of a cemetery advertised as "History Carved in Stone," and self-described quite seriously as:

> ... a park-like oasis in the center of, and owned by the City of Little Rock. Flowering plants, shady trees, berry bushes, and honeysuckle give it a pleasant, restful atmosphere enhanced by a Bell House built around the end of the 19th century.
>
> The four-square-block area was donated to be used as a city cemetery in 1843 by Roswell Beebe and Senator Chester Ashley. It has become the final resting place of such notable Arkansans that it has earned the nickname "The Westminster Abbey of Arkansas." Interred here are 10 state governors, 13 Supreme Court justices, 5 Confederate Generals, 21 Little Rock mayors, several newspaper editors, military heroes, physicians and attorneys.

The lawyers may be last but the poets are unmentioned. Yet one did, somehow, slip past, finding a spot under the rubric of "General Interest." Though ignored by sign painters, he's only a row up from O. Dodd: John Gould Fletcher, winner of the Pulitzer of '36, Amy Lowell's "Imagist" pal, friend of Eliot and Pound, now rests a skull which hosted the best brain on the acre near that of his wife's, Charlie Mae Simon, author of children's books, friend and biographer of Dr. Albert Schweitzer, she lies next to the water ladling elbow of the little Krause girl who had watched the Yankees invade her town in '63.

If Adolphine could but reach again she would touch a husband—John. G., hero of Shiloh, prisoner of war, postwar millionaire cotton speculator;

free-thinking *homme d'affaires,* and furtive reader of Darwin, who sent his strange little poet son off to Harvard, with his share of the fortune pocketed by share-crop fingers, banked, bonded, and bequeathed for a trip to Paris, helping the son to help the unknown Pound with un-repaid loans; then bounding off to London, finding there, Eliot, a border-state boy gone British, the "most intelligent man I ever met," John Gould would say, helping him, too, to publish the *Wasteland*—itself partly, secretly, edited by Pound—a work of three for all to see as one:

> After the torchlight red on sweaty faces
> After the frosty silence in the gardens
> After the agony in stony places
> The shouting and the crying
> Prison and palace and reverberations
> Of thunder of spring over distant mountains
> He who is living is now dead
> We who were living are now dying
> With a little patience.

Now here, arranged in well-tended rows claimed for trees, across from a carwash where nostalgia resurrects an ante-post-bellum past—*fin de siécle* houses rise with high, hard-to-heat ceilings, ex-wood-burning kitchens, nooky side porches, once nice for laying out bodies of the hanged—they keep well in winter—but now are stacked with slick unread magazines and heavy-looking bestsellers lying ponderously among hot weather lounges, couches, and thin-necked modern lamps—morning coffee, iced tea and gin—*frou-frou* bedrooms—antiques—eighteenth century, Colonial Virginia paintings, up-to-date computers, and modulated alarms. Is *Wall Street* up or down? You know, the portfolio is, of course, always more interesting than the Pound.

But the bones are here a-mortalizing across the road in oblong blocks centered by Grand and called Cypress, Myrtle, Jasmine, Cedar, Willow, Rose, Orange, Juniper, Elm, Maple, Magnolia, Locust, Spruce, and Pine, the place sandwiched between Broadway and Gaines, I-630/Eleventh and Thirteenth, as a hierarchy of death whose stories are curled beneath the ground like un-etherized cats lying under a table.

So, let's stroke a few. Peter Le Fevre (1750–1820), a *Quebecois aventurier* looking for fortune on the lower river but finding death instead, who was put down above water it was thought, only to be flooded up again and dropped like a prank in someone else's yard—his dried intact remains remained roped up in a tree, then bleached, washed, and retrieved to a granddaughter's Little Rock parlor till buried near her own moldering self across from Juniper.

Then there is Mary Webster Loughborough (1836–1887), who lived in a cave once with her Confederate husband high along a bluff above the Mississippi—a town founded by a preacher named Vick since it was dry, above Natchez and below Memphis. Here Mary fought a battle by that name—losing it, of course, and with it the war because Lee went off to Pennsylvania of all places and so let her starve. Mary, a writer, founded the *Ladies Southern Journal* in '86, and placing a memoir, *My Cave Life in Vicksburg,* on that infernal list that sells best, lies now on Cedar with lots less room than she had in the cavern above the river and with about as much to eat.

Oh, to be sure, we can't forget poor Sarah "Sallie" Faulkner Trapnall (unknown till '81); planted between Rose and Willow, a debutante whose powerful father named a county and sired a princess to die a pauper   family and money all gone, Sallie, a cripple lamed by a carriage wheel, once lived in mansions before begging in the streets to show what can happen even to a *belle* of the ball who is put out then goes back down.

Then there is Quatie Ross, the Red on Rose, a Cherokee chief's wife, who died in the Rock while on a feverish hiatus from the "Trail of Tears," succumbing on the Arkansas leg in '39.

Not too far, over from her, the O. Dodd boy is on Elm, up from the Fletchers, down a bit on Juniper, while Fagan, the general, who everyone really knew (need Steele have asked) "put him up to it," still keeps his distance on Cypress by the back fence, a defender of slavery, he sleeps a street across from a Negro college with colors of green and yellow, sharing a row with a governor and a state senator near a special sunken hole ever a-waiting victims of bed and bottle as "a plot for members of the Legislature who die during sessions."

Mr. Shall's skull is on Orange.

> The Hanged man. Fear death by water.
> I see crowds of people, walking round in a ring.

Homer Joe was to be buried back at home, "out back" near his family, friends, and animals: Calvin and Luther—that was the plan.

Medora decided that it was good after all, that it was a bad winter. The hard ground and the creeks and rivers would bear up an old wagon loaded with all the new stuff off Markham; a boy in a coffin, herself—a fancy white Tottenburg mare "on permanent loan" and one very tired, reluctant, and generally confused mule, who in the depths of his mule mind longed for the Edenic fields of his now-lost Arcadia. As it stayed cold and Homer kept fine, no buzzards followed them or anything, and Medora made good time without much bother.

That is to say, Ulysses went faster than any such mule ever has, walled-eyed, blowing, bouncing at a fatuous but steady trot; the little group—horse, mule, woman, and dead boy—stopping the night in the forest, camping, warming by a low fire, the air touching zero again after it snowed thick in the dying warmth of a very long day.

But at midnight men came—on horses, fast—lots of them, cursing and laughing as they rushed past. The fire was dowsed and Medora sat listening to the rattling sabers and creaking saddles—Yankee cavalry on the loose, she whispered to Useless and the horse, while holding his nose from a neigh. They came fresh from flaming her Arcadia, she realized, yet still she saw it simmering when she arrived—the cold morning air lifting with mist, frost, and slow circling, yellow, smelly smoke curling above standing chimneys as they pulled in to find no one there.

Yet with the help of some paper under a stone, they found all but one. Rose-In-May had gone off again with the Blue soldiers, Aunt Essie said, "looking for that no-good darky of hers she cain't never git over."

So Medora, Iphigenia, Nora, and Aunt Essie dug Homer Joe's little place behind an Arcadia now only ash and brick. The ground was frozen hard. Then, early, as the sun came up, Homer Joe went down, while Medora recited from St. Paul the same words now etching themselves on a great-great-grandson's granite—another boy killed in another civil war—a love affair with lost causes, it seems—where Elizabeth sat remembering her Grandmother Nora as the old woman of her childhood, with straight wiry gray hair and a tiny, barely visible mustache, lying curled on a bed in Mississippi. Then Medora added, because she felt something else needed saying, "Lord, I done what I could ..." She sighed, then to the others, "Y'all need to learn ... it's hard, I know ... but the sooner the better ... that life ain't nothing but a-learnin' how to say goodbye."

"But I don't want to ever say goodbye," said Nora, crying, "ever, ever, ever."

Medora dried Nora's eyes with hugs, paused, gathered herself, said another prayer and asked God to bless their journey and again to keep her son's soul. Then they loaded the wagon, promoted Useless beside the useful mare, and headed south to Washington.

"They make a funny pair, Ma," Nora said, bouncing on the seat between Iphigenia and Medora, with Aunt Essie in the back, lounging on a sack of feed (bought by Philomena because she had money and allegiance papers), as she smoked a pipe and warmed under a blanket like the one the Yankees stole and never brought back as good gentlemen should but which everyone knew they almost never were. "It jes ain't in em," Medora would say when telling the story well into the next century.

But that day she said, "They do, honey ... a horse and a mule ... shore nuff make a funny pair ... that's a fact ... but I think they'll get us back to our father."

Then she whipped them equally. (Though she didn't know it, Medora was an egalitarian at heart.) So Useless and his female friend lurched forward, pulling them away from Arcadia's ruins without a backward glance.

It was a little before their time but if they had known they might have said John Gould's farewell, which should have been his epitaph:

> You will not wish to follow me
> Across the twisted hills;
> Along the milkwhite streams,
> Adown green limestone sills;
> Where dangling whipporwills
> Cry through the sky at dawn:
> For Into Empty space
> You'll find that I am gone.

CHAPTER NINE

The country seems to have degenerated into bushwhackers. It's hardly safe
to go out of our lines a mile.
　　—Letter to Lincoln from Union general in Little Rock

Medora and her brood trekked through a rough countryside bushwhacked
and ravaged to exhaustion. Their southward journey was a steady meandering
past burned or abandoned houses, uncultivated fields, empty cabins and farms
as they inched along, unsure of friend or foe. Keeping to the woods and back
trails as they were able, entering easily through Confederate lines, trudging
then into the village of Benton, they lodged at an acquaintance's house and
traded some coffee for horse feed and rested. But Medora was anxious to get
on to Washington, so after two short days, she led them down the trail toward
Rockport and the Ouachita River ford.

Despite being behind the lines, this closeness to the Yankee-occupied Rock
created the hazard of a chance meeting with a mounted Union patrol. The cavalry struggle had gotten increasingly savage, developing into a more or less perpetual hell-for-leather game of hide-and-seek that swirled around the
countryside in a great scourge with clashes invariably beginning as a short
screaming, shooting, saber-and-saddle skirmish, followed by a much longer,
lathering catch-me-if-you-can chase back to the Yankee sanctuary, invariably
involving the innocent in some various form of misfortune. In a word, Medora
was worried.

Though, it was generally believed otherwise, the Yankee horse never ventured very far across the Ouachita River, and safety even there was by no means
certain. Too, the woods were chock full of runaway slaves, guerrillas, deserters, and bushwhackers whose numbers and brutality seemed, like the struggle itself, to increase as the war fed fat upon the increasingly lean population
for its third year.

Mindful of this, Medora, being a colonel's wife, arranged from the
Confederate authorities in Benton for a modest escort of Gray cavalry for the
early part of the first day. These riders went with them several miles south of

town but turned around near noon, politely, and with obvious reluctance, leaving this brave woman with her two daughters, an elderly female slave, a mare and a mule, all looking very lonely, standing as they were on a wilderness road surrounded by a woods containing "God knows what menace," Medora said. Staring and waving at their departing countrymen with a most grateful sadness, they all well knew, at least as far as Rockport, Medora's helpless little flock would simply have to take its chances. In short, they now were on their own.

Yet, God provides, as they say, and, almost as soon as the Southern boys reined reluctantly around, disappearing behind them, a new protector emerged—a male Blue Tick hound who, as if very patiently waiting, stepped bravely forth from the forest, following at a slight distance, seemingly taking up his post in relief of the horse guard. Nora and Iphigenia called and whistled but he stopped in mid trot, listened, then trotted again, not quite coming, nor quite leaving. He was obviously tired and his ribs were visible even to Aunt Essie, whose aging eyes, by her own account, were increasingly dim.

But they didn't give up, and by lunch, Nora and Iphigenia squatted in the frozen mud, coaxing the old hound up to a piece of hard cornbread. It wasn't long before they had their hands on his head and arms around his neck, pulling and inspecting his ears and tail and poking dirty fingers into his mouth and eye and smelling his nasty breath. He didn't care, his tail wagged slowly, then accelerated as they sang sweet words in baby-dog talk till one of them got licked on the lips. They missed Calvin and Luther and were very glad of having found this peripatetic hound.

"What's his name gonna be?" asked Medora, watching with amusement.

"Wagon Wheel," Nora pronounced with the authority of one who has given the matter a great deal of mental energy.

Everyone laughed, including, it appeared, Wagon Wheel. The name was perfect. "I like it so much, I think I'm going with y'all to Washington," he seemed to say, smiling as only a dog can. He obviously was Rebel to the bone and going to the Confederate capital was very much to his liking.

That first night they camped some piece off the road in thick brush, about two miles up from the ford at a spot Wagon Wheel, "riding point," seemed to recognize.

"Don't burn nothin' wet, it makes too much smoke. Cut limbs awf the trees or get the ones standin' awf the ground ... they're dryer than that's own the ground ... it's damp from snow and rain," Medora reminded, as they built a small cooking fire, ate, and hovered around its warmth.

As was the routine, they emptied the wagon, stacked supplies around its three sides, made an evergreen bed underneath which they covered with blankets and then stretched a tarpaulin into a half shelter from the edge of the sideboard, pinning it to the ground with crude wooden pegs—a house with one roof, so to speak.

That night, Medora rolled up at one end and Aunt Essie at the other, the two girls snug in the middle, with Wagon Wheel curled at their feet and, bound tightly in blankets and clothes, they stayed warm—except, of course, for exposed things like noses. That night it got cold—very, very cold.

Usually up well before dawn, this morning found them sleeping. It was snowing, and their lair had become a cave of snugness.

But reluctantly, Medora sat up at last.

"Lord hep us, it's almost a foot deep," she said, staring out at the white stuff.

She hesitated, then staggered out and began to labor together a fire. Aunt Essie followed, breaking sticks and limbs pulled off trees. Soon, with dry pine-knots lit, a fire was stoked and coaxed into a great blaze as they put together their morning "glop" in a big black pot to go with hard cornbread and coffee.

Then Iphigenia and Nora crawled out, rubbing their eyes and brushing off the snow before eating.

No sooner had they finished, enjoying that brief unofficial respite that always seems to arise between eating and not, than Wagon Wheel swung his head, stopping in mid-cornbread bite, listening. He paused for a second, then trotted off about fifty yards along their back trail and stopped. Then he bayed a mournful sound that came from deep down in his hound's body and soul.

"Shut him up!" Medora yelled, running to him, but Nora got there first, put her arm around his neck, and clasped his jaws shut as the heavy gallop of riders, creaking and rattling with saddles and sidearms, came at last to the weak human ear, the noise coming louder and louder rushing past for the river, then turning down to the ford. Union, Confederate cavalry, or bushwhackers? they wondered, as the sound faded as quickly as it had come upon them.

"That devil Steele ain't above sendin' patrols this far along for nothing … he's toying with a-marching south, I warrant … come sprang," Medora said, adding, "They won't letem sit thar long no matter how pleased he is at a-doin' it."

"Dem hosses was fresh," Aunt Essie offered, releasing the mare's nose. (Ulysses, aside from a steady, prideful flatulence, was not noisy about really anything, much less Yankee outriders, so had been ignored.)

As they gathered once more round the fire, chatting away their nerves,

Wagon Wheel, still agitated, loped off down to the road, sniffed around, then returned with a look of deadly, uncharacteristic seriousness.

"Yeah," Medora said, unconsciously scratching him behind the ears, "didn't sound like no withered-out Reb nags, did it, Aunt Essie?"

"Noam."

"They'll be back then, Maw?" Nora asked.

"They might, honey, but if'n they're Steele's boys, they'll take another way back ... most likely ... else they might get thumped by ours or bushwhackers, or both, you know, a-followin' and a-waitin' for a mistake like that, shadowin' along like wolves. No, we better sit tight for a little while, case somebody's a-followin' or they circle back right smart. Lucky the snow covered our tracks."

"Our boys wouldn't hurt us none, Maw. I wish we'd find some more," said Nora wistfully, poking a stick in the flames.

Medora had noticed a certain something growing between Nora and one of the pinkfaced riders and now she heard this feeling again in Nora's voice.

"No, but the bushwhackers will, honey ... they're worse than Union Blue ... we best be careful with awl of 'em ... maybe, we'll run into our own but best hide from all sorts, as we can. Cain't take no chances with none of 'em."

They waited for an hour, then broke camp and forded the Ouachita, making slow progress. They passed a wagoner on the trail who told them the patrol was Union and had gone through toward Arkadelphia but "our boys are own thar tail now and they won't have time to so much as stretch thar legs."

Medora, nevertheless, decided to get off the road again and found an old trail still visible in the snow like a small sunken streambed. She followed it to a creek, crossed, and took another, even fainter trail that meandered them through a large stand of pine then led up to a deserted house that appeared suddenly in a grown up meadow like an apparition.

They crept by it then followed along unexpectedly into a small valley that ran about a quarter of a mile more coming finally to a rail fence fronting a cabin. It was a small square of logs with a porch, a chimney of mud and sticks, with a roof cistern collecting on one side. Behind was a slovenly barn, an empty slave cabin, and some out-buildings. In front, the hitching post, a supper bell, and a large shade tree with a nice set of deer antlers nailed proudly head high gave it that lived-in look.

Medora decided to be bold.

"Ho!" she yelled, standing in the wagon, "is anybody about!? Ho! Anybody home!?"

There was silence so she said it louder.

Nothing.

"Don't reckon there's a body around," she said.

Wagon Wheel was busy investigating, first sniffing the yard in a looping circle up to the steps, stopping, sniffing once or twice more before hopping on the porch, smelling the door, backstepping a little, until he paused and with a deep mournful bay said he thought someone was, indeed, home after all.

For a moment things seemed time-suspended—Wagon Wheel hunched down, staring at the door, the women in the wagon with Medora holding the reins and Aunt Essie beside her, black fingers gripping the shotgun, Nora and Iphigenia lying on corn and coffee sacks with their heads just visible over the sideboard, while the horse and even Ulysses gawked with perked-up ears at a slowly opening, creaking door, nudged back by a Damascus barrel side-by-side that slid through about halfway like a curious two-headed snake.

"Hand me the gun," Medora whispered, sitting back down, reaching, as Aunt Essie slid the doublebarrel across Medora's lap.

"Who are you and what do you want?" came a female voice, just loud enough for them to hear.

Wagon Wheel back stepped, bellowing uncontrollably, looking first at Medora then at the cabin, back and forth, making music, then swung in a circle of indecision before sitting on his haunches again, howling crazily.

"Come here, Wagon Wheel!" Medora yelled. "Just here with my Negro woman and two daughters, Mam! Come here, Wagon Wheel! I said come here!"

"I'm gonna shoot that dawg if you don't pull him back!" the voice said, appearing now as a woman, standing full in the doorway, raising the shotgun almost to her shoulder.

"No!" screamed Nora, jumping down.

"Nora!" Medora yelled, standing again, lifting her gun a bit but not aiming.

Wagon Wheel bellowed even more bravely as Nora flung herself around his neck like a calf roper.

"Little girl, take that dawg outta my yard," said the woman, lowering the gun slightly.

Nora grabbed him by his loose neck hide and jerked him back to the wagon where Iphigenia pulled him in as he crawled over the sacks then raised his head over the sideboard and bellowed one more time just to have the last word.

"We got him, Maw," said Nora breathlessly proud, Iphigenia pushing the tail-tucked rear, while Nora, trying to make him hush, wrestled him down onto a sack of corn, making them both disappear.

"What do you want?" said the woman once more.

Medora looked more closely at her. About her own age, wearing a ratty sweater over a dirty calico dress, she was hard but clever-faced, with her graying hair mussed back into a bun. Then the blond head of a very dirty child emerged, staring timidly around a knee, fingers tightly rumpling the calico.

"Go back inside, Heidi," she said, and the head disappeared.

"We don't mean y'all no harm," Medora said, lowering the gun even more. "We're a-runnin' from them godforsaken thievin' Yankees and bushwhackers … took this road to your place … didn't know you were down yar … we don't mean no harm, Mam. Honest."

The woman hesitated, looked them over a bit more, then lowered the gun and said, "Leave your piece in the wagon and come own in."

As Medora's eyes adjusted to the dark she saw a house of only one large room. Half was nearly taken by two beds: a large four-poster with a smaller one beside it; at the other end was a great stone fireplace fronted by a table, some chairs with deerskin seats, a corner dresser, and a bureau. Scattered around were such things as coal oil lamps, candles, crockery, sewing items, clothes, an almanac, faded newspapers, a powder horn, Bowie knife, a child's doll, missing an eye and arm, a big black Bible and even a cavalry sword in its sheath hanging proudly over the mantle. There were no windows, so, the lamps were lit this winter day for heat as well as light.

"My name's Hildred," she said, "Hildred Himmel. My husband, William, is a-servin' with General Price. My daughter yar name's Heidi."

Medora quickly told her story while Aunt Essie and Nora took care of Mary Bell (the mare's new name) and Ulysses, while Iphigenia played with Heidi and Wagon Wheel in the front yard's dirty snow.

"Reckon y'all's hungry," Hildred said.

"I've got cawfee and …"

"Cawfee?!" Hildred interrupted.

"Sure do … from the Rock."

"Well, I'm powerful glad you took the turn ye done … come own, let's rustle something together."

The fire was stoked, then the children called in for stale cornbread, molasses, and very cold salt pork fat with a side slice of venison. The adults had coffee while children drank goat's milk from a pitcher.

Hildred had not stopped talking since she laid her gun on the bed. After eating, the girls went back outside with Wagon Wheel.

"Just like as happened to you, them plunderin' Jayhawkers come thew one day ... eatin' or killin' all the stock they could lay blade to ... a-lootin' the smokehouse and such ... cussin' and hollerin' ... it was them Ioway boys ... them that like to strut with their spurs and swords and talk big and awl ... they's the devil's messengers, I tell ye."

"Sounds like the same bunch'o demons that come thew Arcadia ... a-plunderin' vermin from hell they are," Medora said quietly.

"Yeah, them's the ones ... the very same ... nem and a bunch of Kansas Coloreds ... all fancied up in blue ... mixed right in with 'em, too ... you know, to scare Whites about the darkies a-risin' up and awl ... but that just makes people want to bow thar necks that much more. But our boys, God love'em, was on thar sorry damn tail the whole time and finally run 'em awf like the cowards they is a-fore they could git down to a-burnin' us out. They never found my goats neither ... which I keep hid in a little barn behind the first big field which is now all growed up in cuckleburrs and briars and sech. We worked hard a-clearin' that pasture but I just cain't do nothin' with it as short-handed as I am with the darkies run awf and William in the war. Heidi and I'll manage till William gets back ... on goats milk, squirrel and deer ... and whatever the good Lord sends our way ... we'll manage ... till our boys lick'em good and we'll have our own country then and want have to put up with Yankee interference no more ... just have to start all over again own our place though. Himmel Hill, that's what we a-named it. William thought of that when he seed it ... we was aimin' to go to Texas but he took a shine to this piece o'ground yar and we been own it ever since. That's the long and short of it, we'll jes have to start over when this yar war is over in the Lord's good time ... his time is not ourn ... we have to accept that ... but least ways Heidi and I ain't had no trouble since that last bunch of Yankees come thew and awl ... truth is, now thar ain't that much for no one to steal ..."

"How about bushwhackers?"

"Oh, I know most of them boys ... they ain't no problem if'n you know 'em and handle 'em jes right. I ain't got nothin' for 'em no way."

Medora told her about Titus and then asked, "Do yew know whur William is a-servin' at now?"

"Last I knowed, they's in Warshington ... but I don't yar much these days. He come thew own a spot of leave jest afore the Yankees done ... hid in the woods the whole time he was yar, except at night. I still had one darky left then, never had but four ... she carried food out to him ... where he was hid at and awl ... but awl my other'ns done run off by then and now she done the same. I never expected that outta her ... left out with them big jayhawking Kansas Coloreds who think its thar job in life to stir up awl the others in this yar country ... ruinin' ever last one, I tell you. It's Satan's work, shore is. Well, anyway, Kissie took a quick shine to one of them struttin' bucks in a big hurry ... I seen that right off. I raised her up like one of my own ... shore did ... her mother, Grace, God rest her, died a-birthin her ... I bought Grace awf a free Black that come thew on his way to Loosiana a-fore the war. He wanted to sell her bad and we got her cheap as dirt ... best deal we ever made own one ... good as gold, too ... she wuz ... real sweet natured. Her owner, this free Black, why he just showed up out of the blue one day, like you done ... with his traps and awl, family and his three slaves. He said he was a blacksmith in Missouri ... had learned his trade from a good master who let him work on the side and buy his freedom ... then he went into business for hisself and bought a slave, then another, and was a-doin' rale good ... but decided to move on to Shreveport whur he said his mother wuz in bondage and he wanted to work and buy her freedom too ... said she'd been sold when he wuz jes a boy ... said he had too many mouths to feed on the trail and had to sell somebody awf. So that's how we got Grace. Anyway, I told Kissie, Grace's little girl ... that's her name ... lest ways the one we call her by ... not her Christian name ... the kids give it to her when she wuz just a little thang a-playin' together in the dirt. I told her I'd never sell her nor nothin' ... she'd have a place for the rest of her born days with us yar ... she could live and die with our family for shore ... just live with us till the end of her pilgrimage... have a good life ... just like one big family. See, I promised Grace on her death bed ... she made me promise with her dyin' breath. I held her hand and we prayed over it ... together ... me and Grace a-prayin' durin' her last moment ... then she left this vale of tears fur a better land and I could never go back on that promise, see. I'd die first.

"We got awl a body needs yar ... a good piece of ground ... farm and garden ... raise our own stock, hawgs and such ... row-crop fur some cash ... thar's still some game around ... our smokehouse wuz always full ... we don't need nothin' else. But Kissie run awf anyway ... she was cryin' and awl ... you know a-hollerin' and carryin' on like they'll do when they git awl worked up ... a-thowin' her arms around me and a-askin' me to forgive her and ever'thang ... a-sayin' she couldn't hep it nor nothin' ... that we'd done right by her and but she jes wanted to be free ... it was a turble thang to behold."

"There's no understandin' it, Hildred."

"Naw, after awl we done for 'em ... and that one just up and run awf like that ... not gratful at awl ... it wuz sumppin' to behold ... you're right ... I mean, we never broke up no families ... never sold nobody ... though I had one young boy I should of sold first chance I got ... he done run anyway ... man come thew yar one day a-wantin' to buy him cheap and William wanted to sell but I talked him outta it ... said we vowed never to break up a family ... that ain't rat. I don't hold with it ... it's against God's law. But fact-o'-the-bidness we wuz too easy on 'em in some ways, I guess ... lookin' back on it ... but we believed it our Christian duty to do rat by 'em. But, anyway, first chance they get ... they'll run ... ever last one. It's this Yankee curse is what it is ... corrupts everythang. It ain't rat, they're gonna ruin the whole damn country before it's over, if we don't win this war ... but thar'll be a judgment, for shore, I have to believe that."

"There will be," said Medora.

"But I figure the pieson started a-risin' and Kissie jes couldn't hep herself ... she'll git nuff of them uppity town darkies some day and come home to the only family she's really got."

"She might," said Medora, "you never know about a darky ... what they're really a-thinkin', I mean ... but town shore ruins 'em."

"Town ruins ever'body, in my book. Not just darkies, Whites too."

Medora said nothing.

"Kissie wuz a good girl, though, she really wuz, not like most. Like I say, raised her up like one of my own. I lost my two boys ... one to fever one year and the other to the croup the next ... three and six ... Little William and Wenford, they's buried out back ... where I'll be someday ... Grace's buried not far awf. So, Heidi and Kissie's all the kids I got left ... now Kissie's gone," said Hildred, not noticing Medora's silence.

Then Medora told her about Homer Joe.

"Remember, dear, have faith," said Hildred, "that'll get you thew.".

"Amen ... you got any other family at awl?" asked Medora.

"Brothers and one sister. Brother Raymond, the middle boy, is with the Third Arkansas up in Virginny ... with Marse Lee ... mustered in with that bunch over at Tulip ... he's been wounded twicet ... come home oncet for a short spell after a-takin' a Minié ball rat straight thew the meat of his leg at Second Manassas ... couldn't wait to git back ... beat ever'thang I ever seen ... and another brother ... Rodrick ... he's the youngest. Him and William joined up in '61 with Price. They was at the Elkhorn together. William damn near got kilt thar hisself, come home to mend while Rodrick, unscratched as he wuz, went a-walkin' with Van Dorn, and nem that was left, awl the way to Miss'sippi … too late fur Shiloh. I sure wuz thankful to hear that, I tell ye…. thought he's gonna make it for shore … seemed like the hand of Providence wuz in it, but then he got kilt straight awf at Corinth. I ain't gonna feel rat till I find his grave … gonna go lookin' first chance I git after this yar cursed war is done finished with. Will and I are a-goin' to see if'n we can find it. He promised me that much. I shore hated that … a-losin' him … he wuz the baby of our family."

"Any sisters?"

"Onc, she's married, lives awf in Texas somewhures … don't never hear nothin' much from her though. Husband's a sutler come down from Kentucky … come thew one day … just like that free Black done … but with a big fancy wagon and awl … like a gypsy … a real shirker, that's all he amounts to … a-makin' money on the war sellin' to whichever army's around. It's blood money in my book. I got no use for him and Hilda knows it. They got two youngins now, boys, but they're too young fur the war, thank the Lord."

"Aunt Essie?" said Medora, thinking of her own when Hildred mentioned her nephews.

"Yessum."

"Go check own the girls and Wagon Wheel … they played long enough out there … catch thar death …"

"Yessum," said Aunt Essie getting up from behind the table where she had been sitting, quietly leaving her coffee and going out.

There wasn't really room for them with Hildred, and, while Medora was reluctant, but since no one wanted to sleep outside anymore or in the barn, they decided on the slave cabin. It had a fireplace, crude furniture, and beds. Medora, Aunt Essie, Nora, and Iphigenia were all together with Wagon Wheel curled on the floor by the fire, while Blue Bell and Ulysses were in the barn with the wagon. Medora piled blankets thick over the old beds that still smelled of humans—humans who had been sleeping there before them, night after night, in a constant state of hope and longing—humans, now fled onto roads, camps, and towns, "Contraband," as the Yankees called them—the old chains finally broken—the new ones waiting to be fastened in an invisible un-sever-ability—chained to the land in a new un-slaved-slavery, then to the cities in a un-freed-freedom—a justice forever deferred, kicked down the path in an unending, wandering, wavering, circling movement from town to soil, then to town again, then to big city, owning nothing, always serving, place to place, a shackled people with no covenant or promised land, wandering in an endless desert of alienation and unrealized anticipation.

Heidi, in her innocence, had wanted to sleep in the slave cabin, too, where Kissie had slept, because she had loved and missed her, and now her new friends were there and she loved them in an instant, but Hildred wouldn't have it, so Heidi sobbed in her own tiny corner bed, cried for herself and a father gone away to something she didn't understand, sobbed for her dead brothers killed by fever and the slaves that had run away with the Yankees, which for her was the same as death. She cried a warm wet tear-stained brown circle on her pillow till Hildred let her in her bed and warmed her to sleep next to her own hot, still un-old body buried under layers of heavy blankets in a cabin that often got so cold water froze in the pitcher.

No one could remember a winter like this in Arkansas and it was getting colder, the night slowly brightening with a moon that lit the snow in a white reflection, eliminating any need for torch or lantern, as Hildred, awakened by the creeping chill of an ebbing fire which she usually let go out but fearful for Heidi's health, rose, stoked, added logs, and, low on wood, went out for more. She needed no lamp and quickly succumbed to the thrall of a moon lifting itself over the dark shadow line of trees like a great silver balloon. Pulling her shawl more tightly, she paused under the servitude of blinding snow, stars, and the silver sphere.

"Where will our next winter be?" she thought. It was now possible for her to imagine the unthinkable—leaving Himmel Hill. They had worked, built, cleared the wilderness, put in a garden and orchard, planted row crops year after year till in security they imagined their final days; children raised and gone, grandchildren, themselves resting at last with family and slaves nearby— duty done—the reward of heaven to come. But the war had come instead, a hell, not heaven, burning itself into their lives like the pine knots now raging in the slave cabin, just visible through the chinks like a merciless furnace, forcing Hildred into a frantic despair of losing all. What can a worn-out, nearly middle-aged woman with a small child do? she wondered, shackled as she was by the moon's visage into pausing, despite the freezing air.

For the first time, she feared that heaven held no answers, that in all its hard beauty this moon set above the trees was nothing but a great gray rock floating frigidly in the sky, thoughtless of Hildred Himmel, or her Heidi, or William, her sister in Texas, her brother with Robert E. Lee, or Kissie or anything at all—not of this war, nor peace, or any other human vanity, folly or thing of any kind; all human suffering, joy, love, hate, hope, crime, ambition, and despair

PHILLIP H. MCMATH

passing pompously beneath its blind gaze like every other Lost Kingdom ticking its way inexorably toward its tomb of lost time.

She freed herself from the moon's brightly dull despair, picked up an armload of wood and turned, retreating, as from a thing of horror, in to a fire that would warm her worn but busy hands. After quickly stacking the wood, she squatted in the shadows before the hearth, the flames dancing over her weathered face like an apparition, as she stoked up a great blaze, then rested on her heels, staring hypnotically into its heat, listening to the steady rhythm of Heidi's breathing, then her eyes were at last drawn away from the flame to the angelic face framed serenely by the golden curls of all that remained of her living flesh.

It snowed for two hours in the early morning but stopped at sunrise. But the warming sun brought the bushwhackers like maggots out of a frozen carcass—Sam D. Suggins and his four sorry sons—riding up noisily on lathering stolen cavalry horses, except for the obese in-bred idiot, Deverl, who rode a stout black mule. They carried pistols, sabers, Bowie knifes, and short-barreled carbine rifles. Sam wore a turkey feathered, nearly new Stetson, while the others sported worn-out broad brims, except for Deverl, who, once again the exception, pulled down a filthy woolen sock cap over his large ears and oily black hair.

Moonshiners liberated by war into their more natural instinct of full-blown brigandage, they smelled of filth and, except for the youngest and smallest one, were on an early morning drunk, and a bottle went quickly hand-to-hand as they halted in front of Hildred's cabin fence.

Sam hollered. The door opened as before, the shotgun nosing out in just the same way.

"What do you want, Sam Suggins?" she said, loud enough for Medora and her crouching brood to hear as they stared through the chinks of the cabin.

Suggins dismounted and walked halfway to the porch. He belted a pistol and an officer's saber, which dragged a wiggling line in the snow like a slithering snake in white sand.

"That's far enough, don't take one step closer," said Hildred, raising the gun a little off her hip.

Suggins stopped.

"We're told thar were a wagonload of White women and nigger female come up this-a way ... you knowed anythin' 'bout that, Hildred?"

"I ain't seen 'em."

"Well that's rale funny cause we wuz a-trailin' 'em till this yar new snow covered thar tracks … but it shore looked like they wuz headed up to yore place."

"I ain't seen 'em, I said."

"Mind if'n we look around a little? If they ain't yar it won't do not harm, now will it?"

"I shore do mind, Sam Suggins, you are drunk and I don't want yore kind on my place … so … I'm tellin' ye to leave … rat now … ye yare me … I mean it!"

"You's a might touchy today, ain't you, Hildred?"

"I don't hold with bushwhackers, ye know that. Yew boys ought to be a-servin' in the army a-fightin' Yankees not terrorizing yore own people and scarin' the darkies … so, take yore tails awf my land and git!"

"We killt 'r share of Yankees … and the niggers stay skeered."

"I'm a-tellin' ye to get awf my land rat now!"

Deverl let out a crackling gush of hysterical noise, snorted, freed his feet of the stirrups, and swung them back and forth as if in a swing.

"Goddamn it, Deverl, hush!" yelled Suggins, turning and facing the man-child.

Deverl hushed, stopped swinging his feet, unholstered his pistol then sullenly began to fondle the new colt revolver, staring down its long barrel then fondled it again.

"I see that cabin is a-smokin' … one of yore runaways done come back?" Suggins said, turning back to Hildred.

"Kissie."

"When?"

"Yesterdee."

"Well, well, I guess yore powerful glad of that ain't ye? Must git hard tryin' to keep this place up without no niggers to do the hard work. Will gone and awl … jes yew and that youngin' of yorn, ain't it?"

"It beats a-murderin' and thievin'."

"We're jes a-takin' what comes our way, is awl … jes like all the rest, see? We jes takes different thangs."

Hildred caressed the triggers.

"You must git lonesome without no man around, huh, Hildred?" Suggins said, leering up a big grin, showing his black teeth.

"Sam Suggins, I'm a-gettin' rale tard of this yar little conversation … so, ye and yore sorry lot need to git out of yar rat now 'fore I git wore out a-holdin' this yar scatter gun an decide to use it so I can tend to my chores that needs doin'."

"Naw, we ain't a-goin' jes yet. See, the way I figger, Kissie was the nigger woman in that wagon we been a-followin' and the rest wuz White ... all women a-travelin' by thar lonesome ... that's what we heerd, an' if they wuz White they must have valuables ... ye know a-carryin' family jewels and heirlooms and sech like ... own the run from a burned-out homestead an' awl ... or even gold, maybe ... a-sewed in thar dresses or hid somewhur rale private like," he said, sneering again, "and we jes might have fun a-lookin' for that," he added, laughing stupidly.

Deverl laughed too and swung his legs more than ever.

"Goddamn you, Deverl! I said hush! I don't want to have to tell ye no more!" Suggins said, turning on him once more, flushing red.

Deverl hushed, stopped swinging his legs, and played with his pistol again, then turned to the small rider on his right and said, "Drank!?"

This one, obviously the youngest, slight of build with a boyish face, handed the whiskey with his left hand without drinking. Deverl finished it in several Adam's Apple-bobbing swallows then threw the bottle against the house. It rolled slowly gathering speed till it fell off the porch with a plop.

Suggins faced Hildred once more. "I don't see no wagon or nothin' and since no self-respectin' White would sleep in a nigger cabin, yew musta got yore Kissie in thar and the Whites hid back in that holler maybe whur yew keep yore goats at in the ole hawg barn a-back thar and ye got them hid rale good like ... huh? Ain't that rat ... awl tucked away ... whur ye can look after 'em ... don't ye?"

"That you'll never know, Sam Suggins."

"Or maybe they's in the barn or jes inside behind ye ... all hid like rats under the beds an' all, a-cryin' and a-hopin' we won't look under thar?" he said, trying to peek past her.

"I'm tellin' you fur the last time ... git!"

Suggins quit smiling. "Listen, goddamn yore hide, I'm sick a-arguin' with ye ... we're gonna take a look around, see, and yew ain't gonna stop us, ye yar!" he said, dropping his hand to his pistol.

Suggins big sorrel, Satan, turned his head and whinnied. Blue Bell in the barn whinnied back.

There was a pause, then Suggins smiled.

"Well, if that don't beat awl, thars a horse in the barn, wonder who hit belongs to, huh?"

"He's mine."

"Thought the Yankees done took all yore stock … huh?"

"They left me a horse."

"That ain't hardly like 'em, now is it, Hildred?"

She said nothing.

He turned away to his sons.

"Boys, hit looks like we done come to the rat place, after awl. Dudgert, yew and Delbert take a look see around in that ole barn and then go get that nigger winch outta the cabin and brang her yar!"

"How 'bout that horse?" Dudgert asked.

"Leave it for the time bein' … we'll take it when we leave."

Dudgert started to rein for the barn but Hildred froze him. "Dudgert!" she said. "Son, yew ride in any direction except out that gate and yew'll be a-caughin' up buckshot, ye yar me! And that's a promise!"

Then she yelled even louder, "I'm not a woman to be toyed with and y'all know that much about Hildred Himmel. I've faced down Yankees and Injuns and no bunch o' sorry damn drunken bushwhackers is gonna rob my place while I'm a-breathin', ye yar? So, ride on out rat now and ain't nobody gonna get hurt … understand what I say? Now, boys, I ain't a-triflin', I tell ye!"

Medora inched her shotgun a little farther through a chink to steady it, aiming at the four heads lined up along the front fence.

"I thank I can reach 'em awl," she whispered to Aunt Essie. "Ever last one."

"Lawd hep us," Aunt Essie said.

"Amen," whispered Medora, cocking the hammer, aiming the bead right on Dudgert's floppy black hat.

"Lawd, Lawd," Aunt Essie said, holding the dog's muzzle. "The Lawd keep and protect us."

"We got too many for ye, ye caint hold us," Suggins said matter-of-factly.

"We'll see, won't we, Sam," Hildred said, thumbing back the hammer and raising the gun to a snug shoulder fit.

Then the idiot shot her. In the next quarter beat, Hildred mashed Suggins's head backwards, his Stetson flying, while, slumping in the doorway, with the second trigger, she helped Deverl down off his mule. His new revolver, stolen from a dead Yankee boy freshly arrived from Kansas, fired harmlessly a second time as he rolled off in a great moronic plop. His mule, suddenly unburdened of two-hundred-and-sixty-odd pounds of superfluous flesh, stepped back, straddled a quick reverse turn, and lunged for the gate.

In the next half moment, Medora touched the line of riders with the right barrel, nudging Dudgert neatly out of the saddle. The others whirled away, but she put the second barrel into the nearest one's left shoulder, hoping the shot would pattern out into the farthest—but neither fell, as the horses passed the cantering mule at the far fence by the road.

"Damnation!" Medora said, reloading.

"You gots 'em! You gots 'em! You gots 'em!" yelled Aunt Essie, opening the door, jumping up and down. She watched Delbert slump to the ground, catch his foot in the stirrup, and get dragged into the gate post, untwisting his boot. His horse leapt through, leaving him as the other rider jumped the fence and disappeared with mule and horses into the trees.

"Damnation!" Medora said, seeing Hildred with Heidi shrieking over her and the wounded man rolling in the snow while Wagon Wheel bayed out the door.

"Damnation! Damnation! Damnation!" Medora kept repeating as she reached Hildred. "I'm sorry, Hildred, I'm so very sorry," she said, holding her.

"It's awl my fault ... I shouldn't come own up yar ... forgive me, please. I'm sorry ... it's awl my fault, dear."

"No it weren't," Hildred whispered.

Aunt Essie fumbled open the blouse revealing a small hole at the breast.

"Let's get her in the bed," Medora said.

They lay her in it, then Medora leaned over not knowing what else to do. Hildred's lips moved as Medora pressed her hand into hers.

"Take care of Heidi," Hildred managed.

"I will ... I will ..."

"You promise?"

"Yes, I promise."

"A-fore God?"

"Yes, a-fore God ... I promise."

"Thank ye," she whispered, then died.

They prayed while Medora squeezed Hildred's hand. She prayed for God to receive her soul, to forgive herself for causing her death, and she prayed for the souls of the men lying in the yard and for strength to "do right by Heidi," who was in Aunt Essie's arms crying.

"Stay here," Medora said finally, laying the hand down. "Ephey ... you and Nora take Heidi, look after her best ye can ... Aunt Essie, come own," she said, going out.

The two went around poking bodies and gathering up guns, stacking them on the porch in a clatter. Then she went to Delbert, now dead up at the front gate.

Wagon Wheel had bitten this bootless foot, tugging off the sock to reveal the unwashed, black unmanicured toes. The tattered gray sock lay nearby. Medora stared at the dull face, snarling even in death, and for the first time doubted her own immortality since it made no sense for such as he to be anything but forever dead.

She turned to Aunt Essie. "I'm a-goin' down the road … see if we winged that other'n … no doubt Wagon Wheel's own the trail rat now … he might tree and I need to be thar when he does."

"Yessum."

"Go on back to the girls and hep them with that young-un," Medora said gently, shouldering the gun, and walking off as Aunt Essie went back to the house.

Medora found spots of blood and followed them about a mile till they and the tracks turned into the woods, the horse walking slower while the blood got thicker.

Entering the trees out of breath, she paused, found a log, brushed off the snow, and sat. In another time, she might've gone rabbit hunting on such a snowy windless day. Instead, she was hunting a wounded man. She was afraid, but had to either "kill or tend" whichever God wanted, she decided, sitting there thinking and listening. "When you shoot a body … he's yores furever," she remembered her father telling her once.

Listening to her breathing, the minutes went by in silence. Seeing only the sun and snow, feeling only the solitude, she at last heard the soft flutter and ruffling of feathers, as a sparrow preened on a twig.

Watching it, Medora Pilgrim suddenly realized how weary she was of all the sound and severity of war—and how she longed for its end. Sitting quietly, the sun poking warmly through the chill, she unexpectedly appreciated peace's sweet simplicity and hoped she might live to see its return, yet wondered if she ever would.

Then she heard something else. In the distance. The hound. She got up, went at a fast walk, the barking growing louder with each step as she picked up the blood and horse and dog tracks intermingling through the forest. Then she saw something in the snow that didn't belong—a crumpled hat. She examined it, picturing its owner slumped over, thick coagulating clumps stopping his heart forever. .

Without thinking, she ran down, then across a creek and up a rise. She knew she was very close. She walked cautiously, circling tree to tree, stopping, then moving, waiting, listening. Then she saw it, a form—the dog going round and round panting, whining, and barking. She stepped closer, straining to see. But she waited. Wondered. Trembled. Suddenly there was a crash and something ran past, almost knocking her over, she jumped behind a pine; a riderless horse winding away—disappearing. Now she saw the dog lunging at something, snarling and biting, and she sprinted to him.

"No!" she said, coming up, pulling him back by the hide of his neck. "No! Enough! Enough! Stop!" She kneeled beside a shape lying face down, and turned the body over, its head falling back. Medora fumbled open its shirt where a small breast unfolded into the cold air.

"My God in heaven!" she screamed. "I've killt a girl!"

Medora rigged a tourniquet then, dragging the dog away, went for help. With Aunt Essie, she hitched the wagon to Blue Bell and returned, loaded the girl, and brought her home to Heidi's bed. She was barely alive.

"Don't know if she's going to make it, mam," Aunt Essie said, staring down into the bloodless face.

"We've stopped the bleeding," Medora said, examining the wounds again— one in the left shoulder that had sealed and the other through the flesh of the upper arm that had bled.

They tended both, then prayed, Medora, Aunt Essie, Iphigenia, Nora, and Heidi, holding hands in a small circle at the foot of the bed while Wagon Wheel sat on his haunches nearby, whining in perplexed neglect, listening to prayers of recovery for an enemy.

The next day's task was far from easy but they loaded the bodies into the wagon. Deverl insisted they use a pulley rigged between two saplings to raise him, but it was done, and the four were dumped in a shallow and very common grave behind the hog barn, then covered with dirt, sticks, and snow.

"Them feral hawgs'll dig 'em up straight away ... no deeper than we done put 'em down," Aunt Essie said, as they drove away.

"I cain't say as I much keer," Medora said whipping Useless into something he tried to pass off as a trot.

"How long we gotta stay?" Aunt Essie asked as they pulled up to the big cabin.

"Tomorree we bury Hildred proper like ... then we wait and see what happens with the girl ... we'll take her as soon as we can travel ..."

"If'n she don't die on us."

"I cain't stand no more dyin', Aunt Essie, I just caint, so, I asked God to spare her. Told 'im I'd take care of her for awl my borned days if'n he would. God is just, Aunt Essie. She'll live ... I jes know she will."

"Miz Medora, de Lawd don't always do what we say … you done lived long nuff to know dat."

"He will this time … I cain't have her death own my slate … I done got more'n I can handle now."

"Now, you didn't know dat was a girl …"

"No, I didn't … but I won't be able to live with it if she dies."

"She'll live den," Aunt Essie said, getting out and walking back to unload the pick and shovels to start on Hildred's grave.

That night they washed Hildred and dressed her in her wedding gown found in an old black trunk. They laid her back on the big bed and held a wake with prayers and hymns till they fell asleep from exhaustion.

Then they buried her in a deep grave with a stone marker and some more prayers. But then their attention shifted to the living—the wounded girl who they nursed for several more days till one morning Aunt Essie came in and said, "Miz Medora, de girl's awake and shore nuff talkin'."

"God be praised," Medora said, standing over the big bed and looking into the pale but awake face propped up on two dirty pillows.

Their new addition began by drinking lots more water and eating more soup and bread till she was able to tell her story. Her name was Dagmar, her dad was, indeed, the infamous Samuel Dixon Suggins, bushwhacker and bandit. He had wanted a boy and made her pretend to be one. Her mother had died two years ago of "the fever," leaving Dagmar helpless. "Deverl was the worst," she said. "I sold whiskey and rode on raids with nem boys," she added. "But I hated 'em … ever last one."

"You pore thang," said Medora.

"But I never kilt nobody," she insisted.

"Good," said Medora. "I wish I could say that."

Then Medora told her about the shootout. Dagmar cried but then said she felt worse about "Old Lady Himmel than anybody … she wuz a good woman … we never should a-come up yar no way … we wuz jes askin' fur it. I knowed it weren't gonna come to no good but they never wanted to hear nothin' I ever had to say 'bout nothin'."

She added, "Deverl wuz crazy … and a-shootin' folks when thar wuz no need for it. He kilt a Yankee boy jes las' week who done surrendered with his hands up and awl … jes to steal that damn pistol he shot Miz Himmel with …

said he needed a new one and awl … he didn't have to kill that boy to git his pistol … he weren't no damn good and it wuz jes a matter of time till somebody got him like Miz Himmel done. I'm glad she didn't have a third barrel for me is awl I got to say."

"I'm shore sorry I shot you, Dagmar," Medora said. "I thought you wuz jes one more of 'em. It awl happened rale fast like …"

Dagmar interrupted. "Mam, it weren't yore fault … it wuz bound to happen … they way we wuz a-livin' and awl … they wuz drunk most ever day … drank, gamble, kill, and rob … wuz all they ever wanted … day and night … it wuz jes a matter of time till it awl caught up with us."

"You rest now, honey. When you're able, we'll travel on to Warshington," said Medora.

"To Warshington?" Dagmar asked in amazement.

Medora then told their story.

Dagmar listened intently then pleaded, "Kin I go with ye, Miz Pilgrim?"

"Shore, honey … we'll look after ye till yore able to come back home."

"I ain't got no home to come back to, Miz Pilgrim, except that shack and a few acres of Pa's … and I don't never want to see that agin as long as I live."

"No people at awl?"

"None … you done killt 'em awl … ever last one."

Medora paused. "You can stay with us as long as you like."

"We best leave as soon as we can … these days they's bushwhackers and Yankees all thew this yar country," Dagmar said, sitting up a bit. "Load me up now and let's git today."

"Yore too weak, lay back down, honey … besides, it's late, tomorrow we'll hit the trail … first light … now yew jes rest."

Before sunup, Medora and Aunt Essie loaded Dagmar on a pallet and, along with Heidi, Nora, Iphigenia, and the dog, filled the wagon, then hitched Blue Bell and Ulysses. With Medora driving and Aunt Essie gripping the shotgun, they headed toward the Confederate Capital, leaving Himmel Hill to the goats, graves, and groveling hogs.

After two days, at the confluence of the Ouachita and Caddo Rivers, near the vanished Indian town of Chugate, unbeknownst to them, our little company camped upon the same ground as the Spaniard Moscoso had three hundred years before. But they did not remain so long as he, breaking camp, as was their habit, in the lifting darkness of the next day's morning, then feeling their way onto a trail that merged in the soft light with a road that entered the village of Arkadelphia.

Here they paused, traded coffee for food, and sent word ahead to Washington. An escort soon arrived, but Titus sent not only his soldiers but his surgeon as well. This healer glanced at the delirious Dagmar and, hardened by three years of war and two shots of whiskey, one for himself and the other for the girl, quickly sawed off the left arm.

But Dagmar survived the doctor and, when able, went with them the two days to find Titus sitting bestride his great Pegasus, to Medora's eyes, at least, a husband like a god, waiting along the road under a tree, the sun warming the snow away into muddy patches under his animal's feet.

Hugging first Medora in a long desperate, tearful embrace, and then his brood and welcoming Dagmar and Heidi into the fold, he thanked Aunt Essie, whom he embraced as well, he then led them into Washington. They indeed were a sight as Colonel Pilgrim led down Franklin Street in the little town that now boomed under the false pregnancy of war as a camp city of refugees and an army in the field. People sandwiched into hotels, homes, and haylofts—pouring down the Southwest Trail after being pushed off the Rock, which had fallen in September into Steele's grasp, making Washington the new capital. Before the war it had become a place of mansions and manors and less and less a place of cabins and shacks; more and more a place of lace and less and less a place of leather, as the fashions of the fifties floated their way up the Red River from New Orleans to be worn by folks in fancy buggies intermingling with frontier wagons in front of the five fine hotels, new stores, offices, saloons, and grand houses, where there were balls, theatricals, and even chat about building an opera house. Yet the sixties brought this army that was not yet busy with fighting but more with feeding and simply finding a place to stay.

Washington was West, certainly (with Austin, Bowie, and Crockett, it had hosted the Texas Revolution), but it was also the South too as the cotton plantations had slowly replaced the forests, all, of course, cleared and worked by slaves shipped from the Louisiana market or wagoned over the trace from back east.

Soon there were the Simmes, the Mosses, Holts, Allens, Bensons, Bookers, Martins, Shields, Monroes, Rikes, Duggers, Norwoods, Parsons, Jetts, Montcalms, Clarks, Stuarts, Cheathams, Fontaines, Conways, and Sanders, mostly from the Carolinas and Virginia, who came across from Tennessee or up from Louisiana, to fill the cotton land from the hill of "five trails," which soon they named for the first president as a touching point for these tracks which continued on southward as one bigger road to the Prairie de Roane and Texas.

And so it went till the interruption of Lincoln's election had settled such a gloom that it spread itself into a war that surprised no one but him, as the sons of this small town, like so many other numberless sons across the land, North and South, began to die. Young John Carrigan and Montcalm Simms were among the first from here.

(In '61 their sires went to a place called Wilson's Creek, Missouri, where young Montcalm was found pillowing upon a rock which his father turned into a blood-dried headstone in the Ozan cemetery.) The list got longer, of course, and finally the fetching had to stop and the dead had to bury down where they lay so only the wounded trekked home now to leave again if they could to have another go at a glorious death for The Cause.

Then Steele cut his way over from Helena, and so now Washington had it all: the government, politicians, the armory, and the army while the fleeing people like Medora swelled it into a wartime boom.

It was a crowded place. Governor Harris Flanagin and his First Lady, Martha, were guests over at the Oxleys, but he kept his scattered generals safely close: General Tom Dockery was out at the Moss plantation, while Marmaduke was in town at the High Hotel near "Prince John" Magruder, who held court at the Joneses' nearby. Good old General Cabell was just across the street, while surly Hindman preferred hiding at Arnold's mill; "Granny" Holmes slept at Perdue Springs and the Jo Shelby Missourians were pridefully resting at the "Old Murry Place," with Maxey and his Texans just three miles past. But General McNair, luckiest of all, since he was a Washingtonian, stayed pleasantly at home.

Once General Kirby Smith himself even rode up from Shreveport. And Ole "Pap" Price saddled over from Camden to headquarter at the Muldrow Place from time to time, to chat with Fagan, who stayed with the Duggers on their hill, or court ole ex-governor Rector way out at the Methodist parsonage— to pray, inspect, and cheer everyone up.

Of course, lesser lights such as colonels and below, clerks and legislators above, were scattered everywhere, to sleep on cots and couches, if not in tents or barns or anywhere they could find.

In a word, it was a whirl of sweet adversity, and in the way of sending a sign to Steele they stood to have a ball loud enough to sting his Yankee ears: an orchestra of violins, cello, bass, clarinet, piccolo, and harp was quickly made then added in with a dash from the colorful Colonel Boudinot, a famous Indian lawyer, poet, and soldier, who would sit down at the grand piano to sing as far as Mister Lincoln's old ears could hear.

It was the "Crockett Ball," for the great man's grandson, Colonel Robert Crockett, the guest of honor, and all of Washington in uniforms and hoopskirts danced at the Moss plantation manor house, all bedecked in bunting under its chandeliers of candles, with its sliding doors thrown open and its rooms denuded of furniture, in a bare circle around the great hall and dining room where the ladies and girls danced warmly with their gentlemen and officers in a waltz of joyous defiance of a war that would soon stop their music forever.

But Medora quite simply had missed it. She had been busy elsewhere and today was content to see astride the trail her uniformed Titus, be-sabered and mounted on his Pegasus prancing around their worn-out old wagon hitched forward by a white mare and a black mule, driven by two women—African and Anglo—loaded with the colonel's missing daughters—and a new one sitting up with an arm pinned at the sleeve—a hound following happily—a crowd gathering along Franklin Street, cheering and waving as they pulled into Washington. It was as if the war had been won and the South had gained her independence and all would be well.

But while Medora smiled and lifted a hand, she thought of Homer, Hildred, and Himmel Hill; the choking boy swinging in his dance of a different sort; Arcadia and Arkansas—slain; and again, just as she had that day sitting upon the stump, she longed for peace—wished the war had never come—and, though she put no tongue to it, felt a very great relief but no real joy at their deliverance.

CHAPTER TEN

Well, Prince, Genoa and Lucca are now no more than private estates of the Bonaparte family. No, I warn you, that if you do not tell me we are at war, if you allow yourself to palliate all the infamies and atrocities of the Antichrist (upon my word, I believe he is), I don't know you in future, you are no longer my friend, no longer my faithful slave, as you say. There, how do you do, how do you do? I see I'm scaring you, sit down and talk to me.

——Pavlovna Scherer, a distinguished lady of the court, as said in the first paragraph of Tolstoy's War and Peace

"Well, my dear, how are you? Come sit down right here beside me and tell me everything," said Mrs. George (Matilda) Merrywell to Medora Pilgrim as she sat sipping the wine James May made in the little shed behind his house on the Ozan road. "So good to see you again ... I trust you have recovered from your terrible ordeal?"

These words were uttered in February 1864, in the parlor of one Mr. Simon Sanders, a leading citizen of Washington who was hosting a party (one of many that night) in honor of General James Fagan before the dance at another, larger home, which, like the Moss mansion the night of the Crockett Ball, was all bedecked with flags and bunting.

Medora, who had exchanged a gun for a purse and her rough calico for a hoop skirt, sat with unusual reticence beside Mrs. Merrywell, a stout buxom woman with a round pink face, who would frequently intrude before her companion could speak.

"I have heard it all, my dear ... we all have, of course ... heard every last bit ... your tragedy ... your terrible loss. I'm so very sorry ... and your seein' that awful hangin' of that poor, poor wretched O. Dodd boy ... I jes cain't imagine, honey! Him no more 'n a child ... what an awful crime! It tells us all we need to know about our enemy, doesn't it? They're the very devil?"

Medora tried to speak but was interrupted yet again.

"Oh, yes, Medora, you're the talk of the town, my dear, yes, indeed … your escape from those evil bushwhackers … you have such courage … such grit! We could all learn from you, my dear! And the one-armed girl you and the colonel have so kindly adopted as your own … how so very fine and Christian of you … everyone admires you so for it. I hear she is a scout now … a-ridin' with the colonel on that fine mare he gave her … and no more than seventeen … sportin' a pistol no less … and wearin' a fancy uniform you and your Aunt Essie made for her. Is there another girl like her? I don't know of it, if there is. But she's not the social kind, is she? And you're so wise not to try and make her so."

Medora drew breath but again it was too late.

"And it was so terrible about your Arcadia … What beasts they are! But you still own the land and I hear you buried your silver and hid your grandpa's portrait, then sewed your dollars in a dress. How very clever. These times are so very tryin' … yes, the Lord is tryin' us and he has a plan for all our sufferin' … but if we jes stay brave and fight … he'll guide us to victory in the end. I'm sure of it … yes, indeed. God help us if we lose this war … it will be the very devil to pay … the rule of Mammon and Baal … that's what I say … so the Lord won't abandon us … I'm as sure of that as I am of heaven."

"Whom the Lord loveth he chasteneth," said Medora quietly. "Hebrews twelve, six."

Mrs. Merrywell blanched, hesitated, then said, "Yes … well, dear, I've never quite understood that …"

"Jerusalem suffers worst of all," said Medora, now being a touch sententious. "Purified by suffering … then delivered from her enemies … in His own good time … which is never ours."

Mrs. Merrywell interrupted, saying, "We just have to be brave is all I know … the way ya'll've been … ya'll're such an example, my dear Medora, such a wonderful example … then the Lord will give us victory … I'm sure of it … y'all have shown us the way."

Medora averted her gaze in time to see Titus free himself from a crowd and come toward them.

"Ah, yes, here is your fine husband, Colonel Titus Pilgrim now. So good to see you, Colonel," said Mrs. Merrywell, extending her hand, which he took with a slight smile, a polite greeting and a broader, wordless smile to Medora.

"I was just tellin' your lovely, brave Medora here, Colonel, how very proud of her we all are."

"Thank you, Mrs. Merrywell, but no one is prouder than I," Titus allowed with a nod that was almost a bow.

"Oh, yes, indeed, how you must be so very proud ... and relieved."

"Yes, relieved," he said gravely.

"How are you enjoyin' Washington, Colonel?" she asked, eyeing him with a certain coquettish delight as she noted his dark curly hair, blue eyes, and handsome clean-shaven face set off by the immaculate gray uniform that he wore with such perfection.

"It's wonderful."

"Yes, we've found it pleasurable," Medora finally managed.

"Yes, but you should have seen it before the war. Oh, it was so romantic. We had fox hunts by the moonlight and more dress balls on plantations than you could shake a ridin' crop at. And the weddin's? They were always so very special ... with such parties! Oh!" she gasped, "the candles ... and the rosewood with such silver settings a-shinin' everywhere upon 'em ... such taste! Why, in this very room, just there." Matilda Merrywell swept the room with her little fan. "By the fire ... right under that wonderful portrait of Simon ... there ... there in that very spot his lovely daughter Virginia was married ... you know ... to Augustus Garland. You never met him, Colonel?"

"Only once did I have that honor," said Titus.

"Of course, he's in Richmond now ... in our Congress," she said, leaning a little forward as if to impart a great secret. "I understand he's very close to the Davises ... but Virginia stayed here as you know ... the entire time ..."

"Oh, yes, we've had a nice chat. She says she has no need of a move to Richmond," said Medora.

"I know she's grieved by his absence," said Mrs. Merrywell, "but we need him there so badly. They tend to forget about us out here in the West. They're so preoccupied with Virginia ..."

"Yes, and Atlanta ... but they sometimes seem to forget about us altogether ... always clamorin' for us to send help and sendin' us none. I bet half our men are over the river, but I dare say Augustus is helpin' all he can," Titus said, then added, "It's well known that he thinks we might yet make an alliance with French-Mexico."

"They moved to Little Rock, didn't they ... just before the war?" Medora asked, as if she had not heard Titus.

"Yes, he went in with a very successful attorney there—Ebenezer Cummins."

"Judge Cummins?" said Medora.

"You know him?"

"Oh, yes, Matilda, everyone knew ole Judge Cummins ... and when he died Mr. Garland inherited his practice ..."

"Yes, a very lucrative one, I'm told."

"Yes, he was very busy ..."

"But, as I say, they were from here then ... and all their family."

"Didn't Augustus have a brother?" asked Titus.

"Yes, indeed ... Rufus ... a fine gentleman ... and he fell in love with a Walker girl ... Isabelle ... the doctor's daughter ... then Virginia and her sister Zenobia went back to Virginia as girls to visit relatives ... and low-and-behold they come back here to Washington with their lovely little cousin by the same name ... Zenobia ... a family name they say ... but we all called her Nobia ... to tell 'em apart, you know. Why ... everyone just loved her and it wasn't long afore she set her cap at Isabelle's older brother ... Robert ... actually Isabelle's half-brother ... 'cause ole Doc Walker had him ... by a first marriage ... you know? Why, in no time her father found out somehow and sent a young, dashing army officer ... Captain Joe Brown ... a-lathering hotly all the way out from Virginia as fast as he could to head things off ... but he failed ... lands did he! He had such a wonderful time at the balls and hunts at the Walker plantation. He danced at their weddin' ... a double weddin' it was ... the two couples a-marryin' together ... why our Virginia captain had more fun than anyone else!" Matilda now squealed with laughter and fanned herself in a room that was getting warmer with the swelling crowd.

"What happened to the girls' mother?" asked Medora, quietly.

"Oh, dear ... I'm afraid they lost her when they were no more'n babies. But Simon never so much as looked at another woman ... she was his one and only ... he never really got over his loss ..."

"How did he raise his daughters?" asked Medora.

"A servant ... Aunt Liza ... she's been with the Sanders family ... well, forever ... come with them from North Carolina. She's as fine a human that ever drew breath on God's earth ... she is ... everybody loves her. She raised those two girls like her own ... stood right behind 'em on their weddin' day ... she's in the kitchen now ... with your Aunt Essie ... you need to go and meet her ..."

"I will," said Medora. "I've heard so much about her ..."

"We have such interestin' Negroes here, Medora ... there's even one ... an ancient gentleman who said he was a body servant of General Warshington!"

"General Warshington!?" gasped Medora.

"Yes, but he had such dignity and carriage and seemed to know so much about the great man that folks sorta believed him ... then there was another ... Bob Samuels ... who said he was an ancestor of De Soto!"

Medora laughed for the first time.

"His tale was so strange and complicated that it had about it the ring of truth … and he did look sorta Spanish! I think folks kinda believed him too."

A servant brought some more of the Mays wine on a platter of silver. Mildred took a fresh glass, but Medora, waved him off politely. What she really wanted was some tobacco—or snuff.

"Mam, we have some cider," said the servant, a middle-aged Black man dressed in britches, white shirt, and waistcoat as a kind of livery.

"That'd be fine … thank ye," said Medora.

He fetched the cider. As he left again, a young officer, a captain on Titus's staff, joined them and was introduced by the colonel.

"They say that there's great debate a-ragin' as to what to do about us," said the captain.

"How is that?" asked Mrs. Merrywell.

"Well, mam, it's clear that Grant has to march on Richmond … and Atlanta … take 'em if he can … but out here it's another story. Steele would like nothin' better than to sit out the war all perched on his Rock where he and his boys seem to be havin' such a gay ole time … a-courtin' and a-churchin' … they've never had so much fun … but ole Commissary Banks wants to be the next president so he cain't jes sit … he's gotta do somethin' in a hurry … but what?"

"Will they attack us here … in Warshington?" she asked with alarm.

"It's the capital, mam …"

"But it's not that important," said Titus, "Banks'll go for Mobile, I thank … and let us be …"

"That'll allow General Smith to concentrate all his forces against Steele, won't it, Colonel Pilgrim?" interjected the captain.

"Exactly … we'll whip 'em good then."

"Maybe they'll act together … send Banks up the Red to Shreveport and Steele against us …"

"That saves Mobile," said Titus.

"And if they do that, Colonel?" Mrs. Merrywell asked.

"We'll beat each one at a time, mam," Titus said.

"He's evil," said Medora. "I seen'm hang that boy … it was the worst thang I ever saw … even … well … what happened later … and awl …"

"Folks talk constantly of that O. Dodd boy," said Mrs. Merrywell, not listening closely. "It shows the righteousness of our course."

"They say that Steele ran a pretty good bunch of spies thew ole Pap Price's camp up in Missouri … in '61 … that they gots lots of good information …

back when ole Steele was a colonel ... guess he knows what a spy can do ..."

"I'm sorry, Captain," said Medora forcefully, "the boy's facts ... if you want to call 'em that ... wuz worthless! Besides, he was only seventeen ... it wuz murder, pure and simple!"

"Yessum," said the captain.

"When will we know, do you think, Colonel?" asked Mrs. Merrywell, turning to Titus, after a slight pause.

"The enemy's intentions, mam?"

"Yes, sir ... they won't sit idle, will they?"

"No, Mrs. Merrywell ... Lincoln is up ... if he loses, we win. He must have some victories so they'll move in the early sprang ... late March or April ... but we watch everythin' ... we'll know the minute he goes into motion. He'll have to ford the Ouachita at Rockport with pontoons, the water should be high with April rains ... and the Caddo at Arkadelphia. We'll know his every move ... we keep a sharp eye on awl the crossin's."

"He won't be movin' through friendly country ... you can depend on that, sir," said Mrs. Merrywell, proudly.

"No, mam, and he'll have a hard time with forage ... he'll starve ..."

"They say the Frontier Division ... over ravagin' the Indian Territory ... will probably come down from Fort Smith," said the captain.

"Maybe," said Titus with a hint of irritation.

"Then our Indians will come down to fight with us ... they hate 'em ..." the captain added.

"The Five tribes?" asked Mrs. Merrywell.

"Yessum, the things that've happened over there are ... unspeakable ... they hate 'em worse'n we do," said the captain.

"If that's possible," Medora said, sipping the cider while studying the floor.

The captain was pulled aside by a lieutenant and so excused himself, but they were soon visited by other guests, none as bold as Mrs. Merrywell with Medora, but nevertheless eyeing her with curiosity and chattering away.

"It's so hot," said Mrs. Merrywell, fanning.

"Dinner is served," announced the servant loudly, as if hearing her.

Strolling in on the arm of her husband, Mrs. Merrywell tugged Titus's sleeve and whispered, "You won't forget your promise ... about my Charles?" she said.

"No, mam," he said with quiet impatience. "I'll do what I can ... but the staff's full jes now ... I have to warn you ... but I'll ask, Matilda, I'll ask." Titus spoke without really looking at her as they entered and were seated.

"Oh, my," said Medora, surveying the table with its silver, china, and candles set before her with such fine company. Now Himmel Hill seemed no more than a dark dream, she thought, then said to no one in particular, "Oh, dearest, Titus, when will it ever end?" she said, sitting and turning to him with tears glistening as the servant poured the wine she would never touch, and Titus replied, "Oh, my dear Doddy (his pet name for her), we'll hang own somehow and Lincoln will be defeated ... then there'll be a separation and we'll be free at last," he said with a confident smile, taking her hand under the table and squeezing it tenderly.

Leaving her hand in his, Medora surveyed the table in the candlelight, which set the silver and crystal sparkling, heard the busy rattling of forks, spoons, and glasses by elegantly dressed men and women chatting in that ephemeral confidence engendered by wine and privilege, as Virginia Garland leaned over to her and in a low sweet voice asked how her Arcadia "came by its name."

CHAPTER ELEVEN

Him that's not skinning can hold a leg.
—Abraham Lincoln

A rather sentimental, naive and irresolute Habsburg, one Archduke Ferdinand Maximilian, rear admiralisimo of the Austrian navy, governor general of Lambardo-Venetia, younger brother of the Emperor Franz Josef the First, husband to a frenzied Belgian princess called Carlotta, was soon to be lifted up by the arms of Napoleon III of France and set down hard, square and squirming, upon the cactus throne of tempestuous Mexico. Here, it was hoped by a cabal of reactionary clerics and *hidalgos*, this gentle prince might prove useful in pilfering the fruits of victory picked off the revolutionary tree by one Benito Pablo Juárez, a full-blooded Zapotec Indian lawyer, who, in those days, with his *mestizo rancheros, creoles,* and Indian *guerrilleros,* was three years at war against an alliance of generals and priests. It was a rebellion inspired by this little man who forever dreamed of liberation from the *hacendados* and *gachupines* of his day—replacing them with a constitution conceived by himself—a dream indeed in the Mexico of 1864, but now deferred by intervening French soldiers whose grandfathers had stormed the *Bastille* and proclaimed the *Rights of Man* across the face of monarchical Europe.

Toward this state of affairs Lincoln, at the beginning of that year, cast a war-wearied eye westward. To forestall any French-Habsburg-Confederate alliance, it was necessary "to show the flag in Texas," advised his chief of staff, General Henry Wager Halleck. Known as the "most unattractive man in Washington," "Old Brains," as Halleck was called, was that oddest of birds, the military pettifog, a translator of a life of Maximilian's mentor's uncle,*Vie de Napoleon.* In jealously superseding Grant at Shiloh, he had nailed down his own martial immortality by maundering through Mississippi for a month looking for Corinth. He covered these twenty-two miles, he insisted, much as the Romans had in Gaul in A.D. something or other—inching day-by-dreary-day, a mile more or less at a clip, atrophying a hardened army of 110,000 that could've covered the entire distance in one number of the calendar and fought on the next without so much as taking an extra breath. Instead, Caesar Halleck halted evening to evening to build yet another "fort" in the false anticipation of a devastated half-dead Confederate army of some 30,000 dragging itself out to destroy an enemy that it couldn't defeat when fresh and armed with surprise. In this way did Wager Halleck studiously misapply history by overnurturing that most precious of life's and war's commodities—time—oozing it away in inverse drop-by-drop proportion to the Gray animal's running blood—stanching it, as it were, till it finally recovered and ran away to fight for another three years.

This same grand Caesar now planned a romping dash and conquest across a great flat map of a nation spread out over a White House table that his be-ringed fat little forefinger framed for Mr. Lincoln as Texas.

Many are summoned but few are chosen, as they say, and Fate selects her heroes carefully. One such was Bay State Nathaniel Prentiss Banks, former governor and congressman (Speaker of the House), who (without the bother of experience) had been newly honored by Lincoln as a madeup major general. He was then made-over fresh again after his humiliation in Stonewall's Shenandoah, where he was tagged by the ever starved Confederates as "Commissary" Banks for the beneficent outrunning of his own baggage trains. But he's the one I need, boys, Lincoln had said, sending over the stars, and there it was.

So this new year of '64 found Banks burrowing up yet again, "wested" as governor-general of Louisiana, in relief of another political warrior, one Benjamin Franklin "Spoons" Butler (whose success as a lawyer was exceeded only by his failure as a soldier), who had so pacified the ladies of the Crescent City that they painted his face on the bottoms of their bottoming chamber pots.

It was with such similar grace that Nathaniel Prentiss now found himself favored by being monikered anew as "Mister" Banks by his midwestern farm boys languishing in the hot Louisiana towns, swamps, slow rivers, and bayous of a strange land with even stranger people for an enemy. These lads, everyone knew, craved only to be led by such soldiers as were now afforded their eastern brothers in Sherman and Grant, but they got the Bay Stater who was no better than Butler.

But the other hero honored by fate's smile was, of course, none other that our friend Frederick Steele, an Empire State neighbor of "Mister" Banks. Somewhat effete and high voiced, the dandy Steele busied himself with all the delights of a velvet-collared epicure while basking in the early spring sunshine of his twin glories—a long hot hike from Helena and a humble boy's slow hanging.

Yet the war went on, and on, and on. And so a war that everyone in '61 expected to end by the New Year had been transformed by '64 into something that no one thought would ever stop. Yet, each year needs have a plan, and this year's was simple enough: Grant would be off to Richmond, Sherman to Atlanta, and Banks and Steele were to bestir themselves toward Texas—with the flag. Or as Lincoln put it, "Him that is not skinning can hold a leg."

The South's plan was far simpler—that is, to hang on and hope, in time, they might be redeemed, not by the French-Mexicans or even the English, but once again by the Union general who saved them so many times before, George McClellan, now transformed into a presidential politician promising peace. In other words, they wouldn't get skinned if they couldn't get caught, they'd just run around the barnyard till "the Yankees got all wore out and quit."

But Banks, thinking of '68, was a little disgruntled in finding himself a mere Louisiana leg-holder. Texas was just not big enough of a hindquarter for his commissary, Montezuma Habsburgs or not. Only Washington via Mobile, Alabama, seemed shank enough for one skinning up to the Oval Office. Conversely, Steele preferred Little Rock to Washington—Arkansas, that is, the state's new capital of that old name. And, as he well knew, it was the only Washington in his future. In fact, war was of no real interest to Frederick Steele, despite his martial name and education. He longed simply to remain a gormandizing city boy, preferring hors d'oeurves at table to an abattoir in the field.

Now, admittedly, it was indeed true that the Graybacks roamed his backside with cavalry, guerrillas, and bushwhackers, but still, his army's smokehouse was full, and, if the river would just stay up through spring, and the railroad from DeVall's Bluff would stay open through summer (he built block houses and kept cavalry on patrol), the general and his little army family could live pretty high on this Arkansas hog. "Thank you kindly, Mr. Lincoln, we're happy just where we are," he seemed to say.

See, in the Trans-Mississippi, the great dirty little military secret was that Steele and his boys kind of liked the place. (The "place" is always a pleasant surprise to strangers—then and now.) In fact, they let it be known that the Rock was the *only* place in Arkansas they really did like. Here they were finally meeting decent folks and were parading, courting, churching, and agreeing quietly about the poor O. Dodd boy while generally relaxing and wishing for the end. The thing to do was simply wait—someone else would pull the guts out into the silver bucket, and then they could all settle down. In a word, they'd had enough.

But while one may not be interested in war, war may be interested in one, especially if that one lives in a certain place at a certain time, advertises one-self in a starched new blue uniform, wears a saber, carries a pistol and a musket—sports a plumed hat, shiny brass buckles, and black boots, even if the strutting is only for church or parade or courting. So, ready or not, Texas it was to be, a great Blue convergence at Shreveport, Steele and Banks, then west-ward-ho into, well, glory. There was lots of skinning yet to be done, the hide had to be taken off the South for good and they'd just have to help. That was all there was to it.

Maybe this was the best way to the White House after all, decided Banks upon reflection, finally warming to the subject in a letter to Halleck, pro-claiming:

> The occupation of Shreveport will be to the country west of the
> Mississippi what that of Chattanooga is to the east. And as soon as
> this can be accomplished the country west of Shreveport will be in
> condition for a movement into Texas.

"Old Brains" agreed, so Commissary coiled then sprang out in April with newfound enthusiasm, creeping up the Red, paralleling Admiral David Dixon Porter's 210 guns of thirteen ironclads, seven light draught gunboats, and forty transports escorted by a brigade of Marines. It was so impressive Porter described it as "the most formidable force that has ever been collected in west-ern waters."

Meanwhile, near his brown water creature, Banks crept north by northwest with his 30,000 marching boys in blue, dragging in train a thousand loaded wagons, augmented by the *Corps d'Afrique* —1,500 ex-slaves formed and well accounted for at Port Hudson, much to the surprise and horror of the White South, but now relegated by our politician Banks to escorting a logistical tail stretching out twenty miles behind and pulling up the rear.

But, gliding in, so to speak, fresh and ever alert, was another group—always to be found circling the edges of war—speculators. These flew up from the Crescent City Cotton Exchange and hopped in hungry anticipation on the tops of the boats like black treetop buzzards on a limb at the ready, spreading their wings with pen and paper (letters of trade signed and sealed by Messers. Chase and Lincoln, to make it all legal, you understand). These birds were expectant of a different kind of killing— "contraband cotton" all freed up for the world market. The chirping had not stopped since last year's raid up Bayou Teche where Commissary Banks had stolen 500 bales, fetching a New Orleans price of $5,000,000 clear profit. Now the hope was for 200,000 to 300,000 bales at an even better price. His Massachusetts mills, ever dependent upon slave-plantation cotton, lay idle, and General/Governor/Congressman Banks knew all about the locality of politics, even in 1864.

So, after winning a few shoot-outs at Fort De Russy and Henderson Hill, this two-headed creature wiggled up the river and along its banks, turning and twisting its fangs into roosters, cows, pigs, and barking hounds patrolling half-guarded houses where women, children, old men, and loyal slaves stood in helpless refusal.

Or, in the words of one Yankee general to his Ohio mother:

> Western troops are tired of shilly-shally, and this year they will deal their blows heavily. Past kindness and forbearance has [sic] not been appreciated or understood; frequently ridiculed. The people now will be terribly scourged.

And "terribly scourged" they were. In this American against American version of "search and destroy," the country was plundered and torched, as "Sherman's guerrillas," as the Blue boys tagged themselves, burnt and pillaged while stacking up "Sherman monuments"—that is, chimneys standing mutely over the black ashes of manors and mansions as a symbol of the new Federal-State arrangement they were duty bound to enforce.

Of course, it got out of hand, and at last a tag-along reporter decried that "our noble army" was in danger of "degenerating into a band of cutthroats and robbers."

Apparently the gods heard something, because things started happening without so much as a word from any mortal anyone could find.

First, there was to be no confiscated cotton for the carrion crows to convert to cash. The Louisianians burnt it—every last bale. On plantation after plantation, farm after farm, place after place, it was stacked and torched till the rising flames flew the vultures up in a circling and chirping empty-bellied flock back to their New Orleans roost where they clicked their beaks incessantly to the Northern press about the incompetence of "Mister" Banks and the cruel vicissitudes of war in the West.

Second, the Leathernecks were laced with the pox. Then the river fell while Banks wandered off lost, exchanging a good road near the navy for a bad one near the enemy, angling away out of ear, musket and, finally, gunboat cannon shot. He angled toward a fateful place called Sabine Crossroads—a web of wagon trails exiting for Texas to the west, the Red River to the east, and Shreveport north. Here at about two o'clock on April 8, 1864, in the shade of a large, shady oak, Banks found an unbuttoned youth sitting upon a horse, a leg relaxing over the pommel, puffing cigar smoke into a blue-black cloud that rose languidly into the still air. Everyone said he seemed lost in the inscrutable calmness of one waiting for an old friend.

He was Major General Richard "Dick" Taylor, the Kentucky-born son of Zachary, who had spent his early days in Scotland, France, Harvard and Yale— busily becoming what we once could call a "Classicist." (That is, unlike Titus, he read Homer and Virgil in Greek and Latin.) But since his commander, Kirby Smith, was born a mere botanist/mathematician, Taylor condescended to write him in common English, complaining that, "While we are deliberating the enemy is marching. King James lost three kingdoms for a mass. We may have lost three states without a battle."

His general knew, of course, that if this president's boy was anything, he was well connected. Kin to Madison and Lee, he even had watched a poor sister, dearest "Knox," married off to one Jefferson Davis, only to see her die rather promptly at his "Brierfield" as a freshly blushing but all-too-feverish bride of Mississippi's slow-burning malaria.

So Kirby Edmund Smith just had to put up with him, and, while Davis reflected upon poor ex-brother Dick's slim chances, all could see from Shreveport, or even Richmond, that this young scholar's 9,000 stood not unlike the immortal Greeks barring the "hot gate," one might say, to mix metaphors of time and place from Stewart to Spartan.

That is, Taylor had only two thin divisions of foot, Mouton and Walker, which he had just looped across his middle, end to end; and with his four guns had buckled cannon on his center; then, with his horse (Bee and Major), he had strapped something on his flanks. Then he sat in the shade, waited, and smoked—coolly ruminating out hot letters to Smith of spoiled erudition.

It took a while. He thought they'd never show, but within the hour the Blue serpent slowly wiggled up the hill, and, with the flick of a tongue, sensed danger, stopped, and arched back in a bewildered coil. The tiny brain for this encounter was couched in the skull of a Kansas lawyer cavalry one-star named Albert Lee, whose brigade had only just finished enjoying a running skirmish with his opposite, General Thomas Green, a quiet spoken veteran of the Texas fight for independence, the Mexican war, and countless Commanche fights. Green's slow slashing retreat had resisted till it came to a hard stop here at the Crossroads, screening Taylor with Grayback riders.

The lawyer didn't like his brief. He had an infantry brigade but it was clearly not enough. So he sent for Banks, who hurried up, conferred, then rode back, personally worrying along another brigade to help out. These at last jogged up hotly at 3:30. Still this seemed too little, so Lee rode back in search of Banks again, protesting even harder, saying they would be "gloriously flogged" if they attacked. Taylor, he implied, seemed to be holding something above his head just waiting for Lee to slither down. Politician Banks's insistence now came sugarcoated—a compromise—a deal. In return for an attack, he'd throw in another division. "What do you say?" said the congressman to the lawyer, who blanched, seemed to agree, then rode off without quite saying yes or no, leaving everyone thinking both.

Meanwhile, Taylor bombarded Smith. He fired a barrage of paper that seemed to burn the hands of the riders: to HQ Smith/Shreveport from HQ Taylor/Mansfield—back and forth, the dispatches went, hour to hour, one to the other, in a never-ending battle of well-turned phrases.

Young Richard might've been more sympathetic. After all, four-star Smith found himself *generalissimo* of an area larger than western Europe; that is, Texas, Louisiana, Arkansas, Missouri, and the Indian Territory (Oklahoma), which everyone soon referred to as "Kirby Smithdom"—a Kingdom bound by sea, mountains, swamps, plains, and rivers where, without a navy, neither deep nor shallow, blue nor brown, and with a force of foot hardly large enough to defend Shreveport.

Smith parried as best he could by saying that, while he was, to be sure, no Frederick the Great, he was still a man of some military competence: West Point (class of '45); he had fought in Mexico with Taylor's great father; commanded an army that invaded Kentucky from Knoxville; and, before being "wested" here too late to free either Missouri or New Orleans, he had arrived too soon not to feel Vicksburg's and Port Hudson's fall, and was now enjoying a very pinched isolation with no prospects of help from anyone, including Richmond, much less Habsburg Mexico.

But, he added, while the situation was endlessly desperate, it was by no means utterly impossible. With the advantage of interior lines, he had said, they could slay one snake at a time. To this end, he had stripped Texas of horse (Green) and Arkansas of foot (Churchill), left Price to vex Steele with cavalry at Little Rock, and abandoned Texas to the French, if they would but take it.

So it went for days, but with the steady advance of Banks, Smith was clearly more nervous and Taylor soon grew as fearful of friendly riders lathering down from the north as he was of enemy soldiers sliding up from the other way. It was simple, he thought, sitting under his oak, old Smith just couldn't see from behind his desk way up there in Shreveport and so was in a terrible fret, while

PHILLIP H. MCMATH

he could see clearly from his saddle and was not. He, after all, knew his man. Napoleon Banks was no Frederick either, Taylor having had the pleasure of whipping him with his Louisiana "Tigers" in the immortal Shenandoah of '62. There was nothing for it but to sit now, wait, and do it all over again here on the Red. That is, if Smith would leave him be and Banks would hurry on up before it got dark.

Thus, like most generals, Dick Taylor fought on a double front, and so slowly, imperturbably grew more and more impatient. After all, it was almost four by his watch, and if this snake wouldn't strike he would just have to strike the snake. For this, at last, he reached to his left, grasping the cudgel in the person of a Creole West Pointer, Brigadier General Jean Jacques Alexandre Alfred Mouton, son of the governor, Alexander, who led his Louisiana delegation out of the Democratic convention of 1860, and with it most of the South and any hopes of outvoting Lincoln. But if fathers make wars then sons fight them, and son Jean Jacques survived a wound at Shiloh to pin on a star for La Fourche, Atchafalaya, Berwick Bay, and Bayou Teche. Taylor now swung the governor's boy hard against the reptile's right. Mouton, delighted, landed heavily. The thing curled and struck Mouton a mortal wound, then jerked away, writhing under the general's blow. Quickly Taylor struck again—this time from his own right, with Bee and Walker. Now the thing twisted, rolling in upon itself in that direction, slashed a little forward, then slid a great way backward, as Green's cavalry circled behind and whacked at its head with saber and shot.

But the dying Mouton bravely pressed the staff into the firm palm of his top brigadier: Camille Armand Jules Marie, Prince de Polignac, an elegant six-foot-four Gaul with "Napoleonic" beard and trim mustache; a colorful, dapper veteran of the Crimea where he had fought courageously for his beloved France. The general accepted the flag greedily. After all, he was the son of Charles X's prime minister and his grandmama had been a Lady in Waiting of Marie-Antoinette, a friendly liaison that facilitated her own love affair with the King's (Louis XVI) brother, the Comte d'Artois.

A prince with such royal connections could do little else but rush to the side of France's Lost Louisiana as her "La Fayette of the Confederacy." First, he had to run the blockade for a dining-in with the Davises—was a success—so was soon given a colonelcy and diverted to Corinth for the boredom of a staffing-in with Beauregard till he managed a brigade under his other Gallic friend Mouton, *fils*. But, since French never breaks easily over the Texas tongue, our proud Polignac soon became known as their pet "Polecat." In other words, they liked him.

And so this intrepid striper now lifted his standard tall enough for everyone to see through smoke and shell as he strode his Texans forward for a *touche* with their steel. Then he turned the Yankee cannon round, spraying the critter's back till it was burnt and broken in two.

What followed is best told by someone who saw it all—a reporter standing behind.

> Suddenly there was a rush, a shout, the crashing of trees, the breaking down of rails, the rush and scamper of men. It was as sudden as though a thunderbolt had fallen among us, and set the pines on fire. I turned to my companion to inquire upon this extraordinary proceeding, but before he has the chance to reply, we found ourselves swallowed up, as it were, in a hissing, seething, bubbling whirlpool of agitated men.

Then, a moment after Dick Taylor had unburdened Mister Banks of his dream of ever moving into the Ole Taylor place on Pennsylvania, a rider arrived telling him not to, if you please.

But this time our scholar's response was laconic—Spartan, not Latin.

Dear Sir,
It's too late. The battle is won.
Your Obedient Servant,

Dick Taylor
Commanding General, CSA

By February Dagmar Pilgrim (it was now official) grew into such sufficient health as to become restless, volunteered as a scout, and, sporting a new private's uniform tailored by Medora and Aunt Essie, was soon mounted on one of Titus's finest as an army messenger.

Then February tore away and March, predestined to such hope and apprehension, came, bringing news that transformed a painful anticipation into a kind of strange relief. Banks had bestirred himself on March 18, ravaging his way northwest up the Red River toward brave Richard; while, on the twenty-third, Steele had slipped from his Rock and was, as steadily reported by a stream of riders lathering into Washington, slowly meandering southwest down the old Morosco-Medora trail; first pontooning the Saline at Benton, then the

Ouachita at Rockport, and lately crossing the Caddo at Arkadelphia, camping at our famous spot conjoining with the infamous "Frontier Division," fresh from its recent ravaging of slave-owning Indians in Oklahoma, its blue column trekking down behind De Soto from Fort Smith into another great coming together on the Caddo, unifying some 15,000 Union infantry, cavalry, artillery, countless new wagons, teams of rested, government-bred mules and horses with a horde of hustling civilians, all merged in the anticipated glory of taking Washington before conquering Texas.

Dagmar, who, that day at Himmel Hill, had in a horrible trice seen it all coming as she knew in time it must, DeVerl's bullet entering Hildred's chest, her father's head blown back to her right; Hildred's second barrel, almost instantly, blasting full seemingly into her face but hitting DeVerl instead as his harmless second shot jolted into the ground, the great collapsing form following behind; a thing she could not regret, having felt its hideous heaving mass in the incestuous rape of her innocence; seeing it then falling into the snow liberating her to bolt after the stout, now empty-saddled mule as another blast came from the right stinging away her arm; Delbert curling out of the corner of her eye hard into the fence post like a great rag doll she had once seen a child playing with in the dirt and envying because she would never have one; hearing the merciless hound, falling into darkness and waking in Hildred's bed tended over by a kindly white-haired Black woman and her younger female master as a kind of mother in double harness; this same Dagmar, just turned sixteen, with a fresh name, daughter of a colonel in the famous Shelby division, with a new horse, new pistol on her off side and Hildred's old fireplace saber hanging, clanking proudly from her hard brown army saddle, her reins held deftly in her remaining hand with the hot news of Mansfield fresh upon her ear, came riding up to her general.

Meanwhile, Steele was not meeting very few friendly faces as he entered south Arkansas. Instead, he encountered the same hostile place the Spanish, French, and early Angloes had found, which the latter cleared into fields for small farms and plantations to be always intermeshed as a kind of frontier farm country with thick stands of timber, tumescent rivers, and sinking shallow spots called "bottoms," whose stillness slithered with snakes and 'gators and where existed beautiful swirling birds, flowers, and massive, ancient trees so old as to touch the edge of mortality, penetrated only by a twisting maze of seemingly lost trails tracing themselves faintly to a few bigger ones that eventually become roads that in a storm would "swallow a mule and wagon whole" and cause this newest invader lots of trouble when it took a notion to rain.

Here the Whites treated malaria with a blue backwoods mixture of vinegar and gunpowder. A Confederate battery even had a black bear mascot named "Postlewaite" that they fondled and fed like a loosely chained dog. Here, too, they invented the Bowie knife, plotted the Texas revolution, fought Indians, kept slaves, hated abolitionists, lived, loved, and died short, difficult lives in an independent isolation that forever drew a certain type to the Southern frontier. It was not nineteenth-century Main Street America—there were no railroads, bridges, or manicured canals, no illusions about the inevitability of progress, the perfectibility of Man or even his Brotherhood. Here friends were just too hard to find and General Steele's army would find damn few in a pitiless land that smiled at his torment and cruel desperation.

Because by the time our general had reached Conquistador Moscoso's Caddo camp he had eaten half his rations, and so began to pillage an already pillaged country but with no effect but to harden the bitterness of an embittered, hard people. These, some said, were the hardest and meanest anywhere, made mean by the short meanness of life in the deep woods, cotton and corn fields, and swamps of lower Arkansas, upper Louisiana, and east Texas, now called Arklatex.

Here, shadowed always by the lean, leering, mounted rednecks, loving this chase like hounds upon the hare, Steele fought a continuing, over-the-shoulder, sideways, and frontal nipping series of hot skirmishes that flamed almost into battles before sputtering out, but which turned his head back and forth in a dizzying, spinning circle like a great harried beast burdened more and more with the intruding vision of impending doom, as he ventured onto the cusp of a country he was supposed to subdue but which now seemed instead to open ever wider like great jaws ready to slice and swallow him whole even before he ever got to that hellish infinity of land called Texas.

So, Steele was bitten by these quick fights that tore his flesh as his pursuers darted in and out, nipping and yapping with delight, at places named Hollywood, Spoonville, Antoine, Terre Noir Creek, and Okalona, the latter only a river up from Washington, deflecting him east to a spot called Prairie d'Ane where he fought an even hotter fight. Stunned and bleeding, the Blue beast now searched for a lair, turning away from his hopeful link-up with Banks and the ever-fanciful invasion of the Lone Star, he loped east instead to Camden on the Ouachita, a small settlement that actually was in those days Arkansas's "second city," much older and almost larger than the Rock, settled also by the trapping and trading French as a post called *Écore à Fabri*, because it could huddle above the river with the beautiful Indian name (Wash-tah), and which now rose up large and quite formidable behind abandoned Confederate ramparts where Steele settled in, caught his breath, and bleated out a long shout for help.

One who did hear was Kirby Smith, still busy with Banks in Louisiana, but who nevertheless would gradually slice northward Gray detachments large enough to embarrass Steele into military history as one besieged by a force smaller by half. Thus, that complex vastness of the Southwest, that ever-Confederate bastion, that unique and ever-anomalous country-within-a-country-within-a-country, watched as its erstwhile invader was transformed from lofty ambition to the heaving, baying alarums of two frantic, foundering Yankee armies, that had failed so much as to place one Blue boy upon Texas soil, which stood in all the restless ecstasy of a recently blooming youth, rebelling against the greatest parent power on the planet, straining to be free once again and jealous of all imperial dreams but her own—only weakly allied with her Southern sisters—a vast western Kingdom with Austin as its cap and a trodden Southwest under its boot—the map of Texas laughed at this Federal army bounded ever yet by the buffer states on her eastern border.

Dagmar's grand good new news came loping up to Gray general John Sappington Marmaduke, not that lately of Yale, Harvard, and West Point of '57; the son of a Missouri governor; his father a Unionist and blazer of the Sante Fe Trail with this son now commanding Rebels near Camden. The scion was described by one as "the beau ideal," who "sat his horse with consummate grace … the catch of the river towns," and who, at this moment, indeed, sat a fine chestnut among the smaller horses of his gathered staff, hearing the sound of Richard's Sabine success touch his ear in the form of a shout off the back of a blown brown gelding, ridden up by this breathless one-armed "boy" who managed a sharp salute by biting the reins then pulling out a yellow-papered dispatch from a saddlebag.

"General Marmaduke, sir?" Dagmar yelled, dropping the leather blindly from her lips into the open hand using her blue eyes as a way of fixing those of the general so he'd listen to what she had to say.

"Yes, son, you have something for me?" the general said quietly, with a perfunctory salute.

"I gotta a paper yar from General 'Pap' Price, sir. He says General Smith done whipped the Yankees at a place called Mansfield … Loosiana … whupped 'em good and they're a-runnin' hell-for-leather down the Red! In full retreat … ever last one of 'em!"

"Defeated, you say, son, defeated?"

"Yes, sir, and runnin' like the very devil's own ... down the Red ... to Alexandria, sir ... whupped good by a general under Smith called Taylor ... at a place called Sabine Crossroads, sir! It's all in nem papers thar!" she said pointing.

"Bless you, boy, bless your very soul. And God bless Dick Taylor ... he's a good' un," he said, reaching for the dispatch.

"We got that thar paper with instructions from the general," she added, releasing the message to Marmaduke, who took it, unfolded it, and read quickly.

"You've done well ... Private ... ?" he said, looking up, stuffing the dispatch in his pocket.

"Pilgrim, sir, Private Dagmar Pilgrim ... message rider for General Price hisself."

"Pilgrim? You any relation to the Colonel?"

"Yessir, he's my step-daddy," she said proudly. "I'm powerful proud of that."

"You have good reason to be, son."

"Yessir, I know it, thank ye, sir. He and General Fagan done whupped Steel's rear guard all the way into Camden yesterdee ... shore nuff did, sir," she added, telling the General something he knew very well as if it were the newest of news.

"Well, Private Dagmar Pilgrim, your father and General Fagan seemed to have slammed the door good and shut, yes, indeed, they have for sure," he said smiling. "I thank you with heartiest of thanks, now get something to eat and rest a bit ... if you can ... you'll need a fresh mount for your ride with my reply to General Price. But you'll be going soon. Report to Major Smith here ... he'll see you to it," he said with a nod toward an officer mounted on his right.

"Yes, sir," said Dagmar, saluting smartly again, her gelding stepping away as the reins went slack, trotting off in one tired but still-fluid movement.

Turning to Major Smith, Marmaduke said with a laugh, loudly, as if the whole army were listening, "Gentlemen, I think we got Steele treed at last ... now if we can just whistle up enough dogs from General Smith we can put him in the sack."

Frederick Steele, indeed, was up something of a tree and, though he well outnumbered the hounds (Marmaduke having only three cavalry brigades of about a thousand each), Smith no doubt would soon circle up more.

In a word, Steele didn't know quite what to do. Though a professional of some competence, he, to be sure, was no Napoleon, and Camden, a village of about a thousand, was, of course, no Moscow, but there were, nevertheless, some uncomfortable similarities. Steele was an invader trapped in a place he didn't want to leave or stay in—advancing was suicidal, retreating unacceptable, and sitting but a thing of slow dissolution.

Too, like the Corsican, Steele gave little thought to the hard imposition he pressed upon his hosts. First, he comforted himself in a fine mansion on 710 Washington Street, and then, propping his army's feet, so to speak, upon a sullen population's front porch, he paced and pondered in the painful isolation of Mrs. Graham's grand parlor. There, studying a map spread over her fine dining table that she had ordered at great expense and trouble from New Orleans; up the Mississippi, the Red; off-loaded by Camden's slaves where, unbeknownst to Mrs. Graham, it would become a convenient prop in a grand national drama played upon the stage of her home as headquarters to a Yankee major general, Commander of the Department of Arkansas, who now smoothed his map out along the hard polished surface and reflected upon his dilemma with his worried staff, repeating to them that he had not wanted this expedition, had never understood how he, with but two divisions, one cavalry, the other infantry, mixed in with but a handful of artillery, and sustained by a fragile supply line stretching like a filament up the ever-fluctuating, fickle, and often falling Arkansas River, or, when impassable, up the White and over the railroad from DeVall's Bluff to Little Rock (a nearly indefensible line of track), then stretched even further toward Texas till that filament had finally broken in his crossing of this wilderness; crawling with the roughriding Gray-back cavalry and recently arrived Confederate Creeks from the Indian Territory, raring for revenge against Thayer's Frontier Division, which had ravaged the homes, farms, and families of all the Civilized Tribes sworn to the Confederacy.

How could he? Frederick Steele wondered, a Yankee from New York, with an army of mostly midwestern farm boys and newly enlisted ex-slaves and free Negroes, pacify Arkansas, something no one had ever yet done, whether Indian, Spanish, French, or Anglo, so as to prepare this wild warring prodigal of a place for an orderly and peaceful reentry into an American Union.

Meanwhile, he was being slowly strangled by Governor, now General, Pap Price, who dreamed of destroying Steele so he could steal Missouri away as this Blue army was groping for Congressman Banks's hand like a blind man feeling a wall somewhere in northern Louisiana? This all done to keep Texas away from the Mexican-French while side-stealing some cotton?

Looking at that map in Mrs. Graham's parlor then, it all seemed an order tall enough to daunt Napoleon, and, in fact, it had done just that, since the emperor sold Louisiana (Arkansas) in the deep despair of his brother-in-law's defeat in Haiti—humiliated at the hands of slaves and sickness—thereby, reluctantly releasing France's last American Kingdom; selling it to make war on these same Habsburgs now perched precariously upon a kind of Viennese-French-Montezuma throne thrown across the Río Grande.

Worse, Steele said to his staff, at the other end of this now-fractured filament, which he traced with his finger back the way they came, he had perhaps mistakenly left his best regiment, the Third Minnesota, clinging to his depots on the Rock. In a word, all that the Union had so painstakingly bought in the West by victorious blood at Pea Ridge (Elkhorn) and Helena was now in the greatest peril of being lost and with it New Orleans or even St. Louis.

At last, he sighed and gave his orders: He would wait in his Moscow—stall till Banks won or lost (he knew nothing yet of the Sabine), meantime, reducing rations even more. But, too, he must forage—send a large party west immediately, he said—out where they had seen all that fresh corn but did not have time to stop—at a mill on White Oak Creek, just past another spot with the ominous name of Poison Springs.

CHAPTER TWELVE

It's time to pay for this here Reb corn, boys!
—anonymous Union soldier

With Pap Price headquartered at Woodlawn, fifteen miles to the southwest, Marmaduke, under Price's urging, now sent two cavalry units, Colonel Greene's brigade and the Third Missouri, in and along the Camden Road, shadowing to the east and south, while whistling up reinforcements in the form of Cabell and Crawford's Arkansawyers.

The Union muster was commanded by one Colonel James Williams, the White commander of the "Colored" First Kansas, co-joined with Kansas cavalry as an odd admixture of some eleven hundred pulling two hundred wagons and six cannons. This lumbering line of men and mules lazed slowly past Poison Springs to White Oak Creek where their scouts had previously smelled out the Confederate corn. Here they loaded all that was not previously burnt in the hurried anticipation of their coming, then soon fell into a sleep that brought a morning specially made for a leisurely reverse, raiding return back to Camden.

In this the Yankees were not particular, taking all the food and fodder found in an inching, frogging, half-backward forage—a steal and plunder soaking of the countryside like an inkblot of blood spilling out from the neck of their deep blue column, saturating in every direction.

One Reb recorded that the wagons had "pilferings" from houses of "children and women's clothing," of "baby frocks, shoes, stockings, women's bonnets, shawls and cloaks to take home to their families in Kansas." A nearby lady's farm, like Nora's blanket, was stripped of everything, even bedclothes, leaving only "the drapery of the windows" as consolation for empty drawers and bare cupboards in the farmhouse.

Then Captain William Duncan's Eighteenth Iowa sauntered out of town as a smiling, greeting "covering force," to replace those siphoned off as "stragglers" or "sick"—men lagging behind or lured by that lawlessness lurking in the heart of every unleashed army, peppering themselves about the countryside in raiding parties and individual adventures in and around farms, cabins, barns, and smokehouses, stealing and sacking as had been done to Arcadia and pretty much everywhere the Federal army marched in Arkansas and the rest of the South.

The Eighteenth pressed its way west and soon started a sputtering quarrel with Marmaduke's mounted patrols, seemingly always too near, yet a little too far, appearing and disappearing in and out of the trees and thickets, firing, yelling, and laughing, then camping close and watering their horses at the same creek, as a Confederate mare neighed to her Union sister, lifting her gray head from the slow stagnant pool a few yards away, clearly visible, drooling water in a whinnying final call for a peace that went unheeded.

Then, next day, White Iowa met Black Kansas at Poison Springs, commingling for a moment then separating as Iowa took up the escorting rear in a reverse backward turn toward the fourteen miles just covered from Camden.

Soon, mounted Bluecoats, trotting in advance of the column, encountered some Gray horse, spontaneously gave chase, shouting and shooting for about a mile; then, coming around a slight curve their lark was foreshortened by a Gray group of dismounted men pulled across the road in a ragged line. The riders wheeled about firing an aimless protest, cursing and whooping a face-saving defiance, before scurrying out of range and sending word back to Williams that there was trouble up there in the form of "Johnny" cavalry.

Alarmed, but not surprised, the colonel quickly shuffled Major Ward's First Kansas Colored forward where it found the Indiana Light Artillery fumbling ammunition chests open while busily unlimbering its 2 six-pounders. The major set one battalion right and the other left, before halting them with a sharp snap to load muskets. Then, Williams pushed some horsemen ahead in a tentative test of strength. Guessing the messenger's meaning before hearing his words, the colonel figured he was almost ready, so he curled back into a hard defense, then sent more cavalry up to screen Ward's left and right battalions while simultaneously galloping orders back to Duncan. His rider found the Iowa veterans casually eating and filling their canteens at the infamous creeks, but they knew enough when they saw the panting horse to stop and listen.

"It's time to pay for this here Reb corn, boys!" someone shouted as Duncan formed them to the south, arranged his two howitzers, shook out skirmishers, and waited.

The terrain couldn't have been worse for the Blues—thickets of briars, brush, and bending pine—so Williams decided to "recon-by-fire," as they would say about a half a dozen wars later, that is, hoping to spark a response; and so cannon was shot aimlessly into the tree line, in a staggered series of ominous grunts, its shot rising, then falling in the middle of a rather forlorn and incongruous silence, as the drift smoke floated into a soft white cloud above the trees.

"Maybe they'll shoot," Williams said as an out-loud wish, more to himself than anyone in particular.

"They're holding fire, sir," offered a staff major quietly.

"Both sides are getting better, I'm afraid," said Williams. "But at least it'll signal our foraging parties to return."

"Yes, sir ... or run," said the major.

"They're better off with us ... raiding ain't gonna set well."

The major set quietly, then said, "Sir, I don't believe Johnny's gonna oblige us today ... like you say, both sides been at it for too long."

"No, but send another volley all the same," said Williams.

This was done, again with no effect except to inspire the skirmishers, who had only offered an occasional bang but, now inspired by the big guns, started a steady stuttering quarrel of hide-seek-and-shoot. The battle of Poison Springs, like a fire climbing precariously up dry sticks, was slowly taking hold, cracking and popping its way gradually but steadily toward a rising flame.

As soon as dismounted Southern cavalry was seen snooping toward the Union right, Williams sent Lieutenant Robert Henderson's horse troopers loping forward to screen. Then, a mounted boy, a Reb messenger, rode hard into them and was captured.

"I'm a-lookin' for Colonel De Morse," he announced, panting in bewilderment.

He was brought instead to Colonel Williams. A Texas lad of sixteen, then with thick sandy hair, sporting strips of dirty gray uniform, he now stood under the Yankee colonel's horse instead of the Reb's. When asked, he gushed out that the Confederate army was "under ole Pap Price hisself," who had sent him from Woodlawn, just behind Dagmar, to order Colonel de Morse "to tickle out the Yankee right."

Then, as if prompted, another rider saddled up, only in blue, saying that Ward was "in a hot one" with the Texas Cavalry only four hundred yards south of the road. Williams then shifted forward what he could—a cannon and some infantry—he needed more, he knew that, but could not spare it.

"Take him away," he said with a nod, sending the boy off as a prisoner who would soon escape in the fight to tell of it later to his own children in the quietude of his fire-lit parlor.

"Go to Duncan and tell him he must send up four companies of infantry at once … forward to Ward, you understand, son, it's urgent!" he said, turning to an orderly.

"Yes, sir."

"Repeat it!"

"Captain Duncan must send four infantry companies at once to Ward."

"Good! Go! Go!" said Williams shooing the boy's horse with his hat.

But the Iowa captain could do no such thing. His skirmishers were sparring heavily with a dismounted, snooping, crawling group of Rebs now touching more and more the extremity of his tender right flank. So, changing his front, he moved his infantry forward into Mr. Lee's orchard on the plantation of that name, spreading them out, pushing his cannon in behind, while bending his cavalry into a right flank fish hook, as the colonel's rider lathered up, spitting out orders to help the "Coloreds."

"Please tell the colonel that I'm most heavily threatened and simply can't send anyone to Major Ward's Negroes."

"But, sir …"

"Tell the good colonel if I do as he wishes, he will be flanked! Understand! Flanked by damn!!" shouted the captain, his face turning red.

The messenger turned ashen, saluted, and rode away. Like a cornered wolf, if the Blue army struck in one direction, it could not bite in the other—yet it must strike or be taken by the throat and killed by Marmaduke's pack of circling dogs.

Meantime, De Morse's Texans were intent on doing just that—coming in from the animal's tail—circling behind it while Brigadier Cabell and Colonel Crawford's brigades busied the head. Here the Texans were hindered yet also helped by the terrain of brush, briars, and blinding pine thickets, as, dismounted, they crawled and wiggled forward, always angling more to the left, while dragging cannons across shoved-over saplings, like little boys sliding toys under a just slithered-through hedge.

Sneaking to a field's south fence, they greeted Lieutenant Henderson's north rail-jumping riders with quick demonstration of why the south rail was slightly too far from the Blue column, shooting and unseating some in thudding clumps. Ignoring a dying Henderson, the Blues reined backward, dropping dark lumps of troopers into the high weeds behind them like baggage left in a storm, then galloped back to their own line.

The Texans then rushed forward in a stooping Indian-style race across and through the north rail, as De Morse rode up, dismounted, and dodged the dead and dying, to join the living in their rush to their left.

He still could not yet see the corn wagons stopped single-file, but he could sense them there somewhere opposite his line, not far at all. Then De Morse tried to touch Ward's right but found instead a fronting ravine, which his skirmishers slid silently into, as a ragged Gray wave broke through a tree-thicketed forest and disappeared as if by magic into the earth.

De Morse then re-crossed to find the artillery chief, Captain Butler Krumbhaar, busily shinning cannons over saplings, quickly breaking the fence, pulling away dead Yankees, then dragging his four brutes by the tail, twisting them around and stuffing each snout with powder and ball.

Major Ward's wounded Blue muzzle snarled back into a reflexive arc of infantry and cannon as skirmishers and cavalry shuffled into a gap between the extreme right fronting De Morse and that of Duncan—an obvious, irremediable weakness. Then, a thousand yards toward town, astraddle the road, Hughey's Arkansas and Harris's Missouri batteries (four each) began to lob more pain onto Ward's head while Krumbhaar poked shot into his flank. The Blues tried counter-battery, but it was useless, as they were sandwiched by crossing cannon strokes that got hotter by the second.

This made Ward's people shield down under a pine ridge, while Williams, watching from his saddle, swung his glasses side to side in a gloomy view of the tightening ambush. For thirty minutes the cannon hit his line as he sat calmly sweeping the trees in search of some glimpse of something that he might conceivably give him the name of hope.

One thing he could not see was Colonel Tandy Walker's Confederate Choctaws, a regiment of Red Rebs that had walked four days in an eastward shadowing march of Thayer down from the Indian Territory and were slithering now to Duncan's right, down by the tail of the Blue wolf they'd come to skin.

"It looks like Reb was right," said the staff major riding up closer, yelling. "It's ole Pap Price hisself. His whole damned army!"

"Indeed, it is, Major ... all we can do is hope Steele hears us."

"I think we're a little too far, sir."

"No, but listen to that!" said the colonel pointing to where De Morse's Texans now opened up from their hide of one hundred yards to their right.

"The Johnnies seem to want this damn corn pretty bad," said the major with a quiet laugh. "What say we just give it back," he chuckled.

Now, as he slyly ordered Colored Kansas into silence till the enemy got closer. Tasting weakness, the Texans rose from the ravine and as one assaulted across the hundred yards—but it was too wide by half. The ex-slaves brushed through the field with a sweep of lead, splitting the Texans, breaking their nearly solid wave in two, rolling its pieces into the ravine, while a splinter of it ricocheted onto the cannons as, Krumbhaar, reacting, lifted more fire over the pines, pouring it hard onto the Black's in a steady burn of ball.

Colonel Tandy Walker, watching from the left, now ordered his Choctaws forward and, under cover of woods and a ditch, whooped into a Red frontier fight with the White Iowans a few yards short of hand-to-hand in a dispute that was very close, hot, and personal.

Meantime, Dagmar lathered from Price to Marmaduke and from Marmaduke to Colonel Colton Greene, commander of the Third Missouri Cavalry.

"Colonel Greene, sir, General Marmaduke says dismount and move to Colonel De Morse's flank ... on the right ... fill the gap between him and that road. The Texas boys got thar hands full and need hep quick-like. He says he'll come on down with the others ... Cabell and that bunch ... as soon as he kin, sir!"

Greene shooed Dagmar back with a nod and a yell, then dismounted his Missourians and ran them through the thick woods, arriving east of the same split rail bordering a much wider pasture, lined them along its southern lip in a huddled rim of wadded up Grays, hesitated for a final breath, then assaulted.

Marmaduke, growing ever more inspired watching through a long glass from a little rise, would later write:

> Without bayonets, many of them badly armed, most of them insufficiently drilled, they charged in splendid style through an open field ...

It was Ward's muskets that sparkled the general's fancy by separating out the unlucky from the others who made it to the far rail at a crouch. Now all were in place—Greene, De Morse, and Walker, stretching south along the Blue creature, curled head to tail, snapping out at Marmaduke's heel, who, standing in his stirrups, quickly waved General Cabell's horses in like an axe swinging for the predator's head.

Centering on the road, supported by artillery and the eerie screams of the Rebel yell, the three Arkansas regiments crumpled into Ward's skirmishers, touching his main line with fire, where Ward, denied reinforcements, resorted to unit shifting—stealing from one company to pay the other—a shuffling confused attempt at making do.

Here, on an overly warm spring day at this place called Poison Springs, the war had in a curious way reached a certain consummation—had assumed a final ironic symmetry. For many of these men had met before, dueling each-to-each—Red, White, and Black at a place called Honey Springs—a Union win in '63 that had unraveled the Gray's last ragged patch in the Indian land woven there stitch by stitch by the fat but nimble fingers of Albert Pike: a Harvard Bay Stater, come here to make money, teach, write, buy slaves, build a grand mansion in the Rock to sell later to John Fletcher as a place for his poet son, John Gould, to grow up in, as preparation for Harvard and other foreign places, till he came home at last to stay.

But Brigadier Pike placed his fortune, name, and talent on secession's square in a bet with his adopted state, which, after all, did only what his native Massachusetts had threatened to do over war in Mexico and with the British in 1812.

Pike, a great Mason, good journalist, okay lawyer, and bad poet, had proven a diplomat in treating with the Five Tribes, "civilized" or not, many themselves slavers, allying against the Blue soldiers who had scourged them forever. Thus, in '61, did Pike sew in the Creeks, Choctaws, Cherokees, Chickasaws, Seminoles, Osage, Shawnees, Senecas, Quapaws, and, finally, even the noble Comanches, who declared they would hold "the Confederate States by the hand, and be of one heart with them always."

The great Cherokee chief John Ross said:

> I'm gratified to inform you that the Great-Being who over-rules all things for good has sustained me in my efforts to unite the hearts and sentiments of the Cherokee people as one man ... with one voice we have proclaimed in favor of forming an alliance with the Confederate States, and shall thereby preserve and maintain the Brotherhood of the Indian Nations in a common destiny.

Then in '62, at the Elkhorn, his regiment of ponies, serving under Pike, McColloch, and Van Dorn, arrived early (well ahead of the Choctaws, Creeks, and Chickasaws), soldiering in thousands of braves with names like Samuel Poor Boy, Andrew Rabbit, Daniel Red Bird, Ned Short Arrow, and Moses Skon tah hee, led by their war chief, Colonel John Drew, and his lieutenant colonel, William P. Ross, the chief's nephew, lawyer, farmer, and editor of the tribal newspaper, who had raided Princeton by placing first in his class of '42; these Reds now earned words for Pike at Elkhorn by killing and scalping Yankees in gleeful retribution for all the tears shed on all the trails across *La Florida*.

The *Boston Tribune* was outraged:

> The meanest, the most rascally, the most malevolent of the rebels who are at war with the United States Government, are said to be recreant Yankees.
>
> Renegades are always loathsome creatures, and it is not to be presumed that a more venomous reptile than Albert Pike ever crawled on the face of the earth.

Not to be out-done in cold-blooded metaphors, the *New York Tribune* hooked this Pike by the gills and filleted him on the grill of their public's opinion as a "ferocious fish."

But the folks back East just hadn't gotten the picture. This war had bled out of Kansas long before the fireworks at Sumter; had exsanguinated itself into an ever-swelling, bushwhacking, throat-cutting stream that ran on as ambushes and lynchings, pooled around as raids, and clotted up now and then into things large enough to be called battles.

The Union had formed regiments like the First Kansas from ex-bondsmen and free Negroes, shocking most of the Whites and many of the Reds, including many heretofore Unionist slave owners, with not just the "horror of abolition," but with a war of color. In a word, in the Trans-Mississippi, a nerve had been touched, making its war a *guerre à outrance*—no quarter given or asked.

So, when De Morse's Texans reorganized and (buoyed by Greene) surged again, White Texas and Missouri plunging frantically ahead against Black Kansas, it was clear that Mr. Lincoln, in pitting section against section, had unleashed nothing less than race against race.

Colonel Williams, who had seen a lot, lived to write of its ferocity:

> For another quarter of an hour the fight raged with desperate fury, and the noise and din of battle of this almost hand-to-hand conflict was the loudest and most terrific it has ever been my lot to listen to.

Yes, for these men, Red, White, and Black— veterans of Honey Springs— that day's bitterness was now laced with the sweet venom of revenge at the Springs named for poison.

"You first, nigger, now buck to the Twenty-ninth Texas!" someone cried out in summation of the thing.

Losing most of its crew, the Indiana boys withdrew the one James rifle on Ward's right. The one on his left was quickly out of canister so was taken back about a hundred yards.

PHILLIP H. MCMATH

Ward rode up to Williams.

"Sir, half my men are casualties, three companies have no officers, and without those guns I must have reinforcements or I can't hold!"

"Major Ward, I have none to give!"

"But, sir, the Johnnies are pouring in stronger and stronger! We're gonna break!"

The colonel hesitated, then decided.

"Hang on ... I'll ride to Duncan and prepare him to cover your retreat."

Ward saluted and rode away as Williams loped toward the remnant of his Iowans.

But racing west the colonel felt his mount relax as a Minié ball slipped above his toe and into the horse's heart. He dismounted, allowing the gelding to unwind his feet upward before relaxing to the ground, himself standing, reins in hand, staring downward in surprised grief at an eye gradually unburdening itself of war.

He would remember it as the most stunning death of all—the one with the greatest pain. And, for a moment, the colonel of the First Kansas Colored was out of action. Then he felt a nudge as the major pried the reins of another horse into his fingers, so he could ride away to find Duncan still gripping the trunks of Mr. Lee's apple trees.

With the arrival of the two howitzers, Williams released the Iowans from the orchard, reforming them south of the road, but Walker's Choctaws only slipped closer, increasing their pressure from under the pink blossoms with their sparks of red blazing at the Blues.

"You must hold here and cover Ward's retreat!" Williams yelled to Duncan, who could only nod a glum "yes" as Williams rode east again.

But Ward's front was already collapsing as two companies withdrew and were followed in by five hundred of Crawford's brigade supporting Cabell. A volley slowed them, but Rebel cavalry then turned the left, forcing another retreat of sixty yards, as, on the right, Blues began to leave the line, first in singles, then in bunches, like shingles lurching off a storm-ripped roof—flying away into the winds. Sniffing blood, Arkansas's regiments rushed Ward's center while De Morse's Texans rammed the right again, this time reaching the Kansas flank that turned and broke.

But, as always, a remnant remains, survives to build anew, and it did that day, rallying around Ward, fighting a slow withdrawal back to Duncan, holding there for a moment—a knot of veterans, a semblance of order amid chaos, huddling hard around Major Ward and some wagons, shooting into the Grays.

Yet the wolf had been mortally struck and it was writhing, kicking out and in against itself, and would, in this twisting, turning death, be bitten again and again, punished and killed for all the frustrations and fears that men can endure.

General Steele, standing on Mrs. Chidister's front porch (he had moved from Mrs. Graham's), stood silently, listening to the guns, then, after a time, turned and went inside.

"Are we sending a flying column, sir?" implored a colonel, following him into the parlor like a boy with his father.

"No," snapped Steele, not looking up from a map spread across the dinner table.

The colonel paled.

"They're lost … I'll send no more," Steele said, running his finger across the topography and roads north of Camden while trying not to listen to the guns.

More officers came and went, conferring around their commander, expressing muffled consternation about the Williams command. Then, unexpectedly, a tired and dirty lieutenant entered with news of Mansfield.

Steele listened in silence, dismissed the messenger, looked down at the map again, hesitated, then went back out on the porch, his entourage following.

"The cannons are firing less," said the colonel, softly.

"Yes," said Steele. "I know."

"They're moving them again, I suppose."

"That's not it, Colonel."

"Sir?"

"No, now it's hand-to-hand."

Ward's troops came through the left in a broken Blue wave with the Grays mixing in hard behind, and, as General Steele had said, it was now indeed a thing of bayonets.

An Arkansas colonel described it:

> Away trotted the poor Black men into the forest, clinging to their rifles, but not using them, while the pursuing Confederates cut them down right and left. To the honor of the men, let it be said, that not a man on the left stopped at the tempting train of 200 wagons and mules standing in the road deserted by the escort. Some White men

PHILLIP H. MCMATH

lay dead by the train, killed by artillery, but received only a glance of the victorious troops who were after prisoners, batteries and the mounted men and officers.

The Williams-Duncan-Ward command fell back yet again, now to the Lee plantation's manor house, standing mutely like the South herself, as the men, fought among her rooms, out-buildings, and slave cabins.

Then the Blues abandoned the Lee place and, leaving their cannons, made a hesitant retreat through gently rolling but heavily wooded country, fighting ridge-to-ridge, finding at last a belated but dismal solace in a swamp.

By 11:00 P.M. the first stragglers, some with snakebites, most with wounds, and all with a staggering exhaustion, stumbled into Camden mumbling midnight tales of massacre and murder.

Breaking off the chase in fear of the "flying column" that Steele never sent, Maxey, who ranked Marmaduke, halted his hounds to chew the prey: 4 cannons, arms in stacks, 125 prisoners, 30 wagons ruined and 170 seized with mule teams of 6 still burdened with "corn, bacon, stolen bed quilts, women and children's clothing, hogs, geese, and all the *et ceteras* of unscrupulous plunder," someone noted.

The Choctaws returned to arrange themselves into a rear guard—the tail of a triumphant, winding walk to Woodlawn, which soon looped around a proud Price smiling in the middle glow of a great warming fire.

The Grays had lost but 4 percent, while the Blues nearly a third—the Kansas Colored 182 of their 438—of which 117 were killed—an out-of-proportion ratio raised by the refusal to accept their surrender.

Later, under a truce, burial parties found White officers scalped by the Reds, their bodies centered in stripped humiliation with their dead arranged neatly around them in the unending circle of all revenge.

Steele, otherwise reduced to rumors, had yet received only the one runner on the eighteenth. But it was more than ever clear that Congressman Banks's march to the Oval Office had ended at a dusty crossroads in Louisiana, while for Steele, idling in Camden, the poison of yesterday's defeat was rapidly working its way through his entire army as a Confederate victory. Still, he had no choice but to cut rations yet again while the animals could fodder for just one more turn of the clock. But, though some time was added with the "flying column" arrival of a serendipitous supply train from Pine Bluff, it was clear that

Steele's own ambitions had likewise devolved from invading to evading—from acting to reacting—from destruction to its avoidance.

On the nineteenth, he composed a message to his superior, General Sherman. "It is useless to talk of obtaining supplies for my command," as "the countryside is well-nigh exhausted and the people threatened with starvation," he dictated. Adding a rather forlorn suggestion in the form of "wondering" if the navy could churn its way up the Ouachita with supplies. But the ink had not dried on this wish, than came a dusty Captain Robert Dunham, riding from Grand Ecore with the crumpled words of official confirmation of Banks's defeat, retreat, and, worst of all, a cry for help in the form of an order for Steele to march down to the Red River as his rescuer.

"This is absurd!" blurted his chief engineer, Captain Junious B. Wheeler, without waiting for word from Steele who demurred and, in quick dictation for the rider's dirty hand, penned a lament about being steadily pounded and probed along his outposts, adding that he was low on supplies and facing a force that would do nothing but swell in boldness and power. And because of this, an adventure into northern Louisiana was not to be contemplated. Nor could the West Pointer resist prodding the politician: "The Rebels are said to be very much encouraged by an order of General Kirby Smith, detailing his successes against your command," he added, without, of course, mentioning this same Smith's "successes" against himself.

Meanwhile, Smith parsed Taylor of everything save praise—pinning on a third star and making him Louisiana's temporary military tsar—then, leaving a covering force, the commander of the Trans-Mississippi marched up to Camden with three infantry divisions: Brigadier Thomas Churchill's Arkansawyers, Brigadier Mosby Parson's Missourians, and Major General John G. Walker's Texans.

Arriving at Calhoun, a little south of Price at Woodlawn, Smith reached the end of his telegraph line stretching back to Shreveport, and so began an extended chat with Price by horse as Dagmar and others rode hard in the steady stream of a forty-mile loop between the two. First, Smith nodded assent for Poison Springs, then he pushed Price to go north and east, cutting Camden from the Rock, Pine Bluff, and the railhead at DeVall's Bluff.

With any luck, the future math professor of Sewanee College calculated to his wife, Steele was his, he wrote, as, "Neither man nor beast could be sustained in the exhausted country between the Ouachita and White rivers."

CHAPTER THIRTEEN

I know you will, my daughter.
—Col. Titus Pilgrim to Dagmar

Colonel Titus Pilgrim, staffed to General J. O. Shelby's cavalry brigade, who, as we have seen, always looked imposing in his uniform, saber, Stetson, and sidearm, looked even more so as he rode up on Pegasus—a mount taller even than the large dark horses that Shelby was so superstitious about riding.

Titus hadn't seen his new stepdaughter since Washington, and now, as they had received urgent orders for an interdiction of Steele's supply lines, he wanted to say goodbye and so dismounted behind where she squatted by a small fire—alone as she usually was.

"Dagmar!" he said.

"Papa!" she said, coming to embrace him.

("Papa" seemed to fit, since she had called her real father, "Pa." By comparison "Papa" seemed fancy enough for a colonel, she decided.)

They hugged quickly.

"Papa, you're the only officer they let me hug," she laughed, standing back again by the fire.

"I'm the only one I want you huggin'," he smiled as he stepped near her.

There was a slight, embarrassed pause as they looked at each other in the dancing light, then Titus said, "We're leaving at daybreak and I wanted to see you."

"Crossing the river?"

"Yes, at Matlock's for a swing around in a raidin' ride north and maybe back again toward Hampton and down again to El Dorado landin' ... gotta stop anymore supplies from gettin' in ... we jes 'bout got ole Steele trapped."

"I thought as much ... about time we started gittin' some folks over thar. I figger that Steele's gonna leave this yar hole and run fur the Rock prutty soon like. He cain't stay yar much longer or we're gonna sack 'em for shore."

"You should've been a general, Dagmar."

"Don't take no general to see that, Papa."

They laughed again.

"They've been working you pretty good, I hear."

"We stay at it, I'll say that. But after that lickin' we give 'em at Pieson Sprang, I figger we gonna be a-ridin' lots more. That's gotta be a-settin' on Steele's mind pretty good by now ... thangs is gonna git lots hotter soon ..."

"You're right ... we gotta hold 'em as long as we can, then, like you say, we can drop him in the sack and tie the knot. After that lickin' Taylor gave Banks, it'll be double-sweet."

"I know yall'll do it, Papa, as soon as them boys walks up yar from Shreveport."

"Jo Shelby will ... he's the best cal'very leader this side of Forrest."

"He's a goodun, ain't he, Papa? I wanted to ride with ya'll, but they won't let a one-armed tomboy do nothin' but carry words around."

"I hear you're the hardest ridin' of the lot."

"After you done rode with my kind, you kin ride with most any of 'em."

There was nervous laughter at mention of her old family.

Titus warmed his hands then kicked a burning log. "Dagmar, I want you to do to sumpin for me," he said, pulling out a letter. "Here, make sure Medora gets this ... if I don't live, that is. But if, God willin', I ain't killed in this fight that's a-comin', burn it. I won't see her before then or I'd give it myself ..."

She slipped it into her leather case.

"Shore, Papa, I'll see it done," she said, spitting into the fire making it hiss in agreement.

"It says all the personal thangs ... and tells her to go back to Arcadia ... Missouri, that is, the town I was born in by that name. I have people there. It's my wish to her ... to sell out and go back there." He paused, then added, "Dagmar, honey, I'm gonna rely on you to help Medora and the girls as best you can."

"I ain't no good at settin', Papa, but I'll see she gits yore letter and anythang else I kin do fur her and nem gals ... till you git back ... I promise."

"I know you will, daughter."

Titus reached out, embraced her again, and then quickly turned, mounted Pegasus, and disappeared quietly into the night.

After watching him go, Dagmar squatted, stirring the fire with a stick while staring blankly into its flame, then, with the back of a dirty hand, she wiped away a tear tickling her nose.

CHAPTER FOURTEEN

... the substance of Louisiana and Texas was staked against the shadow
of Missouri and northern Arkansas.
—General Richard Taylor, CSA

It was clear that Price was in danger of being reinforced by Smith's shifting across shorter distances—defeating one army, then turning on the next.

Of course, all of this was over the strenuous and very insubordinate objections of Richard Taylor, who forever gloried in his fantasy of finishing Banks and freeing New Orleans. Smith then, always torn between north and south, was in a dilemma. Which was it to be: Banks or Steele? Taylor or Price? New Orleans or St. Louis?

Taylor would complain in a postwar scribble that Smith sitting in Shreveport gave "much of his mind to the recovery of his lost empire ... to the detriment of the portion yet in his possession"—that "the substance of Louisiana and Texas was staked against the shadow of Missouri and northern Arkansas."

In this way, the South, like most losers, would be pursued unceasingly by lost victories, which could be resurrected only in the grief of unforgettable hopes: Wilson's Creek, First Manassas, Stone's River, Shiloh, Gettysburg, Chickamauga, and that run of days now called Red River. And, since the unrealized always has a perfection with which the realized can never compete, these conjured an awful "if" into the worst anguish of all—a memory of a *never* merging with the dream of an *almost*.

It was precisely this that pushed Kirby Smith into that most painful of choices: Which ambition to leave in undone perfection and which to compromise by the attempt. In the end, Steele's nearer idleness was deemed more of a reality than Banks's receding retreat, which, like a spring pressed downward, might yet grow stronger under the very pressing, while Steele seemed almost unwound in his unattached, seemingly bewildered isolation.

Better, some whispered, for Smith to win at Camden than Taylor take New Orleans. For this he would be harshly judged, but then Kirby Smith was no Prince Hannibal, nor was he meant to be. He played it safe.

Stripping Taylor of three divisions, Smith set them in motion on a northerly forced march. They weaved through Shreveport on the sixteenth to the exhilaration of cheering crowds—bands and flags—some eight thousand marching Gray infantry, dressing it up for the home folks, stepping to the steady stutter of their drummer boys as Louisiana ladies, children, and old men thronged in gratitude, waving along the lads from Arkansas, Texas, and Missouri. Then, to lessen the pressure of forage on an already over-foraged countryside, Smith forked them out of town into a three-pronged route of approach, with General Churchill's Arkansawyers slipping to the west up the Wire road, paralleling the Red, before leaving its valley and crossing the border to Magnolia. Here they converged with General Parsons's Missourians, who had formed the middle prong coming through Rocky Mount, while Walker's Texans were swung to the east toward Minden where, on the eighteenth, these survivors of Mansfield, Pleasant Grove, and the Hill were indulged an overdue rest.

On the morning of the nineteenth, Smith then pushed one-half of Brigadier J. O. Shelby's cavalry division, including the rested "Iron Brigade" of about one thousand horse, across the Ouachita River north of Camden at Matlock's Ford, where they nudged aside a Yankee patrol in a sharp skirmish, then galloped east around Steele in a horseshoeing loop through Hampton and back to El Dorado Landing on the river to the south.

Advised of their arrival, Fagan disturbed the morning darkness of the twenty-second by plunging across Matlock with his remaining three cavalry brigades, two in a division under Brigadier Cabell, late of Poison Springs, and Shelby's other one, under General Thomas Dockery—a double column of three thousand fresh animals swimming through the spring green water like a vast migrating herd, then emerging from the chilled wetness for an invigorating, dashing, circling rendezvous with Shelby, who, scattering scouts like birds from his perch at El Dorado, soon learned from Titus that his Gray riders were shadowing a supply train meandering from Camden to the northeast.

As Fagan crossed the Ouachita, the two divisions of Parsons and Churchill walked wearily into Woodlawn, where, to divert attention from Fagan, Smith nodded a short rest before ordering a feint at Steele in a loud but largely bloodless melee of shot and shouts—done as enthusiastically as could be expected from those who, down in Louisiana at Pleasant Hill—the follow on fight after Mansfield—had just suffered some of the worst violence of a very violent war, thrown into it at full tilt, backing up and being thrown again like an axe against a shield, then, without repose, reverse marched and wielded against the enemy standing some distance behind.

The "serendipitous" supply train that came through earlier had been unloaded, and within forty-eight hours was ready to make a second journey, despite now knowing that Shelby's "Iron Brigade" was lurking around the Moro Bottoms. The train's lambs were 211 wagons shepherded by one Lieutenant Colonel Francis Drake (future railroad tycoon, university namesake, and governor of Iowa), who took command of twelve hundred Indiana, Iowa, and Ohio Blue foot, four guns, and an attachment of cavalry when his superior colonel fell sick in his tent.

The expedition crossed the river quietly in the night, camped, then moved out early on the twenty-third. But the deliberate Drake's morning to-and-fro ride was shocked by the revelation of seventy-five gypsy-like wagons hugger-muggering in his rear as refugees—sutlers, strumpets, and shirkers that stepped ahead of some three hundred runaway slaves moving in hopeful desperation behind a White mob aping the orderly Blue column as its chaotic half-brother.

It was an exodus shuffling off for the Promised Land of Pine Bluff, a small village on a big river, then governed by that great grand Yankee colonel, Powell Clayton, down from Pennsylvania—the future carpetbagging husband of the beautiful *belle*, Adeline. This devoted Rebel spy from Helena, who, as his brief but bewitching prisoner, imprisoned him forever and would be all conquering as the postwar mistress of their new *Linwood* plantation where she reigned in an unofficial, if belated, rich triumph, while he, like all the ravagers who remained, was, in time, seduced by the Southern sweetness of the exposed white breast of getting rich quick—the possessor becoming himself possessed, marrying her as the generalissimo groom of Reconstruction Arkansas, then Republican governor, U.S. senator, intercessor and confidant of Grant, and the eventual ambassador to Mexico.

But today Powell, our soon-to-be millionaire politician, planter, and planner of railroads sat in worried anticipation, not of Yankee customers coming South on his Reconstruction trains, but of columns of Rebel cavalry riding up from Camden toward himself.

"What have you heard from Colonel Drake?" he asked after a moment, raising his head slightly but not directing the question to anyone in particular.

The answer, if known, would have been that the Drake column was at that moment pinching slowly up to the Moro Bottoms, "pioneered" there by the refugees pressed into service as reluctant road builders, corduroying hundreds of wheels over hundreds of ruts and washouts, turning them through rugged, forlorn country which one diarist described as "poor low and flat, mostly covered with pine & cypress [sic] ... the ground is verry [sic] sandy & no improvements to amount to anything ..."

On it went, building its road ahead like a train laying down its own track, till twelve miles out it succeeded in bursting one of Shelby's waiting patrols huddled quietly in a thicket like a covey of nervous quail, shattering the quietude with a sudden heart-shuddering, sharp, but ultimately harmless, skirmish of sabers, shrieks, and pistol smoke, while Gray riders fluttered quickly away in all directions, so the Blue thing could resume its phlegmatic, muddy, yard-by-yard, foot-by-foot, inch-by-inch monotonous march, whose tedium was broken only by the discomfort one experiences when being secretly watched, as unknown horses neighed in the brush, throating Union mounts to a friendly but ominous answering return, while the Blues treaded more and more over fresh circling tracks, mashed under the dropped debris of strange riders: last night's ashes, broken limbs, and flattened-down brush flushed away from by waves of frightened, chattering birds pushed on by churlish crows and ill-humored hawks flying from an invisible but portentous vexation of something moving furtively in the woods.

In short, the column discerned all the disturbances and detritus of a small, but ever-growing horse army prowling around it, and the men were afraid.

All this Titus watched with a spyglass, and, without taking the instrument from his eye, dictated yet another dispatch to Shelby.

> The enemy, in the numbers I have previously reported, has now reached the western edge of the Moro swamp where he has halted for his evening bivouac. His runaway Negroes, under the supervision of officers, however, continue to corduroy into the bottoms and across Moro Creek. Doubtless, they will work throughout the duration of the evening with the intention of proceeding on the morrow. Likewise, the enemy has posted mounted scouts and patrols to the east and west, but, per your instructions, we have diligently avoided contact.
>
> Would advise an approach from the east to affect a junction somewhere near Marks's Mill. There, I have ever confidence, victory will be ours and with it another step taken toward the achievement of

our independence and liberation from Federal tyranny.

Will so proceed till otherwise advised.

Yours Respectfully,
Titus Pilgrim, Colonel,
CSA
April 24, 1864

That evening, after scurrying patrols in opposite directions as Titus had observed, Drake sent one Lieutenant James B. Schrom forward with the burden of answering Colonel Clayton's question. This lieutenant's little band, pulling an ambulance loaded with dispatches, soon found itself wandering into a tree-shrouded darkness none expected to see again this side of the grave. Here they struggled with a morass that needed but a mile to enmesh them into a mired-up halt, and where, guarded by a patrol forwarded by Drake, they gradually huddled into a sun-abandoned world for a sleepless night among the moccasins and mosquitoes of the Moro mud.

To be sure, no one in that war agreed on very much: Why it was being fought? Who was right or who wrong? Why it was won or why lost? But on one thing everyone did agree—the passage of time. It simply refused to move in the normal way. Seconds would be hours, minutes days, days weeks, a week months, and a year an eternity. The war seemed never to want to end, and 1864 was the longest year anyone ever expected to live through—if live through it they did. For the Drake expedition then, it was a long night. Yet everyone seemed to know that Colonel Pilgrim's "morrow" at the swamp's entrance knew it and Fagan's lads loping through the darkness like hungry but happily hunting wolves knew it. The difference was the Grays slowed time with desire—the Blues with dread.

But come the morning did, the sun first making a darkness that no one believed could have been darker than before, yet darker it was, a heavy, smothering darkness that lay over them like a coffin lid nailed down over dead eyes; then, after an even slower hour, there cracked at long last a slight, light-emitting grayness that pulled the great wilderness up in outline against the eastern sky like a mountain of trees to be climbed rather than marched through. Seeing this, Drake's camp began that half-reluctant but ever-restless, noisy, confused, waking that sleepy men and animals make in anticipation of a morning's motion—a hurried breakfast, followed by that boundless sound of thousands of men talking, cursing, and yelling in a packing, saddling, hitching, lifting, loading, and banging nervous cacophony that such an army makes in preparation for simply walking down a small road.

Drake, the future railroader, got everything lined up just so before spreading more cavalry out from his train in a quick overtaking of Schrom, his horses lunging past toward the trace intersections east of Moro but a little west of Marks's Mill.

Next, he moved forward the Forty-third Indiana Infantry with a battery of Missouri cannon, both commanded by one Major Wesley Norris, whose task was to "ride point." But, as is frequently true with point riders, he was not found to be in good humor. His evening reports, passed back from patrols and sentries of "strange goings-ons," had generated a response from the future Iowa governor that went: "Major, there is no enemy in front; you get scared too easily. Go back and go to bed!"

Grumbling ahead of his grumbling regiment, the major, who knew that these "goings-ons" were precisely the thing they were walking toward, led his men in a slogging swamp passage toward the junction of Mount Elba and Warren wagon trails where they were told to halt and, if necessary, hold.

Then the main column, inching behind its pioneers, lunged forward in a swarm, followed into the sunlit forest, and soon found themselves multiplying Lieutenant Schrom's experience by 286 as wagons stuck, stopped, and sank.

Drake would recall that his train "mired down as the mules floundered in the seemingly bottomless slush holes, some scarcely visible except their ears."

Leading this herky-jerky Blue procession were the Indiana infantry boys humping along as they had from the very beginning, starting in Terre Haute, their '61 rallying point, humping down through Kentucky, across the Big River to Missouri for the battle of New Madrid and Island #10, then back over again to western Tennessee for the pounding of Fort Pillow and a move into Memphis, then farther down the Mississippi for the amphibious Yazoo Pass adventure north of Vicksburg, fighting snipers, snags, and snakes; mercifully turning around, churning up and into the yawning mouth near *Poste aux Arcs* on the Arkansas (Cayas), slipping by the sleeping dead of Anilco north of where their murderer, De Soto, bequeathed his swine to the world, his slaves to the wilderness, and his soul to the swirling brown eternity of the Big River's womb; steam-boating silently by there and into a chute for a slow chug up the White, then quickly back down again, they paddlewheeled to Helena for a feverish rest, a nice siege, and a pretty good scrape with the ever-graying general Theophilus "Granny" Hunter Holmes, when he tried to retake the place with Price to help depressurize Vicksburg.

All of this, as it turned out, being a mere tune-up for the longest and hottest hump of all across the Arkansas Delta (just a little south of the route the Spanish had used hotly humping along so they could prop up a great rain-making cross at Parkin to cool things off); resting at the Rock on the river, wintering there in '63 and '64, but reenlisting just in time to watch David O. Dodd hang in his slicked-up Sunday best while Indiana's finest was humped-up in pretty dress-blue uniforms with shiny bayonets and sabers, standing at attention in the shivering sun, while the cherub-cheeked boy choked under a gibbet for the benefit of a mob, including Medora Pilgrim, who had come in the futile effort to save her own son from such an early grave while watching from a buggy as another mother's child swung for some harmless notes made to impress General James Fleming Fagan, Medora's husband's commander, a Kentucky Whig politician and planter turned Arkansawyer who hated all things Yankee, turning, with his first taste of war in Mexico, into a soldier as a lieutenant with Yell's rifles then unsatisfying himself at Shiloh till he had watched with a ravenous impatience the same Indiana Blues warm up for the downward and increasingly hungry and hotter hump to Camden and this morning's hot and even hungrier hump through yet another horrible swamp humping over to a road crossing south of a place they'd, of course, never heard of, called Marks's Mill, a humble clump of log houses and, of course, a mill or two, with a slender sapling stuck out front by one Mr. Hastings Marks as a way of doing something with it after whipping a recalcitrant buggy horse; tending it into a rooted and growing great tree till it stands today on what used to be called the Red Lands, near a line of woods, just to the northeast of the Mount Elba and Warren road crossing where the huffing, humping Indiana Forty-third were finally to end their infernal huffingly humping frustrating war by fighting the hottest and final battle of their lives with the very same Fleming Fagan who had diverted them so in January with such a fine hanging and was now waiting impatiently astride a very big sorrel for them to come up out of a swamp and down toward Mr. Marks's famously immortal tree.

It seemed fitting they should meet, and meet they did, as Lieutenant Schrom, who was beginning to feel more than a little *de trop* standing by his helplessly mired-up fourgon, was relieved with orders to abandon all such wagons while wheeling the others out and into a circle west of the junction. In this way, Drake flanked Schrom's right with the Thirty-sixth Iowa, while the Seventy-seventh Ohio, resting behind, was told to take up an ambling rear guard.

Meantime, our future Arkansas governor from Pennsylvania, Powell Clayton, learning that Drake was inching toward him, dispatched a "flying column" of some 350—cavalry mixed with infantry—under one Major Henry P. Spellman, who, leaving his foot in the Saline to guard his ford, raced down the Mount Elba road on toward the Forty-third, which, seeing his horses rushing forward, gave a great hat-waving hurrah.

Hearing shots, Drake found Norris to begin where they had left off. "Why have you halted, sir?!"

"There are Rebels to my front!" said the major.

"There is no enemy in front!"

"Yes, there is … for I have seen them … and you ought to order up the Thirty-sixth and the Ohio boys to positions on my right and left!"

"Major Norris, I order you to advance your line and feel of the enemy if there is any in the front!"

"All right, Colonel," said the major in that unmistakable "you'll see" tone and, saluting, rode off, dismounting with a command for his men to get up and advance on-line, which they bravely did, taking a mere one hundred yards to make their major's point by giving the Grays the pleasure of seeing an enemy in range and walking. This changed in the instant it takes a Minié to zip in a flat, short trajectory, sent by young-eyed men who can quickly pop out death from the trees as easily as kiss your hand.

Drake relented, ordering Norris to cover and extend his lines while he stretched the flanks even further with dismounted cavalry—his own and Spellman's.

Quickly the fighting rose hotter as the Union Missouri battery began to bark back and, Drake, under this rising heat, melted Norris's other companies into an even thinner line as the Iowans huffed out of the swamp while the Ohioans still lagged back.

As for Fagan, having covered the forty-five miles from El Dorado Landing on the twenty-fourth, he camped at Edinburg, eight miles from the Mill, in time to be overjoyed to hear from Colonel Pilgrim via one Lieutenant W. H. Farrell, a hard-riding scout from the Fifth Missouri, that the Yankee column was camped east of Moro Creek.

"We'll be at ole man Hastings's before those Yankees can ever cross that bottom," Fagan said to Shelby, a broad grin visible in the fire light where the two were standing when young Farrell strode up, fresh off a blowing horse, saluted, and gave the proudest news of his life.

So rosy-fingered dawn soon found Fleming Fagan saddling fast upon the Mill, where, with Shelby in the lead and his scouts squabbling with Blue skirmishers, he pinned the Federals nicely and swung Shelby out of sight wide to the right, arcing him around behind. It was a turning trick threaded through obscure stock trails led by Private William D. Marks, the miller's son, who knew every trace, twist, and track in the backwoods of Bradley County.

Coming behind Shelby's brigade was Cabell's, whose horse regiment, the First Arkansawyers under Colonel J. C. Monroe, rapidly dismounted across the Warren road to nudge back the Blues a bit, while the Second, under Colonel T. J. Morgan, tied in to the west for an unwavering butternut advance through the trees around the Marks's clearing.

Unhitching behind them was Hughey's Arkansas Battery, which unlimbered its four guns into a quick, lifting fire for the Grays to pass under. Then, swinging past the cannon and slithering to the right, a battalion under Lieutenant Colonel T. M. Gunter arrived, dismounted, and slipped forward easily, impaling Spellman while seizing wagons like popping a stopper back into a bottleneck pointing at Pine Bluff.

Meanwhile, on the Reb left, Morgan's men followed him, turning the Blue right, setting teamsters on their heels before pistoling mules as a way of keeping things pretty much plugged up on their end.

Things seemed to be going well for the Johnnies, but the Forty-third Indiana—country boys all—"Westerners" who gave the South so much trouble everywhere—had not huffed and humped so long and hard to reach this spot to run away and, so, now insisted on bulging things up the middle, refusing passage there as Monroe was not just stopped, he was thrown back.

This pressed upon the ground a certain contour, not of a horse track but of a cow or pig of some kind—that is, cloven—pushed down by the Forty-third's curling up in the middle while the Grays busied themselves molding the edges around them.

But the Indianians, with a nod from Drake and a shout from Norris, recovered, then struck back, counterattacking reflexively with that unconscious, uncoiling unanimity only veterans possess.

The First Arkansas staggered, though as they would later insist, "grudging every foot," to where they started. Elated, Drake borrowed a battalion of Iowans newly arrived from his left and pressed them forward. But from this emptiness other Grays poured fire onto the Forty-third's flank, forcing the regiment to turn, withdraw, and stop, allowing the First Arkansas finally also to stop and lay in for a buzzing exchange over the Blue and Gray clumps commingled upon the ground.

Meantime, Gunter, obscured by forest on the Gray right and sensing his isolation from Monroe, wheeled about and traversed completely across the rear middle for a tie-in on the First's left.

Likewise, Morgan, on the other end, done with mule slaying, reached the same conclusion the same way, and so did about the same thing—turning, feeding his people through the trees till they touched Gunter's new flank for a knot-tying there.

Seeing this, Brigadier Cabell decided to try again. He ordered a second advance—on line—toward the Midwestern farmers' sons crouching among the weeds, woods, and works of the Marks's place.

That's to say, with Gunter and Morgan hugging in, Monroe got the lads up, dressed in, pressed out—then forward, Rebel-yelling and shooting through the trees and into the Mill's clearing, brushing Indiana back onto their Missouri battery, where, like children hiding behind a big brother's toys, they unbent into a new line.

"Wait a bit!" yelled Lieutenant Peetz to his crews, their hands nervously fingering the four fire sticks as the Grays, obliging in a way that a self-absorbed age can little understand, charged into the mouth of mortality as Peetz gapped the Grays open with grape, and the lucky fell back.

Soon the battle settled into an hour's scrum as Cabell scooted in his artillery and scrubbed Peetz hard with long-range grape of his own. In short, it became a standoff.

General Thomas P. Dockery, delayed by horse foraging, finally led his belated but fresh brigade up the Warren road. Dockery came up to Fagan, their stirrups nearly touching as Fagan studied his friend. He was always a difficult man not to forgive.

> Neither orders nor cannon-shots seemed to disturb that equanimity which he always carried with him into battle. Jolly, energetic, yet absolutely devoid of nervous sensibility, he appeared to have perfect immunity from both fear and anxiety.

Heaven smiles with the charming, and Fagan's irritation soon faded with an exchange of conventional courtesies considered in those inferior times as an expression of sensibility, followed hard upon with a mute acceptance of the profered excuse, then he responded, not with censure, but a quick outline of events and instructions to go in on Cabell's left.

This Dockery did with a broad, grinning shout, unsaddling his men into a great joy that soon pressed upon the right flank of the increasingly silent Drake.

PHILLIP H. MCMATH

But the thunderclap came not from stage right, with Dockery's entrance, but with a glum-faced messenger entering from Drake's left.

"Sir!" yelled a scout, one of three, loping up to Drake and saluting perfunctorily, riding forward as his two long-faced companions reined back, content to let him speak these heavy lines, riding as they had, seemingly from nowhere, upon mounts a little more than half dead from exhaustion.

This, intruding as it did hard upon Dockery's entrance, turned Drake's head first in one, then into the other, direction, like a bear swinging between the hounds.

"What is it?!" shouted Drake with that "don't-bother-me-now-you-damn-fool" note heavy in his voice.

"Sir, there's a large column advancing down the Mount Elba road!"

A pause.

"A large column, did you say?"

"Yes, sir … very large."

Another pause.

"Cavalry?"

"Yes, sir … led by a man on a big dark horse wearing a plume."

"Shelby!" yelled Drake, dropping his head.

It was Shelby, indeed, with Titus at his side.

Drake said no more. Dockery was tearing at his right, Monroe, Gunter, Morgan his middle, and now Shelby was heaving into his hindquarter.

He stared mutely. The two horses circled nervously, coming fully around, then face to face again as Drake maintained his stare.

"How far?" he asked, coming round after a second circling.

"They should arrive any moment, I fear, sir," said the scout, his manner declining from assertion to a kind of pity.

Drake thanked him and, without returning a salute, rode off for the shifting of a battalion of Iowans to the left, while scurrying a runner to his cavalry leader, Major Mark McCauley, with orders to charge in an "S" pattern through the lead elements of Shelby's oncoming column, "so as to break them up" for the infantry, he explained.

But the messenger returned lamenting failure, so Drake went himself, loping across the battlefield like the bear now strapped to a horse, as a Minié, no doubt dropping a bit at the range, lost the heart but found the hip, sliding below his belt into the bone. He grunted but kept running, riding up to the major, growling out a painful repetition of his instructions—that is, of carving up a thousand with sixty.

McCauley absorbed this.

"We will obey orders, but there will be none left to report," he said, shaking and lowering his head in one motion.

"You will go through them so rapidly that, in our opinion, you will suffer but slight loss," Drake is reported to have responded as confidently as he could.

Yet by now McCauley's lowered eyes had focused his mind upon something else—alive—moving down his colonel's boot. He looked closer as it slipped along the leather like a thin reddish snake sliding down a black tree, slithered around the ankle then onto the stirrup before transforming itself almost supernaturally from serpent to syrup in a slow, sluggish drip to the ground.

He looked at Drake, each realizing what the other knew, as they met gaze to gaze.

There was a hesitation, then the major asked quietly, "Are you severely wounded?"

"Yes," said Drake, waving it off, then returning to the matter at hand, saying, "We will support your charge with infantry," he groaned. Leaned forward upon the pommel and pressing with both hands, he raised himself briefly with a grimace, then settled down again as McCauley watched a face transformed from defiance to desperation.

"Do you understand?" Drake managed at last.

The major looked at the boot again, then at his commander's paling face, thought for a moment, and gave a reluctant half-nod.

Satisfied, Drake wheeled in search of the Iowans, but completed his journey only by half before lolling out of the saddle—like an untied animal—rolling in a faint, his horse shying, slipping the reins from his hand with a quick backward arch of the head, then swinging into a cantering, disappearing run.

A captain came and bent over the colonel, receiving his whispered instructions that Major Spellman should take command; but this was never done, and the Blues were by one bone-finding bullet reduced to a mindless defense.

Shelby's division had warrened its way through the wooded back trails, winding at last upon the Mount Elba road about five miles east of the Marks's place. Here, joyous at scouting reports that no train had passed, he screened a battalion to the right and turned west at a trot.

Coming toward the rising sound of battle, Shelby encountered the flotsam of war—desperate civilians, detached wagons, deserters, and the odd riderless horse fleeing up the highway.

Then, about a mile away, he halted and, after chatting with scouts, threw his regiments into thicker columns of four and advanced, coming soon upon straggler wads and wavering wagoners, who quickly panicked into the woods. He stopped, unlimbered his cannon, signaled Fagan with two booms, spread his thousand horses on line, and charged.

Hearing these cannons, Cabell ordered his men up and into yet another assault.

Gunter, Monroe, and Morgan gave it another go, overrunning Peetz's James guns, capturing them and fifty Blues hiding in a cabin along with Drake, who was found there lying upon the floor.

"I am General James Fagan, commanding the Confederate forces, about eight thousand. I understand that you are Colonel Drake, commanding officer of the Federal forces," said Fagan, leaning over the stretcher and staring down at Drake.

There was no response.

Fagan added, "I compliment you, Colonel, on a gallant defense."

Again Drake said nothing.

"Can you not arrange for a surrender of your brigade?" insisted Fagan.

At last, Drake spoke without raising his head. "I am no longer in command, sir."

So what of the slaves, strumpets, sutlers, and shirkers? Most had taken an early exit—screaming into the swamp—slowly staggering or saddling back through where they found some Iowa cavalry struggling to catch up—grouped at Moro bridge, listening to the firing while letting the flotsam pass.

One remembered:

> The halt had scarcely been made, when a most demoralized crowd
> of cotton speculators, sutlers, refugees, teamsters, etc. mounted on
> mules and horses, dashed past at the "best gate" the animal possessed
> for Camden, followed immediately by a volley from the enemy.

Some few died, of course, and some few others were wounded or went missing, including an unhorsed, bleeding but clever-tongued Iowa lieutenant with the eerily Anglo-Vietnamese sounding name of Silas Nugen, who told the Johnnies he was but a scout for Steele's hordes closing fast upon their heels. Young Nugen was an inscrutably good liar.

Fagan lost 41 killed and 108 others blessed by glory. Yet Drake lost his entire command—a hundred dead, double that in wounded, 1,300 prisoners, 300 wagons with mules and horses, stacks of arms, Peetz's cannons, Schrom's papers and, of course, the colors and himself as a half-colonel lying fully stretched upon the ground.

CHAPTER FIFTEEN

Camden looked like a deserted town, no noise or Yankees ... Oh! what relief to be free of them! We did not know what joy was in store that day—didn't know that our boys in grey were so near ...
—Mrs. Virginia McCollum Stinson

The news of Marks's Mill, newly ridden as it was over the fresh tracks from Poison Springs, had the effect of spinning General Steele's thoughts—like a gyrating compass—from south by west to north by north—and, accepting the ill tidings, he vowed to waste no more energy upon Mr. Banks in the Bayou, or Maximilian in Mexico, rather, henceforth he would focus his attention solely upon Frederick Steele on West Washington Street; that is to say, he had kicked the can down the glory road toward starvation long enough, and, after a grim quartermaster's report and a council of war, he resolved to scrape the south Arkansas mud from his feet forever. But it was a thick, heavy, and tenacious muck that would not come off easily, especially considering how much walking and can-kicking he had done in simply getting to and hanging around Camden town.

Major General Steele, like every soldier's hero, Napoleon, had, indeed, found his Moscow and now had no choice but to take those grudgingly painful back-steps toward his personal Elba. But, God forbid, he said, not through the horrors of the Moro swamp, along that road to Mount Elba for a link up with Powell in Pine Bluff, but, unlike the Corsican, Steele was disinclined to desecrate the smiling skulls of those he had so recently sent to die, but, rather, he would veer left, toward another Rock, upon which he had deposited the Third Minnesota—guarding his rear, his government, and, apparently, most everyone's girls—getting there by crossing the Saline (Sa-leen) at a ford owned by an ancient and irascible Confederate ferryman named Tom Jenkins.

It can be said with some measure of safety that nothing in the general's life became it like his leaving of Camden. His commands were concise, clever, and carried out quickly by men suffering under the logic of a *mot d'ordre* they themselves would mandate had they been in this commander's place.

Indeed, it was done with rapid precision: Those wagons and stores that could not be taken were marked for destruction; rations were issued at two pieces of hardtack and a half pint of cornmeal per man; at 8:00 tattoo was sounded loudly while drums beat even louder; pickets were noisily doubled; cavalry patrolled the streets to keep folks inside; and, finally, instead of sleeping, the army assembled as quietly as 9,000 four-legged and 10,000 two-legged creatures ever could. A pontoon was floated expertly over the Ouachita and a very relieved army then began to slip quietly across to the northern side.

"Perhaps no order was ever executed more quickly or more quietly," reported one private. Adding, "In a few moments we were on the march in the darkness of the summer night."

It was only April 26, but it must have seemed summer warm to the boys from a home where it might yet be spring cold.

But none of this went unnoticed.

One Camdenite, a Mrs. Virginia McCollum Stinson, lived a few blocks from the general in a fine house on West Washington with her three small children, a "saucy Rebel" sister named Kate, who managed to sneak letters to Confederate prisoners, a matronly slave named "Aunt Sallie," and a chore-running sixteen-year-old Black boy, who was persuaded by the Yankees to go with them. He and Aunt Sallie helped "Miz Virginee" busy herself, when not cooking and sewing for the Grays, in caring for her brood. And, after it was over, she wrote her immortality onto the trouble of a few clear pages about all that happened.

Her husband, George, who had been mangled almost blind at Shiloh, was switched from infantry to the supply, while a brother-in-law, John M. Daly, had invested his life in General Earl Van Dorn's failed recapture of his reputation by not recapturing Corinth; while her blood brother, now serving under Price, Lieutenant Colonel Hugh McCollum, would on the Twenty-sixth horse into town in triumph, to eat at her table and sleep in a four-poster bed with clean sheets made up by Aunt Sallie, before getting a jump on catching Steele at Jenkins's Ferry, so as to return a little late but lying quietly in the back of a wagon stolen by his slave along with a mule to bring him home in.

Hugh would not eat at sister Virginia's table again, nor sleep in a fine, clean four-poster bed made up by Aunt Sallie, but would move instead to a peaceful spot on a hill, guarded today with a U.S. flag that rattles gently in the wind against a silver pole, his bones set off as befits a leader, close but a touch distant, slightly above his comrades who came as he had, or, like survivors will, slipping tardily into place in their own good time, one by one, slitting the neatly mowed grass open for a modest tomb tended now to a newness that arrests forever that false thing we mistakenly call the present.

Alas, back in Missouri, Francis Blair Jr., "Frank," whose father was friend enough of Lincoln to be in his cabinet, had tried to tell cousin "Jo" it would happen, and it had, the Federals coming upon the South generally, and Camden and Virginia Stinson in particular, like a calamity of Blue locusts killing, eating, taking, burning, and slaughtering—fighting the men, freeing the slaves, foraging away hers and everyone else's cows, horses and hogs and, of course, emptying the smokehouses, except in her case, two hams were successfully pled for by Aunt Sallie, standing as she did at the open smokehouse door, the keys rattling in her hand like a keeper of a king's treasury, importuning the Yankees to leave something lest she and all her Black and White folks starve.

This ravaging continued till a captain named Rohadaback came more as a boon than a burden. He, unlike most Yankees, she said, had some manners and was "every bit the gentleman." These Blue locusts flew away—at least for the moment. But captains can do little with colonels, and he was powerless against some other visitors, a pair of strange out-of-town tarts escorted by Colonel James M. Williams, of Poison Springs fame, who, it was said, always seemed to have such "nearabouts," appearing after a few days with an unannounced, insistent knocking at the door, before stepping past a protesting Kate and a sullen Aunt Sallie into the Stinson parlor.

No outrage compared with this, but Aunt Sallie was forced to lend the fine room, where Hugh would sleep his last clean sleep and where Aunt Sallie, pretending to do some domestic business, deftly locked the closet, hiding Mrs. Stinson's boudoir by slipping a paper dollop into the keyhole of the door.

"What's to be done?" Miz Virginia wondered, in hand-wringing humiliation at her scullery table, unwittingly anticipating Chernyshevsky's great, and as yet, unanswered question in his unreadable novel of that name, borrowed by Lenin and put by both, not so much to all of Russia as to all the world, the greatest question of all: *What's to Be Done?* which inspired the pages of Harriet Beecher, who scratched out the greatest piece of political fiction of her time. One can just see the black-dressed Mrs. Stowe, sitting at her bench, scribbling forth, according to Mr. Lincoln at least, his army from her pen as from the Blueness of her ink, seeping its dreadful way toward Mrs. Stinson, sitting in her boudoir, dressed in brown, an answer of sorts.

But Kate, Aunt Sallie, a maid, and a slave gave little thought to the "Cursed

Questions" of such remoteness, and a great deal more to the two slatterns upstairs and, so, giddily kitchened-up a solution that, while certainly no answer for a Chernyshevsky, or Stowe, or Lincoln, or Lenin, was fine enough for them, as Miz Virginee encouraged an infant niece into an all-night house-emptying colic, which sent our two red-eyed whores grumping through pink dawn's door in search of some better friends for fornication.

This was funny, when such was in short supply, but the laughter, in time, only released in Mrs. Stinson a lamentation:

> Oh, how thankful I was they had gone. We were kept in such a strain of excitement that we didn't know what would be next. If we could only hear from our dear ones in the army, to know that all were alive. And our father and mother were seven miles from Camden on their plantation with fifty or sixty of their Negroes, we feared to hear from them.

It was, indeed, an anxious time. Then victory, coughing forth from the cannons of Poison Springs and in the breathing murmurs of the Mill, whispered out to her the promised syllables of a sudden change for the better.

First, the good captain shocked Virginia by paying his "bill" with six greenbacks, which he un-wadded on her parlor table with a thanks and a polite exit; secondly, a squad of Blues cooked Aunt Sallie's fingers nearly to that color, while stuffing first their palates and then their packs; thirdly, the "silly" Black boy disappeared; while lastly, and most telling of all, with Rohadaback out, the Blue locust came back in, desperately pistoling around the yard in a last-minute chicken-killing.

But every tragedy has a survivor, and this one's was a venerable laying-hen who hovered herself cleverly under the house, staying and refusing to come out till all the Yankee hordes were gone forever.

Yet chicken-out they did, winding their wheels with cotton and wagoning quietly to the river. And, if any doubt remained, it was allayed by the mockingbirds that, silent from the first, sang from midnight till light. Aunt Sallie said it was a good omen—that God's will would, indeed, be done.

Then their own, a husband and a brother—Hugh and George—came a-knocking proudly out on the porch. They were soon followed by Kirby Smith himself, standing there, smiling, tipping his general's hat and asking polite permission to bivouac on her place.

> Camden looked like a deserted town, no noise or Yankee in town,

Oh! what relief it was to be free of them. We did not know what joy was in store for us that day—didn't know that our boys in grey were so near us, Oh! what joy when our dear men came marching in town—what waving of hands and handkerchief's, women and children greeting their loved ones.

But the greatest shock of all were the Reds sitting placidly in the yard—Confederate Cherokees and Choctaws—dressed in colorful paint and pea-fowl feathers, sitting dignified upon their ponies and asking for food. They stayed for a day, frightening almost everyone into a staring fascination, to which the braves paid no heed as they camped, then rode away as quietly as they had come, back to Oklahoma.

Meantime, Fagan, despite orders not to leave the Rock uncovered, gambled that Steele might yet sit a spell by a river and, so, fatigued by his fight at Marks's Mill, disobeyed his way off glory's page in hopes of finding rest and a little forage somewhere near Arkadelphia.

History might have been kinder to Fagan if he had not fought at all—suffering Drake to pass, empty and unneeded, harmlessly by to Powell Clayton waiting anxiously at the Bluff. In being dashing, Fagan had not been wise—had played the lion in a scene written for a fox.

CHAPTER SIXTEEN

By other windings and by other steerage shall you cross to that other shore. Not here! Not here! A lighter craft than mine shall give you passage!

    —Dante, Divine Comedy, *Canto 3*

Dagmar, newly charged with the news of Steele's unriveting from the village on the river, swam her filly roan across and, cooling wet with nostrils blowing, raced her hard in search of Fagan. Or, using a cliché common to countless matinees, melodramas, prosy plays, and penny dreadfuls, she "rode like the wind."

Skirting Steele's rear, which now bulged out in the Blue form of Brigadier General Frederick Salomon's trudging division of foot, she slippered along its arch, stopping now and again to scout and spell her little mare, until she reached Salomon's head, which she slithered past, along Steele's main column, till she passed it as well, angling slightly west then turned in a slowing trot for roads north.

Here, with the relieved expectation of finding Grays, she found Blues instead and, after a furious chase, was unhorsed and caught.

By the early twilight of April 27, a mere hour before Dagmar's swim, Steele's engineers unburdened the river view by beavering up their bridge, revealing nothing for their Southern friends to follow but a road of quiet relief into Camden. Churchill's Arkansawyers were given the honor of liberation at 9:00, and Walker's Texans the greater leisure of coming at 4:00.

As for the Confederates' own pontoons, stacked idly in Shreveport although much pled for on the Red, they had been summoned but halfway up the river, then, through a comic *contretemps* of confusion, were sent back down, then forwarded again. It was by this contrivance that Smith did deny them to both himself and Richard Taylor, thereby saving what remained of Mr. Banks's navy and serving up to Steele a fairly broad river and a very long and busy day for deftly setting down behind.

By the afternoon of those first glorious hours of Confederates in Camden, as Dagmar was being interrogated by a rather flummoxed captain from Iowa, Smith was busy looking for a bridge.

Richard Taylor said it best but, alas for Smith, he was not a man of easy absolution. While he did in time forgive some few: Jefferson Davis for carrying his beloved sister, Knox, over the threshold of a nuptial tomb at Brierfield; and, too, did in time strive to forgive God for stealing, out of jealously it seemed, his two small sons with scarlet fever. He, busy on the banks of the Red with no time for a rash or to be home with Mimi Bringier, a beautiful and wealthy New Orleans Creole, married at the same star-crossed age as his sister—seventeen—well knew and assumed God must likewise have known that the deaths of Zach and Dixie would soon put his Mimi in grief's early grave, and did, could not, despite his feeling for the folly of Southern secession, ever quite forgive the Yankees for ravaging Louisiana like the Blue-backed barbarians he considered them to be, subjecting his dear *Fashion* to sack and sword, killing his children's two ponies and nailing their hides to a barn as some sort of statement about what had happened at an obscure crossroads near the Sabine, and so now longed for revenge.

His treasured Southern Lost Kingdom, his Arcadia, Prince Richard's *Fashion*—begun while father Zachary was perched as president over a nation in a precarious prewar peace—did, before the war, become one of the great sugar producers of all *La Florida*. His visiting Connecticut Yankee anti-slavery friend, Frederick Law Olmstead, the designer of New York City's Central Park, once chatted up to him over whiskey a model for gradual emancipation and evolutionary Southern development, before he returned North again to describe *Fashion* as a "a capital plantation," needing only to solve its labor problem in a more civilized manner. This plan, pressed upon a quietly listening Taylor in the serenity of *Fashion's* parlor, was far preferable, he insisted, to the violent revolution which Northern abolitionists and their unwitting Southern allies, the Democratic Hotspur "Fire Eaters," were about to visit upon everyone.

But when something is felt more as flesh than fact, it will in time burst to flame; then sensible chats over sherry will have little chance, and fact will soon march as flesh to be burned in the fire of war.

Thus it was, despite a postwar offer of a no-interest loan from some of his more prosperous ex-slaves (refused by Taylor with a polite but foolish pride), that *Fashion* was prevented from ever being put right again—the parlor evening collapsing into the ruin and rubble of the *Destruction and Reconstruction* (as he called his book) of Taylor's beloved but devastated South, and penned by him in peace of what he had seen in war.

Yet, forgiving God, or President Davis, or the Yankees, or being forgiven by one's former slaves, was one thing, but forgiving Kirby Smith was something else. Taylor: *J'accuse!*

> General, had you left the conduct of operations in my hands Banks's army would have been destroyed before this; the fleet would have been in our hands or blown up by the enemy. The moral effect at the North and the shock to the public credit would have seriously affected the war. By this time the little division of Polignac and Vincent's Louisiana Cavalry would have been near the gates of New Orleans, prepared to confine the enemy to narrow limits. I would have been on my way with the bulk of my army to join Price at Camden, enriched with the spoils of a great army and fleet. Steele would have been brushed from our path as a cobweb before the broom of a housemaid; we would have reached St. Louis, our objective point, by midsummer and relieved the pressure from our suffering brethren in Virginia and Georgia. All this is as true as the living God and required no more than ordinary energy for its accomplishment.

In remembering the infantry while forgetting a bridge, General Smith, it seems, had contrived to misplace a war!

But Smith vowed to continue his odyssey by finding his *Homer,* not a book of verse but a hoy of that name, sunk and settled on the river's wrong side, hailed by a swimmer seeing her cabin scuttling out of the green water, darkly stuck there like some freshly dead carapace staring with lifeless eyes through the slime.

Homer's planks were salvaged, rafts nailed, lines swum to pine, and, by pioneering out the day, a bridge slowly emerged, ramshackle but ready, till the next morning found Smith shuttling at last across in a shaky but steady line of Gray—men, mules, and mounts led by walkers; wagons and cannons in a line—the cavalry long since swum away, as Marmaduke's Missourians, now understudy of a part set for Fagan, rode to a place called Bucksnort, where it was hoped they would front Frederick Steele's racing battalions to a bumping, abrupt halt.

Another thing was found as well, a long narrow gilt-framed mirror, dived up from *Homer's* modest room for primming ladies, soon set by naked, leering men as prop for a limb, where it reflected a laughing, prancing joke that, in the spring warm sun for a moment at least, it all seemed to be.

"The Johnnies must be hard pressed if they are reduced to using one-armed boys," said the captain to the corporal, after ordering Dagmar sent to the rear.

"Whar ye takin' me?" she asked her escort.

"To the back of this here column ... they're some other Rebs there and you'll be a-marching with them in this little retreat of ours."

Dagmar was passed down the Blue line of infantry intermingled with wagons, animals, and cannons, all moving "Indian file," generally north at a pace falling just short of a run.

Her interrogation had been brief, done on the move, the captain reluctantly getting off his horse to sit with her on some half-empty sacks of flour in the back of a lurching wagon. He had, of course, come for truth, but that commodity, while occasionally seen, is less often heard, and like most skilled fibbers, Dagmar weaved a fabric of deception and irrelevant debate with the thread of truth, rolling it deftly into a ball so tightly intertwined that it would hold, she felt, for at least an hour, when its unwinding would demand more time and thought than a busy officer was willing to give. He would have to reflect, return, re-cross question again, then she would deny, debate some more, and say she was misunderstood, till the entire matter would be an unraveled, confused, useless mess lying in the ever-shifting mud underneath them.

She said she had no dispatches and was sent simply to tell Fagan of Steele's departure, nothing more, but she really had dropped those papers in the brush, along with Titus's potentially posthumous letter to Medora, all wrapped neatly up in brown cloth, as she swam a creek and sped into a thicket. She told the captain she knew nothing else, not adding that there was doubt as to Fagan's whereabouts or that Smith was frantic to ensure he was somewhere blocking Steele. "Spirits's good," she said and "run up even higher after Pieson Sprangs and word come of Banks." Having said this with obvious pleasure, and sensing his irritation, she pressed her advantage with delight, adding, "Kirby Smith 'spects to catch ole Steele like a ole boar coon changin' trees."

The captain shook his head slightly then asked about the infantry. Dagmar answered that she didn't know, lying, as she made it a point to be well informed and knew all the units and their commanders. When the inevitable question about the cavalry came, she told a half-truth—that she wasn't sure where Marmaduke was—although she had a pretty good idea that he was swinging wide somewhere trying to get ahead. Then things shifted to background questions, taking them out of order more out of negligence than design. Dagmar answered that her name was "Tom," her father and mother were dead but said nothing, of course, of Colonel Pilgrim, using her old surname instead.

This officer, who seemed impatient and uncomfortable off his horse, now tethered in a following walk, accepted her answers without much cross-examination. But with time nevertheless to resent her saucy manner, he told her gruffly, by way of putting her in her place, and thinking she was a boy, that she was lucky to have on a gray tunic and CSA belt buckle, else he would have had her shot as a spy.

Brushing this aside, Dagmar decided to make a joke, smiling and pointing to the bright silver buckle Titus gave her as a congratulatory gift. "Ye know what CSA stands for don't ye, captain?"

"No, what?" he said offhandedly, looking up in irritation from the quick scribbling he was trying to do in the interval of the wagon stopping unexpectedly, but immediately regretting his open-ended question.

"Corn, Salt, an' Apples," she said with a laugh.

He looked at her in astonishment, then frowned, saying, "You doubtless will find yourself wishing for some apples, with or without the salt, before this adventure is over."

"Well, sir, I ain't used to much, no way."

"Where'd you lose that arm?"

"A-riding with Shelby," she lied proudly.

"For that you were made an orderly?"

"J. O. don't want no cripples."

"Where's Shelby now?" he asked, knowing full well he was with Fagan somewhere.

"With Fagan," she said quickly, knowing he would know that.

"What were his casualties at Marks's Mill?" he asked slyly, also knowing from returning stragglers that Shelby was the difference in the battle and wondering what price he might have paid for the honor.

Dagmar thought, then decided the truth would work fine here, replied, "I don't ratly know, but I heerd they wuz prutty light." Adding, "We whupped ye good thar, didn' we?"

The captain frowned again, shifting his weight as the wagon lurched into motion, and, irritated that he had not taken full advantage of the pause, said, "You'll be walking in the rear with some other Rebs and some contrabands traveling along with us."

"Captain, ye gonna put me back thar with a bunch'o niggers?"

"We got to put you somewhere and Johnnies and Negroes are all assigned to the rear," he said louder than he really wanted.

"Us Rebs an' runaway niggers is all of a kind to yew Yankees, ain't it? I ain't no difference a-tall?"

"Just about."

"Whar ye from, Captain?"

"Iowa," he said wistfully.

"Captain, let me put a question to ye. What if I brung an army of Rebs up thar to Ioway an' started a-killin' an' a-robbin' folks an' a-turnin' thar niggers a-loose, what would yew do then, huh?"

His jaw dropped. In his experience, Rebel prisoners were sullen, not given to debate.

"There are no Negroes in Iowa … not to speak of," he said, really without thinking, debating without meaning to.

"No niggers in Ioway! Come on, Captain, they's niggers ever'whur!"

"Listen, Mr. Suggins …"

"I mean, they's some kinda nigger thar, ain't it? Ever place, even Ioway, has some kind o' niggers. Maybe they ain't black nor white but they's thar, ain't they, some color or nuther, ain't I rat? My ole Pappy larnt me that much. He said thars always niggers around a-some kind … it ain't so much the color as yer place own the ladder, he said. Why they's Blacks in Loosiana that own slaves an' big plantations … rich as can be … respectable … they git treated lack Whites … they ain't raly niggers … see … the point is not to be on the bottom rung, ain't it? But with my ole sorry Pappy … see … trouble wuz, he couldn' git more'n one step up and knowed it … yew know, he wa'nt much more'n a White nigger hisself … bein' he wuz sech a screwgutted damn drunk an' wuz treated that a-way by folks ever'whur. That's what that white lightning done to him … it made him black as the devil's beard. Truth wuz there weren't a nigger in the county that didn't git more respect than he done, an' he knowed it too … an' that ate at his ole damn rotten sorry screwguts an' a-made him drank that much more … till his innards wuz damn near eat 'pletely out and would've done jes that till he got put outta his misery with a load of buckshot by a White lady with a side-by-side. That were a-blessin' … fur the both of us … I'll say that much, Captain … a rale blessin'."

The officer was astonished.

She continued, "Hell far, jes' look at me! I'm no more'n a White nigger to yew, ain't I? And if'n I didn't have own this yar gray shirt an' belt buckle ye'd a-hung me up like a dowg frum a tree, now wouldn' ye?"

"You're just another Reb prisoner to me, Mr. Suggins, nothing more or less."

"And that's not more'n a runaway nigger to yew Yankees, ain't that rat? Ye got no more feelin' fur us than that, do ye?"

"Now, son, we're fighting a war with you … you can't reasonably expect us to love you."

"Ye didn't answer my question of a while ago … I mean, if'n we come up to your precious Ioway country an' started a-doin' what y'all's a-doing yar, ye'd fight us too, wouldn't ye?"

"We don't have any slaves, that's the difference. Slavery is an abomination."

"Oh, well, I don't know no ten-dollar words, but I gotta notion what ye mean. An' whur did ye git that thar fine farm land ye got up thar, huh? From the Indians, ain't that rat? Reckon how much did ye pay them Reds fur it, huh? And what'd ye all do if'n we come up thar with a big damn army and started a-killin' an' a-stealin' and a-armin' them Reds and a-givin' em thar land back ye stole from em, huh? Ye'd fight us high and low such-like we is a-doin' ye, yar and now, am I rat?"

The captain blanched. "I'm not here to debate …"

Dagmar interrupted quickly, sensing a rout, "The way I figger it, come to thank of it, them is yer Red niggers up thar in Ioway, ain't they? Ye done thinned a-nuff of 'em out to steal thar land from 'em, an' now yore a-down yar a-lecturin' us on how to trayt folks. See, my ole pappy wuz rat, White nigger hisself, he knowed 'em when he a-seed 'em, everwhat the color … Black, White, or Red … he knowed 'em. It's how they's trated..that's the thang that matters, ain't it? It ain't the color a-tall … it jes' makes it a mite easier … like what y'all done to them poor Reds up thar in yore country."

"That is very different."

"How's that, Captain?"

"We have not sundered the Union."

"Naw, but ye would've 'sundered' it, as ye call it, if'n we wuz goin' a-took yore rats away, wouldn't ye … then took yore farms an' all … kill … steal an' burn … yew'd sunder then, wouldn't ye, afore ye let us give that good farmland back to them Injuns ye done cheated an' killt, yew'ed a-sunder rale good, now wouldn't ye?"

He sighed.

"Guess, come to thank of it, is why them Injuns is on 'r side in this yar little war, ain't it? Ever wonder 'bout that, huh? Why they's a-fighting with us?"

"The Indians on your side are slave owners."

"Not all of 'em, the Comanches ain't and they's own 'r side."

"Young man, I'm not here to argue about this war. You will be sent to the rear as a prisoner. If you try to escape, I will have you shot, you understand?" he said matter-of-factly.

He put away his notebook and pencil hurriedly, nodding to the corporal who had been huffing along next to the horse, listening with some amusement, then the captain ordered the wagon to stop, untethered the mare, mounted, and rode away, happily leaving Dagmar to the guard.

On the day that Smith came into Camden, Fagan, receiving no news of Steele's retreat, had unwittingly horsed across only a few miles ahead of the Union column and had soon fallen into a funk of indecision while looking for corn. It seems that James Fleming, after setting his thirteen hundred captured Blues upon their long walk to a Tyler, Texas, prison, was, as is sometimes the case, struck suddenly by a post-battle depression.

But Shelby, a truer soldier, exhilarated and not depressed by success, proceeded to lecture his commander on the obvious, "Whatever you do, don't uncover the main road!"

However, Fagan demurred, till Shelby, more rankled than ranked, pacing up and down, wrung out a concession, "At least contact Smith!"

Fagan nodded off an officer for a fool's errand that was too late by a day.

As for Dagmar's failed mission, she had searched for a Fagan that simply wasn't to be found—not on any main road, that is, or any place she might have looked. For Fagan's search for food left him lost to all but himself and, not finding Steele, found that same perplexed self standing instead in a flooded river bottom, staring across a swelling Saline. Then, unable to cross, yet crossing Shelby with ease, he turned southwest to Arkadelphia, leaving Dagmar to the surly captain, and the captain's general to the painful but urgent luxury of retreating an unimpeded army as fast as fodder and fatigue would allow.

With such a horde to his south, Fagan might have taken some notice. He did, nevertheless, in the end, manage to note other things: his little village, a little bit of forage, and some friends; but in even shorter supply would be forgiveness, for Taylor could not, of course, ever forgive Smith; Smith, in turn, could never quite forgive Fagan; and Fagan could never, even within his long, remaining twenty-nine years, ever find time to forgive himself.

PHILLIP H. MCMATH

Collared by defeat, Steele had despaired of any such consolation, but by effectively trading coats with Smith at Camden, he had unbuttoned into the softer, less ambitious, comfort of expecting less and less, till he was anxious for little more than moving rapidly up a muddy road to the Rock.

Steele transported a small contingent of prisoners and hordes of runaway slaves, grouped and trudging in a wad near the rear of his retreating army that gradually became a mob.

Late on the evening of the twenty-seventh, as they came at last to a halt, a cohort of guards herded them into a circle for the night. Dagmar sneaked around till she found the end of a wagon and plopped down in exhaustion.

"Hi, I's Septimus," said a Black teenage boy who walked over to where she was sitting propped against the wagon wheel, her face barely visible in a lantern lit nearby.

She looked up in weary amazement at the face appearing out of the edge of the light.

"I's Septimus … Septimus Reymonde," he repeated.

She stared for a moment longer then said quietly, "I'm Tom … er … Tom's what folks call me … Tom Suggins."

"You's a girl, ain't yuh?" Septimus said proudly, putting his hands in his pants' pockets in great satisfaction.

Dagmar looked at Septimus with astonishment. He wore an oilcloth cap and a shirt of Lowell cotton over pants called "hard times," and he had on high-top leather shoes laced up to the ankle.

"Whut makes ye say that?" she said after a pause, scooting herself up a bit.

"Eva ding 'bout yuh says it … you's tryin' to hide it 'n all, but I sees it straight awf."

"Them Yankees don't know it," she said, dropping her eyes.

"Dey ain't looked," he said with a broad smile.

"Ain't many female riders," she said. "Best be 'r little secret, okay?"

"Oh, don't be worrin' none, I's not tellin' nobody. I's a runaway myself … I done runaway from Miz Virginee and Aunt Sallie back daya in Camden. I's gwine to Little Rock 'n freedom now … dem days of slavin' is ova fo me."

"I figger ye musta run from somebody," Dagmar said.

"Lots uh us is … firs' chance … we runs … sho do …"

She thought, then said, "Yeah, thar's niggers a-runnin' wild all over this yar country now."

"Yeah, an' dey ain't eva gonna go back ... no way ... no suh."

"Wuz they bad to ye? That why ye's a-runnin'?" she asked in weary irritation.

"No, Tom ... they wuz real good to me ... but I's always wantin' to run ... I never could get that outta my hade ..."

"Ain't that ... uh ... kindly unfeelin'?"

"Yous means ungra'eful," Septimus said proudly, stepping closer inside the circle of light and sitting down opposite her, crossing his legs and, without thinking, plucking a blade of grass and chewing it like it was the sweetest thing in the world.

"Yeah, Septimus, ain't it kinda wrong of ye to always be a-thankin' of runnin' when awl that time they's bein' good to ye ... awl time a-havin' that in yer head when they's doin' rat by ye ... nen ye up an' run while they's been a-feedin' ye an' a-givin' ye a home an' awl ... an' they a-needin' yer hep round the place, I'm sure o' that ... 'specially now with nem Yankees a-runnin' round stealin' an' a-causin' sech trouble for decent folks? I mean they coulda put ye in nem fields or sold ye or sumpin', couldn' they? Instead, they wuz good to ye ... looked after ye an' nen yew paid em back by a-runnin' first chance yew got ... like ye done ... ain't that jes' wrong as rain, huh?"

"Oh, I knows whats you's sayin'," he replied, spitting out the grass, "but, see, Tom, I jes' wants to be free is awl. Some day I'm gonna make it up to dem ... some kinda way. I done prayed over it powerful like one night."

"Prayed over it? Ye ain't a-tellin' me that the Lord done tolt ye to run awf an' leave yer folks what had been so good to ye and awl? You ain't a-gonna tell me that, now, is ye?"

"Oh yes I is ... Aunt Sallie done tole me to pray ova eva dang I done dat what wuz big ... to pray eva day ... an' de good Lawd done tole me whu I needed to know. Awl I done is whu Aunt Sallie done tole me to do."

"I jes' cain't believe she tole ye to run," Dagmar said.

Septimus drew himself up a bit and looked at the sky above them real careful, paused, and said, "Well, Tom, it ware jes' like dis, see, it were a powerful dark night, jes' like dis one we gots heya, dark as my mama's grave, so den I waits 'cause I knowed de ole moon he be up directly ... I didn't want t'be talkin' to de Lawd in dat devilish dark ... so I waits and waits ... jes' a settin' quiet like ... but den dat ole big moon he come own up ... a big'un ... silver ... an' jes' a-smiling ova at me ova dem big fine ole oak trees Miz Virginee had in de back yard ... an' den I talks to da Lawd ... prays an' prays an' prays till I mos' nigh cried ... an' den ... directly I hears a loud voice ... it's de Lawd ...

a-takin' time outta his very own bu'ness jes to speak to Septimus 'bout whu was a-troublin' him ... a talkin' jes' to Septimus Reymonde ... jes' like he done to Moses ... an' I wuz mos' sceerd to deaf but he tell me to run with dem Yankees as soon as I could an' I don't have to be no nigger no mo' and not be worryin' myse'f too much 'bout dat an' den afta a time it gots awl still and quiet like an' den a big dawg somewheya commenced to howl ... real lonesome-like in da night ... at dat ole silvah moon ... and I knowed de Lawd wuz finished 'cause he wouldn't 'llow no dawgs to howl if'n he wuz still talkin' nor nothin' an' so dat wuz it as sho as I'm settin' yar an' dat's what He done tole me to do fo sho ... up a run with dem Yankees as soon as I could, sho did ... and heya I is a-settin' heya a-visitin' with you ... ain't it de truff ..."

"Ye shore 'bout all that, Septimus?"

"Sho, I's sho, He said it be ok if'n I made it up to my folks someday. He say a-slavin' be wrong an' to be free if'n I wants to. I jes' wants whut de Lawd done give me is awl ... He mades me free dat night ... took de chains away ... I felt dem drop at my feets ... sho did ... dey hit da ground with a turble sound ... it wuz so loud dat I wuz a-freed dat de White folks a heerd dem drop too ... and wake up an' catch me a-standin' der ... but dat sound wuz freedom fo' me 'cause de Lawd made 'em drop ... an' my prayers wuz answered dat night under dat ole moon ... sho was ... den, afta dem chains o' slavery done drop away it skeered de dawg 'cause he hush an' it got real still an' I wuz free ... sho wuz ... may de Lawd strike me iff'n I's lyin'."

"Freein' awl ye niggers is the Lord's work, I suppose?" Dagmar asked. "Then why did He make y'all slaves in the fisr' place, huh, answer me that, Septimus? Huh?"

"Sho ... it's awl His plan ... see ... dem Yankees a-comin' to town wuz de Lawds work, too, see, like de Philistines in de Bible ... de chariots an' de fire an' locus' an' de plague an' de famine an' awl ... dat wuz God's vengeance own His own people fo' what dey done an' fo' freedom fo' His chil'ren ... ain't nothin' happen by chance in dis ole world, no, uh, uh, an' His will be done. So I a-starts hepin dem Philistine Yankees ... kinda sidled up to 'em real close like ... hepin an' awl ... you know ... heya an' der ... an' when de time wuz jes' right I runs. I mean, I knowed dey wuz gwine to leave on der chariots an' cross de river like the chil'ren of Israel outta Egypt an' dat dey would take Septimus Reymonde with dem too..to freedom an' to de Promised Land."

"How long wuz ye with that family?"

"Awl my life ... dey raise me up from a baby. My sho nuff mama died after I wuz born'd ... she wuz a field nigga an' she died a-havin' me ... den dey brought me to de big house in Camden … like dey done Moses an' Aunt Sallie an' Miz Virginee is my real mamas an' dey raised me up to be strong an' learned me de Word …"

"An' ye don't feel bad about a-runnin'? After awl that, huh?"

"I cried when I run … sho did, Tom … it hurt powerful when I done dat … but I cain't hep it. I gots to be free … when I gits to Li'le Rock, I ain't gwine be no nigga no moe. No matter how good dey is to me at dat big fine house … I's always gwine be uh nigga in Camden … dats whys I up an' run like dat. Dey wuz rale good to Moses wa'nt dey, an' he run too, didn't he?'

"Ye ain't no Moses, Septimus."

"No, Tom, but I's me, an' I'z awl I gots. I jes' don't wanna be no slave awl my born'd days an' de Lawd done tole me I doesn't has to be no moe … an' he hushed dat big dawg an' he dropped dos heavy chains away an' sent dem Yankees … so I up an' runs … its de Lawd's will, Tom, sho is … I seen His hand in it … sho as we is a-settin' heya by dis heya fiya talkin'."

There was a pause, then Dagmar said, "I got news fur ye, Septimus. When ye git up to Li'le Rock yer still gonna be a nigger. It ain't no Promised Land … or nuthin' like that."

"No … uh uh … eva'body is free der … ain't no niggas der … Mr. Laycoln done fixed all dat."

Dagmar laughed.

"Ye ever thank whut's gonna happen when them Yankee soldiers up an' leave? They cain't stay furever, any more than they can stay in Camden, they's already a-runnin' as hard an' fast as they kin … an' they're gonna a-leave someday from the Rock … the same way … an' no matter everwho wins this here little war, thangs is gonna be prutty much the same way they wuz afore."

"No, deya ain't eva gwine leave … no..uh uh … no … dey is stayin' foreva … dings is gwine be different from now own … ain't gwine be no more niggas … no more … folks is jes' gwine be folks … awl free … Black an' White … awl free an' de same."

"An' whut're yew gonna do up in Li'le Rock?"

"I ain't gwine worry 'bout dat till I gets der. But I be free der, dats awl what counts … yeah … dats de deng … I won't be no slave no moe. I find sumpin … it'll turn up … de Lawd done tole me dat. Aunt Sallie wuz always a-sayin' dat … an' de Lawd tole me dat Hisself when I wuz standin' der in de moonlight a-prayin' till dem tears come a-wellin' up in my ole eyes like a big riva … He done answer my praya … sho did … an' he ain't eva gwine let Septimus

Reymonde down ... I knows dat for sho ... no ... uh huh ... nevah ... or he wouldn't'o drop de chains away an' hush de big dawg like He done dere undah dat ole powerful moon."

"Well, maybe the Lord will provide somebody as good to ye as Aunt Sallie and Miz Virginee wuz back thar in Camden ... if and when yew ever manage to git to Li'le Rock. Ye'll be lucky if'n ye kin find them two somewhures else, ye mark my words, Septimus."

Then he asked, "An' whatchew runnin' 'way from, huh, Tom?"

"Me?"

"Yessum, you's runnin' from sumpin, dat's fo sho ... I can see dat right awf."

"Well, I been a-runnin' pretty damn hard away from them Yankees ... but they finally done caught me ... or yew an' I'd never met, Septimus."

"You's a-runnin' from more dan dat, ain't you ... I mean how do a girl awl dressed up like a boy wind up a-ridin' 'round dis heya country in de middle of a wawah when all de utter respectable White girls is home a-hidin' with dey mamas, huh? Dats what I wants to know."

"I ain't r'spectable," Dagmar said with quiet defiance.

"No ... I seed dat straight out ... but why's you de only one a-ridin' 'round awl dressed up like a boy, respectable or not."

"I joined the Reb army ... I wanted to ride. I ain't no parlor flower."

"Do dem Rebs thank yew's a boy, huh?"

"Nawgh ... them boys know better."

"Well, I ain't eva heard tell of no Reb females in de army."

"I ain't like them others. I mean, I up an' asked to ride ... an' they said I could run some messages ... 'round camp an' awl, if'n I wanted ... okay ... so, I got good at it, see, better'n most ... them messages started get further an' further apart, till purtty soon I'm jes' anuther dispatch rider ... without nobody a-sayin' nothin', I'm a-ridin' awl over ... and that's that."

"If'n yew so good...how come yew an' I is heya, huh? Havin' dis heya li'le ole chat, Tom ... tell me dat?"

"I had me a little piece o'bad luck ... a-lookin' fur ...," she started to say Fagan. "Fur somebody and found them Yankees firs'. I couldn't out run 'em, my little filly wuz flat wore out and they wuz on nem big strong, fresh Yankee horses. That, Septimus, is why yew an' I is a-talkin' rat now, an' I'm a-leanin' against this yar hard damn wagon wheel a-thankin' I outta git me some sleep. But, I've had 'nuff talkin' fur one night ... I'm plumb wore out, myself, an' I got a-feelin' we's gonna have us a big day a-morrow ... so ... if ye don't mind I'll be a-turnin' in."

Septimus reflected, then asked, "Well, Tom, I's tayaed myseyf ... kin I sleep at de odda end o' dis heya wagon?"

"Suit ye'se'f," Dagmar said, rolling away into an almost immediate doze.

One Blue soldier would write that "never had we seen such haste when a column was moving," as Steele's men were bugled awake at 4:00 and within twenty minutes, before very much coffee or what might pass for breakfast was downed, were columned up in the dark, while the prisoners and ex-slaves, who were given nothing at all, were clumped behind, under guard, for the trek north.

Chasing them with *Homer's* help, Kirby Smith loped his infantry over the Ouachita River, while galloping Marmaduke ahead in the circling hope of road-blocking between Princeton, where Steele would camp the second night, and the town of Tulip, southwest of Jenkins's Ferry on the Saline, with instructions to hold the head until his hurrying infantry could grab the tail and hang on.

Since the Blues had a seventeen-mile jump, the Grays found themselves out-legging their wagons as Churchill, Parson, and Walker pursued at a near run.

"Reckon they's eva gwine feed us?" said Septimus, huffing at Dagmar's side.

"I ain't et since yesterd'y morn'," said Dagmar. "But they ain't seem to have got much tharselves, so I don't figger they'll worry thar heads 'bout 'r empty stomachs."

"Well, I ain't et since you has," he said. "I had me a little pack of vittles, but one of dem soldiers done stole it from me fir'st ding. Now I ain't got nuttin."

"Keep it going, you two!" yelled a guard walking behind them in the morning light.

"I ain't gonna drop back none!" said Dagmar.

"Well, you Johnnies keep it closed up, or we'll shoot the first one that straggles!" said the private.

One prisoner limping beside Dagmar spoke.

"With this heya bad leg, I don't know if I can keep up," he muttered.

"Yew best do it ... I don't thank he's a-kiddin' none," she said.

"Reckon they'll shoot, Tom?" asked Septimus in a loud whisper.

"Why yew's free, Septimus ... whutchew skeered of? Ye kin run if'n ye want to. 'Sides, ye's young and fit ... other'n hunger pains, ye ought'n to have no trouble with this here little stroll ... none a-tall."

"Where is I gwine go? Dem Rebs catch me dey ain't gwine be none too happy 'bout runaways, is dey, Tom?"

"They wouldn't do nothin' but send ye back."

"Tom, I ain't so sho 'bout dat ... cause las' night I couldn't sleep narn ... so I up and walks around some, an' I herd dem Yankees a-talkin' real low like ... seems like some o' dem Blue soldiers what wuz a-hidin' in de woods from dat battle ova by a mill somewheya ... come in an' a-said dey was killin' runaway niggas if'n dey caught 'em with des Yankees ... a killin' dem like road chickens ... is what de say ..."

"Den dey was some slaves dat wondered in las' night, too, comin' in ones an' twos all de night long, an' dey says de same thang too ... sho did ... dey wuz real skeered ... been a-hidin' in de woods awl night an' a-feared dem Rebs was gwine catch dem and kill'em."

"Tall tales, Septimus ... tall tales ..."

"Tom, I don't dink so; dey was powahful skeered."

"I don't know if I'm gonna keep up," repeated the soldier limping at Dagmar's side.

"Hey ... Private!" yelled Dagmar. "This here feller here's got a bum layg ... he ain't gonna make it ... reckon ye could see yore way to a-puttin' 'im in a wagon somewhures?"

"Ain't no Johnnies going to be riding when Union boys is walking."

"But he's plumb wore out ..."

"I don't give a damn!" growled the soldier.

"He'll just have to keep up is all."

"He's a wounded pras'ner," insisted Dagmar.

"Yeah, and I don't want to have to fight him again. Keep up, you!" yelled the soldier's corporal walking back, overhearing, adding, "Or I'll stick you like a slaughter-shoat! Keep 'em closed up, son!" He said to the private and then fell back to the rear.

Soon it was light enough that Dagmar could see the limping prisoner. He wore rags of a gray uniform, was in his mid-forties, extremely thin, balding, and barefoot.

"Lean on me," she said, taking his arm and putting it around her shoulder. "That foot of yers is swole-up bad," she said, feeling his weight.

"Thanks," he said just above a whisper.

"Come on, Septimus, git on the other side yar ... an' hep us," Dagmar said.

Septimus came around and took the man's other arm and the three walked together behind a wagon loaded with Union sick and wounded. The guard moved to their right, carrying his musket across his chest—the bayonet glistening in the sun now nudging up over the tree line.

"Ain't that a sight," laughed a Confederate walking behind them. "It jes' 'bout sums up this whole damn war, don't it?"

"Quiet there, Reb!" yelled the corporal, striding up again. "I don't want no damn lip from you Johnnies ... understand?"

Then he yelled back to other soldiers at the rear. "Keep them Rebs closed up! Don't want to stick no more stragglers than I have to ... I'd rather stick a pig than a damn secessh ... at least I can eat a pig!"

"Speakin' of eatin', reckon yer is gonna find some piece o' leather or other to feed us, or are ye gonna weaken us down so ye kin stick us with a clear conscience when we start a-fallin' out?" asked Dagmar, as the other prisoners began to pass them slowly as they lagged more and more.

"I don't want no sass out of you, boy! Understand! You're a wise'un ... I can see that," said the corporal turning to her. "And keep it closed up, you hear? You're starting to straggle already."

"He cain't ... no way, Corporal," huffed out Dagmar.

"Yes, he will or by heavens I'll give him the steel," said the corporal.

Dagmar was quiet till the corporal was called away, just as the train stopped unexpectedly.

"What's yer name?" she asked, dropping her arm.

"Jim ... Jim Curt ... an' yew?"

"Tom ... Tom Suggins ... the boy yar is Septimus."

"Pleased to meet yew," said Curt, nodding slightly.

"Whur'd ye git crippled up?" she asked.

"Prairie d'Ane ... ball hit me an' my horse ... killt'm ... an' I got left ... captured ... Yankee doctor in Camden wanted to take it, but I wouldn't let 'im."

"Ye's smart ... they'd saw on a dead man ..."

"And yew ... how'd yew lose that arm?"

"Oh, I tole the Yankees it dropped off a-ridin' with Shelby, but it were a lie ... my stepmother took it with a load of buckshot."

Despite his pain Curt laughed and so did Septimus.

"Yo' stepmama done shot yew?" he said, taking the energy of turning his head for the first time.

"Yeah, my sorry ole pappy went a-bushwackin' when the war got turned up good an' he made me go a robbin' an' killin' with him an' my brothers ... though I ain't never robbed nor killt no one ... I seed my share ... an' I knowed it was a-comin' some day. I cain't remember my real mama none ... but my stepma ... the one that loaded me down with that buckshot ... she felt bad about it an' awl ... so, she an' her nigger woman nursed me rale good ... saved my life is whut they done ... an' took me in ... for that I'm pierful grateful, I am."

"Yew's a girl, ain't yew?" said Curt.

"That's a purty impolite question to be a-askin' a feller," said Dagmar, not quite as astonished as when Septimus had said it. "Whar ye from, Jim?"

"Idebelle ... Loosiana. I gotta small fa'm thaya ... wife an' kids ..."

"How long ye been in this yar war?" she asked.

"Oh, I jined up rat at the start ... saw some fightin' ova thaya in Miss'ssippi ... then got hemmed up at Vicksburg with that bunch last yeya ... an' wuz paroled ... come home an' got thangs in prutty good shape 'round the place ... ye know ... afore I jumped parole. But I wanted to stay own this side of the riva this time, ye know, so I could git home now an' nen an' kinda a-look afta thangs. I was a-tired o' walkin' so I come up heya and jined that cavalry bunch ... nen had this piece uh bad luck in that little fite with my foot an' awl. Ye know I went thew awl that damn hard Miss'ssippi fightin' an' didn't get a scratch ... then got hit in that little scrape back theya at the Prairie d'Ane."

"Them Yankees know ye jumped parole?"

"Oh, yeah ... I told 'em in Camden ... wa'nt gonna lie 'bout nothin' ... they's gonna put me in prison when I get up to Li'le Rock ... they say ..."

"Why did ye jine up again?"

"That's what the wife wondered. But I'll tell yew the same thang I tole her. Jes' sheer cussedness, I guess ... I cain't thank of no otha rayson ... don't own no niggers an' don't want narn. I figga we gotta turn 'em loose directly noway ... wawah or no waw ... it's jes speedin' thangs up is awl. So, jes' cussedness, is awl I kin rally tell yew. An', after Vicksburg, I knowed we'd prutty much los' this heya wawah noway ... that was a powerful mistake Davis an' nem made ... a-leavin' us to starve like that ... like rats in a hole ... I tell ye ... I'll neva un'erstand that. So jinein' up agin don't make no rale sense, does it? But, awl the same, too, I guess I caught a bad case of Yankee-hatred ... didn't have that so much at first ... hell, I didn't know narry a-one till this heya war got started ... but I do now ... and I got no use for 'em ... none at awl, Tom. I'd jes as soon stick eva las' one of 'em in the belly if I could."

"Yeah, I know what ye mean," Dagmar said quietly, then turning to Septimus added, "All 'cept Septimus yar ... he luves Yankees mor'n his own folks ... thanks they's gonna turn a-loose eva darky in this yare country ... don't yew, Septimus?"

Septimus looked away.

"Well, Tom, the boy's probably rat 'bout that. I guess if I's a nigga I'd feel the same as he duz."

"You wouldn't fight for em ... them Yankees, would ye ... I mean, even if you wuz a nigger and awl, yew wouldn't do that, Jim, would ye?"

"Naw ... I wouldn't go that far ... but Septimus ain't neither ... he's jes' a-runnin', rite, Septimus? All yew got on yo mind is runnin' ... yew ain't fightin' fo' no Yankees now are ye? I mean a-runnin' is one thang ... they'll jes send ye back ... but a-fightin' is sumpin else agin ... yew un'erstand that, don't yew, Septimus?"

"No ... uh, uh ... no, suh, I ain't fightin' fo' narn ... I jes' wants to be fray, Mr. Jim."

"See, theya it is, Tom ... this whole damn war in a wad. Makes a fella wonder what it's awl about, don't it? ... 'Course all they gotta do is jes' go home, then it'd end then an' theya, now wouldn't it?"

The column lurched ahead again, and the threesome resumed walking arm-in-arm.

"Y'awl, I don't know how much of this heya stroll I'm gonna be able to go on," said Curt, limping worse than before, trying to keep close to the wagon.

"Come own," said Dagmar, tightening her arm around his back while Septimus did the same, making them look like comrades on a drunken spree.

Meantime, ahead of them, Shelby had wrangled permission to send a group under one Major Benjamin Elliot to scout the main road. At 11:30 Elliot dismounted his men at Tulip. Then, at noon, a scout lieutenant cantered up, yelling that a large column of Blue horses—Steele's cavalry probing up from Princeton—was nosing toward them.

Elliot threw a line of horses thinly across their path, but the arriving Blues soon gathered stronger, till by night, exhausted and flanked, the major gave way. It was during this short Tulip halt that Dagmar and Curt wandered into the woods with a guard—a private of nineteen from Iowa, whose mother prayed for him morning and night, kneeling and whispering to the Almighty to keep him safe from death and brutality.

"Ok, but if you try and run, I'll shoot," said the boy, after giving permission to take Jim Curt to the woods. "That's our orders, and Corporal Zahn is a hard man ... you hear me? ... a hard man who hates Rebs."

"Curt cain't go nowhurs," replied Dagmar.

"Naw, but you sure can."

"And who the blazes is goin' a-take keer o' him?" said Dagmar, pointing down to Curt. "Yew an' that high an' mighty damn corporal of yurs who a-thanks he's God hisself?"

"Watch your tongue there, Reb," said the farmer's son—a delight to his parents, a good hand on the place and a better student, who never once disobeyed till he ran away and enlisted. "Zahn's been busted once ... down from sergeant ... for what he did at a farmhouse ... which you don't want to know about ... and he's aiming to get his stripes back, see ... he's a tough'un ... which is why our captain gave him this prison detail. Corporal Zahn hates the ground you Johnnies walk on ... understand? I mean the man's seen a lot of this war ... and it did something to him ... so don't force his hand, okay?"

"Soldier boy, I seed that the minute I laid eyes on 'im ... he's a bad 'un, that's fur shore ... but we cain't go far noway, so don't be a-worrin' none," said Dagmar.

"Stay in sight," he said, following. "I'm not in the mood to let anybody escape," he added, fingering the trigger of his musket.

"And whut durn diffirence would it make, do ye thank?" said Dagmar with a side glance, wandering into a stand of trees, "if'n this yar ole man done run awf, huh ... tell me that?"

"I don't want trouble, understand? So, don't try nothing smart, okay? It wouldn't make me any difference if you all ran off, but I have answer to Zahn, and him to the captain, and him to the higher-ups, see that's the way it works. It's this thing that everyone has to answer to but nobody's really in charge of. I mean, it's bigger'n all of us put together ... bigger'n General Steele himself ... bigger even than Lincoln and he's president. So, it's lots bigger than you and me and your Reb friend here ... and if I was you, I wouldn't tempt it none ... or it'll crush you like a bug."

They moved some distance away from the guard and Curt hobbled down against the trunk of a big oak, leaned back, closed his eyes, rested for a moment, then opened them again, saying, "I'm a-gonner, Tom. Yew don't need to a-waste no moya time a-nu'se maidin' me, yew heya ... jes' leave me to die an' run ... yew can git away if you go quick-like. One step an' yew'll be fray."

"I cain't ratly do that," said Dagmar quietly.

Curt closed his eyes again, his face going pale.

"I cain't keep up no moya," he said just above a whisper, his eyes still closed. "I'm plum wore out."

"Ye gotter ... 'sides the way we done stopped sudden-like makes me figger 'r boys finally done got in front of 'em up thar somewhurs ... Fagan ... 'r maybe

Marmaduke … gotta stop 'em afore they gits to the Saline … with that fine damn bridge they got … they'll git away fur shore … so … maybe we ain't gonna walk no more'n this today no way," she said, adding, "jes' don't give up, Jim … ye kin always take one more step …"

"I cain't … jes' laev me … that boy won't stick me … he ain't the kind."

"He jes' might … cain't never say fur shore a-what he might do … pushed hard nuff … 'sides, if'n he don't that damn corporal of his'n will … he's a bad 'un … believe me, I know bad 'uns when I seen 'em, and he's the very devil."

"Reckon thaya's any water 'round heya?" Curt said after a slight silence.

"Hey, soldier boy!" yelled Dagmar.

"Yeah," he yelled back in irritation.

"How much water you got in that thar canteen of yores?"

"Not enough to share."

"Let me have it … I'm a-goin' to fill it up somewhure."

"I don't see no water here."

"You ain't looked … let me have it …"

The soldier walked over, handing her the canteen.

"I'll go with you," he said. "He ain't going nowhere," he added, looking down at Curt.

Quickly, the two disappeared into the brush.

"They'll be little cricks 'round ever whur … as damp as its been," Dagmar said.

They went through thicker brush, then down a small fold in the ground, coming to a cut among the foliage, where, curling around the roots of large trees, they found a brook.

"Yar," she said, flopping on her belly, drinking, shooing nats away with her ragged hat, swallowing long and hard, then sinking in her face before filling the canteen. The soldier, keeping one hand on his rifle, did the same. Then they sat up, sitting together, the rifle now lying in the weeds besides them.

"Boy, does that feel good!" he said. "I'm about worn out myself."

"What's yer name?" Dagmar asked, removing her shoes and washing her feet.

"Joshua …" he said

"Like in the Bible?"

"Right."

"Mine's Tom."

"Tom?"

"Rat … Tom Suggins."

"You were a dispatch rider?"

"Rat."

"You're a girl, ain't you, Tom?" he said, blushing proudly.

"Now how come ye figger that, Joshua?" she said, turning to him, looking him in the eye.

"I saw your shirt fall away when you drank," he said a little ashamed.

"Now that ain't too polite of a young feller, now is it, Joshua? To be sneakin' a look at a girl like that? Whut would yer mama thank, huh?"

"Well, I didn't know not to look, now did I? I mean, you said you were a boy, didn't you?"

Dagmar laughed, then said, "I'd be mighty grateful to ye, Joshua, if'n yew don't tell nobody ... ain't awl these Yankees is the gentleman yew are ... if ye git my drift."

"I won't say anything."

"I'm much obliged to ye."

"How big a Reb army is chasing us, Tom?" he asked, glad to change the subject.

"I don't ratly know ... ever thang Kirby Smith's got, I reckon, awl walked awl the way up from Loosiana, ye know, after a-whippin' Banks an' awl like Richard Taylor done ... they's in a powerful froth to bag yer general now ... kit an' caboodle ... that's fur shore."

"Yeah ... Steele must think so ... I mean ... the hurry we're in. We came all the way down here, half starved ourselves, lost two supply trains, and are running back as fast as we can go. The men are blaming Steele something awful for this darn mess he's got us in."

"Well, Joshua, the way I figger, it's a race to the river. It's awful high jes' now ... an' if yer bunch kin cross that, ye'll slow Smith 'nuff to git own up to the Rock, 'cause he ain't got no bridge with 'im ... it'll hold him up jes like at Camden. Yew got boys got vittles an' fortifications at the Rock, rat?"

"General Smith doesn't have a bridge, huh?"

"Rat ... that's why they's a day back or more ... but how we's stopped ... looks like maybe Fagan or Marmaduke ... or one of 'em ... is 'cross the road ahead o' us a payce ... a-holdin' thangs up ..."

"If Smith catches us, he'll nail the hide on this whole darn army," he said.

"Then I'll be a-guardin' yew, won't I?" she smiled wryly.

He looked at her in surprise, then said, "Come on, Tom, we better get back." She put on her shoes and they both got up.

"Ye knowed as well as me that ole Jim ain't gonna make it, Joshua," she said, staring at him as they walked together through the brush.

"He won't be the first," he said, turning away. "Come on, we've got to get back in column."

"Kin we jes' leave him a-settin' by that thar tree, huh? He's wore plum out. It won't hurt nothin' … whut ye say, Joshua? Let's jes' leave 'im here a-settin' thar?"

"I can't, Tom; they'd have my hide … I'm under strict orders about all prisoners."

"They don't have to know, if'n we do it rat," said Dagmar, following him back. But he didn't respond.

"Give me the canteen, Joshua," she said, taking it and leaning over Curt.

"Here, drank," Dagmar said, squatting, letting Curt unstop the top, then lifting the canteen with her one hand, Curt taking it and drinking deeply.

"Thanks," he gasped.

"Come on … we gotta get back in column," Joshua said.

"Why, Joshua? We ain't moved none."

"We will soon."

"An' how do ye know that, Joshua? We ain't never stopped this long afore. I'm a-tellin' ye … looks to me like sumpin' has done got ahead of us. I bet they's a purtty good little fight a-goin' own rat now as we spayk."

Zahn, standing in the road, yelled for them to return.

"I've got to go now … get him up and get back in column …"

"Okay, Joshua, we'll be 'long directly …"

Joshua shouldered his musket and walked to the road, talking to the corporal as he went.

"I cain't go, Tom," whispered Curt.

"Ye got to … they won't leave ye. I tried to talk 'im into it but thar warn't no budge in 'im."

"Heya," he said, fumblin' out a crumpled letter from his shirt pocket. "It's fo' my wife … see she gits it … yew heya?"

Dagmar took the letter, stuffing it in her shirt.

"I'll see to it," she said, then shook his hand and walked away.

"Thank Septimus for me, yew heya … I thank he's a good nigga."

"I will," she said not turning round.

"God bless," he said, watching her go, waving weakly.

The column began to fall in with orders for moving again yelled up and down the line.

"Where's the ole man?" asked Joshua coming up.

"I tolt ye, he ain't a-comin', Joshua," said Dagmar now in her most surly of moods.

"He's got to!" he said.

"Well, he cain't an' he ain't ..."

"You go fetch him, right now, Tom!"

"Go fetch 'im yoreself, Joshua, if brangin' that ole man is so damned awl-fared important to savin' yore goddamn Union ... yew go fetch him yoreself!"

"Where's that damn Reb cripple?" Zahn yelled, wandering back.

"He's back there sitting by a tree ... says he can't go any more, Corporal Zahn," said Joshua, looking away.

"Sitting by a tree!?"

"That's right ... too lame to budge ... maybe I can find a place for him somewhere in one of the wagons ... with our wounded ..."

"No Rebs is riding who can halfway walk ... I told you, we don't have room for our own as it is ... got wounded walking that ain't much better'n him. Go back and get him ... and if he don't come ... shoot him!"

"Shoot him?"

"That's what I said. He's a escaped prisoner ... my orders are to shoot Rebs that run ... go shoot the son-of-a-bitch, if he won't come ... or we'll just have to fight him again ... he's jumped parole once ... he'll heal up and shoot you on the battlefield, boy ... or somebody else ... go shoot him if he won't come, I say!"

"I can't do that, Corporal Zahn."

"Why the hell not?"

"It's just not right. He's a defenseless man sitting against a tree."

"By damn you will or I'll have your hide, boy! I'm giving you a direct order! Either bring him back here or shoot him!" said Zahn, turning red and shaking his fist.

"Corporal Zahn ... he's not running or anything ... it's not right ..."

"By God he's the same as running ... pretending he can't go on and all that ... he's been hobbling around Camden all week with no trouble ... eating our provisions when we're starving ... he'll be well enough to blow your damn fool head off! If it was up to me, I'd shoot every one of them damn Reb bastards right now and be done with it! By God, I would! They're every last one's a traitor ... Steele is too damn easy on them which is why we ain't won this war yet ... too easy, I say! You go back there and bring that damn Reb to me or shoot him ... and if you don't, by God I'll do it and I won't waste no bullet ... you understand ... I'll stick him good ... I will ... you want me to do that? Give him the blade ... or after I get back, I'll have you courtmartialed!"

Joshua turned and slowly walked back. Then the wagons lurched forward and the column began to inch slowly north again.

"Come on! Bunch it up, you bastards!" yelled Zahn, herding the prisoners into a reluctant, shuffling group. But Dagmar paused, staring in the direction of the trees.

"You little devil … keep moving or I'll stick you, too," he said to Dagmar, coming over and shoving her.

She stared hard at him, then started walking with a studied reluctance. They moved about fifty yards before the shot. Then an ashen Joshua emerged, gradually caught up with a quick but self-conscious stride as the train disappeared around a bend, leaving an empty road with nothing but songbirds to fill the silence.

Major Elliot, meantime, like a farm boy pressing an unlocked barn door hard against the weight of an exiting bull, finally discerning it was Steele's entire command he was shouldering, at last broke away, and, more in alarm than fear, ran for Pratt's Ferry. Arriving the next day, he found that farmer Fagan had chored off without so much as leaving a note on a limb.

Thoroughly "jaded," Elliot swam the Saline, finding forage in safe abundance on the other side. Yet here he rested under a special burden—the beast was out, and Fagan was simply going to have to find out for himself that it was snorting down the road.

But, as it walked through farm country so fine that it reminded many Midwesterners of home, the creature was thinking of little more than merely swimming the Saline. The morning was sunny, peaceful, almost light-hearted, and the Union column soon tied Princeton to Tulip with a Blue thread of soldiers, animals, wagons, and straggling civilians—most walking, some riding, but all beginning to believe that the worst was behind, that they had at last made good their escape. So the mood lifted into chatting, joking, and laughter amid the jingle and rattle of harness, as animals relaxed to their burden in the loveliness of a fine spring morning.

And then, at noon, there was a change. Clouds gathered from the west and, moving toward them, slowly frowned away the sun, casting the day with a strange green light, blowing dirt, sticks, and leaves in a twisting swirl, as the light changed yet again, like lamps on a stage, suddenly dimming down darkly into an eerie blackness that boiled over them. This premature night fastened away their fair spring sky forever, like a lid closing on a tomb, slid shut by some unseen hand, thundering loudly on its hinges as it was securely sealed and latched somewhere in the east, bolted down with a rumble, the thing smothering over as an amorphous, magically changing pandemonium of cloud, lightning, and thunder, freezing the upward glance of ten thousand heads craning helplessly skyward, wondering when it would finally come down upon them, till it did at last come—first ever so gradually, dryly withholding its power in the torment of an angry anticipation—lighting the sky, then shuddering the ground and air with silver shafts of flashing electric spears of fire, striking on either side, splitting trees, slicing the earth with the taunt loud crack of nerve-shearing near misses like artillery explosions no soldier had ever heard, all the while continually sliding its thunder over them in ever-deafening crescendos, as background to a chiaroscuro of light alternating before their eyes into a kind of blindness. More strangely, the unmistakable fresh rain smell came briefly to their nostrils with an odd pleasantness, then evaporated with base groans, louder, ever closer, like the voice of God speaking in the only language they would understand. Then, as if denied a response, reluctantly, ever so slowly, it released water drops with a slow, but steady increase, striking like fat, hard flying bullets, patter-pittering, then increasing to the smaller more numerous missiles of a shower, thence to a sheeting rain, then, finally, to a river flowing out of the sky itself, flooding the earth with an infinity of water which rolled into the Saline, making it a tributary, not from the earth but seemingly from a nether world, a stream already swollen, forever slipping through swamps, past bottomland trees that no mortal hand had yet touched. This usually greenish, now quickly brown, minor-goddess of a river would normally slip quietly away in search of her bigger sisters, first, the Ouachita, then the Red, then finally, swoon with them into their father-Mississippi's arms and with him run as one to the mother-sea, but now this day, would race to them in a desperate embrace, as from a great fear or passion or both.

Brigadier Eugene Carr, whose mounted legion had been such an encouragement for Major Elliot to go in search of Fagan, now hooved up to Jenkins's Ferry moments before this flood. Here he found, not more Grays as he greatly feared (for there can be little doubt, with Marmaduke swinging in from the right, and Smith's lean Grayhounds beginning even now to snap at Steele's dragging tail, that if Fagan had awakened to his proper role, the Blues would have been destroyed, the battle won, glory obtained, and Gray spirits greatly lifted from the deepening despair of that fateful spring). To Carr's very great relief, he discovered instead a very badly rutted, but utterly abandoned, road wiggling down a slash in the earth like a giant serpent in search of water. He followed its slitherings to the river, where he traced its invisible head freshly submerged into a swollen and ever-rising surge of brown current swirling forth from what one would describe as "the worst swamp in Arkansas."

It was here, not that far above Mount Elba, where Major Spellman had recently crossed his cavalry in his hurried exchange of it for the Calvary of captivity in Texas, and yet a little below Pratt's Landing, where our Major Elliot, having inadvertently switched banks with Spellman, would very soon find himself in a captivity of another sort, that is, on the wrong side of a flood, drowning not in water but in the frustration of what he knew, had been sent to find out, but, Cassandra-like, could not find a listening ear for, until it would be too late for everything but the even harsher ruminations of history—his lonely haven in turn just a little below where the conquistadors had likewise been imprisoned in the confines of the cold of 1541–42, immured in the service of a Habsburg kinsman of the present king of Mexico, a royal line of blood that men have trailed for almost a thousand years—into battles, oceans, prisons, and scaffolds—in loyal search for that greatest chimera of all—the crown of a borrowed glory, a tripartite parure of sin—ambition, avarice, and adulation—set like diamonds upon the leaden brow of folly—searched for and, at last, found within the forbidden depths of mountains, fields, and continents, and, today, in this place of this particular, twisting, obscure river—a conflux contending with itself in a restless inner conflict of current as it debouched from the primitive and eternal innocence of Arcadia into the self-consciousness of the Styx of war, necessity, and time, which these men must cross, no matter from which side to which, but cross they must—from the *inferno* of strife into the *purgatorio* of escape—to the final passage of *paradiso* in the peace of release and repose of death where glory's diadem is at last set aside and a lost innocence regained.

But for the moment they would have no ferryman. If the Ouachita had been their first to cross—their Acheron—nevertheless, today they would be defeated in their second expectation of an easy transit. There had been no mythical keeper, poling across to exact his toll from the dead—a last payment for the unforgivable sin of having lived—an *obolus* laid upon their mortal tongue as recompense—nor would there be today, upon this crossing, such a toll at all, but one of another kind.

Or to say it another way, "usually" is not quite the same as "always," and given the obvious and well-known fact that old man Tom Jenkins, despite rejoicing in his station as a "notorious riparian owner," who, as such, could be well relied upon to be "usually around somewheres," or, "hardly ever far," greedily squirreling his ferry's toll into a mean little black purse that snapped shut, as though

PHILLIP H. MCMATH

with a clicking beat of his heart, in apprehension of some vital force escaping into the foul air, but, to be sure, certainly not retrieving fares from the tongues of dead souls, as in the foolish service of some legend or myth of an ever-uncertain metaphysical salvation. No, sir, this ferryman would not be bothered with such nether-world nonsense. He, Mr. Tom Jenkins, was, after all, a man of affairs and always about his trade: talking, toting, and tinkering with his rusty, half-sunken tug of a scow that nudged against the mud bank when not kedging across like some moribund, captive monster he had snared in the marshy mist and now enslaved in a mass of lines, cables, and pulleys—forever doggered into the wretched service of going from one side of the river to the other, unload-ing, then loading, again and again, over and over—pulling, pushing and poling—backwatering, belaying, and bearing—back and forth, back and forth, in the absurd unending busyness of all business in this world. Yes, it was cer-tainly true, Mr. Tom was "usually around," always "a-vistin' there or the other place," as they said. But, General Carr soon discovered that this particular devil's jack, on this day at least, was nowhere to be found.

Old Mister Jenkins, as it turned out, was no Charon. And this, to be sure, was no River Acheron, or Styx, but the muddy Saline, deep in the wilds of Arkansas where one did not grow old waiting on trouble. Our toothless ferryman, it seems, had heard the guns of Tulip and knew it wasn't thunder. Besides, any fool could see it was "fixin' to rain and the river was already a-floodin'." It was, quite simply, time to leave, and he did just that, taking his lighter with him, sculling slowly down the river like any other amphibious swamp critter looking for a hole.

The general could scarcely disguise his disappointment. The barge might have helped to get a line across, and, too, he had very much wanted to meet so famous a figure. But no matter. 4,000 wheels, 20,000 feet, and 40,000 hooves could never find much purchase on so a small a lugger anyway, nor make any real use of its geezer owner, however renowned.

> By other windings and by other steerage shall you cross to that other shore. Not here! Not here! A lighter craft than mine shall give you passage!

It's not really known if, by man or god, these immortal lines were spake unto the good general's ear, but they, or something very much like, must have been, because he ordered up the bridge.

CHAPTER SEVENTEEN

Country level, heavy timbered. Desperate roads, no improvements, per-
fect wilderness ... Mud no mule's leg can fathom.
    —*Private John P. Wright, Twenty-ninth Iowa*

Captain James Wheeler, Carr's chief engineer, moved up the pontoons, and
by a little past three had stretched them toward the Blue line. But the Saline
was shouldering higher, so Carr stretched a little more, while the bottoms, as
if awakened from a slumber, for two and half miles rolled itself over into an
irritated mash that axled the wagons and bellied the mules.

In the raining despair of the ensuing darkness, Wheeler called a halt. But
Steele, feeling the Grays nipping up now at Tulip, said no. So, once again the
Blue hive jerked forward, corduroying to the sound of whips and curses—the
mules floundering, sticking, surging, unsticking, floundering and sticking again,
as the column crawled through the black wallow toward the bridge, touching
it at last in the darkness, like a blind man reaching for a rope, then feeling and
holding tenaciously, wagon by wagon, animal by animal, man by man, over the
Saline, which surged in the invisible abyss below, over the bridge which was
bobbing up and down like some marsh creature that might break free and swim
off at any moment.

The first was Carr, who, leaving half his division to guard the train, bridled
the rest across, then, swinging into the saddle, loped away in the happy freedom of one unleashed from an unwanted, but inescapable, burden. For him,
like everyone, Gray or Blue, the whereabouts of Fagan was very much a mystery, and his solution was to intercept an imagined thrust from the Rock or
maybe the Bluff.

Meantime, the other cavalier, Marmaduke, spent his early morning slipping
between Princeton and Tulip in the sure and certain hope of blocking a foe fleeing up the road. He found Grays instead—his own Eighth Missouri Cavalry,
previously detached and pushed forward by Price. These riders related tales of
cheering citizens and running Blues at Princeton, but clearly the moment was
lost, and Marmaduke could only chase to Tulip, where he touched Steele's rear

guard at last—the Sixth Kansas Cavalry—quickly recoiling them into a hot exchange until the blowing storm, bringing a turmoil of rain, wind, and fire, crossed both their houses with a celestial violence that soon smothered the Kansas-Missouri fight into silence like the flame of a guttering candle.

In the sheets of this maelstrom, Marmaduke hid for a moment Colonel Colton Greene's brigade in an arching right-wedge hook aimed between the Yankee horse and running foot of the main column. But Kansas rode back, deftly closing the gap, falling onto the infantry of the rear-most General Salomon's Third Brigade (Colonel Adolph Englemann), who suddenly turned and dug themselves into a tired, wet, but determined "T" across the road, connecting the trees and ditches together in a ragged Blue line, letting the Kansas horse through before firing on Marmaduke.

Thus in the afternoon Greene and his general came together again, butting hard against this upper-case letter of Midwestern infantry suddenly scribbled out on the ground by the Forty-third Illinois, the Fortieth Iowa, and the Twenty-seventh Wisconsin. It was too much. The Gray cavalry stopped, dismounted, sent for help, pushed in close for an occasional shot but all the while knew that eventually pontoons would be stretched and the Saline crossed through the shank of the coming gloom of a black-hooded, drenching night.

In Salomon's rear, there had gradually arisen a steady build-up of runaway slaves, camp followers, and the small band of prisoners that included Dagmar. Most walked but some few rode horses and mules and an even smaller number were in wagons. Their fear of being overtaken was never greater than when Marmaduke touched the Kansas horse.

The Africans and shirkers split between those that hurried forward, creating havoc among the soldiers, and those that ran away, leaving wagon, horse, or mule behind, preferring the anonymity of the forest to being seen with the Yankees. Some of the "contrabands" had joined Drake, only to flee from Marks's Mill to Steele, and now to flee once again, not knowing really where to go, finding the Federals to offer an unsettling back and forth combination of safety and danger.

The Gray prisoners, hopeful of release, began to lag and were pressed forward only by the curses and threats of the soldiers.

"Joshua, I tolt ye I'd be a-guardin' ye soon," laughed Dagmar at the sound of Marmaduke's guns.

"Keep moving," he said, pushing her with his musket, "we got to go forward ..."

"Whur to?"

"To the river …"

"River? Damn, Joshua, I'm wore out … cain't we jes' move a mile or two up this yar road an' find a place out o' this yar storm and res' fur the night? We're goin' a-ketch 'r death …"

"All the prisoners got to go to the river … orders is orders," he said, pushing her again, then herding the other prisoners like reluctant sheep.

"We'll have to walk all night to git to the riva," one of them shot back.

"Come on! Keep moving! We'll rest when we get to the ferry!" Joshua yelled, pushing with the musket against the man's back.

The little wad moved slowly down the column of wagons only slightly faster as the guns sounded louder and the rain poured ever harder.

"Whur's Septimus at?" asked Dagmar. "He was a-standin' yar jes' then … now he's done gone awf somewhurs."

"He's run off … I don't know … he just run," said Joshua.

"I doubt we'd be seein' him agin, that's fur shore … he's skeered to death," she said.

"Wouldn't you be?" asked Joshua.

"Hell, they woudn't do nothin' to that boy 'cept send him back," said Dagmar.

"Would you want to go back?" asked Joshua, walking behind, wet and huffing.

"He ain't no better awf, Josh … everwhur he goes."

"You can't blame him, now can you?"

"Naw … I'd run too … hell, Joshua, I wuz nothin' but a damn slave myse'f."

"Come on, let's step it up!" Joshua yelled as they passed a wagon of wounded.

"Keep them closed up and moving," yelled Zahn, coming up behind.

"I am … I am," whined Joshua.

"They're going to try to run on you, now them Johnnies is up with us … in this rain and all. They say it's Marmaduke's devils in our rear now, and the whole damn Reb army won't be far behind. We'll be lucky if we don't lose half of our own before we put that river behind us … keep them closed up, boy … unless you want me to start shooting them!"

"Yes, sir."

"Any you Rebs take a notion to run, you better be a sight faster'n a musket ball … you hear me!" yelled Zahn, but his voice was canceled by a rod of lightning stroking a tree in half.

Every creature, human and animal, jumped. An officer was thrown, his horse running into the woods.

"Move! Move! Move!" shouted Joshua, forcing them into a trot. But now they could hardly see. Joshua tripped, fell, his musket scooting under a wagon that ran over it, breaking its stock.

The prisoners disappeared—all but Dagmar, who stopped to help him up.

Zahn yelled and ran, but now everyone was absorbed in a panic, swarming around the wagons like fish in a flood slipping past rocks.

"Come own, jes' a-well to forgit that musket now, Joshua. It's broke fur shore," said Dagmar, pulling him to his feet.

"Thanks," he said, water pouring over him like an emptying bucket.

"They's done run awf ... ain't no catchin' 'em now ... they're gone."

"Well, Tom, let's go to the river. My orders are to take you there," he said, trying to wipe the water out of his eyes with the back of his sleeve.

"Orders is orders, ain't they, Joshua?" said Dagmar, laughing as they turned and walked together just a little faster than the surging column.

On the evening of the twenty-eighth, General Thomas J. Churchill's Arkansas Division found itself camped several miles south of Princeton. A few more miles back, Mosby M. Parsons's Missouri Division rested, and farther still, the Texans of John G. Walker slept. It had been a long, hard loping day after crossing the Ouachita, but one of rising expectation as the Grays encountered the increasing waste of war—packs, clothing, equipment, abandoned wagons, and all the "plunder and property" stolen as spoils of invasion, spread by the Yankees along the countryside and cast away in the face of an incipient destruction.

But even this was not encouragement enough for the Grays to go on unceasingly, as flesh and muscle, demanded rest. Yet, almost simultaneous with the shutting of their eyes it seemed, Price, commanding Churchill and Parsons, ordered his two divisions up by 2:00 for something he dared to call "breakfast," then set his lean hounds upon the trail again.

They trotted to Princeton, where, arriving at noon, they learned that the Blues were but a few hours ahead, dropping behind them even greater amounts of baggage, which they mixed with stragglers, lending the impression of being ever closer, and evermore desperate, as night found the exhausted Confederates panting happily into the little wet flower of Tulip, only a bit behind Marmaduke—all hot upon the smell of warm blood. Soon they curled into a lay-down bivouac, tiredly sleeping in the rain, knowing well enough that the morrow, in its cornering of the beast against the Saline, would mean that many had slept their last.

A Confederate surgeon recalled the twenty-eight-mile march.

> At 3:00 next morning we were on the road again. Not a living animal was to be seen along the wayside—nothing but ruin and desolation! Women and little children sometimes stood by the road and watched us pass. They did not seem very glad to see us for they were too hungry to be demonstrative, and we had nothing to give them, not knowing ourselves where our next meal was coming from.

> By and by we came to Princeton. The enemy had camped there the night before and had literally sacked the town. They had left nothing to the inhabitants. The ladies with their children and a few old men came out on the square and gave us some flowers and their prayers. It was all they had. Bless the women of that little village! Their patriotism never grew cold nor for a moment faltered in all the night or that horrid nightmare. We made no stop at Princeton. Towards night we reached Tulip ...

By light on the thirtieth, Steele had half his wagons and all his artillery across, but in laying his army athwart the water, the sudden sound of shots, like a stick against a serpent stretched across a log, threatened to break him in the middle.

He urged them on, but the far side proved a disappointment, since there the rising swamp was even worse than the near, and, as the rain still poured with an incessant delight, equipage crossed only to be mired and lost, as mules all but disappeared and wheels plunged stuck, till Steele, like the captain of a sinking ship, lightened his hull by sinking its freight, throwing away baggage and cargo, doubling the teams from the wagons lost, saving one-half by sacrificing the other, in a scene of muddy pandemonium as the animals were spurred by whips and the men by fear.

Ever of two minds, fleeing and fighting, Steele first turned from one to the other—east to west. But now, with the sound of muskets, he turned west, cantering back to find Salomon facing Marmaduke in his rear.

Here Steele found that his brigadier had assessed the ground well. Salomon pointed to their right, there, he said, slithering along north of the road, in mutual search of the river, lay a creek named for one local Mr. Cox. It was over its banks and flooding back toward the track, while to the south, the general's left, he indicated a thick, almost impenetrable, wilderness standing guard for him like an extra Blue infantry regiment. It was, Salomon described later, a "majestic forest, growing out of the swamp, which it was very difficult to pass through ..."

And, hewn in the center, at their front, pasted along the road, one behind the other like postage stamps stuck on a child's playful string, were three fields of corn, harvesting some nearby farmers' names—Jiles, Cooper, and Kelly—into the unexpected fame that war often gives to unknown places. These were three and a half, three, and two and -half miles from the Jenkins's crossing, and, as such, provided the only openness in what was otherwise nothing more than forest bottoms, flooding canebrake, and brush. It was a good position. Salomon thought he could hold, "Long enough," he told his commander. "You must," Steele said quietly, reining away for the Ferry, as Salomon summoned Samuel Rice, leader of his First Brigade.

Meantime, Marmaduke, ever the nibbler, was snipping out ever-larger bites, so, fearing he might take hold, Salomon dragged his skirmishers out of Marmaduke's reach, then withdrawing his regiments, planned to make of them a shield guarding the wagon train snailing in alternating patterns of stuttering and stopping for two miles toward the bridge in a stalling but steady retreat through the mud.

Salomon used Rice's right to touch Mr. Cox's creek; and with his middle he split the fields of farmers Kelly and Cooper along a thick belt of woods; then, to the left of the road, he stretched Rice's left into a sink of swamp that stood mutely before him as the most imposing place of all.

Yet Rice had another regiment, the Thirty-third Iowa, which, playing the role of guarding the rear, he soon discovered, faithfully resting at the near edge of Mr. Jiles's turn rows—too far forward of his new line, he thought. He told its colonel, Cyrus H. Mackey, to withdraw and move back to Cooper's—the next field down—to rest and eat. But just before this stirring, they were gratified by Gray forms crawling out of the morning rain and mist through the stalks and bushes well within their vision and range. It was "I" company of the Fourth Missouri—Colonel Greene's boys, dismounted troopers, inching like Indians in Marmaduke's first tentative probe of the Blues.

To be sure, this modest piece of Iowa had marched a long way, had lately missed the Springs and the Mill, had walked and cursed and starved in summer, snow, and storm—from home to the hellish Helena of flood and fever, then in '63 trekked to the Rock. From there they went hunkering on down to Camden, and then raced to here; along this declension, losing a small few to shot but a great many more to sickness, and now, at long last, like a suffering hunter ever harried by a lurking wolf finally seen in a momentary gray blur through mist and mud, found their fatigue shaken suddenly away by the pleasure only a quick trigger can give at such a time and place—recoiling out a solid, if ragged, rip of Midwestern musketry, exploding more on reflex than command, tonguing a fire of unexpected joy, as, while ramroding powder and ball, they yelled such happy threats of death and damnation that Rice knew, when it was returned by the Grays, with shot and shout, that these men, like fighting schoolboys, would not be easily disjoined.

He did not try. Rather he sent a friend to help—the Fiftieth Indiana, which he placed so as to fist in from the left. With this, the Grays reluctantly let go—snarling back into the trees. Then Rice, after a watching-wait, letting the rifle smoke fog up heavily into the trees like a cotton curtain lifting over a few curling clumps—still or moaning and dying—their brothers gone—Rice paused, exhaled with satisfaction, and quietly relieved the Thirty-third with the Twenty-seventh Wisconsin, marching Mackey's tired Blues proudly back to Kelly's field for "breakfast."

It was, of course, still raining, yet starved and sleepless, these were fed something that could be fisted up in a gulp. When Rice rode by they swallowed out a cheer that sprung his hand into a sharp salute and startled his horse into a prideful, prancing trot. For many, it seemed a culmination.

But, as time will always move relentlessly from one thing, no matter how happy or cruel, to the fateful next, reality intruded in the form of a crash of muskets—sounding with a heavy desperation that can better than words or explanation tell the tale which only those who have heard it will ever know. It was without that desultory sputtering of a game upon a field that war sometimes has, but came rather with the weight of a hand that holds within its fist the stone of death that the sound fell upon the ground, as Colonel Green's Grays struck back at Wisconsin and Indiana hard and sudden, racing in surprise over the clumps in the corn rows and following behind the Blue skirmishers with an unexpected lunge for the throat.

Alarmed, riding forward and knowing without having to see or ask, Salomon ordered Rice again to withdraw from Jiles for a tie-in with the others.

Here, Salomon said, he would wind the Blue string in a tight bow to his left, tying in forest and creek on either end as one taut, impenetrable piece. But this time the Grays knew better and sprang onto their prey before it could flee, sinking their teeth in deep and not letting go. The Blues fought to be free, but the Grays held, following them from Jiles to Cooper, dragged behind as if by

PHILLIP H. MCMATH

a fleeing animal, while others trotted rightward to bite the Union at its tender left flank in the forest.

Turning and fighting in Cooper, the Blues and Grays struggled till the quarry finally kicked its pursuer off begrudging him the second field for the heavy timber behind, finding at last Rice's main force drawn up and waiting patiently in the trees between Mr. Kelly's patch and the one just abandoned. Here Fifty and Twenty-seven passed easily through the Twenty-ninth, Fortieth, Thirty-third Iowa, the Ninth Wisconsin, and the Forty-third Illinois, all formed in a menacing wall of resistance. With the fleeing train and rising river at their backs, here they must stand, so they did, waiting, then blasting the Gray pursuer off in a heavy volley as he appeared, lunged at them in turn, hoping to find the life-spot and kill the creature forever.

Green recoiled—he could do no more. He must wait for the infantry. Meantime, Blue Fifty and Twenty-seven stopped their flight in Kelly's field, regrouping into Rice's reserve. For the moment at least, the Grays were lying, panting in the forest, but all knew they would come again.

Up at midnight, Churchill's Arkansas division, sleepless in the rain, wearily rose from their "rest" in Tulip into a stumbling black-blind night, as his two thousand stretched themselves into a long Gray column in search of Marmaduke's Missourians.

An officer in the Thirty-third Arkansas recalled:

> At midnight we were called into line and ordered to move on. The night was so black that one could almost feel the darkness with the hand. Sounds of distant thunder fell upon the ear, which, as it came nearer, swelled into a roar. In the darkness one could see nothing. Then a flash of lightning would come and reveal a long line of bayonets stretching away down the road and out into the darkness.

Behind them, another group of Missourians, Parsons's foot, broke camp, and, two miles behind, they chased Churchill in hopes of catching him before he caught Marmaduke, who everyone knew, had already caught Steele. Farther back was Walker with Texas hoping to come and make the difference by weighing the weary creature to the ground, buckling its legs to find its neck.

So, while the wet Churchillians threw wooden fence posts into a rough roadbed like a train track relieved of its rails, sleeping upon them in a ragged line a few sodden inches above the ground, their general, his commander, Price, and his commander, Kirby Smith, met in farmer Tyra Brown's front parlor for a chat.

Smith was not happy. While his object was at hand, his fingers were coming in spread apart, piecemeal, not as a fist but a sideways palm when he wanted to wait, swing with all his might one mighty blow. But fearful now that Marmaduke would be mauled, he made ready to thrust in his Arkansawyers more like a fending jab than a hook.

This, of course, was what Thomas Churchill was told to do. This scion of Kentucky plantation wealth, born to the manor, as they say, had after the law been taken from that singular drudgery of other people's problems to that of the more objective plural romance of those in the mass; that is, of war somewhere else, at a distance that is, but where he found the intrusion of a certain reality instead—in a Mexican prison camp, after the war of that name.

Coming home sobered through the Rock, traveling the Southwest Trail into Markham, our erstwhile prince of privilege stopped, rested, circulated, met a federal judge's granddaughter, Anne Maria Sevier, surnamed from Huguenots, who had anglicized it over from Xavier. A daughter of a U.S. senator; niece of a governor and founder of Tennessee and grandniece of a vice president, Anne was, one might say, well-connected enough to charm young Tom from pause to pursuit, and thence to a nuptial permanence, building for her and their quickly arriving brood a plantation castle east of the capital which her proud and happily snared Churchill named with an uncanny prescience, *Blenheim,* in memory of his British family branch. But, alas, such is the briefness of all unbounded bliss in this world, their dream was soon broken by the thing of war that, since glory does not always require some remove, carried the cruel intruding fact to their very door.

In the rapid severity of these times, *Blenheim* was savaged and sacked. Little survived but Anne Maria's grand piano, which was saved as an out-of-tune, black wire trough for the feeding of already over-fed, arriviste Yankee horses, many of whom, leaner and much busier, were this very morning loping northward with Brigadier Carr in search of a certain Fagan, who wasn't to be found by friend or foe, but whom Carr feared was now avenging a thousand *Blenheims* these gate-crashing guests from the North had visited upon their Southern hosts.

Churchill, prisoner to the Mexicans, had in '63, become one to the Americans as well, taken with his little Gray brigade of 5,000 at Arkansas Post (*Poste aux Arcs / Anilco*), only a day downriver from his *Blenheim,* when the political Major General John McClernand and Admiral David Dixon Porter took the place. McClernand, Churchill's brother of the Kentucky bar, who early on had grasped the obvious opportunities of staying Federal and who, in early that same year, floated down from Memphis with 30,000 rifles, fifty transports, and thirteen gunboats, as appendages and instruments of his presidential purpose, to swing up the Arkansas to a place called Fort Hindman manned then by Churchill. McClernand attacked with the escorting hand of Admiral David Dixon Porter firm upon him, a son of a commodore and foster brother to the immortal Farragut. Porter was a Pennsylvanian who had spent his career sailing the West Indies in service of this new republic, but who at this very moment was retreating in mutual desperation with Congressman Banks, dropping his ravaged brown water fleet with the fleeing army down the Red, hastily to Alexandria, one by water, the other by land, in a paralleling, panicking retreat before Taylor's tiny Gray force seconded by a tall, brave, French prince whose fathers had served their aristocratic Louis to overthrow the usurping bourgeois Bonaparte with a Restoration which, through three successive, failing Kingdoms, collapsed then upon a nephew, Louis Napolcon, who had so recently set these armies in motion from his cactus perch in Mexico, all of which had started Banks and Steele in motion in the first place.

It had been at this Hindman, upon the Cayas, at a place where history for a time seemed to have become permanently stuck because it was the first high ground just a tad up from where *Los Conquistadores* survivors, three centuries before, as we have also told, rafted down in the other direction from the Gallic canoers, not to New France at all but for New Spain. They had floated free from the burden of those thousand lamenting slaves who wanted anything but their abolition and stood sobbing among cheerfully rooting swine, each abandoned to a virgin vastness. Now the Bayou Blanc bottoms a little east of Christopher Shaw's grave seems like a chaste presumption stuck into a world ever-busy with sealing itself into a prison of glass, steel, and machines to whom it so readily surrenders its virture for the ready coin of golden gods, and from which, once lost, no Lincoln can ever grant abolition much less absolution. But then, in that little wisp of time which each was granted, these weeping ones were liberated by the Spaniards into the wilderness, wished to have their slavery back again, watched as those masters fled from avarice and ambition to the safe destitution of an empty saline sea for a long and very painful paddle to the city of Montezuma where this remnant from *La Florida* would fill the world with tales of glorious woe. But not one aggot of gold, silver, or pearl would they palm across to king or prince or beggar, nor any new stories of Aztec or Inca Lost Kingdoms would they tell, only unwittingly immortalizing an obscure place hewn upon the banks of the Caya River's woods, intruding into a new world that was not yet quite ruined but where in another little pinch of proud time Porter and McClernand, reaching to pin on their own small ribbon of fame, would charge hard upon to stride and strut and summon the erstwhile master of *Blenheim* to surrender as their new slave—taking him in chains to an Ohio prison, the very center of this spreading brave new world of powerful things, crushing everything like an iron wheel might a flower.

But Churchill, too, is now in Mount Holly mounted on the Grand, just over from his August friend and fellow Redeemer governor now a Garland upon Spruce just a few rows over from O. Dodd and not that far from old man Shall.

By this double honor of being twice imprisoned his time was foreshortened by an exchange, as Churchill found himself swapping the cold food of a penitentiary bench for the warm feast of a president's table in May. And it was here he received the finest fare of all, he would later say—of his life—greater than the double Ohio/Mexico immurement; or thrice leading triple brave men in battle, or the pinning up to major general in '65, or, even in '80, of being elevated leader of his new, poor, and freshly ravaged state, which he, ever faithful to misfortune like so many others there and elsewhere in the South, had followed loyally out of the Union simply because it was home. One could never fight against it, certainly not for some abstract thing that had something sinister about its head—seen by all standing away and feeling its heat, as from St. John's seething, prophetic Ephesian brain—and what through the great suffering and scourge of it, they were always saying things against in holy prayer-like imprecations, like "God will not let us lose this war," or, "God help us if He does," or, "God scourges those He loves," knowing that the South was right in some enigmatic way despite the world's and history's judgment that it was so egregiously wrong.

It was here, at the pleasure and privilege of that memorable Richmond dinner planned so devotedly by Davis's Devina, that Davis himself dropped his request, that is, over a drop of precious wine—blood-like, undried, and very red, safely sailed through the blockade imposed by Mr. Lincoln's half of what he thought of as his "country" upon its wayward lower half, making it, he hoped, tie each-to-one-forever, all in the name of some "metaphysical" principle that had been, like all such metaphysics, at best vague, but really little more than a misunderstood, sewn-together arrangement in which there was simply not room for both—one perforce crushing the other into its other self.

A "country," Lincoln insisted—himself believed—was a meaningless invention of lawyers, a "worthless bit of old parchment" as Thaddeus Stevens had confessed, if not felt in the flesh—bone-of-bone. Meanwhile, the greatest of

PHILLIP H. MCMATH

all wars was being besieged that day between that one Kentucky backwoods teetotaller and another Kentucky sophisticate, each who had come sliding through their mother's hips within a hundred miles of the other; one a sipper of the stuff stowed snugly among bales of cotton, cannon and shot slipping regularly past the abstainer's powerful New England Federal ships, similar to the ones that had formed the capital for Yankee ingenuity by its great New England slave trade, which, even as the war was being fought for "freedom" and "abolition" of the crime that had made them rich, were still sailing out of New York City to Africa and Cuba for some quick and ready cash.

So, the wine came, as it always does, whether grape or human, juice or blood, floating itself deftly upon the tides of easy rationalization—unbottled, decanted, and poured delicately at the Confederate White House table that evening in Richmond, as it was in Boston, or New York, or Philadelphia, or London, or Paris, or Washington, or Havana—flesh turning to blood, blood to money, money to wine in that modern bourgeois communion of capital, whether North or South, Blue or Gray, European or American, cash transubstantiating itself, pressing out at all such special events the manners and manors for gentlemen all, like the fellow-Kentuckian-turned-Arkansawyer, ex-double-prisoner Thomas James Churchill, who swallowed and savored it in a sweetly bitter unknowing dry prelude to his own president's heavy, unanticipated words that it was his wish that Churchill should shoulder the melancholy honor of bearing a newly dead Virginia general to his grave—an unwitting pall-bearer of a Gray prologue-funeral for his brave and tormented country—recently torn from the hands of a parent that quite simply had no more patience for this fighting, half-blind child groping clumsily to find its way free from an only half-realized injustice.

In a word, Thomas Churchill was to shoulder the immortal Stonewall, freshly killed at Lee's most recent masterpiece of Chancellorsville, into his eternity, liberated at last from what Jackson considered a holy crusade commanded upon him by his Old Testament God—Alpha to Omega—Genesis to John—Fall to Fire—Old Adam to New.

"The Lord has been very good to us today," Stonewall had said with quiet satisfaction, surveying the apocalyptic carnage of Sharpsburg.

So, it was this same Thomas Churchill, together with Price and Marmaduke—governors and generals, past and future—who rode like a little troika to a slight rise near farmer Jile's house, surveying the Saline swamp. Here they stopped, reflected, talked, then, without waiting on Parsons, decided to send Churchill in for Marmaduke.

A veteran of the Thirty-third Arkansas described it best.

> After our regiment had stood there in line for twenty minutes it was
> ordered forward and into action. There was nothing of the romance
> of war or battle. No waving of banners; no martial music; no throng-
> ing of women; children and gray-haired men to the battlements of
> a beautiful city to witness the sentiment about this. The rain pattered
> down steadily. The men stood in the ranks, cold, wet and hungry,
> and gazed down into that dismal, cheerless swamp. The ground being
> soft to ride, the officers dismounted and took their place on foot,
> and the regiment moved down across the little field as steadily as if
> it were on drill. The men did not jostle each other even.

Crossing Cooper's trodden corn in the open, these tired-to-the-bone regiments run so far up from Louisiana and the fresh unpleasantness of Pleasant
Hill, who had hustled through Camden's brief glory and along the racing rainy
road to Tulip, were stopped short, then pressed down by Blue fire into a muddy
swale, which, undulating mercifully like a slight swell over the otherwise wet,
flat ground, granted some few the luxury of a later death. To their right, their
other Gray brothers cleared the woods of snipers and skirmishers like so much
underbrush, only, before settling in, to be thrown back by a quick countershift
of Rice's sliding infantry, coming up tree to tree in a Blue serpentine line like
a snake slithering sideways in segments, separating and coming together,
seemed to advance as by some water sloshing magic through the swamp.

The Grays, responding in kind, also came apart and together again in re-
reforming pieces, as first one regiment, then another began to nibble hungrily
at Rice's flanks. With a flinch, Rice intruded upon the exhausted Thirty-third
Iowa's breakfast, dragging it from low cook fires and half-warmed fare to a
post-haste, shoring-up sprint to the left, where they were set stumbling to a
stop by Colonel Shaver's Twenty-seventh and Thirty-eighth under-strength boys
for "a dog-fall" of a standing, slugging, pulverizing exchange, like street fighters pummeling together, a swinging patch of a mutually desperate melee. With
the thicket as cover, and ginned up by the arrival of Marmaduke's dismounted
Fourth, Shaver began to shave Iowa's left slowly away, razoring him into a slow,
shooting retreat of some 250 yards, bending back the Blue left to the point of
a fateful break, facing Rice with a crumpling, flanking rout, and with it, Steele's
annihilation.

Yet, as if waiting for the precise moment, and with a ubiquitous love of irony
that the great, cruel goddess of History adores, she sent in the Blue First

PHILLIP H. MCMATH

Arkansas—yeomen from the unslaved Ozark hills—who lustily charged, impaling their fellow Arkansawyers with the ferocity of all family feuds, running them through with their own sharp judgment of the future. Then she charmed up the Twelfth Kansas, cheering them all together, as Blue Arkansas, Kansas, and Iowa shuffled reluctant Gray Shaver back to where he had begun, then as if for good measure shoved him harder still some three hundred yards deeper into the wilderness of defeat.

It seemed clear, the Grays would say later in the endlessly sighing years to come that surviving a defeat always brings, "Smith should have waited for Parsons!" But there was a deeper reason. For want of understanding, such mistakes are really never more than an extra bite of bitterness choking on the logic of that which decides such things; so rather than a turn-of-chance of an endless heartbreaking, "What if?" it became in time on the lips of many a "had to be."

Ever in pieces, more came in, first Hawthorn's Rebs, who bogged his charging regiment down in the swale, which was becoming more and more a heaving mass, sputtering forth a steady musketry as mingling men loaded, fired, and ducked again at others who leaned and loosed a ball from the comfort of a tree in an unending popping exchange that to the Blue's satisfaction was obviously going nowhere.

The stymied Smith then sent an odd Churchill regiment of dismounted cavalry to the left (Lieutenant Colonel H. G. P. Williams), wading them across Cox's creek to try their luck on the Federal right. This they did as on the other side, with an early victory promising success—wading, pushing, and tangling themselves among the Blues in a deadly, brushy, formless fire-fight, bending the Blues back into another bowing near-break, till Salomon relaxed the pressure with his Forty-third Illinois reserve, rushing them up just in time as he had done with Rice on the opposite end. Then Salomon shored others into the solidifying middle and right, as Williams, like Shaver, had to reverse a gain into a loss.

Finally, Churchill sicked his reserve—the Twenty-sixth Arkansas—which had lain panting in the weeds behind, like a heeling terrier—and with them a young lieutenant of infantry, farmer James Rudd, a veteran survivor of Prairie Grove and Pleasant Hill, who had seen enough to be content in waiting, but when commanded, flung his platoon with all the others in support of Parsons's newly arrived Missourians, charging forward together as Williams was withdrawing opposite, lunging at the middle and left hard enough to give the "Rebel Yell," before bouncing off the centering Second Colored Kansas and the Fiftieth

Indiana, who brushed them rudely back with a shout of their own for a stand-off sufficiently safe for Rudd to descend down on the paternal side as the great-grand sire of a governor who was given the honor of his name on a short little street where David O. Dodd was hanged.

Rudd was faithful to the end, grudgingly surrendering in Texas after Marse Lee said it was all right, going just as Grant had granted in Virginia, with a mount and a gun, limping home on a "pore horse" to "his porer place" in south Arkansas that "had nothin' left but the dirt," to start over, to farm and father himself out of obscurity with a paragraph he would never read.

Parsons's Missourians, who everyone agreed were as fine a fighters as the South had anywhere, of whom, it was said, went about the beastly business of war with such a grim joy that they "never lost a man save by death," almost broke the Blue line in the final, desperate, heartbreaking assault as they mingled with the Twenty-sixth and Rudd's brave boys; then, themselves failing and falling back, as Walker's "Greyhounds" walked tiredly up, after trotting twenty-one miles since 2:30 that morning, and tried it themselves, walking hard in a hot-stepping clash around the Union left as Shaver had done—the going in and coming out being the pattern of a hard, deadly day that went in-point-of-fact, nowhere.

At this time Colored Kansas got its counterattacking revenge by overrunning a battery and bayoneting away the hope of surrender for an unlucky few who paid for what was being said about the Springs and the Mill.

So it was, after such a morning where for many the inexorable weight of the clock had at last lifted with the sun and dropped to an unburdening stop, that the Grays were resigned to a discursive exchange and then to a silence that fell over them all like a pall draping the dead.

In defending the initiative, Smith had wasted each of his states in rotation—first Arkansas, then Missouri, and then he wasted Texas besides. In sending Churchill in without Parsons, he lost them both, for not waiting on Walker, who was lost in his lonely turn; thus all was lost and Steele saved.

And, in a stuttering beat of this denouement, a musket ball purchased General Rice a long, painful exit home before buying him an even shorter passage to another more heroic place as one who lost his life but gained a slice of fame in an affair which by 12:30 dripped to its desultory finish as the final thousands of feet and hooves echoed safely over the Saline in the closing act of General Steele's retreat at Jenkins's Ferry.

Yet there was a kind of epilogue writ by a tight wad of desperate stragglers, as Dagmar and Joshua were rolled with a remnant of the panic-ridden rear guard downward toward the bridge.

"We've got to wait here," Joshua yelled, stopping in a small clearing by the trail within sight of the river, panting, grabbing her shirt, and jerking her back, saying, "The Iowa boys are going over first and then we go … with this guard … but when our turn comes, we'll follow quick, see … before the Johnnies come up, understand?"

"No! Let me go, Joshua! Takin' me won't do no good … jes' turn me a-loose …," she said trying to free herself. "It's over now … it don't matter none, so, jes' let me git back to my own people, Joshua, that's awl I want now! I ain't a-goin' no further, ye understand?!"

Joshua shook his head. "You're the only prisoner I got left and you're going," he said, pulling her with his free hand while holding his new musket, recently plucked from a dead man's tight fingers, in the other.

"It's over, Joshua … y'all won now … so, jes' let me go … let me git back, ye yar!? It won't do no good takin' me with ye … no good a-tall!" she yelled, stopping, pulling away from his grip, and pushing away, falling backward into some infantry rushing by.

"Move out of the damn way, Reb!" yelled a private, shoving her into the mud at Joshua's feet.

Joshua reached for her.

"Let me go, Joshua! I ain't a-comin' with ye," she yelled, rolling away, crawling through the crowd.

"Tom! Come back!" he called, leaning over, reaching after her among the stamping legs.

Then shots came from the trees, and the soldiers hastily formed in a ragged line facing the thicket, separating Joshua and Dagmar on either side of them.

"Stop! I say!" yelled Joshua, as the volley ripped over her and she wiggled under its cloud toward a treeline standing like shouldering stumps, its trunks and tops hidden by the smoke laying lazily across the little meadow like a heavy gray layer of lapping fog.

There was a shout. "Forward!" A yell.

The Blue line advanced tentatively, overstepping her. "Get out of the damn way!" said a soldier, tripping on her leg then kicking her ribs, before being knocked down himself by the surging line, then bouncing up for the explosion from the forest which knocked him down yet again. The Blue line now staggered backward, retreating away from several writhing clumps and exposing a curled-up Dagmar lying by the still soldier.

Dagmar again snaked forward between the Blues and the Grays as Marmaduke cavalry charged from the brush with a scream, jumping her and breaking the Blue line before it could reform and ramrod another volley.

But one horse paused.

"Tom!" yelled its rider, leaning down, losing his hat, "Get on!"

She rose from her knees and, with the rider's arm, swung deftly behind the saddle just as Joshua arrived and, afraid of shooting her, stabbed with his bayonet.

But the horse swung away, and the rider slashed a saber that Joshua parried, thrusting his bayonet again at the circling horse just outside his reach. As the bayonet missed once more, the horse came round in another rapid motion, slashing and rearing on its hind legs as if it were one great creature.

"You!" yelled Joshua, as hooves came down and the saber struck his upraised weapon.

"Joshua!" screamed Dagmar, pulling a pistol from Sergeant Curt's belt, while the horse spun back again, headed for the trees. "Let me go!"

"Yew should-a kilt me, boya!" yelled Curt, whipping the flank of the horse.

"I will now by damn!" Joshua said, steadying himself, raising his musket, aiming carefully at Curt's skull.

"Joshua! No! No!" screamed Dagmar as she saw the rifle shouldering up and quickly shot a little below its line of sight, the rifle kicking away as she and Curt disappeared into the forest and Joshua fell.

CHAPTER EIGHTEEN

Voilà comment on passe un pont sous la barbe de l'enemi!
—Napoleon, upon crossing the Berezina

One might say that old Tom Jenkins's Ferry had been Frederick Steele's Berezina, and like Kutuzov, who should have destroyed the *Grande Armée* there, Smith should've destroyed Steele on the Saline, not, as he did, thumbing away all hope of surpassing Taylor at the Sabine. His hidden, if obvious, purpose, always being to rise jealously level with a victorious junior, he only managed to fall below instead, not knowing the difficult but easy maxim that such subordinates should be shouted ever forward in admiration and never shortened back in imitation.

Thus, Smith had disappointed the South of her hoped-for Trans-Mississippi Cannae, and with stalemate elsewhere, she lost the dream of unsaddling Lincoln off his war horse and landing him hard upon the soft blanket of compromise spread deftly upon the ground by the curling Copperheads ("Crats") beneath their votes of '64.

So, though she won much, in '64 she lost more. As Atlanta fell and Richmond was taken by the throat, the battlefields became little more than a ballot box of fire—Republican versus Democrat—"fight and talk," "vote and fight"—then and beyond—into Lincoln's reelection, surrender, the so-called Reconstruction—past and future—on and on—the great American contradiction working itself ever onward toward its inexorable tragic destiny of avoiding dissolution.

But for a moment, the South had herself a victory. One of her greatest: as in Louisiana Banks fled down the Red and into Arkansas as Steele pulled across his last wagons, stragglers and beleaguered guards. He burned his legendary bridge *sous la barbe* of Kirby Smith's black one, only to find, if anything, that things were not easy on the other side. The "bottoms" were not easy, the weather even worse, and the Gray phantom Fagan appeared at long last, riding through the mist and mud in the person of Major Elliott's little battalion of brave Missourians, pushing the Blues almost to panic hard against the *ravelins* of the

Rock's redoubt, where, still clutching three stands of Confederate colors, the proud Second Colored Kansas led the way in, as the Blues force marched hard upon the smiling, dry, and very well-fed Minnesotans reluctantly waiting to hear all about what they had missed.

They would have heard something like Captain Heinemann of Salomon's staff saying:

> Steele knows that he is a West Pointer, and doesn't appear to know anything about Arkansas, where he is or what he is doing. Damn these regulars! They map out battles on paper, draw their salaries and— smoke cigars.

And Heinemann about the retreat:

> Save our artillery and baggage, run like whiteheads for the Saline bottom, cut through anything that puts itself in our way, and with the river at our back, the bogs at our flanks, face about and fight for our lives.

Or, "a strange and wild time," as one laconic private put it, perhaps best of all, remembering the nightmarishly dark march along a fire-lit road burning with hundreds of abandoned wagons, while thousands of starvlings busily bargained hardtack for two dollars a bite, or a silver watch, or any small piece of looted *bijou* a soldier could find or steal yet again from the pockets of the dead or defenseless, as Steele's army slogged three more swampy, rainy days to a capital which suddenly seemed so strangely like "home" that the Blue army would warm itself there in semi-besieged comfort till told it was safe to come out again in '65.

But let us book the dead and lost: While the Grays had lost slightly more at the Ferry (about 800 plus to 700 plus), in going south, Steele had, of course, not found Commissary Banks, much less Texas, running instead to his barricade on the Cayas, spending his forty days in the wilderness losing some 3,000 men, 10 cannons, 635 wagons, and 2,500 mules, all spun out behind in a swath of depredation and destruction like an erratic storm.

As for the Grays in Arkansas, while they drove off a larger army with two victories and a draw, losing a third fewer men, with hardly any missing, and pitching almost endless stacks of rifles into wagons and hitching up mules for the asking, Kirby Smith quite simply never could find his reputation again— not anywhere among the colors, cannons, and corpses—no matter how long and hard he looked. But he was handed up to the honor of monikering as

"Hydrocephalus"—a promotion from the pen of a president's son whose own elevation to lieutenant general did nothing to tie his tongue or dry his ink. Richard Taylor, being a man who could not only out-fight but out-write his superior, shooed him to his retiring postwar perch on a Sewanee mountain to teach boys numbers that never did quite add up for Taylor, no matter how hard the old eagle did the sums.

Yet, for Banks, it was even worse, and for Richard Taylor, therefore, even better, and yet worse. His French Prince Polignac's paltry Louisiana infantry (2,000), even with such others as he could give (Tom Green's Texas cavalry of 3,000), was still outnumbered five to one as they pushed 25,000 Blues along like feists yapping at Banks's heels, barking loudly always to seem bigger than he was by "by sending drummers to beat calls, lighting campfires, blowing bugles, and rolling empty wagons over fence rails," chasing him in a southward romp from Grand Ecore to Natchitoches to Cloutierville for a good snarling at Monett's Ferry, then following snappingly to Alexandria, as the Union army in Louisiana, from Mansfield to Pleasant Hill downward, lost some 5,500 killed, wounded, and missing—like in Arkansas, a third more—while Porter's paralleling fleet ran the Confederate's gauntlet of guns hiding on the rising riverbank high above Banks's boats floating below on the dropping sandy Red. An admiral who was ambushed from the weeds, losing his best, the 700-ton, *Eastport,* below Grand Ecore, sunk before the holing of his brave little *Cricket* nineteen times, holing her in five minutes, then stroking her with thirty-eight more (losing 31 of her 50) as she floated helplessly back from the shallow brown ribbon past the freshly sunken *Champion 3,* who went down as her broken boiler scalded 175 runaway slaves—killed by what was said to be one of the "most fatal shots fired during the war." Then the little *Cricket* watched as the *Juliet* and the *Fort Hindman* were riddled up as she had been, leaving the sinking transport *Champion 5* to be captured exsanguinating on a sandbar like a shot-through turtle; with all the rest and remainder escaping via the "*deus ex machina*" miracle of engineer half-colonel Jo Bailey's raising of the Red with wing dams like the parting of another sea of that description in a moment of perhaps less divine but no less imploring desperation.

It was, in sum, as one of Banks's staff officers said, "an unhappy affair." So much so that Mr. Banks, in a fit of pique, compounded that unhappiness by burning Alexandria to the ground.

One witness diaried his city's death as:

> There is no use trying to tell abut the sights I saw and the sounds

of distress I heard. It cannot be told and could hardly be believed if it were told. Crowds of people, men, women, children, and soldiers, were running with all they could carry, when the heat would become unbearable, and dropping all, they would flee for their lives, leaving everything but their bodies to burn. Over the levee the sights and sounds were harrowing. Thousands of people, mostly women, children and old men, were wringing their hands as they stood by the little piles of what was left of all their worldly possessions.

Though the Union armies never ventured south again from their rock in Arkansas, or north from their spot in Louisiana, and while Taylor and Smith could rightly claim one of the greatest triumphs of the war, their victory was savored with the bitterness of all such success unseasoned by the spice of conquest.

Taylor broke off finally fighting with Banks but never with Smith:

The fruits of Mansfield have been turned to dust and ashes. Louisiana, from Natchitoches to the Gulf, is a howling wilderness and her people are starving. Arkansas is probably as great a sufferer.

And again to Smith:

The destruction of this country by the enemy exceeds anything in history. For many miles every dwelling house, every Negro cabin, every cotton gin, every corn-crib, and even chicken houses have burned to the ground, every fence torn down and the fields torn up by the hoofs of horses and the wheels of wagons. Many hundreds of persons are utterly without shelter.

So, "the fruits of Mansfield" did, like the Confederacy itself, indeed turn to "dust and ashes" and, in the end, came to little but that very suffering and, of course, sacrifice, conceit and courage, defeat and dissolution of yet another Lost Kingdom—nothing more—nothing less, just as Prince Richard had said.

PHILLIP H. MCMATH

CHAPTER NINETEEN

*The chronic irritation of a hope deferred would be joyfully ended
with the negro, and the sympathies of his whole race would be due his
native South.*
    —Patrick R. Cleburne, Major General, CSA

One can be great without being a genius, and a genius without being great. The South had one great man in Lee, one genius in Forrest—yet they were military and separate; while the North combined genius and greatness in one— where it was needed most, political not military—in Lincoln. And since no army, regardless of how well led or well inspired, can long surpass its political reason to be, the South, absent a stroke of good fortune which it never got, nor divine intervention which could never be granted, was from the beginning doomed.

So on Palm Sunday Lee surrendered and on Good Friday, Lincoln was shot. History was finished with them and the war was over.

Or so it seemed. In the East, that is. In the West, there were others who saw it differently. Here surrender seemed out of place. After all, they were winning. It's one of the war's great ironies that this grandly wild Gray region— half the size of Europe—only just to the left of the Great River—always considered hopeless by Richmond and from which it took much and sent nothing, was the only thing still standing in '65. Now the hiding and running, armyless, almost friendless Davis, by surrendering Vicksburg, had swapped half his dominion in a search for shoes in a small seminary town in Pennsylvania. Davis sent only his dumb, deaf, and debilitated strays to wear their stars west of Memphis as recompense—out of sight, as it were, if not out of hearing. He now hoped that if he could but cross over into this gigantic land of his greatest neglect—touching a Mexico that had no love of a proud nation that had just stolen half its land—if he could but regain this severed portion of his Lost Kingdom, he could fight on—Lee or no Lee.

Suddenly King Davis found all this wide western territory much grander somehow than the paltry little strip between the Rappahannock and the

Potomac in which he had been enthroned so far from the much greater part of his realm, arching out, he now saw as for the first time, above the West Indies—a gulf, a sea, and an ocean splitting a continent—straddling above New Spain—Texas, Arkansas, Missouri, Louisiana, the Indian Territory—and the Mississippi flowing to that Gulf and then to the Cuban Caribbean of his youthful glory breaking out south and westward into a vast new world that had always been *La Florida's* natural destiny—a land of many shades and sounds, tones and tongues, that could have been his, had he but listened to that Cordelia of his nature, as first, Cleburne, and, finally, Lee, said he should, by granting the Africans freedom in return for loyalty, turn the moral and manpower tables on these shopkeepers, who knew little or nothing of anything west or south of St. Louis, or really much cared.

In Georgia, Major General Patrick Ronyane Cleburne, the British Army-trained, Anglo-Irish Arkansas lawyer from Helena via County Cork, who, by saving the Army of Tennessee twice, was described by Lee as a "meteor shinning from a clouded sky," an anti-slavery Southern nationalist who, in urging the freeing of the slaves, penned a petition of desperation for Davis in the post new year of frigid, foreboding '64, pleading from his frozen, dark quarters near Dalton but a few days before David O. Dodd was to swing a little too close to the ground, an outline, as it were, of saving the country and, as if one were needed, of the consequences of "subjugation" to such Republican tyranny, if they did not.

> It means the history of this historic struggle will be written by the enemy; that our youth will be trained by Northern school teachers; will learn from Northern school books their version of the war; will be impressed by all the influences of history and education to regard our gallant dead as traitors, our maimed veterans as fit objects of derision.

And on slavery:

> Apart from the assistance that home and foreign prejudice against slavery has given to the North, slavery is a source of great strength to the enemy in a purely military point of view, by supplying him with an army from our granaries; but it is our most vulnerable point, a continued embarrassment, and in some respect an insidious weakness.

And his proposal:

> ... that we immediately commence training a large reserve of the

most courageous of our slaves, and further that we guarantee freedom in a reasonable time to every slave in the South who shall
remain true to the Confederacy in this war. As between the loss of
independence and the loss of slavery, we assume that every patriot
will freely give up the latter—give up the negro slave rather than
be a slave himself. If we are correct in this assumption it only remains
to show how great this national sacrifice is, in all human probabili-
ties, to change the current of success and sweep the invaders from
our country.

And on the slave himself:

The chronic irritation of a hope deferred would be joyfully ended
with the negro, and the sympathies of his whole race would be due
to his native South. It would restore confidence in an early termi-
nation of the war with all its inspiring consequences, and even if contrary to all expectations the enemy should succeed in overrunning
the South, instead of finding a cheap ready-made means of holding
it down, he would find a common hatred and thirst for vengeance,
which would break into acts at every favorable opportunity, would
prevent him from settling on our lands, and render the South a very
unprofitable conquest. It would remove forever all selfish taint from
our cause and place independence above every question of property.
The very magnitude of the sacrifice itself, such as no nation has every
voluntarily made before, would appall our enemies, destroy his spirit
and his finances, and fill our hearts with a pride and singleness of
purpose which would clothe us with a new strength in battle. Apart
from all other aspects of the question, the necessity for more fighting is upon us. We can only get a sufficiency by making the negro
share the danger and hardships of the war. If we arm and train him
and make him fight for his country in her hour of dire distress, every
consideration of principle and policy demand that we should set him
and his whole race who side with us free.

And the Cause:

It is said that slavery is all that we are fighting for, and if we give it
up we give up all. Even if this were true, which we deny, slavery is not
all our enemies are fighting for. It is merely the pretense to establish
sectional superiority and a more centralized form of government, and

to deprive us of our rights and liberties. We have now briefly proposed a plan which we believe will save our country.

P. R. Cleburne, Major-General Commanding Division;

D. C. Govan, Brigadier-General;

John E. Murry, Colonel 5th Arkansas;

G. F. Baucum, Colonel 8th Arkansas;

Peter Snyder, Lt. Col., Commanding 6th and 7th Arkansas;

E. Warfield, Lt. Col. 2nd Arkansas;

A. B. Hardcastle, Colonel 32nd and 45th Mississippi;

M. P. Lowrey, Brigadier General;

F. A. Ashford, Major 16th Alabama;

John W. Colquitt, Colonel 1st Arkansas;

Rich J. Person, Major 3rd and 5th Confederate;

G. S. Deakins, Major 3rd and 8th Tennessee;

J. H. Collett, Captain Commanding 7th Texas;

J. H. Kelly, Brigadier-General Commanding Cavalry Division.

January 2, 1864

Army of Tennessee, CSA

The plan was suppressed, and Cleburne's promotion to lieutenant general deferred. And Forrest, when he heard of it, asked, "If we do this, what are we fighting for?" If Cleburne and Southern nationalists like him were fighting for independence, Forrest, the old African seller, was certainly fighting for slavery and its harvests; just as Lee, who hated slavery, was certainly fighting for Virginia and her honor; while Smith, Marmaduke, and Taylor were fighting for the Constitution, the "consensual" Union, or at least their version of it.

For their part, Fagan, Price, and Shelby wanted nothing less than a New Kingdom, while Churchill, Medora, Titus, Curt, Dagmar, James Rudd, and the Indians were simply fighting against an invader led by that nonabolitionist emancipator, Lincoln, and his generals—the slave-owning Grant and anti-abolitionist McClellan, who were in it, of course, for the Union; while Porter and Steele were in it from duty, just as Banks and Joshua were in it from desire—the man wanting fame, the boy an adventure off the farm.

And what of Septimus? To be sure, while he certainly would agree that it was indeed a cold winter, even for Camden, none of this cut any ice with him. He agreed with Forrest—it was all about slavery—and as such, like Stonewall, his personal salvation. For him, the war was about freedom, nothing less.

But Jefferson Davis quite simply had been trapped for too long in an eastern Virginia tidewater controlled by his enemies to listen and much too long by an idea that he had always been but a step from embracing, but never quite could, not even as he sat with his lifelong slave and best friend, James Pemberton, together those happy days in Havana (when Cleburne was in Helena), where, after all, *La Florida* began. This slave, who ran Brierfield, had advised him to go after Knox's febrile death, to grieve but also to plan a new Brierfield, a new future, and a new Cotton Kingdom. Now it was too late, with Cleburne dead at Franklin, shot through the breast at the breastworks of a lost battle of a lost war, where he had been foolishly sent by that hopped-up, one-legged, hopping Hotspur, John Bell Hood, who finally had finished his destruction of the Army of Tennessee that was given him by Davis over the objections of Lee, who could characterize a man or thing at a touch, saying Hood "was all Lion and no Fox."

Pat Cleburne, then, becoming but one more commingled, twisted corpse among thousands—Blue and Gray—sleeping in the supreme sacrifice of having transmuted a verb from plural to singular—the United States "*are*" to "*is*"— in what is given out as a necessary but heartbreaking national sacrament of blood-bonding on a spot memorialized today so sublimely by that great American symbol—a Pizza Hut.

A far better memorial is at Mrs. John McGavock's mansion, Carnton, a plantation, where even now upon her surgical parlor floor the blood refuses to be scrubbed away by the endless varnishing of assiduous time. For upon her back porch the bootless Cleburne was unloaded, having been looted of kepe, diary, watch, wallet, sword-belt, pistol, and life by lesser men, the mules wagoning him up with three others to be plopped in a row—crumpled, dirty, disheveled forms of uniformed flesh—three youthful generals—Adams, Strahl, and Granbury—side-by-side near him—lying still in a mute quartet of gray-jawed death's dried gore, flecking dark red over beard and golden braid upon the broad back boards behind the kitchen window near a swing where children used to kick and sing, reposing in that folded-up but powerful way the dead have of possessing us for a moment longer than we would ever really wish or admit to.

And what of the new strategy in the Far West? Davis asked, with Cleburne gone and Tennessee, Georgia, and Virginia done for. The Virginian said, "no"— no savagery—no guerrilla war—which, unknown to the evermore tired gentleman from the Old Dominion, had really been underway from the start and had not stopped because of something agreed upon far away over Mr. McLean's kitchen table.

Yes, after Richmond's fall, even after Appomattox, Davis would not listen and, ever deaf to defeat, heard instead the distant, previously unheard guns of the Far West, because, as one Union colonel complained, "The operations of the enemy guerrillas in Arkansas are far more vindictive and remorseless than anywhere else under my observation."

So "remorseless," in fact, that after Camden, Brigadier Napoleon B. Buford, commander of the Delta, opined from behind his Helena bastion, "Why do we continue to occupy the interior of Arkansas?" and noting to Lincoln in a quick scribble pretended for another, advised him to hold the Mississippi at Helena, while anchoring Steele on the Rock, tethering him tenuously by rail to De Vall's Bluff, then give Fort Smith back to the Red and Gray guerrillas altogether with the Indian Territory; the Grays proving Buford's point by '64–'65, so much so, according to one Mister Sutherland, things resembled another time and place upon another North-South field.

> The situation facing the Federal Army in Arkansas bore an eerie resemblance to that facing the United States Army in Vietnam, for it seemed to men like Steele that while they controlled the towns, most of the Rebel countryside belonged to the Rebel guerrillas.

President Davis saw Kirby Smith safely ensconced in Shreveport and Price, ever dreaming of Missouri, marching unmolested past Steele to Kansas City and, though turned back, marching past again—unchallenged in his going and in his coming by Steele, causing one Unionist to wag of the epicurean supremo:

> General Steele at Little Rock lives quite like an Eastern prince with his harem, wines, dogs, horses, equipages, and everything in great style.

Mr. Lincoln's Little Rock Republican governor, Isaac Murphy, at whose feet the famous fresh flowers fell in '61 from Mrs. Trapnall's hand, had by '65 wilted into saying:

> The feeling is that unless strong reinforcements are soon here, and more energy displayed by the military authorities, Arkansas will be again in the hands of the Rebels.

This was too much.

In December, Steele was removed to Florida.

But Grant was too much, and, in April, Davis was run to ground in Georgia.

Then Lee and Lincoln went home—Lincoln reclining in black and Lee in gray, Lincoln to a grave and Lee to kneel beside an ex-slave and pray.

CHAPTER TWENTY

One equal temper of heroic hearts,
Made weak by time and fate, but strong in will
To strive, to seek, to find, and not to yield.
—Ulysses, *Tennyson*

Major General "Jo" Shelby, after making life splendidly miserable for Steele in the Rock, at last rode north with Price on his famous, dream-obsessed returning invasion of Missouri in '64, where, with Fagan, Marmaduke, and Cabal in tow, according to old Pap's recollection at least, Price's Gray army "marched 1,434 miles and fought forty-three battles and skirmishes," threatened St. Louis, then, turning up the Missouri River, raided west where Shelby, along the way, took Glasgow and four hundred Blue prisoners, then Sedalia, "stampeding" seven hundred more, fighting sharp actions at Lexington, Little Blue River, Independence, Bryam's Ford and, just south of Kansas City, at a place called Newtonia, where Pap finally found a defeat sufficiently serious to hand Shelby's cavalry the final honor of saving the army once again, as, with Marmaduke and Cabal captured, Price reluctantly turned south, leaving Missouri for the last time in the war as he and Shelby cobbled together a mutually desperate retreating run through the Indian Territory which one survivor would describe as "arduous"— swinging wide of the Union cavalry at Fort Smith before dipping back into Arkansas—their glorious, suffering mutuality ending at last in the quietude of a western Ouachita mountain wilderness where Shelby saluted sadly then rode his depleted division away for a winter's rest in the hiding safety of Pittsburgh, Texas.

Here, rapidly regrouped, and more rapidly bored, he soon dreamed of the great "grand" thing Lincoln had long feared someone might—a Trans-Mississippi-Mexican Confederation. For this, the fire-staring Shelby plotted to replace Shreveport's sedentary Smith with a newer, younger, Simon Bolivar— Simon Bolivar Buckner, that is—the Kentuckian who, after Chapultepec, had walked with his West Point mates, Richard Anderson and Sam Grant. Anderson would later survive Seven Days, Sharpsburg, Fredericksburg, Chancellorsville,

Gettysburg, and the Wilderness, and become the hero and savior of Lee's army at Spotsylvania, saved from his old buddy Sam Grant by a night's march, beating the Ohioan to a Virginia crossroads of that name on Lee's right flank in the spring horrors of '64. His old hiking partner had shifted his Blue foot a step too late that very hot May day; but in April of '48 he had stepped in time with Buckner and Anderson—single-filing up the sacred Mexican volcano of Popocatepetl; weathering the rain by sleeping in a "roofless" cabin; curling together as boy-generals into a blanketed innocent ball, before starting up again in wind and snow, climbing above the clouds till, like minor deities, they surveyed the valley sunlit beneath through storm and broken cloud—supernal white giving way to earthy green and mundane terrestrial brown—inspiring Buckner to say, then and later, that "Mexico was the romance of our life," before coming back down again to fight each other even more than they had the Mexicans, but not before a ruined Grant, drunk and destitute in New York, surrendered meekly to Buckner for food and fare back to find his fairer, ever-faithful, Julia waiting patiently for his return. So Grant would indeed likewise return the good deed at Fort Donelson as Buckner surrendered to him in his faithful turn, without fear, his Gray army, then came talking, dining, and laughing in Sam's tent after the tendering to the one he had walked up a different kind of volcano with on the Cumberland River revetments named for an obscure Confederate brigadier who had the good fortune of being Andrew Jackson's nephew. But good Buckner stalled a bit while that fox Forrest made his girt-deep escape through a swamp of ice out the back door, his horses breaking the sheets with pawing hooves, as his freezing infantry followed waist high in a cracking, chilling wake, wading out to meet Sam Grant again the very next year, this time not at a fort but at a church in the backwoods named for peace in Hebrew. Yes, indeed, it was this same old Mexican hand, that Jo Shelby wanted, this self-same Simon Bolivar, Grant's and Anderson's pal, whose head he would crown as regent of his future South West Empire in the land of volcanoes conceived in the hypnotic winter revelries of Jo Shelby's flame-burnt brain that thought never of surrender but only of a fresh new glory and ever-newer Kingdoms.

But these revels of winter slowly gave way to the reality of spring, and the famous Missouri Cavalry Division soon received word from Shreveport to saddle up again for Arkansas, and it did, trotting back there once more where, near the little town of Fulton, the news of Appomattox fell hard upon them like the sound of a distant catastrophe sputtering off the tongues of its fleeing survivors as Sam Grant accepted the quiet, dignified surrender of another Mexican War

West Pointer, Robert E. Lee, in a farmhouse in Virginia. This exploded the other Washington into fireworks and, as if there hadn't been enough noise already, Lincoln asked the band to up and play Dixie loud as possible while his boy waved a captured Stars-and-Bars from an upper White House window.

It was time to "bind up the wounds," Lincoln had said. But they were too deep for Jo Shelby and with a morose and grim-faced determination, he circled his division of horse back into Texas to meet with Buckner and Smith to fight on—in Mexico if need be, with the French or Mexicans, or whoever would have them, he said.

Dagmar decided to go too, and so left Jim Curt to his barren piece of nearly ruined ground in Louisiana, while she rode off with her cavalier hero, Jo Shelby. Try as she might she never could find the brown package by a tree but Titus had survived anyway, so, she strapped on Heidi's husband's saber as a kind of symbol of her newfound independence among men; kissed Medora, Nora, Ephey, and Aunt Essie on the cheek; Ulysses, Pegasus, and Wagon Wheel on the nose, and Titus on the ear and neck, who, after telling her a tearful goodbye, finally gave up on all Arcadias himself, selling one for a loss and forgetting the other, then pilgrimaging his women the other way with Ulysses, Pegasus, and the hound, leading them all deep into the Arkansas Delta to find good land which Titus thought might be just cheap enough to start over again. But, soon disappointed, the family finally crossed the Mississippi instead in '66, a little south of where De Soto had lost his slaves and swine, if not his soul—Titus rafting the other way into the state of that name only to find nothing there either but the same desolation—carpetbaggers, wandering freedmen, Yankee soldiers and scalawags. Then in '67, he turned north toward Medora's poor but, nevertheless, eating family, who took them in. Thus he completed the circle that had begun when they were children and ended with an age, renouncing Paganism forever by selling Pegasus to a carpetbagger for money and a mule to help Ulysses wagon them into the dirty front yard of a long-lost sister. The matching mule team twisted around a big green shade tree loud enough to bestir a hound to bark as if in recognition before sniffing to a snarl at Wagon Wheel till they both got tired and made a tail-wagging separate peace. For them, man and animal, mule and dog, at least, the Civil War was at last over, but, as one struggle ends another begins, so the thing to be known as Reconstruction was thus begun with all eyes now focused on the end of a century that but began another like a finish line that ended and started but another race of another age for their children to run end-to-end—to-and-fro—year-to-year—century-to-century—in all the progress of progress. If you want to call it that; if one can ever believe in such an outlandish Yankee idea—the dead dropping in turn one by one into eternity and out of the melodrama of time and endless flux whose fate had said they should live through for some reason or other. "God's will," Medora would have insisted, and did say as long as she had breath to repeat it to those who might listen and agree because it seemed as good a reason as any, and the only one that ever made any sense to her.

But Shelby was of a different mold and, not wishing or accepting the turning of the drama's final page, could only ask who might improvise with him some newer lines. A few Whites said no and then the Reds—Comanches and Choctaws—said they wanted to go home and so ponied off to fight the Blues some more on the plains till finally beaten. Yet about a thousand remained and so Shelby, leaving Postlewaite the pet black bear behind, trotted his "Iron Brigade," as it had become known, though it was now a division, into Texas to meet at Marshall with Buckner and some others (Smith, though near, was absent), like the Reds, to fight the United States forever—to make Texas a new country again, rather than live in defeat under Federal tyranny and its Blue humiliation.

Jo's "Grand Design" was simple, and, since *les absents ont toujours tort*, the fault was clearly Smith's for being gone, and the right remedy lay, perforce, in his ready removal—so it was done and done quickly, with Buckner set in his place. Spake Shelby thus:

> Gentleman, the army no longer has any confidence in General Smith. We must concentrate everything we have on the Brazos River at once, and the men must have a leader whom they can trust. Fugitives from Lee and Johnston will join us by the thousands, and we will be able, at the very least, to interpose an army of a hundred thousand men between them and disaster. Mr. Davis is on his way here, and he alone has the right to treat to surrender. Our intercourse with the French is perfect. Count de Polignac is our emissary to Louis , and General Preston should go at once to Mexico to learn from General Bazaine whether it is to be peace or war between us. Every step to the Río Grande must be fought over; we will march into Mexico and reinstate Juárez or espouse the cause of Maximilian. It makes no difference which.

Then Jo paused for effect, drawing in his breath as prelude to a dramatic coda, adding, "Surrender is a word which neither myself or my division understand."

There was applause, and then Shelby easily flattered Buckner into sup-planting Smith. It seemed a good start, but Lincoln and Grant stopped the "thousands" with their clever generosity to the gentleman Lee and soon Smith suggested a surrender at Shreveport while Davis, insufficiently covered with a loving Cordelia's coat, got caught cold in Georgia and was quickly chained by an embarrassed upper-half-nation, till he was quietly released to write some tedious memoirs, proving it's sometimes better to hang with a loyal fool than bore the world with scribbling and long living.

Yet Count Polignac did, indeed, make it back to France, but as none's emis-sary but his own, returning to his estates to wait, not for the Mexicans, but for the Prussians, who soon obliged him with yet another glorious war—Bazaine versus Bismarck—Polignac fighting this time not for Sevastopol of the Crimea, nor New Orleans of the Confederacy, but for Paris of his own country, as Bazaine followed him home from bloody Mexico to cover France with the same at Sedan in '71, thus sowing the seeds of sorrow for '14 and all that it has meant till now.

But our lonely paladin, Shelby, persisted and rode his Iron remnant south-west, and, like Moscoso, whose Spanish trail he borrowed out of Arkansas, at last touched the Brazos but, unlike that brave subaltern conquistador, did not turn round again, but kept on riding toward the Río Grande and its Bonaparte nephew's throne built for the setting of a blond Viennese butterfly collector with his beautiful Belgian princess upon, somewhere south of Texas.

Indeed, this poker-playing state of Texas has always been the Joker in the American deck. Consummated in the twin Austin-Houston passion of '36 from a conceiving moment in Washington—Arkansas, that is, Texas was born in the Southern Anglo victory over the Browns; a slaver upsetting the balance. Indeed, Adams Junior had said Massachusetts should walk out if Texas should walk in. But it was only after a wink at Britain that a jealous Uncle Sam, at the risk of divorce (the Bay State ever being a hot-bed of secession), only very reluctantly opened his door and let her in. It was an uneasy adoption as Texas always kept things in a stir, siding with one group against the others, and, knowing she was only half welcome, stormed out in '61 for a more comfortable live-in with those smiling Southern siblings who had always been more friendly.

But because of her the Mexican War had been fought and new territories were soon wombing out as this extended Western family upset the balance before the greatest American war of all.

The North grumped that Quincy had been right after all, it was all because of Texas; or, touching Destouches's axiom the other way, by her presence rather than her absence, was she always wrong.

America's new brood now grew up fast into states—bounding up west and north of *El Paso del Norte* where, if one recalls, Don Juan de Oñate, emissary of one of those other, intruding, Habsburgs, Phillip II of Spain, nailed his *La Toma* to a cottonwood, praying for God's blessing on this new land, but which had in time become another kind of "taking" for the ever-expanding American colossus; taking the upper half of Mexico, and yet, because of that, becoming wildly different from anything east of St. Louis—slave or free—Blue or Gray. Which Kingdom would finally prevail in Manifest Destiny?

In April 1865 Texas, with her Southern sisters ruined, half of Mexico possessed, was, for the moment at least, an independent woman of some means, and, unsullied as she was by Yankee insistence, the question became, "What would she do now that it was all over?"

It was into this vast question mark that Shelby and his faithful flew from defeat and dreamed of finding at last a final, unlost victory. But Buckner was more reluctant than perhaps he had seemed and soon returned to Shreveport to assume command of a reality that could only be released by its quick surrender (always his solution in a pinch) for the more profitable burden of a business in New Orleans. Besides, he had been to Mexico, fought there and hiked around a bit—was a much better tourist with buddies Grant and Anderson than he ever wished to be with Shelby. One Mexican volcano was enough for him. It would be better, he decided, if one simply started over again and got rich, which he promptly did before returning home to become the Democratic governor of Kentucky in '97; honoring himself further by the final favor of lowering old friend Grant's remaining mortality down into an immortal grave, then running himself up for vice president in '96 for good measure.

In letting bygones be bygones, the South's Simon simply proved forever that he was always more Buckner than Bolivar—much better with business than with bullets—leaving his good fortune in one to his family and his ill fortune in the other to his son, Simon, three-star West Pointer Buckner Jr., who, in emulating the wrong side of the matter, managed to become the last American general killed in 1945—putting the final touches on a dying Japanese Empire at a strange island place called Okinawa—the westernmost Pacific outpost, one might say, of Manifest Destiny—dropping more Bucknerian blood upon a field than his father had ever felt really necessary.

No, *Bashido* was not for Buckner Senior, nor any such notion of Samurai honor. Not for him the thing that made the cave so eerily quiet, weighted as it was with the strange patience that waiting suicides always seem to have—the probing Americans finding them all propped dead against the wall's half light—Lieutenant General Mitsuru Ushijima's entire staff—who only moments before had killed Buckner *fils* as a fitting end to the last great battle of the last great war of the last great, Lost Japanese Kingdom—Ushijima saying goodbye "in a fatherly way," a surviving sergeant said. He then took his sword from a second, and straddle-legging down before a clean white ceremonial cloth spread delicately over a ledge above the sea, plunged the dagger in as an atonement for defeat and an incipient dishonor.

Yes, to be sure, Shreveport was much better than any kind of *seppeku*—one simply didn't do such things in the age of chivalry. New Orleans was better still. Besides, one just might get elected in a border state—or bury a president—or bequeath a business in a will—make a comeback.

Jo would just have to go on without him—and did. And, after adventuring with desperados in ordering things in Waco and Waxahachie, saving the Texas gold in Austin, and feasting at New Braunfels while the ever-watchful Dagmar, in sounding the alarm, saved his horses from nocturnal rustlings on the plains, Shelby reached San Antonio safely in June to settle law and order on this bustling, chaotic Anglo-Mexican town of ten thousand, prospering in the crossroads of Confederate contraband—cotton, cannon, and *carne*. Here he set up shop at the Menger—the "Mingos" as it was called—which fronted the Alamo's hallowed facade where Texas found a victory born from defeat. It was a very grand hotel, indeed, where T. Roosevelt would soon recruit his own version of Spanish horseback adventures for a follow-on war in the West Indies—Rough Riders saddling up in the lobby bar to drown old defeats within the depths of the same Irish soldier's song as Shelby's did, drinking deeply of the twin glories of gore and grog.

> Riflemen, shoot me a fancy shot,
> Straight at the heart of yon vidette;
> Ring me a ball on the glittering spot;
> That shines on his breast like an amulet.

Here Jo plotted with the Texas commanding general "Prince" John Magruder, freshly up from the coast; the Gray governors of Missouri, Louisiana, and Texas; and a coterie of Rebel generals on the lam, who, to everyone's shock, soon confronted the dusty figure of Kirby Smith himself descending in disguise from a ambulance whirling up before the Alamo's immortal plaza. Smith, fresh from surrendering at Galveston all that remained of his Lost "Smithdom," had, he said, merely ridden across Texas for a meal, a clean bed, and a chatting drink at the Mingo with his brave boys.

Jo, embarrassed by the sight of such a king so recently usurped, saluted, and offered him his army back. It didn't work. He was too old, Smith said, had now "become a name," and wanted no more war—had only come to say for them to do the same, then smiling painfully at the expected answer, slept calmly on his Mingo sheets, drank and ate a bit more, then said farewell before slipping into the dust again heading ahead for a hide first in Mexico then in Havana to see who might hang and who might not. But fearing that he "might be hanged yet," he tarried still. "Mercy on us! We split, we split! Farewell!" Yet no enchanted isle it was for him, he patiently listened for the storm to pass, then, since "the rarer action is in virtue than in vengeance," was permitted to return "to seek a newer world," he said, where, though much was taken, enough remained, to sire up eleven postwar Smiths, made in a bed with a Miranda who first made him a shirt for his blessed wounds from First Manassas. Here, despite the unending noise of Richard Taylor in page and parlor, prancing upon the world's stage with prince and president, ever pleading, of course, about what had happened on the Red; this unmoving Smith did quietly achieve his greatest glory of all—the Sewanee mountain magic of teaching boys to "follow knowledge like a sinking star" as from a secret book.

In a word, a quiet Tennessee home was enough for him, as it should be for any man—mule—or mutt, to have. And he did till '93.

CHAPTER TWENTY-ONE

*I saw, or imagined I saw, a great empire beyond the Río. This river
they call the great river.*
— *Major General J. O. Shelby, CSA*

General, then Colonel, Powell Clayton, it will be recalled, sender of the
famous "flying column" to the wounded, good man Francis, who, at old man
Marks's Mill was encircled by Fagan and Shelby like hounds around a gut-shot
Postlewaite, while the Pennsylvanian Powell, the future tycoon governor-
generalissimo and, ultimately, U.S. senator from Arkansas, did wait and wonder, till able, under a flag of truce, to retrieve the stretcher-ridden, future
railroad-building (ever-grateful) Republican governor of Iowa into the Blue
lines at Powell's Pine Bluff—our old bear Drake, remember him?

This was all done, of course, out of a sense of duty, laced, too, one supposes,
with the ulterior hope that in the fullness of power and patience, Powell would
get himself moved up by such as Drake, friends bonded by the brotherhood of
war, to higher things, like appointment by William McKinley, ambassador to
the same country in which Jo Shelby, victor at the Mill, now likewise hoped to
cross into for even greater glory than what had happened in Arkansas or
Missouri.

So it was that Shelby's mounted thousand were at last poised to wade into
that tragically exotic Indo-Latin land of the Eagle and Serpent not that far from
where their erstwhile enemy's son, Powell Clayton Jr., major, U.S. Army, in
noble loyalty to the notorious bad luck that all such sons seem to have, would
die honorably attempting a "flying column" of his own while dealing with some
mestizo *bandidos* racing for the same *Río Grande del Norte* that seemed always to
offer refuge, repute, and ruin all at once—dying, not in the quick fatal snap of
a few bullets near where his sire had been *numero uno* for eight years, but in
simply falling from his horse.

Indeed, it was this obscure major's death, more than anything else, even that
of "General C," as Adeline called him, "C" dying it seemed from the shocking
presidential election of a Democrat from Virginia, as any other mortal cause—

that is, it was the death of a son, rather than a nation awash in the deaths of sons, or even a famous husband, that set the good widow Clayton to thinking.

Miss Adeline McGraw, the dedicated Rebel spy from the river hamlet of Helena; daughter of a steamboating Confederate father, who became postwar mistress of Moscow's *Linwood* plantation, which had reconstructed itself a tad to the northeast of Mount Elba where "C" had waded Spellman across the Saline for the Mill; then, just as quick, found herself as her state's First Lady moving to a fine river house on "Carpetbagger Row" in the capital Rock; the houses now all gone, except for one lone survivor compromising herself, like shabby gentility in need of a job, as an office building, straddled as she is between a modern monstrosity on one side, and a mausoleum of computers on the other, but mounted then as one among a string of proud Victorian sisters; mansions set in a victorious line of what the parvenu Yankees promptly, and for them, quite properly, proudly named "Lincoln Street."

It was there Adeline McGraw Clayton hosted Arkansas's first families as a "gin-up" for Washington, so to speak, before Mexico and Europe followed in natural, almost inevitable, succession; all done for the dining in of General C's career on the one hand, and the assiduous marrying off of their beautiful daughters on the other. Charlotte to the Baron Ludovic Moncheur, the Belgian minister to the United States, and Kathleen, to Sir Arthur Cunningham Grant Duff, an English diplomat and man-about-town. Southern girls suddenly becoming "Baroness" and "Lady"—too good certainly for a sleepy Mississippi River slackwater where a saucy mother had been arrested by their stern father for being on the wrong side; too good, as well, for the isolated grandeur of so fine a spread as *Linwood*, or even the bounding nouveau riche of booming Little Rock—nor, in the end, even of that proud but rather provincial Southern "town" on the Potomac—Daisy Millers with much better luck than she, females making money-marriages, not military males majoring in Mexico, but going to Europe and staying there—those were the two daughters Clayton.

Or, put another way, it all turned out rather well, but it was this obscure, swashbuckling death upon this trickling brown *Grande* of a river guarding a country where Adeline had once been America's first mistress in Mexico, that put her to philosophizing about what had seemed maybe, in the end, a bit too grand for a middle-class Helena girl, and had, in her graying days, gradually transformed life from a luxury to a burden.

So, in a friendly letter, she expressed a premonition of the loss of "the closed corporation" as she called her love for the son, Powell Jr., whose dying, coming as it did hard upon the loss of the public corporation of the more profitable life of "General C," in whom she always owned controlling interest, was, as it turned out, indeed, a death foretold:

> Am like an old cat or some wounded animal that wants to hide before dying.

> *Can't you understand me? I love my children, each the same but this coming separation from Powell is positive agony, feeling as I do that I shall never see him again.*

And, like her grieving feline self, she was gone within the cozy curl of a year—buried in England—far from the river, plantation, mansion, and the Mexican *palacio*, and not at the place where she always said she was most happy with the ever-happy name of Eureka, the Ozark village where the open "C" corporation had built a grand hotel on the crescent of a hill—the best place in town still to be—where "C's" new rails connected the "miraculous" but now-polluted springs of the poor, agrarian upper mountain South with the prosperous, ever-expanding capitalist western Midwest, where they went to wait out the Redemption, raise daughters, and make money for Mexico.

Yes, there is, as always, a tie-in. There was another *Bruxelles* Princess Charlotte in the Mexican mix—not an American one gone to Belgium but a Belgian one gone to America. This other Charlotte, ambitious beauty that she was, was wife of another lordly man, Maximilian, the Habsburg younger brother to Franz Josef, emperor of a European Kingdom (not Austin-Houston but Austro-Hungarian) set by that great house upon the Old World's Danube. "A garden of roses, a place of delight, and veritable paradise," a poet had once declaimed about the big place.

Charlotte, the feminine form of Carl, or Charles, was quickly Latinized to the "Carlotta" of a foreign queen. This Carlotta, proud, passionate, and completely pleasureless without a place, intrigued in Paris with her equally charming friend, the Empress Eugenie, the Spanish, quarter-Belgian, quarter-Scot wife of the reigning nephew emperor of the greater Corsican of France, (Louis) Napoleon III.

María Eugenia Ignacia Augustina de Guzman y Palafox y Portocarrero, daughter of the late and very dashing Spanish Count of Montijo, who was wounded fighting for her husband's uncle in the Peninsula War, Eugenia—Eugénie as she became known in Paris—was such an intriguer that the British foreign secretary called her the "intrigante." But this Eugenia was above all a lover of all Napoleonic *gloire* which she learned dandling on the knee of the great Stendhal, who told the future empress of the Second Empire romantic stories about the glories of the First, and who wrote, it was said, the scene of Waterloo in his masterpiece, *La Chartreuse de Parme*, just for her.

It was this Eugénie who, under the double impetus of an ambition born of glory, and a boredom born of neglect, a neglect because of her husband's many mistresses, but whose toleration gave her ever greater power so that in the fullness of its increase Bismarck would say that Louis Napoleon was "a sphinx without a riddle" and Eugénie was "the only man in his government," did she weave together with her sister-soul-mate, Carlotta, a conspiracy with exiled Mexican Creole priests to set upon Max's head a crown of cactus thorns. It was to be a kind of Napoleonic restoration, if you will, of what had been Habsburg all along, and since King Charles of Spain had ridden hard upon the Aztec throne with the saddles and swords of his hard-hearted hero Hernan Cortés and, since the half-Habsburg, half-Bonaparte boy, the only legitimate son of the great Corsican, known to the world as Napoleon II, Max's first cousin on the female side, had died too young to rule but old enough to observe with his dying breath that nothing but "a zero lies betwixt my cradle and my grave," so, they thought, it would be a kind of vindication, you know, for each royal house to have a great Catholic empire of its very own, founded by France and ruled by a Habsburg— a counterpoint to the increasing vulgarity of that democratic Protestant country ever threatening from across the Atlantic.

Eugénie poured into the ear of this lesser Napoleon all the poison of her pompous imperial dreams—of defeating the Liberals in the name of kings, Mary, and God; of a Latin victory over the Anglo; of the resurrection of Mexico upon the hegemonic Cross of her faithful priests (who of course wanted back their property taken by Juárez); of the gold and silver of New Spain taken from the mines for the Old; so that, in the bloody wedge of the American Civil War, Napoleon Number Three would, with Maximilian as titular head of a titled crown, begin to build a New French Kingdom from Texas to the Isthmus.

As for Maximilian Habsburg, the bored archduke listened to his Carlotta, for he knew very well that among the Viennese treasures of his much greater fathers were three most prized: the Holy Grail of Jerusalem; the unicorn sword of Europe's Charles the Bold; and, the most intriguing of all to him, the feathered headdress of America's Montezuma. Was it his fate to add a fourth? More magnificent even than his brother, Franz Josef, the Emperor of Austria, of whom he was always, of course, jealous, for all to see?

PHILLIP H. MCMATH

If Musset could lament in '33, "*Je suis venu trop tard dans un monde trop vieux.*"
One can say with some assurance what a later, second-fiddle Habsburg must
have felt without a throne to fill. Was it, he must have wondered, in pillowed
tête-á-tête with Carlotta, "'not too late to seek a newer world,' my dear?"
Doesn't our vessel puff her sail upon the tide? Isn't there "some work of noble
note might yet be done?" *Allons, allons, toujour allons*! He might have muttered, seeking a greater glory for his declining house in the meteoric rise of
his own name. "I give you Mexico!" Napoleon III had said, "a throne on a pile
of gold!" Hearing this, Max ran to Rome—told his *Holy Papa* he would go—
to do His work among the unwashed of America.

Yet in Aztec times things had been a little different. The marveling men of
the Yucatan had seen ship sails set white against the sea; had found outlandish,
shore-stranded clothes slowly washing up in a sandy box; had spoken with
strange, unexpected Indians canoeing into Tabasco with stranger tales of even
stranger White men who grew from the backs of four-legged creatures; had
wondered at a great light that shone for forty days in the eastern night; had
watched the temple towers of Huitzilopochtli burn while Montezuma
mumbled about a comet with three heads looming ominously over Anahuae.
Did this not portend the coming of the white-bearded Quetzacoaltl of their
legends? it was asked. The answer moored itself at last against the shore as
Hernan's galleons bridled to anchor like the riding of his black apocalyptic
horse upon the sands of Mexico.

But no such portents portended our new Habsburg's second coming; they
were not feted at liberal Vera Cruz, but were soon seated instead upon roads
that broke their wheels; struggled slowly, painfully, through a poverty that even
a visit to Guadalupe's Virgin could not vitiate; then bedded at last in the city
upon a billiard table's velvet since the palace bed was not provided yet for a
Belgian queen. It was too much, and Carlotta moved them to Chapultepec to
live among the green illusions that she grew idly in the pretty pot of her little
mind like the perfumed gardenias of Montezuma.

Here, at least, with the Valley of Mexico at their royal feet—a good view
everyone agreed—snow-crowned mountains with clouds swirling like gun
smoke around the head of a monarch, flowers rising like delicate serpents twisting head-up around a desert thorn, and taciturn servants waiting their turn to
tip a sombrero and bow a knee. It was all very enchanting. They were pleased.
It seemed worth the journey somehow.

Claro! With the people's *pesos,* they refurbished the *palacio* at great expense,
gave seventy wine-laced lunches, multiple lavish receptions, and sixteen balls,

as Max and Carlotta did their *pas de deux* upon their newfound stage; a monarchic *bal masqué* for all the world to see; cantering among the hills for the view, fleeing to Cuernavaca for the air, and condescending with the Indians along the way, while Max, in his laboring hours, wrote endless laws that were disobeyed, and scratched out hundreds of pages of courtly etiquette for the unread. He was bewitched—a prophet newly inspired—a new shepherd for these lost sheep wandering on volcanic hills of this brave new world he was sent by God and King and Pope to save.

But there's a Caliban in every land and, Max and Louis Napoleon were but stems of a greater branch, and, like all such borrowed glory, were grafted to a fate of an ever-budding grief.

Or, to put it another way, none of this went unnoticed. It was seen in *El Paso del Norte* by an exiled, dark-skinned Indian lawyer from Oaxaca, Benito Juárez. An impoverished herdsman's son, he was no Habsburg or Bonaparte prince but a Zapotec peasant, born not in a royal bed but upon a mat of reed thrown across a dirt floor. With hardly a dollop of Iberia in his veins, he was illiterate, growing up impoverished in the mountains with his tribe. This precocious boy, it was said, would languish in a tree and give speeches to his loyal lambkins in Zapotec—because he knew no Latinate.

"Will you teach me Spanish?" he had implored an uncle who knew a little.

"No, I won't," said the old man.

"Why not?"

"I have no whip," he replied.

"I will get one," said the future president of Mexico.

When Benito had exhausted the old man's linguistic lashes, he ran away, forsaking his little village of San Pablo Guelatao with its famous lake, *Laguna Encantada*, and with it, too, childhood's innocence; a lonely twelve-year-old walking the forty-one miles to Oaxaca—the urban anchor of the westward edge of the Isthmus of Tehuantepec—a provincial town rejoicing as the capital of a state bounded on the north by Puebla, the east by Chiapas, and the south by the Pacific. *En route*, Benito traveled among the mountains and down into the great valley given by Mexico's first Habsburg to Cortés, anointing the conquistador as "Marques del Valle de Oaxaca." It was here the Indian lad trudged up the river Atoyac, flowing westward as it does to an ocean that troubles China in the East, rejecting in turn the wayward streams that twist to the West spilling down the divide to water the cattle, corn, and cane of the peasant poor, before converging slowly into a plain that leads to the sea road for Spain.

In Oaxaca, the future enemy of an archduke gained his bread as a domestic;

living *de un día para otro,* till, under the benevolence of a Catholic Creole, who saw something special in this little Benito and smoothed his way into seminary to be a priest, where he, always more of this world than the next, learned just enough Latin to finish Spanish, enough liturgy for the law, and enough theology for politics.

Still, it was, after all, a start, because the Mexico into which he had been born, like the Zapotec himself, was yet a country unburdened by books, and, like him, almost with him, really, Mexico would slowly and painfully awaken, arise, and amble out of the valleys and villages of its childhood and onto the streets of the lost innocence of her urban future.

True, Spain had brought Mexico certain great gifts: faith, language, unity, and culture, but these were bought at a benighted double price—exploitation, extraction, and the elimination of her old civilization by conquest. Thus, for three centuries, she was completely overborne—suffering under the long boot heel of Cortés without benefit of Renaissance, Reformation, or Reason— enslaved by the only country in Europe to have successfully resisted all three, and soon confronted by the very one whose upper half embraced them the most.

Nevertheless, independence, as it must, came in its own inevitable good time in '21, led by that charismatic Hotspur of an army officer, Agustin Iturbide, who, in an unintended comic emulation of his hero, Napoleon I, crowned himself emperor like that in Notre Dame, but whose expense so affronted his country's impoverishment that in three short corrupt years was humbled against a wall and dethroned into a bloody heap upon the ground.

The bullets were mortal to Iturbide but gave life to an endless cycle of conspiracy, corruption, and civil strife in which one dictatorship's palace coup d'état replaced the next, till Santa Anna fought a two-front war with Richard Taylor's father and brother-by-law, who each would build mansions of their own from their victory at a *hacienda* called Buena Vista. In that war Winfield Scott would emulate Cortés, land at Vera Cruz, march past Puebla, and overcome Mexican courage to take Chapultepec and the great City.

Thus would half of Mexico's home be lost, taken by a president named Polk; a dour Tennessean, who inadvertently, split two, not one, houses in twain, collapsing the sawdust Caesardom of Santa Anna ("Napoleon of the West," some bragged), into such a ruin that her conqueror could not divide the rubble without razing his own.

This was all papered together in a thing called the Treaty of Guadalupe Hidalgo, to which the United States said "yes" in '48; and "yes" again to herself in '50 for a compromise of that name and number, digesting the new lands, it was hoped, under a notion called "popular sovereignty" for the new territories that "slave" or "free" were spoiled away at Hidalgo. But this was not enough, and the structure began to sway and shimmer, until a desperate America said "yes" again to a short-lived shibboleth, styled "Kansas-Nebraska," which merely stuttered out the same idle hope of keeping it all under one caving roof, till Lincoln finally said not "yes" but "no" and it all collapsed in the echoes of his mighty voice being answered in turn by the sound of cannon in South Carolina.

In this way did one war led inexorably to the next—each to each, following in train, one hard upon the other, as they always do, in an ever-shifting, spreading cycle of violence, as Mexico and America first fought the other, then themselves.

But Mexico did at last graft a kind of civil overgrowth upon the chaos—a certain flowering rooted in her greatest city, planted by students, intellectuals, and poets like Guillermo Prieto and Ignacio Ramírez, and nurtured by that champion of independence, the venerable Quintana Roo, president of the College of San Juan Letrán, who insisted that there were, indeed, such things called "progress" and "justice," even for a land held in the talons of an Eagle eating a Serpent.

Yet the Indian tribes and Anglo-Saxon filibusters still raided in the north, race war still ravaged the Yucatan, and the *bandidos* were, as always, terrorizing everyone in their usual rape-and-rapine, saddle and smoke, ubiquity. In short, the country was too bitter, broken, and bankrupt for mere words, however poetic or mellifluous, to so easily unburden herself of the flow of blood.

Action was soon the fashion, and it came in an undoing wrought yet again by the landed Creoles, clergy, and colonel/generals, who in their desperation disturbed the exiled Santa Anna from his remote Elba of Venezuela, summoning him from vanity's eternal pleasure of planning one's tomb, and, in a kind of comic opera coup, plopped him once more upon the volcanic throne of Popocatapetl.

Yet as a kind of counterpoint to all this, our runaway peasant's son, Juárez, now forty-one, had become governor of Oaxaca, where he converted not souls from perdition as his kindly mentor had intended, but government receipts from *rojo* to *negro,* while embracing Indians, lifting the poor *Mestizos,* and raising himself up quickly before his country's eyes as a reforming Liberal to be watched with ever-greater attention.

This *poquito* Benito, reserved yet frank, but whose frankness always still retained that famous reserve and whose reserve still retained a certain reassurance, also had perhaps more importantly that rarest of all qualities in a Mexican politician, a complete and unquestioned incorruptibility. To be sure, such a man must always be pushed into exile by such a man as Santa Anna. And he was—to New Orleans, where with his growing family, Benito made his living rolling cigarettes for Americans and stirring revolution for Mexicans.

Of course, Santa Anna, sustained only by a strutting dissuasion, could not and would not last. Soon in the rugged state of Guerro resistance arose, led by the old guerrilla chief, the Indo-African Juan Álvarez, who enticed his Serene Highness into the folly of searching-and-destroying after him with a searching whose futility was equaled only by such destruction's counterproductivity.

But, Santa Anna, always the master of show, celebrated this in his capital as a great victory—standing himself up as a Napoleon Creole bravely atop a quickly stacked up Arc de Triomphe—waving the Mexican flag in the glorious after-breeze of murdering and looting some peasants out of their *pueblos*. It was not Austerlitz or Jena, but it would have to do.

Álvarez heard and saw and merely laughed loud enough for all of Mexico to hear as his riposte. For once Santa Anna was silent and though blinded as always by vanity, he was never deafened by it and so heard Álvarez clearly enough. Knowing full well that he mustn't run of out funds just as his people ran out of *frijoles*, he quickly deposited gold purchased from an American named Gadsen, who dug dollars for him out of some hot sand not stolen at Hidalgo, then, to stack it a tad higher, our emperor undercut the big-shot New York City African sellers a bit and pocketed some more by selling Yucatan prisoner-slaves to Cuba.

But Burnham seemed to move ever so much closer, and the Alamo's conqueror saw himself ever more within than without—the besieged rather than besieger—and, again imitating his favorite Corsican, he desperately patched together a plebiscite of approval, you know, to keep the folks off the walls a tad longer. Still, it did no good, and an obscure law student in Oaxaca, one Profirio Díaz, couraged up a "no," and by this voted out a shout that found an echo in a remonstrance written by a confederate of Álvarez, Ingnacio Comonfort, in the "Plan of Ayutla," he proclaiming a "dictatorship of the revolution" via a new constitution; whereby the trees were made to move closer still.

Thus the names were beginning to fall upon the page in a line: Juárez, Álvarez, Díaz, and now Comonfort—reputations writ into place with that implacability of pantheonic success the ambitious never ignore.

Or, in a word, it was time to leave. So Santa Anna, wanting no St. Helena, secretly sailed away, disappearing fittingly on a ship named *Iturbide*, to strut and fret upon Mexico's stage no more. Like Bonaparte, he had made quite a wind and not a little wrack, but he had no real desire to die, however bravely, with a bunch of useless harness on his back.

Thus began a twelve-year period academicized as "The Reform." And like the French Revolution, which it aped, it wanted finally to kill Feudalism and grow into "Modernity." Make law, a constitution, lop off, if you will, the double-headed power of Church and Army forever.

To this end, always mirroring France (the intellectual and cultural "super-power" of the age), it hoped to swap the hegemony of one for another—the *Mestizos* playing the role of the bourgeoisie standing up against the Creoles as *l'Ancien Régime* trying to save themselves, first with Santa Anna and later with Maximilian, in a kind of desperate book-ending of Bonapartism.

Like most revolutions, it could but take just two steps forward when it really aspired to three, only to be forced reluctantly back one more besides. But there is really no such thing as "a radical departure from the past," as the cliché proclaims; the present always sets itself lightly like a patina over that hard dry thing called History, or as Faulkner said in his immortal, if slightly overstated, fashion, "the past is never dead, it's not even past." The past always kneels at our feet like a secret, unwanted messenger, mumbling what has been done, what is being done, and what will yet be done again.

In the Mexican Reform, then, Feudalism was damaged but not destroyed; property was rearranged but not redistributed; the Indians and masses were still oppressed, not liberated; and the new *Mestizo* class, despite ever-greater energy and efficiency, could do no more than put the old muddy, bloody boots on corrupt dictatorships, one after the other in a slow-stepping march from one century into the next.

But each moment has its actors, and while Ignacio Comonfort knew his lines, he did not know the play; he was a *moderado* with characters who were not, proffering an open hand when the plot called for a dagger. His land reform failed and his constitution was erased; then he was chased from the stage, as the curtain dropped down only to bounce quickly up again for three more years of civil war.

Knock! Knock! Sounds loudly as the curtain rises upon a casino cashier, one Felix Zuloaga, now suddenly promoted to general, who gambled and won by seizing power in the City, overthrowing the Reforms and exiling Comonfort, while Juárez, who had returned to head the supreme court, was awarded a prison for his chambers.

But Benito, now the constitution's accessor via the fall of Comonfort, soon found himself not presiding over a court at all but a country, and so escaped to Queretaro to form a government for the business of carrying on a revolution.

Zuloaga, intent on murdering all liberals in the name of God and His Holy Church, hotly pursued Juárez, who fled yet again, this time to Guadalajara; then, one step ahead of spilling new blood upon an old wall, rode on to Manzanillo, then sailed to Panama and from there looped via Havana back to New Orleans, where he had become something of a *habitué*, till, resting up a bit, by this circle did appear once again in Vera Cruz. Here he remained impregnable—sustained by a people and a parasite—the people of this town, ever the defenders of the constitution, and the lowland *(tierre caliente)* parasite. (Yellow fever was the surprising defender against the Zuloaga's highland, non-immune soldiers who were powerless to hang, shoot, or bayonet a mosquito's microbes sufficiently to disturb such a city and win a war.)

From here Juárez waged an action against reaction (written up as the "War of the Reform") by pitting city against town, Indians and *Mestizos* against clerics, wealthy Creoles, and their generals against History; wading his Mexico, a country seemingly born to blood, through more than it had seen since Cortés, dragging her to the other side of these three years panting in victory for his revolution.

Thus did the United States and Mexico contrive to merge several seemingly independent revolutionary wars into one long, essentially continuous, continental one. And, as one seemed to end in January of '61, so did the other begin. That is, as the little brown-skinned Zapotec lawyer rode unobtrusively in his black carriage, dressed in a dark suit, quietly arriving from Vera Cruz through the back streets of the great capital, so did the tall, somewhat swarthy lawyer from Illinois prepare to lead a country into what Mexico had only just seemed to finish—each connecting History's whorl with what had ended and begun at Hidalgo into a strife renewed.

Yet in a country of military *machismo,* Benito Pablo Juárez came with a certain quiet humility, knowing full well that in the three arrangements of power—Monarchy, Republic, and Despotism—each needs to a degree (depending on its fears) a steady injection into the body politic of a powerful toxin known as *La Gloire!*

La Gloire! With it the entire century seemed blinded, mesmerized by the flames lit by the greatest man of the age, Napoleon Bonaparte. If from him the fires of glory were genuine, if not profound, Benito also knew, in lesser men such as nephew Louis (Napoleon III), this glory was but a distant reflection; for Santa Anna, merely a false light; while for poor Maximilian, alas, a fading shadow in the night.

Put another way, Juárez knew who and what he was. He knew that for a nonusurping, unprepossessing Zapotec lawyer dressed in black, coming not to found a despotism for himself but a republic for others, he needed no such thing as personal glory. The glory was his people's—*las gentes,* nothing less.

So, Benito Pablo Juárez, the shepherd's son from Oaxaca, rode no horse, wore no uniform, braid, sword, or crown, tipped no salute to the adulating crowd, but entered upon power quietly, hidden away in a shade-drawn carriage, the sash drawn over his face but never over his vision—the first civilian president of Mexico.

And as for Jo and Dagmar, one can safely say, they didn't know really very much about Mexico. Oh, they knew a little something, of course. They knew that the French had more or less "taken over" the country, and had chased the little Indian, Benito, away to *El Paso del Norte* where he was hiding and holding out again like he'd done so many times before, and that with his big modern army the French emperor, Napoleon III, had sat a Habsburg emperor named Maximilian to squat upon the throne way down there somewhere in Mexico City.

But they didn't know much else. They didn't know that Juárez had inherited a country so ravaged and ruined with death and debt that it could not make restitution or right from the ruins and was threatened by foreign intervention till the French finally did come to collect, they said, and were, to everyone's surprise, promptly defeated at a little place called Puebla, halfway between Vera Cruz and the big City, on the fifth of May, of '62; were flung back, that is, from there by one Ignazio Zaragoza and the brave peasant soldiers, who drove them to the coast with a thousand Frenchmen short of what they had started out with. It had shocked Europe, but in the clamor and clang of its own war, America had not heard its cannons.

Nor did Dagmar and Jo, nor anyone else realize that this little, furious battle, now known as the national holiday of *Cinco de Mayo*, should be celebrated by both parties of Hidalgo since it almost certainly saved Mr. Lincoln's idea of what a Union ought to be. Then, even though not one Yankee or Reb was there

---

to shoot a single shot, die, or yell hurrah, it was, nevertheless, without a doubt, a point to be penned in with the Elkhorn, Shiloh, Sharpsburg, Vicksburg, Gettysburg, and Atlanta, on the American side of things.

That is to say, had Louis Napoleon won in '63 instead of '64, it was thought, he would have tipped his hat at Davis and brought the British in by the boot. But, by the fifth day of that fifth month of that earlier year, he was grievously delayed and, worse still, embarrassed, and to save his honor had to wait yet one more year besides—to get and send another, bigger army, which upon arriving saw the Yankee wheel had turned in such a crushing way upon the South that Louis balked and was more loath to offend Lincoln than link the other.

Mr. Lincoln, ever watchful, insisted that he wasn't ever really "skeered" at all; but, in truth, he was "skeered" enough, especially after the Grays took Santa Fe; and later he was "skeered" even more when one Mr. Picket, not the charging kind but the Confederate's man at Chapultepec, let it drop over a drop of wine that Richmond might return some of the stolen loot-land in return for a patch-up with the previous lower-half owner. To be sure, the lawyer from Illinois had never approved of President Polk's theft, but he was not much pleased with the remedy of replevin either. He was, in short, always a might more "skeered" than he let on. After all, who was he to disprove Balzac about crime and fortune?

But, as we have seen in '64, he was alarmed enough to put Steele in motion from the Rock down toward Miz Virginee's table and Banks in motion from the Red up toward R. Taylor's tree.

In any case, our Shelby, Dagmar, and their fleeing thousands were approaching the Big Brown River way beyond the Brazos. And now they had a decision to make. Maximilian or Juárez? France or Mexico? Which was it to be?

Meanwhile, old Kirby Smith and some friends, under escort and armed with letters, sped ahead into Mexico without the pause of any hesitation while Shelby's legion stopped in *Paso de Águila* (Eagle Pass) on the Texas side and bivouaced themselves into an unaccustomed lag of thought.

This *Águila* had quickly spread its wings over the same steady commerce of cotton, cannon, and contraband flowing from France and Britain through Mexico into Texas that had made San Antonio fly so high. But, with war's end, *Águila* had just as quickly folded its wings; its CSA Fort Duncan, now stripped of soldiers, left Eagle's streets to American beggars, bandits, and Mexican *bandidos* who were busy picking over its body like half-starved buzzards.

Unruffled outside of town, Shelby spread into his camp, put out pickets, then pointed his cannons across the water at *Piedras Negras* and its Juárista governor, *Adelantado* Andres Viesca, who, most impressed, watched through a glass this strange bird on the other side, till fluttering a white flag and with a guard, Shelby glided over at the call of the *El Comandante* to pow-wow.

This Viesca was described as "polished and elegant," an officer who spoke to the blunt Missourian most graciously and with a "voluble and suave" air, while extending the munificence that only Latins can give when they are in the mood. He extended their chat for two days. What was offered was astonishing—in return for loyalty to Juárez and his revolution, Shelby would be the supremo under Viesca, who, in turn, would serve directly under Juárez. Together they would command the northern states of Nuevo Leon, Coahuila, and Tamaulipas, where, headquartered at *Piedras Negras*, Shelby's force would join with the Viesca's two thousand, recruit even more, then march and defeat Maximilian's men now occupying Monterey. With this defeat, the way would be open to the City of Mexico and these two heroes would be second only to the great Juárez himself. Besides, added the general, with the American war over and Grant sending Sheridan with fifty thousand horses France was doomed by James Monroe. But, of course, for Shelby, if he were at Juárez's side, he would be untouchable, he said.

"It's your only choice ... the road to Mexico City is open, but you must ride there with the Mexicans," Viesca said with a wry smile. "Not the French."

Shelby, for all his great dreaming, had never dared dream such a dream as this. His great Southern Kingdom, as if offered by the gods, was suddenly, almost miraculously, his—proffered now in the open palm of this man Viesca. He had but to accept, and disgruntled Grays would saddle to his standard in the thousands. He would be a Confederate Caesar, a hero-of-heroes to Mexico, Texas, and all the South. He could fight on—impregnable—never to yield! The *Río Grande* was his Rubicon! How would he cross?

But with *El Comandante* he kept his counsel, was coy, said he would ponder then present this thing to his men. "They would have to agree," he added solemnly, then departed to persuade.

Returning, he confided quietly only to a few. When Dagmar heard—herself no student of History—she saw the obvious, and with the intuition and common sense of her race, said, "Gen'ral, I ain't seen a Frenchy 'round yar yet."

Shelby laughed nervously.

"I mean, sir," she added, "to me it's rale simple, the Mexicans ain't got no place to go back to ... the French do."

Shelby nodded, then gathered them all and said as much, explaining the offer and asked they accept.

Then, as noted by Major John Edwards, the brigade poet and scribe, Shelby said:

> If you are all of my mind, boys, and will take your chances along with me, it is Juárez and the Republic from this time on until we die here, one by one, or win a Kingdom. We have the nucleus of a fine army—we have cannon, muskets, ammunition, some good prospects for recruits, a way open to Sonora, and according to the faith that is in us will be the measure of our loss or victory.

There was some desultory discussion, then Shelby said as a closure:

> Determine for yourselves. You know Viesca's offer. What he fails to perform we will perform ourselves, so that when the game is played out there will be scant laughter over any Americans trapped or slain by treachery.

There was some more debate, and then the men huddled to themselves.

But soon, out of Shelby's hearing, they found their tongue in one Colonel Ben Elliot, proud, tall, aristocratic, a VMI veteran cavalryman wounded four times in four years, who came back with their words, stepping forward and saying to Shelby in a somber voice, just loud enough for the assembled thousand, now standing behind him in a stolid mass of Gray silence, each lending an ear.

"Have you reached a decision, Colonel?" asked Shelby quietly.

"Yes, sir, we have."

"What is it?"

Again the words were noted by Edwards. "General, if you order it, we will follow you into the Pacific Ocean; but we are all Imperialists, and would prefer service under Maximilian."

There was a pause. Shelby stood alone, gaping back at his army, and could say nothing but with these words saw reflected in their staring eyes Juárez's palm close at him into a fist. For the first time his legion stood apart from himself, indeed, apart from all logic, just a he had stood in '61, apart from Lincoln. But they were, need it be said, his men; the immortal Iron Brigade, Cavaliers not Roundheads, romantics not realists, who preferred the purity of an unsullied defeat to the easier, more profane, propitiating victory; and in his heart he was not surprised.

Alas, he had half expected it. After all, that was or had been himself, else he would have signed up with cousin Blair and all those well-fed, strutting Union

Blues riding around now in the bright sunshine of their success. Nor had he surrendered, turned in his black plume, adjusted his cap to the new order, but had ridden off to here, to the very edge of his dying country where its implicit hopelessness was only compounded by a new, unexpected hope renewed, offered then lost in this moment.

No, he shouldn't have been surprised. His brigade merely preferred the glitter of a distant Kingdom to the reality cast down before them; preferred it to the mud-hutted poverty of *Piedras Negras;* preferred a blond Habsburg prince with his damsel in distress, the beautiful Carlotta waiting to be rescued, to the poor, dark Zapotec pettifog with his disorganized people ("a bunch of greasers," one had said in the debate) now asking for help across the dirty brown fact of this squalid border town set on a shallow, ignominious river far from home.

Yet for a moment, Dagmar Pilgrim, the one-armed Sancho Panza, had, to her proud, dashing quixotic major general by two quick sentences, forced him to see the Mexican windmill for what it really was. But he, in turn, had been unable to unblind his men. Perhaps it was because he still wore his colorful plume, carried his saber, and rode a big dark horse that was by this vote converted in a wink to a Rosinante.

Or maybe it was his own ambivalence, his own discomfiture with a mere expediency, an abjuration that had been a lifelong passion, nurtured since childhood, held dear, since he and his playmate had horsed around the big yard together, the future, now dead, cavalryman, John Hunt Morgan (killed by Blue cavalry in '64, riding out of the fumes of boyish fantasy to beard him in his full-blown bloom of glorious death). Morgan became Shelby's rival and fellow hobby-horseman, bouncing together in the innocent growing-up glory days of boyhood Lexington—a dusty dream that did not lend itself to the easy awakening purchased by compromise and caution—a burden of youthful visions that had sustained him and these men for four, arduous, bloody but magnificent years and could not and would not be so easily turned into something else by the solace of a scheming success now offered up so logically by Comandante Viesca.

So they voted. And two were for Juárez, his and Dagmar's.

"Is this your answer?" asked Shelby, wearily.

"Yes!" came the response.

"Then it is mine, too," replied Shelby more loudly but with a note of false enthusiasm.

Then he paused, drew in his breath, and said louder still, "Henceforth we will fight under Maximilian! Tomorrow, at four o'clock in the afternoon, the march will commence for Monterey!"

"Hurrah!" throated a thousand voices, which merged into one thunderous shout echoing as a shot across the river into Mexico. It was a cry that defied dishonor, defied History, indeed, defied a world—a cry of the past as against a terrifying and for them, unacceptable, future. Of *Fraternité* against *Egalité!* Of *La Gloire* against *La Nécessité!* Of *Le Panache* against the *Le Peuple!* Of sword, saddle, scabbard, and plume against the machine! And, of course, our cavalier knew it must fail.

But, before disappearing into this tent, Shelby indulged not in a descant but an aside picked up by the ear of the ubiquitous Edwards.

> Poor, proud fellows—it is principle with them, and they had rather starve under the Empire than feast in a republic. Lucky, indeed, for many of them if to famine is not added a fusillade.

The next morning Shelby ordered his men mounted and formed in a line along the river, although, as had been suggested by the amiable Viesca and, in her way, his sensible Dagmar, one should always be mindful of the spell one casts over others and ever ready to exorcise its ecstasy.

But he saw it was too late now—there was nothing for it but to conjure up its charm in some final bit of magic—a last saluting wave of his mystical wand—before crossing from a place called Eagle to a place named for Black Rocks and its fresher but far more forbidding reality—he had to wave it again.

So, early that morning, Major General J. O. Shelby rode before his mounted, lined-up thousand horse of the renowned Iron Brigade, seated on his dark charger, booted and spurred, his dress uniform of butternut-gold appearing fresh in the sun; his famous plume black shining as if freshly plucked from some warlike angel, his unrelinquished sword clattering at his side. He was for a brief moment the last knight of a dying, chivalric myth—an idea that had for so long pranced its poetic path through the hearts of men into this last, panting thousand as nothing else could or ever would again; that had sustained them in a way that their more mundane, modern, prosaic enemy could never understand, then or now.

Saddled in a nervously pawing parade line, horse-to-horse, these doomed knights now saw riding before them their dream's very apotheosis—a symbol personifying itself from abstraction into the flesh and blood of a magnificent steed and rider, trooping their line to a great, spontaneous, last hurrah that rippled from their souls into the crisp air as this splendid thing came cantering by. Their cheer sustained itself ever louder as the rider turned, paused, reared as if to fly, and raised his plum, then touched the ground and came charging past again for the final time—ever.

Yet there was one more martial sacrament to perform. Their large Confederate flag, floating above them as their great talisman of war, which had led them through so much, unsullied and unsurrendered, had to be given its final honor.

Major Edwards rode forward, holding it straight. It was he who had received it ceremoniously on behalf of the brigade, after it was made and tendered by the patriotic ladies of a small Arkansas town.

Then the regimental colonels, Elliot, Williams, Gordon, Slayback, and Blackwell came forward, took the flag, and waded with it into the *Río Grande*. They held it for a moment in the slight breeze, then after a suspension sustained by another great cheer, lowered it in silence, weighted, and sank it into the river's oblivion.

Shelby could stand it no longer. He dismounted, ran into the water, and sank his black plume as in a common grave beside it.

Colonel Slayback later composed a doggerel that expressed the time and moment on the level of the men who felt it:

> They buried then that flag and plume in the
> River's rushing tide,
> Ere that gallant few
> Of the tried and true
> Had been scattered far and wide.
> And that group of Missouri's valiant strong—
> Who had charged and bled
> Where Shelby led,
> Were the last who held above the wave
> The glorious flag of the vanquished brave,
> No more to rise above from its watery grave!

After all this they had no choice but to cross. Following Shelby into the water was the legion of horse with cannons and wagons sporting a small, tattered "Stars and Bars" guidon flying a half length behind to Shelby's left. The men of this brigade, mostly Missourians but well stiffened by Arkansawyers, Texans, and Louisianians, were like the lost tribe of the great Gray army that had for four long years over half a continent, from Maryland to New Mexico, from Mississippi to Missouri, from the Gulf to Gettysburg, fought against a great Kingdom in the greatest battles of the world's greatest war, but now were leaving their own soil which they had defended with such incredible, heartbreaking courage, and were wading into Mexico.

It was the fourth of July 1865.

CHAPTER TWENTY-TWO

I would like to see the clause in Adam's will which excludes France from the division of the world.
— King Francios I of France

Louis had not done too badly for himself, or so it seemed. After all, following a couple of failed power grabs which garnered him a stint in the same prison as the hero of Mansfield's father, Jules Armand Auguste Polignac (repayed for his pains of loyal service to Charles X by being locked in the *Chateau de Ham* by rebels); Louis, now Napoleon III, had been kept there, too, by Charles's successor brother, Louis-Philippe, not for loyalty but for treason, then released in time to overthrow the new, fledging republic in the coup d'état of '51, from which Louis Napoleon at last established himself solidly enough on the new glorious throne of the glittering Second Empire to invade Italy, take Saigon, and occupy Mexico.

But, like his uncle, the chewing of these fruits, sweet in the savoring and quickly swallowed down as victory, could only be digested as defeat. The triumph in Italy against the Austrian Habsburgs, pursued in a self-conscious imitation of his greater name, strengthened Berlin at the expense of Vienna and thereby moved Bismarck ever closer to Paris.

So it would be but a short distance from '70 to '14, and from there to 1940 (Kingdoms falling like pins). The Mexican adventure would become a Vietnam for France in that midcentury, just as success in Indochina would prove in the middle of the next to find in its very name the meaning of failure.

In fact, 1865 had not begun well for Louis Napoleon at all. It was clear, even to him, that his hesitation conceived on the Mexican *Cinco de Mayo* had grown into despair for the American South, and, perhaps, he now feared, for himself as well. His army, so far away as to be almost hidden, was busy jockeying precariously along on the back of the Mexican jaguar, as the Prussian falcon was easily seen morphing into a disturbing new thing called the First Reich while the United States slowly constricted the Confederacy, forming what can only be called the Second American Republic.

Thus, on two sides, Napoleon III was faced with the dilemma of all such adventurers—that is, how to purchase peace with the paltry coin of an exhausted glory and thus prevent a worse defeat; he wanted out of Mexico, the sooner the better, but didn't know how.

Worse still, the year had begun with the portentous and unexpected death of his best advisor, friend, and half-brother, Duc August de Morny, the very clever if corrupt, "love child" of their unhappy and neglected mother, Hortense (daughter of Josephine), and one of Talleyrand's bastards, Count Charles de Flahaut, of whom it was written that "he was as brave on the battlefield as he was in bed," and who was himself the infamous half-brother of the other, more famous Talleyrand bastard, Eugène Delacroix.

The Duc de Morny, who seemed to have his grandfather's disconcerting guile as well as his graceful decadence, had warned brother Louis Napoleon about Mexico, just as his *Grand-Père* had warned his own Napoleon about Moscow, but, unlike him, was denied by death's sudden intrusion the bitter pleasure of offering to undo what he had striven to prevent.

Indeed, the situation in Mexico began to look more and more like one of Delacroix's masterpieces. Not his *Massacre at Chios*, which is oddly placid despite its violence, but *The Lion Hunt*, showing the deliciousness of death that Delacroix so loved even as he denounced it, with its claws sunk deeply into the dying horse's back.

So, what was once said of another master (Chopin) by a poet (Baudelaire) applied really more, it seemed, to the painter (Delacroix) and was now even truer of the politician (Louis), that is, that he was "a bird of brilliant plumage, fluttering over the horrors of the abyss."

Every folly has its instruments. And the instrument for Maximilian were the swords of his general, Marshal Bazaine, Achille-Francois (like Polignac *fils,* a Crimean veteran), former commandant of Sevastopol, and under him, one Colonel Pierre Jean Joseph Jeanningros, who, as commander of four thousand, was the tip of the emperor's cutlass pointing northward from Monterrey toward Texas.

The absinthe-addicted Jeanningros, whose charm was exceeded by his ruthlessness and his ruthlessness by ambition, was seconded by a side-kick sadist, Colonel Dupin, whose department was *contre-guerrilla*. Like Jeanningros, he was elegant with, as one said, "the polished manners of a duelist," and with "an unbelievable constitution" who "possessed every vice but drunkenness." Dupin was fond of saying men cannot bear arms if they have none and so cut them off *Juáristas* as he ravaged the country with his elite five hundred whom he described as "an ancient band of thieves exhumed from the backstreets of Paris."

These two, Jeanningros and Dupin, army comrades of some thirty years, had served in Italy and Algeria, then in the glory days of France's China adventure shared in the looting of Peking's Imperial Summer Palace.

"Ah!" Dupin had waxed eloquent at his courtmartial, "when I saw mountains of gold and precious stones piled up around me, and when I think of the paltry handfuls taken away, by god, Mr. President, I am astonished at my own moderation."

Monsieur Le Président cashiered Colonel Dupin when he should have been shot and passed over Jeanningros's promotion when he should have been cashiered; but because such men are far too useful, Dupin was soon restored and Jeanningros quietly registered again upwards on the list.

Unlike their lords, such servants are rarely burdened by lordly illusions, and these two, of course, were liberated by their knowledge that Mexico's future was Mexican not Maximilian.

Soon, even Bazaine was unblinded by a note passed in Paris from a new bumpkin president (Johnson) to Napoleon. "The sympathies of the American people for the Mexican republicans are very pronounced and the continuation of French interference in Mexico is viewed with considerable impatience."

And from Jeanningros it was clear enough that, in the matter touching upon Mexico, the "jig," whatever its previous position, was now definitely pointing "up." But as he had in Algeria and China learned well enough, the line between the wolf and the wolfhound was easily blurred.

That is to say, he didn't much care—they would continue to pursue, kill, and snarl at their master's enemies till whistled away. For them, the hunt needed no hallowing—it was, after all, the happiness of kings and therefore of themselves, who were content to pant tirelessly before his majesty's horse with need of no reason save pleasure.

But sometimes it's not so clear who or what the quarry really is. Jeanningros had heard soon of Shelby (his spies had told him all), and, too, Monterrey was quickly filling up with a veritable confection of distinguished Confederates: Generals Kirby Smith, Thomas Hindman, John B. Clark, and "Prince" John Magruder, were among the more stellar who wore stars; and, of course, there were the assorted colonels, majors, and men of lesser stripes, many of whom were already in the saddle serving Dupin. Even some politicians joined the ranks: Governor Thomas C. Reynolds and Senator Trusten Polk, both of Missouri, as well as one William Gwin, U.S. senator from California, imprisoned for two years for his Southern sympathies, who had fled to France then returned to Mexico for Maximilian's help in colonizing Sonora with Southerners. Perhaps most interesting of all, there arrived that brilliant mixture of letters, law, politics, and war, which the age seemed to produce, Governor/General Henry Watkins Allen, a Harvard-educated Louisianian from Virginia who had a thing for self-determination, was a veteran of the Texas War of Independence, fighter for Italian liberty under Garibaldi, world wanderer, memoir writer *(Travels of a Sugar Planter)*, Confederate campaigner for Southern nationhood at Shiloh, Vicksburg, and Baton Rouge and, finally, was wounded from saddle to statehouse as governor of Louisiana where, in the consensus of most and the words of one, he became "the single great administrator developed by the Confederacy." But now he was in Mexico and, like a man before retiring who does one more final, busy, little thing, had started (with Shelby's scribe, Edwards) an English newspaper before he died in 1866.

All these merry gentlemen were soon spending their evenings drinking with this soldier Jeanningros, filling their glass with his wine and his ear with their woe while munching a *morceau* of hope about the excellence of the marching knight they all called "Jo."

Their French host soon heard about the offer and its foolish refusal, of the chivalric ceremony with the flag, then the crossing with the one-armed Sancho Panza of a fair-haired, pretty but rough girl riding an Appaloosa, and of a peaceful pact with Viesca, not an alliance but a sale—cannons for silver and safe passage—since Shelby needed money and wanted to travel lightly unmolested over the rutty road to Monterrey. It was this trading of cannon, despite the vow of allegiance, that made Jeanningros so unhappy and undecided.

Of course there was fighting. As Shelby left what today might be called the Trans-Mississippi Vietnam of Missouri, Arkansas, Louisiana, the Indian Territory, and Texas, for the Vietnam of Mexico, he had to fight through Brown guerrillas controlling the countryside as the Grays had so recently done at home.

Major Edwards, in a more somber mood, would sum it up later and rather well, with words describing the essence of all such Vietnams:

> First and last, forty thousand French soldiers were operating in
> Mexico at one time, to say nothing of the native forces enlisted in
> the cause of Maximilian, and yet the very best they could do was

hold the towns while the Juáristas held the country. All they ever owned, or occupied, or controlled, or felt safe in, was the center of the territory which their cannon covered.

Edwards was right. Vietnams are all the same. And, Shelby, by siding with Maximilian, mounted his troops into the unfamiliar mold of Steele meandering through Arkansas, and, like him, struggled along in hopes of succor in some city, fort, or town.

They had quite simply entered a new war, the Mexican civil one, and, like all wars, it has its own peculiar dues, which they soon paid on the *Río Sabinas*, purchasing a victory at a price that wasn't quite Pyrrhic but was dearer even than Marks's Mill. It was here that Colonel Ben Elliot, the VMI aristocrat, paid his poll tax for voting for Maximilian by exchanging a dead horse and a ball in the hip (his fifth wound and the one from which he would never quite recover) for the privilege of being an "imperialist."

On the *Sabinas,* the Iron Brigade had killed more than two hundred, but still the *Juáristas* circled, making them the center of their concern, crowding them along in a terrain, rugged and rocky, yet known to the guerrillas in its every rut, ridge, and ravine from the *Río Grande* to Monterrey.

Then Jeanningros heard more—that the Southerners were ambushed yet again, but bravely recovered, counterattacked, and killed two of the more notorious guerrilla chiefs, a Cuban named Antonio Flores, and a renegade priest, one Juan Anselmo, who had eluded even Dupin; men, who in the insatiable wolfing of this war, had fed more and more upon the "when" and "how" of the killing and less and less upon the "why."

The colonel was impressed. Still, he could not make up his mind. Thanks to Shelby, Viesca now had cannon. He would just wait and see, humor his guests and decide for himself what kind of man this Shelby really was.

Besides, he had other worries. An army that sits slowly exsanguinates, and his was no exception; its vitality was oozing out, and, though the joke was that Jeanningros shot more Frenchmen than the *Juáristas*, fresh blood against the wall only slowed but did not staunch the flow. Now even a drunken lieutenant had run away, then sobered by remorse, returned, as Jeanningros, eyeing the man's warrant before him lacking but his own name, wished the boy had gone for good. He hated shooting officers, so stared and thought till interrupted. The "rider" had arrived, "from General Shelby," said a hatless captain, standing in the doorway.

"Send him in," Jeanningros said, as, unused to indecision, he gratefully lifted his eyes from the discomfort of an unwritten line to see that, through the voices and noise of entry, he had spoken the wrong word.

It was the girl, dirty and disheveled, but "under arms" with a pistol at her side (which the captain had unloaded), wearing a floppy hat and then, with a snappy lifting of her one hand to its turned-up brim, dropped it quickly again, as she attentioned herself before his desk.

"She came in under a flag of truce ... from the Americans ... they are bivouacked about a mile outside the city, sir," added the captain.

"Corp'ral Dagmar Pilgrim, yer excellency, reportin' frum Major Gen'ral Joseph Orville Shelby, commander of the Third Missouri Cal'very, Confeder'te States of Amer'ca, sir," she added proudly.

Jeanningros laughed.

"Is yours an army of women?" he asked in his French-English.

"We got no women, sir," she replied defiantly.

"And you, what are you?"

"I'm the gen'ral's rider, sir."

"Are there others like you in this legion of Missourians?"

"Confed'rate, sir, we's frum awl over the South ... I'm from Arkansas ..."

"Arkansas?"

"Yes, sir, a Confed'rate state."

"The Confederacy is dead ...," he started to say "garcon" but let the sentence end without it.

"No, sir, Arkansas'll always be Confed'rate."

"Even in the new Union?"

"We's still a-fightin', but, yes, even thar, sir."

"And what are you fighting for ... slavery?"

"I don't own no slaves ... an' don't hold with it none."

"What then is your war about?"

"Our rats."

"Rats?" he replied with gentle mockery.

"Yes, sir, them is whut we is a-fightin' fur ... our rats."

Jeanningros smiled sardonically, while looking more closely at this alluring apparition that had arisen out of the desert leading an army. Her blues eyes set off the sun-bleached blond hair matting down into dirty tangles as it fell loosely from under the Stetson to her neck; her wind-burnt brown right hand—held tightly at her side in a relaxed fist—was rough and sliced with countless half-healed cuts, and just touched her torn denim britches exposing a white knee. Her faded, tattered shirt was little more than a collection of patches tucked under a leather belt that cinched around her bony hips suspending a Bowie knife near a revolver which looked about to fall if she so much as breathed. She was a Confederate soldier, to be sure, but the only suggestion of a uniform was a large, silver CSA belt buckle, and the only thing of any *esprit* was a red bandana tied tightly around her throat like a Texas wrangler. Somehow it still looked new, bought or given in San Antonio, he guessed.

Yet the late-fortyish Jean Joseph Jeanningros, on the other side of the table with a large French tricolor standing behind him, without quite realizing it, furnished an interesting contrast, dressed as he was in a fresh, gold-trimmed blue-and-red colonel's uniform with the high, closed collar of the French colonial service, wearing starched riding pants, polished boots, a sword belt without its object, black revolver on his hip, and medals penned over his heart.

"Are all Southern soldiers like you, Corporal Pilgrim?" he asked after a moment, relaxing back a bit.

"I'm the only one-armed still a-fightin' that I know of, sir," she said, daring to look upon the colonel's face, seeing his short dark hair, tanned skin, and hard, slightly dissipated features, set off by cold hazel eyes above a scar running over the right cheek as if rising from the very blackness of a neatly trimmed mustache.

Jeanningros met her eyes, transfixed them, then his gaze fell upon the pinned-up sleeve.

"How did you lose that?" he asked quietly.

"In a' ambush ... but I kin do most anythang."

"Are you the one who rides the big Appaloosa?"

"I didn't know I wuz so famous, sir," she said, matching his wry smile that suddenly reflected an unexpected charm.

"Well, fame is always a shock."

"Is fame good or bad, sir?"

"Both ...," he said quietly, almost sadly.

Dagmar smiled even bigger, then frowned, drew in her breath, and said, "Sir, I'm s'pposed to give ye Gen'ral Shelby's compliments an' deliver this."

She thrust out a paper in a quivering hand. He hesitated, took it, read, then re-read a-loud Edward's message written under Shelby's direction and translated by Governor Reynolds (educated in Heidelberg, fluent in French and German). Shelby would never have sent her to a Mexican, but, he thought, she might bewitch the French. So, with an escort, he patted her off on the Appaloosa, transforming her, with a white flag stuck in her stirrup like a lance,

PHILLIP H. MCMATH

from his Sancho Panza to Joan d'Arc approaching Orleans. She made quite an impression, indeed, as a French cavalry patrol escorted her proudly into the city and through the Mexican crowd that thronged her along the *Calle Central* to army headquarters.

Jeanningros translated for Dagmar.

> General, I have the honor to report that I am within one mile of your command. Preferring exile to surrender, I have left my own country to seek service in that held by his Imperial Majesty, the Emperor Maximilian. Shall it be peace or war between us? If the former, with your permission, I shall enter your lines at once, claiming at your hands the courtesy due from one soldier to another. If the latter, I propose to attack you immediately.
>
> *Respectfully,*
> *Jos. O. Shelby*

Finishing, Jeanningros let go a mirthless laugh, saying, "My dear, Corporal, how many men does your general have?"

"I cain't say, sir," suddenly reminded of riding with the Yankee captain retreating from Camden and wondering why she was so much less frightened then than now.

"Well, you started with a thousand and now have buried at least a hundred ... we can count fresh graves easily enough. You have sold your cannon to our enemy for silver and now you're exhausted, low on food and ammunition, and must assault me with pistols and sabers riding tired horses, no? I have five thousand ... three regiments of Legionnaires ... and the Third Zouaves ... the best there is ... and two regiments of the Mexican Imperial Army ..."

"Legionnaires?" asked Dagmar.

"Yes, foreigners ... under French command ... hard men ... the weak ones don't survive our training, much less the campaigns ... but desperate ... always that ... desperate men are the blood of our Legion ..."

"Whut kin' of for'ners?" she asked, "frum whar?" she added, thinking up to now all the men were French.

"Oh, the usual Europeans ... mostly Germans and Austrians ... a few Swiss and Belgians ... usually homeless ... always on the run ... some eccentric, half-mad English ... and lots of romantic Irish, who, of course, love war and join just for the fun ... and even some renegade Americans with a price on their heads ... then there are the cutthroat Arabs, Turks, and a few black Africans picked up in Algiers. They all ... all ... each and everyone ... will fight you gladly ... not because they have anything against you, you understand ... if you are brave, they might even admire you ... but simply to have something to do. You see, my dear corporal, we are dying more of boredom than of the Juáristas. I even have to shoot one or two deserters from time to time ... just to maintain morale ... but they fight very well, indeed. Plus, unlike you, I haven't sold my cannon ... and have lots of ammunition ... plenty of water, food, and fresh horses ... you haven't a chance."

"Sir," she said, stiffing a bit, her pride touched, "we've been fighting fur four yar ag'inst the largest army in this whole entar world ..."

"I know, my dear Corporal Pilgrim," he interrupted with a wave of the hand, raising his voice a bit, "but now, if you attack, you will die beneath my walls." Then lowering his tone, added, "You cannot turn back ... and I block your way south ... you are quite simply trapped in Mexico ... between Juárez and Maximilian ... you'll never leave."

Dagmar swallowed hard.

"You should have joined Viesca. At least he would have brought along your cannon," he added casually.

"That's what I said," she said without thinking.

"Ah, then you are wise as well as brave," he replied with a smile, paused, then slowly stood up, adding with a chuckle and the flourish of throwing Shelby's note over the lieutenant's death warrant. "But tis no matter ... tell your general to march in immediately. He's the only real soldier that has yet to come out of Yankeedom. My emperor will bid him welcome! Tell him he's my guest, he and the members of his staff. Tell him to come in, my brave Corporal Pilgrim!"

"Thank yew, sir," she said, surprised.

"Ah, besides, you killed the bandits ... the crazy Cuban and the bad priest ... that damned Anselmo and the bastard Flores ... we owe you for that ... though Dupin will be disappointed, he wanted them for himself, of course. But you might be useful and, besides ... I like your courage."

Dagmar lifted a little taller.

"See to your fine horse, then get something to eat yourself. You look famished. I will send an escort to take you back this afternoon."

"Thank yew, sir."

"The captain will show you out."

Dagmar saluted smartly, did an about-face that was more awkward than she wished and exited quickly.

Colonel Jeanningros snapped back an unseen salute as she whirled around.

Watching her exit, he sat down again, relieved not to think about shooting the lieutenant for a moment at least.

When he had first seen Dagmar, standing proudly before him, he had known what he would do about Shelby. Yet the diversion had quickly passed and now he leaned back over the desk and flicked aside Shelby's message revealing the death warrant beneath, then picked it up, hesitated, and put it away—unsigned.

The evening banquet found Jeanningros enthroned as host centering a great table with his counterpart, the colonel of the Mexican Imperial Regiment (who spoke only Spanish), perched like a peacock on his left, chattering with his staff set out in a colorful line running from his sleeve to the end.

On his right, Jeanningros, beginning with Reynolds, honored the American politicians, while facing them, starting with Smith, were the military, each arranged in parallel lines according to rank and station, as the French officers, headed by Dupin, were placed to the opposite left, in a descending formation across from the Creoles—two rows of red, blue, and gold running one way, as the Southerners, in dress gray and gold, ran the other. (Kirby Smith, like the Mexican colonel, even wore his sword.)

Things had gone swimmingly for Shelby since the day before when he had plucked the happy tale from off Dagmar's eager tongue, and he was, for the moment at least, exultant enough to voice regret for his vote for Juárez. But this was lost on Magruder and Reynolds, who were busy cheering, while Major Edwards, never at a loss for a word or gesture, throated out a toast. "To King, Queen, and Country!" he proclaimed, brandishing a bottle of brandy from his hip for a quick trip round lip-to-lip amid a nervous laughter born of relief.

Quickly the eager Grays had saddled in column the final mile through the city gates and along the silent streets to a barracks and the first sheets since San Antonio. Rested, fed, and scrubbed, the men tonight "did the town," while their officers emerged from special quarters for an evening of wine, guitars, and the singing of smiling *décolleté* senoritas.

To be sure, Colonel Jeanningros, stimulated by the company, *absinthe* and the unexpected good news of being begrudgingly listed for brigadier, was exuberant.

Still there was, he insisted, to be one solecism—the freshly combed, strangely attractive Dagmar, who had washed and wiggled herself into new pants, shirt, and polished boots, was now presented with a bright new bandana to bind her throat *à la Texan,* a gift from Jeanningros himself, who sat her between Smith and the French, across from him, eye-to-his-eye, so to speak, conjoining the two.

"Thank yew, sir," Dagmar had said, somewhat taken aback, coming over and leaning slightly as the colonel tied his present into a colorful, broad bow.

"Voilà ... parfait!" he said proudly, leaning away to see it more fully.

"Thank yew," she repeated quietly, blushing for the first time she could remember, touching the bandana nervously with her one hand then going round self-consciously to her seat.

"Wine?" he asked, leaning over, pouring into her glass before she could refuse. She had never tasted it, hated even the smell of whiskey, and now looked at her wine with undisguised alarm.

A senorita, about her own age, came up quickly, ladled soup into her bowl, then, with a coy wink disappeared into the crowd of servants circling the table as they darted in an out of the kitchen.

Dagmar fingered the glass in nervous amazement: to her right was the infamous silver-bearded, brown-skinned Dupin, who, with suave, polished manners, had stood, bowed, spoken French while kissing her hand, then sat down by her with an ironic smile while mumbling something mysteriously to Jeanningros.

The other way she was even more astonished to find herself rubbing penned-up sleeve with General Kirby Smith, who demarked a descending constellation of counter-facing Confederates: Reynolds, Polk, Clark, Magruder, Allen, Gwin, Hindman, and, of course, Jo Shelby, with Major Edwards a bit out of place, stationed at his commander's side, ahead of the colonels, obviously promoted on the strength of being the scribe.

The fare surpassed all but the finest table as the senoritas hovered with bottle, dish, and spoon, while Jeanningros waxed without waning, adroitly moving in and out of three languages.

First, in expressing his Southern sympathy, he displayed a deep and surprising knowledge of the late war—how it was lost and might have been won—lamenting that a Franco-Confederate alliance was not reached in time to save each country from defeat.

But, fearing an indiscretion, Jeanningros skillfully shifted away, eliciting a few odd, but polite comments from Smith on the one hand, and some bantering, friendly, and very fluent French from Reynolds on the other, then chatting skillfully here and there with others, right and left, till he, from the safety of his own creation, soldier that he was, soon became bored and seized the conversation to sally forth with bold pride on his role in helping place Louis

PHILLIP H. MCMATH

Napoleon in power in the coup d'état of '51 known as *le-Deux-Decembre,* in which the cry in the streets changed from the *"Vive la République!"* to *"Vive l' Empereur!"*

He related how the *Elysee Palace* gates were flung open and the newly uniformed Louis rode through with his entourage led by his Uncle Jerome, Napoleon's brother, on one side, and the Count Charles de Flahaut, Talleyrand's bastard and Horetense's lover, on the other, as the Second Republic was smothered like a new puppy under the purple pillow of renewed Napoleonic ambition, and the Second Empire was then whelped out as the natural cur of the First.

But, as Seneca says, "great crimes have great rewards," and Jeanningros boasted of them while sipping his *absinthe: la gloire* of the Crimea, Algeria, Italy, and, above all, of the delights of China. Here his dancing eyes met Dupin's to exchange a smile of delight as in a mirror.

It was a career's culmination, Jeanningros proclaimed, the French and British marching upon Peking in '60, venturing upon the Versailles of the East, the Imperial Summer Palace, a fairytale castle set twelve miles from the great city, yet guarded only by the bravery of stone dragons leering at them impotently from the roof.

"Ah!" he said wistfully, like a man recalling a seduction, "it was filled with ten thousand dresses of silk and satin which we lifted as over the legs of an innocent maid ... revealing her treasures ... jewels ... rubies ... sapphires ... pearls ... ivories ... gold ... jade ... art ... priceless manuscripts ... all the tribute and loot that flattery and fear can furnish for an ancient Kingdom. How could we resist her violation!?"

Dupin offered a suave laugh, adding, "It took three days ... I was court-martialed, as the world knows ... but," he said with a nonchalant wave of a hand, "what did it matter? The emperor left instructions for it to be burnt. We saved it from the flames."

"Those Chinese would have cabbaged everything," interposed Jeanningros.

"What a place to loot," Shelby could not help adding with a touch of envy.

"So said Blucher in London," Jeanningros said merrily at this approval.

Dagmar, silent, but having tasted her wine and sensing her position, ventured a question but was interrupted as it formed on her tongue.

"That first night," Dupin said, not realizing Dagmar had tried to speak, "oh, what a night it was ... like nothing one has ever seen. Indeed, it was like something out of Dante's *Inferno* ... a veritable hell risen into the world ..."

Here he paused and let the curiosity reach the breaking point, then pressed on with a heavy French accent flavoring his fluent English. "You see, my friends, hell always creeps upon us from the simple things ... the simplest desires ... and this one came upon us because the French *soldat* loves his baubles ... just that ... and, like a little boy at Christmas, he fills his pack with all he can carry. So the darkness that first night was filled with the mad cacophony of indescribable noise of these stolen toys ... cuckoos sounding forth in their idiotic cuckooing repetitions ... springing out over and over again from Swiss clocks ... their chimes clanging the hour seemingly every second ... music boxes playing waltzes, quadrilles, and tearfully sad love songs ... endlessly ... tin creatures of all kinds, sizes, and shapes ... wound and unwound on bouncing springs ... jumping up over and over again to the giggles and merry drunken satisfaction of our devilish lads ... winding up hopping rabbits that stood dutifully to play tambourines for their masters ... mechanical monkeys banging cymbals like performing beggars ... metal, flightless birds beating their wings on springs with endlessly repeated cries, chirps, and calls ... all evoking a childish laughter throughout the night as the soldiers' jubilation was played to an accompaniment of flutes, clarinets, and horns in indescribable dissonance ... all done, of course, to the seething roar and buzz of men's moronic voices ... cheering, guffawing, and shouting ... merging together with the disharmony of a great hive ... no, a horde ... a horde of inmates suddenly revealed to the world by the collapsing roof of their asylum ... a bedlam exposing human lunacy to the *blasé* stars ..."

Dupin was entranced, and, so, entranced the others, mesmerizing them into a strange, incongruous silence that fell with a great, unexpected weight over them all. Even the senoritas, who knew no English, were infected by this sudden, heavy mood, and for a few seconds, stood still and listened with spoon, plate, and bottle hanging down like forgotten appendages from idle fingers.

Finally, sensing a self-consciousness that invited release, Dagmar, her vote for Juárez never far from her mind, again advanced her question, "What do you think of Maximilian?" she asked, quietly directing this neither to Jeanningros or Dupin but dragging it in front of both like bait in hopes of hooking either.

But weary of his own silence and wishing to change the humor of the moment that now hovered just above the morose, Shelby intruded. "Yes," he said, pushing the query toward his host, "His Majesty the Emperor, what kind of man is he, Colonel Jeanningros?"

"Ah, the Austrian," Jeanningros replied as reported here word for word by Edwards, puffing a cigar in satisfaction, seizing the chance to lift things a bit and speak on a subject that burdened his thoughts. "You should see him to

PHILLIP H. MCMATH

understand him. More of a scholar than a king … good at botany, a poet on occasion …"

"A poet?" said Shelby, incredulous.

"Yes, indeed … a traveler who gathers curiosities and writes books … a saint over his wine and a sinner among his cigars … in love with his wife …"

At this, Dupin reemerged, laughed, sincerely amused, but by his manner implied he had somehow heard all this before.

Jeanningros winked at him, then, with a turn of his head back to Shelby and a glance at Edwards, picked up where he had left off, saying: "Believing in destiny more than drilled battalions; good Spaniard in all but deceit and treachery; honest, earnest, tender-hearted, and sincere. But his faith in the liars who surround him is too strong, and his soul is too pure for the deeds that must be done. He cannot kill as we Frenchman do. He knows nothing of diplomacy. In a nation of thieves and cutthroats he goes devoutly to mass, endows hospitals, says his prayers, and sleeps the good man's sleep in the Palace of Chapultepec."

He paused for effect, puffed again, glanced at the amused Dupin, puffed some more, then hid himself in a cloud of floating gray, letting his words soak in, glad to have mesmerized as well as Dupin. Noticing the gaze of Edwards, he felt confident that the good major would not let him sink into the oblivion of all temporary renown, and so lowered the cigar and nodded slightly in that direction as well.

"Will he survive?" asked Kirby Smith, surfacing from his reserve, fortifying his words with the advantages of taciturnity.

"Bah!" said Jeanningros, waving away the smoke now as if it were a mirage obscuring reality. Then leaning over to Smith, who, sitting almost directly across, offered a kind of intimacy, so that Jeanningros, with a somewhat lower but still audible voice after glancing at the Creole who was busy chatting, as he had been all evening in Spanish to a major, said in an *entre nous* confidence, "His days are numbered, nor can all the power of France keep his crown upon his head, if indeed it can keep that head upon his shoulders."

"Does he have the confidence of Bazaine?" General Clark intruded, as if thinking only of his own question, and, unlike the Harvard lawyer he had once been, not listening to the previous answer.

"The marshal, you mean?" replied Jeanningros, a little surprised.

"Yes," insisted Clark.

"Oh! The marshal keeps his own counsel. Besides, I have not seen him since coming northward," he said offhandedly, then shifting the subject asked, "Have you journeyed far, General Clark?"

"I have come from Texas ... and hope to see Mexico City," said Clark, politely ignoring the deflection from Bazaine, which obviously made Jeanningros uncomfortable.

"Ah, Mexico City! It is not unlike Paris," said Jeanningros with warmth, "save for the great cows at court, who would never be permitted as ladies-in-waiting at Versailles," he added with laughter, loudly echoed by Dupin, who was equally amused.

"Still, Maximilian is, indeed, a man of virtue?" said Smith ponderously.

"Oh, yes, General," Jeanningros parried, "he is that ... but I find that little sins are sometimes less burdensome than great virtues."

Dupin chuckled, Smith frowned, Shelby smiled, but Dagmar, ever undiverted, after waiting a beat and seeing her chance, quickly thrust into the space trailing this witticism, saying, "So, Juárez will win?"

Now it was Jeanningros's turn to be taken aback. He stopped laughing, looked at her intently, then in a subdued but sincere voice said, "Yes, of course."

"And so the good emperor will lose his Kingdom?" Dagmar replied softly.

Jeanningros laughed his mirthless laugh.

"My dear corporal ... all Kingdoms are lost," he rejoined, as if realizing it for the first time, a painful smile recoiling his scar like a struck serpent.

The dinner dragged on, but the climax had been reached and the evening soon bored Jeanningros into retiring with that depressed irritation that is so often the friend of euphoria. Reaching his quarters, he called gruffly for the captain of the guard, inquiring of the condemned lieutenant.

"He has asked for his pistol and a bottle of brandy," said the officer soberly.

Jeanningros laughed; he was in no mood for mercy.

"Bring me the warrant," he commanded. "It's in my desk. Bring it now!"

The captain obeyed and Jeanningros signed it—the young man would be shot "at dawn." Then the colonel retired, but he did not have pleasant dreams. Restless, he was awakened by the sun illuminating his window, thought a moment, then arose, and sent for the officer.

"Yes, sir?" asked the captain grimly, now standing in the half-light of the doorway, staring at his commander looking rather absurd in his nightshirt and slippers.

"What is going on?" growled Jeanningros. "I have not heard firing."

"The squad is falling out, sir, but they wanted breakfast ... said they could not shoot a man on an empty stomach ... so, I let them eat."

"Good."

"Sir?"

"Cancel it."

"Cancel?"

"Yes, cancel the execution, I said!"

"Yes, sir," said the captain, perplexed, waiting because he knew there would be more.

"Send him the pistol and brandy ... as he asked."

"Yes, sir."

"At least ... it'll save his honor," Jeanningros added, offhandedly.

"Ah," said the captain, understanding. "Yes, sir," he added, saluted, smiled slightly, and quickly turned to go.

Jeanningros followed as the officer stepped into the hall's darkness. "Captain, I'd have given him two bottles if he had asked!" he yelled madly down the corridor, laughed again, turned, grabbed the door, and slammed it shut. Going back to bed, he slept till noon, did not hear the shot or see the body loaded and hauled away to a small hill above Monterrey and buried in a grave dug by campesinos.

Instead, he arose, washed, shaved, put on a fresh uniform, drank a little brandy himself, ate lunch with Dupin, and never spoke of it again.

CHAPTER TWENTY-THREE

*If your Emperor had been serious in this thing, he should have formed an
alliance with Jefferson Davis long ago.*
  —*Jo Shelby to Jeanningros*

Within a few days the ever-restless Shelby, after allowing to Jeanningros that
the alliance should have been made much sooner, but though it was probably
"too late," he, if given permission, might still "organize an American force capable of keeping Maximilian on his throne composed of men delighted to fight
the Yankees again," adding gravely, otherwise, "the French cannot remain," and
clearly his plan was the "only hope."

Jeanningros replied that, alas, Bazaine was expecting any day for Paris to
reduce him, but, still, if the Southerners wished, he did not imagine the marshal would much mind their dying for France, then added, according to
Edwards, with a slightly mordant smile, "You have my full permission to march
to the Pacific, to Guaymas, or Matzatlan, or wherever you choose, and to take
whatever steps you deem necessary to recruit an army for the empire."

Shelby thanked him sincerely, saluted, and said goodbye to the colonel's *au
revoir* then promptly marched his men off to the old capital of mountainous northern Mexico. Here he found the rather large village of Saltillo, nestling in the serenity of its newfound unimportance some fifty miles southwest of Monterrey.

At dusk, a little short of town, his legion came upon the inert glory of Buena
Vista. Here, they camped among its valley of bones and strolled over its stones
like tourists in the eerie brightness of a fat moon that lifted itself over the peaks
of the Sierra Madres Oriental, coming in its double-size—on command—they
whispered, just in time for a moment's reflection among the forgotten skulls of
war.

More had begun here than anyone had ever guessed, and coming back now
under the crush of time's turning wheel—with the gravity of four violent years
upon their backs—the scene was given a special weight that Thomas Hindman
and John Magruder tried manfully to lift with their casual recollection of the
events on those hot two days in '47.

"Here was I, a future 'Prince,'" laughed Magruder, and "over there was the Jove-like King Zachary, whose son Prince Richard, then serving as his squire, had been sent home with sickness, to be saved for the coming of Mansfield's renown. There was the future King Jeff himself with you, Thomas, Knight Hindman at his side." "Yes, you're right, I was there," agreed the "Fire Eater" and former generalissimo/dictator of Confederate Arkansas, and he added, "hidden in the mesquite brush there was Braxton Bragg with his battery."

Then Magruder waxed eloquent again, saying, "Over that little rise were the courageous Kentuckians and the stalwart Indianians; there was Knight Archibald Yell with his marvelous Mounted Arkansas Regiment." And, he might have added, that state's first congressman and second governor who had resigned to form his cavalry upon the Rock to ride away in emulation of Moscoso, presaging Steele and Shelby down the Southwest Trail; surpassing Steele by passing through Washington, the Spaniard by crossing the Brazos, and forcing upon Shelby an emulation through San Antonio, across the Río Grande, through Monterrey to here, where this brave Indian fighter and veteran of "Old Hickory's" New Orleans triumph had, as one of Jackson's brave backwoods "riffraff," sent Wellington's brother-in-law, the foolishly proud General Pakenham, packing home in a hogshead of rum to molder in Westmeath rather than the Mississippi, as Yell had hoped also to do so here to the Mexican *Supremo*, perhaps in a barrel of *tequila*.

This governor/colonel, Sir Archibald, in his half century was thrice married, thrice widowed, thrice buried, and twice unburied, yet could find death but once riding his charger hard upon the lance of one of King Santa Anna's knights, who gladly graced his brain with a sharp mortality. Behind him, over there, said Magruder, looking the other way, "was the ever surviving, ever envious, Lord of the reserve company, the ubiquitous Albert Pike," who later drifted home unharmed to carp forever about being so egregiously unhooked from the lip of such a hoped-for fame which would only elude him again at the Elkhorn.

"But there, over there," Magruder said pointing another way, turning now with awe, his flushed face beaming washed-out white by the moon and his arm swinging like a musket toward the Grand Mexican Army, "it was there, there, where its gold and scarlet lancer's brave charge was broken, just when it seemed about to succeed, deflected by Davis's Mississippi Rifles, yeoman farmers and frontiersmen, kneeling and coolly pouring fire upon the screaming horses and men, flipping them upon the ground like children spilling toys in the sand of play, cruelly turning them aside, then pushing them from the field with Davis and Thomas in furious pursuit."

Hindman smiled at this now, as one George Meade had later related. This Meade was the future hero and savior of Mr. Lincoln's Union, who on that Pennsylvania field did what Pakenham's brother-in-law, Wellington, had proved at Waterloo—that the rising star of talent will often defeat the declining one of genius—thus he did what no one else had ever done, or would really ever do, as the Iron Duke had done to Napoleon, so likewise did Meade defeat the greater man in Lee.

This same Meade, who had seen so much of war, still could say of Taylor's men that day (out-numbered four to one) that the Buena Vista battle was the "greatest feat" ever performed by American arms, "then or ever."

And Magruder, of course, in telling his tale of the good vision, repeated this praise, and might have added, pointing this way and that, "here we can see the night-lit blanching bones of our great glory—a victory conceived in the fury of a battle that bore upon us only an immortal defeat. Because, here now by our side, walking with us in this lunar light are the ghosts of Meade's own great Gettysburg and all the others close behind: Sharpsburg, Bull Run (one and two), Chancellorsville, Fredericksburg, Seven Days, Wilderness, Spotsylvania, Petersburg, Atlanta, Chattanooga, Nashville, Chickamauga, Franklin, Stones' River, Perryville, Shiloh, Corinth, Iuka, Brice's Crossroads, Vicksburg, Val Verde, Champion's Hill, Malvern Hill, Mechanicsville, Port Hudson, Fort Donelson, Fort Henry, Fort Pillow, Fort Smith, Wilson's Creek, Elkhorn, Prairie Grove, Arkansas Post, Helena, Honey Springs, Holly Springs, Poison Springs, Pickets Mill, Marks's Mill, Mansfield, Pleasant Hill, Ringgold Gap, Red River, Jenkins's Ferry, and innumerable skirmishes and engagements which erased men's feeble lives in time and numbers insufficient for memory to record; 600,000 corpses striding here in the night among ourselves and the older skulls whose death their own death did portend; here, my friends, if you listen closely, are the cries of their lost years moaning in the cannon's groan, in the muttering muskets and in the sad singing of swinging sabers; in the shriek of horses, in the wounded wailing and the cries of the dying; the sorrowing of their widows and the weeping of their orphans; all are here—here set upon the dead glory of this half-forgotten, bloody, lifeless, rock-strewn Mexican field. Here two nations were destroyed and two reborn in the strife of all hard births, leaving us as no more than redundant, wretched witnesses whom toying, fickle death has delayed in taking, so as to curse us with the remembering of always trying to forget."

But of course neither Magruder nor Hindman nor the others said this or anything like it. They had returned to Mexico in the hopes of making all the suffering into something else—of reposing upon these restless spirits a shroud of an eternal, immortal grandeur—and had not come simply to cast the dead down "naked upon the earth" in the ignominy of all the final cruelty of oblivious war.

No, indeed. No one said that night upon the field of Mars that they were pursuing an illusion as substantial as the moonbeams that backlit this moment—the "moonshine" of what Sherman said it all was. Instead, they merely chatted happily of its living glory, quietly laughing with all their fellows in the pride of such a victory, seeing it as they wished to see it and no other way, giving those numberless lost years of those men no more value than the wisps of melancholy, white smoke of their morning fire, then turned at last away and simply stumbled off to sleep soundly upon the stony ground, to arise afresh with a bright new sun and trot merrily into Saltillo.

It was still early when the brigade of iron passed quietly through the solemn town to camp on its other side. Here they were soon bedeviled by guerrillas and then diverted by a gulching flood into a western detour to the French garrison at Parras where an alcoholic and overly senior colonel, one Vincent du Preuil, backed with old brandy and a fresh dispatch from Bazaine, rudely explained the countermanding of Jeanningros. It was feared, he condescended to explain, that the Americans might just "switch to Juarez" and so must return to Texas or report immediately to Mexico City. There would be no journey of recruitment to Sonora or anywhere else, he added with a malicious half-drunken delight.

But Shelby remonstrated with enough force to lift this colonel to his wobbly feet cursing with florid-faced words that were returned in kind by Shelby, and thus, in order to avoid bloodying the desk, a challenge was offered and accepted for the morrow—"brandy and pistols at dawn." "With pleasure," each said with the forced bravado of such occasions, then saluted the other stiffly as a seal to the bargain.

But fortunately for one, or maybe both, Brigadier Jeanningros, arriving in the "nick of time" on inspection, said "no" and ordered a sober apology from Vincent du Preuil after coffee and some hot *frijoles* corncakes for breakfast to settle his stomach if not his nerves.

Yet, Jeanningros added firmly to Shelby that, alas, Vincent du Preuil had been correct, and it was, indeed, the marshal's order and must be obeyed. It was home or the capital—there was no other choice.

And so it was, at the cost of a few more lives here and there, and after many more adventures, such as rescuing a damsel in distress, one Inez Walker, from some *bandidos* at a place called La Encarnacion; then afterward riding off to relieve a guerrilla-besieged garrison of French soldiers at a place called Matehuala, whose grateful major turned the town into a "paradise" of saturnalia, which Edwards described with uncharacteristic understatement merely as nearly endless "days of feasting and mirth," which they abandoned only with the greatest reluctance to resume a routine of skirmishing and rescuing on the dusty road south. They arrived at last in the town of Queretaro, well secured by the French Army in a rich valley of *haciendas* and *rancheros*, and riding through there, they passed the magnificent aqueduct built for the ancient Indian capital of the other Tula but which had also served Tenochtitlan, then passed Huehuetoca and Coyotepec, and finally up the rim of the great Valley where, in a fold of land forty miles wide and eighty long cut in the earth like a giant's sleeve, they saw the greatest city that most had ever seen, or ever would see, that of Mexico laid out before them like *Shangri-la* in a dream.

CHAPTER TWENTY-FOUR

*I wear a sombrero when riding. We eat à la Mexicaine, we have a carriage
with many mules and bells, we are always wrapped in serapes, I go to
Mass in a mantilla.*
　　—*Carlotta writing to Eugénie*

When Cortés and his cohort of conquistadors had seen Mexico-Tenochtitlan
in 1519, it seemed a fairy-like land which they knew most men would never
see and they but once. Emerging between the two great snow-crowned volcanoes, standing like guarding gods above the eastern ridge, Iztaccihuatl and
Popocatepetl, smoking ominously straight at them, "like an arrow," one survivor would say, after finishing, as they had, the arduous, fighting, meandering
march of well more than a hundred miles from the base-camp village, newly
found and founded by themselves, at the end of a probing sea sail from the tiny
island of Cozumel where they had first touched land from Cuba, and from
which they had crossed through and over the *Cofre De Perote* Mountain, then
circled the large salt lake to Cholula, to treat and defeat the Indians in that
place, put them to the sword, as it were, while releasing the hostages chained
there for the fattening of sacrifice and ritualistic cannibalism which sincerely
shocked these Christians. All along the way, people of various other tribes,
whom the Castilians simply called *los naturales*, offered to help them out of
hatred and resentment of the conquering Aztecs, and it came to pass, that with
the aid of these thousands, they at last climbed up to see this view of the Valley
of Mexico, which, as one would write, honored the eye with nothing less than
"another new world of great cities and towers and a sea and, in the middle of
it, a very great city."

What he sketched, of course, was Tenochtitlan, whose quarter of a million
citizens lived in a vast capital of pyramids, temples, stone houses, and buildings laced together by a tapestry of streets and boulevards set solidly upon an
island in a large, twenty-five-mile-long lake waving seven thousand feet into
the sky, and served by three causeways stretching like the long, fine legs of a
fat, floating, amphibious spider touching the shore. Here it sustained itself

within a web of satellites checked into a powerful but subservient lacustrine alliance, as peace always is, by the ever-impending threat of war—Texcoco and Tacuba, being the most important—anchoring, as it were, this Aztec Kingdom of a million living in a land larger than Spain, and like her, shouldering two oceans, east and west, as the supreme arachnid of her time and place, while providing to her dominions a kind of order, prosperity, and culture in return for the blood and bounty of slaves, sacrifice, and submission.

Thus, said the poet of Mexico:

> Who could conquer Tenochtitlan?
> Who could shake the foundation of heaven?

But, unknown to most, these Iberians lived in such a heaven shaking time, since, as Cortés had founded the town from which they had just marched, the modern liberal one, Vera Cruz, that would later save Benito Juárez, which Cortés had established for his Habsburg master. In his name, along with gold and God, of course, he had come to conquer all and everyone, for the very Catholic Charles of Austria, the previous Don Carlos I of Spain, who was, indeed, elected in Frankfurt am Main as Holy Roman Emperor on the very same day that Cortés consecrated his new city, on Good Friday, June 28, 1519, as *Villa Rica de Vera Cruz*.

In his election, this god-like Habsburg had become father of the greatest Kingdom of all. Now, unknown even to himself, through this servant, Hernan Cortés, he was about to have delivered unto him a very "New Spain," which like an ambitious son who, with the ever rising strength of youth, would soon grow up to rival the Old.

Nor could Cortés and his men have known, too, that in that very same year a sailor named Magellan (with a father fittingly named Ulysses), after being denied by Portugal, would be enjoined by their far-seeing Charles to go and squeeze the globe until it fit neatly into the palm of his royal hand, to be held, shown, and finally set, for all to see, upon a purple pillow proximate to his throne like a golden orb.

Nor did they know either that an obscure German priest named Luther would, before the faithful Cortés could sail home in his splendorous fame to Catholic Spain with the saved souls of this New World in his pocket, purloined, as it were, from the perdition of Lucifer—tack upon an obscure church door some printed points of protest against the very same power that had ordained Cortés's sovereign Charles as emperor of the empire His Holiness the Pope preferred to call Roman.

PHILLIP H. MCMATH

So, in standing between Popocatepetl and Iztaccihuatl, then, these Europeans and Indians were unknowingly standing between the twin volcanoes of Conquest and Reformation through which, in making a New World into one, they were unwittingly unmaking and dividing the Old.

And, today, as an unintended monument to their audacity, pride, and glory, there stands on the same spot where Cortés sanctified his coastal city named for the "True Cross," as a kind of Golgotha for all of Mexico, the nuclear plant of *Laguna Verde,* a symbol of modernity's own volcanism, that sits puffing its satanic fire and smoke like Popocatepetl and Iztaccihuatl "straight at us" by the sea.

To be sure, our lost legion knew little of Cortés and his great drama with Montezuma; yet, as a group, they knew, of course, that Mexico had been Indian, then Spanish, mixed the two, and now had seemingly lost its independence to France.

Men, through a stubborn disinclination to see the past, are forever condemning themselves to a stolid blindness in the present, and, to be sure, these were no different. Thus, initially, only a few, through a kind of rugged half-sightless, touching intuition, could, despite the martial superiority of the Europeans, now see the feebleness of the French in this part of the Americas.

Yet, Mexico had played such a role in their recent memory that a little of its history had seeped through and was now jogged into view by the vision of this valley that lay before them. In a sense, they all half realized, sitting upon their horses, pausing, and looking across this wondrous sight of a city, mountains, and volcanoes, greater than any had ever seen, that here their country's, and, had they known the word, *La Florida's,* fate, had somehow come full circle and was tied up in History's neat loop through the West Indies, the Confederacy, the Southwest, and Mexico.

Though they did not know in their own Southland of the early Spanish like De Soto, Moscoso, or Cabeza de Vaca and those who followed, nor very much of the French anywhere but New Orleans or St. Louis, they all knew of General Winfield Scott, "Old Fuss and Feathers" as he was called, who had come from Vera Cruz (the route of all such invaders), resting his anxious Gringos at Puebla.

But they did know that Scott had left this Puebla to fight and win battles against the same Santa Anna they had just spoken of at places called Cerro Gordo, Contreras, Churubusco, and Chapultepec. And, further, that Scott had marched in triumph with stellar subordinates shouldering such imperishable surnames as Lee, McClellan, Grant, and Meade, all the way to this same legendary citadel Chapultepec that now lay in the distance, a hard but doable ride from this northern valley view overlooking the city which Scott and his young immortals paraded into along the *Plaza Grande*, past the cathedral sitting upon the very same spot and made from the very same stones of the great Aztec pyramid which Cortés had marveled at when he entered the city peacefully with a few hundred Spaniards, some horses, dogs and a thousand Indian porters, only, after a peaceful but tenuous interlude, to be forced out in the bloody *noche triste*, yet not retreating much past the volcanoes as a lesser man would have done, glad to have escaped, but to halt, rest, make alliances in those mountains and around these lakes, to build brigantines, then lay an amphibious siege for a month-long, violent, desperate house-to-house fight, which for a moment he seemed to have lost, and which he had hoped to avoid, while watching helplessly as his captured men, Castilians, and Indians were marched up and made to dance in full view of the contending barricades to be sacrificed with an obsidian knife thrust, then thrown down to the bottom, tumbling the steep steps made just for that; and for which Cortés vowed conquest, conversion, and the building of a church for Christ in the city he had saved only by destroying.

Most knew, of course, though mostly ignorant of any but the most general thing about the conquistador, that, in the American conquest, Lee had been the most distinguished of all, whom Scott would call the "gallant and indefatigable Lee." Yet few knew that it was he who had found that the key could be inserted into the lock by swinging round, just as Cortés had done, to the south, under the marshes and lakes, skirting Xochimilico, coming in from the west—a maneuver that was not lost on one obscure Lieutenant Sam Grant, who not only saw it but helped do it, then did it again, in the second of these three strikes in '63, at a place called Hard Times, when, like Scott and Cortés, he landed from the water, forgot his navy, then, not with the help of a Bobbie Lee or *los naturales,* but with that of a Black slave, swam ashore just at the right spot, then swung round and under from another direction to unlock Vicksburg, then enter to close the door behind and cut the Confederacy in half.

Grant saw that it could be done, knew too that he could leave the water, move independently in hostile country, live off the enemy's land, and fight a war of movement against a brave foe betrayed by mediocrities who knew not what he would do next, much less what to do against him.

Somehow all their fates, like the country's itself, were bound up with that of Mexico, and Lee, like Meade and Grant, and now Shelby, had first seen the more mundane Monterrey before discovering the city of lakes and volcanoes

---

that spread before them in such splendor that they were shocked into under-standing that Mexico was something other than squalor and senoritas.

Grant, too, had ridden across the vast open wilderness of Texas, describing it so well in his memoir (the best of the war), as plentiful of game and herds of wild horses that enchanted him in their free roaming of limitless spaces. One hears a note of envy of the freedom that he always wanted but never seemed to find amid all of the heavy baggage of glory.

Sam Grant was nothing if not a paradox. Not wanting a military career, hat-ing West Point (hoping while there that Congressman Davy Crockett's bill to abolish it would pass so he could go home), frustrated and ruined in his early career, himself a slave owner to the end, he became one of America's greatest liberators.

So sensitive of soul that he could not bear to shoot so much as a single turkey or deer in Texas, even when his belly demanded it, or stand aside in mute for-bearance when a horse was whipped by a desperate teamster moving wagons at his bidding through enemy Mississippi; Grant could order men to die by the thousands with the coolest of equanimity, or, oddly, never disgrace his tongue with vulgarity through all the bitter vicissitudes and frustrations of alcoholism, ruination, poverty, politics, and war, yet after crossing at Matamoros, simply could not bite this same tongue quite hard enough when it spoke to Mexican pack mules.

In almost invisible parallel of his rival, Lee, like Grant, had ridden across Texas to San Antonio, but in his case, not with a group but alone, leading a fairly worth-less Irishman named Jim Connelly, his manservant, and two Missouri mules, while hurrying along on a cob with the deliciously ironic name of Creole. He arrived in that town like the others, to be staffed to one Brigadier General John E. Wool, commanding an army of reinforcements bound for Taylor. Here Lee rested a short time, before riding Creole the 164 miles to the Río Grande in two weeks, he crossed, as Shelby would at Eagle, into Piedras Negras, coming into Mexico with 1,400 mounted men, some cannon, and 188 wagons.

Thus, Captain Lee, like the others, at last saw Monterrey, Saltillo, and even Parras. But unlike Shelby, was not confronted there by a brandy-besotted Frenchman but dined at a great plantation-like *hacienda,* which, in seeing it and the country around, impressed him into remarking a certain resemblance to his beloved Virginia, lettering home that, "There are some large estates here, on which there is a union of wealth, poverty, plenty, want, elegance, & slove-ness [*sic*] as with us."

Missing the Buena Vista battle, Captain Bobbie was soon ordered to Brazos, loading there on the *USS Massachusetts* to loll about the coast for two dreary weeks while sharing a stateroom with one obscure, seasick colonel named Joseph Eggleston Johnston, who in the fullness of '62, would get himself wounded in time for his junior shipmate to save Richmond.

Still in the salad days of sunny Mexico, Lee had waded ashore at last to find a better sailor than Joe Johnston in a man named Raphael Semmes, a good Marylander who, like Lord Baltimore, was a devout Catholic among lots and lots of Protestants, and was seen sidling up to Lee, suggesting with a sly smile that with the help of a few Marines they might unload some ship cannons for a sandy bombardment of the town they had to take before marching to Puebla and the land of promise among the volcanoes.

It came to pass then that Semmes, the future commander of the *CSS Sumter*, with which he captured eighteen Yankee prizes before abandoning her in Gibraltar for the immortal *Alabama* to take or sink sixty-nine more, till she was finally sunk off France so he could tour Europe then return and fight again at sea, did on this pleasant, if very hot afternoon at the Mexican beach, find himself firing with the High Church Lee, upon a city founded on the very day and honoring their mutual Lord's sublime and sacred martyrdom, till they pounded through its walls so Scott could march in to take this "True Cross" and hold it aloft to heaven, not as a burden of peace, but as a bounty of battle.

Perhaps there was a pang of conscience about it all because the Protestant general soon ordered everyone to attend Mass in the city's Catholic Cathedral where with its fathers they sang and marched in a circle—Scott, Lee, McClellan, Semmes, and all the rest—to a Latin *Te Deum*, wearing not Carlotta's *mantilla,* of course, but carrying candles in a rather self-conscious gesture of reconciliation and temporary counter-reformation of Luther for expiation of all the hell's fire that Lee and Semmes had blessed them with in taking the place.

While Shelby's men in the morning of their memories knew of course about Lee's apotheosis in the late great war, they knew but a bit of him in Mexico and nothing of *Cinco de Mayo*, but they had, nevertheless, come to realize that Maximilian, as Shelby had observed to Jeanningros, could have won it all had His Grace "been serious about this thing" instead of dabbling at etiquette and butterflies in the Palace of Chapultepec.

But Jeanningros's dinner description of the man, recorded as it was by the assiduous Major Edwards (unquestionably bearing, one suspects, given its tone and style, the best the good major could offer), was soon stuck hard upon their minds as a kind of judgment on all their own green hopes.

PHILLIP H. MCMATH

Louis Napoleon, they now realized, quite simply could not have made a better choice for Benito and Abe. But they were also beginning to see something else besides, something much more important—they were beginning to see the power of the powerless. In this, they were quickly growing up from the immortal courage of hot youth to the more mortal wisdom of cooler years.

That is, on the river at that dirty little backwater border village, *Adelantado* Viesca could, despite the powerlessness of his small army in that dreary town, still offer them the future, while the grand Emperor Maximilian, though master of a powerful imperial army, enthroned in a great city, could sit merely upon the weakness of the moment and hand up to them only the very great nothing of his impotent present—the powerlessness of the powerful.

They would not have been able to put voice to this but were beginning nevertheless to understand that if conquest fails, synthesis does not. Cortés had burned his ships; and in so doing, Spain had remained here and through this remaining had created a new thing—a symbiosis of Cortés and Montezuma— the new *Mestizo* race—Indian and Iberian—a blood and culture mixing into one new nation of Mexico.

Yet these French, they were coming to see, were merely intruders—nothing more. Their ships were always at the ready. Scott and Taylor were the same. But the men who had voted so foolishly at Eagle, voting as men might in Eagle and not yet in Piedras Negras, were gradually developing the instincts of the uncanny two among them who had bothered to look across the river—that is, to see where they were going and not merely where they had been.

These mounted hundreds who stood over this magnificent view of what had once been Tenochtitlan, the Aztec capital of temples and pyramids, markets and plazas, now became Mexico City, with its even wider boulevards, greater markets, and Christian churches that had soaked up the lakes like an ever-spreading sponge; these were not the same men as those who had voted back in Texas. They had changed, had begun to become part of the very thing they had so impetuously intruded upon, and their instincts imprinted now by blood and time were also changing and were no longer born of the lust to interpose, to subdue, but a new one—to *interfuse*.

But, alas, there was no voting again. The only hope was to show this Emperor what they themselves had finally come to see. And so Shelby, knowing this, knowing that they now knew what he had tried to say with words and had failed, knew that for such men mere words were never enough, that what comes to them must come seeping up through the saddle into their very backside, after a pause to enjoy the view, at last gave the signal and rode his lost legion down the rim and into the valley, finding the fine road past the old Seminario de San Martín, past Cuautitlan, Tlalnepantla, Azcapotzalco, Tacuba, and to Popotla, passed the Ahuehuete Tree where Cortés had wept for his dead after *la noche triste*, where he had vowed to return and conquer the city, past there, past the cemetery where the American fallen slept after Scott's duplication of Cortés; into San Cosme Calle and down the Puente de Alvarado, across the canal over which the conquistadors had leapt in their last, desperate assault, then past Caballito with its bronze statue to the Habsburg, Charles V, riding past him, and into the Paseo de Burcareli, and at last, after two thousand miles, on September 3, 1865, these Grays entered into the greatest city in the Americas, rode along its streets and grand avenues, galloped along its magnificent plaza and its great cathedral where before them Cortés, Santa Anna, Scott, Lee, Grant, Meade, and McClellan had all marched in glory and Juárez had ridden in humility, then onward to the fortress of Ciudadela near the Habsburg palace, which was put at their disposal by Maximilian, and into the shadow of where he sat imprisoned as much by a name as a throne and who, if he would but have them, they had come to save and by so doing, might, also, somehow save themselves.

PHILLIP H. MCMATH

CHAPTER TWENTY-FIVE

Adíos, Mamá Carlotta!
—Juárista battle cry

The meeting took place in the Palacio National. General Shelby, wearing his dress of gold braid and sword, now stood before the man he had come so far to see—a living, breathing Habsburg, the Emperor of Mexico, the heir of Charles V, standing before him, smiling in full kingly regalia, flanked on one elbow by one Count De Noue, his interpreter, and his general, Marshal Bazaine, on the other. While Shelby, for his part, was seconded by "Prince" John Magruder and Confederate commodore Matthew Maury, the famous hydrographer, inventor of submarines and torpedoes, and, of course, the faithful scribe, Major Edwards, recording all as related herein word for word and standing beside and slightly ahead of him their steadfast aide, Dagmar Pilgrim, who, in turn, was smartly scrubbed and dressed *à la Mexicaine,* to borrow Carlotta's phrase, with leather bell-bottomed riding trousers, whose thigh tightness flared out over her polished new leather boots, silver spurs (a gift), a matching blouse (her sleeve penned with a borrowed diamond broach), a (also borrowed) cowhide sleeveless jacket with gold buttons, leather tassels, and Jeanningros's red bandana bowed broadly around her neck over an ornately decorated black sombrero covering her back while hanging under two neatly knotted blond pigtails.

This one-armed Rebel redneck daughter of a bushwhacking backwoods bootlegger had come a long way. Indeed, she had never seen a real city of any kind, but had now ridden and fought over half a continent to find herself suddenly residing in one of the world's greatest hives and, moreover, now stood before a European emperor in his palace, placed there among generals and counts in the presence of a scion of the greatest family in all the world.

She was afraid, awed, and a little embarrassed. Did he know how she had voted back in Texas? she wondered, as she stood gazing upon a this tall, regal man who greeted them each one with a friendly and familiar cordiality that surprised her, forcing her to curtsy as he gently took her one hand and spoke in his accented English, which sounded so strange, pushing her, as it were, into a dipping down of her knee in a gesture she had never contemplated much less ever performed, but somehow felt she must do as she stared into his deep blue eyes, and thanked him in a low inaudible voice, then, as she arose, that is, dipped up as quickly as she had dipped down, glanced over his large sensual mouth and the thick Habsburg lower lip, the likes of which she had never seen, but which, unknown to her, persevered stubbornly from generation to generation like some pertinacious deformity of their seemingly indestructible destiny.

Her gaze then came to rest upon this strange protuberance, but, fearing he noticed her eye upon his permanent pout, moved in an embarrassed quick retreating glance over his long, flowing yellow head and beard; more blond even than her own hair which had begun, like most Southern Anglos, to take on an auburn maturity, unlike the true Teutonic, which she saw before her persisting even unto age as a thick, deep, unwavering vein of deepest gold.

But with every step of her Appaloosa, Dagmar had become more and more convinced of the rightness of her vote—and now, looking upon his face, with its curious contradictory combination of sophistication, compassion, sensitivity, and foolish greatness, she saw the man was doomed, and she gasped. Maximilian smiled ironically, as if he knew her thoughts and quite agreed, released her hand, then moved away, greeting the others with a formal familiarity that greatly surprised everyone.

It shouldn't have. After all, his charm was famous, and the Grays of all shapes had been welcomed not only with words but with power. Commodore Maury was soon made commissioner of immigration: John Magruder was chief of the Colonization Land Office; General John Causland of Virginia (Lee's top engineer) was made head of such for the Mexican Imperial Railway; Governor Reynolds managed the "short-line" rails which fingered from the city to its environs, while Governor Allen was already publishing a state-subsidized, English-language newspaper, the *Mexican Times*. Generals Price and Smith had also arrived and thousands of lesser names had likewise come to stay, serve, settle, or slip through Mexico to points even further south.

But Shelby, as always, was more ambitious. He wanted to raise and command an army—a Praetorian Guard to serve the throne—be this Habsburg's Shelby-Sejanus, nothing less.

Maximilian finally sat, but with Bazaine still standing at his side, to hear the petition which was at last solicited from Shelby. He offered to raise his legion of expatriates, Gray and Blue, to replace the withdrawing French.

"It is only a question of time, Your Majesty, before the French forces are withdrawn," he said bluntly, looking at the marshal, who, it was reported, blanched into a "sarcastic" smile.

"Why do you think so?" asked Maximilian calmly, not betraying any sense of desertion by the Napoleon who had sent him.

"Because the War between the States is at an end, and Mr. Seward will insist on the rigorous enforcement of the Monroe Doctrine. France does not desire a conflict with the United States. It would be neither popular nor profitable. I have left behind me one million men in arms, not one of them had been discharged from service. The nation is sore over this occupation, and the presence of France is a perpetual menace. I hope Your Majesty will pardon me, but in order to speak the truth it is necessary to speak plainly."

"Go on," said the emperor quietly, with a weary, fatalistic gesture that implied the opposite.

But Shelby pressed on, saying he could raise a Foreign Legion of some forty thousand Gray veterans.

"I have authority for saying to you that the American government would not be averse to the enlistment of as many soldiers in your army as might wish to take service, and the number need only be limited to the exigencies of the empire. Thrown upon your own resources, you would find no difficulty, I think, in establishing more friendly relations with the United States. In order to put yourself in a position to do this, and in order to sustain yourself sufficiently long to consolidate your occupation of Mexico and make your government a strong one, I think it absolutely necessary that you should have a corps of foreign soldiers devoted to you personally, and reliable in any emergency."

Maximilian looked at the other Americans without speaking, and they all quickly agreed with nods and understated assents.

There was a pause then the prince thanked them quietly, and, as they were dismissed, withdrew with Bazaine.

It is not known what was said, but the emperor sent Count De Noue to reject Shelby with a polite, "No, thank you."

"I knew it," Shelby said, who had been waiting in the antechamber pacing betwixt hope and despair.

"How?" asked De Noue.

"Not once could I bring the blood to his face," said Shelby, turning on the Count with undisguised anger. "He has faith but no enthusiasm, and what a man in his position needs is not only enthusiasm but audacity! You have spoken to me frankly. I shall speak to you frankly. Maximilian will fail at any sort of diplomacy."

"Why do you say that?" De Noue asked calmly.

"Because I have traveled slowly and in my own fashion from Piedras Negras to the city of Mexico. You have not one foot of Mexican territory in sympathy with you. As surely as the snow is on the brow of Popocatepetl Juárez lives in the hearts of this people and before an answer can come from Seward to the emperor's minister of state, the emperor will have no minister of state. That's all. Thank you for your kind offices today, Count. I must go back to my men now. They expect me early."

With that the general saluted and turned on his heel and left.

So it was, that what Juárez in his seeming weakness had been strong enough to offer, and they, in their certain ignorance, had so impulsively refused, was now in turn offered by themselves to Maximilian only to be declined by the fading power of this uncertain prince. In this way the Iron Brigade, which had never known a defeat, was by a flick of a sovereign's finger finally vanquished; and a Habsburg—the mightiest of all dynasties—was at last dethroned by a peasant.

The world watched in amazement as the "invincible" French army marched down the road of victory to its inevitable defeat. Under pressure from Bonaparte to withdraw, Bazaine grudgingly pulled Jeanningros from Monterrey and Saltillo and gave Tampico back to Juárez. Slowly, inexorably, the marshal was leaving Mexico to Maximilian and marching from Matamoros to Metz.

In the retreat's destructive wake, Juarista captains flew as from the air, to ride with their lariats of *guerrilleros* in an ever-tightening noose around the unprotected king: Escobedo in the northeast; Ramon Corona and Riva Palacio in the northwest; Nicolas Regules in Michoacán; and Porfirio Díaz, who escaped from prison by roping down a waterspout, then horsed hard from there to Oaxaca to saddle up his merciless men of the south who came together in a circle to lasso and drag the emperor from his throne to a wall.

Maximilian had said no to Shelby since yes would be an admission of his betrayal. Yet, betrayed he was, and Napoleon, who had always promised fidelity, now wanted nothing but a quick divorce.

What did Maximilian do in the face of the looping cries of the *guerrilleros* for his blood? He gave balls, dinners, wrote poetry, chased butterflies, and being something of a Liberal himself, alienated one side without quite propitiating the other (failed to consolidate "his base," as they say today); then, after sending Charlotte fleeing between the volcanoes for help, slipped away to sleep with his *Mestizo* mistress in Cuernavaca.

"Adiós, mamá Carlotta, adiós, mi tierno amor!" went the *canción* that carried Charlotte's mules to Vera Cruz.

But Charlotte, who was at last learning a little something about the land she had presumed to rule, soon found that Mexico is a country often easier to enter than to leave. It rained a flood upon the rutting roads, running her highness through friendless, nearly impassable country, as the Juáristas plucked her mules one by one to the laughing serenade of *"Adiós, Carlotta!"* It was a sleepless dream of evil nights that was but half-awakened by her escort cutting through at last to Vera Cruz and the sea.

Yet, as the girl who had left was not the woman who returned, so, too, the Napoleon she had left was not the one she found. In fact, she did not find him at all. She was seen instead by Eugénie, surrogating at the head of the soldier-lined Staircase of St. Cloud—waiting with the little Prince Imperial, ironically wearing the Mexican Order of the Eagle proudly over his chest, standing in his cute cadet's uniform by his mother, watching in disbelief as Charlotte fell weeping at their feet.

"Where is Louis?" she asked, looking up through her tears, staring into their amazed eyes.

Eugénie apologized and replied weakly that he was "unwell."

Then Charlotte blurted out her tale of woe as prelude to a petition for help. Eugénie hesitated, but belatedly moved, assured her that Louis would consider it well and all.

"No! No! That is not enough! I must see him! You cannot deny me that, Eugénie!" she screamed.

"I'll do what I can, my dear, but my poor Louis really is unwell ... really he is ... but ..."

"I will not leave until he sees me ..." Charlotte interrupted. "I will come again and again. I will never leave. I will scandalize all of Europe," she throated out in a heavy rasping voice. "If he does not see me, he will be a coward and an ingrate," she said, grinding her teeth. And, after more, even weaker assurances, offered by the silent, open-mouthed boy's mother who gripped him by the hand, Charlotte left, but true to her tears, returned in the morning for yet another cold rejection.

But still she did come "again and again," till at last, as she predicted, the whispering world would make Napoleon III, with Eugénie at his side, grudgingly replace his son at the head of the stair of St. Cloud.

Composed at first, Charlotte gushed out their desperation, pleading that Louis leave a French guard, smaller even than the force Shelby had guaranteed,

---

"At least until the American commitment to Juárez can be assessed," she said, mastering her emotions long enough for a moment's good sense.

"I could have done that before Sadowa," Napoleon said quietly, referring to the Hohenzollern's victory over the Habsburgs in July of '65—Prussia's defeat of Austria—Bismarck's vanquishing of Franz Josef, done so decisively because France's army was in the Vietnam of Mexico and could do nothing while Germany marched from Sadowa to Sedan since France had foolishly sent Jeanningros to Saltillo.

Then, Louis added with a sigh, as if even he understood the importance of the scene, "But now it is impossible. You must realize that by leaving Mexico I am inflicting a humiliation on myself. I would give ten years of my life not to do so. But Mexico is an abyss into which I am sliding and I must stop it."

"Then we are lost ... lost," Charlotte whispered angrily

Louis reached to comfort her, but she jerked away. "My dear," he said, "your disillusionment after so many struggles is cruel, but at the emperor's age there is no need to despair ... I beg him to leave Mexico with our troops ... and I count on you to persuade him to do so ... and confound the hotheads who wish to push him to his doom."

"You are condemning him to death ... my beloved Max ... to death ...," she said, sobbing to the floor to kiss his boots.

"No, no, my dear, you do not want to listen to me. I have been planning a throne for him in the Balkans."

"The Balkans? The Balkans!" she screamed. "No ... no, you don't under-stand," she said now regaining control, looking up, staring defiantly into his eyes. "You are not putting him on a throne but against a wall ... Maximilian will die ... he will never run away! Never! A Habsburg does not ever ... ever ... run away!" she shouted, losing control again.

"My dear, giving up an impossible task is not running away. Europe will applaud a wise decision which will spare both blood and tears."

"Blood and tears!?" she shrieked, sitting back on her heels, with a hideous laugh. "Blood and tears, did you say? Blood and Tears! Hah! Both will flow again ... and because of you!" she choked out, pointing at him. "Rivers of blood ... rivers ... rivers of blood will be upon your head!"

Louis Napoleon was frozen into a pale silence, so Eugénie now reached for her, but Charlotte slithered off, convulsing away from her into a coil as if to strike if touched.

"Get a doctor!" Eugénie whispered loudly to a servant while another brought water.

PHILLIP H. MCMATH

"Here, my dear," Eugénie said tenderly, offering the drink, but Charlotte struck her hand, screaming as the glass rolled noisily away to find the wall.

"Assassins! Leave me alone! I won't swallow your poison!" she said, sobbing herself into a ball.

There was a long, staring silence. But there was no doubt—they all saw it—the Empress of Mexico was mad.

CHAPTER TWENTY-SIX

For God's sakes, let us sit upon the ground and tell sad stories about the deaths of kings.
—Richard II

Louis committed his guilt to the pages of a letter. He addressed Maximilian warmly as "Monsieur, my brother," stating that he had received Charlotte "with pleasure" and had entertained her petition, but added, regrettably, that no more help would be forthcoming—not one more "*ecu* or another man," he said, would be sent to Mexico—that "the moment of decision" had come, and urged his "brother" to flee. (There was no more mention of a "throne in the Balkans.")

As for Charlotte, she wrote Maxy letters of her own. But she did not recount the imperial tête-á-tête with the same enthusiasm, rather, "To me the Emperor is the Devil in person and our interview yesterday he had an expression to make one's hair stand on end. He was hideous and that was the expression of his soul," she said, before flying from this "Devil" to God, carriaging in a rush from Paris to Rome, where, in a very private conversation to which all of Europe was privy, Charlotte was politely received by His Holiness (Pius IX), who listened patiently then explained that he, too, was as powerless as any Napoleon ever could be—he had no army to send.

These privately terrible scenes which were played within the palace walls of prince and pope were nevertheless seen by all the world and soon their painful lines were set before Maximilian by a meddling German priest at Chapultepec.

Attentive, and with an ashen look, Maximilian had asked at last, "And what did she respond?"

"Well," said Father Fischer, a Jesuit who had mysteriously appeared in the vacuum of Charlotte's going—a former Texas rancher, California gold digger and, it was said, the father of numerous *Mestizo* bastards; this priestly Rasputin had convinced Maximilian of the Mexican people's abiding love and like Charlotte agreed that the evil was not they but that "Devil" Louis Napoleon.

But Fischer, who never halted or seemed unsure, now hesitated, unsurely answering, "I am loath to go on, Your Majesty ..."

"Please, Father ... I must hear it all ... please proceed."

"Yes, well, Your Grace, upon hearing this, the Empress paused, leaned toward His Holiness and whispered softly that henceforth, out of deep mourning for her beloved husband, she would always dress in black ... that Louis was Lucifer incarnate who had seduced everyone by his diabolical charm ... and, like his uncle, through ambition and vanity had polluted all of France ... and that he would not rest until she was murdered ... of that she was certain ... that Louis had planted someone in her entourage to poison her ... and she must be cautious ..."

With welling tears Maximilian waited then asked, "And what did His Holiness say and do?"

"He said she was tired ... needed rest ... that she would be allowed to sleep that night in the Vatican ... against all protocol, of course."

"Did she?"

"Yes ... the first woman ever ... officially ... that is ... ," Fischer added, unable to resist.

"And?"

"She was received again ... the next day, as she promised, wearing deepest black ... refusing to eat ... and drinking water only from the fountains of Rome."

Maximilian said nothing.

Fischer hesitated, then filled this silence by saying, "Within a few days her brother came and took her home ... to Belgium ... where she lives quietly in peaceful seclusion on the family estate. She is well cared for, I am told."

Maximilian made a little sound, thanked and dismissed him. Then he turned to the great window viewing the city under the volcanoes from the palace of Chapultepec.

"When Bazaine leaves, I will be free," he whispered. "Free ... free ... ," he was heard to say with a sigh.

But the Juárista ring was closing ever tighter, melting under its increasing pressure the Imperial Mexican Army into a swelling river of mutinous rabble. Gradually the Juáristas overran everything and place except the city. But, like a back door, Puebla and a slender corridor were pushed open by Bazaine through the volcanoes to Vera Cruz where the French ships waited impatiently for the emperor.

Vacillating, deciding to leave, then to stay and back again, finally, under the influence of our nefarious Father Fischer, who convinced him that his Charlotte's sacrifice could not go unmatched by his own, he resolved to stay, fight, and win-over his people till granted by them the miracle of victory in the face of an otherwise certain defeat.

In February, he appointed a new cabinet as a counterpoint to Bazaine's pleas to board and flee in March. Adamantly he refused to follow, and the door was closed; so Maximilian was, for a delicious moment at least, "free." Free as he had always wanted to be, to face Escobedo, Palacio, and Corona advancing upon his royal redoubt at Querétaro and Díaz marching to Puebla.

Maximilian, who now had only a few loyal thousand, inquired of Shelby, but the Iron Brigade was no more. It had evaporated into every imaginable corner of the world, but not until a remnant fought one more bloody fight during the French withdrawal, rescuing its old brandy-besotted nemesis of Parras, Colonel Du Preuil, and his besieged garrison at Cesnola, surrounded by Escobedo's advance guard pressing on to them from the north toward the Confederate colony of "Carlotta" settled by Shelby and Price under the grace and favor of a doomed Habsburg prince.

Here, in the increasingly tenuous corridor to Cortés's city, Shelby and Price, successfully at first, almost realizing their old dream of building a newer Kingdom "beyond the Río," in a final defiance against all notions of defeat, charged their handful forward one more time, into the Confederacy's last battle, not to save themselves but the same foolish French army that had "skeered" Mr. Lincoln so badly way back there in '64, in what now seemed another time and another place, far away; but managed nothing more than saving this tearful colonel, who, with words of shamefaced gratitude, apologized "for the rude things done and said at Parras."

In this way did they pass a sad and bloody hour, but the emperor they could not save, of course, because he would not save himself, nor could they even save their own Dagmar, lying suddenly dead on the ground at Cesnola, shot by a Juárista who didn't know or care how she had voted on the Río, rifling her off her galloping Appaloosa, just like Medora had done at Himmel Hill, only aiming a little better than she had and lots better than poor Joshua at Old Tom Jenkins's Ferry, the Juárista killing her even before she was unsaddled and trampled over by the lathering Grays following hard upon Jo Shelby's big black gelding in pursuit of the ever-receding but insatiable addiction of prideful war. Our now-legendary Dagmar rode beside him dressed *à la Mexicaine,* her reins in her teeth, firing her revolver, her tattered sombrero bouncing on her back and Jeanningros's red bandana, her most-prized possession (other than her Appaloosa and Heidi

Himmel's saber), flaring from her neck into the wind; then falling for the final time not that far from her new, and she had hoped, final home near Puebla where her South had lost its war in a fight fought not between Grays and Blues at all but between these same infernal Latins who had decided so much without meaning to; and in her dying leaving her baby son alone in the Southern colony of "Carlotta" where she had found love at last in the arms of a Mexican horse lieutenant who had galloped away, kissing her, saying he would gallop back soon and didn't because he was held in the unfaithful embrace of his newest lover—ever-jealous death that drove her with a little too much grieving desperation toward the Juárista line, abandoning their infant boy to grow up in Cesnola to think of himself always as something of an "Anglo," and (perhaps it was the Spanish blood mingling with the Scots-Irish) to imbibe a mysteriously abiding ambition to be a great poet, but to become a rather bad but nevertheless sincere priest instead and, like his bootlegging redneck grandfather, a dedicated drunk. This orphan, like his dashing *Padre* and courageous one-armed mother, himself became a romantic wanderer, back-trailing his famous mother's twisting odyssey north through the fateful Querétaro, then to San Miguel de Allende, San Louis Potosí, Matehuala, La Encarnación, La Encantada, and the now-portentous Parras, which had served unknowingly as a kind of antecedent landmark to Dagmar's death. And from there through Saltillo to Monterrey where she had once entered through its gates like a liberating saint for her chat with Jeanningros and his disgraced pal, the devil Dupin, himself sacked but restored by Maximilian for doing not what he wished but what he willed; it was this same Dupin who bowed and kissed her hand while staying, serving, and slaying until the very end of the French folly in Mexico before reluctantly leaving just a step ahead of Bazaine for Paris where, it is said, he was poisoned within the year.

Thus this peripatetic young man rode in honor of Dagmar to Lampazos and the Sabinas River and her first but not last Mexican battle, before re-crossing her almost wet tracks at Piedras Negras because he knew about her fatal vote there and what it had meant and wanted to see the place and spot on the north side and where the flag was buried before wandering through Texas, which he did not much like, and west into New Mexico, which he did because it seemed as blended as himself—Anglo, Indian, and Spanish—to settle and take holy orders because he needed a respectable job and a steadying drink; saving a few souls here and there, of course, and writing his essentially bad but very romantic poetry in an archaic, florid Spanish style which he mastered and recited with sips of *vino tinto* to his flock who loved to listen because, for all his sins, they still liked him, were most amused, and went to him for confession and to mass which he did with a marvelous, unique flare in the obscure village church near Santa Fe. They called him simply Father Pilgrim, though his name was José Fernández Martínez y Pilgrim, and joked about his weakness for drink and drama, which he always adorned with the sincere affectation of a *Castellano* accent, lisping the sad but splendid story which he knew so well and no one ever tired of hearing over and over.

In this way Father Pilgrim would tell how the childish emperor dithered away six precious weeks at Orizaba reading poetry and studying butterflies when all of Mexico was collapsing around him like a burning palace onto his almost saintly head when he should have gone home with his mad wife. How, after the loss of his precious Charlotte, the diabolical Father Fischer, who became so increasingly powerful and poisoned his ear with these insidious delusions of success, convincing him he could prevail only if he ceased to trust the *moderados* and rely upon his good and simple Padre Fischer and his reactionary conventicle of humble priests who were the only ones truly dedicated to him and the imperial cause—the cause of *religión y fueros*—of God and his eternal law—that had chosen Maximilian as His divine instrument on earth and Father Fischer as His voice.

"So," Father Pilgrim said, sitting by his fire in his little adobe hovel behind the small church, his face flushing from the flames of wine and fire, "it came to pass, that in February of 1867 this Paladin of Heaven sallied forth from his castle of Chapultepec for the final time to assume personal command of what was left of his tiny army at a place called Querétaro, northwest of the volcanoes ... a little too far from a sea now made placid by its unburdening of French ships."

He was telling the tale to some three youths (two boys and a pretty girl) who had brought a jug as a bribe, along with food and blankets to lie upon while listening to this legendary tale that everyone loved for him to tell.

"It was hopeless ..." he added, waiting a bit, letting it sink in, then, "Escobedo was already outside the gates and the armies of Riva Palacio and Comandante Corona were rapidly approaching. General Miguel Miramón, the emperor's best soldier ... a sincere follower of our Holy Church who saw Juárez as Satan himself ... and General Leonardo Márquez, Maximilian's best shooter of prisoners and killer of Liberals, something he had been doing with the greatest of pleasure and skill almost without stop since the happy days of '58 ... now disagreed and quarreled with Miramón as to what to do next. You see, Miramón wanted to attack Escodeo immediately ... quickly ... before the others arrived ... but Márquez had grown cautious and wanted to wait ..."

"For what?" a young man interrupted. "Wait for what, Father?"

"That I do not know," answered Father Pilgrim, smiling at the good question. "It was stupid … and, of course, it was what Maximilian chose to do … he was brave but no soldier … and always made the wrong decision … and so granted the Juáristas the very great luxury of bringing up all their forces at their pleasure … forty thousand to his eight or … at most … nine … worn-out and discouraged loyalists who had not the good sense to run away. Of course, they were quickly surrounded … were besieged … and soon began to starve."

"Was there anyone to lift the siege?" the boy asked, emboldened by the success of his previous question.

"Some … in Mexico City … and in Puebla, but these were under great pressure from Profirio Díaz. Maximilian sent messengers for help but they were always captured … interrogated … tortured and hanged …"

"Did Juárez approve of this?" the girl asked, sitting at the apex of what Father Pilgrim immediately recognized as the tip of a budding *ménage à trois* forming at his feet.

"Yes … it was war … the Imperialists had done many bad things …"

"That's so terrible … the messengers sound like such brave boys," she added sadly.

"Yes … there are always the nameless brave," he said, proud of this unexpected turn of phrase and making a mental note to use it again somewhere, perhaps in a poem.

"They, these nameless brave, too, believed in their cause," she said gravely.

"Yes … dear … each side always does … history is full of nameless heroes," the Father said, while making a note that somehow "nameless heroes" was not quite as good as "nameless brave" and wondering why.

"And Maximilian … what did he do?" asked the other young man, sitting close to the fire, which now smelled pleasantly as a piñón nut flashed up from its perch on a top log and mixed its odor with the pine.

"Well, he was magnificent … he lived no better than the others … like a common soldier … slept wrapped in a blanket on *Cerro de las Campanas* (Hill of the Bells) … ate and drank no more than they … and, during the day, happily exposed himself to enemy fire … winning their hurrahs … and, finally, what he wanted most … their hearts. He proved Carlotta right when she said 'a Habsburg does not run away' and was at his very best ever. Then, in the evening, he put on his spectacles and read his romantic poetry by the dim fire before scribbling additions to his manual on court etiquette …"

Here, as he loved to do, Father Pilgrim paused yet again, smiling at the contrast of flame and shadow dancing over these expectant faces, then went on.

"Things soon became intolerable even for such *bravata* ... clearly, something had to be done ... and so Marques volunteered to fight his way out ... and race to Mexico City ... for help ... and he did ... slicing courageously through with about twelve hundred ... cutting himself out of the circle with the greatest desperation. Maximilian gave him absolute power as his viceroy ... to dismiss the idiot cabinet ... sitting idly in the city ... and told him to raise an army and return ... and, of course, bring Father Fischer ... some books and brandy ..."

There was laughter—of the nervous kind.

"Yes ... books and brandy ... and even some piano music ..."

"Piano music!?" asked the young lady, in obvious shock.

"Yes, indeed."

"Did he have a piano?"

"I think not."

There was more laughter, but less nervous and more mirthful. Then the one boy nearest the fire, as if to highlight his incredulity, got up and put another log on, adjusted it with a studied nonchalance, and sat back down to finish hearing this tale of such a delightful fool.

Pilgrim poured another glass of their wine, waited for the boy to settle in, then resumed, "But things never go as planned ... in war or life ... or love ...," he added this last with a twinkle in his eye, "they are always different ... and when Márquez got to there he realized how desperate things were at Puebla and so went there without hesitation. Hearing of this, Díaz put his shoulder to the wheel and stormed the place ... taking it quickly. Márquez then spun about, but it was too late and he was overtaken by Díaz and torn to pieces. It was a terrible slaughter ... but with a few horsemen Márquez himself escaped to the City, but it, too, was surrounded by Díaz in an iron ring. The game was clearly lost. there was no hope ... and Márquez, ever the survivor, escaped to Cuba."

"And at Querétaro?" asked the girl.

"They were starving. During the fighting Maximilian would expose himself in hopes of 'the lucky' bullet but God did not grant him that ... and soon Escobedo, out of a grudging admiration he never thought to have, offered him safe conduct if he would only abandon his army ... but Maximilian refused. It was his great moment and he knew it. He was determined to die a glorious death. Then a desperate plan was conceived by a soldier of fortune ... a German who called himself 'Prince Salm-Salm' ... another adventurer who had attached himself to the emperor. This 'prince' suggested their garrison storm out at a weak point he had found ... then take refuge with the Mejia Indians in the Sierra Gorda Mountains. It seemed a good idea ... but Maximilian, surrounded as he was by horrible intriguers, was persuaded by another ... one Miguel López ... a Mexican officer who, in the absence of the Jesuit, seemed to exercise a kind of fatal charm over him. He counseled caution ... again ... as always ... Maximilian took the bad advice ... and did nothing ..."

"Unbelievable," said the boy sitting by the fire, shaking his head.

"*Claro!* ... it is," said Father Pilgrim.

"What else could he do but try to fight his way out?" added the boy.

"Surrender," said Pilgrim.

"Then ... did he?" asked the boy.

"No ... no, he was betrayed."

"Betrayed?" said the girl, shocked.

"Yes ... by López. He was a traitor."

"How?" asked the more pensive boy.

"He wanted nothing so much as to save his own hide. He took that as a bribe ... and let the Juáristas in the town. Of course, then it was all over. Maximilian fled to the *Cerro de las Campanas* with General Mejía but they were taken there ... and surrendered. There was nothing else to do ... the game was up ... the king had been checkmated ..."

"What happened next?" asked the girl.

"Oh the Juáristas, who knew now of Díaz's success at Puebla, sang songs of delirious victory ... got drunk ... danced with joy ... fired their rifles ... rang the bells and repeated 'Adiós Carlotta' over and over ... song and verse ... then ... for fun ... shot some of their prisoners and next day took confession from a priest after shooting another for refusing to give it to them."

There was more laughter, again of the nervous kind.

"Did God forgive them?" asked the girl sweetly.

"Only if they were truly sorry," answered Father Pilgrim, with a kind look.

"What happened to the emperor?" the girl asked, intruding this question into a momentary silence.

"Oh," said Father Pilgrim with an air of nonchalance, as if he had not intended to say anything more, "he was tried by a court of seven officers who, as expected, ordered it done. The whole world tried to save him ... every crown in Europe ... the pope ... even the Americans ... but it was to no avail ... so, Benito Juárez did the only uselessly violent thing of his life ... he ordered the execution. ..."

"Why?" asked the girl stricken.

"To set an example to foreigners, he said ... not to meddle in Mexico ... it was popular ... he did the popular thing ... it was unfortunate ..."

"How was it done?" asked the other boy who had been hitherto so quiet.

"Well, on June 19 he was taken back to the *Cerro de las Campanas* ... to be placed between his two generals, Miramón and Mejia. But Maximilian, dressed in his very best uniform of gold and blue ... with shined boots and meddles glistening in the sun ... performed a great act of chivalry that was applauded by all of Mexico. He ceded his place in the middle ... the place of honor ... to General Miramón as a tribute to the man's courage and loyalty ... then tipped each of his executioners with a gold coin, saying he 'could not have chosen a better day on which to die,' folding the gold coin gently into each man's hand, asking them to please shoot at his heart ... then he slowly returned to the stake ... and with untied hands took his place with the others ... Miramón in the middle ... each standing erect and proud without blindfolds ... then Maximilian, true prince that he was, shouted out loudly before the order to fire, 'May the blood that is about to flow be for the good of this land!' These words echoed till ripped by a ragged volley of fire, but the men did not keep their word. One bullet struck his face and none his heart ... 'Hombre!' he protested in Spanish. There was a horrible pause ... the emperor fell ... writhed in pain upon the ground ... was picked up again ... a few terrible seconds followed into the silence like an eternity none would ever forget ... then, with another volley, the men earned their gold pieces and killed a Habsburg ... *muy triste* ..."

Now there was a very long pause, finally, the girl broke it with a slight sob, saying, "How sad."

"Yes, truly," said Father Pilgrim to see her face now turned away staring blankly into the flames filling with tears. "It was very sad, indeed ..."

"He brought it upon himself," said the boy, standing and huffing up by the fire.

Father Pilgrim sipped, then said, "Yes, you are right ... but no one believed it could happen to a Habsburg ..."

"They did not understand Mexico," said the standing boy.

Father Pilgrim smiled bitterly at this, adding, "You are right again. They did not. They were shocked ... in fact ... the emperor of Austria ... Franz Josef and his wife, Elizabeth, did not hear the news for a long while ... getting it after they had been crowned monarchs of their new Kingdom of Hungary ... which they joined as a two-headed beast with Austria ... the very day after the wonderful ceremony ... it was an omen, I think. Then, of all things, a posthumous letter arrived ..."

"Posthumous?" asked the girl.

"From the grave."

"The dead?"

"Yes, from the dead ... from Maximilian ... as if from his tomb ... as if written by his cold fingers ... thanking them. Then his cook ... himself an old Hungarian who had seen the thing ... the execution ... suddenly turned up... with the emperor's hat and handkerchief caked with his blood ... a memento thrust from out of the coffin, it was ... and all that remained ... it was all very strange. Carlotta was quite mad ... kept a doll she called Maxey with her ... muttered to him constantly ... covered him with kisses and tears ... raving on and on about St. John ..."

"St. John?" asked the girl.

"Yes, she was obsessed with the Revelation ... the apocalypse."

"And the King of France," asked the other, more diffident, boy, "What happened to him?"

"Napoleon the Third?"

"Yes ... him? I must know."

"Oh, he lost a war ... was beaten by Germany ... led by a man named Bismarck ... who devastated his Kingdom ... defeated his army because it had been mired in Mexico ... and was not ready ... so Napoleon was destroyed. Marshall Bazaine surrendered almost two hundred thousand at a place called Metz ... his entire army. He was disgraced and hated in France ... and the world. Paris was occupied and Versailles was taken as the place of surrender. France was humiliated. Napoleon, who did not have one-tenth the courage of the man he'd betrayed, did not know how to die. We come in this world to die, and he did not know that ... was a coward and surrendered to purchase a few more pitiful years ... living in England ... shamed and beaten at a place called Camden ... with Eugénie and the little boy ... the son ... who eventually went off to Africa to prove himself a true Napoleon and was killed fighting the Zulus ... his and his father's dreams come to worse than nothing ... their Kingdom Lost ... the seeds of the Great War planted by what France had done at Tenochtitlan ... in the land between the volcanoes ... *muy triste* ... it was ... *muy triste*, indeed," said Father Pilgrim, weeping over his wine.

BOOK FOUR

CHAPTER TWENTY-SEVEN

If there is no immortality, reason sooner or later would invent it.
——*Chekhov*

The Sangre de Cristo Mountains were set behind the scene—to the east. It was evening and cold with the sun slipping away, the kind of cold that held you close, squeezing through the warmest clothes to your bones. Cripple Bear and Kroner drove to the top of a ridge, a ripple in the desert, rising somewhere between Taos and Tres Piedras. They stopped the truck, got out, and then walked through waning light to a crest that overlooked the valley. It was a cut across the face of high desert, a halfway point out from mountains to prairie.

"There it is," Cripple Bear said in a low voice, pointing.

"Yes, I see it," said Kroner, his words smoking in the air as he squinted for better focus.

Cripple Bear's raised hand seemed to clutch a cabin in a ravine, just visible in a stand of trees. Yellow streaks broke from a window, lifting faintly up, then fading quickly into the immensity above and out toward the emerging stars.

They were quiet for a moment. Then the sun slipped away, hesitating, a ball of burning resistance, before reluctantly dropping behind a mountain, as if pulled down by some impatient, jealous god. In the sudden darkness it was much colder—forlornly cold—and gloomy. Kroner felt as if he had, after a long and lonely journey, been suddenly, unexpectedly, set upon a strange planet. He felt utterly alone, even though Cripple Bear stood near, breathing heavily from their walk.

"Is he there?" asked Kroner in a quiet voice.

"He was yesterday."

"Okay," sighed Kroner, "will you take me down?"

"No."

"Why not?" Kroner asked in surprise.

"Gotta go alone, my friend ... I can't go with you ..."

Kroner wanted to insist, but didn't. Instead, he reflected for a moment, then stuck out his hand. Cripple Bear shook it then turned away.

Kroner stood until he heard the truck starting, revving, then saw its beams slicing through the night in a quick, overhead sweep as if searching for something in the heavens as he stumbled his way down into the chasm.

The motor faded off into silence, leaving him alone under the dim stars and increasing cold. Kroner summoned his courage, buttoned his coat, put on gloves, and felt his way, soon going along the valley floor without falling. Here he paused and looked around. The yellow cabin light seemed fainter as it filtered through the trees.

"Have I really found him at last?" Kroner wondered as he moved cautiously to a ribbon of a stream shining with reflected stars, rippling and slithering before him like a graceful, mythical creature, speckled silver and black.

Wandering … searching … Vietnam … Hong Kong … Arkansas … New Orleans … New Mexico … looking for Monty Poltam … with all its expectation. Here at last, he was just a few feet away, in this tiny wrinkle of earth—in a lair scratched from the desert like a wounded animal gone to ground. In New Mexico—unique, original, enigmatic, and heedless of all claims—he was now perhaps really there.

Kroner stumbled again, jumped the stream, fell short, landing in the mud with water seeping into a boot. He sloshed ahead with a quickened pace.

He was startled by a yelping coyote that was soon joined by a chorus, yelping, baying, and laughing at him, he thought.

Then they hushed. He stopped, catching his breath, looking up at the stars scattered above like diamonds set upon an immense pillow of soft purple velvet. But, like the coyotes, they seemed to mock him, yet in a different way, mocking really everything, not with a chilling animal laughter, but with a hard, ironic silence—defying the world, cruel, beautiful, inscrutable—a beautiful woman withholding her favors, refusing even to speak, smiling mysteriously, always just a little out of reach.

Then Kroner smelled perfume. It seemed to drift on the breeze, but there was no breeze and there could be no perfume. Yet it was there, so strong that he sucked in his lungs trying to make it stronger. What is it? How could this possibly be here, now?

The odor evaporated. Desperately, he sucked air in again, but it was gone. An illusion? He sighed in bewitchment—an unknown something here, some secret casting its spell. It was peaceful … very quiet … yet there was indeed … something … a sense of foreboding embracing him. He was in the presence of some great power, a power with an alien beauty, of … of what?

Yellow now broke brighter through a window, flirting, shimmering through the branches, moving slightly up and down—a window waving in the night; above, the stars, the weight of their radiant emptiness, enveloped the roof of heaven.

Kroner was apprehensive, strangely happy yet sad. His fate was here. The thing searched for, the great something he didn't understand now coming to his side at long last. Nearby, this unknown, unknowable thing he had always wished for, had led him here, almost against his will, was waiting, smiling it seemed, just beyond a few restless trees. Kroner had never more than half believed. But now he was completely, hopelessly in its grasp, fulfilling its command, carried forward by the perfume's sweet message seducing him on the wind.

The stars, their white winking light, the snake-like creek sliding silver and black, the coyote's heralding voice rising on cue—the perfume, the bouquet—the thing itself, its mood and essence—the power of this fate pushing him inexorably halfway across the earth for an answer to a question that had come to him now, at last. He stepped forward.

It was waiting: the smells, voices, sounds of the everyday—a door, a paper falling upon a floor, a thing dropped after becoming unstuck, laughter, an admonition born of routine, the lost sound of a voice trailing away—her voice, knocking, ringing the door of remembrance and laughing away. This was why he was here, alone in a dark wood, a few steps from his goal, stepping forward boldly now through the trees, making his way to a cabin door, knocking lightly, knocking, knocking, and waiting for an answer that did not come. He turned the knob. It opened. The soft light flooded his senses, and he blinked his eyes but still saw nothing. Then he heard it, music, music coming from inside. It was soft, low—a piano—Beethoven floating toward him. It was familiar, ebbing ... then it came up ... in a wave ... music in an empty room ... flooding over him ... past, into the darkness of the open door ... rising ... mixing the pungent smell of piñón and the soft green of snow-damp earth coming through from the night. He now stood on the edge of some numinous Kingdom—outside its gates, waiting for admittance.

He stepped forward, tripping on the raised doorsill, catching himself, then gaining his balance clumsily, then with assurance, stepping into the room, asking about someone being home as he did. But there was no answer.

Inside, the music was, of course, stronger, touching his ear precisely, note by note. He stopped, listening intensely as he surveyed the scene. There were no voices, no movement, nothing but music. He called again, but again there was no answer.

He closed the door and walked around. There was a fireplace, a wooden table with chairs, a small kitchen, an unmade bed in the corner, and books, everywhere there were books, all sorts of books—large and small, hardbacks and soft backs, in shelves, on the table, scattered even on the floor. Then, too, there was a rather comfortable-looking chair by an oil lamp and a radio on a small table nearby.

Beethoven's piano and violins seeped out the radio, visiting the world from paradise—this music, this music in an empty room. It was the Piano Concerto Number Five, the so-called Emperor, in E Flat Major, ending the first movement. Then there was the transition, the usual coughs, shifting of chairs, and clearing of throats—a live performance somewhere—brought to the wilds of New Mexico by "public radio," Albuquerque. Kroner was transfixed—an empty one-room cabin, books scattered—an unattended fire slowly surrendering to the night's strangulating cold.

New Mexico somehow gave one a sense of being lost in space, set upon a vast, unexplored, half-empty planet—frigid, burning, barren, broken by nothingness—crushing one into a state of diffident reverence—the inexpressible grandness—the variegated light in alteration of sun and moon—the miracle of being at all, of seeing at all, of hearing at all in a place where smell, sight, and sound come forth as daily miracles.

This was the mood with which Kroner greeted this music shifting now to the Adagio. He was paralyzed. Coughs and the scooting chairs stopped, muted, suppressed as the piano touched clearly and precisely each note, joined gracefully and delicately by violins in a slow, ebbing, grand wave, grasping then lifting the sublime to him, offering itself up for him to embrace.

Kroner had searched and struggled for this moment, as the music wound its way into outer space, dissolving like smoke. It was a culmination—an atonement.

He sat in the chair by the light, rested his eyes over incipient tears and listened through the Adagio's completion. It was one of the greatest moments of his life.

But there was another object in the room that Kroner did not notice till the movement finished. For him, actually, the music stopped at the Rondo—always a bit of an anticlimax to the Adagio, like so much in life, it comes as little more than a dull necessity. The moment evaporated. His mind wandered and, subconsciously, restlessly, he shut out the music, concentrating upon other details scattered around in a kind of semi-controlled squalor.

The object was a vodka bottle sitting half-empty on the table, among paperbacks and a roll of half-eaten, hard French bread. Where had Poltam gotten French bread?

He went and picked up the *Stolichnaya*. It was clear and pure. Now he understood. He understoood Cripple Bear's hesitation about bringing him—the mystery unraveling—disappointment coming in a flood. He set down the bottle, looking at everything more closely, touring the place.

Kroner thought he understood or, at least, was beginning to understand. Poltam had escaped the "Uncles" by some clever means but not the picture in the passport—that he had not escaped. It was the "something else" Poltam was forever running from. It was this mystery that excited Kroner, not the melodrama of the getaway, which he knew about anyway, or so he believed.

The "Uncle's have a long arm," was the old saw—only when interest wanes is one really safe. "Better to remain uninteresting," he advised.

Kroner studied the bottle again, debated, but though he was chilled decided not to drink. He went instead to the fire, stacking it with logs from a nearby stack.

While warming, his eyes fell upon a newspaper near the bottle. Legs scorched, he stepped away and picked up the old Sunday edition from Sante Fe, the lifting revealing a writing pad. He exchanged one for the other, looking closely. It was Poltam's handwriting ... hurriedly jotted in bold, neat print.

Philosophy of the Common Task, Fodorov, N.

Kroner turned the pages. Blank. Then looked at the front again. It made no sense. Written in Russian.

There was a noise. He froze, feeling suddenly, for the first time, strangely afraid.

Sensing another's presence, he went to the door and listened. He dared not go outside. Hearing nothing he stood staring out by the window but could not penetrate the darkness. He stood for a time, quiet as possible, straining for the slightest sound, but there was only the popping of the fire. Then he walked around like a police inspector looking for clues. It was then he noticed something else, near the sink. He looked closer. It was a piece of paper with more scribbling, stuck under a stone in the window, as if it were placed there as a hurried afterthought—he could just make it out.

> History is always resurrection, not judgment, because the subject of
> history is not the living, but those who have died, and in order to
> judge it is necessary to resurrect ...

> *N. F.*

Here it became illegible till another paragraph under it, in different ink, perhaps written at a different time, appeared.

> Memory is the principle which conducts a constant battle against the

mortal principle of time. It battles in the name of eternity against the mortal dominion of time. It is the fundamental way of conceiving the reality of the past in our false time wherein it endures only by means of memory. The historical memory is the greatest manifestation of the eternal spirit in our temporal reality. It upholds the historical connection to the times. It is the very foundation of history.

N. Berdyaev

The writing continued but he could not make it out. Had Poltam gone mad? Kroner wondered. What was he up to? And who were this Fodorov and this Berdyaev?

He went around the tiny room yet again but found nothing new. He shrugged and sat at the table with the paper, but the fire, now blazing up, quickly forced a retreat to the shabby but inviting chair by the lamp and radio. But the good music was gone. Someone started sawing away at the *Brandenburg Concerto* that he endured without enjoyment; this was followed by some dissonant discussion—someone trying to make a statement. He fiddled past stations. It was always that way—good stuff disappearing, the moment lost. Spanish chattered on one station but the English on the other was worse—it was boring—worse because he understood it. He was trapped between silence, dissonance, and idiocy. He opted for silence. He switched the radio off. But the quiet hung heavy and what had once seemed warm and inviting now seemed isolated, lonely, and a little frightening. The spell was broken. Deciding to sleep, he gulped a large glass of vodka, built up the fire, turned out the lamp, and went to bed, realizing how very tired he was as his body uncoiled its tension, relaxing into the ephemera of all alcoholic euphoria.

After a while, shadows smothered the fire, and a dark quiet was interrupted only by the sound of heavy breathing. There was another sound, like the one before, only louder—outside—but Kroner did not hear it.

He awoke with a start. Not knowing where he was created a sense of panic. Then, seeing the red eyes of a dying fire staring like a tiger, he remembered and sat up. Shivering, he fumbled for his flashlight. Getting up and lighting the lamp, he restarted the fire, making a great blaze, stoking it till the heat made him stand away.

Turning out the lamp he went back to bed and curled up in a ball—relaxed by the heat into a deep, early morning slumber. He had the strange, vivid, distorted dreams that always seem to come at that hour. He heard a loud knocking, as upon a great door, but his mind refused to awake. Then the noise gave way to an image of himself wandering alone as a boy. There was a farmhouse at the end of a long road in some unknown somewhere, but inexpressibly familiar—then he realized it was home, in South Dakota—a farmhouse in the prairie, isolated down a long road from nowhere—surrounded by a barn and cornfields. Then it changed and became a different house of an odd gray color with red trim—subdued and needing paint—somewhere else. There were large numbers in black on the front, over the door, but he couldn't make them out—four large numbers.

He saw himself standing outside himself, walking up a long driveway with unhealthy green shrubs around the edge and a small, junky car out in the yard. He saw himself outside himself walking past it, closer and closer, but not quite ever getting there but getting still closer and closer, but still not getting there, and feeling a rising frustration as he got closer and closer but never quite arriving. Then a vicious dog, barking and snarling, lunged at him but was held back by some unseen force then was silent, speaking as he approached—whining and speaking to him in a way he could not understand. He saw himself pausing to try to understand, leaning over and listening to the animal whose face changed into Monty Poltam's, then quickly to a large silver-and-black wolf, silently watching him with intense, mysterious, dark, alert eyes and perking-up ears. Then the wolf spoke again, telling him to open the door and he did, slowly, silently, revealing a large empty room.

There was something there—he could sense its presence—alive, breathing. The light from the door illuminated the room as he pushed it open, the light spreading across the floor and into the room like an invisible, magic liquid, revealing something on the floor. He stepped closer, crossing the threshold, the wolf at his side, panting, walking near his knee, loyally looking up and down, then forward at an object uncovered in the half-light. It was a form—on a mattress—the crumpled outline of a body. Kroner stepped forward then knelt down by it. The wolf sat on his haunches, his tongue lolling and breathing heavily, slobbering, drooling on the floor. Kroner could not tell if it were a corpse or an inert body. It was dressed in black rags and curled in a ball on this filthy mattress emitting a nasty, mildewed smell.

Then suddenly the room was flooded with light, brightly rushing into every corner revealing bare white walls. But there was nothing but Kroner, the wolf, and the inert body on the mattress; no furniture or windows—nothing. The wolf inched forward, whining, smelling the body, looking at it then looking up at Kroner as if imploring him to do something. Not blinded anymore Kroner saw himself clearly, outside himself as before, the black-and-silver wolf at his side, reaching tentatively for the figure which he could see for the first time was covered in wet red mud, everywhere, hideous mud, then, still outside himself, the figure quickly rolled over revealing the ashen, gray face of a young woman—a Vietnamese—young, beautiful, smiling a sinister smile, her long dark hair matted with blood and the wetness of mud. She opened her dirty black shirt revealing a large wound bleeding between two small, deeply blue bruised breasts, her nipples dripping a steady stream of fresh milk that curled into the blood oozing from the pierced flesh—mingling red with white into a pale pink stream settling into a pool on her belly, then dripping drop by drop to the mattress.

It was Renee. Poltam's murdered lover. She offered up her breasts with a sinister laugh and the wolf began to lap at the bloody milk and caress her breasts gently with its red tongue, whining and caressing the bullet wound. Kroner screamed, turned, and ran for the door but it closed with a slam. He pulled desperately at the knob, pulling, screaming, and pulling till it finally flew open and he lurched into a small, unfamiliar hallway; then ran and ran till entering a living room, ornately decorated but empty; through it and into more rooms, endless, room after room after room, flashing past, then into a great bedroom with a large poster bed, unmade, with fluffy pillows, where a middle-aged man lay in bed reading, the covers pulled up to a pointed black-and-silver beard, tangled black hair and spectacles, with a large cigar obscuring his face in a soft gray cloud of smoke, letting his book fall away, eyeing Kroner, laughing sardonically and mumbling in Russian.

Kroner flew past (laughter peeling after him in loud echoes) out another door into a massive library with books piled to the ceiling, old magnificent books, hardbound and musty, everywhere books, along the walls to the ceiling in shelf after shelf, stacked in pyramids on the floor, ladders running up the shelves on each wall laying siege to a great canon fortress; a solid oaken table centered by heavy wooden chairs, reams and stacks of paper scattered over and around the floor everywhere, written in undecipherable hand, large square leaves fallen on the hills of books. Written in Cyrillic or French. Kroner ran on, stumbling and falling over a stack standing like a funeral pyre in the middle of the room. He wiggled through, crawled into another room toward a massive door that quickly swung open. He darted through. But there was nothing under his feet—his heart slipped choking into his mouth as he plunged downward through a black tunnel, falling faster, ever faster ever faster. In terror he plunged ever more rapidly, screaming, hurtling downward, the laughter of the man in the bed still echoing, the screams of laughter and declamations in Russian bursting his eardrums as he fell endlessly through pitch-black space, hurtling ever faster, suffocating, unable to scream anymore, suffocating and panting, his heart thumping to bursting. Then, suddenly, there was a bright light, a knock, more light and even louder knocking, then he felt something cold against his cheek—and awoke.

There was a slight, cautiously creaking sound that doors make when they are slowly opened but it did not awaken Kroner. Standing in the doorway backlit by the early sun a man silhouetted himself against the delicate light. He stepped in, came quietly and stooped over Kroner. He paused, then placed the muzzle against Kroner's cheek and laughed softly. Kroner moaned and turned over. The man followed the face with the rifle, pressing the bone till the eyes popped open.

"Jesus!" Kroner said with a start, staring at the barrel.

"Killed you," said Cripple Bear, pulling back his 30-30, his laughter filling the cabin.

Kroner sat up.

"One hell of a crazy damn dream, man," he said, rubbing his eyes, acting brave.

"Yeah? 'Bout what?"

"A wolf."

"Lobo, huh?"

"Lobo?"

"Wolf."

"Yeah ... weird ... real weird ..."

"A wolf'd eat you before you got your eyes open," chuckled Cripple Bear, surveying the room, as Kroner slowly got up.

"It's cold," said Kroner shivering into his clothes.

Cripple Bear dumped his pack and stoked the fire. "It's bad to dream about wolves," he said, squatting before the fireplace, stirring, and blowing the coals till flames blazed up, responding to the touch of a man for whom fire building was as natural as walking or hunting.

"Don't tell me that," said Kroner, going outside, leaving the door open, disappearing, to pee, quickly returning and going to the sink, washing from the basin and pitcher combination.

"Any luck with finding your pal?" Cripple Bear asked, standing up and turning his back to the fire.

"No ... he left in a big hurry ... like out the back when we were coming in the front ..."

Cripple Bear nodded his head, then turned and warmed his hands.

"Want some coffee?"

"Sure ..."

They chatted while Kroner fixed the coffee, making a cup for himself and his friend.

"What do you think?" Kroner asked, now standing before the flames, sipping from his cup studiously as Cripple Bear moved away from the heat to sit in the chair.

"He just ain't up to seeing you ..."

"Why?"

"Scared ..."

"Of what?" he asked, sipping the coffee after the question as a kind of emphasis.

"I dunno ... you tell me," replied Cripple Bear, sipping the same way.

Kroner thought for a moment, drank slowly, then said, "He knew we were coming, Cripple Bear."

"How's that?"

"The radio was still playing ... the lamp lit ... like I say, he obviously left in a big hurry ..."

"Then he was surprised ..."

"He must've heard us or something ... just before we got here."

"He saw or heard the truck ... or a noise or something like that ..." Cripple Bear said.

"Okay ..."

"So ... he's gotta come back ... after all, we're in his cabin and this is his gear and stuff ... he ain't gonna leave it or nothing ... he ain't gone far."

"I'll wait."

"He'll turn up. Word'll get out and I'll hear of it. It won't be long till we run him down ..."

"You're right. I'll sit tight ... right here on his pile of crap ... and just wait."

There was a little hesitation as Cripple Bear shifted a bit, put down his coffee cup and said, getting up and going to his pack, "How about some breakfast? I brought some grub."

"Sure," said Kroner moving over to help.

While they cooked breakfast they chatted without let up about almost everything but Poltam. Cripple Bear went on about things on the reservation, about his children, daughters with teenage problems, a son who played high school football, his wife, and the Anglo girlfriend in Santa Fe.

"Anglo, huh?" asked Kroner, as they sat and began to eat at the little table, the cabin warm enough for them both to shed their jackets.

"Yeah..."

"Does your wife know?"

"I think so but she don't say nothing ..."

"Do you catch any guff about her being Anglo from the boys?"

"Naw ... we New Mexicans are a little splash of about every damn thing ... ain't many pure bloods left. I mean, everybody's got some Spanish blood and even a tad of Anglo here and there ... and Indian, of course. I'm a little Anglo myself ..."

"You are?" said Kroner, surprised.

"Oh, yeah ... my grandmother was a quarter ... that and Mexican ... a quarter each ... then pretty much pure blood Cochiti on the other half, I think ... with a little Spanish thrown in there somewhere probably."

"How's that?" asked Kroner, not chewing the bacon anymore but listening intently.

"Well ... there was a bad priest over in the little Spanish village, across the Río, over in *Pino Blanco* ... you know, you drove through there coming in, just before you get to the *Río Grande* ... well, anyway, this crazy priest used to come into our village ... you know ... to hear confession and stuff, but he was a bad drunk and all ... and ... well ... he and an Indian woman got all lit up one night and done it. Then he couldn't stand it no more once he'd started ... he just kept coming back till the Elders finally run him off. Then the tribe made a rule no more priests could come into the village because of him. It's still the rule ... you want to go to church or confession, you got to cross the river ... no damn priests in the village. But it was too late ... she had a kid by him anyway ... that was my grandmother, my grandfather's first wife, you know, the mother of my sorry old man ... he got the bad booze blood, I guess'n give it to me ... it just kindly stays there and won't leave ... seems like ..."

"Was the priest Anglo then?"

"Half on his mother's side ... and half Mexican from his father ... he had come out of Mexico after the Civil War. His White mother had come there with a bunch of crazy damn rednecks out of Texas or something ... who had done run away and all. Father Pilgrim was his name ... folks liked him, Grandfather said ... for all his faults. Indians see lots of good drunks ... but he wanted to be thought of as White ... so went by that Anglo name, I'm told ... least ways that's what folks called him. I dunno really, my grandmother never knew him, and she took her mother's name and was raised as Indian in the village, just like everybody else, was adopted by the tribe. But I didn't know her none neither. She died pretty young having my aunt … and, so, Grandfather married again … but anyway, see, that makes me a little of everything, don't it?" said Cripple Bear, smiling with a mouth full of breakfast.

CHAPTER TWENTY-EIGHT

By means of an image we are often able to hold on to our lost belong-
ings. But it is the desperateness of losing which picks the flowers of mem-
ory, binds the bouquet.
  —Gabrielle Colette

Elizabeth Shaw found that when she "came to think," as she said to herself,
all she did was remember. Remembrance was the sum of her loving and it was
in "the desperateness of losing" that she bound her memories together. She
came here, to this little patch of ground, hollowed out in the hardwood forest
of the Bayou Blanc bottoms, to gather her past into its desperate bouquet:
Christopher, Mother, Nora, the immortal blanket, the house in Mississippi, her
father ... the boy ... the smell of the grass in that night ... all her memories
... clumped together into the closed fist of her mind ... bound by her at a common green middle with the nimble tightness of mentally holding on ... like
Christopher's fondness of stopping smoke rising over a fire with his open palm
or Grandfather freezing a shadow against a barn wall with a finger or her own
holding of her dying mother's hand for a moment longer until death jerked her
jealously away.

It was here in this special place that Elizabeth came to touch gently this precious bouquet into a delicate separation, to look at and love each, then clump
them together again into the vase of her memory unlike those before her in
their pathetic fadings dropped against a stone among the hopeless weeds of all
such gestures for the dead.

She did the things she must—the "have-tos," as she called them with a slight
sigh—the everyday things of looking after Conrad, cooking, caring for animals,
and working according to her role as mistress around "the place," doing things
with friends in town, done with the unenthusiastic energy of a habitual, intelligent diligence born of a mind-numbing routine—the atavistic shell of necessity lying over the wound of her life like a shield against its irredeemable loss.

Yet there was an inner toughness, an ability to meet a thing or problem with a certain ready reflex—she was known as an eccentric but practical woman and, to the world at least, seemed impervious to almost everything. The present was where she existed but the past was where she lived—held together in this stubborn, unrelenting, delicately interstitial, connecting filament of her ever-concentrating mind—notched tightly together in that tender obsession with irrecoverable lost time.

Elizabeth Shaw, then, lived by the implicit faith that by the sheer doing of this thing—that is, the persisting in it—she could at long last somehow breach the separation of one from the other—the living from the dead—to, in the end, form one indivisible world that merged the visible and invisible in which all suffering was finally erased, the past redeemed, and the dead resurrected.

The boy Kroner had come looking for Christopher's friend with that strange Slavic sounding name. Then there had been this letter, gotten out of her "morning box"—reopened and brought by her to read again in solitude, near Christopher. She felt it out then tossed it into her wicker basket beside the hard yellow cheese. The timing of its arrival seemed odd, she thought, as her long fingers now fumbled it out like a message from one marooned soul to the other. She opened and reread.

> Santa Fe, New Mexico
> 1 Nov. 1977
>
> Dear Mrs. Shaw,
>   I came through some time ago, if you recall, looking for Monty Poltam. As you know, Christopher went to see Monty on his leave in Saigon that time ... when he had a few days of leave ... back in '69 ... shortly before he had to return.

There was a noise, interrupting from the woods, which lifted her eyes away from the page. She listened intently, felt oddly as if she were embarrassed to be seen reading here, felt spied upon. A flush of crimson visited her cheeks. She heard the noise again pattering through the leaves, stopping, pausing, and waiting perhaps for her to lower her gaze.

Then there was a very long silence. Either it had slipped silently away, or was pausing, watching. Tiring, she began to read once more.

> As I mentioned, when we chatted that time I came through

Arkansas, I met Monty after the war, after the fall of Saigon in '75, in Hong Kong, after the evacuation debacle. He was one of the last out, riding on a helicopter with Ambassador Martin. It was crazy then, believe me, real crazy. Monty and all the rest were more than a little nuts—he was real strung-out. I mean, Mrs. Shaw, he had devoted most of his young life to Vietnam.

Elizabeth reflected a moment upon the unintended irony.

Then there was the sound again. Knowing it would be impossible to read till she knew what it was, she let the letter drop. Then she realized, as she heard it again pattering in the leaves, that it was a dog. She saw as it emerged, as if called, out of the brush, pausing, seeing her for the first time, lifting a front leg in frozen apprehension—a medium, rather forlorn and somewhat sad, flop-eared Walker hound with a worn-out leather collar hanging loosely around its thin neck, who wiggled its wet nose with a curious quiver and stared with bad eyes at the odd form slumped against a tree.

Their eyes met then the hound made a decision—a formulation. The animal had quite literally been "thinking it over." One can argue freewill, if one likes, in man, but there's no question about it in dogs. This hound weighed things and after some reflection made a choice, decided to take a chance, and trotted over. He came through the gate and since it's a rare Walker that's not wholly for letting the dead bury the dead, glided indifferently over the graves, till he got to Elizabeth, where he paused a few lengths from her feet.

She spoke softly to him, making him smile as only a good hound can, as he bounced over Christopher's bones to accept her extended hand. She fondled his ears, head, and neck while chattering sweetly. It was suddenly good to have company so from being irritated at the intrusion she was now glad of it and was charmed into feeding the creature till she had no more to give. Laughing quietly, she watched him sniff in the leaves, roll upon the ground, and finally relax in this very good fortune for a much-needed nap.

Lifting the letter from her lap she began to read again. Its retelling reminding her.

"Wake up, son, wake up! It's time to go to college!" she had said excitedly that morning in '63, touching her son upon the shoulders, waking him with two fingers and a kiss.

Christopher had moaned, rolled over, and pretended not to hear.

JFK had asked a generation to ask not what it could do for them but what they could do for their country, but Christopher could not seem to get out of bed. For the moment, at least, he seemed to prefer what Frost had said in that frosty air ... something about sleeping in a snowy evening—it seemed more peaceful.

Oh, he had seen the "stuff on television" about that faraway place called Vietnam, the self-barbecuing monks being the most horrific, but it meant nothing to him. In fact, "going to college" as his mother had said meant very little at the moment, since all he really wanted was to sleep. It was early September, maybe the wise thing was not to do any of that at all, just stay here and live in the woods and wait for the deliciousness of fall to fall upon them. He and Barrel would go hunt. He would not burden himself with books and all their attendant grief and uncertainty.

> It was traumatic suddenly to be wrenched out like that, just in the nick-of-time, the NVA literally coming down the streets that always looked so much like Paris in their Soviet tanks, shooting and crushing everything in their way—the whole effort we had given so much blood and money for going up in the smoke of defeat and humiliation. People were past bitterness, they were unhinged. I think worse for them than the defeat was the sense of betrayal, not just of the whole effort but of those left behind—both the loyal Vietnamese who sided with us and those Americans who had given their lives. In the end, Vietnam was a betrayal of everybody and everything.

The Walker rolled awake, turned over, and scratched his back by squirming in the dry grass. Then he paused and spun up and onto his feet, shook for a moment as if he were wet, and came over to Elizabeth again to nuzzle gently under her hand. Obliging him she dropped her letter once more and with that talent for reading the minds of animals country people seem to possess, she, in a kind of sweet baby-talk, gave tongue to what the dog would have said if he could, such as, "I'm lonesome so play with me," or, "I'm really glad to see you," and so on, and in this manner she gave the creature a certain charm and wit he otherwise would not possess.

The hound seemed to agree with all she said on his behalf, licked her hand, scratched his ear with a repeated and somewhat violent urgency, then stood, frozen into a kind of perplexed concentration. He swung his head toward the woods, barked, and ran madly toward it, disappearing into a bush.

There were other dogs now baying through the brush and her friend fell in with them for the chase.

Elizabeth listened till it faded away, then, a little sad for the loss of the company, resumed reading.

Mrs. Shaw, this guy Poltam was only just past thirty and was already little more than a collection of fragments held together by his passion for what had happened. It sustained him like a kind of glue or something. But, like I said, I just didn't want to end up like that myself, so, as they say today, I "split" and I haven't seen him since the Hong Kong days. You understand, as I think I mentioned when I came through Arkansas, I've been looking for him for personal not professional reasons. It's, I have to admit, something of an obsession. I guess we all need one to kind of keep us going, and chasing around and finding Montgomery Poltam is mine.

Anyway, I followed him through New Orleans where he had made contact with a rather sizable Vietnamese community and from there to New Mexico where I have located him living outside of Santa Fe in a cabin as a kind of recluse. I managed this with the help of an Indian friend who seems to know everybody and everything, man or animal, that moves in these parts. (He's a Vietnam vet and quite a character himself. I could write you a letter as long as this one about him, believe me.)

It's hard for me to explain this pursuit to myself let alone to others, but it seems to be a combination of guilt about what happened and duty … yes, duty … Monty Poltam was my responsibility and I guess he still is. I feel like we let him down, let down that whole entire generation and this is my little way of making it up to them, I guess. After all, this country sent them to do a tough job and then treated them disgracefully when they came home. It's a scandal.

Anyway, after exploring around here pretty good, doing some fishing and a little hunting, meeting this Indian, enjoying the local culture and all, I managed to find Montgomery Poltam at last.

There was another noise—a truck rattling and grinding over gravel. It was coming fast, so Elizabeth tossed the unfinished letter into the basket and pretended to tend the grave. The truck stopped and a Black man emerged and walked toward her. It was Christopher's old friend, Barrel Bradford, who used to work for them. Elizabeth had not seen him in a while. When she saw him she always was put in mind of those halcyon days that had ended so abruptly when Christopher had met and literally gone away with the very beautiful Marianne Todd Marsden. A rich Delta planter's daughter, who came to Arkansas via a great-great-grandfather, himself a younger son traveling west through Mississippi from Virginia, looking for land and his own identity but nevertheless only escaped one "dynasty" to merge into another with the Marsdens, who in turn had come from South Carolina, and had settled in and around Helena. This one product of the line, Marianne, whose Christian name conflated two grandmothers with a surname of the father's, was born, she thought, just to meet her Christopher, even though she considered him a little "new rich" because Elizabeth came "out of the hills" (nothing being generally known outside his family of Arcadia, Titus, Medora, Mexico, Mississippi, or any other part of the great story that remained a kind of inner secret to be retold at special times, in snippets and threads till in growing up Christopher was able to weave together the entire fabric into one magnificent tale which, he decided, he would share with Marianne when he thought she was ready). She only knew that father Conrad was the son of hardworking but essentially landless Scots-Irish rednecks, and he had made his own fortune more or less "recently," that is, after the Second War. Yet, in the end, as is always true in America, the having is always more important than the getting and so all that was at last forgiven in the face of such success.

It certainly mattered not to Marianne, because, in a word, she simply fell for the boy, and since she always got what she wanted, that was that. She claimed him and soon took Christopher as a kind of possession away to "the University" as her prize. They planned, packed, and prepared and at long last the very special day had come and they embarked upon what her mother, ever the romantic, called the "great adventure of life."

So it was that in early September 1963, they emerged out of the flatness of their native Delta into what for them was the strangeness of "the hills," driving Marianne's new car "promised by Daddy for college," motoring (pulling a small trailer-load of her clothes) first through the Rock, and up the Arkansas Valley of the "Cayas" (a name that even Christopher did not know), skirting along on the north side as it dropped out of the Indian Territory into a long brown line separating the mountains on one side from those on the other, like Siamese twins splitting from the halves of one into the wholes of two—ranges rendering them forth from the patient eons—among the oldest in America; Paleozoic seabed, inching upward in northern ripples fashioned from millions of years of dying water things folding their bodies over into layers of limestone till they slowly piled up into a rising crust of peaks that protruded out in the oceanless

PHILLIP H. MCMATH

sun for drying of what, as we have seen, the French of late would call the Aux Arcs (Ozark), while the other twin, to the south across the Cayas, with fewer shells and more clay, would encrust themselves into the sandstone hills that the Indians, a little earlier, dubbed the Ouachitas of Arkansas's hilarious and heart-breaking story.

Between these immortal natural pyramids that were slowly rounded by time into a kind of rolling seabed of rock our lovers drove along following the old two-lane black-blue highway, burg-to-burg, town-to-town, shadowing the riverbank that aped the post–Civil War railroad that in turn aped the eternal stream, but, as might be expected even among the exceptional, they proceeded with that insouciance of youth that produced no thought of much other than this delicious slightly warm sunny afternoon not unlike the one Elizabeth enjoyed while reading her letter under an oak before playing with a grateful Walker before watching an old friend approach—giving no mind themselves to anything much earlier than this particular day or maybe the one before, unlike Elizabeth who thought of little else but the past that seemed personi-fied by a White woman standing by a grave watching an African American cross-ing a country road in overalls with "I need to tell you something" written on his face.

No, there was certainly no thought of funny-sounding names like Paleozoic, Mesozoic, Cenozoic, or of drifting continents, or two hundred million years of range-building, or of receding salt water stewing around with hideous slith-ering things in a self-consuming green soupy swirl slopping out as the "Llanoria" ocean, or the rising of the land out of the "Interior Cretaceous Seaway" at some one hundred and something million years before their brand-new little Ford sedan crept above where dinosaurs had tracked in the fossilization of the shal-low marsh mud that froze into a kind of permanent gargantuan chalk step of limestone that still can be seen today only if one bothers to look, which most don't. Nor did they even think any about the more recent lumberings of the sadly powerful mastodons whose great bones still pop up now and again on Crowley's Ridge (the Mississippi's old west bank) to be stumbled over by hunters of their own time and race via jaw or tusk or petrified skull, or even the arrows, pots, and mounds of our Lost Kingdoms of Aquijo, Quiguate, Casqui, Coligua, or even the brave Tula, who hunted these shaggy creatures to extinction, or even of the restless ghosts of sacked Anilco, or the pow-wowing trading Caddoes, or the more recent remnant Quapaws, or their inveterate enemies, the rampaging Osage, who, in consistently murdering French trap-pers and traders, maintained one of the more uncontrollable American Indian wars; or the weeping Cherokees, who came through a century later trailing their way across Arkansas from Tennessee to Oklahoma. No, there was no thought of them or even the ambitious, magnificently cruel conquistadors, or of the little famous frontier fort with its hardy *domicilez du poste* of hunter, merchants, vagabonds, slaves, laboring women, and dying, feverish children, clinging tenuously to their little lives in the White River wilderness below the silently sighing skulls of Anilco, which, after Cripple Bear's ancestors successfully threw out the Spanish in the New Mexican Pueblo revolt, made this little piece of Gaul at the Caya's mouth opening to debouch with the Mississippi as the only White settlement west of there for what man, in his pitiful and fatuously prideful reckoning of time, chooses now to call the seventeenth century.

No, despite its proximity to Christopher's own Bayou Blanc, they knew not of it, nor cared to know, at least not now, and knew only little more of the late-coming Anglo frontiersmen of America's First Republic, of which they were a linear genetic part, touching its Confederate interregnum middle which seemed to impinge upon themselves only with a certain lingering mild discomfort, with its battles of Blue and Grays and names of ancestors not that far removed. Yet, to be sure, they gave it really not much heed at all, and none of a boy of their own age who, instead of going to college, had gone to the gallows, or of a slave, also of their years, named Septimus Reymonde who ran away in the rain, nor of his friend the hard-riding, brave one-armed redneck girl who took her own seventeen-year slice of time down to Mexico to find finally the one thing she always wanted. Here she left the passionate seed of herself in the vastness of the Southwest in the form of a Mestizo-Anglo alcoholic son who had died only a little time after dropping his own priestly sins into the veins of the same Pueblos who had overthrown those Spanish's ancestors of European and Mexican soldiers, and their endless wars and firing squads, tortures, hangings, and absinthe-drinking, alcoholic, mad colonial colonels with their own set of crimes, murders, and executions—all played out in a country positively obsessed with plunders, passions, and prayers—led by that charmingly foolish, but in the end, exceedingly brave, German emperor, who, by his death did what he had never done in life, win the respect of almost everyone, even his killers, and his hysterical princess of a wife who saw the pope after her eyes were opened for a moment by the veil of madness.

And certainly no thought was ever given to the forgotten Confederate expatriates on the lam from History but lost at last to its page as skimmed-over footnotes like lemmings squirming in the vast sand of their own insatiable vanity; nor was there any time spent on immortal blankets, or famous mules with silly classical names, or faithful following hounds, or great gray horses that rode upon the wings of gods flying above splendid war before hoofing down upon the more mundane mud of Mississippi to be Reconstructed by the condescending Yankees of the Second Republic with its new constitution written under the guise of amending the old, or its follow-on Redemption, which was little more than revenge for a defeat and a kind of somewhat mean-spirited if belated victory of its own in which the South, for a time, won everything but her independence; or that Great War that came upon this world from the follies of one of Napoleon's relatives pretending to be great.

War, Reconstruction, Redemption, War, Flood, Depression, and War again and on and on till the descendants of the survivors settled down upon the ever-water-soaked, sweat-soaked, blood-soaked land to sire these two happy, naive lovers driving their red Fairlane along and above these ever-thickening layers of all the what's-gone-befores, simply because it seemed, as it always does, so very special and wonderful and made just for themselves, having only just, a mere seventeen years before, found their way out of that heavy darkness whereby the soul or being, or what will you, of man, or animal, or creature of every conscious living thing, at last is compelled by some mysterious force to push open that fatal door of the world and permit the light to fall gently across the eye.

"Wake up, Christopher ... wake up ..." Elizabeth had whispered gently that morning of their journey. "Wake up, my dear. It is time to go to college," she had said with that unique three-finger nudge of hers and a kiss.

Burg-to-burg, railroads and highways aping a river—Man following a god with a steel line laid down by immigrants (Swiss German, Italian, and Irish) a hundred years before, dropping their children into these new villages like seeds from the iron-bellied beast along the depots and water-stops that budded up into stations and towns as frontier trails emerged as streets, shacks into stores, hovels into homes and hotels, all named by the whims of the earlier wagoning, horse-riding Angloes with names like Morgan, Mayflower, Gold Creek, Conway, Meniffee, Plumerville, Morrilton, Blackwell, Atkins, Pottsville, Russellville, London, Norristown, Piney, Knoxville, Lamar, New Spadra, Clarksville, Hartman, Ozark, and Coal Hill. Their dead plopped in fenced-off patches around quaint churches crowded together in space-saving rows never far from the center of retail, road, and rail of an ever-hiving business of an indifferent world; stuck aside, plotted off into a kind of half-forgotten apology to an eternity that nevertheless impinges upon the tick-tocking clock and the effrontery of each little fragile life by washing it away into a great sea of pathetic mutability.

These rows of protruding dead lying with their stones sitting up like an audience at the "picture-show" on the Square for a life-size execution happening at the rear—near the fence—where Jesus suffers his divine agony for all the world to see, year-to-year, season-to-season, staring through frozen tears at a blinking stoplight—red-to-yellow-to-green, green-to-yellow-to-red—stupidly repeating its mindless counterpoint of His redemption above the blacktop but which seems to slow the Fairlane to an obedient stop across from a lumberyard on the right; the cemetery on the left and a Dairy Delight a couple blocks away where bee-bop bleats out of a Buick convertible with the top down.

Through the open window Christopher smells the blood of rosin bleeding from freshly cut pine, mixing into a blend of gas and diesel fumes from the car and a train, which are both now stopped and waiting as if side-tracked by Jesus propped up between them against that back fence hanging from his cross.

Christopher's eyes fall upon this modern Golgotha where this Christ is alone—uncomforted by thieves. And, as Marianne brakes under the authority of the light, Jesus's face turns toward them in an eye-meeting grimace as he twists his torso in revulsion away from the Mo-Pac diesel—purring away with its diabolical hummmmmmmmm—as it squats behind the wire just across from the garbage filled, bug-buzzing ditch.

There is the smell, the sounds, the squeak of brakes, then suddenly a pick-up wheels through the intersection, comes round, grinds its gears, and whisks past in the direction they have just come.

As it disappears, Christopher listens to the low moan enveloping the silent Savior with the supremacy of a squatting machine that has no grace nor soul or imagination or sacrifice or redemptive power and from which this nailed Christ seems to be imploring Christopher for succor.

It had been hot that day in Jerusalem when the Forty-fourth Legion did its duty, killing the trouble-making Jew, and while the morning had had a hint of cool, it was a hot day now, too, and Marianne, who did not see what Christopher saw, and never did, said something about the weather without noticing the execution.

"It's hot, honey," she said waiting for the light to change, playing her delicate long fingers impatiently upon the steering wheel.

"Yes," said Christopher, still staring out the window.

"I'm hungry," she whined, as the light changed to green and she geared off, then turned without asking into the Dairy Delight, parking by the Buick to order two cheeseburgers, a pair of cokes, and some fries.

He stirs the stream with a finger next to hers, their two fingers playing together in a side-by-side refraction, touching and un-touching, gaming in circles, making them giggle—a tiny pool eddying in a strong back-current behind a ponderous brown boulder mirroring their faces, smiling and kissing and laughing in the clear fluid images of swirling water that reflects the illusion of a double-dreaming permanence making them laugh again and break their fingers at the knuckle to stir the gravel bottom in a delicately tracing floating up of pebbles as a sandy cloud that soon drifts away, gathering speed till disappearing over the horizon of the storming white rapids where it all comes to rest in a newfound oblivion of the lagoon below.

They had turned off the main highway and onto a back road that lifted them onto an upward inclining plateau of pasture and ponds and into a deeply forested Ozark mountain hard-surface trail that had once been nothing more than a path before becoming a winding wagon rut that their defeated and demoralized Gray army had used to retreat down from Elkhorn on the long march to Tennessee and Mississippi in a kind of backward triangulation of Christopher Shaw's own family.

But Christopher today wound the new Ford upward through reversing turns, short straightaways, curving "S's," slowing and speeding, braking and gearing with delight, zooming along under a canopy of over-hanging trees that covered them in the bowing of hardwoods till they came to a place to stop and walk down to this stream to squat and talk and look at themselves in the cold fresh water like Dagmar and Joshua did that hot day filling their canteens during the retreat from Camden.

Christopher and Marianne were hunkered down together leg-to-leg in what is called a "holler" on a "crick" which rushed past their toes, pushing its way through and around these big rocks in a white foamy and blue-bending of curling waves, slithering around the shoulders of stones in a clear sleeve of water just soft enough to allow the sound of birds to rise through the maples, oak, and pine that in turn shook with the surge of a thousand wings of yet green leaves in a late summer wind that demarked one season to the next, as Christopher and Marianne only half-realized what was happening but understood just enough to pause and linger a little longer in the in-between world of woods and water of a not-quite-vanished innocence.

"Let's stay here forever, Chris … just here and go nowhere else … forever."

"I wish we could."

There was a pause as they listened to the brook, the birds, and the wind.

"Doesn't it make you a little sad?" she added, now stirring the water with a wet stick.

"Sad?" he answered, throwing a rock in a swirl so turgid there was no discernible splash, the stone dropping without a trace. "Why should I be sad?"

"I dunno …," she said, staring into the rapids. "I mean … we've left the nest, haven't we?"

"I thought you couldn't wait …"

"I know … I mean, I'm happy and all but it's still a little … sad … isn't it, Christopher."

"Yeah … I suppose … but you'll go home again. It's not like you're gone for good or anything."

"Yes, but it won't ever be the same …"

"You want to go back … turn around?"

"No … we'll have lots of fun, won't we, Christopher … and you'll still love me?" she said with a forced enthusiasm, standing and putting her arms around him.

"Sure … don't be silly," he said, then kissed her.

Then she broke away and squatted again, wiping away a tear.

"I've always wanted to see a stream with colorful rainbow fish in it," she said matter-of-factly. "Are there any here, do you think … in this little wonderful stream?"

"Rainbow fish … trout, you mean?" said Christopher still standing and looking intently at her.

"Yes, trout."

"Not cold enough," he said officially, surveying the brook with a knowing glance.

She put her hand in again for a moment testing the temperature.

"It sure seems cold enough to me," she added, withdrawing it quickly.

"You're used to our old swampy sloughs … but this is still not cold enough."

"Will you take me trout fishing someday, Chris? I want to go up north somewhere or out west … Colorado maybe … see that wonderful country of aspen and birch and snow and trout fish … huh … I've always wanted to go there. Will you take me someday?"

"Yes, sure …," he said, standing and sliding his hands in his pockets quietly, wondering if he ever would.

"Promise?" she insisted, still squatting and picking up her stick again and stirring the water idly.

"Yes, I promise."

But he never took her to Colorado. In fact, he never took her anywhere except back and forth from home and school. But that first year, after a little more patient courting, he made love to her in a borrowed apartment, but in this possessing he lost her—in the beginning there was the end.

"I want something more," she said at last, pushing him away.

"More?" he asked in surprise.

"Yes ... well ... I mean not more ... but something else."

"Something else? What something else?"

"Oh, Chris, I don't know ... it's hard to put into words. Just something else."

"What are you trying to tell me, Marianne?"

"Well, you are going off to do your ... duty ... fight the war, I suppose ..."

"I don't know ... I'm not sure ..."

"You said you were going in the Marines eventually ... that's what they do, isn't it? Fight wars?"

"Sure ..."

"Then what ... what am I going to do? Huh? I don't want to sit around and wait and wonder and worry? What was the term you used the other day?"

"Grass widow."

"Yes, I don't want to be a grass widow sitting around with nothing to do in Frenchman's Bluff, Arkansas."

"Oh, Marianne, you could grow a Victory Garden," he said laughing bitterly, angry yet strangely relieved.

"What's that?" she asked with a slight frown.

BOOK FIVE

CHAPTER TWENTY-NINE

If it costs ten years, and ten to recover the general prosperity, the destruction of the South is worth so much.
    —*Ralph Waldo Emerson*

Septimus stood in the doorway of the slave cabin watching it rain. It was getting colder and colder with the fire now almost out. At first it had been a shock, this out-loud monologue, but now talking to himself had become too much of habit to seem strange. In fact, it was his only comfort, so, looking over his shoulder at the dying fire, as if to another listener, he said loudly, "I'm studying on getting some dry wood."

For four days now the rain had come and gone but never quite stopped and the woodpile found conveniently in the corner was finally smoking itself into coals in the little fireplace. He had run here that stormy night of the big battle at Jenkins's Ferry—when he had left Dagmar as prisoner in the deluge and storm—unexpectedly finding this cabin behind a burned-down manor house whose outbuildings were left standing in a semicircle like grieving children around the cold carcass of their dead mother.

The cannon boom had long since stopped sounding in the distance of more days than Septimus had counted. Since he had not seen "hide nor hair" of any kind of creature, human or animal, anywhere, it seemed to him as if finally, at last, everything had been swallowed up in the wet suffocation of a great second flood that brought some divine wrath upon the long-suffering earth.

Slowly loneliness had supplanted terror to such an extent that he wondered if, like in the deluge Aunt Sallie had burdened him with in her endless Bible readings and preachings and lessons, God had not drowned every living creature in a kind of rising angry expiation of holy disgust, only to leave Septimus feeling like he was alone as a New Adam.

Septimus thought about this for the longest in the ponderous silence of the dripping rain and the more he thought about it the more he wondered if it hadn't fallen his lot to start the whole thing over again. Maybe that was good and he shouldn't complain, he decided—God singling him out as the instrument to get things right this time. It was indeed a very great honor—Miz Virginee and Aunt Sallie would be proud of him at last and even glad he had run away after all.

Deciding this was indeed the case, he felt better about it, and didn't, for the moment at least, seem quite so cold or quite so hungry, and finally resolved not to ever leave this newly made paradise or disobey or fool around with the Devil serpent or any kind of reptile that might be the evil one in disguise lurking in the Saline bottoms. He would remain as God's ever-faithful companion in His new Eden, because, if He were as lonely as the Good Book said, He would always need company of some kind, even if it was only Septimus Reymonde. No doubt this was why the Almighty had committed the colossal mistake of making Man in the first place. It was quite clear that the Good Lord would just try and try again till He got it right and maybe this was it, Septimus decided, as he "studied" the water gushing into the overfilled ditch swirling its muddy course toward the approaching river, which, if it didn't stop rising soon, was going to make Septimus less of an Adam and more of a Noah in the new divine plan for man and His new world.

But, it's important not to make too much of all this. That is to say, Septimus, for all the spare time now on his hands in his little hideout, had yet to work through a complete theodicy, or come to the paradoxical, and, in the end, inevitable realization that the only Paradise ever worth having was one that had been ever so recently Lost. Nor did he otherwise sort through the great mystery of why a Perfect Being would have any need of any kind of world at all, much less an imperfect, fallen one, ever Lost and Regained, cursed and graced, in alternating fits of time and destruction, disobedience and damnation, in the endless playing out of the divine melodrama between Man and his Maker.

No, the matter simply did not occur to Septimus in these terms, but since it was obvious to him that there would always be a world of some kind, as he couldn't imagine nothing at all, crack his brain over it as he would, he thought only that the Almighty would try again and again till He finally found someone like himself who would not mess it all up. And, despite his hunger and cold, he began to warm up a little proud as the chosen one, even though he was a Free Will Baptist and not a Presbyterian, the one and only "elect." That was what he felt, though the word didn't come into his head; he felt singled out and special in that mysterious way—summoned and chosen all at once. He thus resolved then and there to serve God the Father as his faithful and obedient son and servant and, per force, be provided in return from the awful abundance of this New Eden in the Saline River swamp.

No, indeed, it would not be a fallen world any longer, full of slaves and free, Black and White, Blue and Gray, rich and poor, war and peace, want and plenty, but a heaven on earth full of the innocent happiness of a Paradise Regained.

But soon, after watching it rain without cease for at least another seemingly endless hour, his satisfaction was gradually mellowed by a creeping loneliness, and he realized that if the Lord was lonely enough to make Septimus so he would need someone, too, or "go slap crazy" wandering around in "dis here Garden with nuddin to do or talk to but keep God company." In a word, he was wondering if he might not get bored after a time and whether or not, since the Lord was not the best conversationalist he'd ever been around, maybe Dagmar would free herself from those Yankees, come here quick like, and perhaps be his New Eve. Such a thought, he knew, would have gotten him lynched in the old world but not in this brave new one, no, suh. He was convinced, if she found her way here, then it would be God's will and that would be that. He would provide all things and Dagmar had to be one of 'em.

But the cold rain seemed to steel itself to the hard task of flooding the world within the next couple of hours. His feeling of triumph waned in light of the persistent lack of wood and food, and Septimus began to wonder if God was holding it against him for running off from Miz Virginee and Aunt Sallie after all—that is, when they needed him most. Could this be Perdition instead of Paradise? Hell and not Heaven? He, in an instant, went from pride to fear, prayed for a while kneeling by his tow-sack bed, then, feeling better, "studied" on this in the doorway again, deciding that since God had told him that night to run, he could not be angry and would take care of all those folks back there in Camden, Black and White, in His own good time and in His own good way, and he really didn't have to worry his head over it. Anyway, this was what he told himself, after he stood up and gave it some long and careful thought.

Too, "maybe, dey is all drowned by now noway," he said out loud, and with that decided to kneel again this time in the cabin door and pray over it yet again. He asked God to look after all "dem folks back der," alive or dead, body and soul, and with his words of mercy and contrition lifting to heaven he consummated a covenant to be the best Second Adam the Lord ever made, making it unnecessary for Him to ever make a Third, and so on. He prayed and prayed hard, like that night when he decided to run off with the dog howling and the moon rising behind the oak trees over Camden.

But his knees started to hurt and he couldn't stand it anymore and so arose, leaned against the door, and watched the rain, not knowing what else to do while thinking if only some food and kindling would turn up, all would be "fine and dandy." No sooner had he uttered these words aloud than it rumbled thunder as if in approval of his prayers, and Septimus, amazed and suddenly pleased, stood tall and stared at the sky with pleasure, but then it started raining harder and harder and his feeling of holy approval abated until he got lonelier and lonelier and the more it rained, the more Septimus decided that he was being tested and he'd just have to "let it come to pass in de Lawd's own good time," like as Aunt Sallie was always saying. He would just have to be patient and all would be well, and he would soon be warm and well fed like he used to be back in Camden when he lived behind the Big House on the hill on Washington Street till the Yankees came and turned the whole world all upside down.

He thought of rummaging around that black heap of the big dead manor house again, but he'd long since stripped it of what charred wood might burn and was fresh out of any hope of finding more, so the Lord had better hurry or "dey won't be no Septimus at all and de Lo'd will jes have to learn to live by hisse'f," he said, getting a little surly with God.

But the Lord, perhaps in answer to Septimus's anger, sent something else, not a new Eve in the form of Dagmar, who had long since escaped and was now riding with Shelby, or an ark nudging up the Saline, but a heavy, steady drumming of hooves coming down the road. First there was the thudding sound, then the vision and he could see it clearly, a mass of four horses—Gray cavalrymen charging toward him. He ducked inside and quickly threw dirt over what remained of the dying fire, then stripped his bed of the tow-sack blankets and hid under the bed.

The heaving rattle of sabers and tack rushed toward him into the big yard, through it, and stopped outside his cabin door.

Above the sneezing and blowing of tired horses Septimus heard angry Southern voices debating. Had they seen the whiff of smoke? he wondered. If so, he'd surely be found, but he curled the sacks tighter anyway and prayed again. There was more gruff talk, curses, yells, even some hard, mean laughter, then the urging of tired mounts followed a shouted command, as the group lunged into the wet tree line, splashing out of ear-shot leaving nothing to strike the ear but the silence of the falling rain and the gushing ditch outside the door.

He trembled and shook, not with cold but with fear; he wanted to run, but didn't know where. Maybe they'd come back when they got into that deeper water; and if he broke and ran, they'd catch him and surely send him back to Camden; and if he so much as touched a rifle, they'd hang him from the manor house's big front yard tree; and, if he went toward the Rock he'd be nabbed by the Blues, they'd press him to endless work as a contraband serving the Yankee army that had run away to save itself. But he had never been this hungry in his life and was sure that if he did not starve he would freeze. This thought only made the trembling worse, and the desperate idea intruded to go home and "face the music" or whichever group of White folks might catch him if he could only get a meal of some kind out of them and a warm place to sleep.

He got up and went to the door and looked out cautiously. The rain drizzled steadily off the roof and onto the earth in a rushing brown stream, swirling over the soaked ground and scuppering through the small bordering ditch that emptied into a river that had swollen first into a swamp and now into something of a lake. It was like a living thing, a rising, slithering, tumescent, horrible creature that first filled the river over its banks, then the creeks, ditches, and low spots to isolate the little hills before swallowing them whole, lifting at last into the lowest fields and filling the ploughed but barren furrows, till Septimus saw it coming toward him with a sinister inexorability that made him wonder how long he could hold up here in this place that had seemed so safe when he found it all abandoned and devoid of people of any color and lived for a time on the rotten sack of potatoes he found in the corner that had sprouted out green protruding roots in search of the dirty floor like he was doing—that is to say, desperately rooting in the air for some kind of sustenance and security in a cruel, harsh, and fallen world.

It was precisely this sudden return of quietude, empowered as it was by the quick intruding and abatement of the fearful noise of armed men on horses, that awakened in Septimus the painful realization that he was not God's New Adam in a New Eden after all, or a new Noah waiting upon his ark, or anything of the kind, but was nothing more or less than just another desperate, runaway slave in Arkansas.

Septimus had little knowledge of his antecedents—that is, of how he had gotten to Arkansas from Africa. He only knew that he was his mother's seventh child, seen to by the White doctor who had been prevailed upon by the owner "to look in on" the field slave "May" (so named after the month she was born). The old "Doc" riding out from Camden on his big black horse with his even blacker bag filled with dirty instruments strapped across the saddle pommel to find May dying from an untreatable postpartum infection. He did what he could—had the child baptized with that high-sounding name and saw the mother "layed-out" for burying in the little slave cemetery nearby.

Septimus did learn from Aunt Sallie, however, that May had carried him in her belly from Louisiana (sold "up rivah" as they said, "into the wil's uh Arkansaw"), up the muddy Red to the Ouachita, because she was pregnant by a Creole field overseer whose passion for her got himself fired and her sold by the Free Black Mulatto owner, a rich sugar planter with more slaves than just about any pure White man in lower Louisiana. Hence, it was immediately apparent that he, Septimus, was not only African but half Creole—that is, French with a dash of southern Spain and whatever else no one could really say. And it was this somewhat lighter skin, not deep ebony, almost blue like May's, or fair brown like his father's, but somewhere in between, that was his ticket out of the cotton fields and into the Big House on Washington Street, where he learned to polish silver, wait table, cook, tend to chickens and cows, run endless errands, read, write, do some numbers, and be dragged constantly to church to endure endless Bible lessons and sermons from practically all quarters and sides at all hours and times of day or night, Black and White, till, when at last he got God's permission, all he could think of was running to freedom once Mr. Lincoln's army had finally marched down from Little Rock.

No, he didn't know much about the past or really care. He was not a historian. Like most folks, Black or White, the everyday of today was enough for him to think about.

He did not know that May's mother had been sold in the market at New Orleans by the estate lawyers of a kindly, but good and dead, old French doctor named David Dumont, who had fled with his devoted and merry cook slave from the new nation of Haiti, or Saint-Domingue as it had been known, sailing with her to what then was *Nouvelle-Orléans* to escape the uprising of 1791. That rebellion had been led by one Henri Christophe who, like Septimus, had run away to freedom, not from a Camden house supported by cotton but a Grenada plantation supported by coffee, stowing himself away for fate as a lad among the freshly stacked sacks on the three-masted *Le Roi de France,* which had been busy loading at the quay.

Fortunate in his choice of captains, Christophe was dropped into freedom upon yet another island based on bondage—Saint-Domingue. It was a grand isle of jungles, plantations, and towns whose lonely precipitous hills peaked out of the Caribbean over busy harbors, embracing nearly a thousand ships a year with such romantic names as *Louis Quinze* from Bordeaux, the *Terre d'Or* from Nantes, or the *Nancy Perkins* from Boston. Here caravels, cutters, and coracles tacked about like busy waterbugs among merchantmen and men-of-war that lolled upon the sea of the lucrative West Indian trade.

Les Noirs were topped by thirty thousand *Grand Blancs* owning eight thousand plantations prospering in the lower valley folds and flat plateaus. These were tended to by a middle class of artisans and merchants (*Petit Blancs*) of the trading towns, who for their needs employed the working, wage-earning Mulattoes and Free Blacks. Yet, to be sure, all in their turn were sustained by the expropriated labor of half a million *Les Noirs* slaves. They formed a ponderous base of a race-obsessed pyramid of class and commerce priming the pump of an incipient capitalism with eighty-six million pounds of sugar (*muscovado*), seventy-one million of coffee, seven million of cotton, countless hogsheads of molasses; more rum and indigo than British Jamaica, and more imported slaves than any other colony anywhere, per year, in the New World. It was, in a word, the brightest jewel in the French colonial crown, representing two-thirds of her overseas *livres*—her proudest possession that she much preferred even to either India or Canada.

To be sure, the Indians had vanished and there were no machines—it was slavery or nothing. Its fruits fed Henri Christophe's amazed eye as he wandered about the entrepôt of Cap Francais, the "Paris of the West Indies" as it was called in 1779, which in reality yawned open before him like a great gullet for the world's insatiable appetite for lucre.

One would later describe this harbor in those days as "an indescribable medley of noise and color, turmoil and commotion" whose streets were crowded with the "French soldiers from the casernes, in cocked hats, long buttoned tunics, breeches and gaiters; sailors from the men-of-war in pea jackets, petit coat trousers, and buckled shoes, and their officers in blue coats with white facings and gold buttons, over long white waistcoats, white knee breeches, white stockings, buckle shoes, and gold braid. There were planters—European and Creole—dressed in the latest Paris mode. There were the planters' womenfolk in fine muslin dresses with long, pointed waists, laced bodices, elbow-length sleeves frilled with lace." It was, without question, the wealthiest colony of the wealthiest country in all the Western world. Yet, in the words of Mirabeau, its masters were "sleeping at the foot of Vesuvius."

But by Christophe's arrival a slave-owning aristocrat named Jefferson had written something about all men being equal and thus started a revolution he embraced but could never quite hold; till a mob in Paris released a marquis from the Bastille; the estates general erased feudalism in a vote, published the *Declaration of the Rights of Man,* abolished the Nobility in 1790, and in 1791, moved Voltaire's bones to the Pantheon while debating the status of "Free Coloureds" in the colonies. Hearing this question, the Mulattoes rose to shout their answer, but the shout was so fearful that soon the decks of *La Reine de La Mer* arrived from France to yet again echo an annulment of them as men.

In anger, the Mulattoes rose and fell, but *Les Noirs* rose and stood, as Henri Christophe, now a lieutenant under Toussaint Louverture, blew the conch of freedom and the African volcano erupted, exploding the white snow-like *Grand and Petit Blanc* top all about the globe with the good Dr. Dumont and Septimus's great-grandmother floating down like ash into French Louisiana to settle in the greatest port of *La Florida* near the mouth of the Mississippi.

In time, the busy and now very comfortable doctor read over his morning coffee about Louis losing his head one cold January day in Paris. Dumont felt the world tremble at the murder of God's king in '93 as the French Revolution then abolished slavery in '94. Then in April Danton rode the tumbler one especially busy morning before Dumont's *petit déjeuner*, while Robespierre rounded off another *déjeuner* in July, each dropping his head into a basket, which if fit for a king was certainly not beneath the nod of a couple of commoners.

Doctor Dumont was soon given indigestion with Toussaint's ascendancy over an independent Saint-Domingue/Haiti; but he smiled at the grudging propitiation of the plantations with an old slave-like discipline newly imposed and the new dalliance with the French as New World *Realpolitik*.

Then, to be sure, Dumont got busy, did some more surgery about town, sawed a leg here and there, attended a ball, walked to his favorite café for coffee, delivered a child or two, read a little of Voltaire, bought another slave to help in the kitchen, all in time to read on a Saturday of Toussaint Louverture's new war with the notorious Negrophobe, Napoleon, who, in the first year of the new century, sent his brother in-law, General Charles-Victor-Emmanuel Leclerc and his Parisian wife, Pauline, the emperor's most beautiful and favorite sister, along with brother Jerome, who needed something to do, as well an admiral, of course, and another man, who, despite being a staunch proponent of African bondage, had helped win Jefferson's revolution at Yorktown, General Donatien Marie Joseph de Rochambeau, sailing with the Bonaparte family to Haiti with fifty-six men-of-war and twenty-five thousand foot, to restore slavery in the New World and reclaim the colony for the Emperor, as the "Son of the Revolution" and defender of the Rights of Man in the Old. In other words, to get the money flowing to France again and put *Les Noirs* in their place.

Yet, the good Dumont's dimming eyes were quickly clouded by news of the French frustration from Toussaint and Christophe till at last Leclerc was defeated by the slave's mightiest ally, the inoculating mosquito, whose yellow fever with its mortal bite brought from the Bight of Benin as stowaways on the slavers to kill thousands in but a tick of time, including the husband whose corpse Pauline pickled, not in a good Bordeaux, for sure, but in a cut-rate rum bound for there, all the while consoling herself with the Black Toussaint whom she shackled in the lower decks for an early, ignominious death in Gaul.

But Pauline did not flee as the other fleers fled. Not like Charlotte, who left her man to die while riding behind her mules to the comfort of madness with a pope; nor like her "friend" Eugénie, who with the Prussians pressing hard upon Paris, raced from the Tuileries with the cute little ill-fated uniformed prince in hand, running through the Louvre without pausing even a moment before a single masterpiece of timeless art because time pressed itself so cruelly upon her; that is, till she was nearly tripped in full flight down the hall by Géricault's *The Raft of the "Medusa"* floating above, arresting her with its terror of shipwreck, to which, as promised, all temporal power, not just this sinking Second Empire, must come; freeing herself at last with tears of fear to save a cowering husband, who should have saved his honor with an honest fever or fuselage but who instead fled to die in an English bed under the fingering humiliation of surgeons upon his broken penis. It was apt—as every new mistress was undressed in an antechamber to this imperial lover, who waited relaxing as a reclining nude upon a couch for each entering with whispered admonition to kiss everything but his face—that Louis-Napoleon should die of a stone above his scrotum in Camden rather than a ball in his breast at Sedan, Metz, or bravely against any wall in France, was most fitting indeed.

Yes, husband Leclerc's Pauline was made of stuff more stern, since she brought her man with her as she should; rumed him good to pop him in a hole with a quick prayer that did not fret much about a pope; soon remarried a rich prince named Camilio Borghese, no less; then consoled herself with lovers, made herself the "Duchess of Guastalla"; and ruled over the salons of Paris and Rome, till, dying with a smile of satisfaction in her prince's arms, she was kissed an adieu, while he lamented her through his tears as "the kindest creature in the world."

But brother Jerome, ever the lesser man, abandoned his navy in Saint-Domingue, sailed in flight to Maryland where he tarried in time to sire a child, who sired a son, who made it up by running another navy for the man that got the cavalry up the Cuban hill from the Hotel Mingo. But Jerome could never be enthroned in Baltimore, so he returned to the elder Bonaparte, who was fond of making brothers into kings and crowned him such of Westphalia; then he battled bravely at Waterloo and survived to ride with the nephew's army in the *coup* that put Eugénie in power, till her Medusa struck after Metz and

Sadowa and left her racing through the Louvre to see corpses clinging to a raft as copies from the morgues of Paris.

Our good doctor Dumont hesitated, too, before his own grave, as it were, if only to watch the hated British come to Haiti and rejoice a moment longer at their defeat. For once he found himself, to his great surprise, rooting for the Africans as Christophe served up victory for him as a new general, Jean-Jacques Dessalines, before revolting himself into the power of his own northern Kingdom as "Henry I." There he reigned till suicide ended a drama that the good doctor Dumont could not applaud, for having himself turned reluctantly and gone to Meterie Cemetery with a stroke.

Yet, for that brief time, the shocks upon the pages of the morning gazette did not cease to strike the gaze of Dumont before Christophe's death. As his god failed in Saint-Domingue, so, too, did he fail in Louisiana, when seeing the power of the fever and the weakness of his fleet, he sold it all to the same Jefferson whose words had set the Old and New Worlds alike alight.

Thus it was that Dumont's lovely, glorious France first lost her Canada and India and now her Saint-Domingue and then her Louisiana; so he contented himself as a new American, living and moving with his Gallic *savoir faire* as a very brilliant addition to the very best of New Orleans society, helping and healing while lamenting and complaining about the excesses of revolution, ever tended to by his faithful Black *Carib,* who learned no English but spoke to God and sang to others in a friendly patois of France and Africa brought from Cap Francais. But it mattered not as she shopped in the crowded old market of the city that connected the cathedral and *Hôtel de Ville,* so wonderfully described by Richard Taylor's famous house guest and Yankee friend, Frederick Olmsted, who saw it in much the same way a few days before traveling up to *Fancy.*

> I was delighted when I reached the old Place d'Armes, now a pub-
> lic garden, bright with the orange and lemon trees, and roses, and
> myrtles, and laurels, and jessamines of the south of France. Fronting
> upon it is the ancient Hotel de Ville, still the city court house, a quaint
> old French structure, with scaly and vermiculated surface, and deep-
> worn sills, and smooth-rubbed corners; the most picturesque and
> historic-looking public building, except the highly preserved, little
> old court house at Newport, that I can now think of in the United
> States.
>
> Adjoining it is an old Spanish cathedral, damaged by paint, and late
> alterations and repairs, but still a fine thing in our desert of the rev-

erend in architecture. Enough, that while it is not new, it is not shabby, and is not tricked out with much frippery, gingerbread and confectionery work. The door is open; coaches and cripple beggars are near it. A priest, with a face the expression of which first makes one think of an ape and then an owl, is coming out. If he were not otherwise to be heartily welcomed to fresh air and sunlight, he should be so, for the sake of the Sister of Charity who is following him, probably to some death-bed, with a corpse-like face herself, haggard but composed, pensive and absorbed, and with the eyes of a broken heart. I think that I may yet meet them looking down compassionately and soothingly, in some far different pestilent or war-hospital. In lieu of holy-water, then, here is money for the poor-box, though the devil share it with good angels.

Dark shadows, and dusky light, and, deep, subdued, low organ strains pervade the interior; and, on the bare floor, here are the kneeling women,— "good" and "bad" women—and, ah yes, White and Black women, bowed in equality before their common Father. "Ridiculously absurd idea," say democratic Governors Mc Duffie (of South Carolina) and Hammond; "Self-evident" say our ancestors, and so must say the voice of conscience, in all free, humble, hearts.

In the crowded market-place, there were not only the pure old Indian Americans, the Spanish, French, English, Celtic and African, but nearly all possible mixed varieties of these, and no doubt some other breeds of mankind …

It was, indeed, as Olmsted describes so well, a world obsessed by the Black blood that rose from the African bone to skin in a hierarchy of color mandated by the French slavers, and as Olmsted lists in rank: Sacatra (Griffe and Negress), Griffe (Negro and Mulatto), Marabon (Mulatto and Griffe), Mulatto (White and Negro), Quarteron (White and Mulatto), Metif (White and Quateron), and Meamelouc (White and Metif)—in this way the Haitian cook was on the ebony bottom, but her tongue no doubt found favor in this medley of world language which could hear her heart.

No doubt, too, she saw posted notices in the market for runaways, like Olmsted noticed and immortalized.

Fifty Dollars Reward: Ran away from the subscriber, about two months ago, a bright mulatto girl, named Mary, about twenty-five years of age, almost white, and reddish hair, front teeth out, a cut on

her upper lip; about five feet five inches high; has a scar on her forehead; she passes for free; talks French, Italian, Dutch, English, and
Spanish.

ANDRE GRASSO

Yet, unlike Olmsted's runaway, Septimus Reymonde was not honored by a
written reward—there were too many in 1864 for the world to take much
notice of such notices. But, like Mary, Septimus's African blood had come to
Louisiana by indirection, his antecedent being sold by a Black chief in Benin to
a buyer from Bordeaux bound for the profits of Martinique. From there a
human load was plucked by a Bostonian slaver. Was it old Ralph Waldo bent on
a quick profit in Charleston, who sprung a leak in a little squall off Saint-
Domingue and, in the delay of repairing, sold Septimus's great-great-grandfather for something he almost never did—at a loss to the French? For sure,
this was the exception, and the fortunes of abolition were well assured in the
banks of Boston, as were their abolitionist heirs' hatred of the Southern market, born in two generations for "Destruction and Reconstruction" of the buy-
ers of such as Septimus and Mary whose gold-purchase lined the pockets of an
ever-selling but soon sanctimonious, erstwhile secessionist New England.

But, after all, Septimus knew nothing of Haiti and its revolts, wars and
fevers, yellow and black; or of Christophe or Toussaint or Dessalines; or of the
good Doctor Dumont and his merry cook; or the other Mary or what became
of her. Was she free or slave? Alive or dead? Her story cried out for more than
a footnote upon the page. But, alas, he did not know nor could afford to care;
certainly nothing about the sale of Louisiana that was why he spoke English and
not French, and thus walked now upon the ground of the Confederacy and not
that of a colony of Gaul or Spain or Mexico. And, of course, he didn't remember his mother, knew little of his father except the legend of his race. He had
no family except the one he had just run from, which made him feel such nag-
ging guilt despite all his praying at the dog and the moon and to God that night
standing there in Miz Virginee's backyard until he fell in with Steele's army as
just another runaway trying to cross the Saline ahead of rope or chain, running
ahead of Smith's Grays, stowing in a wagon of White wounded not that much
unlike Christophe on *La Reine de La Mer* before starting a revolution, which,
unknown to Septimus, he was doing just as well, only in a different way, not
with sword or gun or conch but with his feet upon a muddy road.

He was White, too, and Black, too, and a little of everything, too, and didn't have any anger at anyone because of color, or hair, or skin, or any such thing. He just wanted to be free himself, that's all; that is, if he didn't get lynched, or shot, or starved, or frozen, or caught, and worked to death as Blue-Black contraband or Gray slave. That was hard to think upon.

It was sure enough a dilemma and it fell hard upon him, yes, indeed it did. But what fell hardest was the mighty weight of necessity—the hated ever-impending thing that, like gravity on a plunging object, waited patiently for the beginning of every sunrise to push folks through the pressures of the day-to-day—the numbing, urgent needs of what just had to be done soon or else; the this or the that of simply living and breathing, whether it was feeding the chickens, fetching, or doing his Bible lesson to propitiate Aunt Sallie, all of which now, standing in an empty slave cabin in the rain, took on the more-compelling aspect of simply somehow living to see tomorrow, which, if he made it, would merely repeat the same exigent problem. And so on. On and on. Over and over, without rest, till he found his way to his humble grave and a little repose. For a moment, in a flash of self-pity, death seemed a surprisingly welcome development, but then the thought occurred that by the time he got good and settled the trumpet would blow and Aunt Sallie would fly over flapping her great white wings to summon him up to the greatest and longest church service one could imagine, yelling and singing and praying and preaching among the angels and archangels with himself no doubt all scrubbed and washed and forced to sit on the front row with her; then condemned, sent back down to earth as expiation for the sin of running off to wait at table for some nearly eternal big Sunday lunch, eating in the kitchen, washing the dishes, and spending the afternoon feeding the chickens and tending the horses, cows, and turkeys before toting and fetching till dark, waiting on table again, eating and washing and praying and singing again before bed with another quick Bible lesson on sin and hell and damnation and burning and thirst and the flames of perdition set up for him by a loving God; then some more praying and preaching to avoid both, then up before dawn to light the fire in the hellish kitchen to help with breakfast; then, a long tedious grace, said by the White master in solemn unctuous, if not self-righteous, tones—as an endless necessity to thank God for not starving them all to death. He, Septimus Reymonde, would be condemned forever as humble penitent at some White folks' house picked out by God himself under Aunt Sallie's urging. At this, the thought of death lost its allure and Septimus resolved then and there to put it off as long as he could.

He sighed aloud, in a way he had and was not quite conscious of, and with all the strength he could muster, resolved he just wouldn't go back to there.

He preferred the Saline River bottoms, even after the horsemen had ridden up and ruined everything—spoiled his new Eden. And though he had not found a garden in which all was provided, but instead an ever-rising, threatening swamp, which seemed always to have the serpent of crime and cruelty crawling around in it, at least he was free. But free to do what? he wondered in the flash of the next intruding thought, his mind never quite able to rest but always leaping quickly to the next logical thing no matter how much he tried to control it. The plain truth was, "I has to do sompin soon or starve." Maybe in the end we are all slaves, his mind said to him, slaves to that peculiar something, slaves to whatever feeds our bellies and saves our hide from ice or sun, wind or flood. That was it, the tyranny of the gut and hide, "dat was de law of dis here swamp," the thing that kept it slithering with the unending cruelty of life and death; and his gut began to rumble and his hide began to shiver in a most terrible demanding and painful way. "No, suh," he might run from Washington Street, but there was no running from this here iron law of freedom—he had to do something, and soon, or he would die. It was simple as that.

So, without really thinking, or reflecting, he found himself running through the rain back the way he had come, racing toward what he knew not, just running and running, splashing down the muddy road back toward Old Tom Jenkins's Ferry.

CHAPTER THIRTY

$200 REWARD

*Will be paid for the delivery to me, of the following described mulatto
boy, and the Thief who stole him, if alive—but, if dead, nothing, for the
villain of a White man; or One Hundred Dollars for the delivery to me
my Negro Boy Edmund, or for securing him in jail, that I might get him.*

*. . . I have dreamed, with both eyes open, that he went toward the
Spanish country; but as dreams are like some-would-be-thought-honest-
men—quite uncertain—he may have gone some other direction.*

—Jefferson County, Pine Bluff, Ark.,
Dec. 3, 1836, Thomas Bayliss

At first Septimus wandered wearily through the muddy backtrack of his own
flight from battle, but then, increasingly encountering the litter and tracks of
odd out-riders, out of fear and with no object save escape itself, veered to the
southwest, away from Jenkins's Ferry, angling toward Tulip. Upon this route,
clinging as he did to the forest, avoiding the roads, he had easily averted notice.

He had no real plan, only the simple hope that something eventually "would
turn up." And there was an increasing damp chill that was almost as painful as
his increasing hunger and fatigue, but worst of all he felt the weight of an even
heavier despair. Occasionally he would stop, pray, and mutter to himself, fight
back incipient tears, then, with renewed courage, summoned once again with
his own voice, he would bestir himself and continue his lonely journey to where
and what he knew not.

Then, coming near the muddy wagon ruts offering themselves up as a road,
he moved away even more, entering a little stand of thick, hardwood timber,
which, in turn, was intersected by a swollen but quietly running stream. He
could have jumped but saved the energy by wading. It did not matter, his shoes,

such as they were, had that morning finally given way to his bare, wet, and sore feet. And, of course, he had long since lost his hat.

It was harder walking that way but he was afraid of the road and so moved carefully through the woods like a stray creature yet new to the wilderness.

He went but a short time in this way then stopped. He thought he heard something above the sound of his own steps. "Oh, well," he said aloud, "it ain't nothin'." So, he moved but then heard it again and froze. It was, indeed, something after all, he was now sure of it, a noise coming from up ahead—among the trees. He stopped and listened as hard as he could, cupping his hands to his ears. It came again, this sound, but it was not like anything he had ever heard a strange, eerie, grinding noise, not animal, for sure, but less than human, too. He stood listening. It came and went. He was frightened and thought of running away in the opposite direction, but something held him fast.

Then, cautiously, without really deciding to, just doing it, he pursued this hopeful-danger by stepping forward, circling, gradually moving closer—like a creature whose hunger impels it to ever-greater peril. But still it eluded him. He stopped yet again, listening. He did not have long to wait. Then, as if sensing his presence, it stopped for what seemed a very long time—as if it were waiting for him to do something.

He moved closer, gingerly placing one foot ahead of the other, making as little sound as possible, his heart racing in anticipation of each delicate step upon the wet leaves. He stopped and moved, stopped and moved, from tree to tree, ducking under limbs without breaking them, furtively sliding through the forest, pausing, listening, looking, getting ever nearer. Then, there, over there, he saw something, incongruous, not belonging, very much out of place, and focusing upon it in the half-light permitted by limbs (between the sun), he brought into vision at first an arm—then a shoulder, protruding past a tree, leaning a little to the right, only just above the ground. It was obviously a man, a man on his way to falling but held suspended by the trunk of a medium-sized oak, a figure facing the other way.

Surprisingly, there was another sound, one that had not been heard before, a deep, low moan, and then the grinding noise came louder afterward, the two seemingly working in tandem as an expression of the deepest pain of body and soul that a human is capable—that is, a little short of a scream, at the other end, as it were, the lower one, of the scale of physical and mental horror.

Septimus hesitated, then, emboldened, approached with the greatest circumspection, swinging a little wide to get a better view.

Soon, in a few more careful steps, all came clearly into view. It was a White boy in a tattered blue uniform, a hatless Yankee soldier, covered in dried blood, head down, slumping forward, grinding his teeth, and moaning. That was it, the noise, the teeth grinding like dry rocks against each other, yet with a hollow sound, coming with each wave of pain and followed with the quieter moan.

Involuntarily, Septimus almost lost his balance, snapped a twig, and the man, lifting his head slowly with obvious effort, opened his eyes as if they were great weights, seeing Septimus standing there, staring back at him in amazement— their eyes, each to each, now locking in a desperate, wondering stare. There was a pause, then the youth moved his lips, made a pitiful sound unlike any Septimus had ever heard—somewhere between a cry and speech—and lifted a hand to him only to let if fall back into the wet leaves.

Septimus, to his great shock, yelled, "Joshua? Joshua, zat you? My Lawd it is!! Joshua!! Lawd, Lawd! It's Joshua!!"

Septimus, with the help of an empty canteen that he lifted from Joshua's belt, managed to get some water, fetched from the creek, down him after a few sipping coughs. Then, somewhat revived, Joshua pointed to his pocket.

"Lawd, Joshua, is dis all yuh has?" he said, retrieving a hard-tack biscuit, then rummaging through his tattered blue jacket for more of anything at all and finding nothing instead.

Joshua seemed to say "yes" with his sad eyes, so Septimus examined the hard-tack, nearly breaking a tooth on it, then he tried and failed to break the biscuit with his hands. It was harder than any rock he had ever seen back in Ouachita County.

"Joshua … is dis whut yuh calls a biscuit?" he said, sitting back on his heels, examining and turning it over in his hands. "I say it's a devil's rock … it's a rock made by ole scratch hisself and put in yo' pocket as uh joke on bof ah us."

Joshua seemed to smile as Septimus scratched around in the leaves like a turkey hunting a bug, looking for something as hard as the hardtack was hard.

"I cain't find nuthin' powerful nuff to break dis here ding," he said idly, then stood and walked back to the creek.

"Maybe dis'll do it," he said, yelling back at Joshua, dropping the biscuit like a stone with a plop in the water, letting it soak for a moment then retrieving it. He dropped it again and scrambled out a small boulder from the leaves, digging it and rolling it over like a dead turtle upon its back before washing it in the creek, then picked it up again, and, raising it over his head, paused, and let it fall on the biscuit with a dull thud. But the biscuit retreated by hiding in the leaves and mud.

Septimus studied it, then dug it out with a small, dirty stick, found another rock and placed it under their lunch and dropped the bigger one on it like a great cudgel. He repeated this twice, not content now to drop it but throwing it till he was out of breath. Then, recovered, he fell to his knees and pounded the biscuit over and over till at last, to his great surprise it broke in two even pieces along an invisible fracture line.

"Lawd God! Joshua, we done it!" he whooped, then repeated this till he had several uneven pieces that he soaked again into something approaching slivers of brown glue.

"Heya," he said, putting a fragment into Joshua's mouth chased with water, "see can yuh git dis down."

Joshua choked, coughed, sputtered, and tired to chew, then swallowed, till finally, with some more filthy water, it washed and stayed in his stomach.

Then Septimus got his half down. It was, he thought, the finest thing he had ever eaten.

He rolled away to refill the canteen from the creek, drank some more, then leaned against a tree, closed his eyes, and fell asleep.

But like Poltam feeling Cripple Bear's rifle barrel against his cheek, Septimus soon awoke to something cold pressing into his face.

"Wake up, nigger!" said a voice.

Septimus slowly turned his eyes to see a red-headed White man standing over him, pressing a pistol within an inch of his nose.

"Git up!" he said, stepping back, the pistol cocked and held in his right hand.

Septimus got up slowly to see three other young White men getting off horses and walking up. They had on pieces of gray uniforms and floppy Stetson hats, and brandished pistols and knifes. One carried a carbine and another a shotgun. They were hardly more than boys—teenagers, except for the red-head, who looked to be in his early twenties.

"It's uh nigger up yar in the woods with a wounded Yankee!" he yelled proudly, as the others came up to them.

"Yew got a knife or anythin', boy? Don't lie to me 'r I'll blow yer head awf!"

"No, suh …" said Septimus, rising and raising his hands. "I ain't got nothin' …"

"Turn 'round," said the older one.

Septimus did so and the man patted him down and the others arrived all standing in a circle except one who went over to Joshua and made an inspection.

"Turn back 'round. Whut's yore name, boy?" asked the man, as Septimus faced him again, his hands still in the air as far as he could get them.

"Septimus …," he replied, meekly.

"Whut?"

"Septimus."

"Septimus? What kind o' name zat fur a nigger?"

"It's de one they give me," he said a little too emphatically.

"Is zat so? Who? Who give you sech a store-bought name as zat, boy, huh?"

"Doctor …"

"Doctor? You wuz borned by a doctor?" he said, incredulous.

"Yes, suh …"

"I ain't never knowed a nigger borned by a doctor …"

Septimus looked away in silence, his hands as high as he could get them.

"Whut's yore las' name?" he asked, squinting and stepping up, putting the pistol closer.

"Reymonde …," he said almost inaudibly.

"Whut?"

"Reymonde," he said more loudly.

"Reymonde?"

"Yes, suh."

"Yew's from Loosiana?"

"Yes, suh … they sol' my mama up heya to Arkansas …"

"Yew's a runaway then, ain't ye, nigger?"

Septimus nodded slightly.

"Whur from?"

He told him.

"Camden? Yew shore is a long way from home, boy," one of the others added.

"Who's yore Yankee friend yar, huh?" the redhead asked, gesturing with his revolver at Joshua.

"He's just 'bout dead, Billy," said the one standing by Joshua.

"Put yore hands down …"

Septimus lowered them slowly.

"Who's the Yankee ye done took up with?"

"I don't know his name … I jes found 'im up heya in de woods and wuz …" he hesitated.

"Tryin' to hep him? Is that whatchew wuz a-fixin' to say? Huh, boy? Yew wuz up yar a-hepin' this yar Blue Belly weren't ye now, huh … ain't that rat?"

Septimus said nothing.

"Yew know whut we're a-doin' with runaways that done thown in with the Yankees, don't chew, boy?"

"I didn't thow in wid nobody ... honest ..., suh ... I's jes tryin' to see ifn he wuz still alive ... dats all."

"Well, Raymond," said the redhead, giving the name the Anglicized form, "we ain't puttin' up with this shit, see?"

Septimus did not respond.

"Tie his hands!" the redhead, named Billy, said, and walked over to Joshua while Septimus's hands were being tied behind his back.

"Joe Nathan, he's looks 'bout dead, don't he?" said Billy looking at Joshua closely. "Lost lots of blood ... it's a-wunder he got this fur."

"Some doc done tended to him somewhure," said Jonathan, whose name was pronounced just as Billy had said it, and who now pulled the shirt back revealing the bandaged shoulder soaked in blood.

"Yup ... yer're rat ... he done run awf from somewhures ... then passed out yarabouts ... till this runaway done found 'im ..."

"What we gonna do with 'im?" Jonathan asked quietly.

"Well, first let's finish with hangin' the nigger then we'll decide that," whispered Billy matter-of-factly to Jonathan under his breath.

"We gonna hang the boy, Billy?"

"What else we gonna do with him, huh, Joe Nathan? We cain't take 'im with us ... an' we cain't let 'im go ...," said Billy loudly.

"Billy, he's jes a skeered runaway. He's not a-fightin' nor nothin'. Maybe we ought to jes send 'im back, huh?" said Jonathan.

"Naw ... we ain't got no time. His owner's way down in Camden ... that's too damn fur with this war a-goin' own ... how we gonna do that, huh? An' if we let 'im go he's jes gonna thow in with 'em Yankees ... like the rest o' 'em ... we got no choice I tell ye ...," said Billy.

"But he wa'n't really carryin' no gun nor nothin' ... I looked 'round and thar ain't none yar nowhures, Billy ... it ain't rat ... if he's a-fightin' ... why ... that'd be different ..."

"Naw, he wa'n't carryin' no gun," Billy said interrupting, "yer rat ... but they wuz a-runnin together ... see, Joe Nathan, we done caught 'im a-hepin' this yar Yankee soldier ... a-runnin' with 'im ... an' he'll hep them others ... if he wuz any good he wouldn't a-run in the first damn place. It's jes a matter of time till he puts own a uniform ... then he'll have a gun shore nuff ... an' yew'll shore wished yew'd done killt 'im while yew still had the chance ... afore he kills yew or one of yore friends ... or family ... after whut we done

sed up-per at the Ferry we got to make a point … with awl these damned niggers … see … we ain't got no choice … they shouldn't a-murdered our boys
up thar … have ye forgotten that, have ye, Joe Nathan … huh?" Billy paused,
then added, "If ye don't want no part of it, ye can leave … ride awf now …
okay?"

"All rat …," said Joe Nathan, "But let's git it over with … do it rat, I say …
quick like … I mean … come own … let's git it over with …"

"Ye kin fix the rope … yore good at knots …"

"We can use that big oak in the curve of the road back thar a piece … it's
gotta good strong branch that'll hold his weight an' awl …"

"Good … now go'n git it ready …"

Jonathan walked slowly to his horse, took the lariat from off his saddle, and
began to tie the noose.

Billy watched then returned to Septimus.

"Whutchayall doin'?" asked Septimus.

"Well, Septimus, son, I'm aferd we're gonna have to hang ye …"

"Hang me!? Whut for? I ain't done nuddin' … honest I ain't! Nuddin' at all!"

"Naw … yew probably ain't … not yet noways … but yew will … it's jes
a matter o' time."

"Listen! Billy! All I done is run … I ain't done no fightin' … no, suh!"

"Load 'im up, boys," said Billy, interrupting.

They loaded him onto Jonathan's horse, and with Billy walking beside him,
leading his own, and Jonathan holding the bridle under the bit, they took
Septimus to the hanging tree. The other two mounted and rode slowly behind.

"Mister Billy … all I done is run … I shouldn't … I knows dat now … but
I ain't heped no Yankees … touched a gun nor nuddin' … I swear it fo' God
… awl I done is run awf frum Camden … I'll go back … jes let me go … I
sorry … I shouldn't a run … no, suh, jes let me go!"

"You're rat … ye shouldn't a-run, Septimus … nem folks wuz good to ye,
I bet …"

"Yes, suh … dey wuz … dey wuz real good to me an' I wuz wrong to run
awf …"

"Then how cume ye done it? See … that weren't grateful, wuz it? Now we
done caught ye a-hepin' Yankees whut come down yare to fight yer own people … ye leave us no choice …"

"Yes, suh … I wuz wrong to run, Billy … jes let me go back home … I
promise… yuh don't have to carry me to no sheriff or nuddin' … I'll walk
back if I has to …"

"No ... you wouldn' do that, Septimus ... jes as soon as I let ye go ye'll run to them Yankees ... see ... I knowed that 'cause we done already caught ye up yar a-hepin' this yar Yankee boy ... then it won't be long afore yew done thown in with 'em ... be wearin' thar fancy blue uniform and a-killin' yer own White folks with them new rifles they done give awl the niggers to fight for 'em ... now ain't that rat?"

"Naw, suh, dat ain't rite ... all I wants wuz to get to Little Rock ... I didn't wanna fight nobody ... no, suh ... please let me go, Mister Billy ... please... an' I'll go home ... I promise ... yes, suh ... I promise ... fo God I does ..."

They reached the tree and stopped under it. Billy looked up, staring at him intently. Tears were running down Septimus's face. Jonathan threw the rope over the limb and began to adjust its length and tie it to the trunk.

Billy kept talking, looking up, saying, "See, Septimus, I got no choice ... this yare is a war ... an' wars ain't pretty ... yew done seen that yurse'f, ain't ye? Oh, folks try to dress it up an' awl ... but they cain't ... not really ... 'cause war is whut it is ... an' war's killin' ... pure an' simple ... an' I got to kill yew 'cause if I don't kill yew today ... well ... tomorrow you'll be a-tryin' to kill me ... or one-a my men ... now won't yew?"

"No, suh ... I don' wanna kill nobody ..."

"Well, see, that's it ... I believe ye ... 'cause I don't want to kill yew nather ... fact-o-the-bidness, I kindly like ye ... but then thar it is ... ye wouldn't want to kill nobody ... but then ye'll be thown in with them Kansas niggers an' ye'll have to start a-killin' Whites ... even though ye really don't want to ... jes to playse 'em ... or, to jes avoid bein' kilt yurs'f ... that's jes the way it works ... then ye'd kill me an' so now I gotta kill yew first ... it's all thar is to it ..."

"Mister Billy, I ain't gonna have nothin' to do with no Kansas niggas, I'm goin' home ... jes home ... I promise ... please ..."

Billy looked up at him, then said, "Septimus?"

"Yes, suh?"

"It's too late fur awl that ... see, 'cause I done promised myse'f after whut them Blue-bellied niggers done over thar at the Fer'y ... murdered 'r boys a-tryin' to surrender ... run 'em thew with thar shiny new bayonets Mr. Lincoln done give 'em to come down yare an' kill Southern folks with ... to 'r wounded that wuz hepless an' awl ... just a-lyin' thar on the ground ... a-begin' fur thar lives like ye is doin' now ... an' them niggers a-stickin' them in thar guts ... I swore after I seen that ... the first'n I found out yare that even looked like he wuz a-runnin' with them Yankees, I'd hang 'im ... an' it's jes yore bad luck that ye wuz the one I caught ... see? 'Cause I don't never break no promises, see? Not to nobody ... least-a awl to myself."

"But, I ain't had nuddin to do with dat ... I'm innocent ... please, suh!" he sobbed. "I didn't kill nobody ... I ain't even had no gun in my hands ... awl I been doin' is runnin' ... please ..."

Billy smiled his way into a frown, then stepped back and said to Jonathan, "Put the rope 'round his neck!"

Jonathan handed it to one of the others, who rode up and fitted it tightly around Septimus's neck.

Septimus had become strangely quiet and had closed his eyes.

"Septimus?"

"Yes, suh?" he answered meekly, not looking down at Billy, who was standing at his boot and still looking up.

"Yew want to say yore prayers?"

"Yes, suh," Septimus said with his eyes still tightly closed.

Billy pulled out a gold watch with his left hand, raising his right in the air as a signal.

"Yew got one minute ..."

"One minute?"

"I needs moya dan a minute ..."

"Yew got one minute ..."

"When?"

"Startin' now," Billy said, staring down at the watch, holding it higher.

"I needs a mow-ah dan dat ... I cain't handle my sins in no minute."

"Ye done used up half of it a-talkin'."

"Give 'em another minute, Billy," said Jonathan, who was now holding the bridle while the other boy, who had adjusted the noose, rode back to the rear, and was ready to give Jonathan's horse the lash the instant Billy's hand dropped.

Billy looked up from his watch at Jonathan, who stared back while looping the reins over his horses's neck.

"I said, give 'em some more time, Billy, or I ain't lettin' go of this yar bit," Jonathan said, firmly. "Man's got a rat to say his last words ... yew cain't deny 'em that ... even to a nigger ..."

Billy looked down at his watch, then up at Septimus, saying, "Okay, Septimus, it's two minutes to twelve, 'most exactly, so ye do whut prayin' ye got to ... now ... see ... 'cause at straight up noon ye gonna hang, unnerstand!" he said, his voice rising and his face flushing red as his hair.

Septimus closed his eyes tightly and began to pray out loud and fast, asking forgiveness for his sins, and for care of the folks back in Camden and to forgive him for leaving them. While he was praying the horse raised his tail and began to drop big green turds and fart. But Septimus kept praying and praying faster and faster and faster, so that even as the horse finished, he was asking God "to forgive Billy an' Joe Nathan an' the others fo' hangin' me ... day didn't know I wuz innocent ... an' to take cayah o' Joshua."

Jonathan looked at the ground, but Billy got angry and said, "Yew got half a minute ..."

Billy raised his hand even higher but, just as it was about to drop, with Septimus praying so fast now he couldn't be understood, there was a loud powerful voice from nowhere, as if God had spoken.

"Cut the nigger down!" it said, as just around the trees, just past the little turn in the road, a darkly bearded White man loped up on a big black horse.

"Cut the nigger down, I said! An' make it quick!" said the man, wearing a Stetson over long hair, and who now raised a Damascus Barrel shotgun a little higher, laying his finger on the right hammer for emphasis but not cocking it.

"I ain't a-joshin' ... I said cut the boy down!"

"Mister Mansfield!" said Billy, walking around from the left but still holding the watch, talking rapidly as he ducked under the horse's neck, confronting the man. "We caught this yar runaway a-hepin' Yankees," he said, emphasizing the point with the watch while his right hand dropped near his pistol but did not quite touch it.

"Billy Jack Stantfurd," said Mansfield looking down, "yore in charge o' this little hangin' detail, are ye?"

"Yes, suh, we wuz a-comin' back frum 'r layve when we caught this yar nigger a-hepn a wounded Yankee ... looks like he done hep'd 'im escape frum sumewhures over at the battlefield ... some doctor done tended to his wounds an' awl ... but he done run an' opened it up agin ... bad ..."

"Whur's he at now?" asked Mansfield.

"Over thar a piece ... up in the woods ... he's a soldier awl rat ... still got own his uniform ... an' this yar boy wuz a-hepin' him to run ... we caught 'im red-handed," said Billy proudly.

"They armed?" asked Mansfield.

"Naw, sir," said Jonathan, still gripping the bridle, "they wuz both asleep when we come up on 'em. The Yankee ... if he ain't dead by now ... won't las' much longer ... done a lot of bleedin' ... but this boy yar says he done run awf frum his White folks down in Camden. He wuz so wore out he wuz asleep ... but he didn't have no gun nor nothin' ... not even a knife ..."

"That rat, son?" asked Mansfield, turning to Septimus. "Ye done run awf from yore folks?"

"Yes, suh," he said quietly, unable to turn his head because of the noose.

"From Camden?"

"Yes, suh ..."

"That's a long way ..."

"Yes, suh."

"What'd ye do ... fawl in with that sorry mob of shirkers an' niggers a-runnin' with Steele?"

"Yes, suh."

"We gonna hang 'em," said Billy quietly, "jes like they done David O. Dodd... he wuz 'bout the same age ... an' O. Dodd ain't done nothin' ... an' the Yankee bastards done hung 'im ... we aim to do the same."

"This'n ain't had nothin' to do with that, Billy," said Mansfield as his horse turned a circle.

"Naw, but this yar hangin' will serve notice," Billy said as the horse came back around.

Mansfield shot back, "It ain't a-gonna serve nothin' ... 'cause I aim to stop y'all ... this ain't nothin' but a runaway ... anybody can see that ... he's jes a boy ... he ain't a-done nothin' to hang fur ... two wrongs don't make a rat and I ain't lettin' y'all go from soldierin' to bushwhackin' ... it's a thin line an' y'all jes 'bout crossed it ..."

Billy's already flushed face now raised to a flame, then he said, "I reckon ye heerd what done happened over thar at the Fer'y ... with them Kansas niggers a-killin' 'r boys ... nem a-wounded an' a-tryin' to surrender an' awl ... an' then them fancy uniformed-up niggers a-cuttin' thar thoats an' a-stickin' 'em in thar bellies with them long shiny bayonets ... an' thar White officers a-standin' 'round not doin' nothin' ... jes eggin' 'em on... an' awl ... ye done heard 'bout that, I reckon, haven't ye, Mister Mansfield?"

"Yeah ... I heerd ..."

"Well ... I didn't hear it ... no suh, Mr. Mansfield, 'cause I seen it ... nem boys a-beggin' an' a-crawlin' around with thar guts opened up like stuck hawgs ... a-cryin' an' awl ... an' nem big black niggers a-laughin' ... yes, suh, I seen that with my own two damned eyes ... an' so did these boys yar," he said, gesturing with the watch again. "Most of nem boys wuz friends o' mine ... an' these boys yar ... together ... they wuz a-servin' with us ... an' I swore the first goddamned nigger I caught a-hepin' nem Blue-bellied Yankee bastards ... I wuz gonna hang if could catch 'im 'r shoot if I couldn't ..."

"Yeah, an' whur did awl that damn killin' start? Huh, Billy? Tell me that? Down thar at Pieson Sprangs ... that's what I keep a-hearin' ... when yew boys an' nem Choctows murdered an' scalped them nigger soldiers down thar ... west of Camden ... that got this awl a-started an' so it a-done come back own y'all ... that's what done happened ... an' y'all know it!"

"I wa'n't down thar, Mr. Mansfield ... all I know 'bout is whut I done seen myse'f ... that I do know ... whut wuz done over thar at the Fer'y ... that's awl I know or need to know ... what I seen an' ain't never gonna forgit ..."

The boy on the horse behind Septimus spoke up, "Mr. Mansfield, we heerd 'bout Pieson Sprangs an' awl ... but it come up like it done 'cause o' whut done happened over at Honey Sprangs ... over in the Injun Territory ... that's done got them Texas boys an' Red Choctaws so riled up like they is ... an' why they come down yar in seech an' all fared-up hurry with blood in thar eye ... else them Injuns ... why ... they wouldn't be yare atall ... an' scalp nor fite so hard ... or come this fur from home. I heerd they couldn't be held back o-ver. From whut we heerd, the Yankees been lettin' nem Kansas runaways an' Jayhawkers do thar dirty work fur 'im o-ver ... against them tribes ... that's whut's at the bottom of it awl, Mister Mansfield ... that's how it awl got started ... but them Blue-bellies done started the murderin' ... not us ..."

"Yeah, well ... that may be awl fine an' dandy ... but, boys, ye don't know the truth of none of that ... ye cain't know ... but I do know one thang for shore ... this boy 'yar ain't had a damn thang to do with none o' that ... noway ... that I do know ... ye'd be hangin' a innocent man ... that's plain to see. He ain't no soldier ... that's clare ... it'd be murder ... that's whut it be ... an' I ain't a-gonna let ye boys turn yoreselves from soldiers into murderers ... un'er-stand me ... I ain't a-gonna do it, so cut 'm down an' turn 'im over to me. I'll see he's a-sent back to his owner ... go on, Joe Nathan, take the noose awf his neck! An' be quick a-fore I lose my temper!"

They all looked away or down but Billy, who glared at Mansfield while still holding up his watch like he was counting the last seconds of Septimus's short life.

Mansfield continued, "Now, I knowed y'all ever one ... been knowin' ye since ye wuz jes boys. I know yore maws an' paws ... they's friends of mine ... awl of 'em ... an' they's proud o' ye boys as soldiers ... but not as killers ... an' they wouldn't 'preciate me a-sittin' by an' a-lettin' this thang yore a-fixin' to do happen ... ye be crossin' a line that ye don't want to cross, believe me ...'cause, fellas, onct y'all done crossed it ... thar jes ain't no comin' back ... no matter how hard ye try ... believe me ...'cause I seen it ..."

PHILLIP H. MCMATH

"He was a-hep'n 'r enemy," said Billy quietly. "He's a traitor ... pure an' simple ..."

"Ain't we a-doin' the same thang ... huh? We got a shed of 'em over thar our doctors is tendin' to now as we speak ... an' I heerd ole man Marks got a hun'red or better Yankees he an' his wife an' daughters is a-nursin' after that hot fight over thar at his place ... at the Mill ... this boy yar ain't a-doin' nuthin' no dafrent'n that ... he's innocent, I tell ye."

"Yeah ... he done he'ped the soldier to run awf ..."

"Ye cain't be shore he didn't jes come up own 'im like you done, now can ye? He's innocent of a-takin' up a gun ... that's fur shore ... the main thang ... he ain't even got a knife ... 'till he done that ... y'all cain't hang 'em ... it ain't rite, Billy ..."

"Maybe ... maybe he's innocent today, but what 'bout tomorrow, Mister Mansfield? He done run onct ... an' now we caught 'im yar a-hidin' an' a-hepin' a Yankee soldier to escape ... a-tryin' to patch 'im up so he can fight s'more ... that's what he's up to. No, suh, it's jes a matter of time till he picks up a rifle ... puts on a uniform agin his own people ... a-turns on 'em like a mad dawg ... starts to killin' our boys ... a-stabbin' the wounded an' cuttin' thar thoats ... then we'd wished we'd a killt 'im when we done had the chance," said Billy, still holding his watch face up, his other hand now touching his revolver with thumb and forefinger caressing the hammer and handle.

"Billy, I say the boy's a runaway ... pure 'n simple ... an' that means he's another man's property ... ye cain't kill 'im no more'n you'd kill his hawg, dawg, 'r horse that got a-loose. I mean to return 'im to his riteful owner ... like the law says," Mansfield said, urging his horse closer with his bootheels.

"It's too late for awl that, Mister Hardy G. Mansfield," said Billy interrupting, his anger barely controlled, stepping forward between Mansfield's horse and Septimus, "the thang's done gone past the law ... thar ain't no more law ... this ain't the war it wuz ... not no more ... it ain't like when it started ... 'bout the rats of the states an' awl that ... like Ganrl Lee an' Prez-dent Davis thanks an' wuz a-sayin' when it commenced. It's done changed ... 'cause when nem Yankees armed the niggers they done made it into sumppin' else ... they shouldn't a-ever done that ..."

Mansfield leaned over in his saddle and pointed his gun at him, saying, "Well, Billy, if I wuz yew I'd a-git to pen an' paper jes as soon as I could an' write Prez-dent Davis an' Ganrl Lee an' explain it awl to 'im ... what this yar war is rayly awl about ... 'cause they need to yar it jes as soon as possible."

"Hell ... someone nads to ... 'cause frum whut I yar they don't un'erstand it till yet ..."

"Git outta of the way, Billy," Mansfield said, waving the shotgun.

But Billy didn't move, almost yelling, said, "Listen! Goddamn it! ... Listen! This yar's either a White man's country or a Black'ns ... thar ain't nothin' in a-tween ... see ... an' thar ain't ever gonna be ... that's whut they don't un'erstand ... least ways if they duz they ain't lettin' own ... awl fine with frills and awl ... it's a new kinda war now till one side or the other finally wins out. An' it ain't ever gonna stop till then ... see ... an' thar ain't ever gonna be no payce no matter whut kind of paper they sign somewhures ... till this damned nigger question is decided onct an' fur awl. Them Kansas runaways know this ... more than nem pantywaste White men back east who started it awl does ... them niggers know what this yar war is awl 'bout ... I'll give 'em that ... but folks like yew an' the other big shots over in Richmond ... an' Warshin'ton ... cain't seem to see it ... that's the daffernce ... an' yew an' nem nayd to un'erstand rat quick if we don't hang this yar nigger today he's gonna hang us tomorrow ... it's that simple, Mr. Mansfield ... we boys that's a-fightin' this war know now ... we done seed it ... seed it up close fur ourselves ... larnt that over thar at Old Man Tom Jenkins's Fer'y ... the niggers, Injuns, an' Whites ... we know whut it's about a sight better'n anybody else ... so you jes as well to git the hell out the way ... go back to yore women an' farmin' an' leave the fightin' to the men that's a-doin' it!"

Mansfield's horse spun in its tracks again then he spoke in something just below a shout, "I don't need ye to prach to me 'bout a-fightin' this yar war ... 'r whut it's about ... Billie Jack Stantfurd! I got thray boys in the thick of it rat now ... as we spak ... one's with Pat Cleburne over in Tennessee ... he's been in the middle of it frum the start ... fact-o-the-damn-bidness ... he's been shot twict. God knows if he'll ever come home ... an' anuther he's a-healin' up after a-gittin' an arm sawed off down thar at Pleasant Hill ... an' he ain't out-of-the-woods by a damn sight ... an' I got a third'n a-ridin' hard with Jo Shelby ... he ain't really old enough, but I cain't hold 'im back no more ... an' he jes finished that bad fite over thar at the Mill ... an' nen I got a little'n that's own his way yar rat now ... he's a-rarin' to go jes as soon as he can shave. So, don't be a-tellin' me 'bout this godamned war ... or whut it's about ... it's purty near a-finished me ... an' will yet if it ain't over soon ... along with ever'body else in this damn country. They done burnt out ole man Tillerman the other day, an' whut they ain't burnt they ruint ... the price of land done dropped to ha'f o' nothin' ... you cain't git no labor with awl the boys gone ... an' the niggers

PHILLIP H. MCMATH

run awf … an' ever'body is aferd of the goddamned bushwhackers who is worse'n any Yankee ever thought 'bout bein' … no more'n wolves is whut they are … a-cuttin' an' a-killin' any an' ever'thang that comes thar way … which is whut yew boys is fixin' to become if'n I let you hang this completely scared, half-starved nigger boy who ain't done nuthin' to nobody … see!? An' I ain't a-gonna let ye do it, son!! Now move out'o the damn way!!"

He spurred his horse right up to Billy, pointing the shotgun in his face and cocking the hammer with his thumb, saying, "Boys, I didn't want a-cock back on ye … but ye leave me no choice … see … but I ain't gonna stand by an' watch this … ye'll thank me later … 'cause, if ye do this, ye'll be dishonorin' whut we're a-fightin' an' a-dyin' fur … it'll put us in the wrong … wrong! An' if this yar war is whut yew say it is, Billy, then it's bad wrong an' I ain't gonna a-stand fur it … that ain't what my boys is a-fightin' fur … an' I don't won't men like y'all a-turnin' my boys into killers … or a-stainin' whut so many other mother's sons done give thar lives fur … I jes ain't gonna a-let ye do that, now get the hell out of my way, Billy Jack, 'r I'll blow yore fool head awf!"

Now he kicked his big horse forward and Billy retreated slightly.

Suddenly a girl-driven wagon, carrying a White boy and a blue dog, came around the bend. The boy lay behind her resting a musket over the sideboard.

"Whoa!" she said, pulling back hard on the reins. "Whoa!"

The wooden contraption, which was little more than a long, four-wheeled box pulled by a pair of horses, rolled to a halt.

The rough-looking mongrel with a curly tail and holes in his ears bounced out and barked, rushing in a circle around Billy and Jonathan and Septimus sitting quietly on the horse, the noose hanging tightly on his neck.

"Git in the wagon, Toughy!" said Mansfield. Toughy looked up and barked some more. "Toughy! I said git back in the damn wagon an' hush!" he said again.

Toughy turned, barked a couple of times, then bounced back in, jumping up to the boy, who lifted his arm off the rifle and hugged him close. He yelped so the boy swatted him and said, "Hush!" He ducked, disappearing, then his ears poked up and his muzzle nudged up making a sound above a growl but less than a bark.

Mansfield looked away, leaned over, and worked the noose off Septimus's neck, speaking while he did it. "I'm tared of arguin', Billy. Ye ain't a-hangin' nobody this mornin', son. Lest ways not today. Now git down, boy! This ain't yore day to die," he said, reining away a couple of steps while keeping the gun trained in Billy's face.

Septimus, his hands still tied, put his foot in the right stirrup and stood up, then threw his left leg over and dropped to the ground, falling in a heap. No one helped, but unsteadily he managed to get to his knees and then to his feet and would have fallen again but shouldered against Mansfield's horse for balance.

"Joe Nathan!"

"Yes, suh," he said quietly, still holding the bit tightly under the horse's slobbering lips.

"Cut 'im loose!"

Jonathan hesitated, then walked over slowly and cut Septimus free, then returned and gripped the bit once more.

"Boy, git in the wagon!" Mansfield said in the same tone as he had spoken to the dog.

"Yes, suh," said Septimus meekly, rubbing his wrists, walking over and crawling through the open tailgate, over the mounds of supplies and onto the wagon floor. As he did, it jerked forward, stopped, and rolled backward from horses impatient of the halt.

The girl said, "Whoa!" once again, and lifted the reins and pulled back hard and reset the brake. Then she lifted a single-barrel shotgun from against her knee and laid it across her lap.

Megan Mansfield, nineteeen, had long, dark, wavy hair almost touching her thick leather belt. Her white skin set off deep blue eyes that stared intently at Billy.

But the team tried to move again so she glanced away, pulled the reins once more, leaning and yanking back harder, commanding them in a strong voice, then leaning forward as the team settled. Now she set her hands back into the lap of a calico dress hanging over black and very muddy boots and wrapped the reins into a taunt fist. She glanced back at Septimus, the dog, her little brother, then at her father and the men, shifted the leather to her right fist and put her left on the shotgun, touching the trigger guard, pointing it in Billy's direction. She frowned at Billy, whose own hand still touched his pistol. He hesitated, then snapped the watch shut and walked to his horse and mounted.

"Whut is ye boys supposed to be a-doin'?" asked Mansfield, after letting Billy settle into his saddle and adjust the reins.

Jonathan swung into the saddle and retrieved his rope, saying, as he wound it again into a loop. "We got us thray days layve ... after the Fer'y ... we wuz a-goin' back when we come up on 'em ... yesterdee we done a little patrollin' cause we heerd of whut happened over at the Tillerman place ... but the Yankee calvery all done swum the river ... skedadled north in a big hurry ... then we seen this boy's tracks fresh in arn an' we follered own up till yar ... he was asleep an' the Yankee 'bout half dead ... yew know the rest ..."

"Well ... y'all better git own back then ... but yew all remember yew boys is soldiers not bushwhackers."

"Yes, suh," said Jonathan quietly, tying his lariat to his saddle.

"The soldier in the woods ... whut we supposed to do with 'im, Mister Mansfield?" asked the one who had not yet spoken, leaning over the pommel casually, like nothing much had happened.

"Let's go see," Mansfield said, and reined that way.

They went back up the road, the wagon following, with Billy riding sullenly behind; then they stopped and dismounted. But while they tethered, Toughy bounced out and ran into the woods, yapping, warning that he had found a Yankee soldier sitting against a tree, and they had all better come quick.

Mansfield remained mounted but sent Joe Boy running after them into the trees with a tarpaulin. As the group emerged, Toughy was leading and barking instructions while they dragged Joshua to the wagon and loaded him. Septimus stood up and moved a pick and an axe aside, then lifted the head of the litter over some sacks, while the others lifted and pushed at the feet till they got him settled.

Megan, from her seat said, "Septimus ... take the canteen an' see if he'll drank some."

Now Toughy hopped back in and began to smell Joshua from toe to head, while Septimus tried to get him to drink from the wooden canteen.

"Here," Megan said to Joe Boy, "hold the horses," she said, crawling in the back.

Joe Boy climbed up and took the reins, Septimus jumped out, and Megan knelt and lifted Joshua's head delicately in one hand and gave water to drink with the other. He looked at her, lifted his right hand, swallowed, and tried to speak.

"There now," she said softly. "You gonna be fine ... jes lie still ...," she said, just above a whisper. Now he closed his eyes and let the hand drop.

"Thar that's better ... we'll try agin in a little bit," she said, softly lowering his head.

Without taking her eyes off Joshua, she put the cork back in and lay the canteen under the seat, then she turned and exchanged places with Joe Boy.

Mansfield spoke: "Okay, boys ... I'll take it from yar ... if he dies we'll bury 'im 'long the road somewhurs ... now y'all git own back to the army ... they'll be a-lookin' fur ye ... so git own back ... you'll be needed in yore regiments."

Septimus quietly climbed in, closed the tailgate, and leaned back, as the four young men mounted and rode off.

Mansfield waited till they were gone, then slipped his gun into its scabbard. "Let's git goin' … we're bad late …," he said, turning his horse and loping off.

Megan released the brake and the team jerked forward.

Joe Boy, with Toughy lying under his right arm, settled in beside Joshua, who faced rearward. Toughy drooled and panted as Joe Boy petted and scratched his head while his left hand careesed the musket.

"Whut's yore name?" he asked, relaxing and staring at Septimus in the back of the wagon.

"Septimus," he said softly.

"What?"

"Septimus," he repeated a little louder.

"Whut kinda 'o name is zat?"

"I dunno … it's jes de one dey give me … when I wuz bo'n …"

Joe Boy, a hatless brown-headed lad of twelve in torn blue overalls, rather bad high-top shoes and a tattered jacket, thought a moment, stared some more and said, "My name's Joseph … Joseph Mansfield … but ever'body jes cawls me Joe Boy …," he said proudly, smiling broadly.

"Please to meet ya," said Septimus, nodding slightly.

"I guess yore shore nuff pleased to meet us," Joe Boy said, laughing.

"I sho is …," he said, trying to laugh back but not quite able.

They rode some in silence, then Toughy stood and licked Joe Boy's face, then dropped back down, laying his head in his lap. Joe Boy scratched Toughy's ears and said, "I bet yew could shore use some vittles, huh?"

"Oh, yes, suh, I sho could," said Septimus, touching his stomach. "I'm powaful hongry."

Joe Boy rummaged behind the seat till he found a small sack and the canteen.

"Yar," he said, leaning forward, then tossing it, "take a plug o' this," he offered, handing first the canteen, then the sack. "Eat all yew want of this yar venison jerky an' biscuits … awl yew want … we got lots o' it …"

Septimus ate and drank in the manner of the truly famished.

"Pappy's named Mansfield, Hardy G. … but folks jes call 'im Mansfield … Maw calls 'im Hardy mos' time … 'at's her light load … or Hardy G. … 'at's a little heavier … or some times … if she's riled, she'll rare back an' shoot both bar'els …" Here Joe Boy raised himself up and said in a low shout, "Hardy G. Mansfield!" He smiled. "'At's buckshot … the heaviest load she's got … but us kids … wayel … we jes cawls 'im Pappy …"

Septimus nodded and said, "My las' name's Reymonde ... after my mammy's owna ... down in Loosiana ... wheya she wuz frum ...," he said, giving his name the French pronunciation.

"Both yore names is funny ... I ain't never heerd such ..."

"It's whu day cawls Creole French," said Septimus between bites.

Joe Boy thought, then said, "I reckon I'll jes call yew Raymond," he said.

Septimus nodded while chewing.

"We's frum up in Ken-tuck' ... Pappy a-left thar an' went own o-ver into Missouree ... but got tard of that an' afore this yar war done got started he took a notion to pull up an' go own down to Texas ... we had an ole maid aint a-livin' with us nen ... Pappy's big sister ... Aint Clar' ... I don't mamber her none ... she never mar'ied 'r nuthin' ... a shore nuff ole maid ... so she didn't have no uther payple to spake of an' she a-kindly took up with Pappy ... to he'p my maw an' sech thangs as zat ... cook an' awl but jes a little payce own down the road to Arkansaw ... why ever'body took sick with bad wale water drank somewhurs ... an' got down rale bad ... an' it killt poor ole Aint Clar' prutty much straight awf ... so they boxed her up rat quick an' wuz a-huntin' a nice church somewhurs to lay her out in ... yew know ... fur awl eternity an' ever'thang ... but it wuz shore nuff hot an' Pappy says thangs got so bad why they jes had to up'n bury her along side the road somewhure ... in a little patch o' timber ... but in a powerful hurry ... then they found a big rock fur a headstone but it don't even have her name own it nowhures ... no fancy sayin's nor nothin' like 'at. Anyways, Maw said some fine words over her grave 'cause Pappy don't hold with religion none ... he lets Maw do awl the prayin' when thars prayin' 'at needs doin'. He says religion is fur women ... but that wuz zat ... like I say, I don't ramamber it none ... but when we pulled into this yar country Maw says Aint Clar's a-dyin' kindly took sumpin outta Pappy ... he wuz powe'ful sorry fur her an' awl ... see she wuz sorta homely an' never could find herself a man ... Maw says she kindly sa'red up over it ... but they wuz rale fond of her an' Pappy wus rady to stop jes a-soon as he found some good country so we stopped yar. Fact-o-the-bidness, if it hadn't a-been for 'at bad wale water we'd awl be down thar in Texas rat now ... an' yew'd be a-hangin' from the limb of that big ole oak back'er ... in the little turn o' road ... yew know that?"

Septimus seemed to say something but Joe Boy couldn't make it out so said, "But it wouldn't be very long a-fore them ole buzzards'd catch wind of ye ... nen thar'd soon be a bunch o'circlin' ... ye know ... to have ye fur thar dinner an' awl ... then a body come 'round that thar little turn ... like we jes done, an' thar you'd be."

Joe Boy paused for effect then pressed the point home. "Fact-o-the-bidness, if'n you'd been thar long nuff they'd most likely a-smelled ye first ... that is if the wind wuz rat ..."

Septimus stopped chewing.

Joe Boy caught his breath somehow, then continued. "They's a heap o' buzzards in this yar country rat now ... mor'n anybody's ever mambers ... even nem ole timers say they ain't seen nothin' like it ... they's a-gettin' so fat they cain't hardly fly awf a long limb ... ye know, a-eatin' dead horses ... mules ... Yankees ... an' niggers ... they'll eat a nigger jes as quick as a White ... they ain't partic'lar. Yew ever been in country 'at buzzards done left, Raymond?"

"No, suh ... I cain't say I has ... no, suh ..."

"Well ... it'll git so bad ye'd wish they'd come back ... an' in a hurry, too ... they kindly keep thangs a-cleaned up an' awl ... like I say ... I mean a buzzard's like anythang else ... he's got thar place? Pappy says its nature's way an' awl. "

"I ain't neva studied own it," Septimus managed.

"Wayel, like I said, Pappy wuz a-tard a-travelin' own after a-droppin' poor ole Aint Clar' in the ground like they done back kar in Missouree ... an' he shore nuff liked this yar bottom country when he come up own it ... it was wil' an' frae an' a fella could be his own man yar, Pappy says. He don't hold none with a-havin' close neighbors ... says if you can see thar chimbley smoke ... why, thar too close ... so we took to a-clarin' land an' a-livin' on 'bout two hun'erd acres ... row-crop some an' raise thangs ... hawgs an' some cows mostly ... chickens an' awl ... 'course we got a big garden an' hunt an' fish ... we got lots of game in that big timber in the bottoms ... lots o' deer ... some wild hawgs ... even a few panthers a-pass th'ough onct in a grate while ... an' some bar is still in thar they ain't got 'round to a-killin' yet ... that deer ye's a-eatin' now was killt by Maygun ... my big sis ... she's up'per a-drivin' rat now," he nodded to her, yelled and rapped behind the seat with a knuckle, "ain't that rat, Maygun?!"

She looked back and laughed.

"She killt it with that thar sangle bar'el scatter gun she's got a-restin' ag'in her lag up'per. She won't carry no side-by-side 'cause it's too heavy ... she won't admit to it ... but that thar's the rayson ... but it don't matter none 'cause she's a shore nuff crack shot ... not as good as I am, o'course, but she don't miss much ... ain't that rat, Maygun? You ain't as good a shot as I am, are ye?" he yelled again but this time she ignored him.

Joe Boy, who hated silences like death, smiled, then resumed.

"Like I say, Raymond, I wuz born'ed a-way up in Missouree ... rat afore we done come into this yar country ... but a-bein' in Arkansaw is awl I kin call up to min' ... awl the rest of us kids wuz born'ed over in Ken-tuck'. Pappy says awl 'r payple come thew them big mountains after that big fite with the British ... a-servin' under Gan'ral Warshin'ton ... out o' Virginee ... a-lookin' fur land an' awl ... always movin' west, he says, my great-grandpappy, his name wuz Joseph an' I wuz named fur 'im, Hardy wuz own the other side of the family ... anyway, Gran' Pappy Joseph wuz indayntured outta Anglan' ... he says bettern half of 'em like 'im died own the boat an' that wuz 'bout normal ... then he wuz a-chained an' bad whipped in Virginee ... weren't' much mor'en a slave hisself ... nen he worked it out an' run into them mountains an' fought them Anglish 'cause he hated them an' awl ... nen he a-married a woman named Hardy an' directly had my grandpaw own a place thar ... afore movin' own into Ken-tuck' whur grandpaw settled an' married an' awl an' had Pappy who wuz a-born'ed thar. He left as soon as he could ... mar'ied my maw ... an' went wes' some more, nen own into Missouree like I said. But I don't reckon we're a-goin' no further now ... least ways, not for a spale. I heerd it's fine country down in Texas, though ... yew ever been thar, Raymond ... to Texas. Ever been thar in yur life, huh?"

Septimus shook his head.

"Naw ... I don't reckon you have. Whur wuz you born'ed, Raymond?"

"Camden ... my mammy wuz sold up riva from Loosiana ... to a big plantation neya town ...," he said quietly. "But I ain't lived no place else."

"Got any family attall?"

"Mammy died havin' me ... de rest I neva see ... dey all's down in Loosiana ... my mammy died ... I wuz seven ..."

Joe Boy studied a moment.

"Septimus, it mus' be rale hard a-bein' a nigger ... I mean I wuz jes' a settin' yar a-thankin ... it don't hardly seem rite ... the Lord, I mean ... makin' one feller White and the other'n Black ... he works in maystar'ous ways, that's for shore ... don't know if I'll ever figger it out."

Septimus met this with silence.

Joe Boy waited, then continued, "I don't see much of my family nuther ... my brothers, I mane ... they wuz awl name for Maw's side ... Johnny ... we call him ... he's o-ver in Tennessee ... in the army ... a-servin' un'er Major Gan'ral Pat Cleburne ... in the Firs' Arkansaw Regiment ... he jined up with them Spence boys from o'ver at Arkeedelphee, an' he's seen a heap o' fightin' over thar ... been wounded twict ... an' always gone back after he done healed up an' awl ... now they done made him an of'cer ... he ain't a-been home in over a yar 'r better ... come home onct fur a spell to git over a ball he a-took thew the meat o' his arm at Perr'ville, ye know, up-per in Ken-tuck'. Pappy said it weren't that far frum 'r ole homeplace ... nen he come own home the secon' time ... with a pace of arn in his shoulder ... 'em rough ole doctors cut it out after Murfraysbor' ... but he went own back jes as quick as he could. Then thars Jeremiah, he's next oldest, he's down in Loosiana as we spake ... a-marchin' under Gan'ral Church-hill ... he wuz in that big fite they jes a-finished with at Pleasant Hill ... ever heerd of it?"

Septimus shook his head.

"It wuz a big-un ... an' Jeremiah los' an arm ... but he's a-healin' up down thar in Loosiana ... in Shraveport ... that's whur they sawed it awf at. We got a letter frum 'im jes the other day ... 'at's one rayson we go o'ver to Tulip ... to get staples an' letters an' sech ... so Pappy kin see a newspaper 'r two ... yew know, that folks is kindly a-handin' 'round. Pappy rades a lit'le ... nuff to git by ... but Maw done tawt all us kids to rade prutty good. I jes 'bout fried my brain a-readin' nem ole primers at night a-next to that far ... nem coal oil lamps weren't good nuff an' I'd git jes as close to zat far as I could ... it'll sure git hot on ye ... two or thray times I thought my har wuz gonna burn slap up ..."

Joe Boy laughed, and Septimus smiled, but Joe Boy quickly returned to the subject, "But, anyways ... as I wuz a-sayin' ... ever'body's worried sick. Maw cain't hardly think o' nothin' else ... a-fore I was born'ed I had a big sister 'at took cow fever an' up an died own us when she wuz 'bout four ... up thar in Missouree ... an' Pappy he says Maw ain't never been the same a-since they put Little Sis in the cole ground ... a'ts whut we cawl her, Little Sis ... that thar wuz extree hard own Maw. Pappy says he don't know a-what'll happen if she loses nomore ... losin' child'en takes sumpin outta a woman he says. Her har done turned completely white over it ... 'n ..." Here Joe Boy swallowed hard and caught his breath and said, "She don't say much but a feller can shore see she's fretinn' over it awl rat powerful ... it ain't never fur frum her mind ...'at ... an' a-worrin' 'bout my brothers an' awl. Firs' thang she'll want to a-know is did we git no letters o-ver in Tulip ... nem's 'll be her firs' words."

Septimus nodded and choked down the last piece of meat and gurgled more of the water.

"Then thar's James ... he ain't hardly fi'teen ... he's a-ridin' with Gan'ral Jo Shalby ... in the calvery ... he jes jined up a while back. Pappy wouldn't let 'im go no sooner ... Maw didn't want him to go none a-tall ... she wuz powa'-ful agin it ... a-havin' two boys gone already ... but James he done worried ever'body 'bout crazy over it till Pappy said he wuz tared o' a-hearin' it an' let 'im go. Maw cried an' prayed over it an' awl ... she don't pray much but when she does she don't fool 'round. Fact-o-the-bidness, I thought she darn near got hard with God 'bout this last un ... a-kindly a-shakin' her fanger at 'im an' ever'thang ... anyway ... he ... James wa'n't gone morn a month'n they had that big fite the other day... he wuz rat in thick of it. Ye know? O-ver at Ole Man Marks's Mill. It wuz a big vactory fur us ... we done whupped 'em good thar ... ever'one wuz rale proud. Then James he come thew fur one nite ... Maw car'ied own over 'im the whole time he wuz yar ... an' he tol' us awl 'bout it ... how nems they didn't kill, they took prasnor ... the whole lot thowed up thar hands ... an' we took ever mule an' horse an' awl thar fancy new cannons an' thousand or better rifle to boot ... he wuz 'bout to bust ... said he wa'n't that fur frum Jo Shalby when they rode in own 'em ... could see his black plume ... an' him own that big fine horse an' awl ... James, he shore wuz proud ... nen he rode awf the very next day ... Maw a-standin' in the road a wavin' an' a-cryin' ... but we ain't heerd nothin' since. Folks says Fagan took Shalby awf somewhures a-raidin' but Pappy says if they'd a-stayed on that road 'tween Tulip an' the Fa'ry we'd a-bagged the whole durn Blue-bel-lied bunch jes like we done o'ver at the Mill. But they done got away ... after a hot'n ... crossed the river an' run plumb to Lit'le Rock ... whur Price an' Smith prutty much got 'em hemmed-up at as we spake."

Septimus averted his gaze.

"Is that whut yew wuz a-doin' ... a-runnin' with nem Yankees an' other nig-gers to hide up'per in Lit'le Rock? Did I hear that rat, Raymond?"

"Yes, suh," he said quietly.

"How come yew to run awf like ye done?"

"Don't wanna be no slave no mo' ..."

Joe Boy mulled on this and said, "Well, Pappy don't hol' with slavery none ... says it's at the bottom of awl this yar trouble ... fact-o-the-bidness, he don't hold with secessh nuther ... calls it 'folly' 'at's the big word he kindly o' bor-rys awf o' Maw ... when she'll let 'im have it ... 'folly,' she says ... an' 'fiddle-sticks' ... nem is the two words she uses when she don't like nothin' much ... but 'folly' is loaded a lit'le heavier ... it's bigger shot with more powder a-hind it ... an' a lot heavier ball ... like Maygun uses on nem deer ... kinda like Maw's buckshot ... an' 'fiddle-sticks' is'r lite load, yew know fur rabbits an' squirrels kindly like ... anyways ... Pappy fars the word 'folly' when he's hard agin sumpin' ... but my brothers wuz awl fur it ... secesh, I mean ... an' Pappy wouldn't stand in thar way ... he says after awl the killin' an' a-sufferin' ... the

Yankees jes as wale to let us go ... too much blood done been spilt over it now ... we oughtta have 'r indepandaynce ... an' go 'r own way ... he says ... we're raylly a sep'rate kuntry, an' it's jes a matter o' time 'till we split up noway ... but he wuz a-hopin' like lots of folks that it wa'n't gonna come to no war. We rode awl the way to Tulip jes so he could a-scratch his mark out fur Douglas ... back'er in sixty ... he said 'r payple'd naver a'cept Laycoln no more'n the Yankees that other feller but Douglas'd keep thangs a-tied up tugether ... but like I said, he don't hol' with slavery none nuther ... my grandpaw ... back in Ken-tuck ... he owned some an' Pappy seen awl that he wanted."

"He gwine send me back?" asked Septimus quietly.

"I don't ratly know, Raymond ... yew'll have to ask him ... nobody spaks fur Hardy G. Mansfield ... but he shore wuz hard agin nem a-hangin' ye back-er ... I'll say that much."

Septimus started to speak but was interrupted.

"See, Pappy won't stand fur no kinda mistraytement ... not man 'r animal ... mule, dawg, horse, 'r nothin' ... he don't kill nothin' less it nayds it ... a varmit ... 'r snake ... 'r it's sumpin to eat ... an' when he shoots a deer, he won't take nuthin' but a rale good shot 'cause he cain't stand to cripple it ... he jes cain't stand it. Raymond, I kin promise ye ... whutever happens he won't mistrayt yer none ... that's fur shore ..."

"Yes, suh," said Septimus so low that Joe Boy could hardly hear him.

"Wuz ye skeered?"

Septimus nodded.

Joe Boy said, "Ye know, we started to stop back thar ... an' if we'd done that, why we wouldn't be a-settin' yar rat now a-talkin' ... jes like if Aint Clar' ain't died ... we'd be in Texas somewhures. But yew shore wuz lucky ... shore wuz ... it's funny how thangs works sometimes ... ain't it, Raymond?"

Septimus nodded again.

"That redhead'un ... why he wuz the shore nuff bad'un ... I seen nem oth-ers afore, but I ain't never seen 'at redhead'un up tale now ... but I'd a true bayd on 'im with this yar piece of mine," (he patted his piece), "rat at his heart ... an' he seen it too ... looked at me hard onct 'r twict. I thank he knowed if he drawed down on Pappy he wuz a-headed to his maker ... rat fast ... but fact-o-the-bidness, my ball wouldn't naver reached 'im 'fore his head was took plumb off with that ole Damascus-barreled side-by-side loaded with buckshot Pappy had cocked back. Billy been dead 'fore my shot ever teched his heart. An' I carry ever grain of powder she'll stand ... whut with awl that's a-goin' own in this yar kuntry now ... a body cain't never tell whut he's a gonna find 'round the next bend ... but Pappy shore saved yore life back thar, Raymond ... don't never yew forgit that ... not many folks a-done whut he a-done ... not now ... not with whut's been a-happnin' ..."

"I'm powaful grateful ..."

"Thank Pappy ..."

"Yes, suh ... I will ..."

"But I wouldn't take it too hard, Raymond," added Joe Boy, "nem boys didn't mean nuthin' parsonal 'bout it ... un'erstand ... they wuz jes awl hot and riled up 'bout what happened o'ver at the Fer'y an' awl ... an' yew wuz jes the first runaway they could catch," said Joe Boy pausing, then adding with a certain self-satisfaction, "tell ye the truth, Raymond ... I'd shore put that hangin' behind me jes as quick as I could."

Septimus nodded.

Joe Boy now busied himself with inspecting one of Toughy's ears, then, satisfied, let it drop and patted his head and started up again. "I guess that back 'er wuz the closest I got to a fight in this yar war ... truth is, I ain't burnt so much as one grain of powder over it ... an' don't look like they ever gonna let me go to it an' burn narn ... it'll be awl over afore then ... an' nen they'll lord it over me the rest o' my bornded days. I can see it now ... folks'll say, why, thar's ole Joe Boy Mansfield, Hardy G.'s youngest, why, poor thang, he wuz too young to fite ... all his bruthers done went an' served but he wuz jes too young ... missed ever last bit o' it. See, I ain't ever gonna live it down, Raymond, naver ... I know that for shore ... it'll be the burden I'll carry to my grave ... pore li'tle Joe Boy ... why he wuz only twaylve ... an' his folks wouldn't even let 'em go as a drummer boy 'r nothin'."

"You's lucky," said Septimus slowly.

"Naw I ain't nuther ... I'd rather die an' a-molder green in my grave than miss this yar war, Raymond ... an' that's the Lord's truth ... there ain't gonna ever be anuther ... not fur me they won't ... I jes' flat missed it ... that's the long an' short of it," Joe Boy said with a long sigh. "Ain't that rat, Toughy?" he added, looking down and lifting his snout gently while talking into the dog's face, then dropping it. It seemed to Septimus that Toughy understood every word and agreed at the tragedy of Joe Boy missing the war. He looked at Raymond sadly and whined.

Joshua moaned and ground his teeth.

"Lord ... whatzat? I ain't never heerd nothin' like kat!" said Joe Boy, looking at Joshua in horror.

Toughy growled, crawled over, and sniffed Joshua.

Septimus said, "Oh ... I ain't neva hu'd de likes of dat myse'f ... but he's steadying doin' it since I found him," he said.

But Joshua was quiet when Joe Boy rolled over and felt for a pulse.

"Reckon he's gonna live?" he asked, pulling Toughy back to their side of the wagon.

"De Lawd done cayaed Joshua dis close to de promise lan' ... I reckon he's gwine let 'em see it ... " said Septimus.

"Joshua?"

"Yes, suh, dats his name ..."

"Yew know 'im?!" asked Joe Boy.

Septimus told a short version of their story, without mentioning Dagmar, and finished by saying, "Dat sho was a coinci-dayence, now wa'n't it?"

"A whut?"

"Coinci-dayence."

"What's zat?"

"Coinci-dayence?"

"Yeah, that's a ten-dollar word I ain't nayver heerd afore ... whut's it mean, Raymond?"

Septimus thought, then said, "Well ... let's see ... er ... huh ... it mean a mighty chancy inci-dent ... sumpin ya wouldn't like to 'spect to happen ... comin' togetha in a way dat ya jes woul'n't figga own ... like in gam'lin' ..."

"Yew mayn ... yew an' Joshua yar wuz a-runnin' tugether with Steele an' awl, an' then yew a-findin' 'im up in de woods agin ... zat wut yew's a-sayin', huh?"

"Yes, suh ... dats a coinci-daynce ..."

"Now, Septimus, whur did a runaway come up with a high-tone, store-bought word like kat, huh, would ye kindly tale me that?"

"My White folks in Camden used it some ... an' I kindly stole it from dem ... dey wuz always a-usin' words like dat ... I used to a-wait own de table in der big house on Washington Street ... an' at dem big fancy dinna's dey had an awl ... well ... while I was standin' daya a-servin' up der food ... dey was a-servin' up dem big words. I's always learnin' 'em ... den I'd use 'em, too ... deyed jes come up into my mind without me a-doin' nothin' to brang 'em up ... an' den I'd find myself a rolling dem outta my mouf ... jes easy as yuh please ... yes, suh ... dey ain't nothin' to it ... no, suh ... not onct you get used to rollin' yo tongue 'round dem ... sho nuff ... it's easy ... sho is ..."

Joe Boy studied Septimus. "Can you read?" he asked cautiously.

"A lit'le ... I picks up some of dat, too ...," he admitted, not wanting to lie

but not wanting to make Joe Boy uncomfortable either, adding, "we house niggas had to larn some ... yuh know ... nuff to run afta ... fetch ... go to the
stowya an' looks for sech thangs in de kitchen an' awl ... so ... dey larned me
a little an' how to do figgas ... jes a lit'le, too ... to hep Aunt Sallie... she 'bout
worked me to def ..."

"Aunt Sallie? Who's zat?"

Septimus told him and added some more about the family in Camden that
he suddenly found himself proud of.

Joe Boy was unusually quiet, then said, "I guess it wuz ...," he paused, got
up his courage, then gave it a try, "a coinci-dayence ... coninci ... coincidayence
... y'all a-runnin' up own one anuther like kat ..."

"Yes, suh ... sho was ..."

"Did I say it rat, Raymond?" he asked shyly.

"Yes, suh, sho did, ya gots yo' tongue 'round it the very firs' time ... rale
nice like ... yes, suh ... jes practice an' it roll off'n yo' tongue pretty as yuh
plase ... folks'll be ayastonished," he said.

"Whut?"

"Ayastonished."

"Whut's zat?"

They repeated the process on "ayastonished" until Joe Boy could say it as
well as "coinci-dayence."

"Raymond ... playse ... don' use no more them big Warshington Strayt
words own me today ... I'm a-gettin' a sure nuff headache," Joe Boy said, rubbing his head with one hand, and rubbing Toughy's with the other.

"Yes, suh ... it do take some gettin's use' to ... I has de same fellin' fo' a
time ... but den it gits easa an' easa ... till it ain't nothin' to larn a new'n."

Joe Boy scratched Toughy, then said, shifting his seat to signal a change of
subject, "So ... yew wuz a-hidin' up'per at ole Tillerman place? We'll be comin'
up own it directly ... it ain't fur ... jes 'cross anuther crick ... nen we'll jes
'bout be thar. Ole Man Tillerman ... well, he had two boys an' a rale purtty
but high-strung green-eyed gal ... they come into this yar country long afore
we ever got yar ... sol' out an' come up frum somewhures way down in
Loosiana with a drove o' niggers an' some mules ... bought lots o' lan' an' done
wale ... nen a-bought some more an' wuz a-steady clearin' more awl the time
... built anuther fine, new house ... the one yew seen whur yew wuz a-hidin'
... 'r whut wuz lef' o' it. Anyways, it wa'n't long afore they wuz a-puttin' on
airs an' awl ... him an' that wife of his an' thar two sorry sons they sent awf
somewhures to colyage ... one is in the army rat now with Gan'ral Kirby Smith

... as a paper scribbler o' some kind, Pappy says ... but the other'n ... the youngest of the thray ... he's shore nuff sorry ... bad to drank ... 'at dab o' colyage done finished awf whut the whiskey ain't ruint. Wale, he done run awf to the Rock somewhurs ... a-hidin' ... 'at's gener'lly whur folks go to a-hide ... Black 'r White ... he put his hand to a-bein' a shirker when he ain't busy a-bein' a-drunk ... while 'at daughter o'thurn done put own airs an' lives down in New Orluns. She went down thar to some kinda high-tone schul fur females. Pappy said 'at thar ruint her fur this yar kuntry fur good ... an' she ain't been back much since ... mar'ed some rich lawyer down thar we heerd. Then, a yar 'r so back, I guess it wuz ... the ole man he took bad sick ... got laid up sumpin awful ... an' so his wife had to run the place awl by herself ... well, she wa'n't use to sech ... an' with nem boys gone an' awl an' ole Mister Tillerman stove up like he wuz ... she started to a-havin' a rale hard time of it. Nen, 'bout two months 'r so ago ... ole Mister Tillerman finally got 'round to dyin'. The oldest boy he got leave to hep out ... come home fur awhile ... but nen he had to go rat back own account of this yar invasion ... an' nen when this yar Yankee army come a-runnin' thew, like a drove locus's, the niggers she had left awl run awf own her ... an' that wuz zat ... the las' straw, ye might say ... an' thar wa'n't nothin' fur it but fur her to thow up her hands an' a-foller rat a-hind 'em ... ye know ... a-take her traps an' skedaddle rat quick like. She sol' everthang she could ... an' give away whut she couldn't ... an' then she jumped in 'r fancy buggy with the one ole darkie she had lef' an' rodeawff ... jes as quick as she could ... like yew done ... a-wadin' up with the res' o' nem a-hind Steele's army. I raykon she's up-per in the Rock by now ... but we ain't herd nuthin'. Pappy says ever runaway an' shirker in this kuntry be thar a-fore this yar war's done got finished with itself ... like ye wuz a-wanten' ... rat?"

"Yes, suh."

"How come? What's up thar, kin yew tayel me that, Raymond?"

"I dunno ... I jes wants to see it, z'all ..."

"I cain't say I un'erstand that myself ... I ain't lef' nuthin' up-per a-tall. Pappy says thar ain't nothin' in Li'tle Rock now but a bunch o' Yankees, runaways, shirkers, painted women, an' sheisters ... don't know why yew'd want to fall in with nem ... reckon you'll ever git thar, huh, Raymond?"

"Someday ... if Mister Mansfield don't send me back ..."

"Well, Raymond ... like I donc tole ye... yew'll have to take 'at thar up with him. I mean this ain't ever come up afore ... ye un'erstand ... we ain't never had no runaways on 'r hands 'r nothin' like kis ... oh, now an' nen some plumb wore-out stray dawgs might come own up ... wore out an' starved an' awl ... mos'ly ole hounds ... half eat-up with ticks if it's the summer time ... if yew feed 'em they won't never leave out ... an' onct in a great while an ole cow that's out frum somewhurs'll wander along ... o' a hawg 'r a horse ... well, we jes round 'em up an' send 'em back ... if'n we can find out who they belong to. Onct we even had a mule down thar in nem ole thack bottoms below 'r place ... a-runnin' 'round a-cryin' like a li'tle baby ... ye know a mule got no sense of dayrection like a horse does ... got no notion of it a-tall ... an' if he gits out he'll jes run an' cry like a los' chil'. We had a-go git 'im an' brang 'im up to our lot 'till we could find his owner an' awl. Pappy don't hol' with mules ... won't have none ... says they kick ye jes to stay'n practice ... an' 'r stubborn nuff to make a feller want a-curse hisself into a fit. We ain't got nothin' but horses... this team that's a-pullin' us yar now ... Hester an' Henry ... why, them's as fine a matched team as in anywhure in this yar county. Pappy is rale proud o' 'em ..."

Then Joe Boy added after a slight reflection, "That mule that wuz a-cryin' back down thar in nem bottoms ... wayel ... while we's a-lookin' fur who he belonged to, we kindly made 'im a payet ... me an' Maygun." He turned and yelled at her, "Didn't we, Maygun?"

"Whut?" she answered without turning.

"Talkin' 'bout Babe ... didn't we kindly make a payet out o' 'er?"

Megan busied herself driving so Joe Boy pressed on.

"Pappy didn't hold with it none ... makin' a mule a payet ... an' namin' her an' awl ... I mayen, he said he weren't a-goin' feed fur long nothin' that didn't work ... earn its keep some kinda way ... much less a sorry ole mule. Well ... he didn't rest none 'till he found out who ole Babe belonged to. Turned out he wuz Ole Man Nester's ... Cyrus Nester ... him an' his wife an' youn-guns lived down own a little playce they a-clared ... sayv'ral miles o-ver it is ... down deep in nem bottoms. But they purtty much kept to tharselves an' folks didn't see 'em much ... onct in a grayt while Pappy'd ride by that cabin an' thar Ole Cyrus'd be ... jes a-settin' in a rockin' cher own the front porch ... but he wuz a little teched an' he'd didn't wave nor nothin', Pappy said, so he didn't stop. Him an' his wife, Nelva, they had three crazy younguns that done mos' o' whut little work got done 'round that thar playce ... nem an the one ole mule they had ... Ole Babe ... but the oldestn up an' run awf to the army jes a-soon as this yar war got good an' started ... an' within a month 'r so his innards gnarled up own 'im, they said, an' he died somewhurs over in Miss'sippi. Johnny tole us 'bout it in a letter we got ... Pappy says the boy mos' likely never heerd a shot fared ... then that youngest boy of thars ... later, when he come of age an' awl … when Gan'ral Hindman was a-pickin' Arkansas clean fur soldiers … ye know … like a-runnin' a comb over a dawg's back a-lookin' fur fleas … why the boy up an' run awf out west somewhurs … said he didn't own no niggers an' couldn't square a-dyin' fur someone else's. They ain't seen 'r heerd frum 'im since … some folks say he's in Californ-i-a. Nen the las' un … that wil' daughter of thars… why she went and took up with a feller that come a-passin' thew Tulip own his way down to Texas … them Nesters went thar to Tulip onct in a grayt while … fur staples an' sech … an' she met this yar feller an' jes run awf with 'im … as purtty as ye playse … ain't been heered from nuther, Maw says, no more'n 'at youngest boy."

He sucked air as best he could and continued, "Well, when that a-happened … ole Mrs. Nester … why she jes put own her Sunday dress like she was a-goin' to cherch … an' one day jes a-turned 'r face to the wall an' up an' died … that's whut Ole Cyrus tole us later … said she wou'dn't take nuthin' nor talk … jes lay thar in that ole bay-yed 'till she a-died … he tole us that when we brought 'im Babe back. I rode her an' Pappy rode Tater … the geldin' he's a-ridin' own rat now … he don't ride no uther … we wuz a shore nuff sight 'cause Babe wouldn't do nothin' an' Pappy had to halter 'im the whole way an' awl with me jes a settin' up thar a-danglin' my lags … a-swagin' an' a-lookin' stupid … layst ways that wuz the way I fayelt. Anyways, it were a long half day thar an' when we fin'ly got to the Nesters we could tayel rat awf he wuz 'bout half drunk … he sol' white lightnin' to sech as would buy it … had a still back-ker somewhures deep in nem ole bottoms whur he worked it at. Fact-o-the-bidness, Pappy said, it was the only rayel cash crop he ever had … yew know … that ever turned nothin'. Anyways, he took Babe an' thanked us rayl nice an' awl … nen went to vistin' with us like he naver did afore … seemed powerful glad to see us … like we wuz awl ole frayends … even give us vittles … an' told us while he wuz a-eatin' how he had to bury Mrs. Nester hisself in the orchard … a nice li'tle orchard back-ker 'hind that ole cabin o' his … it wuz rayl nice … I thank she tended it mos'ly … an' he kindly got teared up own us … said he a-buried her under an apple traey she wuz powerful fond of … 'cause she wanted the blossoms to fall own 'r grave in the sprang o' the yar an' awl … it 'most got to me an' Pappy … his a-tellin' it like he done. I thank it musta put Pappy in mind of pore ole Aint Clar' a-molderin' up-per in Missouree somewhures … yew know … without no proper headstone nor sech like … cause zat was whut Ole Man Nester done too … used a big ole rock … but without her name own it nor nothin'. He said he wuz aimin' to a-go own to Tulip with Babe one day an' buy a proper one fur her with her name own it, an' maybe some fancy words, like frum the good book wrote own it an' awl … if he could find seech … but a'fore he could do 'at ole Babe she got out own him. He said he musta a-lef' the gap open in that li'tle wared up payen whur he was a-cuttin' far wood in that timber a-hind that one big field he's got back-ker. Pappy said later … when we wuz a-ridin' home … a-ridin' double with me a-settin' a-hind with my arms 'round 'em … a-ridin' on the back of ole Tater jes a-talkin' an' a vistin' the whole way. … Pappy says zat the ole man must-a been drunk when he done it … left that gap open, I mayn … so Babe wandered awf on 'im … yew know … a-tryin' to get own home an' a-gettin' los' instayed … he must o' got bad drunk … got down an' furgot to feed 'im, Pappy said … 'cause utherwise a mule he'll mostly stay put … if he's took kir of he's got more saynse than to go awf somwhures like a horse'll do. Anyway, we come home an' mostly furgot 'bout it an' awl … then thangs rocked along thar fur a spayel an' Pappy he had to go back down thar a-lookin' fur some rough ole hawgs rootin' in nem bottoms 'at he thought wuz ahind the Nester place … yew know … out loose an' awl … an' he happened to ride by the ole man's place … sort'o to check on 'im … an' thar he wuz … as drunk as could be … an' when he seed Pappy he squatted down own his front step … put his thumbs up under his arms an' flapped his ole elbows like rooster wangs … up an' down up an' down an' a-crowin' like a big ole red barn rooster. Pappy said it beat anythang he's ever seed and he didn't stop nor nothin' … though he'd aimed to … he said the ole man wuz always a li'tle teched an' now it look like it jes done took complaytely over … after a-losin' his younguns an' his wife… an' eve'rthang … her a-dyin' own him like she done … a-turnin' her face to the wall an' jes kindly a-givin' up own life an' leavin' 'em like kat. But Nester did have an old yeller dawg I furgot to tell ye about … his name wuz Fetch … an' he run out after Pappy a-snappin' an' a barkin' an' a-growlin'. Tater damned near kicked that mongrel's brains out … I wisht he had-uh … he wuz a mean-un … he an' Toughy like to kilt one anuther onct. Pappy says Ole Tater rolled Fetch own over pretty good with one quick lick upside his sorry ole hayed … nen they rode awf an' zat wuz zat."

Joe Boy caught his breath again, studied Septimus for a moment, and then said, "Wayel … we a-rocked along thar fur awhile longer … a month 'r two 'r sumpin like'at … nen low an' behol' yar wuz Ole Babe agin … a-trottin' down that thar road … that wuz how she found us … 'stead o' a-gettin' lost in nem bottoms like she done afore … she jes run down that thar road … had saynse a-nuff to do that … nen … wayel … uh … yar she comes … yew know … with zat stupid lookin' ole rough trot mules has … rat down that road … she could o' cut own into 'r place ... we ain't' got no fayence over the front ... but Ole Babe she jes kept a-runnin' on that road 'till she seen whur it run into 'r yard ... then fallered it ... like she wuz aferd if she left the road she'd git lost, even if it wuz jes to cut 'cross a li'tle payce ... take kindly a shortcut ... it wuz the funniest thang I ever seed ... no, suh ... she fallered that road rat on into 'r yard ... an' rat own up to the front porch an' nen she stopped ... awl sudden like ... with that funny look own her face ... yew know ... that mules has when they want sumpin' bad ... like ... like when they'll come rat over to ye an' stare with kindly a question own thar face ... an' ... that's what she done ... she stopped rat at the foot of 'r sta'rs with that funny look ... we wuz jes a-settin' own the front porch thar a-swangin' an' awl ... it wuz evenin' but stayel lite an' zat's when we a-set thar sumetimes ... if the works done an' awl ... but nen yar a-come Ole Babe ... jes as purtty as yew playes. We awl laught ... but Pappy ... he don't laugh none ... she looked rough ... wuz three-quarters starved ... her ribs a-showin' an' ever'thang ... an' she wuz cut up like she done come thew a barbed-war fayence. We kindly as sat thar a sur-prised an' awl an' stopped laughin' when we seed how bad awf she wuz ... an' nen Maygun an' I guthered arselves rat quick an' went own up to her ... Maygun jes a-talkin' an' a-pettin' own her the entar time. Then Pappy, he kindly saunters up slow-like an' says, 'This ain't good,' that was awl he said, 'This ain't good,' and kindly shook his hayed like when he don't raley like sumpin."

"She got out," said Septimus, "N' run awf."

"Rat ... so, nex' mornin' ... Pappy an' I got saddled up own Tater an' Henry ... zat's the one that's own the rat thar that's a-pullin' us now ... he's a goodun ... wayel ... we rode own back to Nester's ... but we lef' Babe in the lot ... Maygun went to a-feedin' an' a waterin' her an' awl. I ask why we didn't take Babe own back-er like we done afore an' Pappy said it weren't needed ... wayel ... I didn't ask no more ... when Pappy is like kat you jes as wayel to hush ... so ... we rode the whole way kindly quiet 'cause I could tayel Pappy didn't want to spayk none ... like I say, when he gits zatta-way yew jes-as-wayel to stay quiet yoreself. We went a lit'le faster this time 'cause we wuz not a-hal-terin' no mule an' we covered nem ole miles purtty good."

"What'd y'all find?" asked Septimus in a low voice.

"I cain't 'splain it, but I had kindly a funny faylin' the whole time we wuz a-ridin thar ... an' when we finally come up own that clearin' thar at the Nester playce ... wayel, this bad feelin' kindly got worser ... come awl over me like. I mean, Raymond, I knowed sumpin' wuz bad wrong straight awf ... jes a-soon as we wuz thar. We turned in the clearin' an' Pappy stopped an' I done the same

... an' thar it wuz ... jes a-settin' own the front porch ... rat above the top step whur Nester done played rooster an' flapped his wangs an' awl ... only it were a daffer'nt bird this time ... it were a big ole black buzzard jes a-settin' thar ... like they do ... yew know, rayel paytient an' awl ... a-lookin' at us with zat ole red head a-cockin' back an' forth ... that thar done give me a col' shiver up an' down my spine, Raymond, that's fur shore ... an' nen I looked closer an' thar wuz anuther ... sayv'ral ... fact-o-the-bidness, one wuz a-sittin' in his ole rockin'cher an' one 'r two wuz up own the roof an' a bunch in a traye a-flappin' nearby an' more jes a-circlin' 'round up thar in the ar ..."

"Oh, Lawd," said Septimus.

"Yes, suh ... Raymond ... oh, Lawd is rat ... an' Pappy a-knowin' it the whole entar time ... nen he says fur us to go in, an' I said I wanted a-go back home an' he says no that we got to 'see to it rat' an' so we tethered up an' jes 'bout the time we got up the porch ... nem buzzards a-starin' at us funny like the whole entar time ... why ... we a-smayelt. We shooed nem buzzards awf but they didn't go fur ... they kindly hung around ... a-flappin' up-per in nem big trayes in the front yard an' awl ... yew know ... jes a-watchin' us like a buzzard'll do when he's got his min's stuck own sumpin rayel hard-like ... but Lord God, Raymond! That smayel! It ain't like nothin' I ever smayelt afore or since! It haints me still yet ... I mayen I kin smayel it rat now. Raymond, I ain't ever got it entarly outta my hayed since zat day, I tell ye. So I turnt around an' run into the yard an' thowed up ever'thang I ever et in my life ... seem like ... but Pappy, he kindly caught his breaf ... deep like ... an' went own in thar an' nen he come out rayel quick-like ... a-sayin' Nester wuz in thar dead fur shore ... yew know, a-lyin' in his ole bed. Raymond, he wuz bad dead ... stiff an' awl. Thar jes weren't no way 'round it. We wuz goin' a-have to dig a grave fur 'im proper-like ... an' zat wuz zat. Wayel ... so we went own 'round back an' found an ole pick an' a shovel in a shed an' nen walked back to that orchard to his wife's grave. Well, nem wild hawgs had come in thar out'r nem bottoms like they knowed nobody wuz around ... an' ... wayel, Fetch ... he weren't 'round nuther ... never did see 'im ... I wuz a-wonderin' if Tatar hadn't kilt 'im with that lick after awl ... but nem ole hawgs they done rooted 'round ever'whur ... they done knocked her stone over an' rooted under it ... but thank the Lord they ain't dug her up an' et her 'r nothin' ... but thar tracks an' a-rootin' wuz all over her grave an' in that orchard a-eatin' the apples. In thar garden the fayences wuz pushed thew an' the playce wuz goin' to seed ... bad ... an', too, we could see whur Ole Babe done run thew the fayence after a-starvin' as long as she could stand it ... poor thang. But Pappy ... he didn't say much ... wuz rale quiet while we dug Ole Man Nester's grave fur 'em

… we made it good an' dayep … 'cause of nem wil' hawgs … rat thar a-next to Miz Nester … but that thar wuz the easy part, Raymond … the easy part, I tell ye."

There was a very long pause. Septimus noticed that Joe Boy's twinkle was gone.

"How could yuh stand it?" Septimus asked.

"We helt 'r bref as best we could an' rolled 'im in an ole blanket an' dropped 'im thar … in that hole we done dug fur 'im. Meantime, I thowed up some more … but it wur dry, I tayel ye … I didn't have nothin' left … fact-o-the-bidness, I could hardly ketch my breaf … what frum a draggin' Ole Man Nester to his grave an' a-pukin' like I done … but Pappy he never got sick nor nothin' … he wuz jes kindly pale an' rayel quiet-like. Wayel, we rolled 'im in an' covered up with that fresh dirt we jes dug … proper as we could. But we didn't say no fancy Bible words … nor put nothin' over 'im. Pappy a-went back in thar rale quick an' come out with Nester's double-barrel … the oldest boy done took the musket to Miss'sippi. We strapped it on an' rode awf jes as quick as we could. I asked Pappy 'bout a mile or two later if pore ole Aint Clar' wuz like that, but he didn't say nothin' … I could tell it kindly made 'im mad … so … I didn't say no more … that wuz the only thang that wuz said 'till we got home that nite. Inside of that ole Nester cabin wuz a site … lots of ole bottles a-layin' 'round … it wur shore nuff turble … I ain't seen nothin' like it … fore 'r sayence … an' Pappy said … the next day that jes like ole Miz Nester decided to die … why, Mr. Nester he done the same thang by a-drankin' that ole rot-gut whiskey 'till it finally kilt him … it wuz sumpin' I don't ever want to see agin, Raymond … that's for shore … never."

Joe Boy drew in a bigger breath than ever then sighed it out, saying, "Yew know, Raymond … like I done said … I cain't seem to git that thar smayel outta my hayed … it kindly hangs in thar … 'less I can keep busy or sumpin … I mayen … I knowed it ain't really in thar or nothin' … it's jes in my hayed … but still an' awl … an' it's a-put me to a-thankin' … yew know … 'at ever'-body … Black 'r White … rich 'r pore … Confed'rate 'r Yankee… Christian 'r heathen … is a-comin' to that … jes like ole man Cyrus Nester … an' him awl stiff an' a smellin' like-at fur them buzzards an' nen a-molderin' in his ole wormy grave if he's lucky nuff to have somebody to bury him … why, Raymond … it awl a-come to that, don't it? No matter how hard yew work 'r good ye mite be … it's awl the same, ain't it? Can ye square 'at, huh? I can usually make folks laugh at mostly anythang, but I cain't ever make 'em laugh at that."

"Well, Joe Boy, it don't matter none, 'cause the Lawd done make a bettah place fur us awl," said Septimus quietly.

Joe Boy looked at him then said, "That's whut Maw says ... but Pappy, he don't believe it ... he says it's hard on nem 'at's left an' awl but the dead don't ker none ... 'at's his answer to it ..."

"Whichun does yuh thank, Joe Boy?"

"Darned if I know," he said, shaking his head. "First I thank one thang ... nen anuther ... it's a puzzle to me fur shore ... always will be I guess. I mayn, how come it has to be this a-way to start with? How come the Lord done made seech thangs ... yew know ... with buzzards ... an' ticks ... an' rattlesnakes ... an' chiggers ... an' measles ... an' swamp fayver ... an' bad wayel water, an' Yankees an' sech like? Tayel me that, Raymond. Who in thar rite min'd make sech thangs? Huh? Why would a-body make a buzzard 'r a Yankee for that matter? Huh? I jes cain't a-figger it, can yew?"

"Aunt Sallie say it's the Lawd's will ... yuh say yo'se'f the buzzards clean up de country."

"That's what Maw says, too," Joe Boy added quickly. "'Son, it's God's wayel ... she says, rayel proud an' mighty like ... an' its jes yore lot to 'cept it ... don't worry sech over it ... but Pappy he says it ain't no sech thang ... he cain't bayleev no God'd be that mayn an' hard on folks an' animals an' sech an' nen Maw, she says she cain't bayleev nothin' else ... she gets rayel upset an' riled up over it ... an' says her little girl a-dyin' wuz God's wayel ... jes like poor ole Aint Clar' ... an' if she didn't bayleev 'at she'd jes a-turn her face to the wall like ole Miz Nester done an' give up an' die rat awf like her ... that's whut she says to Pappy ... an' nen when she a-said that he hushed an' didn't say no more ... it's the only thang they don't see eye-to-eye own, Raymond ... darned if I know myself ... but I cain't stop a-thankin' own it ... 'specially when 'at smayel come back into my head," he said looking down, scratching Toughy behind the ear, then adding, "but one thangs fur shore ... ole Toughy yar he ain't worried 'bout it none, are ye, Toughy? I sometimes thank mules an' dawgs is smarter'n folks, Raymond ... I shore do ... they shore seem lots happier ... no matter how hard thangs gits ... why they jes put bad thangs rat behind 'em ... why it weren't no time afore Ole Babe was his ole self ... an' Toughy yar ... he don't take nothin' to heart fur very long ... I caught 'im suckin' hen aggs onct ... an' whupped 'im good ... but he jes wagged his tail an' thawght it wuz funny an' awl. He don't take nothin' to heart fur long ... not like folks ... they may be smarter but mules an' dawgs is wiser. I've come 'round to atta way o'thankin' after studyin' good an' hard own it."

"Yuh cain't nevah brayak no dawg o'that onc' he star'," said Septimus, with an air of experience.

"'At's whut Pappy says. But he's a good dawg ... I ain't ever had a better'n," Joe Boy added, rubbing Toughy's head gently while he closed his eyes.

"Yes, suh, I sees that," said Septimus.

"He jes come up one day ... kindly like Ole Babe done ... Pappy won't have nothin' but hounds ... yew know fur huntin' ... but yar comes this ole scarred-up cur-dawg ... blue-like with torn-up floppy urs an' curled-up tail over his back ... weighin' no more'n thirty pounds a-rangin' wet ... awl covered with ticks an' a lit'le better'n half starved. We had no idee wur he done come up frum nor nuthin' ... 'at wuz 'bout year ago 'r better ... an' Pappy ... he wouldn't take a thousand shiny new silver dollars for 'im ... no suh ... we calls 'em Toughy 'cause he can whip jes 'bout anythang livin'. Fact-o-the-bidness, he saved my life onct. We wuz a-hawg huntin' ... an' nem ole hounds of ourn a-hemmed up a big ole Spanish-bred razorback boar in nem cane-brake bottoms ... been a-runnin' 'im the biggest part of a mornin' since early light ... an' we finally a-worked 'im into a corner ... nen directly yar he a-come out ... a-chargin' rat fur me ... a-snortin' far with nem big ole long tusks jest a-slashin' ever-which-a-way. I thought I wuz safe in among nem ole dawgs, but he come thew 'em like one of Maw's sharp kitchen knifes 'at cuts hot table-butter she makes 'at's so good ... jest a-comin' fur me straight like. He wuz a mean un, I tayel ye ... as big 'n mayen as I ever did see, an' I can stayel see his ole blood-red eyes a-fixed rat own me ... he wuz a-bad un fur shore. He field-draysed purtty nar three hun'red pounds. Wayel, Toughy yar jumped in a-tween me an' that hawg ... in a flash-like ... an' it kindly turned 'im so Pappy could git a clare sideshot with bof barrels o' that big twelve gauge he's a-carryin' rat now ... it stopped 'im col' with that buckshot in his boiler room ... rolled 'im over good with Toughy rat on top of 'im a holdin' his th'oat ... nem other hounds jumped rat in a-hind 'im. Pappy says Toughy mos' likely saved me ... that I wuz in thar a little too close ... up a'hind nem hounds like I wuz. Toughy knowed if he didn't turn 'im in a hurry, I'd be kilt. That hawg cut 'im bad afore he died an' we thought ole Tough wuz a-gonner fur shore ... he laid up 'bout a week, but Maw a-prayed over 'im rayel good an' so did I ... though I ain't much when it comes to talkin' to the Lord, but I done it as best I could ... an' Maygun too ... an' a-doctorin' 'im an' all. I mayen, Raymond ... we prayed fur that dawg mornin', noon, an' nite. Maw says 'r prayers wuz answered ... that's what saved 'im she says ... 'r prayers ... that's what done it."

Joe Boy rubbed him gently then added, "He's my dawg 'at's fur shore ... ever'body says zat. If I'm gone he'll run out to mayt me ... jump rat up own me an' awl. If he cain't a-find me, he'll come rat own in the house an' look up own the peg whur I keep this yar payce ... an' if'n it's gone, why he'll run to nem woods an' a-trail me down but if it's thar ... own the peg, then he'll look 'round the place 'till he finds me."

"See this yar hole in his 'ar, Raymond," Joe Boy said, lifting it up and laying it flat in the palm of his hand, "Pappy says its a bullet hole." Then he lifted the other the same way and added, "an' this un ... this payes 'at's a-missin' ... Ole Fetch pulled the meat outta thatn with one bite ... the time they got in 'at big fite ... but Toughy had 'im by the neck an' would of kilt 'im if I hadn't a-pulled 'em awf a-quick as I done ... an' this yar scar ... the long'un," he pointed to a hairless line running along his right hip to his ribs, "wayel, that ole razorback done that ... Nem ole big reddish swamp hawgs is the maynest. Pappy says they come into this yar kuntry with the Spanish. Fact-o-the-bidness, folks say thar wuz a big camp o' nem Span'rds up river a ways ... a long time ago ... more'n two hun'red yars 'r better ... nen they lef' out an' the Fraynch come in yar, a-tradin' an' a-huntin' an' a-slowly a-mixin' in with nem Injuns. We cain't hardly plow no ground without a-findin' thar pottray an' arr'ws an' sech ... it's ever'whur ... they wuz heap of 'emin yare, Pappy says. Nen the Whites come ... a-brangin' thar slaves ... so, we're new in yar, ain't we? Whites an' Blacks ain't been in yar fur ver' long a-tall ... has they, Raymond?"

"No, suh ... I reckons not ..."

"But nen ... we pushed nem Injuns own over thar into the Terr'tory ... but they's a-fightin' own 'r side now, ain't they? They shore hate them blue soldiers like the ver'r devil ..."

Septimus was silent.

"Anyway ... this yar is the finest dern dawg 'at ever lived ... an' the toughest ... ain't you, boy?" Joe Boy said. "The only thang wrong is he sucks hen aggs ... I cain't brayek 'im ... I tried ever'thang."

"An' you won't nuther," Septimus said.

"But he makes up fur it ... an' nen some ... he'll kill a moccasin 'r rattler without even a-stoppin' to thank 'r nothin' ... he jes a-charges rat own in ... strayet awf like an' grabs 'em an' tayers 'em to payces, shakes 'em to deaf in a flash ... thar pison don't even swole 'im 'r nothin'. Pappy says he done worked up to it seech a way that it don't bother 'im none ... bayets anythang I ever seed." Joe Boy caught some air, then said, "You ever heerd of ...?" but before he could finish, Joshua interrupted with a moan and more grinding of teeth.

"Hey, Maygun! Yew better take a gander at this yar Yankee boy ... I thank he's a-fixin' to die own us!" Joe Boy yelled.

Megan stopped, crawled back, and gave Joshua some water, then bathed his forehead. "He's got some fayver," she said, and made a pillow of some salt sacks. "But I thank he might live," she allowed, laying his head down gently.

"Yes'um," said Septimus, smiling at her. "It's in the Lawd's hands."

Megan looked up startled, started to speak but didn't, then got in her seat, and urged the team forward.

Toughy circled around until he found his old spot, and Joe Boy settled in, leaned back and, stroking the dog, thought and started again,"Well, Raymond, I kindly forgot what I wuz a-sayin' …"

"I thank you wereah finishin' up with Marse Nesta," said Septimus, who hated snake stories.

"Oh, yeah … rat … wayel, let's see … uh, we rocked along thar a little … yew know, after a-droppin' old man Nester in his hole an' awl … nen directly the lawyers flopped down rat a-hind nem buzzards. Pappy says one'll a-circle rat over the other … he says the lawyer ain't nothin' but the human form o' a buzzard noway … only he ain't got no faythers …'at's the diff'rence. Oh, he wars a fancy suit an' a tie, o'course … but that ugly bird's more honest. I mayn … whut you see with a buzzard is gen'rally whutch yew git … he's more straight 'bout thangs. I mean, what he's about an' awl … but … a lawyer … a lawyer he's always a-tryin' to make whut he's a doin' a-look like sumpin else … makin' it look like sumpin' besides livin' awf carcasses an' seech … Pappy says nem's the slickuns … better watch out fur 'em. Anyway, we wuz jes a settin' in thar … yew know … after supper … a-rockin' an' a visitin' o' an evenin', yew know, it wuz a-fore that devil Steele done come into this yar country an' got thangs so awl fared stirred up. I mean, they wuz kindly normal yet … so one day this lawyer come down the road in a lit'le surrey with a deputy a-drivin' … he wuz awl slicked out like Pappy says lawyers always is … with a black store-bought suit an' his cute lit'le strang tie an' awl … an' Pappy he got up an' asked whut they a-wanted. The lawyer says he wuz a-hired by that Nester girl … the wil' daughter that done run awf to Texas with the stranger whut passed thew that time. Well, she an' her brother done got wind o' thangs some kinda way … kindly like nem buzzards done … an' he done hired hisself a lawyer an' they wuz a-floppin' over the leavin's an' awl … the land an' seech … he used anuther big word I cain't brang to mind … he wuz always a-doin' that to whur yew cain't hardly un'erstand 'im … an' he done come down yar to … let's see … how did he say it … to 'take possession of the Nester animal' … take Ole Babe 'n 'other words. Pappy says lawyers talk like'at to cover up thar staylin' … anyway … Pappy is quick to rile … an' he got riled … an' he said thar's no need to come down yar with no armed deputy 'r nothin' to

PHILLIP H. MCMATH

git the mule … he would o' brung her own to Tulip onct it wuz clar whut he wuz supposed to do 'bout it. Wayel, the lawyer … when he seed Pappy awl riled like he wuz … wayel, he kindly settled Pappy down an' said if he'd sign this yar paper … he brung a copy … he'd a-give 'im one an' he'd take the mule awf his hands. And they went own inside an' Pappy give 'im Nester's ole shotgun, too. Wayel I seen straight awf that kindly changed thangs 'cause Pappy didn't a-have to ever brang that up … so it got added to that thar payce o' paper he give us to show that Ole Babe done been 'took possession of' an' awl … real legal-like. Now, Raymond, Hardy G. Mansfield done awl his bidness with a handshake … he don't hold with lawyers … but he wuz a-watin' shayed of Ole Babe 'cause he don't hold with hur nuther … an' he wuz a-tard of feedin' 'er an' a tard o' me an' Maygun a-babyin' her … an' we wuz a-beggin' to keep her an' sech … an', like I said … he don't trust no lawyers no-way an' he signed that thar paper. Maw done squirrled it away somewhures rayel safe-like 'cause she's skeered they might come back own us an' awl … but Ole Babe done got 'took possession' of awl the way to Tulip an' that side-by-side rat along with her … but I don't know whut they done with it … sole it, I reckon."

"What happened to Babe?" asked Septimus with sincere curiosity.

"They sole her to a feller fur a-plowin' his big garden … turns out Babe is good at that … an' we go o-ver ever time we go to Tulip an' see her … me an' Maygun an' Toughy… Toughy likes Babe 'bout as much as we do." Joe Boy laughed, "Yew know, Raymond, ever time we go o'ver to see her … Babe'll see us comin' an' she'll run rat own up to that fayence an' wait own us … nen we crawl in thar an' payet on her an' ever'thang. Maygan always kisses 'r nose … she's rayel glad to see us … an' stands thar a-watchin' us till we go plumb out of site … this las' time we had a rayel good visit with her … shore did. I'm a-goin' to buy 'r some day … if'n I ever git a playce of my own. I like mules … an' I'm goin' to a have lots of 'em … an' lots of dawgs 'course,' he added, looking down, scratching Toughy's ears, "thar ain't ever goin' to be a dawg like Toughy … he's the bes' dawg I ever seed," said Joe Boy.

Then Joe Boy leaned back, breathed deeply, and added, "Raymond, I don't ratly know if I answered yer question 'r not … 'bout runaways an' awl. I jes don't know whut to tell ye. But I can say one thang fur shore … Hardy G. Mansfield is a man o' his word … an' he don't hold with a-breakin' it … nor the law … he don't need no lawyer fur that… nor anythang else fur that matter. He's 'honest to a fault' … that's whut Maw says … yes, sir … 'Hardy G., yore honest to a fault.' That's whut she says … an' she's rat," Joe Boy added with pride, scooting a little and tapping his fingers on his rifle barrel.

Now he smiled, pulled up his gun closer than it needed to be, and rubbed Toughy's back, closing his eyes into a light dog-sleep.

There was a very long silence, then Septimus said, looking around, "I done walked ova dis heya ground dis mo'nin ... early... I can see we be up own it soon ...

"Ole man Tillerman's? I mayen, yew seen it an' awl when yew wuz o-ver a-hidin' ... he had a nice playce ... rayel nice ... wayel, anyway ... after Mrs. Tillerman wuz busy a-chasin' a-hind her darkies, a Yankee foragin' bunch rode thew ... they looked 'round an' picked over the leavings ... nen they burnt the big house plumb to the ground ... fur good maysure ... yew un'stand ... an' that's what ye seen ... the smokin' timbers of it awl ... we thought rat awf it mite be bush-whackers done it ... but thar horses wuz shod ... they wuz Yankees fur shore. Nen they turned thurselves 'round jes as quick as they could an' galloped own back up with Steele ... yew know ... man wuz they a-runnin'. I reckon we might win this war after awl, huh, Raymond? Thangs shore has turned round our way yar awl of a sudden like ... ain't it? Pappy says we mite git 'r indepayendence yet ..."

"Yes, suh," said Septimus quietly.

"But ... like I said ... we ain't herd nothin' 'bout Miz Tillerman ... nuthin' a-tall ... no doubt she done took up with that sorry boy of hers ... that is, if he ain't too busy a-runnin' drunk. Pappy says he ain't worth the powder to blow 'im up with ... an' it's jes a matter of time 'till he thows in with them 'publicans an' Yankees up thar. Pappy don't hold with a-drankin' ... his pappy ... my grandpaw back in Ken-tuck' ... wayel ... he wuz an old screw-guts his-self ... used to be he'd a-fiddle an' a dance an' drank an' sang 'till the sun come up ... but nen the whiskey finally a-took hold an' wouldn't turn a-loose. Pappy says he got down with it bad ... says thars a snake in ever bottle ... an' when it a-bites yew yur a-done fur ... wayel, it bit 'im good an' he'd stay sober fur 'bout as long as he'd stand it ... nen yare'd he go agin ... each time it a-got a lit'le worser till it ruint 'im afore it finally kilt em."

Now they came to a small creek.

"Let's lighten 'r load a bit," said Joe Boy, getting up. "It ain't but 'bout half-a-quarter own up to Tillerman's ... I need to strayetch some."

They jumped out, forded, then walked behind the wagon through a forest. Mansfield, who always rode ahead, often out of sight, now trotted back and told Megan to "stop at the edge' o the playce while I take a gander," then he can-tered off but Toughy caught and passed Tater at a run.

"He'll scout own up ahead," said Joe Boy, holding his musket up as they stood a little past the wagon at the Tillerman clearing.

They waited. Then Megan said, "I don't baylieve nobody's rayley 'round ... else Toughy'd done barked ... let's move for'ards some," she said and eased the brake as the horses pulled into the front yard.

Septimus eyed the ruins he had never expected to see again. He watched the blue dog back trail him into the cabin, enter, inspect, and sniff his way out again. But he did not bark.

"I wuz in der only dis mo'nin'," he said pointing, "rat in dat ole cabin whaya Toughy is now. I stayed in daya mos'o dree days ..."

Joe Boy said, "He smells yew ... but he knows ye an' so he don't bark none ..."

"Yes, suh ... an' des heya haws tracks is from dem boys whut tried to strang me up," he said pointing to the mud. "I seen 'em come pas' ... but den dey musta come in a'hind me when I done found Joshua ... slip up own me ... rayel quite-like ..."

"Yew wuz lucky some bushwhackers didn't git yew, Raymond ... them's shore nuff's hard own lonesome runaways ..."

"It were dat high-strung redhead ... he wuz the bad'n ..."

"Like I said, they wuz jes riled up 'bout the killin's o'ver at the Fer'y ... yew herd 'bout that?"

"Naw, suh ... not till today ..."

"But Pappy says it all a-started down at Camden ... yew know 'bout that, don't ye?"

"Naw, suh," Septimus lied, he heard about that before he ran away. The Union soldiers hardly talked of anything else.

"Nen 'r boys say it awl started over in the Injun Territory ..."

"I wouldn't know, Mr. Joe ... no, suh ... I jes doesn't know nuddin 'bout it ..."

They watched Toughy inspect around, then lope over to Mansfield who was riding toward them now, his shotgun lying across his saddle.

"Pappy says it ain't what's true so much as whut folks thanks is true that matters," said Joe Boy quietly, as he watched Mansfield gallop up.

"Yes, suh ... I reckon dats rayat," said Septimus, as Mansfield came, stopped a few yards away, whirled, and signaled them to follow all in one easy motion.

It was dark when they pulled into what the Mansfields called "The Place." Lights winked at them through the trees as they came along the road. Then

Toughy, who had been whining, bounced out and ran ahead. A chorus erupted as the hounds ran out, sniffed, whined, and barked them home in a loping pack.

It was a large frontier house of one story, more than a cabin but not quite a manor. There was a front porch with four small posts under the roof; a big front door into a parlor, a stone fireplace surrounded with crude chairs and tables. This entered into a dining area, but the right side was segmented with several bedrooms.

Standing on the porch were Mary Mansfield and a neighbor woman who stayed with her when Hardy was away. They each carried a coal oil lamp and cradled a shotgun.

"Hardy!" Mary yelled, lifting the lamp higher, setting the gun aside, and rushing into the yard.

Mansfield yelled, rode up, dismounted, and embraced her.

"Y'all're late! I wuz worried," she said, still holding the lamp ever higher, looking at them.

"We had a tech o' trouble … but thangs is fine … I'll tell ye later … y'all alrat yar?"

"Ain't seen nothin' since ye left," she said, then walked up, embraced Megan and Joe Boy, then lit up Septimus's face.

"Who's the darky?" she asked.

"Oh, he's a runaway we saved frum hangin'," said Mansfield, walking over and unsaddling his horse.

"Hangin'?!" Mary said.

"We come along jes afore they strung 'im up."

"Maw … his name's Raymond," interposed Joe Boy quickly. "He done run awl the way from Camden."

"Playse to meetchye, Raymond," said Mary.

"Yessum," Septimus said, nodding slightly.

"Thar's a Yankee in the wagon," Joe Boy added with pride.

"Yankee in the wagon!? Lord! Lord, whure ye a-git him?" Mary asked, leaning over and illuminating Joshua's face.

"We found 'im up in the woods … we figger he wuz a-wounded at the Fer'y," said Joe Boy.

"Lord he'p us! Is he a-livin'?"

"Well, he wuz a-livin' when we stopped last, Maw … I got 'im to drank a little water 'bout twict," said Megan, standing by her and putting her hand to his face, touching his cheek.

Joshua moaned.

"Lord! He's still a-livin'! But he's been shot bad! I can see that!" said Mary.

"Let me feed Tater ... nen we'll move 'im own in the house. Joe Boy?" said Mansfield.

"Yes, suh?"

"Hep Maygun with them horses," he said, leading Tater toward the barn. "That boy's a-lasted this long ... he'll keep 'till we can git 'r stock took care of ... the horses is plumb wore out," he said, disappearing into the darkness.

Mary crawled in and inspected Joshua under the lamplight. "The Lord he'p us," said Mary again, examining the wound that Dagmar had made. Joshua moaned again and ground his teeth.

"My name is Mansfield, Hardy G. Mansfield," he said, ducking through the cabin door. The room was small, with two beds, a very crude table, two old chairs, a battered trunk, some boards for shelves, and a small fireplace. Septimus and Joe Boy had built a fire, and Mansfield found the ex-slave tending it.

"Yes, suh," said Septimus, standing and stepping over, "I know, suh."

"Well ... we ain't really met," Mansfield said, extending his hand.

Septimus stared at Mansfield. No man, Black or White, had ever offered his hand. Slowly he gave it.

"Please to meet ya," said Mansfield pumping it. "Raymond, is it? Septimus Raymond?"

"Yes, suh."

"I'll jes call ye Raymond ... if that's alrat?"

Septimus looked closely. Mansfield was just past fifty, with sprinkles of silver in a thick but trimmed dark beard and long hair. His face was no stranger to sun and wind, and his hands were tough with gnarled fingers. He stood about six feet, with a hard furrowed wrinkle on his brow like he was about to ask a question or offer an opinion. He wore a sweat-soaked, worn-out, gray Stetson, an open leather coat revealing a red shirt stuffed into a leather belt through denim pants covering the tops of very muddy riding boots.

"Joe Boy fix ye up?"

"Yes, suh ... he he'p me wid de faya ..."

"This'll be yore place, Raymond ... make yorself to home."

"Dank yuh, suh."

"Ye got blankets ... there's an axe out in the woodpile... cut whut ye need ... yew come over in the mornin' ... they'll give vittles out the door ... ye can a-take yore food that a-way."

"Yes, suh ... dank yuh, suh," said Septimus, then he paused, summoned himself, and added, "I wants to dank yuh, suh, ... dank yuh fo whut yuh done dis mo'nin', suh ... yuh done saved my life."

Mansfield interrupted, raising his hand, "Thare's no need to speak o' that, Raymond ... no need," he said with a frown.

"Yes, suh ... but ..."

"Thar's no need a-tall!"

"Yes, suh."

Mansfield lowered his hand, then shifted his gaze around the room, "Joe Boy'll be back with sumpin' hot to drank ... but thar's a water well not fur frum yar ... a-hind this cabin with bucket an' ladle."

"I dank yuh, suh ... suh, how's Joshua?"

"The women're a-nursin' 'im ... he's rat wayek ... darn nar bled out ... but if he lives to see tomorrow's sun, I don't thank we'll be diggin' no hole nor nuthin' fur 'im ... least ways not yet," he paused, looked at Septimus, and asked, "but Joe Boy is a-sayin' yew knowed 'im frum somewhures?"

Septimus repeated an even shorter version of the story.

"Ain't that a site?" said Mansfield. "I figger yew saved his life this mornin' ... tendin' to 'im like ye done."

"Yes, suh ... but I has a question."

"What's zat?"

"Is yuh gwine send me back ... suh ... like yuh done tole dem boys dis mo'nin'?"

"Naw ... I wuz jes a-tryin' t'save ye ... I don't hol' with slavery," he paused, adding, "Raymond, yore uh free man now."

"Dank yuh, suh."

"Thar ain't nuthin' to thank ... it's jes the way I look at it ... but un'erstand... all I kin do is fayed ye ... an' put some dry clothes own yore back ... an' a roof over yore head ... but in return ... ye work fur me, un'erstand. My growed boys ... is with'r army ... a-fitein' ... an' I nayed a good hand in the worse way ... un'erstand?"

Septimus's smile went straight.

"But yore fray to go anytime you take a notion ... anytime un'erstand? ... as ye playse ... I'll not stand in yore way. But I cain't pay no wages ... I ain't got it. Us Mansfields live purty good, but we's pore ... but fray ... 'cause we work hard … take ker 'rselves. Ye'll have to do the same. This yare's a hard country ye done run yoresaylf into, Raymond, rayel hard … it makes nem that lives in it hard too. Ye'll jes git room-an'-board … but ye'll have to work as hard as it is or it'll lick ye, see? I got lots a-needs doin' … but this ain't no high-tone Camden mansion … the women do the women's work … yore a-goin' to have to work with the men … in the fayelds … an' round the playce … a man's work … it ain't hard to larn but it's hard to do if a body ain't used to it … but I'll work with ye own it 'cause I knowed you ain't done it."

"Yes, suh."

"An' ye'll do as I say … 'r ye'll be back out thar on that-thar muddy road … see?"

"Yes, suh."

"But ye do that an' I'll trayet ye rat … Hardy G. Mansfield is a far man."

"Yes, suh."

Pause.

"But ye suit yoreself … yore fray to go … like I say, I ain't goin' a-stand in yore way none … but I don't need to a-tell ye how mayen thangs is jes now in this yar country … it wuz never easy … but it's extree bad now … now that folks's got their blood up so bad with all this damn killin' an' war an' whut a-happened over thar at the Fer'y … but if'n yore with me, ye'll be safe, see? They won't harm you none yar as long yore with me."

"Yes, suh," said Septimus.

"Ye want a-go? If so … ye can rest yar tonight an' layev firs' thang in the mornin' … we'll fed ye an' put ye on the road, if ye like …"

"I'll stay, Mr. Mansfield."

"Good … now git some rayest … take 'morrow awf … then we'll git started. Good night," said Mansfield, raising his hand again but lowering it as he turned to leave.

"Yes, suh, good night," said Septimus, raising his hand part way then letting it drop as Mansfield disappeared, closing the door.

He fell on the bed and pulled up a blanket. Joe Boy came, left some hot cider, turned off the lamp, and went out. But Septimus wasn't thirsty, did not hear him, nor need any light because he only awoke when the sun touched his eyes gently through the little window.

CHAPTER THIRTY-ONE

*Thou shall not deliver unto his master the servant which is escaped from
his master unto thee: He shall dwell with thee, even among you, in that
place which he shall choose in one of thy gates, where it liketh him best:
thou shall not oppress him.*
—Deuteronomy 23:15–16

Joshua recovered from Dagmar's shot, and by June Jeremiah came home
from Louisiana on a borrowed and very worn-out horse. He was, of course,
missing his left arm, was gaunt, sallow in body, and morose in spirit. He did
not relish sharing a room with "the enemy," and so Joshua obligingly moved in
with Septimus.

James, who wrote seldom and came home less, was busy raiding and riding
with Shelby in the Arkansas run-up to Pap Price's Missouri invasion, while
Johnny was in Georgia with Cleburne, trying to stop Sherman. He had been
promoted to captain and everyone was proud. He wrote more often and much
more interesting letters than any of the others and, like his general, Cleburne,
whom he worshiped, he expressed the hope that Lincoln would lose the election if they "could a-hang on to Atlanta and Richmond, while threatening New
Orleans and St. Louis." He mentioned Cleburne's January petition to free the
slaves in return for service, saying he thought it "were a good idee but that most
weren't ready for it yet. Though even them will do whatever the general says."

Jeremiah, unknowingly echoing Forrest, said he wasn't sure what they were
fighting for if they "freed the darkies"; while Mansfield thought Cleburne was
right because it would only make official what was happening anyway, that slavery was "a gonner an' good riddance" and Free Blacks would provide "fresh
men ... they'll fite ... we've seen that wayel enough." Adding, "We got a-take
'r foot awf thar neck sometime ... an' the sooner the better ... it ain't too
steep a price fur our own fraydom." And Joshua, for his part, who had been listening quietly, ladling his soup, offered last that if the South had taken
Cleburne's suggestion sooner the North wouldn't have had a chance, but now
it was too late, saying he "more or less agreed with Jeremiah," that is, if the

South had been willing to do that in the beginning then he wasn't sure what the war would have "started over." He then predicted the fall of Atlanta and Lincoln's reelection. This upset Jeremiah, who was obviously angry at Joshua's rising status in the household, but his objections were quickly "hushed" by Mansfield, saying Joshua "has a rat to his opinion."

It was quite clear that Mansfield was increasingly interested in Joshua's ideas and pressed him quickly about who his family had supported in '60. Joshua said he had been too young to vote but confessed his father, like most folks he knew in Iowa, was "a Lincoln man."

"I ain't surprised," said Mansfield, after some reflection. "I wouldn't rally 'spect nuthin' else ... but I don't hold with Laycoln ... he's the cause of all this yar sufferin' ... his 'lection, I mayen. He didn't know what wuz 'bout to happen ... whut yore northern folks don't un'rstand is that the lower end of the country cain't no more'a accept Laycoln than the upper end could Breckinrayedge," said Mansfield, remembering the other Kentuckian's name that Joe Boy couldn't, adding, "why Laycoln wa'n't even own the ballot yar in Arkansas ... I rode all day to git to Tulip to a-mark fur Douglas ... he wuz the onlyn that could hold thangs together ... either way wuz war ... an' that's whut we got ... war with Laycoln ... I seen it a-comin' ," said Mansfield with that same frown he always had when offering an opinion, whether it related to mules or Republicans.

"Well, sir," said Joshua quietly, swallowing, and lowering his spoon, "most folks didn't think it would come to this either ... least ways not in Iowa. Pa and most others thought that Lincoln was the better man ... that's all ... and ... like you, Mr. Mansfield ... they wanted shed o' slavery ..."

"It's a-dyin' ," interrupted Mansfield, "an' has been fur a long time ... the South is jes a-goin' a-have to git rid o' it in its own way ... without Yankee in'er-fayrence. It cain't go no further west noway ... even if it wanted to ... the conditions ain't rat ... I never un'erstood all the fuss 'bout that." He paused, sipped his coffee, which he drank at every meal when he could get it, and added, "Laycoln's saycond big mistake ... after a-gittin' hisself 'lected ... wuz to ask us fur 'r boys to fite agin 'r own kind ... demand ... ordered aginst 'r wayel ... I should say ... that wuz it ... 'cause we jes cain't fite against 'r own kith an' kin ... he give us no choice but war ... an' that's what he got, ain't it? This yar's Mister Laycoln's war."

"No one thought it'd come to war," said Joshua quietly.

"Nawgh but ye got one now ... that's fur shore!" said Jeremiah, rising out of his seat.

"Jeremiah! We're a-havin' a gentlemanly tawlk yar ... ain't no cause to git riled ... sit down, son!" said Mansfield.

Jeremiah sat slowly back in silence.

"Joshua?" chimed in Mary from her end of the table, opposite Mansfield.

"Yes, mam?"

"Do you thank that ole sow is a-fixin' to have her litter?"

"Yes, Mrs. Mansfield ... most any time," he said quietly, relieved of the change of subject.

Thus the discussions went at the close of the day, sometimes, to what country people, who would rise and rest with the sun, would consider "all hours." And, of course, it was always stimulated by any news or the arrival of a precious letter, usually from Johnny. Megan and Mary spoke from time to time, while Septimus was absent, taking his meals, as always, alone in his cabin.

Joshua, after moving in with him, had eaten there for a time, but his absence was resented, and he soon returned to eating "with the folks."

Septimus, upon Joshua's return, would always grill him, and the family's discussion, in abbreviated form, would be repeated and rehashed around their little fireplace before bed.

The cabin folks, of course, had a different take on the war, and Septimus, though he never said it, nodded when Joshua said he thought Atlanta would fall and Lincoln would win. "It won't take long after that," he added. "It'll take hope from them," he said gravely. "That'll be it."

Most of the dinner talk in both places, however, had more to do with their daily lives; less with politics than with necessity—work, crops, and animals— that is, about the corn (planted earlier and now high) and its harvesting, the wood cutting, water hauling, the garden with its hoeing, picking, and canning; the care and feeding of the horses, cows, chickens, hogs, and, of course, the attendant slaughter of the latter three and the care ("smoking") of beef and pork; and, to be sure, the weather (hot or cold, rain or fair), the Saline River (which Septimus had yet to cross) and its endless creeks (high or low, clear or muddy); the eternal debate about the virtues and vices of mules as against horses (Jeremiah wasn't as sure about horses as Mansfield, while Joshua attempted a defense of both and Septimus, from the safety of his cabin, said he much preferred mules); and, to be sure, dogs, that is, what Toughy had killed that day and what the hounds were running. Did Ole Red really prefer coons to deer and would he switch from one to the other was never quite settled to anyone's satisfaction. And when was Rose to have her puppies and how many this time, and what would they do with them all? As for cats, if there was any domestic animal that Mansfield disliked as much or more than a mule, it was a cat. And, though one or two were badly needed around the barn for mice, he preferred to let the black snakes take care of these and would shoot a cat on sight, rather like any other varmint.

And, of course, there were the other snakes: water moccasins, timber rattlers, blue racers, garden green, barn black, and the pretty and very mysterious kings (left alone because they were cannibals). Then there was the eternal question of whether water moccasins would bite under water and would they come after you? Everyone finally came round to the view that moccasins would go out of their way and rattlers wouldn't. And which one was the most poisonous and what was the best remedy for either bite?

Then there were the wild hogs in the bottoms—the razorbacks—what happened to the old big boar the hounds ran into the river the other day? Deer—where was that big buck hanging out these days? Bear—how many are in there now and what happened to the one missing a toe? Reckon somebody finally killed him? Panther—did you hear it scream the other night, a little after midnight? Mary said she did and Megan thought she dreamed it. And, to be sure, there were the usual passing references to the lesser Kingdom of rabbits, squirrels, possums, coons, quail, hawks, crows, jays, mockingbirds, various sparrows, or any small bird, turtles, insects and, the lowest of the low, skunks. (As of late, talk of buzzards at supper was strictly taboo.)

Joshua, fearful of traveling, did, nevertheless, through Mansfield, manage to contact some wounded Iowa men recovering at Marks's Mill. Through them he sent a letter home and within a month, to his tearful delight, got an answer. He had been reported as "missing" and, of course, his family had feared he had perished.

Mansfield told the Confederate authorities, such as they were, that he had possession of a lone Yankee soldier too sick to move but that he would send him when he was able. In this way, Joshua was easily forgotten and allowed to remain. Jeremiah did not approve but was never able to dispute Mansfield on anything, and so Joshua stayed on their farm as an unofficial prisoner of war, but, in time, he became more and more a member of the family.

They, of course, had been curious about his escape, and he simply said he

---

had been wounded, taken, tended to, and then had run away in hopes of finding his regiment. This was accepted. But it was but a half-truth and he dared not tell the whole story—even to Septimus—at least not yet.

But the storm of war had for the moment abated, and matters settled into a kind of peaceful routine made all the more pleasant by the contrast of a destructive unpleasantness having just passed by, like a storm leaving behind pretty weather. And, while there was constant anxiety about Johnny and James that fed an insatiable appetite for news, the tempest of Steele, it was plain to see, dared not blow out of Little Rock, and so none seemed concerned by that cataclysm's return.

Thus it was, with Jeremiah able to do more as he regained his strength and morale, matching up with little brother's increasing maturity and confidence as Joe Boy was making that painful passage from boy to man, working in turn both with Joshua's example of solid experience and with Septimus's similar boy-man transition, the Mansfield place began to pull together under the steady hand of its master who, as it were, held it firmly, steadily—but always with the lighter touch of Mary and Megan resting upon his gnarled hand—molding it into a completed, harmonious thing that now surged forward like a good team—like Henry and Henrietta—plowing and pulling them toward an unanticipated prosperity and hoped-for happiness that is itself a kind of bliss.

In a word, they all, men and women, Black and White, Yank and Reb, worked, hunted, laughed, and lived together in a short halcyon time of late spring and summer barely interrupted by the distant strife of war.

Mansfield was especially proud of Septimus's progress from a domestic slave to a "free laborer," as he called him, and watched with great satisfaction as Septimus moved easily to the harder but more "manly" work of the field that he now took to with such pride. Mansfield, who had never seen a slave who could read and considered most to be "shiftless and lazy," was impressed both with his education and his character; and he soon saw in him a kind of special project placed in his hands by fate. It was if he, Mansfield, were himself solving the whole terrible problem faced by the Reconstruction South—of race, labor, and land—now with Septimus—and he more than once told Joe Boy he needed to learn to read as good "as that Septimus." Adding, that, contrary to the general belief, "it ain't ruint 'im as a hand nuther." Joe Boy would laugh and try harder. He was not jealous of Septimus as Jeremiah was of Joshua but was glad to have someone his own age as a hunting and work companion and listener of his endless stories.

As for Joshua, everyone was impressed with his education, his skill as a farmer, and his Lutheran devotion. He and Septimus read the Bible they borrowed from Mary after dinner each night in their little cabin. During these sessions Joshua would help Septimus improve his reading and knowledge of scripture and even tried to get him to pronounce his "th's," but Septimus demurred, saying that other Blacks would think he was "acting White."

Septimus, who had resented the endless devotionals and prayers of Washington Street, soon confessed to Joshua that a change had occurred since "my hangin'." Had he known the word, he would have said an epiphany had come over him while he was sitting on Jonathan's horse waiting to be lynched, that "de Lawd done answered my prayers dat day. I wer'a prayin' ha'd as I could ... a-cryin' an' a-prayin' ... an' de Lawd He heayad my praya ... an' He done save me foya some udder pu'pose, Joshua ... yes, suh ... to do His work an' His will heya on dis earth ... I knows dat fo sho," he said quietly.

Joshua studied him closely; it was clear he meant it. He said, "Well, Septimus, I've wondered the same thing. I mean, by all rights I should have died from that shot Dagmar put through my shoulder ... but I was spared ... then you found me ... me and you coming together like that ... a coincidence ... then the Mansfields ... and being brought here when so many others found early graves ..."

"It weren't no coincidayence, Joshua ... it were de Lawd's will ... like wid me ... a gif' ... an' He meand fo yuh to do sumpin' wid it ..."

"Yes, but how do I know what it is?" he asked, looking down, fingering the Bible unconsciously.

"Simple ... pray own it ... jes as hard as yuh kin ... an' in His time de Lawd'll reveal it ... yuh know den fo sho' ... uh huh ... sho will ..."

"When did you know it, Septimus?" asked Joshua, looking up.

"When I seed Massa Mansfield's face ... de firs' time ... a-liftin' dat rope off'a my neck ... he wuz rat der ... next to mine ... an' I looked close ... rat into his hard blue eyes ... an' he looked like de Lawd hisself, sho did ... I knowed it den ... fo' sho' ... uh huh ... de Lawd done sent him to fetch me away from def ... sho did ..."

However well this back cabin devotional was known in the house, out of respect for Mansfield's attitude, no mention was ever made of it. Though Mary prayed some quietly on her knees before retiring, mostly for the end of the war and the deliverance of her sons, and Megan did the same, Jeremiah and Hardy G. both quietly considered it all very weak and "womanish" and prayed not a word.

Of course, because of this, there was no grace at table, so each night

Septimus and Joshua spoke their own before they read the big black King James and talked about it till their eyes got heavy and they fell asleep.

But they always found room to give thanks for their deliverance by the Mansfields; and they'd ask that they be kept well, too, and that their boys, Johnny and James, also be kept safe in a war which they implicitly hoped, but did not pray for, would soon end in Union victory.

And now, after the confession of his epiphany, Septimus would add a kind of intercessory plea for Joshua: that is, for God to "let 'im know" about his mission "heya upon dis ole sad earth." It was nearly always the last thing Septimus would say before their final "Amen" and bed. It was such a special kind of request that he saved it for then.

So for them these days of late spring and summer of 1864 were, in a word, happy and peaceful times and, as such times always do, went quickly by. But, as they existed in the eye of the greatest storm ever visited upon the American nation, they did not and could not last. Indeed, in late July, like a storm that's been slowly building in fair but hot summer weather, there was a very great, unexpected thunderclap of news that raised their heads in wonderment—not near, but far away in the east, over the trees and across the horizon of the Mississippi, all the way to Georgia.

It came in the form of an old gray-headed man in a buggy coming to see about a lost calf, and, while he left without her, he did happen to mention that Davis had switched generals —Johnston for Hood—"after that redheaded dayvel Sherman done nudged rat own up nex' to Atlanta."

This wasn't done echoing and rumbling through their minds, when Private James Mansfield appeared unexpectedly trotting down the road the next day on a worn-out but usually spirited horse named Dandy.

"I wrangled a few days layev," he said, bouncing off and into his mother's arms.

"How long?" beamed Mansfield, standing behind.

"Oh, a wayek 'r better," James smiled back still holding Mary with one hand and Dandy with the other.

"We're a-fixin' to invade Missouree an' take St. Looee an' win this yar war," he announced excitedly that night after supper, adding that Pap Price had his entire Reb army assembling at Princeton and was going to join up with the Iron Brigade and march north and take Missouri back for the Confederacy.

"Yew cain't, son ... ye don't have the strangth," Mansfield said. "The best ye can do is stay yar ... an' keep Steele hemmed up ..."

"Naw, Pappy ... ye don't un'erstand ... thar's thirteen stars in'r flag an' one of 'em is Missouree an' we aim to a-take 'er back. Steele ain't a-goin' nowhurs ... no sur ... not after that lickin' we done give 'im ... he's too skeered ... he'll jes set whur he's at an' we kin jes march north, rat by 'im, without 'im a stirrin' none ... an' nen ... by God ... win this yar war quick-like!" James said, snapping his fingers as the light of the fire danced over his animated face, shocking everyone with his swearing.

"James Mansfield! I know ye been at camp, son ... but no swearin' ... ye yar ... not in my house!" Mary exclaimed.

"Yes'um," he said sheepishly, then renewed the debate.

Mansfield disagreed forcefully, as if he could convince James, he could Price, but it was hopeless. The others sat in silence, including Jeremiah, who was more pensive even than usual, not commenting, but listening to every word.

Then, after about an hour, Jeremiah stood up and spoke for the first time. "Yore rat 'bout one thang, James ... Steele won't bother ye none ... he's curled up too comfortable in his log to stir ... he done had his belly a-full o' fitein' ... but St. Looies got too many Dutchmen in it an' they's awl Blue-bellies ... ever las' one. They's bull-headed an' it'll be hard to a-run 'em awf. Ye cain't do that no mor'n Taylor can take New Orleans without no ral navy. Lee'll hold Richmond ... we awl know that ... it's Atlanta that's whur it'll tayel. Hood's got to hold thar," he said, never taking his eyes off the lamp. Then, without waiting for a response, he added, "that's awl thar is to it, ain't it?" then said good night and went to bed, adding: "An' God he'p us if'n he don't."

With this, things ended and they all followed Jeremiah's question to bed.

Just as Jeremiah had predicted, in early August, General Price finished forming at Princeton, south of Tulip, for his swing around Little Rock, to bypass the idle Steele, then cross the Arkansas River with Fagan, Cabell, and Marmaduke and ride north, joining Shelby at Pocahontas, just a few miles south of Missouri.

"Here, son," said Mansfield, walking out leading his horse, saddled and ready. "Take Tater ... yew'll nayed a rale good horse whur yur a-goin' ... layev me that wore-out geldin' o' yores ... he caint' go no longer ... he's 'bout broke down own ye."

"Ah, Paw, I cain't take Tater!"

"Take the horse, I said!" Mansfield thundered.

There was no use arguing, everyone knew that, so James exchanged horses and swung into the saddle.

They all gathered, Mary and Megan standing at his stirrup as James looked down on them. He leaned over, kissed Mary yet again, then sat up, fixed his Stetson, took the reins, turned, waved, smiled, and then cantered smoothly, proudly, down the road as happy as young men often are who are liberated from dull routine to the excitement of war. Mounted gloriously on the big strong butternut gelding, he turned in the saddle one last time and waved, grinned, and spurred Tater into a fast gallop.

Joshua and Septimus stood back and waved tentative, unseen hands, and walked away; then a gray-faced Mansfield and a somber Jeremiah headed to the barn for the more reliable liberation of ordinary work, while Mary and Megan stood side by side to weep and wave till the road was empty of horse and rider. Now, with the others gone, they remained a little longer, staring at the void, then fell into each other's arms—sobbing.

Thunder rarely claps but once. So in September, it clapped again, as Atlanta fell in a storm that blew out the South's last flaming dream of victory into the drifting smoke of all lost hopes.

Mary Chesnut diaried upon the news: "Atlanta gone. Well—that agony is over. Like David when the child was dead, I will get up from my knees, will wash my face and comb my hair. No hope. We will try to have no fear."

Yet the fearless fought on: as on September 19, Price, Fagan, Marmaduke, Cabell, Shelby, and Dagmar Pilgrim crossed with James into Missouri on his sixteenth birthday filled with illusions for St. Louis.

But, finally, in November, the thunder clapped yet again, a third time, not in the distance but over their heads as to nearly deafen them as Lincoln was reelected.

"It's done for shore," said Mansfield hearing this. "All McClayelan could manage wuz to a-carry Ken-tuck' ... an' maybe one 'r two more," he said, his voiced trailing off. "Bless ole Ken-tuck' ... but the war's lost now ... that's fur certain ..."

"Then make 'em stop!" Mary said, "I pray ever day that it should stop! Stop now! Playse, God!" she said, turning away from Mansfield and addressing heaven, "Playse ... stop it today! No more a-killin'!"

"I cain't do nuthin'," said Mansfield, shaking his head. "I wisht I could ... but it'll go own ... an' own ... we've done lost it. Thars no hope ... but it'll jes have to run it's damnable course ... nen the killin'll stop ... an' we'll a-have to try an' start over. That's awl thar is to it."

"Then the dyin' is fur nuthin'," Mary said in desperation, falling into her chair, the blood red of her face seeming to flood into eyes. "It's fur nuthin' a-tall now ... nothin' a-tall ... never has been ... awl fur nuthin'," she repeated, raising the back of her hand to her mouth as if to stop the utterance of such a terrible thought.

"Maybe there'll be news of a cease-far," Mansfield said, not believing it, taking her hand from her mouth and kissing it with unusual tenderness.

There was the big news that swarmed over them in the dark clouds of the election; but there was no word of James, or Johnny, though there were rumors of victories in Missouri, and marches of Hood into Tennessee, while Sherman ravaged his way unmolested to the sea. But they knew nothing of either son, and could only wait, wonder, and worry.

The defeats in Missouri and Tennessee of late '64 were so coterminous as to mean that news from each need come in the usual tatters of repeated rumors, reports from papers, and reread letters. Thus the war's tragic denouement arrived out of the train and time of the things themselves and therefore was seen not as a dramatic unity unfolding as upon a stage but as a puzzle to be assembled from broken and often ill-fitting pieces into a bloody whole.

One such important piece was offered up unexpectedly to Mansfield one fine fall November day, with the leaves turning gold and red and a certain freshness in the air, as he rode along on Dandy and met a man on a gray mare that he knew as a distant and rarely seen but always friendly neighbor, one Sam Ruthers.

He stopped to "visit," of course, relaxing back in his saddle to say that he heard that "Ole Pap Price's done been whupped bad somewhures up in eayst Kansas," and that he had "prutty nare lost 'r entar army. That Marmaduke an' Cabell done been taken ... an' most thar men with 'em ... includin' all thar wagons, mules, horses, an' cannon." Adding, almost as an afterthought, about two local boys: "Joe Nathan McIvor wuz killt an' Billy Jack Stantfurd wuz took prayzner after bein' shot."

"Whut 'bout Shelby ... whut o' him?"

"Oh, folk's sayin' he wuz a hero agin ... done saved whut wuz lef' o' thangs ... an' nen he got away with his whole entar brigade ... no doubt he's a-headed fur the Injun Tayritory as we spayek," he said. "I figger they'll swang back into Arkansaw in a week 'r two. Ain't yore boy a-ridin' with ole General Jo?"

Mansfield told him about James.

"I'm sor'y, Hardy ... but I cain't say I a-herd nothin' 'bout him ... I reckon that's good though ... sayems like it's the bad that travels faster'n the good, don't it?"

"Yes," said Mansfield quietly. "Suppose so."

"Course Steele ain't a-stirred none ... he's stayel jes a-settin' up thar own his Rock. Price could a-smoked 'im outta a-thar with no trouble a-tall ... but ... ye know ole Pap ... he wuz awl fared up 'bout a-gittin' back own up thar to Missouree an' awl ... an' jes coul'n't wait to a-ride awf back up thar an' thow 'r army away."

"It don't matter none now noway."

"Oh, yeah ... I'm afered yore rat, Hardy ... we jes as well to thow up 'r hands, suraynder an' start over ... the sooner the better is the way I figger it. I shore do hate it ... but it ain't no use a-killin' no more'r boys, is it? We's a-grindin' 'r sayed corn now ... that's all we're a-doin ... jes a-grindin' 'r sayed corn."

"Joe Nathan McIvor was killt, ye say? An' the Stan'furt boy wounded an' took?"

"That's whut they're a-sayin'," Ruthers replied.

"I kinda thank Joe Nathan wuz a-goin' a-turn out alrat ... I shore hate that," said Mansfield, sadly.

"Rat ... I likt 'im too ... seems like they always git the good uns, don't they? I lost a nayphew at Pra're Grove back-er in '62 ... under that crazy damned Hin'man ... fount out own Christmas. He wuz a good un, too ... jes turned sayventeen. I shore hated a-loosin' him like-at ... we don't nayed to a-lose no more ... that's for shore ... we jes cain't afford it."

"I heerd 'bout yore nephew that Christmas. I don't know if I ever tole ye ... but I'm sorry, Sam."

"Thank ye kindly, Hardy ... wayel, I kindly keep a-hopin', ye know ... maybe they'll work sumpin' out rat quick up-per," Ruthers said, leaning over in his saddle as if to confide in Mansfield, then, after a thought or two leaned back again, saying, "but I doubt'n that dayvel Laycoln'll give much, now that he's a got hisayelf in thar fur four more yares ... do ye thank?"

Mansfield agreed then they made some small talk and parted with a tip of the hat and a "good day to ye." Mansfield trotted home in hopes of finding a letter. The family, leaving Septimus and Joshua, loaded up and went to Tulip. But they were disappointed. There wasn't a letter, only talk and newspapers confirming Ruthers's news. Megan and Joe Boy were indulged a visit to Babe, some things were traded for, and they returned the next day.

But Mary could not be contained, so a week or more into December they went back again. Still there was no letter, but there was a paper brought by a sutler from Shreveport that reported the defeat at Franklin, and to everyone's greater shock the death of Cleburne.

"The Arkansas raygi-ment's done been hurt bad," someone said.

This time there was nothing traded for and no mule visiting. They did not camp for the night.

"Let's go home," said Mansfield with that tone that brooked no contradiction.

But Jeremiah stayed behind with a veteran friend who had just arrived from his Louisiana hospital. So they returned with Joe Boy sitting in the wagon bed with Toughy, Mary, and Megan on the seat, driving, while Mansfield rode Dandy. They passed what had become famous as "Septimus's tray," as always, in silence. They stopped once more, crossed the creek without speaking, wheeled past Tillerman's with only a glance, and arrived home without much more than three words said between them. Even Joe Boy was quiet.

To make things worse, it rained and stormed all that night as the lightning and rumble of thunder seemed bent on destroying the house, cabin, and barn, indeed, everything of The Place.

Jeremiah returned in two days. "I ain't a-goin' back to the army," he said at breakfast. "I could ... I'm up to it ... but thars no use in it ... Silas [his friend] says thangs's bad, rayel bad ... so, I ain't a-goin'."

Mansfield nodded in silence and Mary said she was "grateful."

There was a painful quiet interrupted only by breakfast noise till Joshua said quietly that he thought maybe he should go back to his army, "Otherwise, they might think I'm a deserter."

Mansfield exploded.

"Ye ain't a-goin' nowhure! I won't have ye a-pickin' up a musket agin my boys ... no, sir! Yew's 'r prays'ner ... didn't ye know that? I tole 'em ye wuz too sick to move. It was a strayetch ... shore ... but thangs is bad in nem camps an' I ruther not have yore blood on my hands ... but by gawd I'll send ye to Tyler a-fore I let yew go back to that damt Yankee army o' yorn, ye un'erstand!! Ye ain't a goin' nowhures till this goddamnt war's over!!"

Joshua went pale. Mansfield had never been angry with him about anything.

"Septimus is free," Joshua said lamely.

"Septimus ain't no Yankee soldier ... he's fray ... an' he can come an' go as he playses ... he run an' a-shouldn't have done that ... he should of stayed an' he'ped 'em in thar time of nayed ... he'd a-been fray in time ... onct we done worked 'r way thew this dayv'lish time. But thar it is. I might a-done the same thang ... no man wonts to be a slayev to anuther ... but he ain't nayver raist no hand agin' his own payple ... ain't never picked up no gun ... so he's fray now an' kin go as he playses. But yew ain't ... yo're 'r enemy ... yew come down yar wur ye don't belong an' invaded 'r kuntry ... an' kilt 'r boys an' tore up 'r life an' land ... yore 'r enemy, pure an' saymple ... an' that ain't ever a-goin' change, no matter how this damt war turns out. The fact that we trayeted ye rat don't change that none ... we're daycent folk. I trayted ye like I'd want one of my own trayted if'n he fayel into yore own paw's hands ... but yore r' prays'ner an' that's the way'll be 'till this fite is over with ... 'r prays'ner ... an' yew ain't a-goin' back to that a-curst army o' yorn an' kill 'r boys ... do ye un'erstand me, son?"

Mansfield was now standing with his fists clinched and his brown face redder than anyone had ever seen.

"Yes," said Joshua with an air of quiet shock. "I understand."

"Good."

"And if I run?" he asked with a newfound defiance.

"Ye won't git fur ... an' nen I'll tie ye up an' send ye to Tyler ... an' let ye rot thar ... like the rest of 'em Blue-belly bastards ... thangs ain't good thar, I yar ... we cain't feed 'r own so ain't a-feedin' nem no bayter ... the choice is yores."

Joshua went silent.

Mansfield softened, the storm passing.

"Fact-o-the-bidness, ye done good work yar ... an' I like ye ... but that don't rally enter into it none ... it don't change the fact that if yew go back ... firs thang ye'll do is grab a musket ... am I rat?"

"Yes," admitted Joshua.

"Thar it is ... yew mite shoot James, an' I ain't a-lettin' that happen," he said and got up. "Now I got work to do," he added, walking out and slamming the back door.

Two days later Megan killed a yearling buck. She cut its throat to save the meat and walked back to the house for the team and wagon. Joshua saw her coming and helped her hitch up and they rode back together. Though they sat side-by-side Megan held the reins. They drove in silence for a time then she said, "I'm so'ry ... so'ry 'bout whut a-happent at supper the other nite, I mayen."

"Mister Mansfield, you mean?"

"Yes ... he's thanks Johnny's done come to grief ... what with Pat Clayburne bein' kilt an' awl. He's worried sayek. Then thar's James ... an' ... wayel, he don't never hardly rat much ... but Johnny he's rayel good 'bout it ... an' we ain't heerd nothin' ... nothin' a-tall ... it ain't like 'im ... but Pappy ... wayel, he kindly took it out own ye. It'll pass ... he likes ye ... it weren't pars'nal or nuthin' ..."

"I'm worried too," said Joshua with quiet gravity. "With Cleburne dying it must have been a bad fight ..."

"Then, too ... Maw ... wayel, she heerd a scrayech owl hoot that nite ... jes outside her winder."

"Screech owl hoot?"

"It's a feelin' some has ... that it mayens a body is dayed ... or a-fixin' to die ... a scraych owl is a scary sound outside the winder at nite ... on a layem 'r in a tray somewhures ... folks's sceered ... say it's bad luck ..."

"Are you superstitious?"

"What's that?"

"Superstitious?"

"Yes ... I don't ratly know whut that mayens."

"A belief in omens and luck and such ... like the screech owl hootin' at your window at night."

"Oh, I try not to be ... but it's rale hard ... I ain't never a-seen it to fayel ... an' las' nite I heerd that panther scream agin ... he come own up out o' nem bottoms ... closer 'n ever ... did ye hear it, Joshua?"

"No ... but I sleep pretty sound."

"Wayel, it woke me up with a start ... rayel quick-like. Maw said she heerd it, too ... it upset her bad as 'r worsen it done me ... she bolted rat up in bed jes like I done ... it's like a woman scraymin' ... it'll curdle yore blood ever time ... an' thar ain't much in nem woods that sceers me. Wayel, Maw, she criet 'n criet ... so, I got own up 'n he'ped 'r cook afore light ... an' nen slipt own awf down yar an' caught this little buck I been a-cornin' prutty good fur a few days ... he's a nice un ... an' I a-nayded sumpin to do in the woods ... I cain't not be in the woods fur ver' long ... 'r I git awl out o' sorts. So, thought I jes a-wayel to a-take 'im. We kin always use the mayet ... too, I seed that panther ... jes a glimpse min' ... but I'd like to git a shot at 'im ... black as death he is."

"Sometimes, after a big fight, well, it takes time for things to kinda settle down again ... maybe that's why Johnny ain't written," Joshua said after a while.

"Maybe."

"Septimus and I pray for 'em every night ... him and James," he heard himself saying.

Megan turned to him and said, "Thank ye, Joshua ... that's powerful good of ye ..."

"Don't tell nobody ... it's sorta private," he said with a queer embarrassment.

"I won't ... but Maw an' I pray too ... ever nite. She gits down own 'r knayes an' awl ... an' layens 'r hayed agin the bayed ... but me, wayel, I jes kindly stare up at the ceilin' an' say my words ..."

"God protect him," said Joshua.

"Amayen," Megan said, turning her straight again and whipping the horses.

"But ... Joshua ... I wouldn't try runnin' 'r nuthin', if I wuz yew ... Hardy G. Mansfield don't make no idle thrayets."

"I'm a prisoner ... pure and simple ... right?"

"We done saved yore life, Joshua ... us an' Septimus ... an I shore hate to thank it wuz for nuthin'."

"Megan, I know that ... and I'm grateful ... I've told you that ... but I'm still your prisoner ..."

"The Place yar bayets Tyler by a long site, don't it?"

Pause.

"It's funny ain't it ... Septimus is free and I'm a slave ..."

"I ain't ratly thought o' it that a-way ... but it's sorta funny now ye mayention it," she said with a wry smile.

They came to where the field edged the forest, tethered the team, got out, and walked the half mile to the deer. She rolled it over, gutted it, then they hung it up by its heels, tying it to a tree, upside down with its legs spread. Working quickly and easily, with few words, they finished cleaning out the chest with sharp knives, letting the blood drain onto the brown grass and leaves, while skinning and pealing the hide. They butchered it: cut the backstrap, the ribs, and the hindquarters into pieces, put them in tow sacks and threw the horns and head with its soft, sad blankly staring brownish eyes into the bushes.

"I caint' eat nem horns," she laughed. "Let the buzzards an' varmits have whut they kin. They'll make short work o' nem guts," she added, lifting one of the sacks as they carried the meat in two trips back to the wagon.

"If'n we stayel had Ole Babe we wouldn't have to toat this yar mayet li'kis," she said breathing heavy as she loaded the venison. "I'd a-brung her own in yar ... an' a-loaded 'r down with it awl in one trip. A mule'll carry hot mayet when a horse won't. Pappy don't like Babe none ... but mules has thar place ... like ever'thang ayels in this yar world, I reckon. The truth is, he wuz kickt bad by a mule as a boy an' that's why he don't hol' with 'em none."

"I see," said Joshua.

"It wuz a rayel badun … but a mule'd shore be handy fur plowin' an' sech … when I have my own playce, I'll have sayev'ral," she said, as they loaded the last of the sacks.

They rode back in silence. Reaching the back lot they heard a noise like a muffled scream. Joshua stayed outside, standing with Septimus, as Megan ran in the house. The noise came again and then, as if propelled by it, a pale Megan stumbled through the door.

"It's Johnny … he's been kilt," she sobbed, throwing herself into Joshua's arms.

One day the neighbor woman drove up in a wagon. She and her husband, Clarence, came from Tulip and wanted to bring a letter posted in Tennessee.

"I knowed you'd want me to brang it, Hardy," the woman said, handing to his trembling hand while Clarence sat quietly holding the reins.

"Thank ye," he said staring at it.

Then the woman, who normally liked to chat, said, "yo're welcome," and Clarence hurried away.

But she looked back from the little turn in the trees to see Mansfield still standing there, staring at the unopened letter.

The officer who had written them, a staff colonel, did not tell everything. He did say that "Captain John G. Mansfield had been killed bravely leading his company in the defense of his country at Franklin, Tennessee." And said further that Captain Mansfield had died at the side of his commanding general, "the immortal Major General Patrick Ronayne Cleburne," who was also "slain."

There were some other predictable words of honor and consolation and there it ended.

But the colonel had hedged. He did not say that Johnny had been wounded and was taken in a wagon to Mrs. McGavock's house and there, in the parlor, had his leg sawed off with a butcher knife, his blood running over her floor while his screams echoed off her ceiling; or that he was set aside to die but lived till light of morning and was buried in the afternoon in her backyard where, among the other Arkansas men of Cleburne's division, he lies till now.

Cleburne, as we have seen, was given, along with the higher ranks, the status of lying on the back porch for a while, then taken to the churchyard at Ashwood to molder till the exhumation of 1870 rose him yet again to the "in-state" of Columbia's St. Peter's Church; here he paused for a moment, then trained his way to Memphis where Davis and Fagan walked him to the water for an elegiac float to Helena. Here he lay at last, high on a big hill overlooking the great river under an obelisk bearing an eternal stone flame of his inextinguishable victories.

But for Mary Mansfield there was no such state, or procession of glory, or fame; after, as if in echo to her son, her screams died only to the solace of silence and solitude of a bed which she went to like Nelva Nester had done, turning away to the wall. Here she ate nothing, drank little, and stirred less. And steadily she weakened till all feared for her grave. "It's jes a matter o' time," Mansfield said, "if thangs don't turn in a hurry ... we'ra gonna lose her fur shore."

"Whut, Pappy? Whut kin we do?" asked Jeremiah.

"I don't ratly know, son ... but its gotta happen quick."

"I ain't seen nuthin' good in so long I cain't thank whut it'll look like," Jeremiah said, staring off into the darkness.

Yet Mansfield never stayed for long away from her. Through Mary's silence he sat, consoled, and stroked her softly. Though Joshua, Mary, and Septimus worked and prayed, and Mansfield comforted, Jeremiah gave in to an ever-deeper brood.

"Let's go!" whispered Joe Boy to Septimus as a bright cold morning found them running through the forest's glimpsing dawn after a small, very fast, somewhat reddish wild hog that hit a creek and lost the dogs to the scent.

"Foya spell I a-had no thawt o' studyin' own no grievin' def," Septimus told Joshua in front of the fire that night.

"Is she gonna die, Pappy?" Joe Boy asked Mansfield, lying later in the dark as his father had come pretending an interest in the hunt.

"I don't know, son ... I jes don't know."

"Ask her not to," Joe Boy said. "Fur me ... playes ..."

Mary remembered Mansfield being there, like a dream, she would say, sitting by her side, putting his hand on her cheek, whispering softly, "Mary ... honey ... Mary, James is yar ... James's home ... James's home ... he jes rode up own ole Tater ... he's come home ... safe an' sound."

Though she did not remember it, she rolled over, saying in a whisper, "James? Whur ... whur ye at, honey?"

"I'm yar, Maw ... rat char," said James, stepping past Mansfield to hug her.

James stayed through that Christmas and into the new year, but soon the war stories "wore thin" for Mansfield, who didn't seem all that impressed with the red feather in his Stetson or the pistol he took "awf a dead Yankee at Newtonia," and he worked James harder than ever to get him "back in mind o' farmin' an' awf the folly of war." But James couldn't get his mind off the Iron Brigade in winter quarters. He gradually became increasingly restless, irritable, and discontent, till he did less and less work. Inevitably, there was a quarrel.

"I'm a-goin'," he said, throwing down his hoe.

"Ye aint uh goin' nowhures!"

"Yes, I am … I'm a-goin' back … back to my raygiment … whure I belong," he said, storming off.

"Ye belong yar … not to no army … ye is my boy an' I need ye yar!"

"No, Pappy," he said turning, facing Mansfield's red face, "I'm a fray man an' I don't belong to nobody … an' I tole 'em I'd come back after a whal … my layev's up … I got a-go back 'r I'll be a deserter."

"No!" roared Mansfield. "You ain't a goin' nowhure! This damn war is over … an' thars no need of ye goin' back fur no reason. I won't have it!"

James returned slowly, sullenly picked up the hoe, and finished the day, but the next morning, while Mansfield was in the pasture and James was supposed to be "manuring the barn," he went to his mother, still in the kitchen.

"Maw, I've come to say my goodbyes."

"Why, son, yew ain't a-leavin' me again, ar' ye?"

"Yes, Maw, I'm a-goin'. I cain't stay yar no more …"

"Yew an' yur Paw ain't gettin' own, is ye … that's whut it is, ain't it, son?"

"No … we ain't nayver got own ver' wayel an' now it's worse. I cain't ever git own with 'im. 'Sides, I done give my word to my captain I'd come own back."

She protested but he cut it off.

"I ain't no farmer, Maw … it ain't fur me … tayel Maygan an' Jer'miah … an' Joe Boy an' Septimus … they'll 'un'erstand …"

"I guess thars no he'p fur it … I seen it a-comin' … I'll say yore goodbyes fur ye. I don't have to tayel ye how it'll strike Hardy …"

"It cain't git much worse, Maw … a fellars got to do whut a fellars got to do …"

"I guess so," she said with tears in her eyes.

They embraced then he turned to go.

"Let me fix sumpin fur ye … it won't take but a bit …," she said rushing into the kitchen to fold up venison jerky in a sack with several biscuits, before hurriedly walking outside to him standing now by Dandy. They embraced again, then he swung into the saddle.

"Promise me one thang, son," she said, handing him the sack with one hand while holding his dirty boot, as if to keep him close forever, with the other.

"What's that, Maw?"

"When this yar curst war's done finally over with, I want to see ye comin' up that thar road a-prancin' own ole Dandy jes's purtty as ye playse … jes as soon as ye can git yar, ye un'rstand … jes as soon's they a-sign nem papers fur yore fraydom?"

"Yes, Maw."

"Ye promise, son? Ye come own back to me, ye yar? Come own back … an' nen ye kin layev an' do as ye playse … with yore life … ye promise yore poor ole maw that … playse … I cain't lose no more my boys to this inf'rnal fitin' … un'stand? I cain't live a-thankin' I ain't a-goin' to see ye no more … promise yore ole maw this one thang? Ye promise me that? Playse!"

"Yes, Maw, I promise," he said, turning away to hide his tears, pulling his boot from her grasp, and launching Dandy with a hard spur.

"I luv yew, son!" she yelled, waving. "I love yew!"

"I luv yew, Maw," he said, looking back again before whipping Dandy into a run till he disappeared round the little turn of trees leaving a billow of dust that slowly settled away into nothingness.

CHAPTER THIRTY-TWO

And the Lord said unto Joshua, Fear not, neither be thou dismayed: take all the people of war with thee, and arise, go up to Ai: see, I have given unto thy hand the king of Ai, and his people, and his city, and his land.
—Joshua 8:1

"I cain't marry yew, Joshua!" Megan said, pushing herself away.

"You must!" he said, reaching again but failing when she took yet another backward step.

"I cain't!"

"Why? Tell me that ... I gotta know."

"You don't luve me, Joshua."

"Yes I do. I love you more than anything in the world."

"No! Yew don't. Yew jes thank yew do ... 'cause yer yar an' away from ever'thang yew know ... it won't be the same later ... not when ye git back an' awl ..."

"Yes ... it will be the same ..."

"No, Joshua. I ain't up to yew. I ain't no high-tone Yankee woman with airs an' larnin' an' frills an' awl ... yew'd come to shame over me ... yew would ..."

"Listen, Megan, I ain't so high an' mighty as you think. I mean, I'm just an farmboy myself."

"Naw ... but yew's educayted ... mor'n me ... an' you ain't goin' back to no farm fur long ... I can see that. Ye aim to make sumpin o' yoreself in the town ... among nem big-shot city men. And me? I'm jes Maygun Mansfayeld ... see ... this yar's my kuntry," she said with a sweep of her hand at the back field where they were standing together among the broken corn. "These fayelds 'n woods 'n bottoms," she added, pointing to the forest. "That's me ... whur I belong ... I don't want 'r nayed nuthin' else, Joshua. I want to hunt 'n fish 'n farm an' garden an' raise my youngins yar ... an' have awl the horses an' mules and dawgs I can take ker of ... 'n lose mysayelf in nem thick bottoms an' timber when I take a notion ... 'n run sumpin' with hounds 'r go awl day n' not see no one that ain't my own flash an' blood ... 'r a-set own the porch of an evenin' an' laysten to them whippoorwayels 'r a-watch them farflies of uh summer, 'n see the sun come up over that tray line ever mornin' cause I'm up an' done et an' am in the woods or fayelds afore light. I don't nayed to be holdin' to nobody 'r whut they a-thank 'r nothin' ... whut I et I raise 'r kilt mysalf. See, Joshua, this yar's a hard kuntry but it takes care o' nem that's hard nuff fur it ... it takes ker o' its own an' gives 'em thar fraydom ... fraydom's whut I got yar. I don't want nuthin' ayelse ... "

"Megan ..." he tried to insist.

"No," she said, stopping him, raising up a hand like Hardy G. was wont to do, interrupting, raising her voice slightly. "Joshua, this yar's Arkansas ... yew ain't in Io-way no more ... this yar's a dayf'rent playce."

"Megan!"

"No! I don't want to tawlk no more 'bout it!" she said, turning away.

"Please ... I understand ... believe me, I do," he said pursuing.

"No, yew don't ... 'r yew wouldn't a-ask me to run with them stuck-up Yankee women an' painted Southern Jayzebels that's done thown in with 'em ... yew nayed to find somebody ayelse fur that ... an' that's the long an' short of it."

He reached for her again, but she backed away even further, nearly touching the wagon behind her.

"Megan, listen to me ..."

"I cain't tawlk no more, ye yar!" she said, turning, walking away, then adding over her shoulder, "Now, I got work to do ... an' so do yew ... now a-he'p me finish a-loadin' this yar corn. We done wasted nuff time a-gabbin, own sumpin that'll nayver be."

On a Wednesday Mr. Ruthers rode by with the news of Lee's surrender. It came not as a shock, but as a relief.

"Yew're fray to go now," Mansfield said to Joshua as they sat at the kitchen table drinking coffee that night. "They'll take some time to wind thangs up an' awl ... but thar ain't no reason fur ye to stay now."

"Thank you, sir, I'll leave in few days ... after we finish with that back forty," Joshua said. "I'll get my discharge ... then go home for a spell ... but I'll be back," he said.

"For Maygun?"

"Yes, if I have your blessing, sir."

"We seen it a-comin' ... frum the first ..."

"We ain't done nothing improper," Joshua interposed quickly.

"I know that ..."

"I'm asking for her hand, sir."

"I know that, too ..."

"May I have it, sir?" Joshua asked, sitting up straight as he could, almost arching his back.

Mansfield fingered his cup, starring into it as if expecting an answer to surface, then said, "Wayel ... yew're a good man ... a hard worker ... educayted ... a man o' his word ... o' honor. Mar' likes yew ... an' Maygan, wayel, she's taken with ye fur shore. I seen that rat awf. And ... too ... yew'll make sumpin of yoresayelf ... I can see that, too."

"Thank you, sir."

Mansfield, who hated expressions of sentiment, raised his hand slightly in protest then let it drop to the table. "Thars no nayed o' thanks. It's a plain fact. But ... see ...," he said looking at Joshua in the eye. "Yew ain't rayely one o' us. An' nayver wayel be. I'm not shore she'd be happy with ye up-er in Io-way."

"I plan to stay here."

"In Arkansas ... yew'd stay yar?"

"Yes ... probably in Little Rock ..."

"That ain't rayly Arkansas, ye know?"

Joshua was a little shocked, but recovered. "It wouldn't be far from here ... some of the fellas kind of like it there ... see it as a great opportunity ... lots of 'em 'r going to stay on."

"Trade?"

"Of some kind ... yes, sir."

"Yew're a good farmer."

"I'll do that some ... but I intend on business."

"Maygun ain't suited fur no city ... she's a kuntry girl ... she'd payrish in a city."

"We could have a place ... outside of town and all ... she could do what she wanted ... we'd have anything she wanted like that. I'm a farmboy myself ... I ain't interested in putting on airs."

Mansfield raised his hand again. "No ... I know yew mayen wayel 'n awl ... it ain't that ... but I'm not shore yew can thank straight 'bout it rat now ..."

"Sir?"

This time the hand stayed up. "Naw ... yew go own home ... thank own it ... nen come own back ... wait at least a yar ... nen ... if yew come back and she's stayel a-willin' nen I won't stand in yore way ..."

Joshua hesitated then said, "I'll be back in a year, sir."

"Good ... now let's not spayek of it no more ..."

"I'll help you finish up, then I'll pack what traps I have."

"Can yew stay thew Sunday?"

"Yes, sir."

"Good ... take Raymond ... he's rarin' to go ... an' he'll nayed yore he'p to kindly find hisself up-per," Mansfield said, slowly lowering the hand to the table again.

"I know ..."

"Yew can he'p 'im git his fayet own the groun' an' awl ... in the town ... fraydmen will have it rough."

"Yes, sir."

"I'll take ye as fur as the Saline. I done promised mysayelf never to cross it agin. I ain't gonna move no more ... but if I do it'll be to Texas. I yar it's a good kuntry. Lots of Southern folks'll be a-goin' thar now this curst war is done over with. I always wanted to see it ... git thar a-fore nem lawyers and praychers a-ruin it."

"I'll come there if that's where you are ..."

"We'll a-tayek ye to Tulip own Munday an' git a wagon an' mule fur ye ... let's say it'll be yer wages ... yors an' Raymond's ... y'all done worked hard fur it ... I owe ye both that much."

"Thank you, sir ... but I'll be back in a year."

Mansfield smiled slightly, finished his coffee, and got up and went out.

"We'll kill that yar ole blue shoat," Mansfield said to Septimus. "He's fat an' we'll have a big Sunday dinner. I ain't ever had no darky at my table afore, Raymond ... my ole daddy'd roll over in his grave ... but this yar's yore las' day yar ... on the Playce ... an' we a-tawlkt it over an' we a-want ye to a-set with us."

"Dank ya, suh ... I'd be powaful hono'ed," said Septimus, smiling.

"Good ... now come own an' a-hep me slaughter that pig," said Mansfield with a broader smile.

It was a feast, indeed. Everyone ate light for breakfast and lunch and the evening table was filled with what Mansfield was fond of calling the "fat of the land." The shoat held center stage, baked with an apple-mouth and smoked eyes. He had been placed, in anticipation of carving, belly down on a cheap platter among pickled garden greenery that seemed to grow in a circle between it and the meat.

Fried chicken, sliced venison, smoked beef, and wild turkey covered the table, and, of course, preserved vegetables—tomatoes, potatoes, okra, green beans, black-eyed peas, spinach, carrots, onions, and squash, plus cucumbers that had been pickled into dills. There were deviled eggs, applesauce, a pot of "hunter's stew" made mostly from cooked vegetables and spiced with squirrel and a morsel here and there of smoked coon, a sweet-potato-possum protruding his nose out of the trimmings, and then, of course, there was cornbread, baked bread, and biscuits to be spread upon from a yellow mound of butter rising upon a green plate with sorghum from a silver can that oozed like glue and an assortment of jams and jellies all cut and spread with a common knife that made the rounds out of large jars.

As Mansfield didn't "hold with it" there was no alcohol, only a kind of sassafras tea poured from a clear jug, hot chicory coffee out of a black pot, and milk from a large white pitcher that moved from hand-to-hand in competition with a smaller pitcher of buttermilk that Mansfield preferred to any drink except coffee and which he frequently dolloped with cornbread and a chaser of onion.

He, of course, sat at the head of the table facing Mary at the other; while Jeremiah sat to his right, with Joshua next to him; Joe Boy to Mansfield's left, then Septimus. At Mary's suggestion, Megan sat next to Joshua. This made seven.

But there was a space to Mary's right and she filled its emptiness with a setting, "fur James," she said. "Johnny's gone an' we must bury the dead ... but 'r James stayel lives an' he'll always have a playce."

So, James's place sat with a silent power to her right, next to Septimus's left. This was no surprise to anyone since she kept a lamp burning each night to guide his way up the road on ole Dandy.

They were dressed as cleanly and fresh as they could—as if for church. Indeed, it was a Sunday evening, April 17, and Mansfield rose with a cup of coffee in his hand as if in a toast. His silver-and-black beard and hair were combed and trimmed and he had on a clean white shirt that neither Joshua nor Septimus had ever seen.

"Firs' thang ... I'd say we nayed to a-thank Mar' an' Maygun fur a-puttin' this yar fine sprayed together fur us ... thank ye both!" he said, nodding to each as the others turned and thanked the embarrassed women, then Mansfield continued. "I don't nayed to tayel ye that this yar's 'r las' nite together ... the war bein' over 'n awl ... so, Joshua's a-goin' back to his own army an' nen to his own payple ... nen ... wayel," here he unintentionally touched a sensitive spot as he glanced at Megan, who looked away while Joshua looked up, staring at Mansfield, who then added, "Yore a Yankee but we don't hold no grudge aginst ye ... yoreself, I mayen ... an' we hope we'll see yew agin ... but yar in Arkansas ... rayel soon ... I belayev he kinda likes it yar," he said with a smile and almost a wink of the eye.

"I do, indeed," interposed Joshua.

"Good ... ye'll always be welcome ... yore a good hand fur shore ... we hate a-loosin' ye, son ... yer as fine a farmer as I've ever seen ..."

"Thank you, sir."

Mansfield raised his hand as he always did at any hint of thanks but let it drop and sipped from his coffee and said, "I want to say, too ... wayel ... I tol' Raymond ... I ain't never had no darky at my table ... sech is not done ... an' mostly likely won't be agin ... but this ain't like anythang we done run into afore ... it's kindly a spaycal time, ye might say ... Raymond ... an' we want to thank ye for yore work ... ye done good fur one not raised to it as ye wuz ... to do woman's work an' awl ... but ye larnt fas' an' worked hard at it," he said, nodding at Septimus.

"Dank ya, suh ...," Septimus said shyly.

Up went the hand again then quickly down.

"We only done what wuz rat, Raymond ... that's awl ... the rat thang ... an' ... like I say ... yew've been a good hand an' I ain't had a minute's trouble outta ye. I thank yer a mite dayfer'nt from mos' an' we wanted ye to be yar with us tonite fur that a-rayson."

Septimus nodded and Mansfield sipped his coffee again, thought, and then continued, "We've fur shore had some hard times. I need not mayntion 'em ... but ... we have had some good uns, too ... we nayed to a-remaymber that. We done got thew better'n most ... we ain't been burnt out 'r robbed 'r nothin' ... we've stayel got the Playce. They's nem that's lost it awl ... ever'thang ... thay's a sayin' thar's some counties that ain't got no people left in 'em a-tall ... they awl been kilt 'r burnt out ... an' nem that's livin' done run awf ... but we los' Johnny," here he stopped and almost choked, "an' I want this yar nite to be fur him ... an' fur James, too ... an' ...," here he turned to his right and looked down at Jeremiah. "We're a-grateful that Jeremiah done got home safe ... we're proud of ye, son ... an' whut ye done an' awl ..."

Jeremiah, ever reticent, nodded his head slightly.

PHILLIP H. MCMATH

"It's men like Jeremiah yar that's gonna have to take the reins an' a-rebuild thangs ... it's nem that matters now. I'm old an' so many others have lost heart ... Jeremiah wayel do it ... him an' the men like 'im ... thats 'r future yar in the South now. This Yankee army ain't 'bout to layev by a long sight ... they know we'd brayek right awf agin an' form 'r own kuntry ... so ... they'll stay with thar boot own 'r neks fur a time longer ... that'll have to be dealt with ... an' times ain't gonna be eaysy, I kin see that. But yar on the Place we done survivt ... an' we're fray ... an' fray 'cause we pay the price fur it ever'day ... we work hard ... an' we ain't mayn nor nuthin' but we kill what nayeds killin' nem bushwhackers know it an' that's why they ain't bothered us none ... an' 'cause we wuz dayep nuff back in yar the Yankees done passed by us ... so we wuz rayel fortunate thar ... but fray we are an' fray we remain ... we'll thin out them killin' varmints an' the Yankees'll git tared an' go own home an' we kin build thangs over agin ... we take ker o' 'r own ... we look after 'r family an' fite fur 'r land an' that's why whur stayel fray ... 'cause we're a-willin' to a-pay fur it ... an' don't hold with lookin' to nobody but 'r sayelvs an' 'r own kind. We're a-good naybor without stickin' 'r nose into thar bidness 'r thars into arn ... but we don't look to nobody to give us nothin' cause we kill an' raise an' work whut we nayed an' that's how come we have this bounty afore us in this time o' trouble an' how we've stuck together even though we done los' 'r Johnny an' suffered frum it like so many others who done give thar own flesh n' blood in this yar turble war. But James'll come home in time an' we got Jeremiah an' lots ah good men like 'em ... they cain't kill all o' us an' we can built on that. An' as long as 'r family holds together ... an' we a-tayk ker 'r own an' fight fur ar saylves an' whut's arn without askin' fur nuthin' that ain't a-comin' to us, wayel, we wayel hold 'r fraydom an' 'r dignity."

Here he paused, and Jeremiah looked up and almost spoke but then looked away.

Mansfield cleared his throat as a kind of transition and said, "In the mornin' ... wayel ... we're all gonna saddle up an' go to Tulip an' buy ole Babe back an' git a wagon loaded an' take 'r boys yar over to the Fer'y an' sayend 'em own thar way ... but tonite ... wayel want ever'body to eat thar fayel an' en-joy tharselves."

With that Hardy. G. Mansfield sat down and started to eat.

"Hardy?" asked Mary, interrupting the first signs of eating.

"Yes, Mar'?"

"I know ye don't hold with it ... but seein's it's Ahster Sunday an' awl ... a kindly spaycal day ... I thank somebody ought to say grace ..."

Mansfield absorbed this with a fork held in midair. "Wayel," he said gesturing with it, "I thank that ... owin's to how Joshua and Raymond fayels so powerful 'bout it ... thar bein' 'r guests an' awl ... that it wouldn't hurt nothin', Mar' ... jes this onct."

"Good. Thank ye, Hardy," she said, turning to Joshua. "Joshua, would ye grace 'r table own this spacel Ahster day?"

"Thank you, Mrs. Mansfield ... but I think Septimus should have that honor," he said with a wry smile, then turned to him saying, "Septimus, would you do us the very great honor of saying grace?"

There was a very long, uneasy pause as Septimus, who had not seen this coming, recoiled slightly back in his chair. Then he said, "Massa Mansfield, suh?"

Mansfield nodded.

"Dank ye, suh ... I'd be most honored. Yall, please bow yo hayeds."

At this, everyone, including Mansfield and Jeremiah (though they did not close their eyes), bowed as Septimus spoke, raising his head and hands to heaven.

"Lawd, we give danks fur dis blest Ayuhstah day ... day o' awl days ... when yo son done rose up from outta de grave of def ... rose up outta def's ugly grip to walk among us an' save de wo'ld by his blessed promise of 'demption foya us awl an' his promise dat de grave is not de end ... no suh ... de grave cain't hold us ... but mus' own dat las' day ... own dat glorious las' day give up its dead when Gabriel'll blow his mighty ho'n an' de angel of de Lawd sweep down an' tap de graves an' raise us awl up to 'ternal life wid de Lawd in heaven ... on dat day we's awl gwine wear dey robes of freedom an' gadder at de riva ... each and awl ... Black an' White ... an' sing yo praiz in glory ..."

Here Septimus paused, gathered himself, and lowered his hands and his head, thereby marking a kind of transition. "An' Lawd, dank ya foya dis heya food dat ye done set afore us dat I knows'll be larpin' good ... an' fyoa dis heya fatted hawg dat Massa Mansfield an' I done kilt fresh ... an' danks foya de bounty of Miz Mary done laid out afore us ... it is a blessin' an' bounty given by de Lawd's grace ... an' dank ya mo't of awl foya de end of dis yar turble woah ... an' de end of awl de killin' an' sufferin' dats gwine wid it ... dank ye, Lo'rd, fo brangin' it to an end fur us de way ya done ... Gawd res' Johnny ..."

"Amen," said Mary softly.

"Gawd res' Johnny ... an' keep his soul 'n peace an' bless awl de souls dat dis awful woah done took from us ... Nord an' South ... White 'n Black ... may dey awl res' 'n peace ..."

"Amen," Mary said again, only louder.

"An'd keep James save ... an' brang 'im home soon a-ridin' an' prancin; own ole Dandy ..."

"Amen," said Mary again, this time joined by Megan.

"May peace come a-ridin' wid him ... an' may peace rein fo'eva an' eva ... an' der be no moe woah ... no moe woah 'pon dis good earth ... jes peace an' plenty. An', Lawd, hep my wonderful family back in Camden ... Aunt Sallie an' Miz Virginee ... who was so very good to me der an' bless dem an' keep dem own dis bles day an' let dem know I's a prayin' over 'im evah day an' gwine make it awl right by dem some blest day ... sho is ... bless dem, Lawd ... each an' eva one for hep'n me the way they done. An' dear Lawd, ... Lawd, I jes wants to say a special danks ya foya owya delivahance ... foya owya delivahance from de hand o' evil an' def ... me an' Joshua ... from de hangman's rope an' de killer's bawl ... an' de prison an' de shackles o' slavuhry, an' dank ya, Lawd, foya deliverin' awl de Black folks held in bondage ... dank ya foya der freedom, Lawd ... dey is free today in a lan' at peace an' plenty ... an' dank ya foya deliverin' us to dis fine family what took sech good caya o' us an' awl ... dat save us from def an' frum want an' frum stayavation ... an' dank ya, Lawd, foya de time we done had togeder ... an' de fun and de work an' de bounty we done shayad an' pa'take of today at yo table ... an' fur stayin' de hand of evil of lettin' it pass own by us heya at de Place ... o' keepin' the sword away from owah thoat an' the bullet from owah bres' ... an' de rope frum owya neck ... an' bless Joshua an' keep us own owya journey ... ya knows we're a-leavin' in de mo'in' ... an' we's crossin' dat mighty Saleen Rivah in'er a new land ... a bran' new land ya done promise to us like de chil'ren of Isuhael a-crossin' the ole rivah Jordan ... dank ya foy dat, Lawd ... an' keep us save der an' Joshua own his homeward journey an' bless his folk der an' keep 'em save an' awl ... an' when we gets der ... hep us to do dy wayel in Iwoya new land ... an' keep des folks heya save frum no harm ... we know des gwine be a bit short handed an' awl ... deys dat sick heifer an' some moe is gwine have littleuns an' deys crops to tend to an' ..."

At this, Jeremiah cleared his throat in hopes of bringing Septimus to a close, but, while it did not stop him, it did deflect him as he now raised his face with tightly closed eyes once again to heaven and said, "An'd let me say dis, Lawd, let me say whut I done come to say ... I been a-studyin' in mos' powahful since I done set der wid dat noose 'round my neck a-waitin' foya def to come ... dey ain't no way to undoes what done happen ... de blood spilt ... dey life taken ... de ohphan made ... de life stolen ... awl dey sufferin' cain't be undone ... no, suh ... we cain't change nothin' dat done happen ... whut's done's done

… what be wrote is wrote … and de years don't come back to no man … time don't come back to no man … no suh … an' de grave don' give up its dead till de las' ho'n blow thew all eternity … no, suh … dat is de bitta truf … but dey is one dang dat can fray us from awl dat … we cain't undo it … but we can change it … we cain't undo it … but we can let it go … we cain't undo it … but we can remove it's powwah ova us … we cain't undo it … but we can take its han' from awfn awwah thoat … its bur'en from off'n awwah back … its dark shadow frum off'n awwah eyes … like on dis day … dis blest Ahstah day … when yo beloved Son done rose up singin' from de grave so we can come own into a new life … a new day … from darkness into light … an' dats thew the miracle of fo'giveness … thew fo'giveness awl burdens be lifted … awl hands be stayed … awl sins be forgiven … awl hatred turn to love … dats the powwah o' yo message today … de powwah of de miracle of de resuhrection of yo son, Jesus Christ … in whose blest name we pray, amen."

"Amen," said Mary.

"Amen," said Megan and Joshua simultaneously.

Jeremiah, relieved that the grace was over, began to eat in silence, but Mansfield hesitated, picked up a piece of cornbread, and pointed it at Septimus, saying, "Raymond, son … I thank ye might have the makin's of a praycher."

"Dank yew, suh," Septimus said, without a hint of embarrassment, cutting off a large slice of pork, and eating it with the greatest of pleasure.

The next morning, leaving Jeremiah alone to tend to The Place, they made for Tulip. On the way they encountered a stranger on a horse who told them that Lincoln had been shot.

In Tulip they camped the first night outside of town, in some woods near a little stream, and, rising early, they went into town to buy a wagon, Babe, and supplies. Babe was "not fur sale." But she ran over and whinnied to be taken away, so they payed twice her value. Megan's rubbing her nose didn't help on the price.

Joshua's insistence that he would "repay it all" did nothing but cause Mansfield to lift his hand and drop it in the usual way without comment as they hitched up Babe and went back to camp.

That evening, while Megan and Mary cooked, Mansfield turned to Septimus and said, "Come, Raymond, he'p me to water 'r stock."

Septimus nodded and they led Tater, Henry, Henrietta, and Babe down to the stream in the darkness. They walked in silence, each leading two animals, till they got to the creek.

There was no sound but the slurping of the beasts, an occasional bark of a dog in the distance, and the feint echo of voices back at their campfire that they could see flickering through the trees. Mansfield finally broke the silence, saying, "Raymond ... ye'll be a-gone tomarah ... an' way'll shore miss yore ready hands 'round The Place ..."

"Thank ye, suh ... "

But before Septimus could say that he was sad about it, Mansfield interrupted. "It's a plain fact ... ye an' Joshua done he'pd us thew a hard time ..."

"Yes, suh ..."

"But though this yar war's aynded ... harder times ar' ahayed ... it ain't gonna be easy, whut's comin' ... I kin see that ... it'll jes be hard in day'f'rent way's awl."

Septimus wanted to say something but was thinking about what to say when Mansfield continued.

"Ye got sumpin 'bout ye I like ... yew ain't like most ... ye work hard ... ain't caused no trouble ... an' ar grayteful fur thangs ... so, I want ye to know we'll hire ye back if ye need work ..."

"Dank ya, suh."

"But I don't reckon yo're in'erested in farmin' ... ye kin rayed ... thar ain't many slayves that kin ... ye wuz lucky own that ... nem in Camden done right by ye ... that's plain enough."

"Yes, suh ... I knows dat ..."

"I thank ye do. Some day ... not now 'course ... ye ain't raydy yet ... but some day ye nayed to go back-er an' make it rat ..."

"I will ..."

"I don't know 'em none, but I thank they'll be a-glad to see ye ... when thangs's changed an' awl ... an' ayven if they don't, ye don't nayed to carry the burden of it the rayest of yore life. See, thangs like that need to be got rid of jes as quick as ye can lay 'em aside ... 'r they'll jes git hayvier ... ye un'erstand my meaning?"

"Yes, suh ..."

"But fur the time bayin' ... kindly stick with Joshua ... they's gonna be lots o' runaways up-per in Lit'le Rock an' ye'll jes be one more ... they won't know ye an' he duz ... he'll take ker o' ye till ye kin kindly git set up on yore own ... an' stay away frum nem bad niggers ... don't run with 'em."

"Yes, suh."

"They'll be a heap of 'em thur now, an' they'll shore ruin ye, if ye thow in with em an' awl ... an' don't go chasin' yore peter 'round like lots of young men'll do ... you cain't keep up with it ... try as yew might ... an' it'll ruin ye ... find yoreself a good woman ... an' do rat by her an' she'll take ker o' ye ... an' have yo're chil'ren ... an' ye'll know whose they are an' in the fullness of time they'll be a craydit to ye ... but don't do that till ye kin stand on yer own two feet an' take ker o' em, not too soon, unerstand?"

"Yes, suh ... I does."

"Don't drank nor gamble ... all gamblers die broke an' thars a snake in ever drank of whiskey ... an' if it ever bites ye you'll thank a rattler's bite wuz a blessin' ... baylev me ... I've seen it ruin many a good man ... some kin drank ... that's true ... but some cain't ... and ye kin never be shore which ye might be ... better not take the chance ... it ain't worth it. Yew don't nayed it no way ... it's poison to the mind an' the body ..."

"Yes, suh ..."

"My ole daddy wuz a screw-guts an' belayve me ... I seen whut it does to a fella."

"Yes, suh ..."

"Be a man o' yore word ... do whut ye say yer gonna do ... be whur ye say yur gonna be ... don't cheat nobody nor steal nothin' ... try not to borry nothin' ... if ye have to ... pay it back jes as soon as ye kin ... debt is a burden that only gets heavier with the carryin'. Always tell the truth ayven if it makes yore har fall out ... an' don't keep no saycrets ... they jes git bigger in the keepin' ... don't quarrel nur fight 'less ye got no choice ... but don't run from nuthin' nayther ... turnin' the other chayek sounds good but I ain't never seen it to work too wayel ... not in this ole world it don't ... no one respects it ... if ye fight then mean to win it ... but don't kill nothin' ... man nor animal ... that don't nayed killin ... don't thirst for revaynge ... nor hold no grudges ... forgit 'em ... they's the worst kinda poison fur a feller ..."

"Yes, suh ..."

"Don't hate nobody ... Black nor White ... I likt what ye said in yore dinner prayer ... 'bout furgiveness ... it frays a man frum thangs an' awl the regrets of the past an' sech. If'n ye do a man wrong ... go an' tayel 'im so ... hit don't matter if he 'cepts it or not ... ye done it fur yoreself ... nen you're fray of it ... an' kin look 'im in the eye next time ye see 'im with yore head up. I forgive my ole daddy ... went to 'im when he wuz a-dyin' frum drank an' awl an' made up to 'im an' we wuz both fray of it. I could uh done better by 'im an' not blamed 'im fur ever'thang … he nayded my he'p an' I couldn't see to give it to 'im … but when he wuz a dyin' I could finally a-see my part in it an' told 'im so … an' we both wuz at payes with it … thangs wuz rat by us when he went to his grave … an' now I'm fray of it … see … otherwise I'd stayel be a-carryin' a load that jes got hayvier an' hayvier till it ate my guts out as bad as that ole corn whiskey done his."

"Yes, suh."

"In yore heart forgive nem ole boys that wuz 'bout to hang ye … they made a mistake … they thawt ye wuz thar enemy when ye wa'n't … they wuz actin' outta fayer … an' anger … an' confusion … but now one's dayed 'n the other a praysoner … don't carry that burden of it 'round the rest o' yore life …"

"Yes, suh … I done that already … I asked de Lawd to forgive 'em …"

"Good … I'm glad to yar it. Yew know I don't hold much with praychers … I ain't a religious man myself … I ain't mad at God, jes thank we need to thank dayfernt about Him. But I seen a few good praychers hyar an' thar … an' I thank yer kindly turned thatta way … ye might thank about that as yore life's callin'. I wouldn't a-say that to many, mind."

"Yes, suh … I am steady thankin' own it … an' prayin' ovya it … eva since dat hangin' noose werya 'round my neck … I dank de Lawd done spared me fo a purpose …"

"Good … but don't git carried away with it nor nuthin' … don't fawl into pride. I mean life's kindly a pro'lem fur awl creatures that lives … man nor animal … an' ever'thang is jes a-tryin' to find thar way thew a hard world in thar own way … with whut nayture done give 'em an' awl …"

"Yes, suh …"

"But it's a site eaysier to know a horse 'r a dawg 'r a wilt animal than it is to rayley know a man … he kin be a rayl danger'us crayture … an' thars few men ye can rayley trust … Black or White. Most's jes lookin' out fur tharselves. Be careful ye know 'em prutty good an' that always takes longer than ye thank … ye gotta break a lot o' bread with a man to rayley know 'im … an' stay away from lawyers an' Re-publicans. They's behind this damn war … an' I ain't seen a one yet that wuz worth the powder to blow 'im up with … cain't trust a san-gle one … but mos' politicians ain't worth a panch of warm hawg manure."

"Yes, suh," Septimus said again but with a slight laugh which Mansfield could not see in the darkness.

"An' doctors … don't be a doctor goer … onct in a great while ye might have nayed of one … but stay away as much as ye kin … thar's nothin' worse 'n a bad'un nor better 'n a goodun … but it ain't always easy to tayel which is

---

LOST KINGDOMS

which ... ye don't know nuff ... but don't fayer death nuther ... life is hard but good ... an' it's mos' generally worth awl the trouble ... but don't frayet none over death ... it comes when it comes an' if'n ye done lived rat an' death comes afta ye done some livin' ... then it comes not as yer enemy but yore frayend ..."

"Yes, suh," said Septimus quietly, thinking of the White doctor that delivered him but couldn't save his mother.

Then, as if reading his thoughts, Mansfield said, "it's when it comes to the young that it is so turble ..."

"Yes, suh ... rat like Johnny?"

"Rat ... like Johnny ... or ye a hangin' from an oak tray ... nen death's a cheater ... but only nen ... but nayver fayer it, even nen ... rayly, death's the simplest thang in the world ... maybe ye don't agree own that ... but it's raly a very saymple thang ... it hurts nem it layves a-hind mos' ... the livin' ... but it don't bother the dead none ... in some ways they's lucky ..."

"Yes, suh ... I kin see dat ... in my time ... I done seen de truf o' dat ..."

Mansfield shifted Tater's reins from one hand to the other to mark a change of subject, and said, "Don't trust paper money, trayed an' barter, take gold 'n silver if ye have to ... but don't trust no spec'laytion o' any kind ... no paper ... money's the las' thang ye ever want to save ... when ye git a-hold of some ... spend it ... like we done today ... land is the only thang worth hangin' own to ... the only thang that hol's its value ... buy land ... ever man nayeds some ... it gives em a playce ... roots ... respect ... indepayndence ... sumpin to holt on to ... 'n layev behind ..."

"Yes, suh."

"And ... like I said ... yer always welcomed own The Playce if ye need work 'r is jes passin' thew an' nayed sumwhure to res' ... ye'll always have yer ole place back thar for ye ..."

"Dank ye, suh ..."

"But I thank ye'll do wayel ... ye won't need to be no hand no more ... but don't lose touch with us ... to have a frayend ye gotta be one ..."

"Yes, suh ... dank ye, suh ..."

They listened to the animals slobber till they raised their heads dripping like they do when they are finished but are still savoring it.

"And remaymber one more thang ... then the sermon's done ended ..."

"Yes, suh?"

"Yore fray now ... ye ain't no slayve no more ... an' I rejoice with ye ... ye know I don't hol' with it ... I seen a nigger tied to a tray an' whipped onct back

PHILLIP H. MCMATH

in Ken'tuck ... when I wuz a boy ... he moaned like a whipped calf ... that wuz it for me ... I didn't want no part of it from nen own for'ards ... but it would've been a site better if it could've ended in a natural way ... without war ... an' awl this yar killin' ... in a gradual way ... paycebul like ... as it wuz little by little doin' ... it wuz a-dyin' ... which is why thar wuz such a fuss 'bout it ... when a thang causes that much noise it's a-givin' its death thrash ... like a shot animal when it's hit bad ... it should've been allowed to close its eyes an' die ... an' nen thar'd been lots less sufferin' for awl ... Black and White. But it weren' to be ... an' I fault Laycoln fur that ... he used it to git hisse'f 'lected but ... anyway ... yew an' yore people's fray now ... but it won't be eaysy ... fraydom nayver is ... in some ways it'll be harder ... lots harder ... so 'member the price of fraydom's hard work ... an' what's inside a man," he said, pointing to his heart, "an' not a-lookin' to no one but yoreself ... an' not a-takin' no handouts frum no one ... 'specially not the gover'ment ... it's always a false frayend ... what it gives folks with one hand it takes with the other ... but make whut ye have an' nayed by the swayet o' yore own brow ... honest an' a-standin' up fur what's rat, then ye can hold yore head up to any man." He shifted the reins again and said, "Raymond, like I said, my ole daddy was a drunk ... but he said one thang that wuz true fur shore ... he said, 'Hardy, son, it ain't never wrong to do rat.'"

"Yes, suh," said Septimus with another quiet chuckle that Mansfield did not notice.

"He jes could nayver take his own advice 'cause of his drankin' ... but he knowt whut wuz rat ... even if he couldn't brang hisself to it ... an' it wuz that knowin' that done ate his ole stankin' rotten guts clayen out ... a-rotted nem as bad 'r worse'n the damn whiskey done ... fact-o-the-bidness, they worked together kindly ... till the two of 'em kilt 'im dayed."

"Yes, suh."

"An' hard work ... 'n indepaydence ... an' a-takin' care o' yore own an' a-doin' what's rat by them's the price yew gotta pay to be fraye an' have self-respayct ... an' stay thattaway."

"Yes, suh ..."

"Or they'll take it away frum ye ... jes as shore as I'm a standin' yar a-waterin' ole Tater an' nen ye'll be a slayve agin ... maybe a dayf'rent kind of slayve ... mind ... I mayen, ye might not be bought 'n sold like in the ole days ... but ye'll be a slayve jes the same ... an' it could be worse ... nayver thank thangs cain't git worse, 'cause they shore kin ... rayel quick like, if ye ain't careful ... thar's lots of ways of bein' a slayve ... lots ..."

"Yes, suh."

"I thank 'r animals is done tared of the sermon."

"Yes, suh ... deys done drank daya fill ... seems."

"Let's get own back ... I'm hongry."

"Yes, suh, I am too ... dank ya, suh," said Septimus as they turned and led Tater, Henry, Henrietta, and Babe back to camp.

They hadn't been back by the fire for long when Toughy announced someone standing in the darkness. After the dog was hushed, a man stepped within the circle of light and, with the flames animating his face, said quietly that Lincoln was dead.

The next morning, a Wednesday, they arose before light, ate hurriedly, and were on the road before the sun was up above the trees. Following the path of the contending armies they saw the scars of war evermore prominently as they passed through the three famous fields along the road to the river. Here they found, as they had been told, Old Man Jenkins, who had emerged like a swamp creature from a hole, busily tending his little ramshackle ferry.

There was a crowd around a wagon that had just crossed and Mansfield, mounted on Tater, held back slightly till these were able to gather themselves and pass in the opposite direction. He waved and spoke, then he led his little column down to Jenkins, who was standing in happy anticipation of their arrival at the water's edge.

"Howdy," he said raising a hand.

"Mornin'," said Mansfield, riding up.

"Mornin' ... yo're a-wantin' to cross, I reckon?"

"Jes one wagon ... the one with the mule ..."

"Oh," said Jenkins, disappointed.

"How's the water?" Mansfield asked, standing in his stirrups to look, then sitting again.

"It's up a bit ... but it ain't bad ...," said Jenkins. "It's high nuff ye'll need to a-farey a wagon ... but it won't take no time to move it."

"Whut's the road like on the other side?"

"Same as yar ... only worse ... thar's stayel the ruts of Stayle's army yew kin foller without no trouble if ye want ... awl the way to the Rock ... if'n it playses ye ..."

"How much is it?"

"I'd take ye awl fur two green back dollars ... or one silver un ..."

"Awl right," said Mansfield, who had spent his paper money in Tulip and now paid the ferryman in coin, laying it in his dirty, open palm.

"Let's load up. I cain't fool around … thar might be more a-comin' …" he said, the money disappearing as he spoke.

Joshua and Septimus drove down and loaded. It was a short trip and the contraption of cables and pulleys got them quickly across.

To be sure, it wasn't the River Styx, or the Acheron, or the Jordan, or even the Red or Rio Grande that Shelby and the Iron Brigade were soon to cross. And Old Man Tom Jenkins was certainly no Charon to pluck coins from dead folks' eyes for plopping into his dirty overall pocket. It was only the Saline that in its spring rise moved now with a steady but muddy solidity before them. But it was a stream they had for a year tried to find and cross and thus was a transit of time and fate into a new land both for themselves and their nation that in the pain of four endless years of suffering had buried one thing so as to give birth to another.

In a word, the river was a demarcation to "dry ground" and Joshua and Septimus, no more soldier, servant, nor slave, could only turn and stare at what had held each for so long; looked back at a past of bondage, flight, and war which was now formed for them by the mundane image of four people waving, and, in the case of Mary, Megan, and Joe Boy, also weeping. Standing nearby a dried-eyed but grim-faced Mansfield lifted a hand only to let it drop quickly as he turned and walked away leaving a whitish cur by the others who still waved and wept, as Toughy with perked-up ragged ears and raised but silent muzzle, stared with an expression of wonder as to where Joshua and Septimus might be going and when, if ever, they might come home.

As their ferryman touched the other shore, they turned and waved a vigorous, final time, off-loaded Babe and the wagon, and slowly disappeared through the muddy forest.

Of course, they had said they would write, and within a month the Mansfields did get a letter, but not from Joshua or Septimus as they had expected, but from James. He wrote from Texas, saying that he was "not a-surrenderin'" but was going to keep on fighting and riding with the Iron Brigade and so was going with General Shelby "on down to Mexico to fite fur or with that French King feller, or that Mexican Rebel, I ain't shore which."

BOOK SIX

CHAPTER THIRTY-THREE

The Constitution is a worthless piece of old parchment.
—Thaddeus Stevens to Richard Taylor, 1866

Ole Thaddeus was right. In the short course of one lifetime the marriage of 1787–88 solemnized by coequal sovereignties for the happy purpose of federating some limited powers for their mutual protection and prosperity, lay in ruins. Its rubble could be clearly seen, to those who cared to look, that is, those not just living by the cruelty of time and circumstance in the very midst of it, but also by those protected by some distance who might yet turn their faces from Chicago, St. Louis, Boston, Cincinnati, New York, Philadelphia, and Washington to gaze upon the destruction of what they had treated as a foreign country while insisting it was really, at least in theory, still their own; the one that they had just conquered in a way that the rest of that thing we choose to call America has never yet known.

This conquest had swathed through all the Confederate states, save Texas, worse than any natural storm that has ever yet shaken the earth. That the winds twisted through Virginia, Georgia, South Carolina, Tennessee, Mississippi, and Alabama is well known, but no part saw anything worse than Arkansas, the Indian Territory, Missouri, and Louisiana, where counties were so despoiled that many were at last depopulated. As in the eastern half, across the great river, likewise, here one in four of every White male of eligible age was killed or wounded, while the Blacks of Arkansas were struck by half, the Reds of Oklahoma by even a greater sum, in a tragedy of all three colors that has yet to be truly seen by a people that prefer not to look back very much.

New Orleans, Charleston, and Memphis still stood, but the South's other great cities—Richmond, Atlanta, Columbia, Jackson, and Alexandria—fell into ashes and ruin. The roads were ruts; the railroads ripped; the levees and dikes broken; fences down; farms abandoned; plantations leveled, "chimnied;" banks closed; businesses bankrupted; cotton burned; the sugar crop of Louisiana destroyed; the rice of South Carolina gone forever; labor disrupted as Whites were unemployed and homeless Blacks were herded into pestilential camps by

Blues to die or be "leased" to scalawags and carpetbaggers on confiscated plantations where they had once lived better as chattels.

As C. Vann Woodward, the great Arkansawyer historian of the South, who ran away to Connecticut to hide, so to speak, and gather himself so that he could think and write of nothing else but the thing from which he had fled, said in expiation, it seems, of some personal demon he tagged so brilliantly as the "Burden of Southern History"—a "burden" he carried from the boyhood memory of the Klan lynching a Black outside the Conway County courthouse—after a life's reflection said:

> In the Civil War the Negroes who crowded into Union lines were made to order for the role of scapegoat. The treatment that they often received at the hands of their liberators marks some of the darkest pages of war history.

Or, as so many others would echo, like Richard Taylor that:

> The world cannot properly estimate the fortitude of the Southern people unless it understands and takes account of the difficulties of under which they labored. Yet, great as were their suffering during the war, they were as nothing compared to those inflicted upon them after its close.

And didn't the bondsmen welcome their "liberators" in Blue? If so, why did it shock so that only one in five, like Septimus, fled while the other four remained, or, of equal amazement, that they did not want the crops destroyed, the houses and cabins burned, or their masters murdered, but insisted instead that these were "our crops," "our houses," and "our cabins," and often as not, "our White folks." In this they seemed to say that like the Russian peasant unserfed in '62, we may belong to you but you and your land belong to us—to possess is always to be possessed and to be possessed is always to possess—and so the South was then and now thus ever possessed in a concentric circle that it has never quite been understood.

But some questions were simple. How would they live? Where would they go? What would they do now? Blacks wanted freedom, of course, but also they needed and wanted land, and, in the end, got only half of one and very little of the other. But they never wanted revenge and took little against property and almost none against people. The Haitian volcano did not erupt. Why? Because the South and Haiti were similar without being the same, the South was less of a suppression, though it was that, of course, than a slowly evolving symbiosis,

PHILLIP H. MCMATH

which, in all its ambivalent complexity, was never seen so by Blue and only half so by the Gray. And, in blindly trodding in upon it, the ignorant invaders could only disturb it into a different but equally complex and in some ways even more unjust "Reconstruction."

The North made the mistake of thinking the races were enemies, but they were not, not really, though every effort was made to make them so; and at times, as at Poison Springs, Fort Pillow, Jenkins's Ferry, and then during Reconstruction it seemed that they had succeeded in setting one color against the other.

Woodward says it better:

> The ironic thing about the two great hyphenated minorities, Southern-Americans and Afro-Americans, confronting each other on their native soil for three and a half centuries, is the degree to which they have shaped each other's destiny, determined each other's isolation, shared and molded a common culture. It is, in fact, impossible to imagine the one without the other and quite futile to try.

It was not that few White Southerners owned any slaves or that fewer wished to. Many, like Lee and Cleburne, who stayed loyal to the Confederacy, longed for slavery's elimination, while some few Blacks and more Indians were themselves owners of men. But of the masters, most, though not all, were good people who offered paternalism as justification both to themselves and to the world with a sincere sense of "Christian duty"—and, of course, too, for the other, more obvious motive of preserving the institution for their own profit.

So by 1860 all agreed that materially, at least, the Southern slave was superior to all the Russian serfs, most of the European, and many of Europe's workers. And, in America, the comparison was favorable to much of so-called free labor and most of the Irish.

This fruit of paternalism was eagerly accepted by the slave, but for different reasons; first, as an obvious and ready improvement; second, as "his due" for work done and liberty lost; and, third, as leverage for great the thing implicit in it—emancipation—which was always an amelioration touching its logical conclusion.

Septimus Reymonde fled then, not from any ill treatment (though, of course, some did) or want, but from the simple and very understandable desire not to be the property of another. But, finding himself in the shivering liberty of an empty Tillerman cabin, Septimus soon saw that one remains bonded to whatever sack of rotten potatoes happens to fill the belly.

Ezra Adams, a former slave, summed it up.

> De slaves on our plantation didn't stop workin' for old marster, even when dey was told dey was free. Us didn't want no more freedom than as was gittin' on our plantation already. Us knowed too well dat us was well took care of, wid plenty of vittles to eat and log and board houses to live in. De slaves, where I lived, knowed after de war they had abundance of dat somethin' called freedom, what they could not eat, wear and sleep in. Yes, sir, they soon found out dat freedom ain't nothin' 'less you is got somethin' to live on and a place to call home. Dis livin' on liberty is lak young folks livin' on love after they gits married. It just don't work.

Put another way, Southern slavery gave the African bread while it took his freedom, and Northern liberation gave him freedom while withholding his bread. It was, indeed, an "unfinished revolution."

But in its paternalism the South was in reality half-blindly evolving toward its other symbiotic self, not something foreign, nor even toward an implacable enemy as some feared, and many, like Billy Jack, fervently believed, but toward the endemic other half of its own culture and consciousness; toward an inevitable, if slow, resolution of the excruciating contradiction of the Christian assertion of human value and its simultaneous reification as property. Hence, the hysteria of the "Fire Eaters," who, seeing as they did the moribundity of slavery in the Border and Upper South, spreading ever deeper toward them, used Northern abolition to light the flames of secession as a stanching and ever-desperate cure.

Yet what the South was offering in 1860 was far too slow for a Northern revolutionary engine that just had no patience with Mansfield's hope of evolutionary waiting. And in the event, while Lincoln's political genius saved a Union that his ambition almost destroyed, he brought nothing to the South in the end but suffering and destruction. Problem was, he knew it. And it was this knowing that frowns out from the ever-grieving, ever-aging face of care that the photos so painfully show. But, as he always said, he would make it right in the end; would round off the edges in those four remaining years after Septimus and Joshua had at last crossed the Saline. And he knew that this would be the hardest and the most important task of all, and without him, it could only be left to those least equipped to take it in hand.

In their time of travail that fell upon them, the Southern people of all races, if they could but lift their heads the other way, that is, to the North, could see from the remnants of their own devastation, a view of a vastly different scene.

The other half of that compact of which had made such terrible war upon them was now booming, not by the sound of cannon but in the blooming boon of peace. There were no burned cities, no broken roads or rails, no lost crops, nor closed banks, and a working class of immigrants was readily laboring for easy exploitation and ever coming in boatloads from Europe to be used in the simplest terms of work and money.

Here were expanding industries, improvements, roads, canals, prosperous farms, and newly tracked railroads that chugged people and their things from town to country and ever westward to new virgin land and back again. Telegraphs linked cities and cables continents to carry their words, while newspapers, books, universities, and schools opened their minds.

Within five years of Lee's surrender every industrial record was broken by the side he surrendered to, while his old agrarian nation stagnated in the distress of defeat, his enemy's steel was forged, its coal dug, copper mined, textiles spun, oil refined, flour milled, hogs and cattle slaughtered, shipped, and eaten, lumber sawed and nailed and made into great new cities as output increased by 80 percent and the value of its goods by a hundred. Fortunes and dynasties were bred into a new aristocracy of heroes; a pantheon not based upon courage but upon capital.

The South could canonize her heroes in gray and gold—from the cannon of war and defeat and lost victories—Lee, Jackson, Longstreet, Stewart, Forrest, Shelby, Taylor, and Cleburne, but they arose from the glorious pages of a bitter past, while the North sanctified her new heroes in the black and white of the fresh, quick pages of the daily news—of peace and victory and prosperity—with names like Vanderbilt, Harriman, Rockefeller, Stanford, Swift, Armour, and Carnegie as the new "knights of industry" who led a triumphant army of money to a great "Gilded Age."

Germany and Japan would get rebuilt, but the South got "Reconstructed," then, like a half-mad, penurious second cousin, she got pushed out of sight, down the stairs, and into the basement of the American Second Republic. But first, never let it be forgotten, she had to be punished. In '66, Isaac Murphy, the hero from the hills who caught the Blue bouquet from the lady in the gallery and the wartime governorship from Lincoln, tossed by wire across half the country to Little Rock, soon found himself facing a Confederate legislature of Democrats who called themselves "Conservatives."

These soldiers came not in their erstwhile defeat but in a newfound, caustic victory. First, they voted their veterans pensions and new limbs and stipends for their widows; secondly, they stood and hollered "nay" to that centerpiece of the new Republic, the Fourteenth Amendment, which in effect repealed the Tenth; and, under the urgings of one Jeremiah Mansfield, himself a sleeve-pinned and powerful member of his Dallas County delegation, voted out of committee a resolution of thanks to President Davis for his "leadership during the war."

This same derisive shout was hurrahed by all of Arkansas's rebellious sisters, and it was heard across the land and by our old friend Thaddeus, who, over Johnson's veto, disenfranchised them all eleven; prorogued their legislatures and constitutions as "illegal"; gave their ex-slaves the vote (while it was still denied in the North); ordered new elections and new constitutions; required the ratification of the Fourteenth Amendment upon pain of "readmission" and set them under a Blue military dictatorship commanded by a brigadier or better.

Then the Grays yelled a retort: Why do we need to petition for "readmission" since the war has proven we never left? And if truly "out," then our leaving was legal, and you were wrong, which you now implicitly admit; and, if "out," then how can we ratify anything not being a state, much less number fourteen, which we have already rejected? And, if "in," and coequal, there is no need to petition for anything and surely your sacred Constitution is not amended by bayonets? It is you who are acting unconstitutionally! Our legislatures are our business and our constitutions cannot be changed by Congress! See! So we never left, the slaves are free, your precious Union saved, you have won, it is settled, and there is nothing more to discuss! Take your army away and give us our rights, and we can live in peace as fellow countrymen!

Lincoln had said that such arguments were "metaphysical" but it was precisely over such metaphysics that he had made war in the first place. But soon it did not matter. He was gone and Johnson overridden, so Thaddeus's army rattled its bayonets louder and louder till new "elections" were held, new "constitutions" written, as the carpetbaggers, scalawags, and ex-slaves saddled in, riding upon the semi-dictatorship of Governor/General Powell Clayton who rode in behind Murphy in '68, now with his own "Unionist" (Republican) assembly, of which Joshua replaced Jeremiah as a member and said "yes" to number fourteen and all the Grays again were outcast.

The Republicans were there for justice, Union, and freedom, they said, but also for cheap land, newly laid rails, and fresh cotton for the "Satanic Mills" of Merry England Old and New. From this speculation Clayton bought *Linwood* at a bargain for his Rebel bride and manned it with "leased" Black labor to prime the boiler of his railroads till he carriaged from Lincoln Avenue as governor to that Washington near Maryland and thence to Mexico with his own Charlotte; rising ever higher as confidant and friend to presidents of two countries, Grant, Hayes, Harrison, McKinley, Roosevelt, and Taft in one, and Profirio Díaz in another, who had helped put in and then followed Benito Juárez, as Mexican despotism followed freedom through the door of yet another failed constitution.

None of this was easy. With the un-vetoing of the Union Democrat Johnson, the Republicans won something they could not count away by voice or a show of raised hands—the sound of strange men on horses riding through the night with covered faces, with torches and guns and hanging ropes, so that the governor/general met them with "militias" of Blacks led by Yankee or scalawag Whites and the new war was on—or the old one never really stopped.

In this clash soon rose the moans of murder, rape, and plunder as the Klu Klux Klan, freshly arisen from Tennessee, "fought back"—and all excesses against one race were set against it and those against the other set to the militia. "Reconstructing the South" soon swung to the tune of the alarm of guns and noose as vote stealing became *de rigueur* in a strife that rode upon fear and bitterness under the lash of disappointment and desperation.

Then Tilden beat Hayes, but a deal was struck so the loser could raise his hand, and Reconstruction ended. Then Joshua quickly left his seat and Jeremiah plopped down behind again as White Supremacy marched in. It was called "Redemption," riding in upon the coattails of a Democrat named Augustus Garland, a smart lawyer married to a gentle lady from Old Washington, herself raised by a slave who had stood faithfully behind in her parlor under the portrait of a father who kept the slave but gave away the daughter, his picture still seen today, smiling down upon so propitious a match to such a fine counselor who so obviously was leaving for elsewhere to counsel others—the erstwhile Confederate senator and advisor to Davis, and after Appomattox, like a sensible advocate, he sued for himself and the South to win (5–4 among the Robes) for his rights in *Ex Parte Garland,* a victory without a shot of ball or blood, as important as any other for his Cause.

Our Augustus, followed hard upon the brief coup d'état of erstwhile "Governor" Brooks and the short interregnum of Baxter, the old North Carolina Unionist slave owner who, one supposes for not hanging him when they had the chance, now winked at the Democrats and left the gate open behind with the vote to give Garland Powell's old chair. Now Garland could, within a term, follow the carpetbagging general once again, but staying on the train this time at Richmond, he rode a little more up the line, covering with amazing quickness the distance that once had been so dear and so fatally far for so many. He soon arrived at the other Washington and senate of a country we call the United States, in her new Republic, to advise yet another president, a Democrat called Cleveland, not a lawyer, but a fat middle-aged sheriff from Albany who once did his own hanging and now hung a Garland in his cabinet as attorney general because he needed a Confederate deputy to ride with him South of the Mason-Dixon to find a few White votes.

In this way the Confederacy sent her men to take Washington as they never could before, and even Missouri fell at last as she sent General Marmaduke riding off to seize Jeff City like Pap Price failed to do and Ambassador Clayton, like Jo Shelby, Dagmar Pilgrim, and James Mansfield, retreated to Mexico to recoup the vain hope of fighting yet again.

For sure, none of this was what Washington, Hamilton, and Madison had in mind when they chatted and scribbled that time upon the Delaware and Schuylkill; nor Lincoln nor Grant when they talked and fought upon the Potomac; nor Lee, or even Jefferson Davis, when they did the same upon the James, but it is indeed what happened on either side of the Mississippi and the Río Grande.

How could this have happened to what they had dreamed as becoming something else? Where had it all gone awry?

> Sovereignty is the highest degree of political power, and the establishment of a form of government, the highest proof which can be given of its existence. The states could not have reserved any rights by articles of their union, if they had not been sovereign, because they could have no rights, unless they flowed from that source. In the creation of the federal government, the states exercised the highest act of sovereignty, and they may, if they please, repeat the proof of their sovereignty, by its annihilation. But the union possesses no innate sovereignty, like the states; it is not self-constituted; it is conventional, and of course subordinate to the sovereignties by which it was formed.

It would have been hard to find a Founding Father who would have disagreed much with Virginian John Taylor's assertion of what they thought they had done and dreamed of in those propitious days at Philadelphia.

Indeed, Jefferson and Madison, in the "Virginia-Kentucky Resolution," insisted that what they had done and dreamed allowed the states to protect themselves from tyranny by disobeying what was unconstitutional. Moreover,

PHILLIP H. MCMATH

they had appended the Tenth Amendment, which reserved to the States all powers not specifically granted to the Federal government, as the "foundation of the Constitution," Jefferson explained.

It was to be the keystone. But fourteen trumps ten, and the "foundation" of the First Republic was no longer the "foundation" for the Second.

But approval of Fourteenth, some still insist (take away the gunpoint votes and it fails), was illegal. This is idle. War, our eternal "midwife of history," is also its mortician, and had buried the old dream to give birth to the new. It was, in a word, a revolution of violence and not consent; and by its blood it blotted out forever the old "foundation"—John Taylor's sovereignty of 1789 written in as the number 10, was therefore forever struck off the page— "parchment walls collapsing."

What is sovereignty? Is it not the power to compel willing, *internal* consent of the governed? Not an *external* consent bought by fear, but a willing consent that men recognize as legitimate, however burdensome or unjust. A true king may be hated, but his authority is never in doubt.

Sovereignty, then, must come in the end from something bigger than men themselves. They will not respect what they alone create and can only willingly bow to some idea of providential omnipotence and grace—but not downward to weak Man upon the earth, for whom they have self-contempt, but upward toward God and his sun. It was from this the colonies derived their sovereign life—as the king's property—partially loaned to them upon his authority in the New Kingdom.

But a king's sovereignty, or the First Sovereignty, if you will, was destroyed by America and France in revolution, leaving the former with but a diffuse, Second Sovereignty, as a derivative from the First, and, after her king's fall, France was left with none at all.

Yet, in America for unity's sake, and in France for substitution, each made an alliance with a Third, or new, "People's Sovereignty" or "Popular Sovereignty." This, it was claimed, arose from "Natural Law" and therefore was likewise legitimized by providence, without which, everyone acknowledged, no true sovereignty of any kind exists at all.

In this way is understood John Adam's insistence on "Divine Providence" and Jefferson's declaration of the "Truths to be self-evident" that were "endowed by their *Creator* with certain unalienable rights"—a new and workable providential imprimatur was offered for the problem of legitimacy as well as a self-conscious nullification of "Divine Right" with "Divine Liberty." In a word, Man for King but not Man for God.

Yet, the States, nevertheless, having destroyed the unity of the First Sovereignty, found themselves in need of inventing a new unifying head upon which to place something, but not quite, like a crown. A president was born, striding forth rather like an ersatz king, not in robes but in breeches, and Washington would do nicely because he seemed to wear the latter like the former. But, it was insisted, his power must arise from and be limited by some fading ink scribbled upon Thaddeus's old parchment that invented co-equal but "balanced" and "checked" branches governing the unifying but "limited" new Federal power. It seemed a stroke.

Thus the First Sovereignty is set down by the Executive sitting in for a King, and is lifted heavenward a bit by electors from out of the popular muck; and as for the Second, there would be a Senate for the States, chosen by their assemblies, not quite heavenward but still somewhere above the ground; and then there's the lowly, earth-bound House, the democratic, Third Sovereignty, directly picked by the People, from out of the mud, if they liked, or by the mob, if they wished.

Yet there was to be another, an additional creature, the unelected life-tenured judiciary; sitting like stern bishops in black, ruling as a kind of Fourth Estate, an elite that, under the Second Republic, would in time limit the First, usurp the Second, and dictate to the Third through the power of the Fourteenth Amendment with a political potion that was never dreamed of by anyone, even those like Joshua who had shouted "yea" and not "nay" like Jeremiah to its ratification.

But it did not quite fit. No nation (and there are few true nations), to echo the immortal Joseph de Maistre from his seat in St. Petersburg where he gazed with horror upon the monstrous face of modernity, "can ever have a constitution that it does not already possess." And, since it must arise from a collective, if unconscious, understanding that is *antecedent* to its creation, the more it must be written, the weaker it becomes. Every line diminishes and every amendment leads it ever closer to a crumpling into the trash of time.

And, as for presidents, they never quite do; are always a little too much the fish of a king and never enough the fowl of a prime minister, or the reverse, what you will. They sit, or seem to sit, as slightly ridiculous, somewhat tattered politicians upon a golden stool pretending that their feet are not in fact touching the ground.

In truth then, America, in decapitating its First Sovereignty, was left with a sovereignty of thirteen tatters that were then sewn together till they were shredded again by the most vicious of civil wars, and France, poor France, was left with none at all and fell with the head of her king into the basket of chaos and the catastrophe of Bonapartism, and Gaulism, its bastard child.

From 1791 until 1795, the French National Assembly, the Legislative Assembly, and the National Convention labored forth two constitutions and 15,479 laws. But they were able to create only Robespierre and the Corsican. It's the same, everywhere and always, whether Left or Right, of this time or the next, of Lenin or Louis Napoleon, into a vacuum despotism needs must march with the infernal stench of illegitimacy hanging like a soiled cloak upon its back no matter what posture of glory or pretense of goodness it may have crowned upon its head by pope or proletariat.

Yet the British? Why is the British constitution immortal? Because as a *natural antecedent* it is deathless, and in its wordlessness is un-needful of any superfluous scratching upon a page. It could no more be hatched out by an assembly of politicians than could its language, its common law, or its literature be made by a din of shouts, votes, and niggling, committee-sitting lawyers. It is the Sovereign Crown of Tradition and Time set carefully upon the brow of the Popular Will, and nothing less.

But, too, Britain is not a sham, not a false nation, with false laws and failed constitutions that live shorter lives than the fools who create them. Those are mere self-conscious pieces of paper that arise from nothing, are illegitimate, and are quickly tossed aside by History into the can with all the rest.

America was somehow in between, not yet quite great or even grand, but was a collection of thirteen little legitimacies with a greater ambition than simply to remain small—a collective idea, which, however vague, already existed as a unifying thought. But in this ambition there was a flaw. Like their erstwhile king, who, in giving a pound of sovereignty, rather than lending much more than a penny of autonomy, had thereby Lost a Kingdom, they did not see that power once given is never ever willingly returned, and that sovereignty is ever jealous and, like a lover, does not happily share its beloved with another.

So, in enthroning a federalization in place of a Crown, however "limited" they wished it to be, the states had unwittingly created not a friend but a foe who quickly saw its creator as a rival—a political *ménage à trois* between two governments and the people—unhappily matured with the lust for power as its beloved object and its curse.

It would, of course, come to blood, as most great things do, not over slavery that was but its device, but over this inevitable political passion. Or, as one has said another way so well, "the fundamental cause of the war was a difference of views on the matter of sovereignty, but the immediate occasion was the matter of slavery."

Thus, the First Revolution destroyed the First Sovereignty; the Second, the Second; and the Third, for the moment at least, now stands in unsteady triumph upon the ruins of each.

BOOK SEVEN

CHAPTER THIRTY-FOUR

"History is the process of resurrection ..."
—*N. Fyordorov,* Philosophy of the Common Task

The reporter came in the hotel bar and sat down tiredly upon a faded red stool. It was a hot late summer day in 1941. The war news interrupted the radio music crackling away but he wasn't listening. Without asking, the bartender scooted a mug of beer forward, the foam drooling from either side, but the reporter didn't touch it. Instead, almost in one motion, he loosened his tie, took off his Fedora, plopped it on an empty seat, then, seeing a white napkin with *The Marion* gold printed on a corner, pushed it near the beer. He paused, studied the foam, then with a certain, if somewhat odd, pleasure, lifted the beer and gently set it down on the napkin. But still he did not drink.

"How are things, Brady?" he asked, his hands gripping the mug loosely.

"Fine," said the bartender, wiping the spillage with a dirty rag, getting close to the napkin without quite touching it.

"Turned off hot, huh?"

"Right," Brady said, tossing the rag into some secret out-of-sight spot and rubbing his hands on the apron worn over a short-sleeve shirt. "We'll have a couple a-more weeks yet ... then it'll break ... it's always the same in September," he added, "ever'one wonders ... complains ... an' it's always the same. August is over but it's still hell in Arkansas."

The reporter turned his eyes down again to the beer and, as if studying it, hesitated for a moment longer, then gripped the mug tighter and gingerly, almost ceremoniously, lifted it slowly to his lips and drank deeply.

"You got the best brew in town, Brady ... you know that?" he said, lowering it delicately onto the napkin, arranging it underneath.

The bartender smiled, leaned back against the counter, and lit a cigarette.

"You always say that, Jake."

"That's cause it's still true."

Behind Brady, just above his head, a very long, fierce-looking fish swam in a tank of dirty greenish water, back and forth, back and forth, in a monotonously futile search for escape, turning and swimming, turning and swimming, back and forth, propelled only by the slightest movement of his tail.

"Brady?" asked the reporter, after watching this ritual with an almost hypnotic fascination, "tell me, what the hell do you feed that gar, huh?"

The bartender smiled even broader, like a hitter seeing a curve hanging above the plate, then powering it over the fence, he said, "I feed 'im wise-ass, nosy reporters who ask dumb questions ... that's whut."

The reporter laughed loudly, then drank again, only with less ceremony, almost without thinking.

"Come on ... what the hell do you feed that poor bastard?" he said, mopping idly with the wet napkin, then wadding and dropping it into an ashtray where it slowly unfolded into the gray ash.

"He don't eat nothin', Jake ... he just swims round an' round ... without stopping ... backerds an' farerds ... you know, a-lookin' for a way out ... always lookin' but not findin' it ... like most damn people I know ..., 'specially the ones that come in this place an' get all good and snockered a-lookin' at him for hours an' hours on end 'cause they ain't got nothin' else better to do with their dirty rotten lives ... and, like him, just cain't find no way out. But he's too damn busy to eat. I ain't ever seen 'im eat a damn thang ... he just ain't interested ... he just circles and circles."

"Come on ... as long as you've been here ... you must've seen him eat something for Christ's sakes," said Jake, pulling a fresh napkin from the pile and slipping it smoothly under the beer.

"The night shift feeds 'im ... I never work nights ... ask them."

There was silence then Jake asked, "How long's he been in there?"

"Long? Hell, Jake, I don't know ... he was in that filthy damn tank when I got here ... that's been two years 'r better ... no doubt he'll be there long after I hit the road."

"He's an institution, Brady ... that's what he is ... a goddamn institution," said Jake, as the alcohol touched his brain, lifting his mood into laughter.

"A whut?" Brady said, exhaling smoke as a defense screen.

"He's an institution in this place ... hell, in the whole damn town ... they'd declare a day of mourning if anything ever happened to 'im. It be front page ... black borders and all ... we'd have to write a big damn obit like a big-shot croaking or something," Jake said, drinking and chuckling at his own wit, feeling better all the time.

Now Brady, catching the joke, laughed. "You're right, Jake ... if he died they have to shut this crummy bar down ... or sneak a new one in on the night shift

... but, if it was up to me, I'd throw 'im in the river where he belongs and give 'im a damn break."

"You wouldn't be doing him no favors, Brady ... the biguns'd snap his ass up for sure ... there's some monsters in that son-of-a bitch, they say ... some real monsters."

"Maybe ... but I bet he'd go for it, don't you reckon? Wouldn't you? Make a break if you had half a chance? I mean, what's he got to lose," Brady said, sticking the Lucky Strike to his lips, turning and looking at the gar. Then he turned around, saying with an exhale, "Shit, I seen that damn thang so long it gives me a headache."

Jake laughed.

"Want another one?"

"Sure," said Jake, finishing in a gulp, pushing the empty forward, as he waited for the refill to slide across.

"You think our other fish is coming ... Mr. Smith ... what's his first name again?" Jake asked, looking at his watch.

"Gurston ... Gurston Smith ...,"said Brady, emptying the ashtray and setting it near the reporter.

"You figger he's gonna show, right?" Jake said, putting a fresh napkin under the beer.

"He'll show ... but he's kinda funny ... careful you don't lose 'im."

"I'll do my best ... rich, you say?"

"He ain't worried 'bout nothin' ... I'll put it that way."

"Real estate? Isn't that what you told me?"

"He's in it all."

A young man came and sat a few stools down. Brady waited on him, returned, and shook his head at Jake. Soon a very attractive woman came and sat with the young man. He bought her a beer, and they retreated to a booth in the corner.

The radio music replaced an advertisement with "I'm Crazy about My Baby" crooning away, but no one seemed to notice.

"Things are picking up," said Jake with a smile, fiddling with the napkin's edge then tearing it into a little ball and dropping it into the ashtray.

"Yeah ... they're new ... I don't know 'em," Brady said, studying the couple with a squint through the bar's half-light. "They ain't guests."

"How do you know?"

"Guests like them two always come in together ... they're meetin' ... they ain't got a room."

"Not yet," said Jake with a wink.

"Yeah ... I'd hate to think it's going to waste," Brady said, looking down and busying himself with envy while washing a few glasses.

In a few minutes, two young men came in and Brady took care of them and, a moment later, an older man walked in.

"Here's Smith," Brady whispered urgently with a nod, pretending to be busy.

Jake Storns swung around on the stool then got up as Smith approached with a confident stride. Brady introduced them and they shook hands.

"Can I buy you a beer, Mister Smith?" asked Storns.

"Call me Gurston ... no, thanks, a co'cola'll do."

"Bottle, right ... with a straw?" asked Brady.

"Thanks," Smith said, pleased.

After Brady handed him the coke with a straw sticking out, Storns said, "Let's go to a booth ... huh?"

"Sure," said Smith, following him to a stall two empties down from the couple.

Sitting opposite, they exchanged pleasantries as Southerners often do, that is, avoiding the business at hand, chatting about the weather, sports, in this case, baseball (they liked the Cardinals but didn't think they'd win the pennant), a little harmless local politics, and, finally, the war in Europe. Storns thought Russia would fold eventually, like France, and Smith said they'd "find a way to hang on." But both agreed it was just "a matter of time till we got in it," as Storns put it, adding, with a knowing air to Smith's nod, "that's what Roosevelt really wants, but he just cain't say so yet."

At this, Brady, on his way to taking the whispering couple two more beers, dropped off Storns's Fedora with some snacks. Then he went over to the radio, sliding over stations, till he found some soft swing that seemed to glide to the easy rhythm of the swimming, turning fish in the tank.

Storns, at last, himself tired of circling, and sensing the moment was right, decided to drop in a hook.

"I understand you're from Dallas County?" he said bravely, watching the question sink a bit.

Smith, as if anxious to follow it, said, "I left when I wuz a boy ... my dad come here to find work ... he weren't no farmer ... his folks wuz kindly rough ... livin' in the backwoods farmin' an' huntin' but I grew up here mostly ... graduated from Little Rock High," he said proudly.

Storns looked at him a little more closely. Gurston Smith seemed about forty, and he wore a neat, expensive but conservative cotton suit and a broad tie knotted tightly despite the heat. He was large and burly, with thick black hair, brown skin, and deep blue eyes that pierced from under a furrowed brow.

"Ever go back?"

"Oh, sure ... I got kin there ... I see 'em regular. Why?"

"Well, I'm a reporter ..."

"Yeah ... Brady said as much ... for the *Gazette?*"

"Right ... well ... see ... I've ... we've been doin' a little piece every Sunday ... on our history ... a special you might say ... have you seen it?"

Gurston nibbled the snacks and sipped his coke through the straw. "I musta read over it ..."

"Well, the editor, my boss, thought ... well, you know ... with war clouds gathering and all ... we're gonna need heroes real soon ... that folks might be interested in the heroes of our very own past ... as examples ... see, right here in Arkansas ... the frontier wars ... Indians ... Texas ... Mexico ... the War Between the States ... Spanish American ... and the Great War ... all of them ... you know, patriotism ... leading up to what's happening now ... and, like you say, is surely comin' ... 'Arkansans at War' that was the title ... see?" he said, waving his hand a little above his head.

Gurston Smith watched the hand impassively, didn't speak but just kept nibbling and drinking, waiting for some more attractive bait to flop in the water.

"Well, anyway, we're doing the state section by section ... period by period ... and we're up to the War Between the States and I'm gonna do south Arkansas ... Steele and all that ... that's my beat for this little piece ... always been sort of interested in history myself ... and I got to to diggin' round and I found a fella named Jeremiah Mansfield ... found out he was in the famous '66 legislature from Dallas County ... you know, the bunch that caused ole Isaac Murphy so much trouble before they took the vote away from the Rebs. The guy was a one-armed veteran ... a Confederate ... a sure 'nuff real Arkansas hero and leader in those days ... and ... well ... one thing led to another and I found out later that he had a brother killed serving with Pat Cleburne over in Tennessee ... another real hero in the family. And I got to snoopin' some more and heard about you. Brady says he's known you awhile, and you might be able to tell me more about Dallas County, might be able to help me out some ..."

"Oh, yeah, Brady and I 're good friends ... I sold his brother a house ... 'bout a year or so ago."

"You ever hear of this Jeremiah Mansfield fella?" Storns asked, sipping the beer then leaning forward a bit, feeling a little uncomfortable with this cool, collected Coke drinker.

"Heard of 'im, you say?" said Smith, as if a little deaf, which he wasn't.

"Yeah, sure … I understand he's kind of famous down there."

Gurston forced a smile. "Oh, yeah … I've heard of 'im … you're right … most down in Dallas County has … they all know the Mansfields, they come into that country before the war … as I thank you know."

"Lots of them still down there, right?"

"Sure … lots of 'em …"

There was a pause. Storns felt Smith was playing with the bait without wanting to swallow it, so he decided to jiggle it a little. "Can you tell me something about this man Jeremiah… know anything about him at all? I mean he's a real interesting fella … and you can't always get what you need out of a history book or an old newspaper … I mean, historians put the skeleton of things out there but they usually leave out the heart, if you know what I mean … that's what I'm interested in, Gurston, the heart and soul of it. Can you help with that at all … any at all? I mean, the ole veterans are all gone now and we need real-life personal-interest stories from somewhere, huh, what do you say?"

Gurston Smith stared closely at Jake Storns, hesitated a little, finished the Coke with a sucking sound, set it aside, then said, "Well, see … Jeremiah … he … he was my grandmother's brother … Granny Megan … Megan Smith … my dad's mother's brother. Uncle Jed the older kids called 'im, but he died jes afore I was born and, o'course, I never knew 'im none."

Storns tried not to sigh out loud then he reeled hard as he could for almost half an hour but couldn't land him. Finally, the whispering couple left and Jake Storns was nearly drunk with Gurston's evasions and circling.

"But look … Storns," Gurston said finally, a little tired of the fun. "I don't know this story nearly as good as ole Uncle Joe Boy," he allowed at last. "Why don't you ask him?"

"Ole Uncle Joe Boy? Who's that?" Jake said, astonished.

"Yeah, like I said … Uncle Jed died a little afore I wuz born … an' Granny Megan didn't hardly like to talk about it much … but Uncle Joe Boy's Uncle Jed's younger brother … he knows it all … ever bit of it and he's good at tellin' it."

"You mean to tell me your uncle Jeremiah Mansfield's got a brother that's still livin'?"

"Yeah … he's up-per a ways though … in his high eighties somewheres, nearly blind an' all … but he's still sharp … loves to talk an' he could tell a lot more an' better than I ever could. To tell you the truth, I never paid that much 'tention to it …"

"Where does your Uncle Joe Boy live?"

"On The Place … he stays there with my ole maid sister who keeps house for 'em both. I own it now … jest to keep it in the family an' all … but it belonged to my great-grand-pappy…Hardy … Hardy G. Mansfield … the G. is for Gurston … Granny Megan's paw … he come in to that country from Kentucky an' Missouri… settled in the fifties … nen the war come along … as you know … he's buried there in the family plot along with his wife, Mary, Uncle Jed, an' an aunt of mine, Granny Megan's daughter, Aint Clare, named for one of Hardy's sisters I think it was … Granny Megan ain't buried there … she's a-layin' with her husband, my grandfather, next to him in the ole Smith cemetery … an' my dad an' mother along with 'em … they wanted to go back home and be with all the folks for eternity … but Aint Clare she wanted to be buried with the Mansfields for some reason. Oh, too, there's a dawg … he's in there too … in his own little spot."

"A dog?!" gushed Storns.

"Yeah … named Toughy … he was Uncle Joe Boy's a way back yonder … he never had no family of his own an' he wanted that dawg buried there … he's got a headstone an' ever'thang …," laughed Gurston. "Uncle Joe Boy … is real sentimental 'bout thangs … an' a little crazy … but you need to talk to him … he knows a lot more an' that, and like I say, he's a heap better at tellin' it."

"When can I see him?"

"What you doin' tomorrow?"

"Tomorrow?"

"Sure."

"It would be a pleasure, Mr. Smith, … er, Gurston."

They shook their goodbyes and Storns went to the bar to pay.

"How'd it go?" Brady grinned.

"Pure gold, Brady, pure goddamn gold," Storns said, putting the Fedora on the back of his head and fumbling out money.

"Good … I'm glad," Brady said, making change.

"No change," said Storns putting up a hand. "Keep it … you earned it, pal … but someday you're going to tell me what y'all feed that poor damn fish, okay? I gotta know, promise?"

Brady pocketed the change.

"If you wanna know so bad, I'll tell ye what we feed 'im right now."

"Okay, what then? Come clean, Brady. No crap. Huh, whatta you feed 'im?"

"Hell, Jake, we feed 'im fish food."

"Wise guy," Storns said with a laugh, turned and headed for the door.

The radio played Duke Ellington's "The Rose of the Rio Grande," as the reporter disappeared into the heat and the whispering couple got a room.

As for Brady the bartender, he lit a fresh Lucky and fed the fish. In the spring, he went to sea like he always wanted and drowned off Novia Scotia after his ship was torpedoed.

Gurston picked Jake up in his new De Soto sedan. It was as hot as ever but the rolled-down windows helped once they got rolling along the blacktop.

They wore lightweight cotton suits with Fedora hats but Storns loosened his tie and folded his coat onto the back seat.

"We'll be there in a few hours," said Gurston, shifting the column gear and driving in silence. Sensing Gurston's reticence, Storns said little. After they got out of town Gurston set his hat on the seat and loosened his tie. This seemed to mark a change so Storns fell into the error of trying a few pleasantries, like in the Gar Hole.

"Cards won yesterday," Storns ventured.

"Yeah ... I caught the last inning on the radio," Gurston said.

"But they don't win on the road like they should. What's the old saying, win at home and play five hundred on the road," Storns said, forcing a smile.

"Right ... sounds easy."

Storns talked some more about baseball without much comment from Gurston, who finally said, "You hang out much at the Marion, Jake? ... that your beat?"

"Some ... it's where the action is .... I mean, the truth is, Brady's got the slow shift but it jumps at night and there's always something going on upstairs ... the lobby is where it's at ... if you'll just sit and listen. You ever hear of Spider Rowland, the columnist?"

"Yeah ... sure."

"Ever read 'im?"

"Some."

"Well, I'll tell you a little secret ... ole Spider ... he'll pretend to be drunk ... or asleep ... or something ... up in the lobby, I mean ... kinda slumped over in a chair ... there, you know right smack dab in the middle of everything ... with his eyes shut and all ... listening ... see, folks will talk ... chatter ... all kinds of stuff around 'im ... that's how he gets most of his scoop. Go in there some time and watch 'im ... it's funny as a barrel of monkeys ...," Storns said, trying to get a laugh out of Gurston by slapping his thigh.

Gurston did laugh, but only politely.

"Yeah ... it's the truth ... ole Spider says the whole damn state is run in the Marion Hotel ... in the lobby ... in its rooms ... the restaurant ... the bar ... in its beds ..."

Now Gurston's laugh was nervous.

"Ever try the buffalo in the restaurant upstairs?" Storns asked, resolving to press on.

"Buffalo meat?" said Gurston, accelerating around an old pickup. "I didn't know they could git any."

"It's the specialty of the house ... a real delicacy ... John ... the Black guy that runs it ... he serves it fried ..."

"Fried buffalo?"

"Yeah ... only it's the fish, not the humped animal with horns ... it's great. I like it better than catfish or anything else that swims ... you ought to order it next time you're in there ... really, it's the best thing in town."

"I will."

Another pause.

"Ole John runs a tight ship ... let me tell you, pal ... he's got a cook back there that'll make you go home and throw nails at your wife," Storns said, laughing uproariously with another knee slap that was followed by another uncomfortable pause. Still, Storns pressed on.

"Whatta you think they feed that gar down in the Gar Hole ... huh?"

"I dunno."

"Fish food ...," said Storns, laughing in a loud silly way.

Gurston drove in an almost sullen silence, passing another car as they crossed into the next county, going south. The country now became heavily wooded with few but very poor houses and an occasional modest farm. They crossed a slough that hardly moves, misnamed Hurricane Creek, drove about ten more miles, then crept through the village of Sheridan, so named after the war, and sped down a highway supported by "bar ditches" pushed up like dikes in a swamp.

Storns was resigned to silence as they bridged a river in just a few seconds.

But now Gurston said gravely, "That there was the Saline. We're in Dallas County now. You're not really into south Arkansas on this road till you've crossed it. We're a-turning here," he said, slowing almost to a stop and turning to the right, the sedan bouncing and rocking as they traded blacktop for gravel.

Gurston loosened his tie even more and said, "Last time I wuz down I told 'em I'd be back today so they're kindly expecting us. Uncle Joe Boy don't go nowhere much anyway ... no, doubt, he'll be jes a-settin' on the front porch rockin' when we drive up."

"What's the home place like?" asked Storns, relieved at Gurston's conversation.

"It's little more than a hun'red acres o' ground ... mixed timber an' cleared land ... I harvest the lumber an' rent the rest to a fella that farms it ..."

"Sharecrop?"

"We don't like to call it that," smiled Gurston. "I mean, he don't live on it ... he has some land of his own, so he don't like to think of hisself as any sharecropper. But I gotta make money on The Place if I can ..."

"Sure."

"Uncle Joe Boy lived there all his life ... inherited it from his paw ... Hardy G. My grandmaw Megan had a share in The Place ... that's what we call it ... The Place ... an' Uncle Jed, 'course, but Uncle Joe bought 'em both out over time ... but nen ... why he got up in years an' he jes couldn't do it no more so I bought it to keep it in the family an' all ... an' to give him an' my aint Clare ... the ole maid, remember? ... a place to live out their days."

"You say Uncle Joe Boy never married?"

"No ... he courted some, folks said ... but basically he just lived there by hisself with his pack of dawgs ... horses an' mules ... he loves most animals ... used to always have a good saddle horse 'r two ... he rode till he jes couldn't get on one no more ... he was great with any kind of animal ... wil' or tame ... an', like I say, he always had a bunch o' dawgs around ... big Walker hounds ... that could run all day ... sometimes they'd catch a deer ... jes run 'em down ... an' some mutts of all kinds ... he'd take care of anything that happened up. Farmed an' hunted ... that's all he done ... or ever wanted to do ... he loved to hunt mor'n anybody I ever saw ... 'less it'd be my grandmaw Megan ... she hunted up till the day she died ... nearly. Lots of time she an' Uncle Joe Boy'd hunt together. She had some great hawg-dawgs ... Blue Ticks mostly ... and a few Red Bones ... she didn't hold with Walkers like Uncle Joe Boy ... they wuz faster but didn't have the nose the other'ns had, she said ... they never settled that argument ... fought over it till she went to her grave," said Gurston, laughing sincerely for the first time, then continued, "an' 'o course, she farmed some ... an' fished ... an' gardened ... they all done that ... slaughtered their own meat ... hawgs an' steers an' deer ... an' lived in nem bottoms pretty much free as you please. But it takes a certain kind to live there ... Grandmaw Megan said 'the bottoms knows its own,' she'd say, and it sure knew her and Uncle Joe Boy."

"As I think I said, this fella she married ... James Smith ... she married into the Smiths ... but nem two together were kindly rough ... even for this country, an' its rough as a cob. And, my paw ... he grew up thatta way, too, but, like I tol' you at the Gar Hole yesterdee, he didn't take to farmin' much ... he kindly wanted something else ... so he left jes as quick as he could. He married a neighbor girl ... my maw ... she an' him were teenage sweethearts an' never dated no one else in their entar lives ... used to sneak off nights an' meet in the woods an' hay barns an' such ... ever'body knowed it an' all ... an' their folks tried to keep 'em apart but it was no use ... cain't fight Mother Nature, as they say ... so they run off an' got married an' moved to Little Rock for work on the Missouri Pacific ... he become an engineer ... had a good job with 'em ... but he retared after thirty years an' they both wanted to come home to Dallas County ... to die, I mean ... to the ole Smith family plot to be buried ... down in Princeton ... it's old ... an' well tended ... each by the other ... with all their folks and all ... an' so I brought 'em ... each in their turn ... within a year of their a-leavin' ... they jes couldn't face the world without the other'n in it ... so, I done that for 'em ... me an' my sister Sarah ... the whole family come. See, my paw, he went over this entar country nearly ... a-ridin' on the railroad ... but I don't think he ever got that bottomland life completely out of his blood ... Maw neither ...Grandmaw Megan put it in her kids pretty good ... she was a sight ... fact-o-the-bidness, I think they'd a-moved back sooner if he didn't have such a good job thar an' all. So, I mean, we come back a lot 'cause my folks never lost touch with their family on either side ... Smiths nor Mansfields ... ever'body gets along pretty good."

"How many children did Grandmaw Megan have?"

"Five ... one died of a fever ... a boy ... Little Hardy they called 'im ... he died when he was about two or thereabouts. He was her first ... nen there was Uncle Johnny, he went in the timber business an' done purtty good here in Fordyce ... James, my paw ... 'n Aint Clare, she's the youngest ... the baby ... who you're fixin' to meet in a little bit ... an' then there's Little Joshua ... the fourth boy."

"Any of them living ... aside from your aunt, I mean?"

"Yeah, Uncle Johnny, he's in his seventies an' o' course retared from his business. As you probably know, after the war, the railroad come thew ... but it bypassed Tulip an' Princeton ... they was pretty good-size towns up to then, but that pretty much kilt 'em ... nen Fordyce ... the railroad town ... sprung up like a weed ... an' Uncle Johnny moved down there for the work ... nen he saved his money an' got into loggin' an' timber ... an' bought hisself a lumber yard. Like I say, he done real well, he an' his wife had a bunch o'kids ... my cousins, o' course, ... they live over there now ... scattered all down thew that end o' the county. Once in a while we'll have a reunion an' I'll see 'em ... our family's still pretty close ... considerin' ..."

"And Little Joshua ... what became of him?"

"Oh, he was kilt in the Great War ... in France. I was a little too young for it ... the Great War, I mean ... an' my paw, he was too old ... but Little Joshua went in the army jes as quick as he could and was making it a career ... he was a sergeant ... ... but he got kilt in '17 ... died for France, as they say ... machine gunned by the Germans, o' course."

"Why for France? Why not for America?"

"What dawg did we have in that hunt? Huh? Tell me that, Jake? It was for France ... the way I look at it ... even though they talked like it was for America and all. I mean the Yankees invaded us ... now that was an invasion, shore 'nuff ... an' upset our country something terrible ... we still ain't got over it ... but the Germans ... when're they gonna get to Arkansas, you think? They'd jes stopped in Paris, don't ye reckon ... an' that'd been that ... it's too bad they didn't take that place when they first started ... in 1914, I mean ... it would've been a lot better ... that'd been the end of the whole damn thang, the way I got it figgered ... an' Little Joshua wouldn't have died like so many of them million or so fine boys ... on both sides ... an' we wouldn't have all this trouble we got now with this crazy bastard Hitler. I mean he never would-a come along now if Germany had-a won then, right?"

Storns laughed in an odd way and could only say, "There were a lot of Germans in the Union army ...," Gurston's point was a surprise, and he was thinking about it.

"Yeah, but they didn't have on no spiked helmets, now did they, Jake," laughed Gurston. "But don't get me wrong ... hell, at the time, I wanted to go so bad I could taste it. I wanted to be a Doughboy ... so did Paw ... but they wouldn't take him 'cause of his age even though he tried to fool 'em ... it's in the blood, I guess ... to go ... we always do ... we Mansfields and Smiths ... and we was shore proud of Little Joshua when he went ... we're still proud of him."

Gurston gathered his breath, went around a very slow model-T, and added, "Anyway, he got married a little afore he left and his wife had a baby ... a boy ... but we ain't seen 'im but once and she ... his wife ... was from up in Ohio somewheres ... a Yankee ... some said that's what comes of marrying one ... anyway, and she didn't stay in touch or nothin' ... never hear from 'em a-tall. I thank she musta remarried or sumpin' ... but we don't know."

"I see," said Storns, wiping the dirty sweat off his brow but glad to listen.

"Losin' Joshua like that ... really ... it put Grandmaw Megan in her grave ... I'll always believe that ... with all she'd seen and the hurt she'd done felt ... with all that had happened to her in the war an' all ... an' in 1919 when that damn flu epidemic come thew the way it done ... after the Great War ... a-carryin' folks off right an' left ... why it took her away, too ... her that ain't ever been sick a day in her life. I'll never forget it ... seein' her in that casket ... in the only nice dress she ever owned, I reckon ... all dressed up pretty like. I stood there lookin' at that ole worn-out face which they'd tried to fix up with makeup an' all ... I mean, on her that ain't never had none on in her entire life ... she still had a certain ... well, grace about her ... they couldn't ruin that ... an' I thought about all she'd seen ... an' done ... an' been thew ... suffered 'n all ... so, I said to her, well, Grandma Megan ... you're a great one, that's for shore ... an' your dyin' is a kind o' victory ... the only victory worth havin' in a fallen world ... that's what I told her standin' there by her before they put her into the cold ground."

Storns was shocked at this unexpected expression of sentiment. This Gurston Smith who came alive after they had crossed the Saline River was not the same laconic Gurston Smith who lived in Little Rock, sold houses, drank Cokes in the Gar Hole from a straw, and wore expensive suits and cinched up ties on hot summer days. Even his speech had changed—his very being seemed transformed south of the Saline.

"I'd like to learn more about her," Storns said, after a few seconds.

"Ask Uncle Joe ... he's good at tellin' her story," Gurston said, looking at Storns with a strange look then back at the road. "But ... the way I figure it ... she died from that war in France jes like Little Joshua done ... I mean, that epidemic was caused an' spread by it, wa'n't it?"

"Right ... Gurston, I read somewhere they figure it killed more people all over the world than the war itself ... the fighting, I mean," Storns added, glad to throw a punch at this guy who had him so off balance.

"Really?" parried Gurston, looking at him again, "I didn't know that ... but I ain't surprised," he said, looking back again, shifting and speeding up under a canopy of leaves that overhung them with a mixture of shade and light. "It's less than an hour now ... The Place, I mean ... we'll pass thew Bismark in a minute ... then to the Tulip-Princeton road," he said, as they left a trail of dust billowing behind like a stream of yellow smoke.

Soon they wound through some shacks at a railroad crossing with the grand name of "Bismark," honoring the founder of the First German Reich and conqueror of Louis Napoleon.

"Tulip's not far," Gurston said, turning right, accelerating. "They almost made it the state capital once," he continued as they rolled into a squat of houses and a Baptist church.

"What? Tulip?"

"It's true ... in the frontier times ... it almost beat out Little Rock ... like I said, this used to be an important place ... killed by the railroad ... this was the main road before that ... down to Camden ... which was a busy river port in them days."

"I had no idea," said Storns, who fancied himself something of an historian of the state.

But Tulip evaporated easily as they turned east again through heavily timbered, field-spotted country interlaced with summer slow streams that they crossed on rickety, rusty iron and wood-planked bridges.

Storns was struck by the lack of people, and, other than a lone car passing behind, he saw no one at all. Oh, there were a few houses and an occasional cabin, but they all, in their way, seemed each stuck in a kind of tree-shaded secret.

Then Gurston, grown mysteriously silent again, surged them over the empty stage of an old drama—Fagan's dereliction, Steele's retreat, Marmaduke's dash—battle and flight—Septimus's escape, Dagmar's rescue, and Joshua's wounding. And behind the De Soto, back to the left, was Princeton where Pap Price had formed an army for his ride into Missouri. Riding easily upon the springs of iron rather than a horse of a conquistador or cavalryman, there seemed now more life in war's death dance than in the dullness of this stolid peace.

In abject silence they plunged ever deeper and through more and more woods and fewer and fewer fields, past fewer and fewer houses. The De Soto bridged at last a dry creek and, though Storns didn't know it, skirted for about "half-a-quarter" the old Tillerman Plantation, which now was a pine forest bordered by bobbed-wire-like briars, standing as backdrop to a cabin and a barn set in gray dilapidation among a field of sunburnt cotton.

"We're not far now," said Gurston, at last, unknowingly echoing Joe Boy to Septimus that day after they had waded across behind Megan and the wagon.

Gurston sped up, hurrying till he turned upon a nice white house trimmed in green with a silver tin roof that came down a little too far upon four posts standing as short, but solid rock columns.

"This is The Place," Gurston said, stopping a little in the unfenced yard. "The ole house went in the twenties ... a marble'd roll four or five different direc-

PHILLIP H. MCMATH

tions before findin' a wall, so, we give up ... tore it down and I built this new'n," he added. "Uncle Joe Boy didn't want to ... but I got tired a-patchin' it."

As they got out, two hounds and a mongrel greeted them but were quickly called back by a diminutive woman dressed in black. She was standing on the porch by an old man sitting in a rocking chair who waved but did not rise.

"That's Uncle Joe Boy there," Gurston said, speaking and waving lazily as they approached.

"High, y'all," said the old man, dropping his hand on the last word as if it were just too heavy to hold up any longer.

Storns was introduced and they chatted about the trip as Gurston fetched another chair and Aunt Clare brought ice tea without ice.

A medium-sized mutt of incredible ugliness hopped up to accept a few languid strokes from Uncle Joe Boy before lying at his feet, listening with sad attention to everything that was said.

Gurston explained Storns's mission in sympathetic tones, then Uncle Joe Boy asked a few polite questions as Aunt Clare, a dour middle-aged woman, quietly rocked on the periphery.

"What's the dog's name?" asked Storns, trying to get things started.

"Ricochet," answered the old man proudly.

Storns laughed. This made everyone smile so he pressed on. "As Gurston mentioned ... we're looking for stories ... stories about heroes ... your family's got lots of them ... a real inspiration for the people of our state ... folks look up to men like Johnny and Jeremiah ... and I'd be honored to tell their story ..."

"And James ... don't forgit him ..."

"James?" asked Storns. "Oh, yeah, he's the one who went off to Mexico ... after the war ... with Shelby?"

"To my way o'thankin' ... he wuz jes a great a hero as any of 'em," said Uncle Joe Boy, rocking a little more for emphasis.

"I'm sorry ... right ... he rode with the Iron Brigade, didn't he?" said Storns.

"That's rat ... jes as soon as Hardy G. ... that's my pappy ... an' Maw ... her name was Mary ... would let 'im ... I mean, he wuz 'bout to run 'em slap crazy to go an' awl ... so they let 'im on his sixteenth birthday ... he made Marks' Mill rat after that ... then he rode own up into Missouri an' down agin ... come thew a couple a-times ... a-vistin' ... nen stayed a while longer ... but then was awf to Mexico ... 'course they didn't want 'im to go thar ... but thar wa'n't nuthin yare for 'im ... he weren't no farmer ... didn't have the patience fur it ... so he up'n went ... he jes couldn't give it up ... a-ridin' with

Shelby, I mayn … he wuz kindly hooked own it an' awl … couldn't thank of nuthin' else … 'bout ran ever'body crazy over it."

"Did you ever hear from him down there in Mexico?"

"No … not a single word onct he got thar … I'll never furgit it … him an' Maw a-standin' rat yonder whur yore De Soto is parked at now," said Uncle Joe Boy, pointing to it then dropping his hand again, "her a cryin' an' awl … she didn't know I wuz a-watchin' 'r nuthin' … he an' Hardy G. … wayel, he wuz a hard man in his own way … brought up hard … wayel … see … he … like I tole ye … didn't want James to go … so he kindly wuz a-runnin' awf."

"I see," said Storns.

"The war then wuz jes as good as over an' Hardy G. couldn't square his goin' back to whatever wuz left of it. We done lost one boy to it … an' Jeremiah had buried an arm down thar in Looisiana. But thar weren't no holdin' 'im an' he run awf. I'll never forgit his a-kissin' an' a huggin' Maw like they done that day … him a-settin' thar on ole Dandy, a-leanin' down out that saddle of his an' holdin' her kinda long an' hard … them not knowin' I wuz watchin' an' awl … then his ridin' awf round that little bend in the road thar," Uncle Joe Boy said, raising his hand again and pointing, "till he was gone like the puff o' hot summer dust he left behind."

The old man's eyes glistened as he let his hand drop again.

"I don't mind a-tellin' ye, I cried then an' I still choke a little now when I thank about it," he said.

There was a long silence interrupted by a large black fly that lit on Uncle Joe Boy's face. He shooed it and added, "That wuz the last we seen of 'im … never laid eyes on 'im agin."

"Did you ever hear anything … anything at all?" asked Storns. "A letter or something?"

"We got one letter … from down thar in Texas somewhures. We still got it. Maw kep it in the big Family Bible … but it don't say much … James weren't much own writin' … now Johnny … he wrote good uns … yew might want to look at nem some … but, like I said, James he jes weren't no good at it … not a-tall … awl he said wuz it wuz after Lee done give up o-ver in Virginee … that they wa'n't about to give up … Lee an' nem boys could, but they weren't … that they wuz a-goin' own down to Mexico … to fight fur the French … ur that Mexican … whose name I cain't call. Wharez! That's it." Joe Boy said this snapping his fingers to catch the name. "Him 'r the other … ye know … to keep a-goin' … 'course that wuz plum crazy, they had no kinda chance down thar … but that wuz what they done … thar wuz a heap of Rebs

PHILLIP H. MCMATH

that went down thar with 'im … Kirby Smith hisself went down thar fur awhile … ye know … to kindly lay low an' awl afore he come back to be a skool taycher … but yew knew that, rat?"

"No … I didn't."

"No? Well, I thank some wuz afeered of bein' hanged … I thawt fur awhile they wuz gonna a-hang President Davis … they kept 'im in prayson ye know … fur a pretty good while, lot's 'r boys wuz in praysons … it ruint mos' o' 'em … they come back meaner'n they went an' some wuz pretty mean to start with …"

"Hangin' Davis would've just made things worse," opined Storns officially.

"Yeah … wayel, I reckon yer right thar, but thangs shore got bad anyway … but, I larned the hard way that thangs kin always git worse … but I don't know how they could uh got much worse than they done … after the war, I mean … thangs wuz worser in some ways nen when the war wuz a-goin' own … lots worser … them wuz hard times, I'll tell ye that, Mister Storns, hard times."

"So, you only got the one letter?" said Storns, bringing the story back on course.

"Yeah, but nen, he never come home … an' we didn't yar nuthin' for several more yares … Maw, 'course, wuz worried sick … bless-her-heart, she kep' a light a-burnin' ever night to light his way home … ever night, she'd light it up 'n set it in that winder thar," he pointed again at the window, forgetting that it wasn't the same. "Hardy G. 'n I figgered the wors' … so done Jeremiah … thought he never said nuthin' … but then he wouldn't … but Maw she never give up … never," here Uncle Joe Boy sipped his tea, then set it down, away from Ricochet, who ignored it.

"Wayel, thangs kindly rocked along thar fur a few yares nen we yared that Gen'ral Shelby wuz back in Missouree … his fayences in Mexico had kindly done fallen down own 'im an' he thowed up his hands an' done come own home …"

"When was that?" asked Storns, sipping the tea then following his example setting it on the porch. "May I write this down, Mister Mansfield?" he asked, taking out a small notebook and pencil.

"Nawgh … go rat ahead," Uncle Joe Boy said with a slight nod, thinking a moment, then added, "I'm gonna say it wuz along in '68 somewhures … we heerd that … thar wuz sumpin' in the paper 'bout it, too … see, Jo Shelby wuz a legend fur folks back nen 'n awl … a rayel hero … ye ought to write sumpin' down 'bout him, too … in yore paper on a Sunday … some say he wuz, next to Forrest, the best darn calvery officer on either side of the war …

an' nen his goin' awf to Mexico 'n awl ... they way thangs turned out ... looked better'n better to lots of folks awl the time ... 'specially west of the Miss'sippi whure thangs wuz always jes a little meaner than on the other side, fur some rayson."

"Shelby's never got his due," said Storns sententiously.

"That's rat ... he wuz on the wrong side o' the river ... but anyways ... nem Mexicans finally got 'round to a-shootin' that French feller an' Shelby 'n the boys had no choice but to high-tail it own home ... which he done not awl that long after that happened, wayel ... when we got wind o' his comin' home ... quite naturally ... we wanted some answers ... 'bout James 'n awl, so Maw an' Maygun ... that's my sister ... Aint Clare yar is her daughter ..."

"I know," said Storns.

"I kindly told who folks were," intruded Gurston from his rocker on his uncle's left.

"Good ... then ye know ever'body ... as I wuz a-sayin' ... we wrote up this yare letter to Shelby ... ye know, rayel careful like ... ever'body kindly pitchin' in ... nen sent it care o' him whurever it wuz we heerd he lived at ... up-per in that little town in Missouree somewhures ... I cain't call it rat now ... but the one mentioned in that paper story ... mailed it own up'er to 'im. That wuz the best we could do, see?"

"Y'all weren't sure he'd get it, though?" said Storns.

"Nawgh ... or that he'd answer ... but he did ... he done answered purtty quick ... we got the letter in thar ... in that Bible ... rat thar next to them that James done sent us ..."

"You've got a letter from General Jo Shelby?" asked Storns, astonished.

"Shore as yore a-settin' thar ...," Joe Boy said proudly.

"Can I see it before I leave?"

"Shore ..."

"It's valuable as all get out," Storns said with boyish enthusiasm.

"We wouldn't take no amount of money fur it ...," said Uncle Joe Boy.

"Oh, sure, I understand that ... so ... what happened? What did Shelby say?"

"He jes thanked us an' awl ... rayel nice like ... fur the letter an' awl ... he said it wuz an 'honor' ... that wuz the word he used ... an honor to a-yare from one of his own men's folks ... that James wuz a brave soldier ... that he wuz rayel proud to ride with 'im. He talked 'bout him a-bein' brave at the Mill an' up-per in Missouree ... his 'devotion to duty' wuz one way he put it ... nem wuz his very words ... 'devotion to duty' ... how he could ride an' shoot ... an' go awl day without no food nor nuthin' ... ye know, without complainin' none ... an' nen he tole us he wuz kilt in a prutty good fight down thar in Mexico when they wuz a-tryin' to cross some river somewhures an' got tharselves ambushed by a bad bunch of Mexicans ... that he rode for'ard an' fought 'em hard an' saved the lives of his 'comrades' ... that wuz anuther big word he called up ... he found them big fancy words li'kat somewhures ... an' that James wuz kilt with a Mexican bullet rat thew the heart ...", the old man rocked back a little and pointed to his heart with a long, bony finger, then added, "he said that he didn't suffer none ... an' wuz buried with full 'milit'ry honors,' he said ... with some words over 'im, proper like from the Bible ... in a grave dug thar outside of that Mexican town an' left thar ... that he 'died bravely' in the service of his country' wuz the way he ended it ... like I say ... ye kin read it fur yorese'f ... but I thank that makes 'im a hero to put on yore list, don't it, Mister Storns?" said Uncle Joe Boy, rocking just a little forward now and fingering for the tea glass.

"It sure does, yes, siree-bob," was the answer Storns gave as he scratched in the note pad. "What happened then?"

"Wayel, sir, my maw she took that thar light outta the winder an' went own to bed an' turned her face to the wall an' died ... that's what happened."

Storns stopped writing.

"We buried her within a month of a-gittin' that thar letter from Gen'ral Shelby," Uncle Joe Boy said, rocking back and sipping the tea. "I'll show ye her grave when ye git done a-readin' nem letters ... if ye want ... that is, if ye can afford the time."

Storns was silent.

Uncle Joe Boy went on. "It wuz kindly queer how it turned out an' awl ... 'cause ... after Powell Clayton done finished with us yar in Arkansas he went own down to Mexico hisself with that boy an' nem high-tone girls an' wife of his ... folks said she were purtty nice but put on airs an' awl even tho she weren't nuthin' herself but a steamboat captain's daughter who fought fur the South an' the boy ... his only son ... they say he got run out of the country fur not a-fightin' a duel with a Mex'can awf'cer ... that ain't good in that country ... an' I heerd he couldn't stay down thar in Mexico ... but he wuz in the army ... kindly tryin' to foller after his paw an' awl ... I mayen ole Clayton wuz a rayel soldier ... ever'body knowed that ... an' his boy got hisself promoted own up to major but died in Texas a-foolin' 'round with nem Mex'cans, too ... jes like James done ... only he didn't git shot but fell off his horse, I'm tole.

"Then that brother of his ... John ... who run his plantation fur 'im fur awhile … went to the legislaychore and got buckshot in the face fur tryin' to move own up to Congress … ye herd of that, I reckon?"

Storns nodded. "They stole the election in Conway County …"

"Rat … an' it wuz the Klan that kilt 'im … they say … then that Klansman who done it wuz kilt by a nigger an' the Klan turned rat around an' lynched him … but ole Clayton hisself he winds up down in Mexico too … only later … I mean … wayel, Mister Storns, I kindly studied up own it awl an' I found out that the whole entar Yankee invasion … up the Red an' down to Camden … Banks 'n Steele wuz jes 'cause the same gol darn thang … Mexico. Laycoln wuz skeered we'd link up with them … that Fraynch king feller that they sent down thar to rule an' awl … we'd hitch to his wagon an' awl … an' win 'ar indepayendence. Then James dies a-goin' down thar a tryin' to he'p … to do jes that very thang … an' that damn Clayton … he winds up down thar too … a-losin' his own boy … then his brother … John … gits hisself kilt by the Klan … you know, after the war an' awl."

Storns was writing as fast as he could get it down but Joe Boy didn't wait.

"What I guess I'm a-tryin' to say is … it awl kindly starts the ball a-rollin' … 'n we git invaded by the Yankees to skeer off the Fraynch 'n Shelby goes awf down thar to Mex'co to do too late what Laycoln feered we'd do sooner 'cause Shelby seen whut Davis was blind to way awf in Richmond … an' 'r James dies down thar a-fightin' fur the Fraynch agin the Mex'cans … an' nen 'cause that Frawg army is thar … so fur from home … they ain't ready fur whut that German Bismarck was a-fixin, an' he whips 'em good an' awl an' he whips 'em good an' the sayeds ur done planted jes rat fur the Grayet War that kills Little Joshua … that's what we called 'im … Little Joshua … an' he's kilt in France an' is stayel thar yet jes like James is still somewhures down in Mexico a-molderin' … an' Johnny is over thar in Tennessee a-doin' the same thang … an' this yar last'n … the Grayet War, I mean … up an' brangs the flu down thew yar an' awl over the whole entar world which puts Maygan an' God knows how many other poor folks in thar graves … 'cause the veterans is a-braythin' that contagion with 'em which they done brung home. But that ain't the end of it … 'cause the seeds of that thar war is furrowed in fur the next-un … an' yar we are jes a settin' yar a-rockin' in nineteen an' forty-one a-gittin' ready to have anuther'n o-ver in France looks like … with them dang Germans agin … a-pickin' up whur we left awf … with the sons of nem that kilt Little Joshua … an' the grandsons o' nem that kilt the ones that James an' nem wuz a-tryin' to he'p … but each war's a little bigger 'n the one afore it … each one a little meaner 'n the lastun."

PHILLIP H. MCMATH

The old man drew breath but when Storns seemed speechless, he said, "So, they jes a-well to move Little Joshua an' nem other Doughboys he's with own over, 'cause they're gonna be a buryin' a heap more along side of 'em ... purtty soon. Awl seems kindly linked up, don't it? Queer, how it awl comes 'round together ... like one big wagon whayel, ain't it, Mister Storns?"

Storns rocked forward about two inches and said, "Gosh ... Mister Mansfield, I've never quite thought of it like that ... in that way, I mean."

"That's cause yew ain't lived quite long enough ... see, I'll be ninety next birfday ... if I make it ... an' frum my front porch yar I seen it awl ... some of it purtty darn close, like James a-kissin' my maw goodbye whur Gurston's De Soto is a-settin thar rat now ... an' seein' Johnny go awf an' not come back ... an' Jeremiah come back with a payce dropped awf somewhures ... an' Big Joshua an' Little'n ... an' the so-called Reconstruction, an' the Redaymption an' awl the rest of it. I tell ye, I seen my shar an' have kindly stuck it together in my mind so I can git a-hold own it good. I mean, I ain't educated, Mister Storns, 'r nothin' ... cain't hardly read 'n write too good, but I seen awl this clar enough."

"Yes, it is interesting ... what you say ... it's definitely food-for-thought," Storns said, turning to his little notebook again and placing the pencil against the paper. "You said something a minute ago about Big and Little Joshua ... who are they? Big Joshua ... that is? You told me about the one that died in France ... who's the other one?"

Uncle Joe Boy looked around the porch.

"Tell 'im, Uncle Joe Boy," said Aunt Clare, speaking for the first time. "He come fur a story ... why don't ye give 'im one."

"Sure," added Gurston. "Tell 'im the whole thang."

Ricochet, as if in anticipation, stood up on his front paws and lay his head in Uncle Joe Boy's lap to be petted gently.

"Okay, y'all. Ye got time, Mister Storns?"

"Sure, please ... this is what I came for," Storns said, putting the notebook and pencil away, pushing his hat back, and rocking rearward a little in his chair.

"See ... it wuz a-durin' the war ... I wa'n't no mor'n twayelv ... Johnny wuz o-ver in Tennessee, with Pat Cleburne an' nem boys ... he jined up with the Spence brothers ... an' Jeremiah ... he was stayel down in Loosiana ... wounded we come to find out ... after that bad Playsant Hill fight ... an' a-servin' under Gen'ral Thomas Churchill ... 'cause of his hurt ... a-losin' the arm ... he didn't come up yar fur Jaynkins's Ferry ... see ... James, why, he'd jes a-started ridin' with Jo Shelby ... got in the saddle jes in time fur Marks's

Mill. We awl gone up over to Tulip fur some staples an' hopin' fur a letter ... news ... Maw she wuz always fit to be tied fur that ... we left her own The Playce with a neighbor woman who could spit tobaccee 'bout as good as she could shoot a side-by-side ... see ... thangs wuz purtty rough ... thar wuz bushwhackers to worry 'bout an' Yankee calvery a-prowlin' like wolves awl thew this yar country ... it was rat after the Fer'y fight an' thangs wuz shore nuff stirred up ... wayel, see, we wuz a-comin' back ... Pappy wuz own that fine geldin' he had, a big horse named Tater, 'n an' I wuz a-ridin' in the back of the wagon with the traps an' sech, a-holdin' my loaded payce. I kept her primed with ever grain she'd stand ... me an' Toughy ... my dawg ... with Maygan a drivin' the wagon ... hitched with Henry an' Henrietta ... the best darn team in Dallas County ... 'cause Hardy G. Mansfield don't hold with mules ... see ... an' yar we a-come 'round this yar little corner in the road an' thar wuz a nigger boy a-settin' own a horse with a rope 'round his neck ..."

"Rope around his neck?" said Storns, startled.

"Yeah ... Billy Jack Stantford an' his boys wuz a-fixin' to hang 'im, for shore ... but Pappy saved 'im."

"Saved him? How?"

"I'll tell ye in a minute, but first ye need to know thar wuz a wounded Yankee soldier up thar in the woods name of Joshua, he's been wounded up-per at the Fer'y by a one-armed Confed'rate praysoner ... a girl ..."

"A girl?!" Storns said.

"Yup ... a girl ... she'd been a-ridin' fur Price an' wuz cawt ... she got away an' shot poor Joshua while a-runnin' ... I cain't call her name ..."

"Dagmar," volunteered Aunt Clare.

"Yeah ... that's it ... Dagmar ... she shot 'im an' rode awf an' he nearly died ... one-a 'r doctor's patched 'im an' then the next day 'r so he wuz taken in a wagon toward Praynceton ... whur thar wuz a hospital set up ... with a bunch uh other wounded praysoners, but he was skeered he wouldn't make it to Tyler ... an' run when they stopped near Tulip ..."

"Tyler?"

"Yeah ... Tyler, Texas, whure ar prison wuz at ... thangs wuz known to be rough thar ... an' he wuz skeered he wouldn't live thew the trip 'r die thar even if he made it ... so he run awf ... a-hopin' to find his own payple some-whures, but he jes opened up that shot shoulder agin an' darn nare bled out. Wayel, this boy ... Septimus was his name ... why, he done run awf hisself ... awl the way frum Camden ... a-follerin' ahind Steele's army like so many of 'em wuz a-doin' ... fact-o-the-bidness, he remembered the one-armed girl ...

wayel, these Confed'rates … Billy Jack Stantford, he wuz thar layder … they wuz hot 'bout whut had done happened o'ver at the Fer'y when nem Kansas Coloreds kilt … murdered … 'r boys … an' when they caught Septimus a-hepin' the Yankee soldier they wuz fixin' to strang 'im up … that wuz when Pappy come along an' us rat a-hind 'im."

Now Uncle Joe Boy rocked back, played with Ricochet's ears, and drank some tea for the first time.

"What then was the relationship between Joshua and Little Joshua?" Storns had to ask.

"Well, it's a long story … but I'll tell ye," said Uncle Joe Boy, who then told the story the next hour, bringing Storns up to where Joshua and Septimus crossed the Saline together. Here he paused and said, getting up, "Excuse me, Mister Storns, but I'm a-goin' to take a little brayek, if ye don't mind," he said, disappearing into the house with Aunt Clare a step behind.

Storns looked at Gurston for help and he said, "When they git back, I'll show you."

They returned and Gurston and Storns took their turn.

Uncle Joe Boy rocked back in silent relief, while Ricochet, who had hopped down to a shade tree, came back and lay down again.

"Anybody want anythang?" Aunt Clare asked, hollering through the door.

No one did so she returned to her rocker.

"It's kindly gettin' late … I guess y'all better git on back," Uncle Joe Boy said quietly, taking out a gold pocket watch, looking at it then putting it back.

"No, Uncle Joe Boy, I done planned on 'em stayin' fur supper … yew're goin a-eat with us, aren't ye, Gurston?"

"That's the main reason I come, Aint Clare," Gurston said. "I heard the story … but your cookin' I never tire of."

"Good," she said, adjusting her long, very hot-looking dress over her knee and rocking back. "I'll put it own in a bit … y'all jest as wayel to stay the night."

"How 'bout that? Can you stay, Jake?" Gurston asked.

"Well, Gurston, I can't leave till I hear what happened, now can I? Who could? Sure, Miss Smith, I'd be honored … if you all have room … thank you very much."

"Oh, we got room enough awl right …" she said. "But jes call me Aint Clare, if ye please … ever'body does," she said with a little frown.

"Yes'm, Aint Clare," Storns said a little obsequiously.

"We're glad to have ye …," she added. "We don't want nobody to ever leave The Playce hungry nor tared."

There was a little pause. Uncle Joe Boy showed no inclination to proceed. Finally, Storns said, "Mister Mansfield ..."

"Jes call me Uncle Joe Boy ..."

"Yes, sir, Uncle Joe Boy ... but I have to know ... did Joshua ever come back for Megan? Huh? Did he keep his promise?"

Uncle Joe Boy leaned back, then forward to find the hound's head with a hand, then said, "Shore he did ... he wuz in love with her ... he come rat own back in the sprang of '66 ... jes as soon as he come back from Ioway to see his folks up thar an' awl ... jes like he promised ... only he brought another feller with 'im ... an ex-soldier ... thangs wuz none too safe then ... but still Maygun wouldn't marry 'im ... said he jes come 'cause he wuz a man of his word ... 'n didn't rally mean it 'r nothin'. That thar kindly made me thank more'd happened between nem two than anyone ever said."

"Now Uncle Joe Boy ... you cain't know that," said Aunt Clare with the little frown reappearing.

"I know ... but Maygun she kindly thought he wuz jes bein' a gentleman an' awl ... I mean ... she never talked much 'bout it ye understand, but that wuz the take of the thang ..."

"How long did he stay?" asked Storns.

"Thray days ... but she wouldn't budge, so I thank he got kindly uncomfortable an' awl. He an' that feller he'ped Pappy some 'round The Playce, nen left ... went own back to Little Rock whur he went into bidness ... cotton exchange ... thew in with nem 'publicans an' carpetbaggers an' got rich. He an' the damn Powell Clayton wuz close ... an' he done lots of politickin' with him ... heped 'im git elected governor and awl."

"Yew might mention Jeremiah," suggested Gurston.

"Sure ... rat ... see ... Jeremiah an' him never wuz that close 'r nuthin' ... 'n when he ... Jeremiah ... got hisself 'lected to that Democrat legislature back in '66 ... the one that got 'em so stirred up ... 'cause they got a good bunch of Confed'rates in thar, but Joshua he come by to see 'im one day ... an' even though he wuz own the wrong side uh the fayence ... offered to he'p 'im. Hardy G. didn't hold with lawyers no more'n he done with praychers but Jeremiah had a hankerin' to be one ... an' so Joshua he'ped 'im ... he took 'im to one up'per an' he went to a-studyin' in this ole lawyer's office an' ... Jeremiah, he wuz always smart ... an' after they took the vote away from us up-per in Warshington ... along in '67 ... yew know ... undone awl we done got in '66 ... wayel, Jeremiah stayed own an' finished his work ... an' got swore in."

PHILLIP H. MCMATH

"Did he come back to The Place?" asked Storns.

"After a spayel ... he kindly liked it up-per ... but he wuz hot 'bout whut they'd done to us an' he come own back yar an' opened an office over in Praynceton. It wuz the county seat in nem days ... an' a busy playce ... yew know ... afore the railroad come thew an' killed pore ole Princeton an' Tulip damn nare stone dead. When that happened ... wayel, he thowed up his hands and went own down to Fordyce ... but that's gettin' way ahead uh thangs. Even though he hated Powell Clayton an' nem ... he never forgot what Joshua done to he'p 'im an' awl ... he come own home an' tole Maygun she ought to marry 'im ... that he ain't took up with nobody nor courted nor nothin' ... an' she wuz a fool not to say yes."

"What happened?"

"She wuz bull-headed an' wouldn't change her mind ... an' by then Mason Smith ... Gurston's grandpaw ... he wuz a-courtin' her rayel good ... an' nem wuz successful folks ... farmers an' rayel good ole time Democrats ... frum in an' around Praynceton whur they'd done settled wayel afore the war ... an' even though she kept gittin' nem letters an' sech frum Joshua ... an' they come purtty steady like ... she never answered a one ... an' up an' married Mason Smith jes as quick as she could git herself a new white dress."

"Wayel, she had them boys o' hers rat awf like, Little Hardy who died nen ... Johnny an' James ... named fur her dayed brothers, 'course ... an' long in nen ... Powell he had got hisself in thar after a-gettin' rich ... directly the Yankees thowed up thar military gover'ment over us ... a-takin' ar rats away ... yew know ... a-treatin' us like a colony an' awl ... fur punishment, see ... we wuz goin' t'be punished. Hardy G. said none o' this wouldn't a-happened if Laycoln'd lived ... he said Laycoln come when we didn't need 'im an' left when we did ... but, anyway, this ... as I thank yew know ... made fur rayle hard feelin's ... rayel hard ... an' directly the Klan come in yar prutty good ... an' thangs got shore 'nuff rough then ... they'd done took the vote away from the Confed'rates an' set up thar carpetbaggin', scalawag gover'ment up-per in Little Rock ... an' they was a-stealin' ever'thang that weren't nailed down an' traytin' the folks worsn dawgs, so like I say, thangs got rougher an' rougher. So Clayton, he sets up these yar nigger militias with them bad Whites in charge of 'em ... fancy bushwhackers is whut they wuz ... an' they went to robbin' an' killin' an' some women even got molested. Powell called it by the name o' 'martial law' ... but thar weren't no law to it ... it were supposed to be jes o-ver in Bradley County ... ye know, rat next to us ... an' 'bout eleven others, but thar warn't no line to it a-tall ... it sprayed out ever'whur. The fat sure nuff rolled awf into the far nen, I'll tell ye ... they never should uh done that ... so the Klan swole up big then. It weren't fur me nor Hardy G. but we un'erstood it ... but Jeremiah he jined an' wuz a Grand Dragon ... him an' Billy Jack Stantford ... he wuz the Grand Cyclops of the local bunch ... 'member ... he wuz the same feller that tried to hang Septimus back-er in '64 ... that's rat ... he'd done gone sure 'nuff crazy up-per in that Yankee prayson ... an' like his ole sorry bootlegger daddy o' hisn ... he took to a-drankin' rayel bad ... he wuz meaner'n ever ... but it wuz a mean time an' him an' Jeremiah they put together a prutty good-sized den in yar an' rode hard aginst nem militias ... hard ... they hurt 'em ... hurt 'em rayel bad."

"It's still in here ... the Klan, I mean?" asked Storns.

"Oh, yeah, some, but it ain't whut it wuz in nem days ... not by a long sight ... then it wuz the army of the Democratic party ... the 'publicans had thar Blue army an' nem damn militias an' we had the Klan ... it wuz war, pure an' simple ... fact-o-the-bidness, the war never stopped ... oh, thar wuz a little pawse thar along in '66, but then it a-started up agin. In some ways it wuz worse."

Uncle Joe Boy finished the tea then set the glass down like he always did, opposite Ricochet. Then he continued, "But, see, Clayton wuz 'bout a-lose control of thangs an' he nayded more guns ... he never had 'nuff. He couldn't git awl he wanted from the army who had thar hands full o-ver in Miss'sippi ... they done give 'em awl the hep they could ... so he bought some Belgian rifles with state funds ... ten thousand 'r better ... with plenty o' ammahnition ... an' it got loaded onto a staymboat up'per in Me'phis ..." Here Uncle Joe Boy laughed. "But ole Nathan Bedford an' his boys got wind of it an' they got a staymer uh thar own an' way-laid it out thar in the river ... they say 'bout in the place whur ole De Soto crossed own over into Arkansas. They boarded her ... an' took nem guns an' bullets an' ever' last one of 'em got dumped into the Miss'sippi ... ever las't one went rat down to the muddy bottom ... shore did ... them militias got nary a one."

"I didn't know about that," said Storns.

"They shore did ... Jeremiah tole me awl about it ... though Clayton an' nem Blue-bellies could never prove it. Jeremiah said it wuz Forrest fur shore ... see ... he wuz the one that put the Klan together ... o-ver in Tennessee ... Forrest wuz ... it wuz his idee ... fact-o-the-bidness ... I thank he 'n Jeremiah worked together ... though he wouldn't talk 'bout it none ... 'less yew wuz in it ... they didn't talk much 'bout it ... yew had to be in thar den ... or they wuz rale shut-mouth 'bout ever'thang."

PHILLIP H. MCMATH

"That's still true," said Storns quietly.

"Oh, yeah, like ye say ... it's still 'round an' awl but not like in nem days ... it ain't nothin' like then by a long shot."

"Right," said Storns, leaning back and rocking slightly.

"Then Clayton ... he kindly got into trouble ... he'd made jes ever'body mad ... he wuz high-handed an' tried to rule like the gen'ral that he's been in the Yankee army ... even nem 'publicans wuz tared of 'em bein' governor ... an' he got hisself impayched but they didn't have the votes to finish 'im awf an' he made a deal to layve if they'd send 'im to the U.S. Senate, so, the same damned bunch 'o folks that impayched 'im turned rat 'round an' sent 'im awf to Warshington ... jes to git rid of 'im ... if ye can believe that?"

Everyone laughed.

"He high-tailed it ... nen ole Baxter fought his little war with Brooks ..."

"Brooks-Baxter war," said Storns knowingly.

"Rat ... 'bout seventy 'r so folks got kilt while them two 'publicans fought it out ... but Baxter won, 'course, an' he had some good boys behind 'im, ex-Confed'rates ... Gen'ral Newton an' nem ... ole Baxter had been a Democrat an' a slave owner back in North Carolina afore the war ... but when he come into them hills he wuz a stomp-down Union man. He seen rat away that thangs had to change ... after Clayton, I mayn ... thangs wuz bad ... an' he got rid of them damn militias an' he'ped us git ar vote back an' nen Garland ..."

"Augustus ... he'd been in the Richmond government for Arkansas ... Democrat," said Storns, showing off.

"Rat ... him an' Davis wuz close, Jeremiah said ... anyway, Garland, he wuz a lawyer ... a good 'un an' up as sues over that ... whut do they cawl it?"

"The Iron Clad Oath Law ... that prevented ex-Confederate lawyers from practicing ..."

"Yeah, wayel, that wuz it ... I see yew knowed it purtty good ..."

"The United States Supreme Court ruled in his favor an' he got his license back ... it made him a hero in the South."

"That an' he got ole Grant to kindly calm down the Brooks-Baxter shoot-out ... an' that got 'im 'lected governor an' the Democrats wuz back in the saddle for good."

"Redemption."

"Rat ... Redaymption ... ole Hayes he pulled out the Yankee troops to git hisself in the White House ... but fur a-while it looked like that wuz a-comin' to anuther war ... I mean, they stole the 'lection frum Tilden, didn't they?"

"Sure," said Storns.

"That's whut Jeremiah said ... he wuz in it thick ... he worked fur Garland hard an' fur Tilden too ... he wuz doin' prutty good o-ver at Prayncton ... an' went back to the legislaychore ... but afore that sumpin' else happened."

"What was that?" Storns asked.

"I thank I'd better git dinner on," said Aunt Clare, getting up and slowly going inside.

"Should I go own, Gurston?" asked Uncle Joe Boy, looking at his nephew for help.

"Sure ... that's what he come for ..." Gurston said.

Uncle Joe Boy cleared his throat, and said, "Let me put it this a-way ... Maygun never had no 'tention uh marryin' Joshua ... least ways that's the way she acted an' whut she always said ... to him an' ever'body else ... not that she never cared for 'im 'r nuthin', 'cause she did, fact-o-the-bidness ... an' Gurston knows it, so I don't mind sayin' it ... I don't thank she ever got over Joshua but her raysons wuz her own. She never answered none'o his letters ... not a one, so fur as anyone could ever tayel ... so ... Joshua, after awhile, he give up a-writtin' 'em ... but she kept ever one, afore she burned 'em later ... after whut happened an' awl ... but nen he didn't know she done married own 'im nuther. Jeremiah ain't seen 'im to tayel 'im ... an' ye'd have to say he still had hopes ... an' ... wayel ... Mister Storns, see ... he tried to come back down yar one more time to git her to change her mind an' awl. It wuz when Baxter had done got in thar good an' thangs had kindly settled down a bit ... thar warn't no more martial law 'r militias no more ... they wuz done fore. Joshua come down yar without us a-knowin' it ... he wuz a-passin' thew with a bunch o' high-tone folks that wuz comin' thew Tulip an' he took a detour frum 'em over this a-way by hisself ... a-ridin' a nice saddle horse."

Storns rocked back a bit, the notebook and pencil at the ready.

"Well ... Pappy come up own Joshua ... like he done Septimus that day ... but this time it wuz too late ... he wuz a-hangin' fresh frum that thar same tree ..."

"Hanging?"

"Rat ..."

"Dead?"

"Dayed."

Pause.

"Who did it?"

"Billy Stantford an' his sorry boys ... they come up on 'im an' recognized 'im ... we found out later ... an' Billy ... he'd been a-drankin' o'course an'

PHILLIP H. MCMATH

wuz purtty fur gone ... an' he said he'd seen Joshua a-headin' up one o' nem militias fur Clayton ... 'course it were a damn lie ... an' when Joshua said sumpin' ... course he wuz close to Clayton an' awl but he never wuz part 'o nem damn militias but when he spoke up they knowed rat awf he wuz a Yankee an' so they jes strung 'im up ... an' that wuz how Hardy G. found 'im. He wuz a-ridin' with a hired hand, and they had done wrote the word 'revaynge' on a payce of paper an' penned it to his shirt. He cut 'im down ... come home fur the wagon an' sent the hand fur Jeremiah. He went back up-per an' brought 'im home an' we ... I wuz home a-lookin' after thangs since Pappy wuz gone ... an' we buried 'im in 'r family plot ... ahind the house ... I'll show ye his grave if ye like ..."

"Where was Megan?"

"Well, Pappy tole me to watch The Playce an' they went to trailin' 'em ... him an' Jeremiah caught up with 'im ... he knowed rat whur he wuz a-headin' ... like I say ... he had done rode with 'em ... an' nem boys split awf an' Billy Jack wuz by hisself an' they caught 'em long 'bout dark. It weren't nuthin' to it ... Jeremiah said ... he wuz drunk ... an' asleep in an ole cabin whur he hid out some ... wayel, they got the drop on 'im ... he tried to splain hisself but it weren't no use an' they tied 'im up an' brought 'im back to that very same tray ... whur he'd done hung Joshua frum an' nearly strung up Septimus that day. But ye asked 'bout Maygun ... she come home to look in own Pappy ... to visit an' awl ... she done dropped them two boys o' hers awf with Mason's sister an' come a-ridin' own over fur a visit ... like she done lots ... 'o course I couldn't do nuthin' but tell her ... she wuz own that fine little black mare uh hers ... Midnight ... an' she turned rat round whure she wuz at, jes as quick as she could, an' rode awf hard an' fast. I couldn't let 'er go awf by herself. I saddled up an' caught her ... she wouldn't wait till I got a horse saddled ... but, like I say, I rode rat own after her ... but she wuz a-ridin' that Midnight narly to death an' she come up own 'em a little afore they got back to that damn hangin' tree ... I come up when she wuz a-puttin' the rope around Billy's neck herself ... she said sumpin' to 'im that I couldn't make out an' then she slapped that hangin' horse ... with her very own hand ... an' I seen Billy a-dancin' his death dance with her jes watchin' thar starin up at 'im as that rope chocked the life out o' his sorry body."

There was a long pause.

"Billy Jack stayed up thar fur sayveral days ... the buzzards an' crows come an' finished 'im awf ... finally he fayel to the ground ... but nobody'd touch 'im. His ole paw wuz long since dayed ... an' the rest of his folks ... sech as they wuz ... done left out fur Texas ... they said ... so he didn't have nobody as fur as anybody knowed. After a while, Pappy he an' Jeremiah went own back up thar an' buried his bones up in nem woods somewhure."

"Gosh!" said Storns, going pale.

"Maygun didn't hardly speak to nobody 'r nobody else fur better'n a yar 'r better after that. I thank she'd a died if she hadn't had nem two boys o' her's ... Gurston's paw ... James, an' his uncle Johnny ... to live fur. After that she found herself praygnant with Little Joshua then, a few yars later, she had Clare yar ... her only girl. She wanted to name a boy Mason but never got around to it ... Clare wuz her last'un ... so, I guess ye can see why losin' Little Joshua in France took her straight awf like it done ... I mean, when she got the flu ... she died straight awf ... weak as she wuz. I figgered it wuz a blessin' ... she'd suffered enough in this ole sinful world."

"They wrote the word revenge, you say?"

"Yeah, for them militias ... an' that O. Dodd boy, they said ... but he didn't have nothin' to do with Joshua ... no more'n nem militias done. But I'll tell ye sumpin' else ... that 'xact same day as O. Dodd wuz kilt ... within hars, they say, 'nuther boy with the same name ... Dodd ... Ephraim Shelby Dodd ... cousins, some say ... both come out'o Texas ... wuz strung up o-ver in Tennessee by them Yankees fur bein' a spy, too ... an' jes like David he had morse code on 'im with saycrets awl wrote down 'bout enemy guns an' pickets an' sech ... each had a military trial that folks tried to stop an' both wuz not kilt straight off ..."

"The rope was too long," said Storns.

"Rat ... an' pore Ephraim's rope broke an' he had to be hanged twict ..."

"The Lord's hand wuz own nem two," said Aunt Clare softly.

"Or the Dayvil's ... it ain't clare which ...," said Joe Boy, rocking. "We didn't know nuthin' 'bout that other Dodd boy fur yars ... it come to light later ... but thangs never wuz the same ... like I say, Maygun never got over it ... she blamed herself quite natur'lly an' Jeremiah, too ... fur some rayson I never figgered out. He quit the Klan rat awf after he found out who them others wuz an' they said that Billy done lied to 'im an' said that Joshua wuz one of Clayton's militia men ... he knowed 'em awl ... an' I kindly thank that wuz why he felt it wuz his fault ... see, he come to like Joshua up thar in Lit'le Rock in a way he never done when he wuz yar with us back in nem war yars ... but ever'whure he went, he tole folks that after the Redaymption thar weren't no more need o' the Klan ... that we never needed to a-take the law into 'r own hands agin ... that what them Yankees done to us wuz bad wrong an' illaygal but now thangs'd changed. But folks knowed what happened an' chalked it up to that ... even if Joshua had been a Clayton man ... they knowed he weren't mixed up none with them militias ... an' they felt bad 'bout it. Pappy says ever lawyer is at least half politician an' Jeremiah he weren't no dayfernt ... but he never wuz loud 'r flashy ... jes kindly quiet an' hard workin' ... folks liked 'im ... after a spayel he come to hisself an' got hip-deep back in politics agin ... workin' lots kindly a-hind the scenes an' awl ... but he stayed in the legislay-chore. Like I say, the folks awl liked 'im ... he wuz a vet'ran with a pinned-up sleeve an' that counted for sumpin' in nem days ... an', too, they kindly felt bad 'bout Joshua onct they larned the truth an' awl ... nen Jeremiah went to work hard fur Governor Garland, an' nen Tilden when he run, and fur Gen'ral Churchill the two years he wuz in thar as governor ... him an' Jeremiah wuz rayel close 'count 'o his a-servin' under the gen'ral an' awl ... he stayed close to his vet'rans ... but the Democrats they smayled blood fur the White House 'n ole Grover Clayveland finally got in thar ... didn't he? He wuz a goodun ... honest ... and pig-smart, was the way Pappy put it, not fancy smart but ..."

"Clever," said Storns.

"Rat ... clayver ... the smarts whut counts. Too, he wuz a friend o' the South ... but some Yankees helt it agin 'im that he hired a substitute to go in his playce durin' the war an' awl ... but the South figgered it wuz 'cause he jes didn't want to fight agin us ... he weren't no co'ard ... an' nen, too, he had that bastard kid ... but he'd been a sher'ff up'er somewhures in New York an' done his own hangin' ... so folks kindly liked 'im ... those thangs kindly canceled thar-selves out ... Jeremiah raly worked hard fur 'im ... he wuz in the legislaychore still ... 'o course ... an' head o' the Confed'rate Vet'rans an' awl ... yar in Dallas County ... 'n the 'lection wuz closer even than afore, wa'n't it? Fat ole Grover won out, an' we had a good Democrat at last. Wayel, Jeremiah who never showed no kind o' feelin's o' any kind ... an wuz always rayel quiet an' steady ... why he done a jig. I seen it with my own two eyes ... a rayel jig ... rat thar whur that sedan is a-settin' rat now," Uncle Joe Boy pointed a bony fin-ger again. "He made Pappy laugh like I ain't heerd in yars ... I laughed, too, but nen I laugh a lot ... at mos' anythang ..."

"The first elected Democrat since the War Between the States," stated Storns, pulling himself up a bit.

"Rat ... boy, like I say, it shore felt good ... an' Grover ... he nayded to patch thangs up an' reward the hard work done fur 'im in the Confed'racy ... so he put Garland in thar as attorney gen'ral o' the whole United States ... that made lots of folks proud ... felt like we had 'r citizenship back at last ... we could hold 'r heads up agin. But by then, Jeremiah'd done give up on Praynceton an' moved own down to Fordyce … an' done wayel down thar … nen he took a trip to Warshington … D.C. … I mayen … ole Governor Garland wanted 'im to come up-per an' so he done it. Myself … I ain't ever been out'a Arkansas in my life an' only a few times out'o this yar county. But Pappy he wa'n't doin' so wayel … an' he a-nayded me to stay yar on The Playce to kindly look after 'im an' thangs … so, Jeremiah, he went up-per by hisself … own the train. 'Course … he tried to git Maygun to go, but she wouldn't … she said it weren't fur her no more than Lit'le Rock wuz … fact-o-the-bidness, she never been nowhure much nuther … anyway … Jeremiah went own up-per an' Garland took 'im by to mayet the pres-i-dent … Jeremiah Mansfield shook hands with Grover Clayveland in the White House … hayel, he come home an' hept name a county after 'im."

"Gosh," said Storns.

"They sawed the top out'o Bradley … so Marks's Mill is in Clayveland now … Jeremiah hept with that some. But afore he come home he went by Franklin … o-ver in Tennessee … it wuz out'o the way but he went over thar an' found Johnny's grave an' put a flo'er own it an' awl … he tole us it wuz wayel took care of by the women of the Confed'racy who looked after them graves an' monuments 'n such … he said it's rat thar at that big plantation house whure awl them boys's bur'ed who died a-fightin' with Pat Cleburne. Hardy G. was rayel proud with that … rayel proud … he said Maw'd be happy over it, too. An', later, the boys even managed to git ole Jo Shelby … he wuz a-livin' up in Missouree somewhures … 'pointed as a U.S. marshal … Clayveland done that fur 'em … boy wuz we shore proud o' that. It made awl the papers awl 'cross yar … folks in the South wuz 'bout to bust over it … 'specially in Arkansas an' Missouree … it wuz only far … ole Grant'd done made Fagan a marshal might as wayel as pin a star on ole Jo Shelby."

"And Mister Mansfield … Hardy?"

"He took sick an' died a yar 'r so after Jeremiah moved from Praynceton … the first o' April, in '94. He jes got sick an' we lost 'im within a week … he's buried back'er with Maw, o' course … rat next to her … side-by-the-other … jes like they wanted … together fur awl eternity … out thar with Jeremiah rat next to 'im an' Joshua aside 'em … awl of 'em in a row.

"Wayel, after he done went own over to Fordyce, Jeremiah'd married a widder woman he'd been a-courtin' down thew the yars … kindly late in life, yew might say … I don't know why they waited so long, but Jeremiah wuz rayel funny 'bout thangs an' kindly kept to hisself an' awl … I mean he raly wa'n't like nobody'd else 'bout ver' much ... oh, he wuz a good lawyer an' awl, done wayel ... like I said, folks liked 'im an' he liked them, but he kept a part of hisself sorta tucked away kindly ... he weren't awl that easy to figger ... even fur his family. Maygun she said he was kindly a 'mayst'ry' ... that wuz the word she found somewhures ... I don't know jes whure ... a 'mayst'ry'. Now don't git me wrong, they wuz close an' it wuz shore hard own her when we lost 'im ... but she said that the war an' awl'd done somethun' to 'im deep down inside ... he come back changed ... like when that arm wuz sawed awf sumpin' wuz sawed awf with it ... she said. I wuz jes too young to notice in nem days, and, anyway, they got marr'ed ... him an' that widder ... but damn if she didn't up and die within a yar o' that thar marr'age an' he los' interest in eve'thang rat quick as he put her in the ground ... closed his office plum down an' jes sat thar on the front porch a-starin'. Then, within a short spayel, he wasted away into nuthin' but hide, hair, an' bone, nen fell rat in thar beside her ... but, 'bout a yar or so later, we ... me 'n Maygun ... we dug 'im up an' brung 'im back yar to The Playce ... a few yars afore Gurston wuz bornded. We done it 'cause the widder's family, without a-tellin' nobody, done moved her o-ver to be with her firs' husband so Maygun an' me hitched up the wagon an' loaded shovels 'n picks an' went own o-ver an' shoveled 'm up with ar own two hands an' brought 'im own home ... we wuz a-pullin' that wagon with two fine matchin' horses ... jes like Henry an' Henrietta ... an' folks come along an' thowed flo'ers in thar with 'im ... an' the vet'rans stopped us at Tulip an' put a purtty new Confed'rate flag over his box. Them boys awl wuz from the Jaynkins's Fe'ry Camp ... it's a big un ... an' they rode out 'n tacked it down tight ... they'd heerd we wuz a-comin' with his cawfin in the back an' awl. Mister Storns, it wuz covered in nem purty flo'res 'cause it wuz in the sprang of the yar, fresh an' with all kinds o' colors. We sent word own to Septimus whut we wuz a-doin' ... he wuz a praycher then, marr'ed with a family an' a big church ... an' we kept Jeremiah in the parlor till he got yar ... then he follered along ahind us a-sayin' the Word an' we took 'im own out to the plot ... it's about half a mile back-er ... an' by then more an' more 'o the boys an' friends an' vet'rans come to The Playce ... most'd follered ahind us own horses when we brought 'im from Tulip that day a-fore ... one wuz a playin' a harmonica rayel purty like ... an' ole Septimus, why he walked, a-readin' an' a quotin' out'o the Good Book. It wuz quite a sight, Mr. Storns, shore wuz. I ain't ever seen nuthin' like it, like I say ... an' Septimus he done the service an' awl ... we felt good 'bout it, shore did ... rayel good. So Jeremiah ain't o-ver by hisself no more, he belongs yar, an' The Playce ... whur I'm gonna be soon nuff ... an' thar wuz sumpin' 'bout it that made it better'n his firs' fun'ral. Ever seen a body get two funerals, Mister Storns?"

"Not right off, no, sir."

"Well, I got my fun'ral awl wrote up an' my playce picked out rat thar with 'em … an' my stone already laid an' wrote up own … rat next to Jeremiah's … awl a body's got to do is fill in the date. Like I say, I'm 'mos' ninety … an' it won't be long now, Mister Storns … I'll show ye rat whure I'm a-goin' res' … but I ain't gonna miss it much, oh, I'll miss my folks that's livin' … an' ole Ricochet yar, an' the frost of a fawl mornin', an' the turnin' leaves in November, an' the sound o' a hound a-runnin' in nem ole bottoms 'r a big buck a-standin' in the timber 'r a whippoorwayel of an evenin' … but thar ain't nuthin' much else in this yar world o' tears worth a-stayin' fur, Mister Storns. I'll jes be thar with my payple side-by-the-other till the end o' the Lord's good time … ye know … till when we're awl gonna gather at the river own that las' day."

Storns noticed a softening in Uncle Joe Boy's eyes and felt a little in his own. After a very long pause, Gurston said at last, "You done give all yore wishes to Aint Clare, I suppose, Uncle Joe Boy?"

"Rat … she knows ever'thang … an' she done wrote it down in the big Bible … she knows ever'thang …"

Storns stirred uncomfortably.

Uncle Joe Boy helped him by saying, "An', too, I want Septimus's son to do my fun'ral … not in no church, mind ye, I ain't 'sossiated with none … asides, thar ain't no White church 'round yar that'd allow sech … it jes ain't done … but, see, I ain't awl that religious nor nothin' … oh, like I say, I believe in God, Mister Storns, fellers got to do that, or go slap crazy … but it's religion I cain't abide … an' praychers … it's a rare'un that's any count. I'm like Hardy G. thar … but I like Septimus's boy … he's the only praycher I raly hold with an' I want him to do my fun'ral, rat like his daddy done for Jeremiah's second'n that I jes tole ye 'bout … the White praycher that done his first'n weren't so hot. Ole Septimus, Mister Storns, he done it rat, I tell ye, rat."

"What did he say?" asked Storns.

"He praychhed like he always done … own 'forgiveness' … like that prayer he made that Ayaster Sunday … rat after Bobby Lee done surrendered …"

"Prayer after Lee surrendered?" asked Storns in amazement.

Uncle Joe Boy summed it up as best he could, then added, "He was always praychin' own 'forgiveness' … that … 'r prayin' own it … he said it wuz the only hope fur a fallen world … only way to break the cycle o' thangs … yew know … uh war an' killin' an' awl … he spread that word ever'whure he went

... awl over Arkansas ... Black an' White ... he come thew yar later ... after Joshua died ... and some time afore Jeremiah ... an' wuz own his way to Camden, see, ... wayel, he wuz in a wagon with a pair o' fine white matchin' mules an' with his entar family an' awl ... he wanted us to go ... so we awl loaded up ... every last one of us ... Maw wuz gone by then ... but Pappy, Jeremiah, Maygun, an' me ... we went with Septimus own down to Camden ... in ar own wagon, 'course ... they wanted him thar ... see ... his ole Aint Sallie had done died ... the ole slave woman that had took ker of 'im ... raised 'im an' awl ... like her own 'cause he didn't have nobody ... he wuz a-doin' her fun'ral ... his ole family had called fur 'im to come ... said that wuz her last wish ... 'fur baby Septimus' ... that's what she called 'im ... he said ... wayel ... we went ... it wuz in a purty good size darky church an' it wuz jes full o' folks ... Black an' White ... a-standin' along the walls ... an' a listenin' outside the winders ... we awl sat thar own the front row with the Black family an' the White family whut she worked fur ... an' Septimus done run awf from ... he felt bad about that ... runin' awf durin' the war when thangs wuz so hard ... but they wuz awl thar ... his Miz Virginee and awl of 'em ... she was thar too ... ever'body done dressed in thar finest ... an' his ole Aint Sallie wuz laid out in her cawfin in'r Sunday dress an' the choir it wuz a-sangin' like they do ... they wuz sumpin' ... an' Septimus he prayched agin own forgiveness ... said it wuz the only hope ... that we couldn't change the past, but we could thew the power of forgiveness give it a diff'rent turn ... how'd he say it, Gurston, ye remember, don't ye?"

"Meaning ... give it a different meaning."

"That wuz the big word he found somewhures ... Septimus wuz always a-findin' nem words like at ... but, afore it wuz over, had mos' ever'body cryin' ... it wuz sumpin' ... shore wuz ... I ain't ever seen nuthin' like it ... afore 'r since ... and Miz Virginee, why she run over and give Septimus a big hug; cried and awl, and he cried with her. It was wonderful."

"What did people say?" asked Storns.

"They awl ... ever'one thought it wuz wonderful too ... shook hands an' hugged one anuther. Oh, ye know, it wore awf and they went back to doin' whut they always done ... but ... but ... later ... when Jeremiah's time come ... like I said, it shore made me an' Maygun proud when we brung 'im own home in that wagon ahind nem two fine horses with that parade o' folks we never 'spected an' him awl covered in the Confed'rate flag an' awl ... and we wanted Septimus to do his funeral too, like he done Aint Sallie's down thar in Camden that day ... an' we wuz po'erful proud when he done come an'

praychyed like he done jes like fur her an' said awl the same thangs ... see ...
ole Septimus ... back'er when he wuz a-sittin' own Joe Nathan's horse ... ye
know with that rope choked 'round his neck a-fixin' to hang ... he said later
that God talked to 'im spaycial like ... kindly like when ole Sant Paul wuz
knocked sideways off that big mule he was a-ridin' that day ... ye know an' it
changed his life an' awl the world with it ... wayel, it wuz the same with him,
with ole Septimus ... he said that the Lord done saved 'im thew Pappy ... that
it wuz a mir'cle an' awl ... fur a higher callin' ... to a-carry the word, like he
done, ever'whure awl the rest of his bornded days."

"Is Septimus still livin'?" asked Storns quietly.

"Nawgh ... he died yar a while back ... but he wuz one o' the finest human
bein's I ever come across ... as fine as ever drew breath in the clay o' this ole
sinful body ... that's whut I thank of Septimus Raymond, Mister Storns. Him
an' Pappy ... they wuz the finest I ever seen ... though, o' course, they wuz as
different as day an' night ..."

"You say he had a church ..."

"Yeah ... like I say, he had one of the biggest AME churches in Lit'le Rock
... but I cain't cawl the name ... ever'body loved Septimus ... Black or White."

"You said he had a family ... what happened to them?"

"Except for the boy, who's a praycher, I don't know, but Gurston knows ...
don't ye, son ... he tried to keep up with 'em and awl ... what happened to
Septimus's family?"

Gurston stirred, rocked forward a bit, and said, "His wife died ... they was
three children ... two boys ... one went north ... ain't been heerd from ...
the other preached ... he took his daddy's ole church ... and then there was
the one daughter ... she married a man ... an overseer that worked for Scott
Bonds ... o-ver in the Delta ... but when he ... Mister Bonds died ... seems
like they moved on to Forrest City. I don't even know if they're still livin' ...
but they had several kids of thar own ... but I know only of one son that done
pretty good ... the rest scattered up north ... Chicago ... I hear ... but he ...
the one boy ... went own into farmin' ... workin' for various big planters in
Wattensaw County ... in the Delta."

"What's his name?" asked Storns, making a note.

"Bradford," said Gurston.

"Bradford?" said Storns, scribbling.

"Mose Bradford, is what folks call 'im, but I kinda lost tech. I see the one
boy around town from time to time ... I'll ask 'em, if you like ... he'll
know ..."

"What's the preacher son's name?"

"Joshua ..." said Gurston with a slight smile. "The other son's name I cain't remember, he was the oldest ... I didn't know 'im too well ... but like I say ... he run off ... to Chicago, seems like."

"But those in the Delta are named Bradford, from the daughter, right?" Storns asked.

"Right," said Gurston.

Storns wrote it down.

Aunt Clare came out and announced "supper" and they went in for it. Then, afterward, when he was too tired to read much, Storns saw the letters and, too tired to talk, he was shown the rebuilt cabin used as a kind of guesthouse.

"This is where Joshua and Septimus stayed in nem days ... we've kindly kept it up ... you'll be comfortable in here," Gurston said, showing him a few things then retiring.

Storns retrieved a drink of whiskey from his little bag and quickly unfolded along the bed into a deep sleep. Still clothed, he awoke at midnight, undressed by moonlight, then crawled under the sheets, lulled to sleep by the crickets, tree frogs, and a whippoorwill, till the sun touched his eyes like it had Septimus that first morning, and he awoke to a summer dawn.

There was coffee and breakfast, a quick visit to the cemetery, and a long ride home.

"Did you get what you needed?" Gurston asked as they crossed the Saline.

"And more," said Storns.

"Good," said Gurston. "It's quite a story, ain't it?"

"Yes ... indeed, it is," Storns said quietly.

It was indeed "quite a story." Trouble was, the editor told Storns he couldn't use it. "Folks just aren't ready yet, Jake," he said with a painful look.

The next Sunday there appeared under the headline, "Arkansans at War," a rather predictable feature, "as told by Uncle Joe Mansfield of Dallas County," with gratitude to his great-nephew, Gurston Smith, about the heroics of Johnny Mansfield at Franklin with General Pat Cleburne, Jeremiah Mansfield at Pleasant Hill with General Thomas Churchill, Joshua Smith in France with General John J. Pershing, and a quick sketch of James Mansfield in Mexico with "Jo" Shelby, but nothing at all about Hardy G., Mary, Megan, Joshua, Dagmar, Billy Jack Stantford, "Jo Nathan," or Septimus.

Nor, need it be said, was there a single mention of a horse, a mule, or a dog.

Nor could they have told yet of a woman standing herself by another grave, there, like Little Joshua and James, because some emulating nephew of greatness had meddled in the Mekong as well as Mexico. The woman standing in a wood waiting for a man named Barrel Bradford, Septimus's grandson, to bring a letter, thanking him and reading it as he drove away, was, of course, the great-grandchild of Medora Pilgrim, the woman who changed everything that day by shooting Dagmar in the arm and thus spun the world in another direction.

In the letter Barrel Bradford brought, Kroner told her of the Anglo-Mestizo-Cochiti who found the man looking for her son's friend who had been "looking for the truth," and in a kind of drunken madness had decided he could accept the death of no one and worked through some "strange ideas" in which he was always talking about "History" and it being "Necessity, Freedom, Memory, and Grace," which he tried to explain to Cripple Bear and Kroner during one drunken long, late-night coversation in the cabin where Kroner had at last found him, till the Indian had replied in a kind of nodding agreement "just to keep it simple," adding, *"Sólo dios basta,"* he said, handing his friend a family homily from a "bad" priest who had loved his grandmother one passionate alcoholic night when he was supposed to hear her confession but sinned with her instead. "If eternity isn't, nothing is," Poltam mumbled before passing out.

It was true, he agreed at last, as Kroner now reported in his letter brought by Barrel, only a God can save us—only that is enough—that or nothing, just as Cripple Bear preached to all his drunks. That now or the Iron Machine, which, Poltam insisted had enslaved the South and now was doing the same to the whole world—this being the worst slavery of all—the "everything" that "conspires to enslave the flesh and the soul." But his Cochiti friend told Poltam he simply needed to do a few things differently and he would help if he wished but that he was making it all much too complicated, adding, "You need to save yourself before you can save the world."

Then Kroner set the story upon the page, as he had said he would. That his man had come west, into the Sangre de Cristo Mountains, looking—like the mythical lost mines of the Spanish said to be there, hidden by the Indians, or the buck with the sacred white stone in his neck which, when found, would mean the end of time—searching for just such a thing, like, from home, written upon a hide, the lost treasure of De Soto, sold to a now long-buried "bad" priest. He would come home and tell it, and soon, he said, to his friend who he found in his cabin where he told him the great thing he needed to know at last.

There the letter ended, and Elizabeth folded it gently into her basket, left a note upon the grave, and came back to Conrad, who had wondered when she would return from where, to her surprise, he had always known she was.

PHILLIP H. MCMATH

But Uncle Joe Boy Mansfield never looked for any hidden treasure scribbled upon a hide, nor had he ever read the words of it by a poet named Fletcher, whose father had served with his brother, dead at Franklin.

> We, Arkansawyers of a different race, are the heirs of his legendary legacy. Now and again, we too go off seeking forgotten gold—in the market place of some great Northern city, or in the blue shadowed, deep wooded Ozark hollows. Whether we find it or not does not matter. There is always a map, drawn on deer or buffalo hide, left behind in somebody's hands, showing how, amid the densely wooded ridges, the narrow trackless hollows, the lost path that leads to that remote burying spot can somehow be found.

Uncle Joe Boy never went looking for a conquistador's gold in such a place, but he had, indeed, "kept it simple" by finding it where he was, and, in finding that which he had never really lost, surprised himself by living longer than he thought; dying in his sleep just before Jake Storns and Conrad Shaw, unbeknown to the other, landed in France on a stormy, cold June day in 1944.

As they waded upon the sand, back in the parlor of The Place, a few miles south of the Saline, there was a quieter scene—a short service said over an open coffin in songs and sighs—soon ended by the closing of a lid upon an old man black-suited for taking to softer ground.

Here, on a somewhat hot, but fine day, among fair trees near a field, the birds sang to words said upon a new grave dug as number five after the older, other four.

As hoped, a prayer was offered by a Creole-African, an aging man the deceased had met but once, Joshua Paul Raymond, Septimus's son, who spoke quietly of "forgiveness" then read I Corinthians 13. Their treasure had been found at long last and was buried there—all together as one, at last known, revealed, and resurrected.